MW01490668

Thank you for supporting
me. I love you so much.
Twin Flames for life ♡.

For Shadow and Chance

Rest in Peace, Sweet Boys

Credits:

Cover Design: Sean Galbraith

Editing: Susan D. Kerr

ISBN: 9798372009592

First Published: 2023

Strength List

Amy Blavins, Strength: Recovery—she can heal any wound no matter the permanent damage, but cannot heal common sickness or disease. She uses her own natural healing factor to heal her patients, so over-healing can rapidly drain her energy.

Hazel Sparks, Strength: Phantasm—using the illusion of a demon, she can increase all parts of her body with a set of shadow parts. The parts she can increase include: all limbs and their strength and all senses. She can even gain new abilities such as night vision and the ability to stretch out new limbs up to fifty feet.

BloodShot, Strength: Inflation—when he cuts someone, he can forcibly make the wound slowly expand after two minutes of the first injury. The expansion only continues if he is in a twenty-four-foot radius, but the pain rates as one of the top ten in the world.

Alex Galeger, Strength: Angel— from any body part, he can conjure a bright light that is hot to the touch, hot enough to cause blemishes when in contact, depending on how much light is produced. He can also control the brightness of the light, ranging from blinding like the sun to as dim as a lightbulb. Along with this light, he has angelic wings that perch on his outer back (special clothes are made for individuals with wings).

Anya Lokel, Strength: Mechanics—using any material present, she can create any kind of machinery or armory immediately or at most within five minutes, depending on the item she creates. The machines are powered by her sweat, which contains a small dose of oil, and at will, or after thirty minutes at most, the creations crumple back into the basic material.

Jaxon Call, Strength: Sargent—using a gas that seeps out of his mouth or nose, he can control anybody who breathes in the smoke. He controls who is affected by the smoke, and the spell can be broken by immense pain or loud noises, or it can fade. The smoke dissipates after one minute, and the effect dispels after five. Both can be increased with training, and he can control up to twenty-five people.

Steven Mallnen, Strength: Cyborg—he can transform any body part into robotic at will, but only two body parts at a time (can be increased with training). The feeling of a robotic part for him is that of ice being pressed against your skin, and his robotic limbs can get rusty or lock up.

Camilla Xavier, Strength: Wind Control—as it sounds, she can control any wind or oxygen by the sway of her hands. When used correctly and trained, Wind Control can nullify natural tornadoes and hurricanes.

Tonuko Kuntai, Strength: Ground Control—he can bend and manipulate any surface in any way, but only from the ground. He cannot manipulate walls or ceilings, and he does not create new material, he only stretches the objects he manipulates.

Jessica Alter, Strength: Growth—she can grow plants on any surface and amplify the amount of water in the air to make them grow instantly. As well as this, she can control her plants by a mind link with each one and command them to do nearly anything.

Donte Gavinson, Strength: Enhanced Speed—as it sounds, he can move at inhumane speeds. Not only do his legs move faster, even though he has shorter strides, all his movements are increased when he activates his strength. Like many strengths in society, activating his requires an extreme tense of his body, then when it feels like his body pops, the strength is activated.

Kyle Straiter, Strength Three: Fire Control—not only can he control any fire in his vision, but he also can conjure fire from any part of his body. Having fire on his body for too long will cause burns, and he can control the temperatures of his flames.

Kyle Straiter, Strength Four: Enhanced Strength—on command, his muscle mass will rapidly increase. Depending on how much of an increase is pushed for, his muscles may physically grow.

Khloe Basken, Strength: Intelligence—she can increase her I.Q. to three times its natural state (100). This specific type of I.Q. strength gives her a better strategic awareness and she uses this to her advantage by calculating her foe's and her own attacks.

Cindy Theon, Strength: Agility Enhancement—when holding her two specialized shotguns, she can increase her speed and agile ability ten times her normal rate. This effect has no backlash and can last for an entire day.

Rake Clause, Strength: Snake—he can remove his fingers like fastening tape and turn them into snakes almost instantaneously. The snakes are venomous, but the venom is fed through his blood so he can control the potency. As well as this, these special snakes can burrow through any surface and grow wings within one minute of detachment.

Scarlett Yalvo, Strength: Potent Perfume—she can change her body's smell to control people in certain ways. Examples are to change people's emotions about others or herself, cause people to obey her or others, and decrease the power of others' strengths. Depending on the effect and how much a person inhales, the outcome can last up to three days.

Cora Wavice, Strength: Boost—she can dramatically increase anybody's senses or strengths at will just by the touch of her finger. For example, this can dangerously increase someone's hearing, give someone a bloodhound type of smell, or even increase a person's strength so dramatically that they would be on the same level as the number-one hero or villain. Obviously, accomplishing such a large feat requires years of training.

Iris Blavins, Strength: Recovery—because she inherited her mother's one-of-a-kind healing strength, she can heal any physical damage to one's body. This healing is renowned as the top heal strength in the country at the very least, and Nurse Blavins is the top healing hero in the country.

Zayden Attack, Strength: Shark—half shark, half human, he can swim through the ground as if it's water and through small slits at the bottom of his palms, he can create and shoot shark teeth.

Diana Palkun, Strength: Build—using a piece of anything broken, she can rebuild the entire structure or parts of it. For example, if she has a scrap of a car, she can recreate the car the scrap is from.

Bobby Mamien, Strength: Illusion—he can create and reincarnate dead animals into ghost-esque creatures that can't be hurt by most physical attacks. They have extreme strength yet are very fragile and can be extremely damaged if even slightly hit.

Stafer Candreon, Strength: Amplify—he can copy any person's strength and amplify it to an extreme using a dark power. If one of the people he copies is weak, he can combine a strength he has copied before to create one attack, such as the monster of Bobby's illusion and Camilla's wind.

Hunter Sanders, Strength: Cancel—he can create spheres of magic cancellers out of his body and nullify almost any strength or attack. These spheres cannot be thrown and take a lot of stamina to use.

Jeremy Hunderaks/Catastrophe, Strength: Rumble—he can create strong earthquakes in specific spots that can reduce a person's ability to focus. They can span to a mile radius. It takes a lot of muscle and focus to create these, so he must keep a powerful body and serene mind.

David Blake/Care-Giver Weaponsmith, Strength: Weaponry—using anti-matter found in his stomach acid, he can form any weapon and throw it up through his widened mouth. His teeth are reinforced to not be affected by the stomach acid, his esophagus is hardened as to not get punctured by any sharp items, and his tongue is razor sharp and long to guide the weapons out of his mouth. If David creates too many weapons over a few hours, he will start to vomit blood and feel very ill.

Kane Ine/Care-Giver Animal Creator, Strength: Life Form—he can create any animal from his shadow, and depending on how big his shadow is, the bigger his beasts will be. If it is nighttime, he has no limit to the size except for what his body can handle (that currently is forty feet). He hears the thoughts of whatever animals he creates, so creating too many will tire him out and make him go crazy.

Zach Taling, Strength: Laser—he can create extremely powerful lasers that burn anyone or anything that comes within six inches of contact. He can shoot them by making a gun formation with his fingers or he can create walls of laser at will.

Rose Valington, Strength: Stomp—when she stomps her foot on the ground, she can create powerful waves of energy that shoot in all directions. She can only stomp to activate them, and how hard she stomps computes the power of the waves.

Danielle Kuntai, Strength: Root—she can bend dirt into cylinder shapes, hence the roots, and manipulate them in any way she can think or move with her hands. The roots can only be made of dirt, can dig through stone, and can seep through any hole no matter the size.

White Reaper, Strength: HellFlame—she can create white flames and creatures out of thin air. After burning for a while, the flames spawn the creatures, which look like beetles with the same fangs as hers. She also can turn her bones into long claws that pierce her skin and shoot out like more limbs. She can control them as if they are arms or legs, depending on where they come out of her body.

Fallen, Strength: Distraught—he can read anyone's mind and use their insecurities as a power source. The power he creates forms into beams of pure energy that can vaporize any matter at will. Depending on how strong the victim's insecurities are felt will range the power of the energy. For example, someone with little insecurity will cause the energy to leave burn marks and scratches, but someone who is very insecure will cause the energy to completely vaporize any matter, living or not.

Fallen, Real Strength: Transformation—he can conform anything caught within his pink and orange essence into whatever he pleases. Although he is powered by insecurity, he can control the power of the conformation. As well as this, he can store the power he's gained from an individual's insecurity, but he will slowly start to feel insecure about the same thing the person was if he contains it for too long.

C.J. Dane, #7 Hero, Strength: Leak—he can leak acid from all parts of his body, and he uses a special cloak to prevent it from spilling. When he takes off the cloak, his entire body is surrounded by acid and it gives him superhuman abilities such as the capability to slide on the acid-like ice and the skill to latch a string of acid onto any surface and swing on it. Also, he can form solid structures and items out of acid.

Aubrey Tato, #6 Hero, Strength: Color Bomb—she can shoot out bombs of multi-colored molten fluids, and the more colors the hotter the fluid. She has two types of bombs: ones that shoot out her left hand and ones that shoot out her right. The left-hand bombs are more pastel colors and rapidly cool at any temperature outside her body. She uses these to capture villains or seal holes. Her right-hand bombs are rainbow colored and heat up over time. This liquid can heat to 500 degrees Fahrenheit.

Eleanor Dainey, #5 Hero, Strength: Hologram— she is a holographic person who can make clones of herself. The clones cannot be hurt by physical attacks. They carry the weapons Eleanor carries and have the same martial skill as her. The most clones she can make without overworking herself is ten.

Maverick Case, #4 Hero, Strength: Lightning Bug—harnessing the power of electricity that he can create out of his hands or feet, he can unleash powerful bolts of lightning or bursts of electricity that are like waves of power. Through training, he's mastered his electricity control to such an extreme that his lightning has turned from yellow to black, and the electricity potency is particularly destructive and powerful.

Dame Qualin, #3 Hero, Strength: Angler Fish—a light dangling from his head can shine as bright as the sun and he can breathe and swim quickly underwater. The strength gives the user a thirst for blood, but he counters this by drinking animals' blood daily and building up a resistance over time.

Kaliska, #2 Hero, Strength: Native—they can use dead cells from the ground to summon zombified animals that are much larger and stronger than the animal was before it passed. They can also use the power of a Native Bible to unleash beams of pure power, eradicating anything within twenty feet of the book.

Zane Kinder (Puppeteer), #1 Hero, Strength: Puppet—he can turn his soul into a transparent puppet that is controlled through his fingers by a very, very slim black rope. The puppet's mouth is always open and can mimic the strength of multiple people within a mile in each direction. The puppet cannot be harmed by physical attacks, but any attack that lands on Zane or damages the puppet's strings affects both Zane and his puppet.

Skye Harlem, Strength: Demon—contrary to Alex, she can create a substance made of pure darkness that is freezing to the touch. She grew demonic-looking wings when she developed her strength. On top of that, she can grow her nails out at will and she has four fangs.

Violet Dedge, Strength: Turtle—because she developed an animalistic strength from spending so much time with her pet turtle, she has a large shell that attaches to her back and can be pulled off by only her hand. It is impenetrable by most attacks, having the ability to nullify fire, water, winds, etc. She also can swim abnormally fast and breathe underwater.

Daniel Onso, Strength: Hidden—he can become invisible at will, but when he's invisible he can only see people by their skeletons. His vision is like an x-ray when he's in his invisible state, and he becomes two times stronger. An advantage to his x-ray vision is that he can see through walls on command.

Xavier Kinder, Strength: Puppet—like his father, he can turn his soul into a transparent puppet that is controlled through his fingers by a very, very slim black rope. The puppet's mouth is always open, and it can mimic the strengths of people within a two-mile radius. The puppet cannot be harmed by physical attacks, but any attack that lands on Xavier or damages the strings affects both Xavier and his puppet.

Nervous Hero: Gladiator/Gerald Hatkins, Strength: Warrior—he can immediately sharpen any item he holds in his right hand and any shield he holds cancels out all strengths that attack it. Though he's a nervous *wreck, he has unbelievable swordsmanship and martial arts skills.*

Kerry Teravan/Lady Antress, Strength: Ant—she can carry up to fifteen times her body weight and has antennas on her head that wiggle when she senses danger. She can swiftly dig through any surface with ease and she is unusually shifty.

Ashlyn Gray, Strength: Blizzard—she can create compact snow that can withstand weight up to that of a semi-truck. The snow can be broken with strong pressure or heat and will weaken over the course of just a few minutes. Ashlyn can also create snowflakes that have little to no effect, as more of a sight to see. Finally, she can create ice out of any part of her body and spread it on surfaces. She can control it as she pleases, like Tonuko's strength. The ice shatters quite easily and can melt in the sunlight, but at night it's at its strongest.

Grey Anadam, Strength: Statue—he can turn his skin into stone. He can also increase his skin's durability. It takes more energy to make his skin harder, and the feeling of his strength being activated is that of tensing his entire body.

Adrian Ken/Gravaton, Strength: Guilt—like the metaphor "the crushing weight of guilt," he can convert one's guilt into an increase of the gravity they feel. This increase in weight affects the person's strength and physical body in a spherical shape around them. Others inside the sphere won't feel the effect of the gravity, only the person under his control will.

Annabelle Claire/Muscle Hero, Equal, Strength: Muscle Growth—she can transform white blood cells into muscle fibers, which has benefits and downfalls. She gains massive muscle mass based on how many white blood cells she uses, but over time she loses the ability to tell who is

*friend or foe. She is also more vulnerable to any kind of
sickness.*

*Crocodilian, Strength: Reptile—symbolizing the
metaphor "Chaos is a friend of mine," he can morph his
body into a large reptilian state at will. In this state, he has
armored scales, claws, a long snout filled with sharp teeth,
and extreme muscular strength.*

*Adrian Cate/Faithful Hero: HolyWater, Strength:
Aqua Hands—he can create large hands made out of
water and extend them or grow them at will. The fingers
on his water hands can shoot water like a hose, and the
hands have abnormal strength.*

*Alyssa Vern/Shard, Strength: Glass Control—she
can control any glass in the area and harden any air she
touches to make it a glass-like substance. Whenever
anything rests on the glass she creates, it's like a solid
floor that can hold up to a ton of weight. However, if the
glass is hit, it has the same sensitivity as regular glass.*

*The Child/Kidnapped Boy, Strength: Poison
Shard—the boy can create rough, poisonous shards out of
all parts of his body. The shards can be broken or pulled
out of him but are not poisonous when they aren't
attached to him. The poison flows through his blood—but
only when at least one shard is connected to his body—
and flows into the tip of the shards.*

*Monte Anderson/Testing Hero, Loam, Strength:
Measure—he can create highly durable clones, out of any
substance, that show a number measurement at the spot of
death. The number scale is one to one hundred, and one
hundred has never been reached. Based on research of
similar strengths, reaching a power level of one hundred
would need a combination of all strength-enhancing
powers and amplifying strengths. The clones' athletic
abilities are based on his own.*

Ryuu Kimura, Strength: Dragon Spirit—with the powers of a dragon—including inhuman strength, scaly arms that act as armor, fire breathing, flight through wings, and a special power: vision increase—he can focus his eyes to such an extreme that he can see the power flowing through a person's blood and their next move. This the most sacred strength in Japan.

Tanner Raith, Strength: Hard Zoom—with the touch of his hands, he can willingly harden the oxygen of the surface he imagines, creating discs. He can turn this effect on and off. The discs are as big as he can calculate the circumference or area of the shape. He also can control the speed of anything his hands or feet touch. This is like an on/off switch and the speeds increase or decrease according to how long he keeps the effect going.

Amy Lay, Strength: Domestic—with all abilities of a dog—including super speed while on all fours, sonic hearing, super sniffing, an advanced sense of direction even in unknown areas—she can increase strength in her legs and can gradually lift others' moods over a twenty-minute period.

Kyle Straiter: His Own World

Prologue
The Fateful Day

The world is a twisted, dark, cold place but some have an easier time surviving in it than others. I, Kyle Straiter, know this all too well. Ever since humans developed superhuman abilities, the world has evolved into an everlasting battlefield, split between heroes and villains. Everyone in this world has the ability to evolve a part of their body based on their surroundings—or, very rarely, genetics—and this evolution has been known as strengths. It is what makes us strong. People are only able to unleash and use one strength; for if they use more than one, their bodies would use so much energy that they would begin eating away at themselves to keep up. One man in particular attempted to develop and use more than one strength, and his story was the most known ... for now.

The man's hero name was HotSauce, and he was the top hero in society for many years. He gave the people hope, saved civilians with his lava strength, and overall fit the definition of a "hero." However, all men have imperfections. HotSauce wanted to be stronger, to save more people, so he trained toward unleashing a new, second strength. He spent his days at bodies of water trying to control the water, completely abandoning his heroic deeds. One day, his efforts were rewarded with a second strength: the ability to control water. With this, HotSauce thought he could finally defeat the monster on top of the underworld, who we will discuss later.

*In this battle of the century—the devil versus the hero—HotSauce's body failed him, and he was massacred by the villains' corrupt mob boss, **Tyrant.***

Tyrant ruled the criminal society for as long as HotSauce and used his strength, Devour, to keep it that way. Devour gave Tyrant the ability to eradicate any person's strength at the taste of their blood. Combining this with his inhuman athletic abilities, he was an unstoppable force.

Stories said Tyrant had no family connection, was abandoned at birth, and had lived in the shadows all of his life; this was untrue. They said he had no wife, no children ... a complete fabrication. Tyrant had a wife, Gem Straiter, and he murdered her in front of his only son, Kyle Straiter.

Tyrant was a bloodthirsty bastard who acted only on his desire for power. Like his societal name, he wished to rule the world in fearful tyranny. Tyrant attempted countless times to force me into villainy, to train hard so I could continue his actions, but I refused. I could never fall to the depths of villainy, not after all the trauma he'd put me through—abuse, neglect, ridicule ... every horrible act in the book. Because of my constant refusal, Tyrant one day took matters into his own hands. He murdered my mother, then abandoned me. That day, I vowed to kill him, no matter what it took.

That's exactly what I will do.

The story of my abandonment was something out of a nightmare.

Tyrant barged into the house, as usual, and broke the door off the hinge. This sudden action scared my mother and me, making us jump out of our seats on the couch. He stood in the doorway for a few moments, clenching his fists and gritting his teeth, then he took a step forward.

"Kyle, it's time. You must come with me to my base of operation, now," Tyrant demanded as he stomped over to me. He grabbed my forearm, then dragged me toward the doorway. Tears dripped down my cheeks and, although full of fear, I took a stand. I stomped my foot, halting our movement, then ripped my arm from his grasp.

"No, I won't!" I shouted. "I don't care about my stupid future in crime or whatever, I want to be a hero! Why won't you just listen to me?!" Tyrant's eyes didn't show disgust, but instead a sorrowful rage.

"You are seven years old; you will do as your father tells you!" he erupted as he slightly pushed me. He glanced over at Mom, who was standing with her hands by her chest, and after she nodded Tyrant crouched in front of me. "Kyle, this is what's best for the family. You must come with me, please."

"I don't want to be a villain! I don't want to hurt people like you, I want to help them! Why do I always have to do what's best for the family; what about me?!" I retorted with a shaky voice. Tyrant's calmness was quickly fading, and then and there, I saw true hatred for the first time.

"Dammit Kyle, *you live under my roof so you'll do as I say!* You can't become a hero; you have nobody here to support you!" Tyrant erupted as he stood.

"That's not true, I have Mom! She'll always help me! I'll get super strong, go to the best hero school, be the most perfect student anyone has ever seen, then be a real hero and take you down!" I exclaimed. I could feel my cheeks and ears burn due to my building rage. Tyrant looked up at Mom again, but this time his eyes looked distraught. His jaw shook, then Mom walked over to him.

"I do appreciate a goal and planned future, I really do, but there's just one problem with that," Tyrant vaguely stated as he stared at Mom. I was confused, and looked down at my fingers, then started counting off the steps.

I'll train super hard, get good grades, study a lot, help Mom with work to get enough money to go to the best hero school, then become a top hero ... What could be the problem?

"Honey, please just forget all of this. We can let our son grow up happily, live a better childhood, and have better opportunities than you had. Isn't that what you want?" Mom asked as she grabbed Tyrant's hand and caressed it softly.

He clenched his jaw and looked at the floor, not responding. "You know you don't have to do this. Please, don't do this," Mom pleaded with a cracking voice. Tears welled in her eyes, then fell down her cheeks. Tyrant was now crying as well, and he squeezed her hand harder. With the crack of a broken finger, he swiftly drew his pocketknife, a ten-inch switch-blade, and stabbed Mom through her chest. She didn't cry out or anything, but instead looked at Tyrant with the most remorseful, heartbroken expression imaginable. "I love you," she quietly whispered before falling to her knees and coughing.

"M- Mom?" I whimpered as my hands dropped to my side. Blood stained Tyrant's body and dripped onto the floor, then Mom fell back. "How could you?! Y- You just killed her; *you killed my mom!*" I screamed as I ran toward him, then I began punching and grabbing at Tyrant's clothes. He lifted his right foot up, then kicked me in the stomach. I stumbled back and fell onto my butt, then Tyrant whipped his knife into the ground as he swiveled to face me.

"This is the world, Kyle! This is what happens when you act out of line! People die, your loved ones die, everyone's life ends at some point!" he erupted ferociously. "Happiness is a filthy lie, and you'll learn as you grow up: anything you do, anything any of us do, *will always end in someone getting hurt!*"

"So what?! I don't care if it hurts someone if they're a monster like you! *Heroes take down people like you and bring happiness to everyone and justice to the people who deserve it!*" I screamed as tears poured down my cheeks. Tyrant looked as if he was about to explode with anger, then he screeched.

"Shut up, Kyle, shut the fuck up! I hate you; I hate you with every ounce of my being! You've done nothing but hurt this family! Your selfish attitude is going to get you killed!" Even if I hated Tyrant for all he'd done to me, those words broke my heart. Hearing my father curse me out and

tell me how much he hates me was just as painful as seeing my dying mom on the floor. Tyrant marched toward the front door, then stopped before walking out. "Make me a promise, Kyle. For once, just listen to me: be the best there ever was. Ace all your finals, get into the top school, and be the best prospect in history, then, once you're ready, come kill me." I stared at my mom, then looked up at him with cold, unforgiving eyes.

"I- I promise. I'll be the one to kill you." Tyrant didn't smile, but instead wore a frown. He walked out the door and left my life for the rest of my childhood years. I swiftly scrambled over to Mom and held her head as I stuttered, "M- Mom, you're gonna b- be okay. You can't die, it's not possible!"

"Kyle, listen to me." She softly grabbed my hand with her left hand, then reached over, ignoring the pain, and caressed my face with her right hand. My lip quivered, but I didn't wail. "You're going to do great things, I can tell. You're a gift to this world, never forget that. You'll always be the light of my life—this family was my light."

"M- Mom, please don't leave me! I don't wanna be alone, please!" I pleaded. I couldn't contain it anymore; I placed my face on her chest and cried loudly. She continued crying as well, then looked at the ceiling. She gave the world one last smile.

"I love you more than anything." With that, she took her last breath. I lifted my head, staring at her dead face in disbelief. A pool of blood was spreading from under her, soaking my pants. Unexplainably, while in my arms, her body began shattering into beautiful shards that looked like stained glass. They shimmered in the light, creating a rainbow on the ground as they floated into the air.

"No, Mom, *please don't leave me! I don't want to be alone! I'll be better, I won't be selfish, I'll be a villain, just please stay! Mom!* **Mom!***" No matter how loud I cried, the shards continued floating into the sky, then through the ceiling. Just like that, she was gone.

I don't know why she disappeared like that, vanished into the sky, but what's done was done. I trembled on the ground, then punched and broke the wooden floor. I glared up at the door, seething with murderous eyes, then exhaled sharply.

"Tyrant, *I'm going to fucking kill you.*"

That day was the fuel I needed for the rest of my life. That day was the kick start to the joy, rage, pain, and suffering of my life that led to the end.

Chapter 1
Not as Planned

The mailman knocked on the door and dropped off some mail at my house. Usually I don't receive any, so it was surprising to actually hear the noise of a paper packet. The house was dark and messy, and after standing up off the couch, I had to maneuver past trash and broken furniture to reach the front door. I opened it and stared at a large packet with a fancy, cursive &.ℋ. I raised an eyebrow, then picked up the papers and took them inside.

What the hell is this?

"Greetings heroes of the future," I read, scratching my head. "Seeing all the students who are shut down financially by private hero schools in the area breaks my heart, so I've decided a change needs to be made. My name is Simon Lane, and I will be opening a new school named Eccentric High. It is a public school, no tuition required; however, there will still be the usual entrance exams, both written and physical." My eyes lit up, and I held the packet in the air.

No way, there's no fucking way.

"I CAN GO TO HERO SCHOOL!" I laughed giddily and continued reading the introductory letter. The important details I noted were that the entrance exams were next Wednesday, the school year would start three weeks from today, and all students were required to live in a dorm system on campus to ensure their safety or some crap. My excitement was unmatched, and I immediately called a certain hero to help me train.

The week and two days went by fast, too fast. I guess what they say is true: time flies when you're having fun. I wore an ordinary blue tank top and five-inch inseam white shorts. My shoes were originally white but were now an eggshell white from dirt, and I tied around my head the last gift my mother had given me: a faded black ninja headband. I opened the front door and stood tall. Today was the start of a rocky road toward a successful hero career.

The walk wasn't very long, just ten minutes. For some reason, my palms were sweaty, and I felt sick to my stomach. I was actually nervous for the first time in years. I shook it off and continued on. The school was massive, and the campus covered three blocks worth of land. My eyes sparkled with amazement, then I felt a bump from behind. I stepped forward, looked behind me, and saw a boy and girl standing with each other while facing me. I gave the boy (who obviously was the one to hit me) a side eye, then he apologized in an innocent tone.

"Sorry, I wasn't paying attention!" He rubbed the back of his head and smiled nervously, but through my scowl I could see him shaking. I assumed he was just anxious like me, so I forgave him.

"Yeah, whatever, it's fine." We stood in silence for a few minutes. I couldn't tell whether they were waiting for me to introduce myself or something, so I started walking away. They were both surprised and glanced over at each other, then back at me.

"Wait, are you a freshman?!" the girl yelled. I nodded and stopped, then she explained, "Oh, we are too! We came from Edith!" Edith was a very popular private school in the area, and the student population was around two times the number my unpopular public school had.

"Oh, that's a pretty expensive school." Apparently to them it wasn't. I could tell by the expressions they gave me. "Well, I'm from Trinity Plus, it's a mile or two away." They both immediately cringed.

"So, you're a part of that famous odd-squad grade?" I raised an eyebrow, then realized what he meant and quickly denied.

"Oh hell no, that was the grade below ours. We were the grade with the ninth-ranked student in the country, Cade

Skizz. I think he's going to B.E.G. (pronounced beg) or something." B.E.G. was also known as Bade's Exceptionally Gifted and was the top hero school in the country.

There was a large line forming, so I walked over to get in it. Sadly, they followed and talked my ear off the entire time we waited. We reached the front, and there were five teachers sitting at a long, foldable table. I stood in front of a very muscular man with a large sword at his side; he couldn't help but gulp.

"Your name and strength?" he questioned. I took a deep breath, and after remembering the long consideration I'd given it during the past week, I let out my breath and smiled confidently.

"Kyle Straiter, my strengths are Enhanced Strength and Fire Conjuration." The teachers stopped and the students signing up stared. The man with the sword crossed his arms and glared at me.

"Are you pulling my leg, kid? You're telling me you have two strengths when nobody has ever, in all of history, developed two?!" I nodded and didn't back down with fear. I knew if I wanted to be a great hero like I promised, I would need to reveal from the start what makes me so special. From a young age, I constantly developed new strengths. Ever since the age of five, I randomly gained a new strength every so often, then it abruptly stopped after the age of ten. In total, I ended with ten strengths, two a year. However, even though it was technically telling a lie, I could not tell them how many I have altogether. For now, having two that work well together and give me the opportunity to be the strongest front-line attacker ever was good enough for me.

"Cross my heart and hope to die, sir, I have two strengths." He whispered to the woman next to him, then wrote down my name and strengths and called for the next student. I walked over to the building and leaned on the wall, waiting for the exams to start. The girl and boy didn't follow me this time, but instead started talking with a big group that gathered a few yards in front of me. I closed my eyes, but after a minute, everyone went silent. There were whispers all around, so I opened one eye to see what was going on. A boy was marching up through the line and stood in front of the sign-up table.

"I don't believe it; you're here to attend our school?" the teacher with the sword asked, standing up and looking down at the boy. His hair was spiked in the front in a middle part with one crooked bang sticking out the center. One half was earthy brown while the other was sky blue. In the middle where it parted, the two colors faded. He was wearing a long-sleeved shirt, a pair of plain black shorts, and thick boots instead of regular gym shoes. I closed my eye again, but after another minute I heard footsteps approach and stop a few feet away.

"So, you're the multi-strength kid I've been hearing about?" the boy asked after sticking his hands in his pockets. I moved off the wall and wore an antagonizing leer.

"What of it? Who are you anyway?" I interrogated. The tension between us was already thick, and people started gathering around, expecting either an argument or fight. We stared at each other for a few moments, then he broke the silence.

"Surprised you haven't heard, I'm ranked the top of our grade level nationally. Didn't think I'd need to introduce myself to anyone, but the name's Tonuko Kuntai (Tuh-new-ko Kuun-tie)." He held out his hand for a handshake, but I didn't give him one.

Instead, I responded, "I mean, those dumb rankings don't matter until hero school anyway. Number one or number one thousand, doesn't matter to me." The teachers were calling us over, so as I passed him I smirked, "Either way, I'll kick your ass ten out of ten times." He gritted his teeth then followed the rest of the group. There were around fifty first years, but only thirty-two would make it in. We were split into five groups of ten then led to the classrooms where the written exam would be held. In my group, to nobody's shock, was Tonuko Kuntai. Clearly, they would have us battle, which was perfectly fine with me. After we were seated, the woman who led us stood behind the podium and smiled brightly.

"In front of each of you is the one hundred question written exam. You will have one hour to complete it. Good luck!" She was very cheerful and wore what I estimated to be a gallon of makeup. I opened the exam, grabbed the provided pencil, and got to work. The test was actually very easy; so easy, in fact, that I finished it first, in ten minutes. After flipping the last page, I thought,

Wow, I guess that school actually taught me something.

I was confident enough I didn't make any mistakes that I didn't bother checking my answers. After I turned my test in, there were whispers all around the room, but the teacher shushed them. She graded my test because there was so much time left, and I rested my head on my desk. Finally, after what felt like an eternity, the hour was over. One girl had turned her test in just ten minutes after me; she had long, brown hair in a ponytail and bangs. Tonuko finished at the halfway point, and a few others followed soon after him. At this point, I was very unimpressed with the supposed "top of our grade level" kid.

"Very well done. I'm impressed everyone finished on time. That was the council's test that every school in the nation uses, including Bade's Exceptionally Gifted! Good luck to you on your physical exam, and I hope to see every single one of you in my homeroom class, freshman honors!"

Oh, so this is the freshman honors' teacher. I would have definitely thought that big guy with the sword would be

the honors' teacher. Is this teacher really stronger than him?

She clapped cheerfully as we walked out, and over the speaker a man announced, "All students please report to the Dome for your physical strength test battles. Each of you will be assigned a partner to duel with when you walk in. Please stay in a single file line to give the instructor an easier time. Thank you for your cooperation."

We walked in an orderly fashion, following the other groups that were led by the sword man. One at a time, a man with bulging muscles and longer hair—half of it in a short ponytail—assigned each student their duel partner. He held a clipboard with a list of all the battles that would occur. Tonuko was in line in front of me, and when he walked up to the teacher, the teacher grinned.

"Tonuko Kuntai, you'll be facing your pal behind you, Kyle Straiter. Good luck boys, I'm very intrigued on how this battle will turn out." We were seated on a balcony that had a view of the entire stage. After reluctantly sitting down next to Tonuko and the short girl from earlier (whose name I had already forgotten), I took a deep breath.

"Tsch, already scared Straiter? Don't worry, I'll end you quickly, then you won't have to see me, and I won't have to see you ever again." I looked at him like he was crazy, then snorted.

I retorted, "I'll knock you out in ten seconds flat. That's not a threat, it's a fuckin' promise."

He was shocked at my statement, then looked forward, irked. The first fight was between a boy named Donte, who was short and had spiky, light blue hair, and a boy named James, a plain looking boy with longer black hair. When the battle started, Donte dashed around the stage at lightning speed, overwhelming James. Donte took out James' legs from under him, then punched him as he was

26

landing. James launched outside of the stage, giving Donte the win.

Few battles really caught my eye, whether it be because I was confident of my own abilities, or because I just thought less of all the wannabes around me.

None of these kids have a goal, want it as much as I do. They're all looking to be just heroes, not real heroes. I'm looking at the big picture, I'm carrying somebody's will with me, I'm better than all of these posers.

Finally, my time was up. The last battle of the day was between Tonuko Kuntai and me, Kyle Straiter. He took the stairs down to the main floor while I decided to be a little flashy and jump from the balcony. I landed, and around my feet a flame wheel sputtered. I marched proudly to my side of the stage, and Tonuko stood nonchalantly on his side. I cracked my fingers while letting little flames ignite in my pupils. The teacher announced for the battle to commence, so I wasted no time.

Ten seconds flat, that's all the time I need.

I leapt at him and used flames as boosters on the soles of my feet. Tonuko stomped his foot on the ground and bent the cement, creating a dozen spikes in front of me to block my path. I jumped off a few of them, then charged directly at him.

Five ... Four ... Three ...

He created a massive wall, but I wound up a punch and smashed my fist through the wall. It shattered upon impact, and through the falling rocks, I wound up again and punched at him. He threw up his forearms to block, but I was too strong and hit him out of the stage just as I counted the last second in my head. He skidded across the white line painted onto the cement—signifying the stage boundaries—then fell onto his butt. I stood in the spot he used to be in and held my smoking fist in front of me. My knuckles were split and bleeding, and behind me, the spikes Tonuko had created crumpled down back into the ground.

"Did that random kid just beat the Tonuko Kuntai untouched?" a girl in the stands asked as people stared in awe. I put my hands on my head and walked toward the stairs. Tonuko held his left forearm, the one that took the blunt of the hit. The bone was shattered. The nurse who had attended the event to heal injuries knelt by his side and used her powers to heal Tonuko's arm. She was, surprisingly enough, the most famous healer in the country: Nurse Amy Blavins.

Amy Blavins, Strength: Recovery—she can heal any wound no matter the permanent damage, but cannot heal common sickness or disease. She uses her own natural healing factor to heal her patients, so over-healing can rapidly drain her energy.

"Well done all who came to join my school. As you may have guessed, I am the principal of Eccentric High: Simon Lane. Being forced to not take all of you in truly hurts me, but I was very impressed with the display of strength I just witnessed. Letters of acceptance shall be mailed one week from today, and school starts the Monday after that. I am ecstatic to be able to meet all the promising students who will attend the first-ever freshman class at Eccentric High." The kids applauded the principal with the ponytail, not sure why, but they did. I walked out first, hoping to avoid any conversation. Apparently, it was my lucky day because nobody stopped me, so I was able to walk home immediately.

Unsurprisingly, a week from that day, there was a knock on my door. I answered and a letter with a cursive &.H sat on the welcome mat.

Chapter 2
Brand New Life

"Kyle Straiter," the letter stated, "you are hereby accepted into the pristine hero academy of Eccentric High. Words cannot describe how overjoyed we are to be able to teach such an anomaly, but phenomenal prospect. Not only did you manage to beat the national top student of your grade level in only a few seconds—in addition to destroying a two-yard-thick wall with a single punch—but you also received a perfect score on your entrance exam. Coming directly from your principal, I cannot wait to see you on our campus." I dropped the letter and smiled brightly. I looked back at my disgustingly messy living room, then my eyes were drawn to the only untouched spot in the house: the spot where my mother perished.

"So, I punched through a two-yard-thick wall, eh?" I looked down at my scarred knuckles and smirked, "Figured as much. Combining fire power with enhanced muscles will break some thick-ass walls." I clenched my fist and my smile turned to a stern stare at the spotless area.

I promised Tyrant and my mom that I'd be the top of my class. No matter what it takes, I'll be the strongest, the smartest, and the best in the nation. The Hero Olympics is the ranking event, right? When it comes around in January, I intend to win with flying colors.

The Sunday night before the start of school I packed any clean clothes I had, and even some I'd bought that day. I went to sleep early that night to try and calm my nerves. I wasn't nervous about being the center of attention or Tonuko maybe getting accepted, but more so nervous about the expectations set upon me. Even though I felt like I wanted to throw up, I was still extremely happy. I would finally be able to go to hero school and fight bad guys like all the famous heroes do. I guess I let my guard down, one of my many mistakes ...

Tyrant's Facility, an Abandoned Factory in the Middle of a Field:

"What a pleasant surprise, you've impressed me yet again. Killing the eighth-strongest hero, not an easy feat, but you've accomplished it flawlessly! I'd assume you put in most of the work, Kaci?" Tyrant asked, a smile stretched across his face. Kaci had white hair with one long spike of a bang going down the right side of his face, and he wore a seemingly expensive watch.

"Actually, sir Tyrant, the new guy took care of it all by himself. All I had to do was sit back and enjoy the show." The new guy Kaci was talking about was a man with red skin. His hair was in a heap of curls that accentuated his large and twisted horns, and he wore a black and gray trench coat that covered his sheathed sword. He licked his lips, then devilishly, almost psychotically, smiled.

"That's true, I did it single handedly. Did it with ease, in fact. If that's what the heroes are made of, taking them down one by one will be nothing more than child's play." Tyrant clapped his hands joyfully, then stood from his handmade throne, built from animal bones.

"Why don't you go scout my boy's new school? I trust you with all my heart BloodShot, and as of now, you are the leader of my posse. Not only have you recruited someone else with an unreal strength, but you have yet to lose a battle. Go out there and give little ol' Kyle a warning shot." BloodShot's grin stayed, and his eyes scrunched.

"I will happily do so!" He walked off seemingly looking for someone, then Tyrant sat back down and sighed. He crossed one leg over the other and rested his head on the back of his chair.

The Next Day: Monday, August 19th:

I slowly opened my eyes and blinked a couple times. I sat up in my bed, yawned, then checked my phone for the time: 7:50 a.m. My eyes widened, then I swung my head back and groaned.

I swore, "Shit, I'm gonna be late!" I rushed to the bathroom, brushed my teeth while showering, then dressed, grabbed my phone and wallet, and ran out of the house with my suitcase. After all that, it was 8:20 a.m., just ten minutes before the introduction day started. I noticed that the boy who ran into me during the entrance exam was across the street, also running. As much as I wanted to laugh at him, I was in the same boat. We both arrived with minutes to spare but we were still the last ones. I didn't recognize a single kid to be from Trinity Plus, whether I should have or not. I was panting with my hands on my knees, and the other kid who ran was right next to me.

"Man, I guess we both slept in late, huh?" he chuckled through his deep breaths. I shrugged then saw he reached in front of me for a handout. "My name's Alex, nice to meet you again, Kyle." I stood up straight after catching my breath, looked down at his hand, then walked away.

"Oh, no you don't! We're all classmates, and that means you have to get to know us!" the short girl from the entrance exam shouted as she grabbed my arm. Dumbfounded, I looked down at her as she forced me to shake Alex's hand. "Now my turn, I'm Cindy!" She shook my hand, then she and Alex talked about classes.

What just happened? Get to know them? Why the hell should I care at all about them?! Just because we're classmates doesn't mean we have to be best buds; it just means in the field of battle you're an ally I don't have to fight.

"I figured you'd have made it in, you cocky son of a bitch," Tonuko muttered walking up to me and crossing his arms. We stood facing each other for a couple of seconds, then a very peppy girl whistled, grabbing our attention.

"Welcome all you freshies! I'm a junior here in the honors' class, and I'll be giving you your dorm assignments. Each floor will have twelve people, but the top will have eight. They're sectioned off into hallways of six or four, so whoever is in those will be your floormates for any future training groups!" Tonuko and I ignored her, then I smirked.

"I didn't think they'd take somebody who got babied like you did. I mean, ten seconds flat, I predicted that perfectly, didn't I?" I taunted, causing him to tense his fist and clench his jaw.

"My ass you predicted that perfectly. I wasn't even trying; I didn't want to waste so much energy on someone who I thought was at the level of a preschooler. I can admit I underestimated you, but you better believe that won't ever fucking happen again." My smirk turned to a frown, and I balled my fist. It looked like we were about to start fighting, so the junior walked up and stood between us.

"Woah, take it easy guys. I've heard of both of you, and you're both insanely strong for first years. Shouldn't you be happy to have such powerful allies? You're classmates, you're on the same team!" the junior explained.

"I came to this random ass new school to be the strongest one here! I'm the number one, I'm the national favorite. Now, this random kid thinks he can strut right in and boast about being the strongest?! To hell with that!" Tonuko snapped. He pushed the junior away with one arm, but then she reached out and out of her arms, two massive, muscular, pitch-black, translucent arms grabbed our torsos and trapped our arms in the process.

Hazel Sparks, Strength: Phantasm—using the illusion of a demon, she can increase all parts of her body with a set of shadow parts. The parts she can increase include: all limbs and their strength and all senses. She can even gain new abilities such as night vision and the ability to stretch out new limbs up to fifty feet.

"The hell?! Let me go! He's the one being a sore loser, I was just standing here!" I argued while squirming around, then she dropped us on our butts.

Hazel commanded, "Get along, and I don't ever wanna hear that kind of talk again. I don't care what your rank is nationally, don't ever patronize your classmates!" Then, she turned to me and pointed, "And you, don't egg him on by being cocky! You won one fight, big whoop! The real training hasn't even started yet, so don't go pissing yourself with confidence!" She took a deep breath, then smiled again and shouted, "Alright, everyone, let's get on into the dorm!"

Tonuko and I sat on the ground while everyone else left, then he stood first and followed the group. I looked down at the grass, my face full of fury.

Who the hell does she think she is? Pissing myself with confidence; I have all the right to be confident! I'm probably stronger than her! Whatever, if they want me to prove myself, I'll happily oblige.

On the first floor of rooms, Hazel scanned the piece of paper in her hands. "Camilla, Donte, Claire, Steven, Jessica, and Jaxon, you'll all be on the left side. On the right are Rake, James, Bryce, Ana, Rebecca, and Anya!" Hazel read off. The twelve students headed for their rooms, then the rest of us walked up to the next floor. Hazel announced, "Oh boy, on the left we have Cindy, Khloe, Iris, Alex, Kyle, and Tonuko! On the right ..." She continued naming people, but I blocked her voice out and went straight for my room.

I put my hand on the doorknob, but then Tonuko groaned, "Why the hell do I have to be on a floor with him?! Can't somebody change up the arrangements or something?!"

In response, I chirped, "Do you think I wanna be on a floor with you, Moody Earth, and the clumsy ass kid over there?!" I was referring to Alex. "Just shut up and deal with it!"

"Moody Earth, who the hell are you calling moody?! I swear one win and you already think you own the place!" Tonuko yelled. I snorted and gave him a mocking grin.

"Maybe I do." He squeezed the handle on his suitcase. Our floormates clearly did not want to deal with our bickering.

"Would you two just shut up already? God, you're like a couple of little kids! If you're both so high and mighty, act like it!" Khloe seethed walking past Tonuko. She was the girl who finished the test shortly after me.

Iris added quietly, "Yeah, we can all get along if we try!" She was so innocent, if I so much as raised my voice at her, she'd probably break.

I rolled my eyes and shook my head, then entered my room. It was dark, but with the flick of a switch, the room was actually decently sized. It had a desk, full-sized bed, bathroom, and wardrobe. After unpacking, I took a nap for a few hours. Today was just move in day, so the name "Introduction Day" was pretty misleading. Tomorrow started the first school day, and I had no idea what the hell we'd do. When I awoke, I decided to take a walk around campus to see what it was like.

When I opened the front door, I could see the path that connected us to everything. I followed it and walked up to a forest-looking park. It had a little river with a waterfall coming out of an artificial rock, fish in the pond, and a ton of trees. I stood on top of the bridge that connected to sides of the park and smiled while looking down at the beautiful coy fish. It seemed like nothing could go wrong, but everything did when I heard someone running up to me. I turned my head, then threw my arm up to block the sword the red man just swung at me. After the blade dug into my skin, he smiled.

34

"Little Kyle Straiter, son of Tyrant, I'm so glad to finally meet you! The big man up top said I could give you a warning, so I'm here to do just that!" I jumped back and ripped my arm out of his sword in the process, then tensed my fist. No matter how angry I was at Tyrant, I couldn't help but shake with fear. The man's aura was disturbing, and with the tree shadows blocking out sunlight, he looked like a demon. "Look at that, you're shaking like a frightened child! If I didn't know any better, I'd think you were one!"

"I- I'm gonna take you down!" I stuttered, but we both knew it was just an empty threat. He took a step forward, I took one back, then he darted faster than I ever could have predicted. With one swoop, his sword was through my stomach and out my back. Blood soaked the grass we stood on, and after he tore his blade out of my body, he licked the blood off of it. I feared for my life thinking that his strength had something to do with the taste of blood like Tyrant's, however, nothing happened. I coughed a few times into my hands, soaking my fingers with spit mixed with blood, then a pain worse than I'd ever felt struck.

"There it is, the most beautiful form of murder. I'm sure Tyrant won't mind if you die, not like you were gonna join us willingly anyway!" The wound in my stomach ripped more; it was expanding. My flesh tore apart slowly, and the gash in my arm did the same.

This is it, I'm gonna die already? I made a promise to my mom, I can't go out yet! I just- can't! Her death will be in vain, it'll be all my fault. Tyrant killing her was because of me, now I can't even man up and accomplish what she asked of me. How pathetic am I?

My savior came in an instant. The principal swooped in and stabbed at BloodShot a few times, but he dodged each one. After thinking for a moment while avoiding the principal's weapon, BloodShot verbalized his decision, "Not worth it to risk death here. Good luck, little ol' Kyle!"

35

Before passing out, I noticed that the principal was using a massive nail as a sword. After he dropped it, it shrunk back to its regular size. Then I blacked out. Once BloodShot evaded the teachers and was a certain distance away, the wound expansion stopped.

BloodShot, Strength: Inflation—*when he cuts someone, he can forcibly make the wound slowly expand after two minutes of the first injury. The expansion only continues if he is in a twenty-four-foot radius, but the pain rates as one of the top ten in the world.*

I was rushed to the nurse's office, and Nurse Blavins, after half an hour, healed me to perfection. Supposedly, the strength BloodShot had caused damage that was meticulous and time consuming to heal, as well as energy consuming. She had to sleep for the rest of the day, while I woke a few hours later.

Some students entered a few minutes after I woke. I recognized Alex and Cindy, but there was one I hadn't talked with yet. "Oh Kyle, this is Rake! He's in the honors' class and Alex and I have known him since we were little!" Rake nodded with a smirk.

He commented, "Wish I could've met you when you weren't in a hospital bed, but y'know, gotta take it as it comes." I couldn't help but chuckle, then looked down at the sheets. There were a few red stains, and my left arm was wrapped with bandages.

"I feel so bad, I wish we could've helped!" Cindy whined as she looked out the window at the attack site. There were guards and a man with a white jacket inspecting the area.

Alex nodded in agreement, but Rake thought otherwise. "It's best we didn't, honestly." Cindy and Alex were stunned he'd say something like that, but I understood where he was coming from. "Just think about it; is it better to have one student injured and the teacher's help, or countless casualties and no one able to call for backup?"

"Yeah, he's got a point. I do feel horrible though, you've got to be in a lot of pain. I'm sure your parents are devastated to hear about this," Alex sighed. I shrugged, then looked at Nurse Blavins.

My parents ...

"No, I'm really fine. Since Nurse Blavins was able to heal me so perfectly, I'm sure I'll be able to go to class tomorrow for the first day." Principal Lane walked in the room and clapped his hands.

He happily stated, "I talked with Nurse Blavins before she went to sleep, and you are able to return to the dorm at any time. Your injuries are all healed, but you will be sore for a few days."

The three were happy for me, then Principal Lane asked, "Would you three excuse us for just a few minutes? There's something I need to speak with Kyle about." They waved and left, then Principal Lane pulled up a chair next to my bed. "Kyle, we need to have a talk about your strengths and connections."

"What about them? I have two strengths, sure, but what kind of connections do you mean?" He crossed his arms and leaned back in the chair.

"You don't need to put on an act for me Kyle. Gem Straiter died eight years ago at the hands of her husband, Samuel Straiter, also known as Tyrant." I clenched my jaw, thinking the worst.

What are these heroes going to do with me? I want to be one, too. I'm not like Tyrant. Don't take me down just because you're superstitious.

"Listen, I'm not here to do you any harm. Others might, but I want you to grow past your ... well your past. I know your family doesn't define you, but it does influence

37

you. A strong hate for Tyrant, that's what drives you, isn't it?"

"Yes," I responded, "I'll do whatever it takes to end him. He's taken everything from me: a normal life, a normal family, my mom. Even if it kills me, I'll kill him first." Principal Lane nodded, then exhaled deeply in disappointment. "Who on the staff knows about my family?" I asked.

"Just the vice principal, the leader of our security, and I know. We felt it wouldn't be right to spread this information about you to the rest of the staff without your approval." I thought for a moment, then gave him my answer.

"I'd prefer the teachers don't know. I want as few people as possible to know I'm the son of the top villain before I've done any major heroic deeds." He rubbed his chin, understanding my reasons. "I'm assuming since you know about Tyrant, then you know how I have more than two strengths."

"No, I didn't know that actually. Just how many do you have, and how were you able to develop more than one when the strongest hero ever couldn't handle two?"

"For your first question, I have ten total strengths developed over a five-year span. As for the second, I can't answer that because I'm not sure how I was able to develop so many." Principal Lane was dumbfounded and counted out ten on his fingers.

"That is absolutely ludicrous. Ten strengths, ten?! I am extremely overjoyed that you chose to attend our school, and I hope eventually you will be able to use all ten of those gifts publicly." He sat for another second, then stood and said, "Well, I'll let you go now. I'm sure you want some rest in a comfortable bed, not one of these hospital cots." He left, then, shortly after, I did as well. I quickly headed to my room to avoid any confrontation and slept immediately. I didn't even realize I hadn't eaten in more than a day.

The next morning, I woke an hour and a half before school started and went for a run around campus. I avoided the park this time and went around it instead. After my run, I showered, then finally ate something. It was noted in the acceptance letter that for now we would have no school or training uniforms, so we were allowed to wear any clothes we wanted. I wore a white t-shirt and black shorts but kept my ninja headband in my pocket for when training started. For breakfast, I ate an apple and some yogurt the school provided. I walked to class ten minutes early, and to my surprise, Tonuko was already there. We were told to stand and wait in the front of classroom so the teacher could give assigned seats when everyone arrived. Tonuko crossed his arms and looked away, then muttered, "I heard what happened. I'm- glad you're not hurt too severely." I looked at him and laughed. "I'm only saying that cause I want you to be full power when we fight again! Don't get the wrong idea!"

"I'm glad I'm not hurt too." We waited for the rest of the class to arrive, then the teacher stood and smiled.

"Welcome freshman honors' class! I'll be your teacher for the year, I'm Ms. Palkun! Let's get started by getting everyone seated!" She picked up a piece of paper and took the glasses off the top of her head. She put them on correctly, then read names for the front row from left to right. "Alex, Anya, Jaxon, and Steven! Next row: Donte, Jessica, Tonuko, and Camilla! After that, Rake, Khloe, Cindy, and Kyle. Finally, the fourth row, Zayden, Iris, Cora, and Scarlett!"

We took our seats, then the girl in front of me looked back with her head upside down. Her bright blonde hair, very similar to mine, hung low. "You're Kyle Straiter," she bluntly stated, still staring directly into my eyes. I awkwardly smiled and nodded.

"Yeah, that I am." She lifted her head and looked forward, leaving me utterly confused.

The teacher leaned on her podium in the front of the classroom and looked at all of us. She exclaimed, "Now for the fun part! I want each person to stand and introduce themselves, then describe their strength!" The class got all giddy, but I put my chin in my hand and looked out the window. The campus was bare now, unlike earlier when I was walking to school. I had a direct view of the park, and near the area where some trees were cut down because of the incident, I could see a red patch of grass. I tensed up, then heard the first person introducing themself.

"Hey everyone, I'm Alex Galeger! First off, I can't wait to spend the next four years with you all! Anyway, my strength is Angel!" Clearly, he was the pretty boy of the class, since all the girls were already fawning over him. He was tall, not very muscular, but defined, tan, and his hair parted to the left. The end of his bangs hung freely on the side of his head, like a little wing.

Alex Galeger, Strength: Angel—he can conjure a bright light from any body part that is hot to the touch, hot enough to cause blemishes when in contact depending on how much light is produced. He can also control the brightness of the light, ranging from blinding like the sun to a dim lightbulb. Along with this light, he has angelic wings that perch on his outer back (special clothes are made for individuals with wings).

We clapped, then Ms. Palkun stated, "Very interesting Alex, interesting indeed." Her presence was bizarre, neither evil nor good, but obsessive. She looked at the next girl, who then stood.

"My name's Anya Lokel, and don't you forget it! My strength is Mechanics, pretty awesome right?!" Out of the corner of my eye I could see Tonuko snort, so I assumed they already knew each other. Her skin had a slightly gray tint, and she had long, straight black hair.

Anya Lokel, Strength: Mechanics—using any material present, she can create any kind of machinery or armory immediately or at most within five minutes, depending on the item she creates. The machines are powered by her sweat, which contains a small dose of oil, and at will, or after thirty minutes at most, the creations crumple back into the basic material.

We clapped again, not me specifically, but the class did. The teacher didn't comment this time. Instead, she checked her watch and looked at the next person.

"Uh, I'm Jaxon Call." He clearly had a perm, a new perm in fact, and one of his eyes were purely red. He was skinny, not very built, but stood tall. "My strength is Sargent."

Jaxon Call, Strength: Sargent—using a gas that seeps out of his mouth or nose, he can control anybody who breathes in the smoke. He controls who is affected by the smoke, and the spell can be broken by immense pain or loud noises, or it can fade. The smoke dissipates after one minute, and the effect dispels after five. Both can be increased with training, and Jaxon can control up to twenty-five people.

Ms. Palkun complimented, "That's pretty unique, don't think I've heard of that strength before. Anyway, you're up Steven!" Steven stood and stuck his hands in his pockets.

"'Yo, I'm Steven Mallnen, the Cyborg! If you didn't know me yet, trust me, you will after our first fight!" He was pretty muscular, but average height. I rolled my eyes.

Bold claim coming from someone who defines themselves as a hunk of metal.

41

Steven Mallnen, Strength: Cyborg—he can transform any body part into robotic at will, but only two body parts at a time (can be increased with training). The feeling of a robotic part for him is that of ice being pressed against your skin, and his robotic limbs can get rusty or lock up.

The teacher stayed quiet again, but we were finally in the second row. Up first was the blonde girl in front of me. She stood and said plainly, "I'm Camilla Xavier, and my strength is Wind Control!"

Camilla Xavier, Strength: Wind Control—as it sounds, she can control any wind or oxygen by the sway of her hands. When used correctly and trained, Wind Control can nullify natural tornadoes and hurricanes.

It seemed we were taking longer than Ms. Palkun thought we would because she wasted no time and moved on to the next person. Tonuko stood then boldly stated, "You all know me, I'm Tonuko Kuntai. My strength is Ground Control."

Tonuko Kuntai, Strength: Ground Control—he can bend and manipulate any surface in any way, but only from the ground. He cannot manipulate walls or ceilings, and he does not create new material, he only stretches the objects he manipulates.

When he sat down, the next girl immediately shot up. She had curly, short brown hair, and a sunflower was perched at the front right side of her head.

"Hello everyone, I'm Jessica Alter! My strength is growth, and my beauties can take down anyone!" Out of the tip of her hand, a rose grew rapidly, then she tossed it up at Alex. He caught it, and she blushed happily.

Jessica Alter, Strength: Growth—she can grow plants on any surface and amplify the amount of water in the air to make them grow instantly. As well as this, she can control her plants by a mind link with each one and command them to do nearly anything.

She sat down gracefully, then the next boy stood. I recognized him from the day of the entrance exams, mostly because of how easily he wiped out his opponent.

"Hey all, I'm Donte Gavinson. As you all saw during the entrance exam, my strength is Enhanced Speed!" His pinkie nails, I could see, were painted sky blue.

Donte Gavinson, Strength: Enhanced Speed—as it sounds, he can move at inhumane speeds. Not only do his legs move faster, even though he has shorter strides, all his movements are increased when he activates his strength. Like many strengths in society, activating his requires an extreme tense of his body, then when it feels like his body pops, the strength is activated.

When he finished and sat back down, I sighed out of relief to myself.

Finally, two rows done; just two more and we're finished with this boring introduction crap. Man, I'm starving too. I wonder what kind of food they serve on campus.

It was my turn, so I stood and put my hands on my head.

"You should all know me, I'm Kyle Straiter, the kid that beat Tonuko. My two strengths are Fire Control and Enhanced Strength." People still seemed surprised to hear I had two strengths, but I took no notice of it. It was flattering, quite frankly.

Kyle Straiter, Strength Three: Fire Control—not only can he control any fire in his vision, but he also can conjure fire from any part of his body. Having fire on his body for too long will cause burns, and he can control the temperatures of his flames.

43

Kyle Straiter, Strength Four: Enhanced Strength—on command, his muscle mass will rapidly increase. Depending on how much of an increase is pushed for, his muscles may physically grow.

"Gosh, two strengths that work so well together. It's so amazing, I must say, Kyle Straiter," Ms. Palkun gawked. I awkwardly smiled then sat back down. I looked out the window again as the next girl went.

"Hey, I'm Khloe Basken and my strength is Intelligence."

Khloe Basken, Strength: Intelligence—she can increase her I.Q. to three times its natural state (100). This specific type of I.Q. strength gives her a better strategic awareness and she uses this to her advantage by calculating her foe's and her own attacks.

We moved on to the next girl, Cindy, who was obviously eager to go.

"Hey everyone, I'm Cindy Theon! My strength is Agility Enhancement!" Her hair was somewhat short, but her two ponytails hung low at the back of her head. Her eyes were big, and she had had a smile since I first saw her. For some reason, my cheeks felt hot.

Cindy Theon, Strength: Agility Enhancement—when holding her two specialized shotguns, she can increase her speed and agile ability ten times her normal rate. This effect has no backlash and can last for an entire day.

"Wow, that's pretty cool," I said, not realizing I spoke out loud. She blushed and smiled at me, and I blushed too, but not because I was happy, more so embarrassed. I saw a couple of people around the room giggle, even the stern Khloe. I rolled my eyes, then the next person saved me by going.

"Yo, I'm Rake Clause; kind of a weird name, I know. Anyway, my strength is Snake as I'm sure you could tell." It was pretty obvious—his hair looked like it had the texture of scales, but when he ran his hand through his long bangs, it looked soft and normal. Also, his pupils were not circles but instead small, thin lines.

Rake Clause, Strength: Snake—he can remove his fingers like fastening tape and turn them into snakes almost instantaneously. The snakes are venomous, but the venom is fed through his blood so he can control the potency. As well as this, these special snakes can burrow through any surface and grow wings within one minute of detachment.

"Bro, that's so badass!" Steven shouted in awe. Rake grinned and sat down, then the girl behind me stood. She leaned over her desk and touched the back of my neck. A shiver went down my spine, so I turned around. She had big, red lips, scarlet hair, and she stood boldly.

She smirked, "Hey boys, my name's Scarlett Yalvo, and my strength is Potent Perfume." She was staring directly in my eyes as she said that, and honestly, it was very intimidating. I didn't cower though, but instead stared right back, causing her to blush.

Scarlett Yalvo, Strength: Potent Perfume—she can change her body's smell to control people in certain ways. Examples are to change people's emotions about others or herself, cause people to obey her or others, and decrease the power of others' strengths. Depending on the effect and how much a person inhales, the effect can last up to three days.

"Strange, but pretty interesting!" Ms. Palkun complimented. The next girl took a moment to stand. She had long purple hair and looked as if she hadn't slept in a few days. Quite honestly, she looked pretty dirty and smelly.

"I'm Cora Wavice," She sounded like she could fall asleep at any second, "and my strength is uh ... oh yeah, Boost."

How the fuck can you forget your own strength?

Cora Wavice, Strength: Boost—she can dramatically increase anybody's senses or strengths at will just by the touch of her finger. For example, this can dangerously increase someone's hearing, give someone a bloodhound type of smell, or even increase a person's strength so dramatically that they would be on the same level as the number-one hero or villain. Obviously, accomplishing such a large feat requires years of training.

She sat back down and rested her head in her arms. I even noticed that her eyes blink one at a time. The next person stood, but she was shaking a lot.

"I- I'm Iris Blavins, and m- m- my strength is recovery!" It seemed like she was trying to yell those last words, but her yell was about as loud as someone's regular talking.

"Eh, what did you say? Speak up!" Steven complained giving her the stink eye. Ms. Palkun threw a piece of chalk at his head, then she looked back at Iris. Iris, like her mother, had long, wavy white hair and her eyes were a pink color, almost fuchsia.

Iris Blavins, Strength: Recovery—because she inherited her mother's one-of-a-kind healing strength, she can heal any physical damage to one's body. This healing is renowned as the top heal strength in the country at the very least, and Nurse Blavins is the top healing hero in the country.

Finally, we're at the last one. This better have all been worth it.

"Hey guys, I'm Zayden Attack! As you can tell, my strength is Shark!" As he said, it was painfully obvious. He

46

had sharp teeth, dark gray skin, and small gills on his cheeks. A dorsal fin sat on the back of his head as well.

Zayden Attack, Strength: Shark—half shark, half human, he can swim through the ground as if it's water and through small slits at the bottom of his palms, he can create and shoot shark teeth.

"Amazing, you are all just so amazing! Now, the moment you've all been waiting for, training! Let's have a little fun with it, shall we?" Ms. Palkun gushed. I lit up, and smiled, but some others were more nervous. Most notably, Iris.

Chapter 3
First Training Tournament

We blindly followed Ms. Palkun to the Dome, which sat next to the school. It looked as magnificent as ever and

Kyle (1)	Cindy (8)	Steven (5)	Camilla (4)	Rake (6)	Alex (3)	Jaxon (7)	Tonuko (2)
Khloe (16)	Cora (9)	Scarlett (12)	Donte (13)	Zayden (11)	Jessica (14)	Anya (10)	Iris (15)

smelled like a freshly cleaned car. The stage was fixed up from after Tonuko's and my short fight, and it seemed slightly bigger as well.

"Welcome to the place where we will host our training tournament! Principal Lane decided we should start a new tradition, so this is it—the Freshman Battle. Pretty cool, huh?!" Tonuko rolled his eyes and crossed his arms. "We'll be having a tournament with preset standings, and whoever wins will be seated at the top of your class! To win, you must get both of your opponent's feet out of the stage lines, knock them out, or immobilize them! This doubles as experience with real, unpredictable fighting and a ranking system!"

"So, we're gonna be the entertainment for your little show? Fantastic," Cora snarkily remarked while rolling her eyes. Ms. Palkun was saddened by our lack of enthusiasm, but I cheered her up. I flexed my arm and smirked.

"Sounds like there are some pussies here who are scared to face me. Don't worry, I won't beat you too badly!" This lit a fire under everyone, and the entire mood changed.

"How do we know who we're facing?" Alex asked. The teacher muffled her chuckle, then pointed to the giant screen perched at the

top of the back wall. It turned on, then the bracket appeared:

"How the hell am I a five seed?! I should easily be top three!" Steven yelled at the teacher. Donte was just as shocked, as was I.

Surprising that they put him at thirteenth even though he won just as fast as I did. Makes you wonder how weak that other kid really was.

"Khloe, how are you sixteenth? No offense Iris, but your strength is just support, so it seems like you'd be ranked last considering we were ranked on the physical exam," Scarlett asked standing with the two. Iris smiled.

"Don't worry, none taken!" Khloe twirled her ponytail in her fingers, then dropped it.

"Probably because during her fight Iris continuously healed herself to keep fighting. Smart strategy, but unreliable and reckless. However, it made her last way longer than I did."

Cindy hopped up to me, and that's when I noticed Alex standing next to me. "Kyle, if we both win, we get to face each other! Don't you dare lose, I really wanna battle with you!" Cindy exclaimed. I blushed and rubbed the back of my head.

"Would you lovebirds quit it already?! Kyle and Khloe, get on that stage! The rest of you come up to the viewing deck with me!" Alex nudged my arm and giggled, but I slapped him away, then walked up to the stage. Khloe stood on the other side with her arms crossed. Ms. Palkun began the match, and I decided to let Khloe get the first hit in considering how unfair the battle was. While I tied my headband on my head, she thought for a moment, then grinned.

"Are you gonna go all out in this tournament to try and impress Cindy or something?" I felt my cheeks get hot again, and before I could respond, Khloe used the opportunity of my distraction to try and get a blindsided kick in. I caught her foot before it made contact, then shoved it back at her. She fell over, so I knelt on her stomach and let some flames dance in my palm.

"Easy fight, easy win," I boasted looking down at her. She kneed hard into my thigh, giving me a cramp. I stood back up gripping my thigh, but she stayed on the ground, and kicked my feet out. As soon as I landed, she flipped up onto her feet, ran over then sat on my stomach. She grabbed both my hands and stuck them together, then smiled.

"Look at that, I just upset the top dog that was gonna kick everyone's asses. Oh well, easy fight, easy win!" I sighed, and forcefully pulled my hands apart.

"I was gonna go easy on you, but-" I kneed the back of her thigh, then while she was distracted slid my feet between her legs and kicked her stomach as hard I could without enhanced strength. She flew off me and skidded on the ground after landing. I stood, ran over, and jumped into the air. Fire swirled around my feet, and I swung them around in the air before landing over her head. My feet grazed the sides of her head, then she stuttered, "I- I tap out!" My fire burned out and I walked away.

"Great first fight kids! Now, Cindy versus Cora, get down there!" They walked past me as I walked up the stairs along with Khloe. Alex called me over, and I saw the open seat next to him. I sighed as I sat down.

He complimented me, "Nice win, man, you really made her think she won, then just kicked into a whole new gear!" I shrugged while looking down at the arena.

Cindy held out her hand for Cora, who shook it. "Good luck, Cora!" Cora nodded, then the match began. Cindy immediately drew her guns and fired off a round each at Cora.

Cora tapped her legs and muttered, "Boost." She dodged all six of the bullets (each of Cindy's guns shoot three bullets at once), then tackled Cindy. They wrestled on the ground for a moment, but Cora was stronger and eventually pinned Cindy down. She cupped her hands on Cindy's ears, saying "Boost."

"That's not good. Cindy's gonna pop an eardrum with her ears boosted," Alex analyzed while running his hand through his hair. I agreed and sat up in my chair. The room was silent, but Cora leaned in next to Cindy's ear, then screamed as loud as she could. Cindy cried out and headbutted Cora. As she reached for her head, Cindy swung a gun and hit Cora in the side, knocking her off. Cindy jumped up then ran to the opposite side of the stage.

"Look," Rake nudged my arm, "her ears are bleeding." I squinted and saw he was correct. A small blood trail dripped out of her right ear, and it was safe to assume that since her left ear was the one Cora's mouth was next to, it was bleeding as well.

Cora practically hugged herself and stated again, "Boost." Cindy blinked a few times, then her face softened. She shook her head, then spun the guns around in her hands a few times. Cora's arms grew bigger as she ran at Cindy. She punched at her, but as soon as her shoulder slightly moved, Cindy leapt into the air, flipped backward, and kicked Cora down. Cora turned to get up but was met with two shotguns in her face. "I tap out," she sighed after putting her hands up.

"Good game, that was close!" Cindy smiled; she put her guns away and reached out her hand to help Cora up. Cora took it with a sigh, then the two walked toward the stairs.

"Great fight you two, very entertaining indeed! Now, it's eh ... oh right, Scarlett and Steven! Scarlett, do me a favor and show this boy why he wasn't ranked top three!"

"I thought you were supposed to be unbiased!" Steven shouted as he walked past. The teacher shrugged with a grin.

"I am, for everyone except you! Now, you two can begin once you're both ready!"

Steven cracked his fingers and Scarlett stood with her hand on her hip, the same seductive smile she'd had earlier stretched across her face. A pink smoke crept out of her body, then flew back in. Steven took a deep breath, then he tensed his arms. The noise similar to metal bending came from his arms, and they faded to a gray. Wires snapped out (his veins) and he punched his fists together. He charged in, but Scarlett put one finger up, letting the pink smoke shoot out and cloud Steven's face. He punched at her a few times, but she dodged each one.

"Sorry little boy, but this is game over." Steven's face turned purple and although he tried hard to resist, he was forced to gasp for air. He inhaled almost all of the pink smoke, then fell over. "Do me a favor and leave the stage. I'll do anything you want if you do!" She put her finger on her lip and gave him the puppy-eye look. Steven hopped onto his feet, then practically ran out of the stage.

"Does that mean you'll love me forever?!" He screamed while gawking at her. She gagged, and the effect wore off a few seconds later. Steven blinked and was visibly confused. "How the hell did I lose?!" He stomped past Scarlett toward the stairs while thinking, *Dammit, if only I could turn my organs robotic. That would be so useful.* Scarlett's name was moved up in the bracket and Steven's was crossed out. She happily skipped back to her seat, then Donte and Camilla were told to take the field.

Donte stretched out his legs and hamstrings, then Camilla smirked. "Donte, don't worry, you'll be just fine!" He raised an eyebrow, but his confusion was answered by her saying, "I'll end this real quick!" Donte grumbled to himself as the fight began; he started out like he did against James. However, this was clearly a mistake. His constant motion created power gusts of wind that would knock anyone to the ground, except Camilla. She swayed her hands, and the winds wrapped around her arms. After a second, the winds shot out in a spiral and intercepted Donte's path. He was blown off his feet into the air, then crash landed and skidded across the building. He hit his head on the wall and took a few seconds to get up.

"What a quick match! Well done, Camilla, very nice! Donte, you should try to do this useful thing called using your brain!" Ms. Palkun mocked while clapping. Donte was blushing and clearly embarrassed as he walked toward the stairs. Camilla's name moved up on the large screen, then it was time for the next battle: Rake and Zayden. Rake stood from behind me and took a deep breath. He was clearly very nervous.

"Ay," I said, "You have a clear advantage over him man. All you gotta do is realize it." Rake's eyes showed confusion, but he smiled at me and nodded. He made his way down to the arena along with Zayden. The two shook hands and took their places, then Ms. Palkun announced for them to begin.

Zayden immediately leapt straight up and dove into the ground. The noise of his ground swimming sounded like a jackhammer, but he left no tunnel. Suddenly, he popped out of the ground behind Rake and kicked his back, then flipped backward and dove right back into the ground. Rake stumbled forward, then pulled off his pinky. In Rake's hand, it grew longer and skinnier and grew a head. A green snake formed, and it crawled out of his hand then burrowed into the ground. Rake focused on his mind link with the snake, but Zayden released an onslaught of unpredictable attacks from all over.

"Dammit," Rake huffed while hunched over and resting on his knees. "Clear advantage? What fucking advantage do I have against someone who can hide in the ground?!" Zayden's barrage of blows stopped, then he jumped from the ground across the stage from Rake. He wiggled off the snake that had bit onto his finger, then dove right back down. "That's it. That's what Kyle meant!"

Rake scurried over to his pinky snake and put it back on his hand, then ripped off all five fingers from his left hand. He squeezed them in his right hand, creating a ball that had a similar texture to clay. Rake dropped the ball, and when it touched the ground, it stretched on its own. After a few seconds and a few punches from Zayden, the ball became a seven-foot-long, very thick snake. I couldn't believe my eyes. How could a strength cause just a few fingers to transform into such a large animal?

Rake continued taking blow after blow, until Zayden didn't come up. The arena was silent, and the students around me were watching intently. I rolled my eyes with my arms crossed, then took a deep breath and stretched my arms above my head.

"Why are you so invested? It's obvious, Rake won," I stated with a mocking tone. Tonuko glanced at me and grumbled something to himself. Like I said, Rake won. Out of the ground came Rake's large snake, which was gripping Zayden in its mouth. However, to my surprise, Zayden wasn't upset or angry, but was instead laughing and smiling.

"Man, I thought I had you! This thing was just too big to maneuver around and, damn, it's fast!" Zayden exclaimed. He hung from the snake's mouth in front of Rake, and his head was upside–down.

"I'm lucky I figured out your weakness, or I would have collapsed! You hit pretty damn hard man!" The snake dropped Zayden, then he stood and shook Rake's hand. People around me clapped. Why? I have no fucking clue.

The next battle was Alex and Jessica. They took their positions, but the battle ended as quickly as it began. When the teacher yelled for the fight to start, an extremely bright light blinded us all. After a few seconds, the light dissipated, revealing Alex standing over Jessica. She was breathing heavily, and there were burnt flower petals all around her.

"What just happened?" Rake asked me. I shrugged, genuinely confused.

Did Alex's light produce heat-like flames?

"Your power is beautiful! You had so much control too! It's a shame it wasn't enough though," Alex smiled while reaching a hand to Jessica. She hesitated, then blushed and took his hand while slightly smiling. He helped her up just as her name was crossed off on the screen and his moved up in the bracket. Anya and Jaxon were up, and as they made their way to the stage, I snorted.

"What's so funny, Straiter?" Tonuko asked with his arms crossed.

"Nothing really. It's just that this will be another fast battle. That Anya girl doesn't stand a chance considering all that guy needs to do is breathe out some of that mind-controlling smoke crap," I stated. I put my feet up on the railing in front of us and closed my eyes, but apparently my statement annoyed Tonuko.

"No, Anya has a plan. She wouldn't go out that easily. Don't act like you know what's gonna happen." I was confused and slightly angry by his sudden insult, but instead of arguing I rolled my eyes and watched the fight.

After it commenced, Jaxon breathed out his smoke, which, contrary to his green style, was pink. It swiftly moved and swarmed Anya's head. She moved quickly down to the ground and created something so fast none of us could see just what she did. Then, Anya stuck her hands into the ground, and when she pulled them out, concrete in the shape of boxing gloves came with them.

"You can't hold your breath forever!" Jaxon mocked while running his hands through his permed, black hair. However, Anya didn't let his words get to her, but instead

55

charged head on. He dodged her first punch, then Anya swung her right hand back, which she used to punch at him, hitting Jaxon in the side of the head. He stumbled a couple feet, then Anya took a powerful step and punched him in the stomach. Jaxon coughed as he flew backward and landed outside of the stage. He skidded on his butt and after a couple seconds collided into the wall underneath the balcony. The smoke disappeared, revealing Anya's small secret to winning.

"With these nose plugs, it was so much easier to not breathe that stuff in!" Anya informed everyone after taking out a rock from each of her nostrils. Jaxon swore as his name was crossed out and trudged back to his seat.

The final battle of the first round was very one-sided, Tonuko versus Iris. They both made their way to the stage, but before the teacher could yell for the fight to commence, Iris revealed her thoughts. "Wait, I forfeit!" Iris shouted with her soft voice, shocking some of the students.

"Iris, this is your chance to show off what you can do!" Scarlett yelled, standing from her seat. Iris rubbed her arm and looked down.

She had a surge of confidence and proudly stated, "I have shown what I can do! I've been healing everyone who got injured! That's my purpose, to heal the people who can fight! Trying to fight with Tonuko wouldn't help me or him!"

I, for one, thought her little testament was painfully obvious. Of course someone with a strength to heal shouldn't battle to show off her strength; that would be ridiculous.

"Works for me. I honestly would have felt bad fighting someone who isn't training to be a fighter," Tonuko admitted with a sigh. He stuck his hands in his pockets and walked with her back up the stairs.

"This first round has been absolutely amazing! You are all performing as I expected, excellent work! We will take a ten-minute break before beginning round two, then you'll perform the semi-finals and finale in front of the whole school tomorrow!" Students began standing up and stretching out their legs, then communicating amongst themselves. I continued resting in my chair with my feet on the railing, but I opened an eye to look to my right. I saw Tonuko, Alex, Anya, and Cindy all talking and laughing.

I strongly considered getting up and joining them, but it was as if someone was telling me not to. I felt as if I could hear a voice commanding me to stay seated.

You have a job to do, you are more important than these people. Do not stoop to their level and start socializing for fun. But what if I want to have fun? There is no time for fun. While you're out having fun, Tyrant is destroying another family. He can't be killing more people at every moment. He has to have some kind of a heart. Tyrant isn't like everyone else. He has his toys that can kill at every moment. You aren't strong enough to stop them, so you aren't strong enough to care for others.

So I kept myself distanced for the ten minutes. Instead of meeting new people and connecting with students who had similar goals as me, I focused on beating Cindy in the next match. I would have to be nimble and unpredictable to avoid her bullets and keep up with her athleticism.

After a few more minutes, Cindy and I were told to take the stage. I stretched in one corner, and mentally prepared myself for another victory. I was so focused I didn't see Cindy walk up and reach out her hand. "Good luck, Kyle! Let's both do our best!"

I couldn't help but slightly snort as I shook her hand. I could tell she was confused, so I decided to tell her what I found so amusing. "I mean, I don't think I'll be needing any luck. Thanks though." Her smile faded to a slightly angry frown. She nodded, then walked back to her corner.

Ms. Palkun announced for the match to begin, so Cindy drew her guns and I stood ready to dodge any bullets coming my way. Cindy shot a few rounds at me, but her aim was a little off and I was able to dodge them without a scratch. I charged in and tried to land a few punches, but she was inhumanely nimble and bent her body in ways I didn't know a person could. After my last punch, she jumped up and kicked off my head as she leapt across the stage.

"Wow, that's pretty embarrassing," Zayden chuckled. He was sitting next to Steven and Donte, Scarlett and Jessica were sitting behind them. Steven joined in on the laughing, but Donte scratched his head.

"How is Kyle going to win when Cindy's specialty is dodging up-close attacks? Kyle doesn't seem smart enough to figure out a way to beat her," Donte thought aloud. Instead of other's joining him in thought, they laughed at him.

"No offense, but you probably shouldn't be the one to call someone else dumb. You literally lost because you created wind for your opponent when her power is manipulating wind!" Scarlett mocked. Donte grumbled to himself and turned to face the stage.

I continued avoiding bullets, but I found myself getting very tired. I was quite surprised; my endurance usually exceeded my peers'. I didn't realize it at first, but this downfall in energy cost me greatly. Cindy reloaded her guns and fired off a couple more rounds, and I was able to dodge only half of the bullets. Three bullets embedded themselves into my left arm, two into my left thigh, and one hit the back of my neck. I fell onto my right knee and felt extreme pain throughout the left side of my body. Clearly Cindy didn't think that many of her bullets would land, so she stopped fighting and looked shocked.

58

Like hell I'm gonna lose to a nobody like this girl! I gotta focus, I can't let any more bullets connect or I'm done. How can I stop a bullet when I'm this tired and weak? Maybe, if I can focus hard enough, I can control the firepower of the guns ...

Cindy seemed to be getting worried about my injuries, so she wanted to end the battle quickly. She decided to try and immobilize me swiftly by out-speeding me. She ran around me in a circle for a few seconds, then lunged at my back. While panting, I surprised everyone by flinging a quick punch with my injured left arm. I focused all of my super strength into that arm, causing her to fly out of the stage and crash through the wall. She laid on debris and grass outside; since Cindy was outside of the stage, I won. Iris began healing me first, but I waved her off.

"Go help Cindy, I'm fine for now." Iris was too scared to argue, so she ran over to Cindy and began healing her wounds. I was officially in the semi-finals, and after we were all patched up, Ms. Palkun repaired the wall. She picked up one of the scraps of wood on the ground, then tossed it toward the hole in the wall. The piece expanded and after mere seconds, the hole was repaired as if there had never been a hole.

Diana Palkun, Strength: Build—using a piece of anything broken, she can rebuild the entire structure or parts of it. For example, if she has a scrap of a car, she can recreate the car the scrap is from.

The next battle was Camilla against Scarlett, but the one-sided fight was almost laughable. Scarlett's strength relied on her opponents breathing in her scents, but Camilla could wipe away all the scents with her strength; The battle ended quickly with a Camilla win.

Then, it was the fight I was most interested in: Rake against Alex. They were both on a whole other level of combat compared to most of the class. I would say they were on the same level as Tonuko, but obviously nowhere near me. My first thought toward Rake and Alex after seeing their fights was how great of assets they could be.

When the match began, Alex did the same move as before. He created a blinding light, causing us spectators to not be able to see the fight. "Man, I hate watching this kid fight. I can't see anything!" Tonuko complained.

"Yeah, but I guess it is what makes him strong! If we can't see anything from up here, imagine how bright it is down by Rake!" Zayden noted. For Tonuko being ranked number one nationally, he was pretty dumb.

Rake threw four of his finger snakes out at the direction Alex used to be in, but he couldn't seem to navigate his opponent even with the snakes. Suddenly, Rake felt a burning sensation on the knuckles where the four finger snakes use to be, and the light faded. Alex was standing a few feet behind him and all four snakes found their way toward a body part of his.

"Wow, I was not expecting that! Great job!" Alex complimented. Even though he was being slightly detained, and didn't know how much venom each snake contained, he still had a wide smile. I could not understand why.

"So, does that mean I win?" Rake asked with a slight grin. Alex shook his head, then both his arms lit up. This time, the light wasn't nearly as bright. However, two snakes let go of his arms, then the other two let go from his waist. When the snakes returned to Rake's hands and morphed back into fingers, they were burned horribly. Alex let out his wings, then flew full speed at Rake. In response, Rake bent back, then swiftly threw up both hands and touched Alex's stomach. All his fingers fell off and the newly formed ten snakes latched onto Alex's gut. His wings stopped flapping and he fell to the ground, skidding near the stage line but never crossing it. "Now, I definitely won!"

Why is he so quick to jump to conclusions? Use your head a little more, Rake.

"Relax man, you didn't win! Gosh, you have no faith in me, do you?!" Alex's stomach glowed brightly, and all the snakes were burned off. He leapt to his feet and charged at Rake before the snakes could crawl back. Rake blocked a slew of punches and kicks, but once Alex began using his light as a power increase, it was over for Rake.

Alex punched with his right, and as soon as Rake reached to block, Alex swung his body and kicked Rake in the side of the head. Rake stumbled to his left, then Alex led with a fist into Rake's stomach. He soared off the stage, landed on his butt, and skidded a few feet. "Now I won!"

"Damn, I really thought I had you!" Rake sighed while still sitting on the ground. Alex walked over and helped him up, then the two walked back up the stairs.

Anya and Tonuko headed down to the stage, but they shocked me when they hugged each other before the match began. "Let's both do our best, alright? I don't want you to hold back just because it's me," Anya stated while looking Tonuko directly in the eyes. He smiled and nodded, then the two took their places and the match began. Behind me, all I could hear was Khloe and Camilla discussing strategies on how Anya could win.

"Well, Tonuko is going to be constantly bending the arena, so that should give Anya the advantage because her strength uses rock, right?" Camilla asked Khloe.

Khloe nodded, then responded, "Anya should gain an advantage that way, but Tonuko is smart enough to know that. He won't give her enough time to create anything big. Since they know each other, they know how the other fights."

Please, would you two just shut up?

For some reason, I bit my tongue and didn't ask that out loud.

"Hey Kyle, I was wondering; Why do you and Tonuko hate each other so much? You're always bickering back and forth," Khloe asked with genuine curiosity.

I snorted, then responded, "It should be pretty obvious: we have very similar personalities. We're both cocky and think we're the best. Obviously, two individuals like that would butt heads." Khloe and Camilla nodded, satisfied with the answer. The two of them distracting me so much caused me to miss most of the fight, but I did catch the ending.

Tonuko created a barrage of sharp spikes and attacked Anya with them. Previously, she had created stone boots with a sweat-powered spring that let her perform a super-jump. She leapt into the air and landed directly above Tonuko. He swung his arm, bending the ground below him to create a barrier. Anya landed on the barrier, then flipped off it. She continued jumping back and took a large piece of each spike as she passed. Anya lifted a large clump of rock and wore a large, eerie smirk.

"I've been working on something since summer started! You can be my first test subject, Tonu!" The clump of rock had a hole down the center that began glowing. Tonuko readied his finishing move as well, and when the gun shot out a large spike, the ground underneath Anya flowed like a wave, then launched her backward. The spike–bullet pierced through Tonuko's shoulder, and there was so much wind pressure that he was thrown back. They were both barreling for the out-of-bounds lines, but Tonuko managed to brush his foot against the ground and create a massive spike above him. He grabbed onto it, saving himself from touching out of bounds, but Anya was unfortunate and landed butt first a few feet out of stage.

"Wow, that was pretty close," Rake stated while cracking his back. I nodded, surprised that Anya gave Tonuko such a run for his money. Tonuko let go of the spike and fell onto the ground. His shoulder was gushing blood, but besides that the two were relatively unharmed.

After Iris healed Tonuko's shoulder, the first day of the training tournament was officially over. It was a good thing that it ended, too, because clearly Iris was on her last leg for her strength today.

"Alrighty students, that was a blast to watch! You're all so ... talented! I can't wait to see the semi-finals and finale tomorrow, and neither can the rest of the school! You four will perform in front of all the other classes, as well as the teaching staff!" It seemed Alex was feeling the pressure, but Cindy comforted him. Alex honestly shouldn't have had anything to fear, it wasn't like anyone could see his battles anyway. "Also, before you leave, I should let you know that we will be going on a little field trip this weekend! A permission slip has been sent home to your parents, and the permission slip will allow you to go on all trips that take you away from school!"

Shit, so I have to go to my house to get that thing tonight? Man, I'm already tired ...

We were dismissed, and all the honors' class students wanted to have a little get-to-know each other party on the main floor of the dorm. I thought it would be absolutely useless, so I went straight upstairs to my room. I took a long nap, and after three hours, the sun was setting when I woke. I checked my phone and saw it was 8:00 p.m. I prayed to my mom then planned to sneak out to grab the permission form.

"Hey, mom, it's been 2,369 days since you died. I really miss you. It's been kind of a weird first day if I'm being honest. The students here are so sensitive and emotional, it's confusing. I don't understand why they make efforts to talk to each other and make new friends; friends are just a burden. They make you feel like you really have to protect them, for if they get hurt, you'd feel so much more pain than if it was a civilian you don't know getting hurt. I

63

don't know, I'm just really confused. I wish I could ask for your advice ... but I can't ..."

"Hey, what's he saying?" Camilla asked Tonuko, whose ear was pressed to the small crack in my door.

"I can't tell!" He responded in a whisper–yell. Tonuko, Cindy, and Camilla attempted to look into my room and listen to what I was saying.

Chapter 4
Smarter

I could feel the eyes watching my back while I prayed to my mom, so I stood and closed the door. Through the small crack, I couldn't see anyone spying on me and, quite honestly, I didn't care who it was. Since this dumb teacher mailed my permission slip to my house, I had to escape the walls of this school and go retrieve it so I could get it signed. Obviously, neither of my parents would be happily waiting at home to sign a form for their son. I opened my window and jumped out.

A few minutes earlier, Alex saw three people peering through my door. Two girls and one boy: Cindy, Camilla, and, surprisingly, Tonuko. "Hey, what are you guys doing?" Alex asked in a slight whisper. Whatever it was they were doing, he could tell they were snooping and didn't want to get caught.

"We're trying to see what this kid is doing instead of having fun downstairs with everyone else," Tonuko explained while looking through the crack in the doorway. In the room, they could see me kneeling before my bed with my back turned to them. Alex sat beside Tonuko and looked up at the ceiling, not necessarily interested in spying on me, but more so just wanting to spend time with the group.

"Tonuko, I have to ask: why do you and Kyle hate each other so much even though you barely know each other? Is it really just because you want to know who's stronger or something?" Camilla asked with genuine curiosity.

Tonuko thought for a moment then concluded, "Well, for me, it's that I just can't stand his little mystery boy act." Tonuko stopped peering through the door and sat against the wall like Alex was doing. "For someone to have two strengths, that's unheard of, and now he beats me so easily even though I'm the number-one ranked prospect in our grade level? It's all just fishy to me, I don't know. I wouldn't be as against him if it wasn't for the fact that he's that strong and unranked as well as unheard of."

"It is a little weird. Makes you wonder if he's hiding something more," Cindy added with an uneasy expression lingering on her face. After the words left her mouth, I shut the door and left the building. The four were shocked at the door suddenly closing and sat for another minute before building up the courage to open the door.

"Where the hell did he go?!" Tonuko shouted after entering the room. Camilla pointed to the window, making the answer obvious. In the distance, they could see me run through the front gate and leave the campus.

After jumping out the window, I landed on the ground, causing my ankles to sting quite a bit. I ignored the pain and began running as fast as I could without any strengths. If I did get caught leaving, it would be better to get caught at just that rather than also at using a strength unknown to others. I ran through the front gate unnoticed, not sure if that was a good or bad thing.

This school's security is pretty weak. Especially considering BloodShot was able to sneak right in on the first day. No, he snuck in on the damn day before the first day.

I crossed the street and made my way to my house. Unfortunately, nothing went smoothly for me. Lagging a block behind were my four classmates who had been watching me in my room. If I hadn't known any better, I'd think they were obsessed with me. I managed to lose them two blocks before reaching my house, hopped the fence to my backyard, and entered through the back door. I never locked the doors to my house when I left, what point was there to doing it? There was nothing to steal anyway.

"There it is!" Sure enough, slipped under the door was the permission form. I grabbed it, brought it to the counter, and signed it with my mom's signature, which I had forged so many times I had practically perfected it. I folded up the piece of paper and stuck it in my pocket, then looked around the dark room. I looked at the clean space where my mother died, took a deep breath, then walked out. Suddenly, I heard a voice behind me, one I had heard many times.

"Happiness is a filthy lie." There stood Tyrant, with crossed arms and a large smile. On the ground in front of him was my mother in the spot where she perished. She sat up, then her neck cracked as she turned her head to me faster than I could blink. She whispered something, but I couldn't hear it. Water formed in my eyes.

"YOU FAILED ME!" Mom screamed. The screech was extremely loud and barely comprehensible; I stumbled back and tripped over some garbage. After falling, I looked up and didn't see the two anymore. My hands shook and a shiver crawled up my spine, so I left the house through the backway.

Should I go find the four just to make sure they get back safe? Who knows who or what is creeping around out here.

I walked down the block and passed by one of the many large alleyways around town. The city of Camby was relatively large and divided into two areas: suburbs and city. The city part was smaller than the suburbs but had large skyscrapers and a dozen hero businesses. Since Camby did not have anything of importance; it was not generally a target for criminals. However, with the new addition of a hero school, a strong worry plagued the townspeople that villains would migrate here for easy crime considering the few heroes in the area.

In the large suburbs of Camby, there were ten alleyways that stretched for miles. An old friend and I used to use this alley near my house, called Cat Alley, to travel to each other's houses. However, he moved to a different city four years ago because his parents' hero business was going bankrupt due to the lack of crime in the area. They moved to Parane, the next city over, and I haven't heard from them since. My memory is hazy, but I think my friend's name was ... Daniel? All I can remember about him was his long, brown hair and that he was never seen without a big smile.

As I passed the alley, I saw my four classmates looking around, confused. Camilla squinted as she looked through the alley, then saw me. She waved and shouted, "Guys, I found him! He's right over here!" I walked toward them with my hands and the form in my pockets. A trashcan near me shook. I assumed it was a cat—strays were all over—but the shaking became much more aggressive. My classmates stopped walking as well, but not for the same reason. From where they were standing, they could see a man standing behind me. Only his silhouette was visible because of the shadows and streetlights, so all they could see were his magenta eyes, top hat, and long jacket.

"Kyle, watch out!" Tonuko warned after taking another step forward. The man leapt at me and reached out his hand, but I quickly reacted by ducking. As soon as I could see the attacker's fingers, I reached up, grabbed his wrist and forearm, then threw him on his back. The attacker grunted when hitting the ground, then let out a small, sharp whistle. Out of the trashcan burst a large, muscular arm that appeared to be made of shadows.

What the fuck is that thing?

The beast that emerged from the trashcan was extremely muscular, but its body parts were misshaped. Its arms were much longer than its body and its legs bent inward at the knee joint. The creature's head was very small, and the only facial feature was two, small magenta dots for eyes. I stared up at the creature, wide-eyed, and watched as it swung a punch down at me. Tonuko ran up and slightly pushed me as he swiped his arm up. Tonuko bent a part of the concrete and wrapped it above us. The creature continued punching the concrete wall, starting to crack it.

"Everyone, we need to get out of here! If we can make our way over to a main street, there might be police force or pro-heroes around to take care of this guy!" Tonuko commanded. However, I wasn't one to back down from a fight. I was too scared last time and was nearly killed by BloodShot. This time, it would be different.

"Hell no! I'm gonna kick this no-name's ass!" I argued. My fists engulfed in flames and more fire spiraled around my feet. I used the flames as boosters to launch myself into the air, then I released an explosion of burning fire onto the creature. Tonuko frowned watching me fight and was more distressed to see my attack had no effect. The creature was unfazed. It launched a counterattack by punching my side. I tried to block the punch with my forearm but was instead thrown into the wall to my left. I fell off the wall and landed flat on the ground. My entire body ached and my head was pounding.

The creature moved to step on Tonuko and his weakened shield, but Camilla created sharp wind blades that pierced the creature's translucent skin. With the small amount of wind created, it surprised us to see the creature fall over and vanish. The attacker stood while chuckling and ran back to the end of the alley. He held his hands up and out of the shadows rose two more of his creatures.

"You children should leave now! I only want him!" The man pointed at me, and after a few seconds, I pushed myself to stand.

"Who are you to make demands?!" Cindy argued while reaching for her guns. The man laughed hysterically, and actually wiped a tear from his eye before answering.

"You heroes-in-training are always amusing. Who am I? Why, I am one of the majesty's loyal followers, one of his Care-Givers! I am Bobby Mamien, the crawler in the dark!"

Bobby Mamien, Strength: Illusion—he can create and reincarnate dead animals into ghost-esque creatures that can't be hurt by most physical attacks. They have extreme strength yet are very fragile and can be extremely damaged if even slightly hit.

I recognized the name; he'd been a Care-Giver for as long as I had known them. Tyrant talked a lot about him to my mom. "You heard the man: get back to school! I'll take care of this runt!" I smirked boldly and marched past Tonuko. Out of the corner of my eye I saw his dumbfounded expression, so I decided I needed a little more force in my words if I wanted them to listen. "Do I need to repeat myself?! Get the fuck out of here! I'll take care of this!"

I stomped on the ground, making a large crack toward Bobby. Flames danced on my hands up to my forearms and up my feet to my calves, then I charged in. I dodged the creature's two attacks, then wound up ready to punch Bobby. He ducked under my fist and swiped my feet from under me, then the creature on his left stomped down at me. I formed a square of flames above me and let the fire roar out at the creature. I could tell it was affecting it, but not enough.

So, I need hotter flames, huh? Fine by me!

I focused on the temperature of the flames, which started turning blue. The extreme heat of the fire caused the creature to dissipate into thin air, then I hopped to my feet and stood ready to attack again. Bobby was shocked to see his creature get erased by fire but tried to hide his doubts. I charged head on toward him, maneuvered my body to the left to avoid the remaining creature, and threw myself at Bobby's side. He turned to defend but was out-powered by my super strength. After I punched him, he soared into the wall behind him. I gave him no time to think by charging into the wall, ready to give a finishing blow. Bobby dodged the attack while breathing heavily and holding his ribs.

"Damn, he's good," Camilla complimented while watching in awe.

Alex tried to take charge by saying, "We really should get out of here! This is way too advanced for us!" Tonuko agreed and backed up to the group, but none of them could bring themselves to stop me. Was it fear holding them back, or did they want to keep watching me fight without restrictions?

To attack both Bobby and his creature, I decided to make myself like a bomb filled with flames. Through my bright smile, an orange light glowed brighter. I ran at Bobby, and when the creature jumped in to defend its master, fire poured out of every hole in my body. Tonuko bent the ground up to create a large wall to defend himself and his friends, but the pure wind pressure from the large attack nearly swept them all off their feet. Even though Bobby was down and nearly unconscious, I still wanted to fight. I stomped toward him with a large grin smeared across my face. I could see the burns all over Bobby's body and could tell he was in great pain. However, something inside me wanted to inflict more pain on him. After taking a few more steps, I felt someone grab my arm.

"Kyle, stop! He's already too hurt to fight any more, we should just call the police and get to a safe place in case Bobby has backup!" Alex yelled while trying to hold me back. I pushed him off, causing him to trip and fall onto his butt.

"I'm not done yet," I stated sinisterly. The four continued trying to stop me from getting closer to Bobby, but I continued to push them out of the way and stomp forward. When someone strongly grabbed my arm and stopped me, I turned to look and saw the four faces. Alex was desperate, Tonuko was angry, and Cindy and Camilla were terrified. I stopped walking and stood dumbfounded.

N- No, no why are you looking at me like that? I'm saving you, I'm taking the bad guy down; so why ... why are you giving me that look like I'm a violent villain?

I let Tonuko drag me down the alley away from Bobby and saw a blue and purple portal form near the Care-Giver. BloodShot stepped out of the portal, threw Bobby over his shoulder and smiled at me before walking back into it.

Why is he here again? Don't come near me ... please ...

A police car drove by then stopped and reversed when the officers saw the fires in the alley. We were scolded for reckless behavior and taken back to campus in the cop car. The officer told Principal Lane to punish us all, but I spoke up and admitted I did all the fighting. I told Principal Lane and the officer that the other students wanted to leave and get help but I wanted to fight back. My punishment was having to clean the Dome's seats tomorrow morning before our ranking tournament. We were escorted to our dorm rooms, then the police left.

After the excitement, I couldn't sleep—I was haunting my own nightmares. In the first-ever battle against a villain when I was able to fight back, I went overboard. Tonuko, the top kid in our grade, watched as I mercilessly beat down a man who had already fallen. Tonuko wanted to run away and find help; is that what I should have done? I beat the bad guy, right? Isn't that how these fights should end? Good beats evil and saves the day! It's not like any of us are gonna die fighting, we're too young. People this young don't just die, that's not how it works. Maybe I am right, and everyone else is just too scared ...

The next day, I woke an hour early so I had time to clean the Dome's seats. It didn't take very long, mostly because the principal had me just wipe them down, and even stopped me halfway through so I could go to class. The janitor apparently finished my job. I was the last person to my seat, and the teacher was impatiently waiting for me.

"Took you long enough Kyle Straiter," Ms. Palkun seethed while everyone watched me get settled. Ms. Palkun rolled her eyes, then looked at the papers on her podium. "Today is the second and last day of the training tournament. All other classes are gonna be watching you four, and our class rankings will be announced on the big screen after the final battle. That's about it for today." The students began talking with kids around them about the fights happening today, but I just leaned back in my chair and looked out the window. I felt Scarlett tap my head, so I looked back at her.

"So, do you think you're gonna win it all?" Scarlett asked while leaning on her right hand.

Without hesitation I responded, "Yeah, I'm going to one hundred percent win it all. No doubt about it." I heard Tonuko grumble in his seat, so I smirked and asked, "What, got something to say Moody Earth?"

"I'll see you in the finals," he retorted quickly. Tonuko's confidence shocked me; it shocked me so much, in fact, that I didn't respond and just nodded. I heard a couple people's snickers, and my cheeks and ears felt hot: embarrassment. I hated the feeling of embarrassment, it made me feel inferior to others, even though I know I'm not. Ms. Palkun took us to the Dome, which was filled with students and staff. Four benches were against the left side wall underneath the seating balcony, and at each bench was a person holding a headband. Tonuko, Camilla, Alex, and I walked over to the benches, and one of the four walked up to each of us. Hazel walked over and handed me the black headband, which had a bold, white "four" in the center.

"What's this even for?" I asked while looking at the thick headwear.

"I picked you in a bracket to win it all, so I get to give you this headband that signifies you are an elite of your grade. The highest-ranked boy is known as the king and the girl is known as the queen, but the number-one spot is saved for the class representative!" Hazel informed me as we sat at my bench. I scratched my head while looking at the headband, confused about a few things.

"What does a class representative do, and what's the point of having a king and queen for every grade?" I asked.

"Well, a class representative is more so just a title. You don't have any extra work or anything, but you will be known publicly as the top student in your class. This means that students all over the nation will know your name more than any other student at E.H. for your grade. That's basically the same point of the king and queen, and there's one for every grade to allow the top guy and girl of each grade to have their own spotlight." I nodded, telling her I understood.

Then, a man spoke over the speakers, "Hello ladies and gentlemen! I am your very own E.H. Guard Captain, Fox-Tails. Welcome to our most exciting event: the freshman final four!" The crowd roared with excitement, and when I looked over at Alex, who was sitting on the bench to my left, he looked nervous and paler than usual.

Fox-Tails is the tenth-ranked hero; what is he doing here at E.H.? Why would such a strong hero care to protect a public school like this?

"Today we have quite the battles for you! First, the strong Kyle Straiter will face off against the careful Camilla Xavier, then the quick-witted Alex Galeger will face off against the one, the only, Tonuko Kuntai!"

74

Why does Tonuko get to be the "one and only?" I beat him already, he's not even that strong!

"Alrighty folks, let's get this show on the road!" Fox-Tails was very cheerful, and he had a good announcer voice. "Kyle and Camilla, go ahead and take the stage! The fight will begin in two minutes on the dot!" I stood and looked back at Hazel, who gave me a reassuring nod. I don't know why, but her nod gave me more confidence. I smiled, then turned and walked to the stage while putting on the headband. Camilla stood staring at me, then held out her hand.

"Good luck, Kyle. Let's both do our best!" She gave me a smile, but my smile faded as I looked at her hand.

"Good luck? I don't need any. This shit's a warmup for the finale," I stated, then turned to walk to the other side of the stage and stretched.

The audience apparently didn't like my statement because a wave of ridicule and anger swept my ears. I rolled my eyes and continued stretching, then, on the big screen, Camilla's first day picture and my first day picture appeared along with a thirty-second countdown. I took a deep breath to collect my thoughts, then wound up both my hands and slapped my cheeks hard. I heard some gasps from the audience but ignored them as I was finally mentally prepared to battle.

"Let's go, Kyle! Keep on being the badass you are!" Rake yelled while smiling big. Anya, who was sitting next to him, looked over with a confused expression.

"What's got you on the Kyle Straiter train all of a sudden?" Rake continued looking down on the stage with sparkles in his eyes.

"Kyle helped me with my first fight and actually got me the win! I don't think I've ever had a friend like him before!" Rake looked at Anya. "It's kinda cool to know you're friends with someone so advanced and a clear future top hero, don't you think?" Anya was utterly shocked by Rake's enthusiasm for me.

"But what about Tonuko? You've been friends with him for years; don't you feel the same around him?" Anya asked, sadness lingering in her voice. Before Rake could respond, Steven spoke up from behind them.

"Honestly, Tonuko and Kyle seem so different. Sure, Tonuko is super strong, but Kyle just gives off a whole other vibe. I mean, he beat Tonuko in ten damn seconds! I watched it in person and still can't believe that happened!" Steven exclaimed. The final ten seconds began counting down on the big screen, and when it hit five, Fox-Tails joined in the countdown.

"Yeah," a boy who sat at the edge of the advanced class stated, "Kyle is pretty damn awesome." When the clock hit zero, the boy's deep blue hair sparkled in the light and my arms erupted in flames.

Chapter 5
My Place

On the roof of the Dome, a figure lingered in the window. She had long, strawberry blonde hair styled into pigtails, and a constant, closed-mouth smile. She peered into the arena, then squealed when the timer began.

"I can't wait to watch Kyle fight! He's so dreamy, and so strong!" She sighed happily, then sat down with her legs crossed. "I'm so happy Tyrant let me come to watch these fights!"

After the Timer Struck Zero:

I waited a moment before striking, trying to lure Camilla into using her winds. The flames on my arms danced and roared, encouraging her to attack. I could tell from her personality the first couple days that she was easily provoked. She swayed her hands, and that's when I struck.

I ran at Camilla and threw from both hands; fireballs landed just outside her hands' reach. The flames combined with the winds Camilla was manifesting, causing them to rapidly increase in power and throw her off balance. I slid in front of her and punched her right in the stomach. Then, as she was soaring backward, I used flames to increase my speed tremendously and swiftly ran behind her, landing another punch on her back.

She was launched around twenty feet in the air, and as she was landing I announced, "You've had an easy path here Camilla, but it ends now. Don't feel bad, it's not fair you had to face me. Life isn't fair though." Winds exploded on the ground and blew in every direction. I stomped my foot, sticking it into the ground so I wouldn't be swept off my feet.

"Come on, Camilla, prove that cocky bastard wrong! He's all bark and no bite, trust me! He's just trying to get into your head!" yelled the guy who sat on Camilla's bench, trying to encourage her. The guy's hair was very long and black with white lines that strongly resembled a spider's web. His bright green eyes contrasted his earth–brown skin, and his dark, baggy clothes looked dirty and rugged. I looked to my right and saw Hazel smirk as she glanced at the man.

"Don't listen to Devin, just focus on the fight! You've got her weakened, so don't fuck up; finish the job! You got this, Kyle, I believe in you!" I nodded and slightly smiled again. For some reason unknown to me, Hazel's words of encouragement always put some kind of smile on my face that was hard to conceal. I turned back to Camilla, who had successfully formed two tornadoes when my head was turned. I tried to take a step back, but I apparently grounded my foot deeper than I thought. My foot was stuck deep in the ground, and as hard as I pulled, it wouldn't budge. I slightly panicked as I heard Fox-Tails over the intercom.

"It appears the tides have turned for Camilla! Kyle's foot is trapped in the ground, and he has two powerful tornadoes heading straight toward him! Can you feel that wind pressure folks? It's nauseating!" I continued my attempt to pull my foot out, and only successfully did it when it was too late. One of the tornadoes sucked me up, then threw me into the sky. They dissipated, then Camilla soared toward me and landed a punch on my face. My body was turned in the air, and I hit the top of the glass dome face first. The glass sizzled, and I was enraged. I pulled my feet under me and pushed hard to send myself flying toward the ground. With my feet under me again, I flipped in the air and landed upright on the ground. My landing caused a rumble and a divot formed in the concrete beneath me.

You're gonna regret that big time, Camilla. I thought this would be just a simple warmup match, but you made it personal!

I stomped toward Camilla, my fists balled and my eyes locked on hers. I rushed toward her, and she slowly backed up while raising her arms. She threw a blade of wind at me, but I ducked underneath then swiftly punched her hard on the cheek. She fell to her right, then I kicked her stomach, sending her sliding a few feet and leaving behind a small trail of blood from her mouth.

"What a powerful hit from Kyle! It appears blood has been drawn, meaning this fight is getting interesting!" Fox-Tails shouted into his mic after standing up from his seat. I heard countless people booing and screaming at me.

I ignored the ridicule and stepped toward Camilla. However, when I saw her eyes closed and how peaceful she looked ... I stopped dead in my tracks. Her face reminded me of my mother's after being stabbed. I looked down at my hands, then held my head and fell to my knees. I trembled, then a large gust of wind sent me flying into the air. Almost instantly, another gust of wind threw me to the ground. The impact sent cracks across the floor of the Dome, then a black hand made of sharp winds picked me up again.

"Oh, wow, what an amazing creature created by Camilla! That thing is as tall as the entire building!" Fox-Tails' smile faded slowly as he looked down at Camilla, who hadn't moved since my punch. "Wait a second, Camilla is unconscious on the ground. If that's true, then who's creation is this?!"

The wind titan lifted me to its head, then slammed me into the ground again. I gasped for air when it lifted me yet another time but was quickly thrown into the ground once more. My right arm shattered, and blood was pouring from my head.

"Students, stay in your seats! The staff will handle the attack! Please remain calm!" Fox-Tails commanded. I faintly heard screams from the crowd and looked at my frantic class before being slammed into the ground yet again.

"Quick, Devin, we gotta save the kid!" Hazel screamed after jumping from her seat. Devin crossed his arms in front of his chest as he was running, then threw spider webs at the being's feet. It tried to take a step forward but fell and dropped me in the process. As I was falling through the air, Hazel reached out with her demon arms and caught me. The being vanished after it fell. I breathed heavily as Nurse Blavins and Iris ran to my aid, and my vision was hazy.

On the Roof:

"How could you attack him like that Stafer?! Tyrant specifically told us we aren't allowed to attack!" the girl who was watching the fight yelled at the man standing next to her. He continued peering into the arena, then turned around and yawned.

"Sorry little girl, but I was bored as hell. I wanted to see that kid in action—he intrigued me. Sadly, he couldn't handle my strength though," Stafer commented.

Stafer Candreon, Strength: Amplify—he can copy any person's strength and amplify it to an extreme using a dark power. If one of the people he copies is weak, he can combine a strength he has copied before to create one attack, such as the monster of Bobby's illusion and Camilla's wind.

"Don't you mean the girl's strength? You're just a phony who's entire being relies on the strengths of others," the girl retorted before crossing her arms. He looked back at the girl with cold, ruby eyes.

"Don't insult me Laci, unless you wanna end up like Kyle. I'd suggest you keep your mouth shut with that weak ass mace of yours."

Laci pouted, then threw her hand in front of her and flung a mace at Stafer. The mace appeared out of nothingness, and it flew straight toward Stafer's face. He caught it with his bare hand, and one of the spikes pierced directly through his palm. Stafer stared at his palm and watched as the wound healed itself. The mace fell to the ground, then sizzled and faded. "How dare you attack one of your fellow Care-Givers?! You can trust me that BloodShot will hear about this."

"Go ahead and tattle to that asshole, you lapdog!" Laci hissed as Stafer turned and walked away. He made his way to the side of the building, then jumped off. In the air, a swirling black and yellow portal formed and sucked him up, then sucked in on itself. "I hate him!" Laci turned back to the glass dome and saw the event was cleaned up.

Back in the Arena:

I sat on my bench feeling very sore. The Blavins' healing can heal wounds, but not cure the damn soreness. Yet, I was still very grateful for ... the both of them. Hazel put her arm around me, then sighed.

"Well, that was a scare. Thankfully, whoever attacked you is gone now it seems." I felt safe in her arm, and sighed as well, then smiled. "You're lucky to have a friend (and a friend's mom) with such good healing powers, Kyle; otherwise, I don't know if you would have survived!" I looked at the floor and squeezed the end of my shorts.

"Phew, that was quite a scare! However, the show must go on! Tonuko Kuntai and Alex Galeger, take the stage. Know security is searching campus for the attacker, and you two are completely safe!" My eyes were watery, but I wasn't sure why. Hazel noticed my lack of response, but I spoke before she could ask anything.

"Do you really think that people think of me as a friend?" There was a painful silence, so I knew the answer.

What am I thinking? Why would anyone be my friend. Hell, I barely even know what a friend really is.

"Did you really just ask that dumb of a question? Of course there are people who think of you as a friend! I mean, I'd say we're becoming friends!" Hazel yelled after taking her arm off me and turning to face me. I looked at her, then back at the ground. Even if I tried to hide it, my smile was growing.

There're people who think of me as a friend ... I can't believe it. Even though I'm cocky, even though I'm an asshole about my goals, there are still people who ... care ... about me.

The screen counted down the final three seconds, then Alex and Tonuko's battle began. Tonuko immediately stomped his foot, and the entire layout of the stage changed. There were random hills, spikes, tunnels, and objects.

"Why did he do that? What's his strategy?" I asked.

"Well, now he knows the terrain he just made, and Alex doesn't. It gives him an advantage by knowing all the nooks and crannies of the stage." I nodded and stared at Alex, who was analyzing his surroundings. "Either way, I think Alex can outsmart Tonuko. He's pretty bright, both literally and figuratively."

"Yeah, he does seem to be pretty smart, and his strength is amazing," I added.

"Well, not necessarily. For raw fighting skills, sure, but in missions where heroes need to be stealthy or hidden, it is actually a hindrance. In any dark situation—like nighttime or in a dark building—Alex can be seen fighting from a mile away." My eyes widened, and I glanced at my hands. I squeezed them into fists, then looked at Hazel.

"I never thought of it like that. It's the same with my fire. I can be seen fighting almost anywhere in a dark situation." Hazel nodded and crossed her arms while leaning on the wall behind us. My eyes sparkled with amazement, then I complimented, "Woah, you're so smart Hazel!"

"Thank you, but don't count yourself out in dark situations. You also have that enhanced strength, which is a powerful and versatile strength on its own. Once you learn how to control and use your strengths here, you will be able to use your strengths in separate instances." I smiled and looked up at the sky through the glass dome.

"I can't wait to be able to control my strengths more. I'll be able to handle myself and save those around me. I'll be able to fight better than I could against BloodShot, and Bobby in the alley, and- now this wind user-"

"Boy, these villains are really coming after you, huh?" I swiftly looked away and nodded, then clenched my jaw.

Shit, thanks for making it obvious you're after me Tyrant; you jerk.

"It must be because of my two strengths. Not trying to sound cocky, but having two strengths that work this well together sure makes me a threat to villains like Tyrant, right?" I bluffed.

"Yeah, you know that is true. Let's discuss this more after the tournament; it seems like this battle is getting really intense!" She was definitely right, because when I looked up, I saw Alex flying at Tonuko, who had a large chunk of the ground stretched with him while he was about twenty feet in the air. The cement on his torso also stretched onto his fists, creating concrete gloves. Alex used his wings combined with the power of his light to beam at Tonuko at speeds I don't think I would be able to react to. However, Tonuko swung a quick punch at the same time as Alex. They punched each other (Alex hit Tonuko's face and Tonuko hit Alex's hip), then both flew in opposite directions. The cement around Tonuko's arms and torso shattered, and one of Alex's wings dangled and was broken.

83

Alex used his other wing to glide back to the ground a few feet away from Tonuko, who had stood and was breathing heavily.

"Damn, you're strong Alex," Tonuko panted.

"Yeah, but this earth manipulation makes it so hard to get a solid hit on you. No offense, but it's pretty annoying," Alex said with a closed-mouth smile. They both chuckled, then Tonuko reached out a fist.

"Let the best man win," Tonuko stated, offering a fist bump. Alex fist bumped him and nodded with an even bigger smile than before, then Tonuko stepped back and took a deep breath. Alex did the same, then he exploded into a mess. The light still helped increase Alex's speed, even with its weakened power, and he was able to speed around then punch Tonuko in the back of the head before Tonuko could react. He stumbled forward, then Alex swiped Tonuko's feet out from underneath him and let him hit the ground hard.

"Th- That's it, I win," Alex gasped as he struggled to stay standing then fell. The ground beneath Alex wrapped around him from the feet up, eventually reaching his neck. Alex was clearly in pain as the cement's grasp grew tighter, so he shouted weakly, "Y- You win, you win!"

Tonuko stayed on the ground but I could see his grin as he stuttered, "Don't c- count your chickens before they h- h- hatch." The ground let go of Alex, and he fell face first at Tonuko's feet.

"Wow, what a fight! These two are very skilled. Well done boys! But now, the moment we've all been hoping for! The rematch of the century: Kyle Straiter versus Tonuko Kuntai. We will be taking a thirty-minute hiatus before returning for the finale!" Fox-Tails announced. He put the mic down and hit the mute button, then took a swig of water. His happy expression faded to a stern stare as he looked over at Principal Lane, who was seated next to him.

84

"Well, what do we do about that attack? This is the second on-campus one on Kyle in just the first three days of school, and the third in total."

"Well, we must increase security around campus and look for any weak points in and around the walls. As well as this, we must contact the Seven Influential about perhaps a teleporter within the Care-Givers. I'm unsure, but I have a feeling that they aren't just waltzing in over our wall. Instead, these criminals are being placed in specific locations where Kyle is," Principal Lane answered while looking toward Hazel and me.

Hazel went to talk with Devin, so I took a breather and sat on my bench. When I looked at the sky, I saw a man looking down at me. He had sky blue eyes and blonde hair that glistened in the light. We made eye contact, then I snapped and ran out of the arena before anyone could stop me.

What the fuck are you doing here, you bastard?!

A Few Minutes Before:

Tyrant stepped out of a portal extremely similar to the one Stafer jumped into. He ran his hands through his hair, then looked over at Laci. Tyrant wore a magenta dress shirt with a solid red tie, and sleek black dress pants along with black dress shoes. He fixed his tie, then spoke.

"Laci, what's this I hear about Stafer attacking Kyle, and you attacking Stafer?" Tyrant asked while staring intimidatingly into her eyes.

She gulped, then explained, "W- Well, Stafer came out of nowhere and a- attacked Kyle. I was so mad that he d- disobeyed you, so I threw my mace at him to scare him off." Tyrant slowly walked over to her, then raised his hand. Laci flinched and exclaimed, "I only did it because I don't like when people disrespect you! Stafer and BloodShot don't give you the respect you deserve!" Tyrant lowered his

85

hand and put it on her head. She looked up and saw his comforting smile.

"Laci, you don't need to be afraid of me. Thank you for protecting my rules, but don't resort to violence on your own allies. They are both new, both need time to grow and learn to trust us and themselves. Never forget, with great power comes even greater responsibility." Laci relaxed and smiled, then Tyrant peered into the arena. He and I made eye contact, and he smiled as I ran toward the doors of the Dome. "Looks like we're going to have a little visitor."

I made my way up the ladder to the roof, then jumped from the last step and stood ready to attack. Never in my life had I been so close to killing someone.

"Wh- Why are you here?! Get the hell away from this campus!" I screeched before igniting my hands. Tyrant put his hands up, clearly not wanting to fight. "Don't try and pussy out on me now! You abandoned me seven years ago, and now you show up and just look at me from a distance?!" My voice croaked as I shouted, "You ruined my life, took everything I loved away from me!"

"Kyle, listen to me: If you draw too much attention to us up here, then someone is going to find us and hear you talking like you know me," Tyrant stated after taking a step closer. I backed up and trembled more violently.

"You took *everything* from me! I don't care who knows, *I just want to kill you!* If you're gone, then nobody else will have to suffer like I have my entire life! If you're gone, then I fulfill my destiny! If-"

"If I'm gone, then *what will that make you?!* What will you do after I'm gone, what's your plan for the rest of your life?!" Tyrant cut me off. I stood wide eyed, and my lip quivered. "You're so focused on me all the time, how about you focus on yourself for once?! Look down there!" Tyrant pointed behind him, then shouted, "There are people down there who are going to be with you every step of the way for the next four years! Why can't you open your eyes and stop obsessing about something that happened seven years ago?!"

"I don't care how long ago it actually happened; I think about it every fucking day! You don't get to tell me what to do, nobody does! Only my parents can, and tell me, Tyrant, were you really a parent to me?!" Tyrant clenched his jaw and gave me the same dirty, intimidating, furious look he'd given me all my life. "You ruined my life, dammit! For once, leave me the fuck alone!"

"I ruined your life? Are you serious?! Ever since you were born, you ruined mine! You are the reason the only thing I loved is gone!" Tyrant erupted while stomping his foot at me. My eyes widened, and I took a step back.

"Wh- What do you mean?! You killed my mom; you took away the only person who loved me! What right do you have to say I ruined your life?!" Tyrant's fists were shaking, and he pointed at me after he let out a huff.

"The only reason Gem is dead is *you!* If *you* weren't born, I wouldn't have had to kill her! If *you* weren't born, I wouldn't have been blackmailed into killing her. If *you* weren't born, my wife would still be alive, and everything would be normal! But no, since *you just had to be here, she's fucking dead, and you're the only one to blame!* Kyle, **you killed your mother!**" My lip quivered and my head spun.

"N- No, you're lying. You're a villain, you killed her. How could it be my fault?! I was innocent, the victim!" I responded, on the verge of tears. Water brimmed my eyes, then a tear dripped from each one.

"You were so rebellious; you just wouldn't listen to me. God, you made me so angry, I didn't know what to do! Pressure was building, rumors were spreading: my son was going to be a hero, he wouldn't join the Care-Givers! I don't know, or care, about how heroes would treat that, but criminals threatened me, my wife, my home, my family! And no, that does not include you, I couldn't care less about what they did to you! I hoped they would kill you so Gem wouldn't have to stress anymore!"

He's lying, he has to be. I couldn't have killed my mom. So why, why does he look so certain?

"Kyle, the criminals were going to kill her. They would ransack the house, burn it to the ground, and trap her inside; I couldn't let that happen to her! They would find her; there were eyes watching my every move, so I did the only thing I could to give her a peaceful death. Now look at you, I'd hoped you would have just killed yourself by now," Tyrant explained. I stepped back, shaking my head and crying.

*Stop, please stop. It's not my fault, it's not my fault, **it's not my fault.** It's your fault, it's your fault, **it's your fault.** I hate you, I hate you, **I hate you!***

With one more step, I fell off the roof. Tyrant didn't bother helping me, he just turned and yelled, "I'll be watching. Don't disappoint me like you disappoint everyone else." While falling through the air, I hoped I would hit the ground and not wake up. However, I was caught by Fox-Tails. We landed and slid a few feet, then he looked up at the roof. I stuttered, at a complete loss for words. Fox-Tails sighed.

"I know Kyle, I heard some of it. Don't listen to him, he's manipulative and pure evil. If you let what he said go to heart, then he's already won." I nodded as Fox-Tails put me down, then took a deep breath and calmed myself. After a moment, I walked past Fox-Tails. "Are you okay?"

"Yeah," I stated, "I'll be fine. Right now, I just need to win this fight." I marched through the doors of the Dome and made my way to my bench, then sat down. Hazel walked over and sat next to me.

"What was that all about? Are you alright?"

"I'm fine!" I snapped while looking at the ground. Hazel clearly didn't believe me but nodded and put her arm around me. I felt goosebumps form and moved away from her reach. This worried her more, but before she could say anything Fox-Tails cleared his throat while on the mic.

"Well folks, the break is over! Time to reveal some little fun facts about our contestants!" Everyone looked over at the screen that flashed Tonuko's grade-school picture. He looked much younger, his hair was shorter and straight, and he was much skinnier. The picture moved to the top-left corner of the screen, then a list of information appeared:

Name: Tonuko Kuntai

Age: 14

Parents: Danielle Kuntai (Vice Principal of Eccentric High) and David Kuntai (Pro-Hero the Savior)

Strength: Ground Manipulation

Age of Control: Seven years old

Elementary School: County Elementary

"Tonuko gained control over his strength at the young age of seven and was named the top prospect of the incoming freshman class! He comes from the great school of County Elementary, and his parents are our very own vice principal and the famous hero Savior!" Fox-Tails informed the crowd. Everyone cheered, shouted, and whistled, all seemed to be rooting for him. Tonuko's information faded, then an old picture of me popped up on the screen. I had hair a little longer than my current style and two black eyes along with missing teeth and a few band aids plastered on my face. In the background, a man who could be seen only up to the stomach was wearing a black tux and holding my shoulders.

Name: Kyle Straiter

Age: 14

Parents: N/A

Strength: Fire Control and Enhanced Strength

Age of Control: N/A

Elementary School: Trinity Plus Elementary School

The crowd's cheering was gone at this point, and confused whispers could be heard all over.

"Uh, well, Kyle Straiter is a generational talent with two strengths and … he came from Trinity Plus. That is … all the information we have on him," Fox-Tails stated nervously. The crowd turned angry and started yelling; they were confused and scared of me. "Well, I don't know about you folks, but I love a battle between the popular boy and mysterious boy! Let's get this party started!" Fox-Tails screamed, trying to change the mood. The crowd almost instantly cheered again, and I took a sigh of relief. I stood and looked over at Tonuko. He gave me a smirk, then walked toward the stage. I did the same.

"Hey, Kyle, let the best man win," Tonuko said while holding his hand out to me. I looked at his hand, then shook it.

"Let the best man win, Tonuko." He looked surprised that I actually shook his hand. We then went to our corners. Fox-Tails announced for the fight to begin, and the boy with blue hair jumped out of his seat.

"Come on Kyle, you got this bud!" the boy shouted happily.

"Just who are you? You keep talking as if you know him," Khloe asked snarkily. The boy with blue hair didn't need to introduce himself because Jaxon had him covered.

"That's Daniel Onso. He, Kyle, and I went to the same elementary school. I don't expect Kyle to remember us though; Kyle and I grew apart last summer, and Daniel moved cities a few years ago," Jaxon explained while leaning back in his chair. Daniel nodded but didn't take his eyes off the stage.

Tonuko changed the entire scenery of the stage again, bending the ground to make weird hills, spikes, twists, walls, and holes. I analyzed the area I was in, then saw a ripple in the ground to my right. I leapt into the air, effectively dodging a wave in the ground Tonuko had created. Fire burst out of my feet, allowing me to keep levitating. Tonuko growled then smacked his hands on the ground. Spikes flew at me, but I dodged each one then charged in at rapid speeds. Tonuko swiftly threw up his hands and created a wall late enough to stop me before I could charge a strong enough punch to break it. I flipped back, landing a dozen feet away from where he stood.

I was really hoping to knock him out in one hit again. Oh well, now I know most of his tricks. He changes the environment to gain an advantage, uses spikes and waves to attack and walls to defend.

"What great defense by Tonuko! We know Kyle was able to beat Tonuko swiftly before, so let's see what Tonuko can cook up this time!" Tonuko became angry at the statement and ran toward me. He created a few spikes to distract me, then dodged my punch and dragged his hand on the ground before swinging at me. When he dragged his hand, he created a concrete glove and socked my right cheek, sending me flying to my left. I skidded a few feet and hit a wall hard. Tonuko didn't stop the onslaught; a pillar flew through the air before hitting me on my stomach and chest. I coughed blood, then wound up and punched down on the pillar, causing it to shatter.

"This won't end like last time Kyle; I'm prepared this time! I know how you fight, and my senses are much more on edge now, ready for you to blindly attack whenever!" I slowly stood; my chest hurt with every movement. Tonuko punched me in the face, then kicked my side. I hunched over, and he stated, "You're too cocky for your own good, and if you become a hero, it's gonna lead to someone getting killed." I briskly grabbed his head, then smashed it into the ground. The ground cracked, and bits of rubble flew everywhere. I panted heavily while looking down at him. My face was full of rage.

"Just shut the fuck up already," I seethed before throwing him into the air. His body spun around, then I jumped and crashed into him, leading with my shoulder. He flew into the Dome's glass, and I followed up with a kick and pushed him through the glass. We landed on the roof of the arena, and there, a dozen feet away from us, stood Tyrant and Laci.

Chapter 6
Building Trust

"Oh my, it looks like you brought me a new toy, Kyle! Thank you so much!" Tyrant laughed while looking at the two of us. Tonuko was shocked and looked over at me. I stood to the side of him but stepped to block Tyrant's view of Tonuko. I moved my left hand back toward Tonuko and my right hand in front of me toward Tyrant and Laci.

"S- Stay back Tyrant. Leave us alone, don't hurt us." It took all my might to not tear up thinking about our earlier interaction, and it felt like something was stuck in my throat. Tyrant cackled and took a step forward, but I didn't back down. "You can do whatever you want to me but leave Tonuko out of this."

Tonuko was shocked to hear this and couldn't form any words. He just stared wide-eyed at the back of my head, then glanced at Tyrant. Tyrant's smile was gone, and he instead looked at me bitterly.

"Look at that, Kyle Straiter acting all noble. The same kid who everyone hates, who is violent and disobedient, is acting like a hero again. You aren't a hero Kyle, you're a violent criminal waiting to conform. Once you do, *you're mine.*" Tyrant ran toward me, and though full of fear, I punched at him. He dodged my fist, then pushed me aside. I fell and hit the ground hard, then looked up and saw Tyrant staring eye-to-eye with Tonuko. "You are a nuisance. Maybe I should just take your strength now so you don't get stronger for the future."

I can't let him hurt Tonuko. Tyrant is my responsibility; I won't let him hurt anyone else!

I tackled Tyrant, then stood and pushed Tonuko through the Dome's glass.

"Laci, attack him!" Tyrant commanded while pointing at me. Laci threw out her hand and let her mace fly at me. I looked Tonuko dead in the eyes while a couple of tears dripped down my cheeks, then Laci's mace hit my back and I fell face first through the window. Tonuko was shocked and Hazel's arm caught him. Hazel missed me though, and I fell to the ground. A loud crash was heard throughout campus, and the ground rumbled.

Before I hit the ground, two black tentacles shot out of my chest and absorbed the blow. When I had landed, I was relatively unscathed from the fall, but there were multiple holes in my back from Laci's mace. I breathed heavily, stunned from what just happened.

"Kyle!" Tonuko screeched after being put down. He ran over to me, but I looked up at him and put a finger over my lips.

"Don't tell anyone about what happened up there. I'll explain it all later, I promise." Tonuko stuttered, then closed his mouth and nodded. Hazel and the guy who was at Tonuko's bench ran to make sure we were okay. Once they deemed us fine, we continued the fight; Fox-Tails had told everyone we had been fighting on the roof and fallen. Thankfully, Tyrant's name was not mentioned.

Tonuko and I seemed off our game. We were both making simple mistakes: missing attacks, letting our guards down, and moving slower than usual.

"What's up with them?" Rake asked with a yawn. He leaned back in his seat and rested his hands behind his head.

"They must have said something to each other while on the roof that either pissed them off or confused them. Also, I'm sure Kyle isn't feeling great after that big fall, even though he was healed," Khloe analyzed. She was much more focused on the battle than her peers.

"You're way too smart Khloe, it's kinda scary. You're so perceptive," Scarlett stated as she acted like a

94

shiver crawled up her spine. Khloe giggled and sat up straight.

"I mean, it's just how my strength is. Anyway, looks like those two might finally be waking up a little," Khloe excitedly informed Scarlett as she pointed at the stage.

I avoided three pillars that Tonuko sent after me, then ran at him. He sent a pillar at my head from the ground next to him, but I slid under to dodge it, hopped back up, and socked him in the face. He soared back but managed to mauver his body in the air so his feet were up and his head was near the ground, then he dragged his fingers on the ground and swiftly threw his hand behind him. A piece of the ground curved up and caught him before he fell out of the stage boundaries. Usually, he would jump off the bent ground and gather himself; this is what I expected. Instead, he threw himself at me using a pillar to boost his speeds, and we collided heads before falling to the ground. I laid on my back for one-too-many seconds. Tonuko used the ground to throw me into the air, then created two huge fists that soared at either side of my body. He used his own fists to control the concrete hands and punched the right side of my body. I soared into the other hand's palm, then it threw me back into the air. My vision was hazy and I felt very weak. Tonuko wound up his fists over his head, intertwined his fingers, then swung as hard as he could. The concrete hands punched me extremely hard, and I went flying down and crashed into the ground. The entire campus rumbled, then the two concrete hands crumpled on top of me.

"Oh my folks, that might just be it! Tonuko unleashed a beautiful attack that must've left Kyle feeling sore! I'm calling it now; this fight is ova'!" Fox-Tails screamed in the mic while standing up excitedly. Tonuko panted and stood with a hunch, trying not to fall over.

"Come on Kyle, you have to get up! Don't lose!" Daniel erupted his feet. Some of the students around him were shocked by the random scream, and Steven laughed.

"Sorry fanboy, but I think that's it! Kyle is done!" Steven contained his laughter and looked over at Daniel. Daniel was staring back with cold eyes, and he smiled.

"Nah, you don't know Kyle like I do. He's not done until he wins," Daniel stated boldly. Steven choked for a retort, then rolled his eyes and looked back at the stage.

The rock pile moved slightly, then it exploded in a fiery mess. Tonuko was swept off his feet and exploded rubble bits rained down on the stage and crowd. I weakly stood in the crater made by my fall; my head was gushing blood, my jaw and left arm were broken, and my right eye was swollen shut. Tonuko looked at me wide-eyed and tried to stand.

Stay down, asshole.

Out of my right foot, a wisp of flames shot at Tonuko and covered his legs. He fell over again and wrapped concrete tightly around his legs. When the concrete fell off, the skin on his legs was horribly burned and he had bleeding blisters all over his legs. When Tonuko was down and in agony, I went in for my finishing blow.

This is it, time to finally end this. Everyone here will know I'm not to be messed with ... everyone.

Flames erupted out of my right hand and I slowly raised it above my head. The flames roared above me and grew bigger while forming into a blade-figure. I took a step forward, then swung my hand down toward Tonuko. The blade of flame landed directly on him. The bottom of the stage was covered in flames, then, when the flames touched the ground, there was a massive explosion between us. I was thrown off my feet but used fire as a booster again and stabilized myself in the air. Tonuko, however, flew out of the stage boundaries and hit the wall behind him, then slid to the ground. Since he was outside of the stage, I won.

"What. A. COMEBACK! KYLE WINS IT ALL!" Fox-Tails screamed while jumping up and down like a kid.

There was a mix of cheers and boos all around, then I fell onto my back and looked up at the glass Dome. I didn't see anyone looking into the building anymore, but I still pointed to the sky, then tensed my fist.

I know you saw me Tyrant, you saw how much I've grown. Be afraid, this is me, this is Kyle Straiter. I will kill you; I will avenge Mom. I didn't kill her, you did. I'll take down the villain society you built step by step. Just you wait.

Hazel ran onto the stage and knelt beside me. She put her hand behind my head and looked down at me.

"You alright Kyle? You have some pretty serious injuries," Hazel asked before waving over Mrs. Blavins.

"Of course I- I'm fine, I won!" Iris was healing Tonuko, and Mrs. Blavins began healing me.

Principal Lane announced on the mic, "Will all freshman honors' students please make their way to the stage. The rankings will be listed on the screen in one minute." My classmates walked down the stairs and after I was healed enough, I stood and walked over to Tonuko. He looked up at me with a stern, but defeated, expression. I could tell he was expecting me to insult him.

If I want to be a hero, and not be like Tyrant, then I have to start acting like one. Everyone else did this, so maybe I should too.

"Good fight," I said while reaching out my hand. Tonuko snickered and shook his head, then took my hand and stood.

"Yeah, yeah, good fight," he responded. His legs were shaky and he fell over again. Alex grabbed Tonuko's other arm, then we helped him stay stable and straight while the rankings appeared one by one. In order from last to first, our class rankings were as follows:

Donte Gavinson, Jessica Alter, Jaxon Call, Zayden Attack, Iris Blavins, Cora Wavice, Steven Mallnen, Khloe Basken, Scarlett Yalvo, Anya Lokel, Cindy Theon, Rake Clause, Camilla Xavier, Alex Galeger, Tonuko Kuntai, Kyle Straiter.

"No way I dropped five places! This is so dumb!" Steven complained with his arms crossed. Khloe snickered and shrugged.

"Maybe just be a little smarter, then you would have moved up majorly like me!" Steven growled and turned away from her. Donte looked down, clearly pretty upset with his ranking. He looked at his hands, then tensed his fists.

"I'll just have to work harder and be smarter. I won't make a dumb mistake like I did against Camilla ever again!"

He looked up and smiled, then Rake threw his arm around Donte. "You got this man! Just start using your speed in ways you haven't, and you'll get crazy stronger!" Rake smiled at Donte, then looked up at his name. "I gotta say, fifth place is pretty nice but I can be better!"

I did it, I actually fucking did it. I did it for you Mom, I fulfilled one of my promises. I'm number one.

"We are very happy with this freshman class. You all are amazing and have so much potential! I cannot wait to see you grow over the next four years! As your principal, I will protect you, guide you, and be someone you can look up to and go to if you have any concerns! Good luck with your training, and work hard!" Principal Lane's speech was motivating. I kinda wished he'd said something motivating before we fought, but, y'know, it was still a nice gesture.

The classes were dismissed and we were sent to our dorms to recover and prepare for our tomorrow, when our first day of real training would begin.

While I laid in my bed, I heard a knock at my door. I stood and looked through the peep-hole; Tonuko was standing in front of my door with his arms crossed. I opened the door, and asked, "What do you want?" He looked me dead in the eyes, it was pretty intense.

"So, you said you would tell me later about Tyrant. What the hell was that on the roof?" I felt a pit grow in my stomach, but I didn't let my nervousness and fear show.

Instead, I explained, "It may sound cocky, but since I have two strengths, I'm pretty valuable to both heroes and villains. That being said, Tyrant has been out to get me since he discovered me. He acts like I'm a criminal, and like I'm just a destined criminal. I'm not, I'm a hero. I didn't want you to get involved, so I pushed you back into the arena, away from the villains." Tonuko nodded while I told the fake story, then sighed.

"Alright, that makes sense. I'm gonna go out on a limb and say you don't want people knowing you have a vague connection with Tyrant, so I'll keep it on the d-l." I smiled slightly and nodded.

Wow, he's actually being pretty understanding about this. What if I told him the truth, would he act the same? No, of course not. If anyone finds out that Tyrant is actually my dad, not just a villain who wants me in his posse, then I'd be arrested and probably put to death.

"Let's tear down Tyrant's society. We're both really strong, we're both destined to be highly ranked heroes. Let's be the ones to finally defeat him," Tonuko suggested while holding out his fist. I looked at his fist and felt slightly offended.

"I appreciate the offer, but I won't be needing to team up with you to do it. I'll kill Tyrant, that's what I'm meant to do." Tonuko raised an eyebrow as he put his fist down. "Tyrant will die at my hands; I promise you that. That's all I'm training to do." I turned around and walked

99

back into my room. I tried to close the door, but Tonuko stopped it from fully closing.

"We're literally wanting to do the same thing. I've watched Tyrant terrorize heroes for years and it pisses me off so much. I hate that man, I hate everything related to him. I'm not saying you need my help, I'm saying let's both work hard to beat him. You get it?"

I took a deep breath, then stated, "You must have not heard me; *I* am going to *kill* Tyrant. It's *my* destiny, it's all *I'm here for.*" Tonuko felt unease with that last sentence. Before he could say anything, I pushed him back and closed my door while looking down at him.

Tonuko won't take this from me, no one will. I'll be the one to kill Tyrant, I have to. If I can't do that, then why the hell was I even born?

I laid on my bed and closed my eyes.

Mom, people are weird. They keep trying to make relationships with me, but what's the point? Why get close to people when I'll just lose them eventually? No, I'm gonna train myself, get stronger, and live out what I'm meant to do. That's all life is, living up to expectations. People are going to have very high expectations of me now, and I'll live out them all.

I fell asleep within minutes and was terrorized with nightmares about Tyrant.

For the next few days, my schedule was the same. I went to class and had two separate training sessions for two hours each, slept between sessions and maybe ate something, then trained more on my own and went to sleep. I barely talked to my classmates, but they were all beginning to bond with each other. I felt like an outcast, but I didn't care.

I'm not here to make friends, I'm here to kill Tyrant. The less people I know along the dangerous path, the less I'll have to hold me back.

On Friday, we packed our bags and waited for Ms. Palkun and the advanced teacher to get us so we could leave for Veena. The school bought two buses for us, each with barely enough seats to fit both classes when we were doubled up in the seats. Ms. Palkun told us two juniors and two sophomores would be joining us, so we'd have extra supervision since Veena wasn't a very safe city.

Veena was the wrestling capitol of the nation and about a four-hour drive from E.H. Wrestling was the most popular sport in the world because people love watching others fight with their strengths in a controlled environment. We would go to the most nationally renowned fighting tournament where the famous new fighter, Foul Odor, would take on Catastrophe, an older and stronger fighter. While I waited on the couch in the dorm, a boy with blue hair sat next to me. When I looked over, my eyes widened.

There's no fucking way.

"Hey Kyle, long time no see!" Daniel exclaimed with a big smile. I stared at him with a heavy feeling in my stomach, and I let out a small gasp.

"D- Daniel, you're here? But you left me four years ago, why are you back?" Daniel and I dapped each other and smiled, then pulled in and hugged.

"Sorry we moved away, but I'm back! We still live in Parane, but since this is a public hero school my parents sent me here! Isn't that great? We can be best buds again!" I chuckled and looked at his blue hair.

"So what the hell is this about? You dyed your hair blue?" Daniel nodded and his smile faded. He looked over at the other kids who were downstairs to his right.

"You remember my sister, Abby, right?" I nodded, now a little worried. "She was flown out across the country to track the Care-Giver's Strategist because he was making suspicious moves involving drugs. That was four years ago and she hasn't been heard from since. We were sent her sunglasses from her hero costume two years ago and told she had passed in battle. So, I dyed my hair the same color as hers so she could be with me every step of the way on my hero journey!" I could tell Daniel was still sore about it, but he wasn't going to be all sobby and would keep pushing forward. I respected that but didn't understand how he could do it.

"Let's go students, we gotta get on the road! Everyone pick a seat buddy, or whatever, and give your bags to Excalibur at the buses!" Ms. Palkun demanded after opening our dormitory door. Daniel and I agreed to be seat partners so we could catch up on the bus ride. After handing our bags to Excalibur, we made our way onto one of the buses and sat in the second to last seat on the right. I sat in the window seat and looked out at campus.

After everyone was on a bus, Ms. Palkun climbed aboard the bus I was on and Excalibur took a seat on the other one. Tonuko and Anya were in the seat across from Daniel and me, and Alex and Rake sat in front of us. Behind us was Hazel and a sophomore girl I had never seen before. She knelt on her seat and looked down at me, then held out a hand.

"Hey hotshot, I'm Kate! I'm Queen of the sophomores and the top of the sophomore honors' class! Nice to meet ya'!" I looked at her hand and shook it, then she pulled me up and put me in a headlock. "I'll keep you in check during this trip! Don't need you having any freakouts or anything like that! Let's all just have a nice, villain-free trip!" I pushed her off me and rolled my eyes, then sulked in my seat. It would be a long, long four-hour drive.

Once we arrived at the hotel, we unloaded and grabbed our bags. My eyes sparkled as I looked at the deluxe hotel. I heard Excalibur inform some students, "This is the same hotel where all the pro-wrestlers will be staying. You should all be thanking Kyle Straiter and Tonuko Kuntai for getting us this amazing hotel. The owner is very ecstatic to meet the two of them!" Tonuko walked up next to me while sighing.

"Welcome to the fame, Kyle. This is gonna happen a lot," he stated. When I didn't respond, he looked over at me, confused. "Kyle?"

"What did you say? Sorry, I was just in such a trance looking at this massive hotel. It's so much nicer than my house!" I exclaimed.

"Really, this is way nicer than your house?" Hazel asked, walking up to Tonuko and me with Kate, Devin, and a sophomore boy. The sophomore boy leaned on Tonuko and ruffled his hair. I was shocked at his height, he had to be around six-foot-eight. Tonuko and I were pretty similar in height, around six-foot-two.

"Get off me Jon!" Tonuko grumbled, pushing Jon's arm. Jon chuckled, then walked past me with Kate and into the hotel. I entered as well with Tonuko, and a familiar-looking man walked up to us. He was no older than twenty and had slicked-back auburn hair and short, wide silicon tubes sticking out of his arms.

"There they are, Tonuko Kuntai and Kyle Straiter! It's a pleasure to meet you two!" I recognized the man now—it was Foul Odor. I shook his hand and smiled, and Tonuko did the same. "Follow me, the big man wants to meet you!" We followed Foul Odor to an office in the back of the hotel. When the three of us entered, there was a very large man sitting in a big chair. He had long, golden locks and he wore a tight button-down shirt.

"Ah, Tonuko Kuntai and Kyle Straiter, nice to meet you. I am Mr. Clarence, I run the show. You two are very strong." We both nodded and stood tall. Compliments were pretty damn nice. "Now, have fun and enjoy the tournament. Be careful wandering around town though, there have been a lot of kidnappings lately."

Kidnappings? I had heard about teenagers and young adults going missing around the area. I've wondered who's in charge of it though ...

"We'll be sure to watch out, thank you for the warning," Tonuko said with a smile. We said goodbye to Mr. Clarence, then walked out with Foul Odor.

"Yeah, it's pretty dangerous around here right now. I'm kind of surprised your class was allowed to come here. The kidnappings have gotten way worse over the past month, and I've heard it's got something to do with Tyrant." A pit grew in my stomach. "Oh well, I'm sure you will all be fine. Just don't go out too late, alright?" Foul Odor held out his fist, offering a fist bump. I gave him one, then he walked away.

"That can't be good. An increase in the number of kidnappings in the area, but no one is in a rush to solve the problem? Really?" Tonuko thought aloud while looking around the hotel lobby. It was vast and very open. You could see all the doors to the hotel rooms if you stood in the middle of the lobby. There was a water fountain and the elevator walls were made of glass. Tonuko looked at me for an opinion, but I just shrugged at him. "Oh come on, you can't tell me you're not curious about solving this kidnapping problem." I walked toward a couch and waved for him to follow. We sat down and my leg started bouncing.

"I didn't wanna show it around the director since he's such a professional, but holy shit I wanna solve this so badly!" Tonuko smirked and crossed his arms. "We can act like real heroes and stop the kidnappers! What do you say?!" I held a hand out to him. He shook my hand while smiling with a closed mouth. He let go of my hand and flipped one of his bangs out of his face, then sighed.

"I completely agree with you, but we're gonna need to get some backup. As confident as I am in myself, the two of us are amateurs and this is a major scandal. There's no way we could beat the kidnapper, or kidnappers, by ourselves."

I rolled my eyes and scoffed, "Oh come on, of course we could. You back me up with defense and I charge in and beat them down, piece of cake!" Tonuko tensed his fist. He stood and grabbed his backpack.

"Use your brain a little Straiter. This isn't training, these villains would want to kill us if we tried to fight them. I'll talk with the juniors and sophomores then get back to you." Tonuko walked toward one of the three elevators and started talking to Alex, who was waiting for the elevator as well. I shook my head, pissed off with Tonuko.

Whatever, I could beat those villains all by myself if I wanted to. I thought you were confident like me, what the hell is this backing out bullshit? I'll find and beat down those kidnappers, especially if they have a connection with Tyrant ...

I entered an elevator a few minutes later with Daniel, and he sighed loudly after we took off. "Man, my parents have been assholes lately. They were so disappointed in me when I was put in advanced instead of honors. Like, c'mon, give me a break!" he complained. I rolled my eyes, a little annoyed with him.

"Relax Daniel, they're just setting goals and expectations for you. If there was no one to set those goals or expectations, then no one would get anything done."

He looked through the glass and muttered, "But they set goals not even you can reach. They're assholes." I clenched my fist and closed my eyes, absolutely furious.

"At least you have parents! Don't complain when you can go home to a loving family!" I screamed at him.

"I get it Kyle, I really do. I feel horrible about what happened with your family, but that doesn't invalidate my problems! Not everything is about you!" Daniel erupted, shocking me. The elevator door opened.

Before walking away, I stated, "Don't take your parents for granted, and do not tell me about my past problems. You left, the fuck would you know?" Daniel was sweating bullets, and I could somewhat tell he didn't exactly mean what he was shouting. However, what was said was said.

Daniel is selfish now too. What the hell is wrong with people?! I should've never been friends with him in the first place if he's gonna act like that.

When I entered my room, I laid on my bed and fell asleep within minutes. I needed a nap and wouldn't get much sleep for a while after tonight ...

Chapter 7
Involvement

Around 8:00 p.m., there was a knock at my door. I answered after a couple of minutes and was met with Tonuko, Hazel, Kate, Jon, Devin, Alex, Camilla, and Anya.

"Come on Kyle, let's get a bite to eat. There's a nice restaurant down the block," Hazel suggested. I looked back at the dark hotel room.

"I guess I'll stop having *so* much fun to hang out with you guys," I retorted with a grin. Hazel giggled, and we left for the restaurant.

The place was a classic inn with booths and round tables, along with a long table in the middle of the room. We sat in a booth and asked a waitress if we could pull up an extra table to seat us all together. After she agreed, we settled in and ordered drinks.

"Well," Hazel started with a sigh, "we all know what we need to discuss here. The fighting tournament starts tomorrow, so we need to have a plan on how we're going to approach tracking down the kidnapper." A couple of people nodded, but I just sat back in my seat and took a deep breath.

Lame, why do we need to come up with a strategy?

"Let's just sneak away while the fighting is going on since everyone will be distracted, then start our search from there. It shouldn't be too hard to track down the kidnappers with the strengths we have," I suggested before yawning. To my surprise, the group agreed.

"Yeah, if we leave while the fight is getting intense, no one will really be paying attention to us. Even if we do get in trouble after, when we have the kidnapper captured, they won't be too mad at us," Jon agreed with a smile. I'd never seen this sophomore around school, surprisingly, but I liked him already. He had a rough, dirty blonde mohawk, but he'd worn a bandana over his head most of the time I'd seen him. He also had ear piercings.

"Since when did you think so logically Jon?" Tonuko snickered in his corner. Jon grinned and held up his hand, allowing electricity to aggressively flow throughout his fingers.

"I can kick your ass Tonuko, so don't be makin' too many jokes over there!" Jon laughed. We all agreed on the plan and decided we'd leave at the climax of the first fight. It would be the biggest and would give us the opportunity to be gone the longest. If we didn't find the kidnappers before we got caught, we would get in serious trouble.

"This is gonna be pretty dangerous; can we even pull this off? How are we gonna find kidnappers?" Alex asked, clearly nervous. Devin rolled his eyes while taking a sip of ice-cold water in a fake-glass cup.

"You first years are something else. Jon's strength allows him to sense reverberations in the ground, so if they have some kind of an underground lair, we'll be able to find out where it is. Combined with my acid webs and Kyle Straiter's super strength, we'll be able to find their base in no time." Alex, Anya, and Camilla still seemed a little on edge so Devin assured them, "If things get bad, we can tell Foul Odor or Catastrophe. Foul loves Kyle and Tonuko, and Hazel and I had a nice talk with Catastrophe about the kidnappings. They trust us, and Catastrophe said to put our trust in them. Now, who's in?" Within the minute, everyone agreed with the plan and cleared their doubts.

After we ate and refined our plan, we came up with a way to find a lead. Since we were heroes-in-training, and all have some form of fighting skills, we would send out Tonuko, Hazel, and me during the night to see if we could find anything suspicious.

"It's always good to have a lead," Jon said. As we were walking back into the hotel, I was stopped by a duo.

One of them had spikey, black hair, a black sweatshirt, and red shorts; the other guy had long blonde hair with immaculate flow, and he wore a flat-brim hat, a black and white windbreaker, and gray short-shorts.

"Ay, you're Kyle, right?" the spikey-haired one asked. I nodded, so he put out a hand and smirked, "I'm Hunter, and we're pretty similar if I do say so myself!"

"Oh yeah, how so? The top kid of the honors' class is similar to some random advanced kid?" Hunter was clearly a bit frustrated, and he crossed his arms.

"Hot shot of honors, hot shot of advanced, we're pretty similar in the sense that we're the best of our classes by a long shot!" I couldn't help but chuckle and I stood tall with my chest puffed out.

"The key to being able to call yourself a hotshot is having skill to back up your claim. I can already tell, you clearly don't. Maybe fix your style first before going around boasting about yourself. The hell is your strength anyway?" I heard a few snickers from behind me, most notably Kate.

"Mine? Oh, just a little thing called Cancel. It's pretty similar to my Queen sister Kate over there!" Hunter boasted.

Hunter Sanders, Strength: Cancel—he can create spheres of magic cancellers out of his body and nullify almost any strength or attack. These spheres cannot be thrown and take a lot of stamina to use.

"Oh wow, *so* cool. You're really the best of your class with a defensive strength like that? You kinda sound like a sidekick to me," I stated in a monotone voice, expressing the sarcasm in the first statement.

"Why yes, I am! This is Zach, the third best of our class! How about the three of us become a little trio, then we can be the strongest group this school will ever see?" Hunter suggested while holding up his right fist and flexing his arm. I tried to contain myself, but I burst out with laughter, embarrassing Hunter.

"Really, are you being serious? Why would I associate with advanced kids when every single honors student is stronger than you? Come on man, think a little!" Jon walked up beside me and leaned on my shoulder, chuckling as well.

"Yeah, he makes a good point Hunter. Valiant effort though, and great confidence!" Jon complimented. Hunter's cheeks and ears were bright red, so Zach decided to speak up.

"No disrespect, but if that's true, then why do you hang out with Daniel?" I thought for a moment, then shrugged.

"I've known him for a long time and he helped me a lot when I was younger. It doesn't really have anything to do with strength." Zach nodded, then held out his hand.

"Well, uh, I'm Zach, as he said. Pleasure to meet you, Kyle." I shook his hand with a smile.

"Maybe you should do the talking for your duo. You're much more approachable than little anger issues over there." Zach giggled while looking back at Hunter, who was even more flustered now. We walked away from them and agreed to meet down here at midnight.

I went straight to my room and sat on my bed while clicking through the channels on the T.V. I saw a news report about the kidnappings and saw the picture of who was supposedly behind the crimes. There was a weirdly built thing, and a tall, average-looking man. The thing had very long arms, inhumanely long in fact, a very short and stocky torso, skinny legs, and no hair. The man had a cloth tied around his neck and right bicep and wore a t-shirt and baggy pants. I noted their appearances, then continued to scroll through the channels.

Midnight came faster than I expected, and at 12:02 a.m., I made my way down to the lobby. Everyone was waiting impatiently for me.

"Finally! Do you have any sense of urgency Kyle Straiter?!" Camilla yelled angrily. I rolled my eyes and walked up to Jon, Hazel, Tonuko, and Kate.

"Alright you three, make your way outside and keep us updated through call. Hazel has two wireless earbuds connected to her phone, so Tonuko and Hazel will wear them while we're on a call. You ready?" Kate asked looking directly at me. I nodded with a smirk, then Devin put his hand on my shoulder from behind.

"Kyle Straiter, I don't like you, but I'm trusting you."

Why doesn't he like me? I feel like I've never talked to him before.

"I won't let you down, Devin," I responded.

The three of us went outside and waved to the others. We started walking in the same direction as the restaurant we had eaten at earlier. The city was quiet and peaceful, there were barely any sounds. We made our way down a few blocks, then passed a dark, massive alleyway. Since Camby had so many alleys, I was used to them, but this one was weirdly bigger. Hazel stopped before the alley, then put her hand in front of my chest.

"Stay back, I'll look to see if there's anything suspicious." I rolled my eyes and moved her arm away from me.

"Thanks, but I don't need your precautions. If they attack me, I'll beat them." I walked out in front of the alley and put my hands up. "Well, if you're in there, come and get me!"

"Kyle, what in the actual fuck are you doing?! Get the hell back here!" Tonuko exclaimed angrily.

"Oh yeah, and what are you gonna do about it?!" I retorted while turning to the two of them. Hazel was looking down the alley, then her face turned to fear and she swiftly looked back to warn me. However, she saw I was looking to my right with just my eyes into the alley. "Come and make me move why don't you?!" A rock flew out of the alley, but I reacted quickly and caught it, then chucked it back at the man who threw it at me. He narrowly dodged it. The rock crashed into a dumpster and exploded into rubble.

"You shouldn't be out here kids, it's dangerous. There are ... kidnappers on the loose," the man sinisterly stated in a deep voice. I could see the outline of the thing behind him creep up slowly, then two stretched arms shot out at me. The fingers looked like claws, and as they stuck into the ground, the thing's body flew at me.

"Kyle Straiter, it really is you! I'm the Creature, it's my pleasure!" the Creature creepily exclaimed while sitting on my stomach. I swung a punch at its face, but the Creature's legs stretched and it jumped high into the air. "I can't take you yet, that would be boring!"

"Dammit Hazel, tell Kyle to get out of there! We know what they look like and Jon knows their reverberations! Get the fuck out of there!" Devin screamed into the phone.

"I know, I know dammit!" Hazel shouted back while stretching her demon arms. The arms were absolutely massive and muscular; her right hand grabbed the Creature. I crouched, then went to jump at the Creature, but the ground beneath me bent in a curve above my head, causing me to hit my head hard and fall back to the ground.

"What the fuck are you doing Tonuko?! I had a clear shot on him!" I angrily yelled while turning all my focus to Tonuko. I stomped toward him with my fists tensed.

He argued, "We aren't here to fight right now, we're here to get data and go! Think a little, Straiter!" I sped up my walking, then punched him in the cheek. He fell over and the earpiece fell out of his ear, then the other man walked over and stomped on it, breaking it.

"Oh no, you won't be getting any information back to your posse. We knew you would come searching for us Kyle Straiter, it's in your blood to be near villains." Tonuko was confused by the statement, but too frustrated and flustered to even think about what it could mean. I punched at the man, but he tackled me by my waist and slammed me into the ground. The ground took me in and wrapped around my body.

What the fuck, what is his strength?! It's so similar to Tonuko's, right?!

Tonuko tried to hit the man's blindside, but when the man had his hand on the rocks and me, more rocks crashed onto his hand and created a boxing glove. He socked Tonuko square on the nose, then looked back at the Creature. The Creature's arm stretched through Hazel's demon arm and pierced her hand; it followed through and dug its claw into her shoulder. She grimaced with pain. The Creature's arm was striped black and white, and when it pierced Hazel's shoulder, the white part turned purple. It looked like something was pumping into Hazel's body, then she passed out. My eye's widened and I broke out of the rock around my body. Hazel's demon arm disappeared, then the creature wrapped its arm around her body like a rope and, while its legs were still stretched, walked back into the alley. Its strides were so long that it traveled a block in a second. The man looked down at the two of us, spat at us, and ran away. Tonuko was shaking, but he stumbled to his feet and grabbed my shirt.

"Come on, we have to go before they come back for us!" Tonuko commanded. I knew he was right and didn't argue this time. I knew I fucked up. We ran back to the hotel, panicked and panting when we arrived. Tonuko was consoled by Anya, Jon, and Alex. On the contrary, Devin stomped up to me and punched me on the cheek. I fell over and looked at his face. It was filled with pure rage.

"What the fuck is the matter with you?! While in the middle of a fight with strong villains, you go over and punch Tonuko?! Are you fucking kidding me?! Were you trying to get Hazel kidnapped; did you purposefully sabotage the mission?!" Devin screamed while looking down at me.

"N-No, I-"

"Just shut up, I don't want to hear your excuses!" Devin looked at the rest of the group and commanded, "We will continue with the original plan regardless of what happened. Now, instead of just capturing the villains, we have to save Hazel as well! Also, the teachers are going to be asking where she is. I'll cover for her. Got it?!" Everyone said yes then went to bed.

Before Devin and I left, I yelled to him, "I promise I'll get her back and take down the kidnappers!" Devin stopped when I shouted, then shook his head and entered the elevator. I went up to my room shortly after and sat up awake in my bed.

"Were you trying to get Hazel kidnapped; did you purposefully sabotage the mission?!"

No, I wasn't, I swear. They're wrong about me, I just made a mistake. I'll get Hazel back; I'll save everyone and take down those kidnappers. **They're as good as dead.**

In the morning, both classes met up and we headed over to the arena, which was about a mile walk. Like Devin said he would, he covered for Hazel. Actually, Ms. Palkun didn't ask any questions about her disappearance, but Excalibur did. We arrived in the arena, which was absolutely breathtaking. The stage was in the center and above it pipes spelled out "CHAMPIONS," the name of the arena. We sat in our front row seats and the seven of us waited anxiously. Our school was introduced as special guests, then Mr. Clarence introduced the first two fighters.

"FIRST OFF, WE HAVE THE BEST UPCOMING FIGHTER IN THE NATION: FOULLL ODOR! IN THE OTHER CORNER STANDS THE MAN, THE MYTH, THE LEGEND WHO'S BEEN ON TOP FOR THE PAST YEAR! GIVE IT UP FOR CATASTROPHE!" Catastrophe was a very muscular man who had a shiny bald head, wore a cape and no shirt, and had skin-tight pants yet no socks or shoes. The bell rang, starting the fight.

A purple mist seeped out of Foul Odor's tubes and filled the bottom of the stage. Catastrophe activated his Earthquake strength, causing Foul to stumble.

Jeremy Hunderaks/Catastrophe, Strength: Rumble—he can create strong earthquakes in specific spots that can reduce a person's ability to focus. They can span to a mile radius. It takes a lot of muscle and focus to create these, so he must keep a powerful body and serene mind.

From the crowd across the stage from us, a man with a cloth mask stood and clapped loudly, then a couple of crows made entirely of shadows swarmed Catastrophe's head.

"Marvelous, just marvelous!" the man who was sitting next to the masked man applauded. "You heroes are just so amazing to watch up close!" The man stood, and as he did so a large hawk made of shadows formed out of the ground. He hopped onto it, then flew into the air above the arena. The other man actually ate his mask, revealing an eerie sight. His mouth was very wide, he had no lips, sharp teeth, and a long, pointy tongue. His hair was brown, messy, and long, drooping in his bloodshot eyes. He wore a black track suit and big, black boots. The other man in the air

115

wore a gray and black trench coat, a top hat, and black pants with a gray-collared shirt.

"Kane," Foul Odor grumbled.

"Nobody moves, or else my good buddy David over here will shoot the place up!" David jumped onto the stage holding two automatic rifles he had hacked up seconds earlier. There were a few screams from the crowd at first, but everyone was silent now. Catastrophe snapped out of his daze and activated his strength on Kane, causing him to fall off his hawk.

I stood, looked to my left toward the others who were supposed to leave, and looked for confirmation. Devin nodded, so while commotion and worry were happening around us, I led the group and ran out of the main stage room and into the short hallway. I panicked and ran into the boy's bathroom and the others followed. David didn't try to stop us; instead, he let out a snarly chuckle and turned back to Foul Odor.

"Kyle, what are we doing in here?! We need to hurry!" Tonuko shouted at me before running his hands through his hair and looking out the bathroom door at the main stage. Alex washed his hands, then walked over to use the hand dryer. Tonuko and I continued arguing, then a weird warping noise filled the room and Alex was gone. Kate was staring at the hand dryer and gulped.

"Alex just got sucked into that thing ... It must be some kind of teleportation device built to kidnap people," Kate stated while walking toward the hand dryer. Tonuko and I followed. A plethora of gunfire came from the main stage area, then Devin took a deep breath and took charge.

"We said we're doing this, so we're going to follow through! Camilla and I will stay back and help against the Care-Givers, and you go save Alex and Hazel!" Devin's confident, straightforward attitude gave us a little bit of courage, but Kate still had her rational doubts.

"Devin, these are freshies you left me with! Jon didn't follow us so we can't track the reverberations of the kidnappers! You're expecting me to watch over all of them and make sure every one of them doesn't do something stupid that will get them killed?!" Devin turned back to face us and walked toward Kate and me. He looked me in the eyes, then grabbed the collar of my shirt.

"Kyle has a big promise to uphold Kate. He's stronger than you, faster than you, and has a higher battlefield awareness and intelligence than you; you are not alone. Tonuko is smarter than you, and Anya will keep Tonuko in check so he doesn't get killed. All I'm asking for you to do is make sure Kyle doesn't go berserk, or make sure he knows his limits. The other two will help you, I trust them." I was angered by his last statement and pushed him off of me.

"So, you don't trust me; you don't think I can do this?!" I glared at Devin, and he glared back at me.

"No, I don't think you can beat criminals with powers unknown to you by yourself! Wow, isn't that a fucking shocker! Listen to Kate and don't get yourself, or anyone else, killed!" I didn't argue. I decided my fists would show him that he couldn't order me around.

Devin looked at Kate and nodded, then ran to the bathroom door and tapped Camilla as he ran by. The two left, leaving Kate, Tonuko, Anya, and me in the room. I stood in front of the hand dryer, cracked my knuckles, then took my headband out of my pocket and tied it on my head. Tonuko put his hand on my shoulder to stop me, but my skin was extremely hot and it slightly burned his hand. I reached my hand toward the heat fan then it felt as though my body was stretched and suddenly, I was in a tunnel barreling into the darkness. I hit the ground and rubbed my back. Tonuko fell on me, Kate followed, and Anya was last. We stood and I saw a wooden beam on the wall, so I threw

117

some fire at it. The torch lit up a portion of the corridor we were in.

"Everyone stay close; we don't know who or what is down here," Kate commanded while standing in front of the three of us freshmen. In the distance, a bright white light glowed, then vanished from the bottom up, signifying Alex went down something.

"Alex!" I shouted, pushing past Kate and running.

"Kyle, what the hell are you doing?!" Tonuko yelled, taking a step. Before any of them or I could react, a man covered in rough, cream–white scales ran out from the darkness, lowered his shoulder, and rammed me into the dirt wall to my left. The ceiling rumbled and dirt and dust fell to the ground. Along with the man, a teenage boy and young girl walked toward us. The man who had hit me smirked, then his mouth and nose grew into a long dinosaur snout and jaw and his fingers grew longer and sharper. Bones in his body cracked and creaked, and eventually his knees were bent in the opposite direction and his arms were twice as long as before. Sharp spikes stuck out from his spinal cord, and he was standing in a slightly hunched position.

"Looks like I get a go at the almighty son, huh?" The man snickered as he raised his right arm, then swiped down and clawed my right arm, which I had used to block his attack. A pillar of dirt flew toward the lizard man and knocked him off me. Kate ran over and grabbed my arm, dragging me back toward the group. "The name's Spike, Kyle Straiter. You will be mine; I'll be the one to take you back to him."

"Kyle, who is he talking about?!" Anya yelled at me while I was still sitting on the ground.

"I- I don't know! This is some psychotic kidnapper; he's probably just talking out of his ass!" Spike slowly walked toward us, letting his sharp claws drag on the ground.

118

"You know exactly who I'm talking about. Once I bring you back to my bosses, they'll take you to where you belong ... the base of-" Without thinking, I activated another strength and sped at lightning speed at Spike. I landed a punch square on his snout, then, as he was soaring backward toward the other two criminals, I blasted flames at them. The little girl hopped out in front of the two guys, then stretched and expanded into a massive blob with a normal-sized head and small limbs. The fire was absorbed by her body, then she shrunk back down to her usual size.

"Did you know that rubber absorbs fire! So cool, right?!" the little girl informed me while wearing a large smile. I was sweating but my fear was detained by the raging fury that grew every time I thought about Tyrant.

"Kyle, watch out!" Kate screamed as Spike charged in and swiped at the left side of my body. I was too angry and lost in thought to notice, so Kate quickly stepped in and formed two cancellation orbs. Spike's claws clashed with the orbs, creating a loud static noise, which ejected the force Spike had used back onto his arm, causing him to spin around in a circle. I snapped out of my daze, jumped up, and kicked Spike in the head. He flew into the wall on the left side of the hallway, then a huge pile of dirt fell on top of him. I stepped backward toward Tonuko and Anya, but Spike leapt out of the dirt pile and on top of me. Anya ran to my side while dragging her fingers on the ground. She formed the same gloves she had during the training tournament and punched Spike in the side of the head. He tumbled into the teenage boy who had yet to make a move.

"Dammit Pete, are you going to do something?! I'm getting quadruple teamed out here!" Spike shouted furiously. Pete nodded then popped a blue piece of gum in his mouth. After chewing for a couple seconds, he blew a large bubble that began floating toward us. The bubble split into multiple tiny bubbles, then Anya reached out her finger and touched one of the blue bubbles. It popped and covered her glove in a sticky acid that melted the dirt around her hand. Anya let the dirt glove fall off, then she nervously backed up to Tonuko's side.

Spike's nose was broken and bloody and one of his claws had ripped off in my skin. I hopped to my feet and took charge of myself. I cracked my shoulder and tensed my entire body. After tensing hard enough, an audible click echoed throughout the hallway, and a bright yellow layer of electricity raged around my body. With a quick step, I launched myself into Spike. We hit at such high speeds that I bounced off his body. However, I used this bounce to grab his arm, twist around in the air, and throw him into the ground. The entire tunnel rumbled, but I ignored the danger signs and punched down on Spike's stomach. He coughed and his eyes widened, then I kicked him into the wall in front of me. Another large mound of dirt fell onto his body, but this time Spike didn't get back up.

Kyle Straiter, Strength Five: Energy Conversion— he can convert any energy in his cells into a speed boost that is represented by the layer of electricity that covers his body. As well as this, Kyle can absorb the energy from other's or natural lighting sources. Of course, using this strength takes a massive amount of stamina and can have deadly side effects since it is taking energy from necessary processes in Kyle's body.

"Wow, you're so amazing Kyle Straiter!" The little girl yelled with a sparkle in her eyes. I turned around and blasted fire at the girl, so she stretched out again and absorbed the flames. What I didn't know was that Anya and Tonuko were charging up a special attack. Anya had a suit of hardened dirt, a near rock material, and Tonuko used a hand he formed from the ground to wind up and throw Anya at the rubber girl. Anya led with her hands flat, palms pressed against each other. When she hit the girl's stomach, it stretched far, then Anya's body ripped through the girl. Blood splattered on my face, and Pete's eyes grew very wide as the hole in the little girl's body hissed and spat out a sprinkler of blood. Her body was thrown all over because of

120

the wind pressure escaping her inflated body, then she hit the ground hard and laid unconscious. Her blood was everywhere.

"N-No, no Katrina, it can't end like this. We were gonna escape with the heroes and be free!" Pete screamed after dropping to his knees and looking at Katrina's dead body. Anya tumbled a couple feet, then lifted her head up and looked back at the girl she just killed.

"I- I just ... killed someone ..." Anya stated quietly while staring with a horrified expression at the dead body. Kate rushed over and knelt at Pete's side.

"Is this your sister?" she asked. Pete nodded with tears streaming down his face

He explained, "W- We were just normal students, like you guys. We dreamt of being heroes, getting in the action and beating up bad guys, saving the day, y'know? One day though, we were kidnapped before we made it to the bus stop ... by those monsters. I was beaten and nearly killed every day for a month before the Creature finally gave us an ultimatum: join their side or be put down in the most painful way we could think of. I was ready to die right there, finally have it all end, but Katrina spoke up and saved my life ... Now ..."

Pete swiftly looked up, causing tears to fly off his face, and he looked over at Anya. "You're a hero, right?!" Pete screeched as he got up and ran at Anya with his hands out and full of gum. "Then how could you fucking murder a little girl?! She was only seven years old, you monster!" Before Pete could reach the shocked Anya, I led with a knee to the side of his head and hit him into the wall. This crash was much larger than any of Spike's and was the limit to what the tunnel could handle. The ceiling began collapsing behind us.

"We gotta get the hell out of here! Come on!" Tonuko commanded. We all ran down the tunnel, but I used my energy strength to speed ahead of them.

"That asshole was hiding another strength, are you serious?! Just what else is he hiding, who was that Spike guy gonna bring him to?!" Anya shouted frantically with fury lingering in her voice.

"All that matters is he's on our side. I don't know what secrets he's keeping, but if all these criminals want to bring him down with them, we have to stop them," Kate stated trying to hide her frustration and panic.

The three continued sprinting after me but saw I had stopped at the edge of light. Above me was a bright blue sky with many clouds, but below me was a dark pit. I looked back and saw the tunnel continue to collapse behind the three, who were running as fast as they could, but it wasn't fast enough. I rolled my eyes, then activated my energy strength and sprinted back toward them. I pushed them forward, sending everyone stumbling toward the edge. Tonuko extended the ground, catching Anya and Kate, then looked back at me. I was holding up a large rock that fell from the ceiling, but the ground beneath me cracked. Suddenly, the ground crumbled, sending me downward into the unknown.

"Kyle!" Tonuko shouted, but before he could make a move to save me the tunnel collapsed the rest of the way. The platform Tonuko had made cracked—the floor was now gone because the tunnel was filled in. Tonuko placed his hand on the wall and looked down at the darkness beneath the three. He focused hard, his bangs dripped sweat, and he panted heavily.

"That idiot Kyle is gonna get us killed now! He should have known you can only bend the ground! All he's done is create more problems for us!" Anya complained while frantically looking around for a way to save the others and herself.

Tonuko clenched his fist, then turned and erupted, "That 'idiot' Kyle just saved our asses back there and now he might be dead because of it! We don't know how far that drop was! It could have been all the way down to wherever the hell the ground is!"

Anya was surprised by Tonuko's sudden explosion of anger but stood her ground as usual. "We don't know that he saved us! We were outrunning the dirt; we didn't need his help! He just created another problem for us to solve because he was trying to be the big, amazing hero!" Anya shouted at Tonuko while walking closer and pointing her finger at the newly formed dirt wall.

"We just killed someone! Kyle didn't create that problem for us!" As Tonuko shouted, his voice croaked and the ground they were standing on continued cracking. "That little girl is *dead* and the guy probably is as well because *we* left him in the collapsing tunnel to save ourselves! *That's not what heroes do!* Kyle ran into death and saved us, *now he's gone!* Don't you understand Anya? *We've done nothing, we're doing nothing, and we're going to die just like Kyle, like Hazel, like Alex, and like **the child we just killed!**"* With the last words, the ground shattered and the three were sent falling into the abyss.

Back in the Arena:

Excalibur stood from his seat and demanded of the classes, "Stay in your seats! This is a real villain battle; I don't want any of you making a dumb decision and getting hurt!" Excalibur grabbed his large sword from behind his seat and jumped onto the stage. He swung at David, but a shadow hyena leapt and took the hit. Excalibur was surrounded by a group of hyenas. Suddenly, multiple blades of wind exploded around him and took out all of the hyenas.

123

Excalibur looked back and saw Camilla and Devin standing at the top of the arena stairs.

"Don't worry Excalibur, we'll back you up!" Devin exclaimed while running down the stairs. Excalibur shook his head, then Camilla floated into the air and created a mini tornado between Kane and David.

While they were distracted, Camilla announced, "Everyone evacuate the building! We'll distract the Care-Givers while you leave!" Civilians poured out of the exit, and every time David shot at them, his bullets were absorbed by the tornado. He seethed to himself, then coughed and threw up a large sniper.

David Blake/Care-Giver Weaponsmith, Strength: Weaponry—using anti-matter found in his stomach acid, he can form any weapon and throw it up through his widened mouth. His teeth are reinforced to not be affected by the stomach acid, his esophagus is hardened as to not get punctured by any sharp items, and his tongue is razor sharp and long to guide the weapons out of his mouth. If David creates too many weapons over a few hours, he will start to vomit blood and feel very ill.

David aimed quickly and shot a heavy-duty bullet that avoided the tornado and pierced Camilla's stomach. She fell out of the air but was, luckily, caught by Devin. David eerily giggled and on pure instinct ducked. Foul Odor's fist flew over his head, then David shot one of his assault rifles straight up and wounded Foul's left arm. Following Devin's command, Iris ran to Camilla and Devin, then Daniel stood from his seat, ready to fight.

On the stage, David aimed his rifle at Foul Odor, causing a distraction that allowed a group of hounds to pounce on Foul Odor's back. He tried to wrestle the beasts off, but only succeeded when he managed to release his strength-weakening gas.

*Keith Stratop/Foul Odor, Strength: Stench—he
can release many different odors from the silicon tubes
coming out of his arms that correlate to different defects
for the opponent. He has learned four different smells so
far, as he is a very young fighter, only twenty years old. He
can emit a purple stench that temporarily blinds people, a
green stench that makes it difficult for people to breath, a
blue stench that causes people to lose their sense of touch
and taste, and a yellow stench, which causes other's
strengths to weaken to half of what they were.*

Kane covered his mouth after breathing in some of
the foul-smelling gas, then he was rammed from the side by
an unknown force. Daniel fell over and hit the ground hard,
revealing his position. Kane jumped to his feet, then kicked
Daniel in the chest, sending him flying into the stands. Kane
formed a large boar at his feet, letting it charge at Daniel.
"What a nuisance," Kane sighed.

*Kane Ine/Care-Giver Animal Creator, Strength:
Life Form—he can create any animal from his shadow,
and depending on how big his shadow is, the bigger his
beasts will be. If it is nighttime, he has no limit to the size
except for what his body can handle (that currently is forty
feet). He hears the thoughts of whatever animals he
creates, so creating too many will tire him out and make
him go crazy.*

The boar leapt at Daniel, who was no longer
invisible, but a red laser wall formed from the ground and
caught the beast, causing it to sizzle and disintegrate. "Don't
worry Daniel, I gotcha," Zach calmly stated while walking
up to Daniel. He reached a hand to Daniel, who thanked him
and used his hand to stand.

*Zach Taling, Strength: Laser—he can create
extremely powerful lasers that burn anyone or anything
that comes within six inches of contact. He can shoot them
by making a gun formation with his fingers or he can
create walls of laser at will.*

Foul dodged a few bullets nimbly, then released more of his yellow toxin out of his right arm and some of his blue stench from his left arm. More dogs tackled him and ripped the flesh on his arms. Suddenly, Steven collided with one of the hounds, lowering his bionic shoulder, and made it crash into an empty part of the stands before vanishing. After that, Donte bolted in quickly and broke through the other dog's exterior, causing it to disappear.

"Get away boys! This is too dangerous! Where the hell is Diana to keep you safe?!" Excalibur erupted while stepping between Donte and Kane. Kane smirked, then shrugged.

"Oh, you mean Diana Palkun? Silly heroes, that's the Diana Palkun of the Care-Givers, better known as Lady Patch!" Excalibur's eyes widened and he stared in awe at Kane.

"Are you serious, this entire time a Care-Giver has been this close to our students?! What if she kills any straggler students who will trust her as their teacher?! *Dammit!*" He charged in at Kane and swung his massive metal sword. The sword's blade burst into flames, but Kane flipped into the air and jumped down on the blade, causing it to get stuck in the ground. The blade's form changed to water, and Excalibur was able to easily rip it out of the ground. As he swung it again, the blade hardened back into metal and sliced a cut across Kane's upper chest, narrowly missing his neck.

David aimed his assault rifle at Excalibur, but an invisible Daniel knocked it out of his hand, then Zayden burst out of the ground, uppercutting David. David led with his elbow into Zayden's head, and proclaimed, "Silly kids these days, you think you have a chance. No, none of you do, except Kyle Straiter. However, he'll be dead by night!" He began cackling but while lost in psychotic laughter, he ate a knuckle sandwich from Rake. Cindy shot a few bullets; one of them managed to burrow itself into David's forehead right above his nose. Blood dripped down his face, over his lips. He licked the blood all the way up his nose and smiled horrifically. "Thanks for the snack, little girl," David stated in a low, scratchy voice.

Rake ignored the creepiness of this Care-Giver and threw five of his fingers at David. A snake molded while in the air and latched on to David's head. "Venom, 500 mL," Rake smirked. "If you move, that snake will seep all 500 milliliters of venom right into your bloodline, stopping your heart. The choice is yours, you fuckin' freak." David began gagging and gargling. "Snake, be ready!" yelled Rake.

David opened his mouth with a smile and sitting on his tongue was a grenade. He used one of his teeth to pull the pin, then the grenade fell out of his mouth and onto the stage. It exploded, causing people to be swept off their feet and throwing off the entire battle. Rake collided into Zach and they crashed into a couple of seats.

While on the ground, Zach looked up and saw a wolf pounce on Steven. He created a laser box around the two, then swiftly threw up a wall when the wolf tried to bite Steven. The wolf backed up and whimpered, then the box around the wolf shrank instantly, killing it. A couple of crows tried swarming the three boys, but Steven took out two and Zach shot down three more.

"Damn, you're pretty good for the advanced class!" Steven smiled while holding a robotic thumbs up to Zach. Zach smiled back with a snicker.

"Thanks, you're not too bad yourself robot boy."

Hunter ran to Zach's aid, calling for Iris. Iris, though out of breath, ran over and began healing Zach. Zach winked at her when she looked up at him, causing her to blush and look right back down at her hands. While Iris was healing, dozens of shadow snakes burst out of the ground and crept at the group. Zach shot countless lasers at them, but they were too nimble and little for him to hit. However, an advanced girl stomped on the ground a couple of feet away from them, and her stomp created a wave of air pressure that killed all the snakes.

"Thanks Rose," Hunter said before high-fiving her. The girl grinned and looked over at the injured Daniel.

"Ugh, I hope he's okay! He charged in blindly!" Rose complained.

Rose Valington, Strength: Stomp—when she stomps her foot on the ground, she can create powerful waves of energy that shoot in all directions. She can only stomp to activate them, and how hard she stomps computes the power of the waves.

"Iris, go help Foul Odor! If he goes down, we're screwed!" Scarlett yelled while hiding in the stands. Iris gulped then slowly made her way over to the knocked-out Foul. She began healing him while crouching in hiding next to the stage. After a few seconds, Foul opened his eyes and jumped up. He ran to Kane and swung a kick, but Kane ducked and swung his fist, punching Foul's airborne leg and throwing him back. Foul flipped over in the air and landed on his hands, then pushed hard and jumped back onto his feet. After dodging a few crows, Catastrophe grabbed Kane's head and smashed it into the ground, but a leopard jumped out of Kane's chest and tackled Catastrophe. Yet, Catastrophe had enough time to activate his strength on Kane again.

"Fuck you, Catastrophe, and your stupid strength! You will never be anything in this damn hellhole of a world!" Kane erupted. He created dozens upon dozens of crows that swarmed the few actual heroes on the stage, then threw a knife he had picked up from David at Catastrophe. It stabbed through Catastrophe's stomach, causing him to fall over while shaking. A giant acid spiderweb fell on top of Kane, burning his skin. David was thrown into the air by an electric explosion and Jon collided into him at high speeds, sending him crashing between the stage and the spectator seats. Foul managed to fight off the crows around him and stomped onto Kane's back, who coughed up blood and wheezed for air.

"You're through Kane. Stand down," Foul Odor stated while releasing his purple stench. Kane tensed his fist and clenched his jaw so hard his face turned red.

He screeched, "David, *kaboom!*" David's eyes turned from bloodshot red to all black, and he marched toward the stage with a giant smile.

"Boom, boom, boom," David chanted. He opened his mouth, and countless grenades poured onto the ground, all ready to be detonated. David hacked up a large bomb, and when he threw it up, blood fell from his mouth onto the wires, detonating it. *"Boom, boom, boom!"* Everyone nearby began running away, but there were still some students knocked out and others severely injured. There was too much commotion for anyone to escape, then every explosive blew up. The explosion sent a quake for miles and the entire arena was damaged. It was so damaged, in fact, that the ceiling cracked and started crumbling. David grabbed Kane and hid under the stage while Kane created giant manta rays to cover them from the falling debris. Within a couple seconds, the entire ceiling fell.

Chapter 8
Real Combat

Tonuko's stomach dropped when the ground broke, and the sound of the wind as the three fell was deafening. Suddenly, a bright light swooped in and grabbed the three, then they hit the wall hard. Tonuko looked up and was met with Alex's bloody face.

"Alex, you're alive?!" Kate screamed with relief. Alex smiled, pushed off the wall, let go of the three, and fell to the ground. He was breathing heavily and one of his wings was bent a weird way. The bright sky contrasted the dark environment around them, and a faint light grew in the distance. Tonuko heard a click, then torches all around the box they were in lit up. The concrete walls were pale black; the floor was still a rough dirt and gravel mix. Across the large room in front of the four was a grand, golden throne. In the throne sat the horrifying creature who stole Hazel, and next to its thrown was his accomplice.

Anya's eyes welled as she stared at the man, who in return was equally shocked at seeing her.

"D- Dad?" Anya whimpered before standing. Anya's dad took a step forward, then the Creature's arm stretched out and stopped him.

"Don't even think about it, Lokel. That's not your daughter anymore, remember? You're a part of my lovely family now, not that braindead hero's!"

Lokel took a deep breath and nodded. As he sighed, his facial expression swiftly changed from distraught to stern. The Creature's stomach grumbled, so it reached its hand toward the group. Alex grabbed Tonuko's arm and pulled him out of the way. The Creature reached into an inground pool behind the four and pulled out a large, live cod fish. Its arm was quickly sucked back toward its body and returned to its normal length. The Creature then opened its large jaws, revealing sharp, red-stained teeth. It ripped off the fish's head and gulped it down before continuing with the rest of the body. "Ah, much better!"

"That was fucking disgusting ... what am I even looking at?" Tonuko stuttered with a shaky voice. Alex held his shoulder, then revealed bite marks.

"I don't know what that thing is, but don't let him near you. We need to escape quickly; it moves fast and is unpredictable with those rubber limbs," Alex informed the group as he breathed deeply.

The white stripes on the Creature's arms faded to a rich magenta, then it stood and cracked its fingers. The Creature's arms stuck into the ground and it launched itself at terrifying speeds toward the group. Tonuko stomped his foot on the ground, bending the dirt in front of the group upward and creating a thick wall between the soaring Creature and the group. In an instant, the Creature maneuvered above the wall, stuck both hands into the ground on either side of Tonuko, and threw itself into him. Tonuko crashed into the ground along with the Creature. While Tonuko was down, the Creature injected him with a purple liquid through the claws on its hands.

"Tonuko!" Anya shouted while crafting her gauntlets again. To her and Kate's surprise, a bright light shone and the two were swept off their feet before the Creature stabbed them.

"Look at that Lokel, my poison worked! In no time, these four will be my little puppets!" Alex's already purple eyes glowed brighter and Tonuko's yellow eyes faded to a bright magenta. Lokel stood stiff and sweated while looking at his daughter. He didn't fight or argue, he quietly stayed in his place.

After the students fully converted to the kidnappers' side because of the poison, I burst a hole through the wall behind the fish tank and stood in the opening with Hazel.

Directly After Kyle's Fall:

I hit the ground hard and groaned in agony. My back was broken and my head was pounding. After around a minute, my body swelled with a deep, rich darkness. I couldn't see for a moment, then my pain went away. I was scared, but happy to feel no pain after falling such a distance. My eyes adjusted to the darkness and I could see vague silhouettes moving on the walls around me. My stomach dropped, then I heard a familiar voice call out, "Please, whoever's there! Let us free!"

Wait a minute, is that-?

"Hazel?!" I shouted while frantically looking around. "Is that you?!" I heard chains rattling, as well as moans and groans—ranging from children to adults—crying out for help. I ran around blindly, then heard her voice directly to my right. I ran to her and broke the chains that attached her to the wall. Hazel fell and breathed deeply through her wheezes.

"Holy shit, what did they do to you?!" I asked.

"Y- You don't wanna know. For now, we need to get out of here and alert authorities that all the kidnapped people have been found."

I hesitated then stated, "No, we have to save Alex first. The kidnappers got him too, he was taken by one of their traps."

We heard the loud commotion of the Creature fighting Tonuko, and then a massive explosion went off miles above us.

"Alright, but let's hurry. That explosion can't be good."

"Yeah, it must be the Care-Givers. David and Kane attacked the arena before we left," I explained while looking upward, though I couldn't see anything because it was so dark. Hazel took another minute to gain the energy to stand, then we walked toward where we heard the commotion. I wound back my fist and punched through the wall.

Through the hole, I saw my classmates sitting around while the Creature laughed at them. Confused, I shouted, "What the hell are you doing?! Come on, Tonuko, stay focused!" To my surprise, a bright beam of light zoomed at my face, and Alex tackled me to the ground. "Alex, what are you-?!" Alex punched at my face but I caught his hand and rolled over on top of him, restraining him. "Snap out of it!"

"Kyle, something is up with them! Their eyes all changed color!" Hazel informed me while backing up to Alex and me. I looked back and saw the other three slowly approaching, then looked back at Alex and quickly thought.

I need to get whatever is controlling them out of their system. It must be about the same thing the Creature used to make Hazel pass out, so some kind of liquid. Maybe, if I use Infection, I can suck the juice out of their bloodstream and allow them to regain consciousness!

My fingertips lost all color, and small, extremely thin white tubes seeped out of my fingernails and crept toward Alex. My eyes also lost all color as I stared at the struggling Alex. I could see faint purple cells swirling around his bloodstream.

Kyle Straiter, Strength Six: Infection—this strength can create tubes out of Kyle's fingernails that act as syringes to take out any bacterial cells found in a person's bloodstream. This strength also allows Kyle to see any system of the body and any infectious cells. This strength has been used by doctors in this society to see infectious diseases such as cancer cells.

When the tubes were mere inches from Alex's heart, we were both thrown into the air by a dirt pillar, then I was punched in the back by Anya, who had built more rock gloves. I wheezed and was sent flying into the ceiling, which was much closer than I anticipated. My head spun as I fell, but Hazel caught me and swept Tonuko and Kate off their feet.

Hazel and I backed away from the group, then Hazel whispered, "I don't know what that strength was, but if it's gonna stop them from being controlled, then use it." I looked at Hazel and nodded.

"Can you promise you won't tell anyone about my other strengths? This stays between us, right?" I asked earnestly. Hazel nodded while taking a deep breath; this meant I would be able to fight unrestrained. I smirked as I cracked my knuckles, then crouched and put my hands on the ground. My Infection tubes stuck into the ground, then four replicas of me rose from the dirt on my left; they were all connected to Infection tubes.

The clones charged at the mind-controlled four and dodged their attacks. I ran in directly behind them and tackled Kate. She struggled on the ground, but I was able to easily overpower her and stick an Infection tube in her chest. The tube sucked out all of the poison in her blood system, allowing her real conscious to reawaken. Kate blinked a few times, then looked around in a dazed state. I smiled at her and said, "Morning sunshine!" Right after those words left my mouth, Tonuko tackled me off of her. We rolled a few feet and before I stopped I morphed a clone out from underneath him that grabbed and wrapped itself around his body.

I've got him now. With Tonuko and Kate back on my side, I'll be able to get Alex and Anya out of that state in no time. Thank the Lord nobody is dead.

One of my clones managed to restrain and convert Anya. To my surprise Tonuko destroyed the grasp of my other clone before his transformation could be completed. The ground suddenly burst into a giant square underneath me, sending me flying across the room. I crashed into the far wall and slid down, then saw to my right a very malnourished boy, who looked no older than the rubber girl from earlier. I was determined to save these kids; I could only imagine what they'd been through. Considering how the Pete guy I'd encountered reacted when talking about leaving and being free, I assumed these kidnapped people would be used as henchmen for the two bosses. I stood but was struggling to stay upright and the world was slowly spinning around me.

I've gotta convert Tonuko and Alex quickly. I don't know how much longer I can stay conscious, but I still have to beat the kidnappers and the Care-Givers too. Oh man, it's gonna be a long day.

White tubes crawled out of all my fingers on both hands, then I charged at Tonuko. Alex tried to ram me out of the way, but Anya punched him with a dirt glove, sending him crashing backward. To my surprise, Anya shouted, "Come on, Kyle, save him!"

I ran at Tonuko, ducked under the pillars he sent toward my face, then grabbed him and body slammed him into the ground. He swung a punch at me, but I grabbed his fist and bashed my forehead into his. Tonuko was stunned, allowing me to finish the conversion. Tonuko blinked a couple times, then groaned and held his head.

"Fuck, you didn't have to headbutt me so damn hard!" he complained but grinned immediately after. I chuckled, then stood and held out a hand to him.

He took it and stood, then I stated, "As soon as I convert Alex, we can go and beat those kidnappers! Let's do this ... together." I held out a hand to him as I smirked. He smiled with his eyes closed and shook my hand, but then we heard:

"GUYS, WATCH OUT!" Hazel screeched while throwing her demon arm at us. I turned my head and was met with Alex's hand covered in light as it stabbed through my body. He punctured through next to my stomach and

135

pushed his hand out the other side. I coughed blood and hunched over after he ripped his hand out of me.

"Alex, you bastard!" Tonuko yelled while punching Alex in the face. Alex stumbled back, then lunged at Tonuko. Tonuko and Alex fell, then Alex stood over him and held out his hand with the intention of blasting Tonuko with a laser of light. Before he could, I swiftly tackled him. We rolled on the ground then I threw him into the wall next to me—the one that separated us from the kidnappers.

"Tonuko, trap him!" I shouted. Tonuko moved quickly, and wrapped dirt mixed with rocks from the ground around Alex, successfully trapping him. Since he couldn't move, I was able to convert Alex from his mind-controlled state. At this point, Alex's head gushed blood, one of his wings was broken, and his right arm was soaked with my blood. He panted as he glanced around, then he looked at me with complete shock as Tonuko freed him.

"Kyle, I'm so sorry," he whimpered while walking toward me. He hugged me and I returned it while wheezing.

"D- Don't worry about it Alex. It wasn't your f- fault," I stuttered, then I looked back at everyone else. "You all should get back to the arena and-" Before I could finish, we heard a monstrous explosion that caused dirt to rain down from the ceiling. "Get back to the arena and provide backup there. I'll take care of these guys."

"Kyle, are you mad? We're not leaving you alone to take on two villains when you're that injured. We should get you to the surface safely and inform any heroes or police around the area that we found the kidnappers' base," Kate argued.

I stood my ground. "By the time the Care-Givers are defeated these kidnappers will be long gone. It's now or never. I'll be fine, a little cut won't be the end of me." I turned to walk toward the hole in the wall to meet the kidnappers, but Tonuko interjected.

"How about we send Alex to the surface, since he can fly, and the rest of us will fight down here? We know the kidnappers' powers so we can adjust accordingly. We don't need to defeat the kidnappers, just stall long enough for backup to arrive," he suggested. Although I really wanted to beat down the kidnappers myself, I agreed along with everyone else.

We ran out into the main room where the kidnappers sat. The Creature clapped and giggled. "Well done, Kyle Straiter, very well done! You are so interesting; I can't wait to take you!" the Creature snarled.

Hazel told Alex to go, so he charged up and flew into the sky as fast as he could. "Oh no you don't!" The Creature roared while sending its arms flying into the wall. It sling-shotted itself at Alex, but I used flames to jump high and fast into the sky. I intercepted the Creature and crashed into it. We were both falling toward the ground, but I managed to get another kick in before Hazel caught me. The Creature soared into its throne and broke clean through it.

"Nice one Kyle!" Kate cheered while I was being lowered.

The Creature shot up from the rubble while facing away from us, then turned and looked straight at me. "Lokel, I want you to get Kyle! I'll provide backup by taking out the others!" Lokel and Anya met eyes, then Lokel closed his eyes and nodded.

"Yes, sir."

Lokel put his hands on the ground and formed two swords. He held them by his waist as rock boots formed around his feet. The boots had springs in the back sole that allowed him to produce super-jumps without a jump-increasing strength. They also let him run faster than usual.

Lokel charged at me and tossed one of his swords. Confused, I grabbed it out of the air, then our blades collided. The rock was strong and surprisingly sharp. "I used metal alloys from the ground to form sharpened rock swords," Lokel explained while locking eyes with me. My stomach was hurting badly from Alex's stab, but I ignored the pain and smirked at Lokel.

"Interesting, also an interesting strategy to give your foe a weapon. Respectable, but risky," I expressed aloud. Lokel smirked back at me, but I stopped his smile by asking, "So tell me, why would you leave your family for this kind of a life?"

"What the fuck would you know about family?!" Lokel angrily erupted while pushing his sword into mine. I stumbled back, then he spun around and swung his sword at my head. I deflected with my sword in my right hand and spun it around a few times while backing up. To my left, Tonuko was holding off the Creature.

"Everyone, just hold them off until backup arrives!" Tonuko demanded.

I rolled my eyes and leapt in for another attack. Lokel and I clashed swords a few times, then I landed a cut. I sliced a gash across Lokel's cheek. It wasn't deep but it was enough to anger him. Lokel threw his sword at me and it exploded mid-air into countless pebbles. I held my arms up to cover my eyes from the barrage of rocks, then I was tackled off my feet. It wasn't a regular tackle though; Lokel used his boost-shoes to send us flying across the room. I landed on my back, then Lokel flipped me over, knelt on my back, and grabbed the back of my head. He pushed my head straight into the pool of fish. I opened my eyes and saw fish swim away. I tried to get up, but I couldn't. Lokel was creating a thick barrier of rocks from his shoes, making it impossible for me to move from my position.

Fuck, I can't hold my breath for very long. If I stay like this, I'll drown.

I struggled and splashed around, but Lokel didn't budge. He gripped my head tighter and pushed his kneecap into my stab wound. I screamed underwater, then breathed and swallowed a mouthful of water. I began coughing and my lungs were burning.

"We have to get him off Kyle!" Hazel yelled while reaching for Lokel with her demon hand. The Creature swung around the wall Tonuko had created and threw itself at Hazel. Its legs stretched and wrapped around Hazel's neck, then it flipped and threw her into the sky. Hazel was already weak from her earlier kidnapping and spinning around while soaring through the air caused her to black out. Anya used her own boost-shoes to catch Hazel and she watched as her dad drowned me. I began feeling very heavy, and my peripheral vision faded.

I feel ... so weak. Please, someone save me.

At the Fallen Arena:

A laser wall held up a majority of the debris. Zach was breathing heavily down on one knee while his hands held up the laser wall. His arm muscles were bulging, and he was sweating bullets.

"C-C'mon guys, get out of here! I can't- hold on to this for much longer!" Zach gasped through his wheezes. Steven used his robot legs to run in and out of the fallen building, grabbing as many students as he could. A few others joined him, but only about ten students were brought out before the laser wall vanished and all the debris fell on the remaining students and civilians.

"Zach, no!" Hunter screamed while running toward the debris. He started throwing small pieces of the ceiling behind him, then saw a leg and pulled on it. Hunter dragged Daniel's unconscious body out from under a large pipe. He dropped the leg and put his hands over his mouth. Police sirens grew louder behind him, and ten police cars along with ten S.W.A.T. cars pulled up to the scene. A couple heroes jumped out of the cars along with dozens of police officers.

"We'll get the civilians from the rubble; you get to safety!" a hero commanded to Hunter. Hunter nodded and ran to a group of students. After the safe students were grouped, Alex soared into the sky from the pit next to the crashed building. He floated in the air like an angel, but then he tumbled down and crashed into the ground—he couldn't control his flying because of his broken wing.

"W- We have to send help down there. Kyle, Tonuko, Anya, Kate, and Hazel are fighting the kidnappers! They need help, Kyle might die!" Alex screamed as he slowly stood. A hero looked over, shocked.

"Y- You students found the kidnappers?! Are all the kidnapped people down there too?!" Alex nodded, then the hero looked back at the police cars. Out from one of the cars stepped Principal Lane and Vice Principal Kuntai.

Mrs. Kuntai looked at Alex, then stated, "We will not be sending any more of our students down in that hole. However, I want Daryll's unit to go and fetch our students who are already there!" Daryll was the head chief of the Veena police force. He had very long blonde hair and held an automatic rifle in his hands. Daryll nodded, then looked over at his unit of five police officers.

"Let's retrieve those students immediately. As of now, we will not be going for the kidnappers. Do you understand me?" His voice was deep and scratchy, as well as intimidating. The members of his unit nodded then ran over to the pit. Daryll peered over the edge, sighed through his nose, and looked back at one man in his squad. The man was already setting up a rope system so they could safely get down the hole. "Damn Kyle Straiter is down there. That boy has been nothing but trouble since the day his daddy ran away," Daryll seethed to himself. "I'll get you up here, Kyle, and get you fixed."

Meanwhile, other police officers set up a line of riot shields between them and the Care-Givers. A police officer shouted, "Expand!" then the shields grew to twenty times their original size. Kane regained his sense of sight, something he lost from Foul Odor, and David scooped up a pistol he had previously spat out. David aimed the pistol at Zach, who was crawling out of the rubble, and shot a round at him. Zach saw David shoot and retaliated with his own laser at the bullet. The laser sliced the bullet in half, impressing David.

Heroes stood in front of the riot shields now, ready to attack the Care-Givers. Kane smirked and cracked his neck. When the crack was audible, two giant hounds formed out of Kane's large shadow. The hounds pounced at the heroes and managed to take out two of the seven. The heroes in this city were known for being from the bottom of the barrel, so two Care-Givers would clearly be too much for them to handle on their own.

Lucky for them, Danielle Kuntai was there. Roots made of dirt crawled out from the cracks in the cement and wrapped around both hounds' legs. The roots seeped up the hounds, causing them to whimper. When the roots were all over the hounds' bodies, they squeezed, killing the hounds. "Ugh, those things were seriously grossing me out," Danielle cringed while taking out her ponytail.

Danielle Kuntai, Strength: Root—she can bend dirt into cylinder shapes, hence the roots, and manipulate them in any way she can think or move with her hands. The roots can only be made of dirt, can dig through stone, and can seep through any hole no matter the size.

"Mrs. Kuntai, please let us go down in the pit to help our friends!" Cindy pleaded. Seeing Alex so injured worried her about the state of the rest of us. Mrs. Kuntai shook her head, but her eyes watered.

"Trust me Cindy, I'm just as worried as you are. I don't even want to imagine what could be happening to my baby boy ... but I will not allow heroes-in-training to be sent into a life-threatening situation." She looked over at Jon and Devin, who were both inching toward the pit. "That goes for you two as well! Nobody is entering that pit except Daryll's squadron!"

"You're such a bummer!" Jon groaned while trudging away from the pit. He leapt into the air above the police officers and unleashed an electric attack on Kane and David. Bolts of lightning shot out at the two Care-Givers and created a mini explosion on impact. David was thrown into the sky, but he landed on a newly created hawk that was flying through the air.

David grinned devilishly, then gagged out another assault rifle. He unloaded on the cops on the ground while screaming, "Thanks for the help kid, now I have a clear shot on these coppers!" Devin calculated swiftly, then intercepted the hawk with a small acid web. The hawk vaporized, sending David falling to the ground. David reacted swiftly while still in the air and coughed up another grenade. He chucked the grenade, pulling the pin as he let go, and it fell into the center of the group of cops. It exploded, sending chunks of men and women flying everywhere.

"Students, you should get out of here. Go back to the hotel, this is a horrific fight. I don't want you seeing this!" Principal Lane ordered while stepping in front of the small group of uninjured students.

"Principal Lane, we can help the heroes! We know enough to fight these Care-Givers! Who knows, maybe we can take them down!" Camilla exclaimed with passion.

"No, it's way too dangerous for freshmen!" Principal Lane snapped. Camilla sulked, then, to their right, they heard Tonuko's screams.

"Medics, we need medics, dammit! Help!" In Tonuko's hands was an unconscious Kate. Anya followed, carrying Hazel over her shoulder.

"W- Wait, where's Kyle?!" Steven yelled. Tonuko looked down and shook his head, then marched toward his mom.

"Mom, we need medics urgently! Kate is badly hurt!" Mrs. Kuntai nervously looked at Kate, then nodded and called for the medics who had just arrived.

In the Pit, Moments Before:

I woke coughing up water and gasped for air for a few seconds. Kate was kneeling next to me and pumping on my chest. She stopped C.P.R. when she saw I had awoken.

"Thank the Lord you woke up Kyle! We thought we lost you!" Kate cried as she hugged me tight. I hugged her back, then slowly stood. My adrenaline kicked in, alleviating most of the pain I'd felt.

The Creature grabbed the sword I had dropped then lunged at me. I dodged it but it was clear I wasn't its intended target. The Creature stabbed Kate through her stomach and a loud crack echoed before the blade pierced through her back. Kate immediately fell to the ground. My eyes widened. The Creature cackled loudly and licked the blood off the sword's blade.

"Down goes one, down goes one, *down goes one!*" it repeated.

N- No, why did you stab her? Don't you want me, why would you hurt her? Take me instead, stop hurting my friends.

I yelled out angrily and tackled the Creature. It continued giggling as we rolled on the ground, but I kicked its stomach, knocking the wind out of it and finally shutting it up. The Creature soared into the air, then I leapt up at it and kicked it into a wall. The entire mountain side rumbled, then the Creature stretched its hands and launched them at me. The hands flew past my face, then stuck into the wall behind me. The Creature pulled itself at me swiftly and we collided. We both began falling to the ground, but the Creature used its arms to swing to safety. Meanwhile, I landed on a hard concrete pillar Tonuko had created to save me from falling to my death.

"Kyle, you gotta relax! We'll get her to safety! You are on the verge of death; you need to conserve your energy. Help is comin-" Tonuko said, trying to calm me.

"*I don't give a damn about the help coming! This bastard is killing my friends, so **I'll kill him!** He's not gonna hurt another person, I swear!*" I screeched furiously. Tonuko was shocked as he began lowering me to the ground. Lokel leapt at me again and we started fist fighting.

"*Kyle doesn't sound like what he did just a day ago. He was yelling before about how he would beat the kidnappers and him this and he that, but now, he's saying he's going to defend his friends. I see you Kyle, I see you!*" Tonuko thought.

I had successfully thrown Lokel into the wall, then landed in front of Tonuko and turned to face him. I put my hands on his shoulders and looked him dead in the eyes.

"Tonuko, take Anya, and Kate, and Hazel and get the fuck out of here!" I demanded.

"Are you crazy?! I don't know what goes on inside that head, but I'm not leaving you here to die!" I closed my eyes as I shouted in response.

"Tonuko, my life is worth so much less than all of yours! I don't have a real reason to keep going, but you all do! Don't let me be the reason you die, get out of here with yours and everyone else's lives, dammit!" Tonuko was completely stunned. He had no response. Tonuko stood looking at my frantic face for a few more seconds, then nodded his head.

"Alright, but when you make it out of here alive and a hero, we're gonna talk about what you just said." I nodded, not really hearing what he said, then turned back to the two kidnappers. Tonuko grabbed Anya's wrist and told her to get Hazel. The Creature was going to stop them, but Lokel grabbed his shoulder.

"Let them go, it's fine. We have the Kyle Straiter here and weakened. We'll get a much greater compensation for having the son of Tyrant rather than a bunch of nobodies," Lokel explained quietly. The Creature stopped moving forward and smiled widely.

"A wise man you are, Lokel." Lokel smiled, then looked at Anya and frowned.

"Goodbye, my darling. I love you," Lokel yelled to Anya. Anya stopped in her tracks, but didn't turn around. She instead continued walking away with Tonuko. Tonuko was carrying Kate and Anya was carrying Hazel, then Tonuko created a large pillar and sent the four up toward the surface. That left me alone with the two kidnappers.

"Come and get me," I snarled while standing defensively. I didn't notice right away, but my arms and legs had grown slightly more muscular, and my hands up to my forearms had a darker tint to them ...

Chapter 9
Two Equals Four

I stood in a face-off for a few moments with the kidnappers, then Lokel ran at me again. He pounded me with punches, but I dodged each one and caught his fist on the last punch.

"You miss your daughter, don't you Lokel?" I asked, trying to connect with him. Lokel became angry again and pulled his fist toward himself. He headbutted me, but my head was so hard it hurt him more than it hurt me. "You want to reconnect with your wife too, right?"

"Shut it, Straiter! You don't know me, so stop acting like you do!" Lokel yelled. He dragged his hand on the ground, creating a glove around his fist, and punched at me. I threw my left arm up to block the punch, but his glove was so dense it broke my arm and sent me flying to my right. I crashed into the concrete wall and my head bled.

I was fed up with his denial, so I screamed, "Snap out of it, you're her father! You should be there for her, not hide away with this creep! Help me beat the Creature, then we can both go and face everyone, face our families!" Lokel's eyes widened and the glove crumbled off his hand.

He's so similar to me. He can't face reality; he can't face the fact that he's not stuck in villainy. Lokel can get out of it though, he's not too far gone!

"Come on Lokel, work with me!" I shouted while holding out my hand. Lokel looked at me and walked toward me. I could tell this made the Creature frantic.

"Lokel, you're with me! Don't listen to Tyrant's son, he's a manipulator just like his father!" the Creature screeched. Lokel seemed to ignore the Creature and continued walking toward me.

Sadly, Lokel created two more swords and tossed one to me again. Our swords clashed, creating large sparks that flew out everywhere. We were sword fighting like before, but his movements were slower. Maybe I was moving faster, but I could predict what his moves were going to be before they occurred. After a few clashes, we each charged at the other. Lokel hopped off the back wall on the opposite side of me and super-jumped at my head. I slid underneath him, and let my sword do all the work. The edges were burning because of my flaming hands, and the sword cut a deep, large gash from Lokel's forehead down to his waist. Lokel crashed into the wall behind me and fell onto his back. He was breathing heavily and staring up at the bright sky.

What did I do? Oh fuck, there's no way I just killed him. Please God, don't let him be dead!

"Lokel!" I cried while running toward his body. The Creature was laughing in the background, but I ignored him and slid to Lokel's side. I held Lokel's head on my right forearm as my tears dripped onto my lap. "Lokel, I'm so sorry. I didn't mean to cut you, I thought I would miss. Oh fuck, what did I do?" Lokel reached his hand up and my wiped tears away.

"Kyle, you did nothing wrong. I purposefully acted recklessly so you would kill me. I can't face Anya, I just can't do it. Anya and Beth, they don't deserve the suffering I've put them through ..."

"Don't give up on me, dammit! You can still go apologize; you have to! You owe it to her!" I screamed at him. Lokel was now crying as well, and his smile was gone.

"K- Kyle man, I didn't want to go. I loved my family so damn much; they were my everything. That thing kidnapped me, and he threatened to kill my family if I left. I- I had no choice! You have to believe me; they have to believe me!" Lokel sounded desperate now and tears poured down his cheeks.

147

"They'll only believe you if you tell them! We can make it out, I can get you to a healer and-"

"I won't make it in time. You still have to defeat that thing so no other family has to go through what mine did." Lokel could see the uncertainty in my face so he continued, "You're a great kid Kyle. I'd be proud to be your father. Just, let Anya know that I loved her with all my heart."

"Don't you die on me, dammit," I shakily demanded. Lokel weakly reached to the ground and pulled out a sword. He handed it to me with a smile.

"As long as I'm breathing, I'll help you beat that thing. You got it, I believe in you." His words gave me courage. I stood and gripped the sword tight. My arms faded to a pitch black, and lightning roared around my body. I shut the Creature's laughing up by leading with a knee to his face. The Creature crashed into the wall above its fish pool, then I led in with my sword and stabbed through the Creature's stomach.

"*I'll make you pay!*" I screamed with all my might. The Creature gasped when the sword pierced its body, and it kicked me off. Its leg stayed connected to me as his pushed me into the wall across the room. I rose my arm above my head, then sliced off the Creature's foot. It squealed like an animal and the remainder of its leg shot back at the Creature's body like a tape measurer. The Creature was wobbly now and blood was pouring out of its amputated foot. When I gripped the wall behind me, a large crater exploded out of it. I jumped at lightning speed at the Creature and it flung itself at me, screaming psychotically while it did so. I swung the sword at it, but the sword crumbled when it hit the Creature, doing no damage. I fell to the ground and tumbled a few feet, but I wasn't done. I turned around as a thick mist seeped off me and charged up my final attack.

I combined my fire power, which for some reason was gray now, with as much super strength as I could muster. My right arm absorbed all the darkness on my body and grew to three times its original size. I leapt at the Creature and collided into it within the blink of an eye. I punched the Creature in the head, and as I swung down, I felt its skull cave in. When its head hit the ground, a large explosion occurred. I was thrown into the air, then landed hard several dozen feet away. The explosion created a mini mushroom cloud along with a bright light. Lokel's body hit the wall again at high speeds, finishing him off.

Kyle Straiter, Strength One

I could barely keep my eyes open—one of them was bloodshot and the other was heavily swollen—but I still managed to crawl over to Lokel. I cried as I reached his body and yelled for him to keep fighting.

"Don't leave me, Lokel, don't leave her! Fuck, I'm so sorry Anya! I'm so sorry!" I cried out. My crying was interrupted by a hand smashing my head into the ground.

"Quit your wailing for God's sake!" Daryll yelled while kneeling on my back. I continued to cry, so Daryll screamed, "Shut the fuck up you annoying runt!" Daryll punched me in the back of my head with the barrel of his gun. All the adrenaline faded, making the pain of my injuries flood me all at once.

"Captain, please relax! Let's get him and these bodies to the surface!" a lady interrupted while looking down at Lokel.

"Shut yer mouth! Kyle Straiter, did you murder these two?!" Daryll screamed. I nodded, then he took out handcuffs and cuffed me. "Did you also murder the Nomeres?! We found a brother and sister dead in a tunnel, was that your doing?!" I thought for a moment because it wasn't. Tonuko and Anya killed the little girl, and they left Pete behind. However, I nodded, taking the blame for their murder. "You've killed four people today Kyle, *four fucking people!* You're just like your daddy, a criminal scumbag!"

149

Daryll grabbed the back collar of my shirt, picked me up, and slammed me into the ground again. "Hero in training my ass! You are a good-for-nothing waste of oxygen! You're lucky I don't kill you right now and say you died to one of these two *worthless assholes!*"

"You shut the fuck up!" I erupted while kicking Daryll across the room. I hopped to my feet, still handcuffed, and continued gasping for air as I yelled, "Lokel was forced into this because he was kidnapped! He loves his family so much, so keep his name out of your dirty mouth! How come on the first day here, my friends and I found the kidnappers while you and your squadron did jack-all! Fuck you!" Daryll stood then shot me twice. He shot my thigh and my shoulder, successfully taking me down.

"Let's go everyone, take that asshole and these other assholes to the surface!" Daryll marched across the room and stomped on my stomach. "Don't ever touch me again, you worthless runt." The lady who interrupted before gingerly picked me up and harnessed me to herself, then began the climb back up the rope. That climb was the longest ten minutes of my life.

On the Surface:

David and Kane were at a standstill with Danielle and Principal Lane, along with Foul Odor, who had woken. Since Foul's stench was decreasing the Care-Giver's strengths, David and Kane couldn't land a solid hit. David vomited a puddle of blood for the fourth time before he yelled, "Kane, let's leave! I can't keep going, I'll die!" Kane sighed and agreed.

A portal formed behind the two and Kane waved as they passed through. Foul ran at the portal, trying to stop them, but it was gone as quickly as it formed. Some who were conscious cheered that the Care-Givers were gone, but many were worried about the injured. Heroes and police alike rescued the injured from the collapsed building. About the time the hurt students and civilians were rescued

Daryll's squadron came back to the surface with me and the lifeless four.

"Mrs. Kuntai and Mr. Lane, your student is hereby under arrest for the murder of four legal citizens. He will be tried in front of the Seven Influential as an Angel Criminal," the woman officer informed Principal Lane and Vice Principal Kuntai.

"We understand," Principal Lane concisely stated.

"Anya, Anya, I'm so sorry!" I yelled to Anya, who was crying while looking at her deceased father. Tonuko hugged her tight, then looked over at me with soft, understanding eyes. "Fuck, I'm so sorry! I didn't mean to, I swear! He loved you so fucking much, he was forced into villainy! Please Anya, believe him! He loved you!" I was quickly cut off by Daryll.

"Didn't I say to shut your mouth?!" Daryll hit me with the butt of his gun again, causing my blood to splatter. Tonuko was infuriated by this and had to be held back by Jon.

"What the hell do you think you're doing?! That's a hero you're hitting!" Tonuko roared at Daryll. He walked away, chuckling to himself. Daryll escorted me to a police car and began filling out paperwork.

I'm a murderer, a complete failure. I'm sorry everyone, I failed ...

My knees were weak, and my vision was shaky and hazy. After a minute or two, I collapsed onto the street, completely unconscious. I was carried to an ambulance and driven to the nearest hospital.

"If that jerk goes to jail, I swear I'll kick his ass!" Tonuko yelled furiously. He turned around and kicked a rock a dozen feet away, then looked over at the pit. "*I trusted you Kyle, you said you could handle it. What happened down there? Why is Anya's dad dead?*" Tonuko was dying to ask me questions but knew he might never be able to.

Alex sat in the back of an ambulance while a nurse taped up his mangled wing. He took a deep breath, then an officer he recognized approached him. "Officer Daniels?" Alex asked. One of Alex's eyes was swollen shut and blood covered his face.

"Alex, it's a shame to see you like this. We found your teacher down the street, but it turns out she's a fresh Care-Giver. Diana Palkun was an alias; her real name is Angelica Haslem, otherwise known as Lady Patch." Alex's eye widened, then Officer Daniels handed him a paper. "She's been taken into custody, but we found this on her. Please make sure to give this to your principal whenever you see him." Officer Daniels ruffled Alex's hair and gave him a big smile. "I hope I can have dinner with your family again soon so I can see you in a better condition. Rest up, big guy." Officer Daniels left, and Alex opened the folded paper.

"Hey Alex, what's that?" Tonuko asked while walking over along with Anya, Camilla, Jon, and Devin.

"It's Kyle's field trip permission form ... it says he lives at 10853 Western Sydney Drive. Isn't that the abandoned house in town?" Alex asked while looking up from the paper. Tonuko snatched the paper from Alex's hand, he couldn't believe his eyes.

"That house has been abandoned for like six and a half years. You're telling me Kyle has lived there all his life? And who's Gem Straiter?" Tonuko asked rhetorically. "*Kyle and Tyrant have some kind of a connection, he has multiple strengths and Tyrant erases strengths, the introduction said Kyle's parents are unknown, but his mom is Gem Straiter here on a school form, and Kyle has lived in an abandoned house for almost seven years? Something's up,*" Tonuko angrily speculated.

"What are you doing reading a personal paper?! Shame on all of you! Follow Vice Principal Kuntai back to the hotel immediately!" Principal Lane demanded after swiping the permission form out of Tonuko's hand. The uninjured students followed Vice Principal Kuntai down the street, and Principal Lane ran his hands through his flowing white hair.

"Mr. Lane, we need to send Alex Galeger to the emergency department for surgery on his wing immediately," a medic informed Principal Lane. He waved the medic off, signaling for the ambulance to take Alex.

"Mr. Lane, you're the principal of Kyle Straiter, correct?" a short, plump man in a black tuxedo asked while walking up to Principal Lane. His fat, red tie contrasted the white undershirt, and his hair was black and greased back. "I am George Johnson from the Villain Investigation Association (V.I.A.) and I'll need you to come with me for some questioning about relationships with Kyle Straiter."

"I'm sorry, but I'm only his principal. I do not know of his connections," Principal Lane lied.

"Wrong, you're lying. You can't get past me; my lie detector strength is unmatched. Please just come with me, we are on the same side for Kyle." Principal Lane reluctantly obliged and followed George to a black V.I.A. van. They drove off to the nearest V.I.A. station.

On the Way to the Hotel:

"Mom, when can we visit our hurt friends?" Tonuko asked. Mrs. Kuntai sighed as she put her hair back into a high ponytail.

"I'd guess you can visit your friends freely tomorrow, assuming they're awake. However, as for Kyle, you will most likely not be able to visit him since he is an Angel Criminal," Mrs. Kuntai explained.

"What's an Angel Criminal anyway?" Steven asked, completely confused.

"You are such a nimrod. Kyle is technically a murderer by law, but he killed four villains. With that in mind, he did what a legal hero would do, but he's not a legal hero yet. Even though he killed two of the most-wanted kidnappers in recent history, he still killed legal citizens. Multiple heroes have had things like this happen with crimes, and they're classified as 'Angel Criminals.' He will have to go in front of the Seven Influential," Khloe explained, cutting of Mrs. Kuntai before she could speak. Steven still looked lost, so Khloe sighed, "You don't know the Seven Influential?! They're the seven most-powerful heroes in our current society. They handle all Angel Criminal cases!"

"Oh, that makes way more sense. Thanks Khloe, you're the man!" Steven smiled as he softly punched her arm. Khloe rolled her eyes.

"If Kyle is found not guilty, he's free to continue training to be a hero. However, if he's guilty, well, that's the end of his hero career," Mrs. Kuntai informed the group solemnly.

Everyone went silent, then Devin stated, "He'll be not guilty." A couple people looked at Devin, confused on how he could be so certain.

"Yeah, that kid is pretty damn amazing. First off, they'll want him as a hero so he doesn't turn to a villain if he's jailed. On top of that, he just defeated the most elusive kidnappers of the century. That little man will be just fine," Jon chuckled while resting his hands behind his head. They reached the hotel as Jon finished, and Mrs. Kuntai turned to face the group.

"Very true, there's nothing to worry about. Now just try and get some sleep," Mrs. Kuntai concluded.

154

She'd begun walking back toward the fight scene when Tonuko blurted out, "Mom, do you know Gem Straiter?" Mrs. Kuntai stopped dead in her tracks and didn't give an answer. "It said in his introduction before our fight that Kyle's parents were unknown, but on a school official form it listed his mom as Gem Straiter. What's that all about? You guys do know his mom?"

"Tonuko, I will not give you personal information about another student. How did you even get that form?" Mrs. Kuntai retorted.

"An officer gave it to Alex. He said he got it from our evil teacher. It had Gem's signature and everything," Tonuko added.

"Her signature? How's that possible, she's-" Mrs. Kuntai stopped herself from finishing the sentence.

"Mom, is she dead?" Tonuko asked bluntly.

Those words hovered in the air.

Nobody knew how to respond, except Mrs. Kuntai. "I am not in any position to talk about Kyle's family," she stated. Tonuko tensed his fist, and his eyes watered.

"We already know he hasn't been telling any of us the truth! We know he has more than two strengths. All these villains know his full name and keep talking about bringing him 'back' to some guy! Hell, I wouldn't be surprised at this point if Kyle wasn't even fourteen! Can't we just be told the truth for once?! Can't you tell your own son something?"

Mrs. Kuntai looked wide-eyed at Tonuko. Tears brimmed from his eyes, then Anya hugged him and looked up at Mrs. Kuntai with her own watery eyes. "W- We're all scared. Please, just tell us something," Anya whimpered. Mrs. Kuntai took off her glasses and wiped her eyes. She put them back on, then cleared her throat.

155

"Listen, I know how worried and frightened you are, but I can't spread private things about Kyle to his classmates. That's for him to decide when he's ready to tell you."

"That's the thing, he'll never be ready! He keeps his emotions all bottled up and only bursts in small spurts of anger and frustration!" Camilla shouted. Mrs. Kuntai hesitated, and bit her lip.

"Alright, alright fine. Gem and I were best friends throughout high school, but she got with a man I couldn't agree with her dating. However, she was madly in love. As much as I hated the guy, they were adorable, a dream couple. Then, the bad came. She and I drifted. I found out she had passed ten years after graduation and Kyle was alone. I had the option of taking Kyle in, it's what Gem wanted if anything bad happened, but they couldn't get him out of the house and gave up. I honestly didn't know if he was alive until Fallen took Kyle under his wing years later," Mrs. Kuntai explained to the group.

"So that night, when we chased after him, he was getting the permission form and forged his mom signature," Cindy thought aloud.

"I guess so, but that's all I'll tell you. I've already said too much ..." Mrs. Kuntai bit her nail and looked around, lost in thought. She snapped out of it and looked at the group. "Get to bed, all of you! Don't you dare even *think* about wandering out of this hotel until morning!" She left, leaving the students confused.

"Something still isn't adding up. Where did his dad go?" Khloe asked rhetorically. Obviously, no one knew the answer—at least that's what they thought. In reality, Tonuko knew the answer.

"Everything's adding up. Kyle's mom died because bad things happened in her relationship with a man my mom didn't like, every criminal is trying to bring Kyle back

to a 'boss', *Tyrant knew him ...*" Tonuko thought with his hand on his chin. He knew the answer, and he was furious. Tonuko stomped off and went straight to his room. Everyone else shrugged it off and went to sleep.

Kyle's Mind:

I woke up in an abyss where I was floating. It felt as if I was in water but I could breathe. However, when I tried to speak, nothing came out. I looked around, very confused, then saw a man float out of the darkness. The man was Tyrant.

"Kyle, what is this? Is this your doing?" Tyrant asked, genuinely confused. I shrugged. He rubbed his chin while thinking out loud, "This must be one of your ten strengths. Anyway, I heard you killed Lokel and the Creature. Well done, well done indeed."

"*Shut your face,*" I thought. Apparently, he could hear the thought because he laughed. "*How do you already know I beat the kidnappers?*"

"My boss was watching with BloodShot. Along with always having eyes on me, I have eyes everywhere." My stomach dropped when he said this. My eyes opened so wide they hurt, and my head spun.

"*Y- Your boss? You're the most powerful villain in history, why do you have a boss? You never told me about a boss before!*"

"You see, Kyle, my boss is nothing but a child, a teenager in fact. He's three years younger than you, eleven years old. He is so strong, though, that he was immediately placed above me when his strength was developed. A new, horrifying, deadly strength. Son, just because I'm the mob boss of villains doesn't mean I can't be- be scared."

I was speechless—to think, the man I've hated, one I thought had no emotions, was afraid ... of a teenager.

157

"How can he be so strong? What the hell is his strength?"

"I believe it's called sickness, or ill or something along those lines. His name is Plague, and he is being trained under BloodShot and me. With one move, he can end the world as we know it. I will not give you the exact details, because I can't trust you, but if he was as careless as the Creature, we'd all be dead right now."

I still couldn't believe my ears. Someone that strong is alive? A sudden pounding filled our ears and my head felt as if it was about to explode. "Don't you dare tell anyone a word about Plague or I'll have BloodShot eliminate you! I'm fucking warning you Kyle!" I blinked a few times from the bright sunlight and opened my eyes. It was daytime and I could hear beeping from the heart monitor. I groaned in pain, but I was happy to be alive.

"Thank goodness you're awake," the doctor sitting at a desk next to me sighed. She was lanky, tan, and had big bags under her eyes. Her hair was long, brown, and curly.

"Wh- What day is it? What time is it?"

"It's Tuesday, September 2nd. It's about four days since you were brought in."

Shocked, I looked at her and yelled, "Four days?!"

"Keep your voice down please, and don't talk too much. You need to conserve your energy. You lost a lot of blood; you were just running on adrenaline and hysterical strength in that battle. Also, you have a hero visitor from a nearby city whenever you're ready." I nodded, and told the doctor to let the visitor in.

In walked a man wearing a red cloak and a plain, white mask with one eyehole. I couldn't see any of his face. The doctor walked out.

"Kyle Straiter, my favorite cocky son of a bitch! You surprised me; the Creature and Lokel weren't an easy duo to take down." The man's voice was easily recognizable. My heart hurt and I started hyperventilating. "Yes Kyle, it's me, BloodShot."

"I swear I haven't told anyone about Plague! I just woke up from a four-day coma!" He nodded, seemingly happy with my response.

"I know, that's not why I'm here. I just wanted to pay a visit to my future partner in crime. I saw the dark force unleashed inside you when Lokel died. Something is living in you, and it will take over your very soul when every single one of your friends die." I looked at him angrily and gripped the hospital bed sheets. "You will join me eventually, it's your destiny." I felt a shooting pain in my left arm, leading to my chest. I grasped my chest, then the heart monitor began beeping very fast. BloodShot let out a muffled, evil chuckle as he slowly backed up. The doctor rushed back into the room and yelled for nurses. BloodShot escaped easily, and I was given medicine that relaxed my heartbeat. A police officer walked in an hour later, took off his hat, and bowed.

"Kyle Straiter, you have a court date in front of the Seven Influential next Wednesday, September 10th. Your hero career will be decided on if you are not guilty and let free, or guilty and sent to jail."

I was terrified, more scared than any time I'd faced a villain. The reality was really setting in.

My hero career, over? It hasn't really even started yet!

"I- I understand ... sir." The police officer put his hat back on and sighed.

"I would also like to apologize for Daryll's behavior. I don't know what came over him, but it was unprofessional. Also, thank you for your service," the officer stated while giving me a smile. "Even if you are convicted as a murderer, you are a hero in the eyes of the families whose loved ones were returned to them. You are a hero, Kyle."

The man held out a photo of a boy whose black hair was in a bowl cut. I could vaguely recognize him as the malnourished boy I saw in the dark room. "My Logan is home because of you. Truly, from the bottom of my heart, thank you." The officer was tearing up, but he wiped his tears and composed himself.

"No need to thank me, it's what a person should do. I'm so happy to hear Logan is home safe now." The officer nodded with a smile, then left the room to go and talk with the front desk staff about the intruder.

I'm a hero ...

Back at the Hotel:

"Mom, it's been four days! Can we please go visit our friends now?!" Tonuko pleaded. Mrs. Kuntai sighed and shook her head.

"You heard to police: you aren't allowed to visit the hospital until Kyle is officially placed under arrest!" Mrs. Kuntai yelled. "I'm so tired of repeating myself Tonuko!"

"Actually, I managed to convince the police to let the kids in! You should be grateful Officer Daniels is such a good guy!" Principal Lane happily informed the group. Everyone was excited to see their friends, and Tonuko led the squad to the hospital. He reached the front desk at the same time as Principal Lane, and the man at the desk immediately knew who they were.

"Down that hall are all your students, Mr. Lane. You students are allowed to see everyone except Mr. Straiter. Only the principal and vice principal are allowed to see him." The slightly disappointed group didn't let what they'd already known get them down. Jon immediately went to Kate's room, Devin found Hazel's room, and the rest went down the hall one room at a time. Alex's room was the first that they entered.

"Alex! I'm so happy you're okay!" Cindy squealed while running up to hug him. Alex hugged her back, then looked over at Tonuko. He gave Tonuko a smirk, then held out his fist.

"We did it, we did it," Alex said, sounding both relieved and proud. Tonuko grinned, then fist-bumped Alex.

"Hell yeah we did." People questioned Alex; Tonuko stayed silent.

Tonuko's rage at me was growing by the minute, and not being able to talk to me, maybe ever again, to find out why I lied was pissing him off even more. Tonuko and his friends visited everyone else; they even checked on Kate and Hazel. When Tonuko entered Kate's room, the environment was completely different than earlier. Jon and Kate were embracing each other while crying, and Principal Lane and Mrs. Kuntai were sullen and teary-eyed. "Wh-What's the matter? Are you going to be okay Kate?" Tonuko asked, concern lingered heavily in his voice.

"*I'mnotgoingtobeahero,*" Kate admitted through her hyperventilating. Tonuko stared blankly and balled his fists. Though she said it like gibberish, he deciphered what she was saying.

"The doctor said that a section of Kate's spine was shattered. She will never walk again," Mrs. Kuntai explained while taking off her glasses.

"But Kate was a top prospect of her class, top twenty in the country. This can't be it!" Tonuko exclaimed. His mother hushed him and gave him a hug. Tonuko never cried, but he felt like something was lodged in his throat. After a few more minutes of comforting Kate, Principal Lane and Mrs. Kuntai left for my room. "Why are you guys allowed in there but we aren't?!" Tonuko asked angrily.

Mrs. Kuntai shushed him again, but more aggressively this time.

"Tonuko, we are in a hospital!" She whisper–yelled. Tonuko stayed silent, allowing her to explain. "Since we are his principal and vice principal, we are allowed inside briefly to talk to Kyle before he is sent to jail. Have a little respect for him, he is in a very dark place right now!" Tonuko rolled his eyes, stuck his hands in his pockets, and walked away.

Mrs. Kuntai shook her head with a stressed expression, then turned to Principal Lane. He gave her a slight smile and shrugged, then Mrs. Kuntai walked past him into my room.

"Oh, I didn't think anyone from school could visit me," I stated when the two walked in. Principal Lane waved to me, then gave me a handshake before he and Mrs. Kuntai sat in the chairs by my bed.

"How are you feeling, Kyle? You had some very serious injuries: a broken arm, two stab incisions, a broken nose, a popped blood vessel in your eye, trauma to your back and head, and a serious stress fracture near your heart. If that fracture was any closer, you would have been gone." I looked down at my hands and tensed them.

"It doesn't matter, I'm a criminal now. I'm no better than my father." I looked over at the two with a distraught, terrified expression. My lip quivered, my eyebrows drooped, and my cheeks and eyes were red. "I killed Anya's dad, ruined her family. I'm a monster!" The two comforted me for a few moments, then they stood once I was calm again.

"Kyle, I have a quick question: how long have you been forging your mother's signature?!" Mrs. Kuntai asked with slight anger in her voice.

"Well, how else am I supposed to get things signed by my parents? How about I ask a question: why is stuff

162

getting sent home when you both know about my situation?!" Principal Lane sighed and looked out the window.

"That was Lady Patch's doing. She sent it to your house so you would be trapped into fighting Bobby the Care-Giver." I nodded. I couldn't be angry anymore since it wasn't their fault. Principal Lane crossed his arms and glared at Mrs. Kuntai, then loudly asked, "Well, since we're asking so many questions, why did you blabber to students about Kyle's personal life, Danielle?!"

"How did you find out about that?" Danielle questioned while looking both shocked and guilty.

"Devin told me. Now, do you mind telling Kyle what you told that group of students?" I looked confused and was slightly worried. Danielle bit her lip, then took a deep breath.

"W- Well, I caved in and told them how your mother passed," Danielle admitted. My mouth dropped. I was enraged.

"Are you fucking joking?!"

I swung my arm to punch the bed post, but I hit my heart rate monitor instead and sent it flying into the wall. It made a loud bang, and when I looked up at the two they looked slightly scared, so I took a breath and relaxed. "Sorry for losing my temper, b- but it's … now they're one step closer to finding out about Tyrant." They nodded, then Daryll burst into the room.

"C'mon you criminal, time to go to the doghouse!" Daryll shouted as he marched up to me. The nurses had disconnected the wires and bandaged me up earlier, so I was ready to go. I was still very sore, but Daryll didn't care. He grabbed my broken wrist—which had been healed by a healer yet was still painful to the touch—and ripped me out of the bed.

"Officer Daryll, take it easy on him! Christ, what is the matter with you?!" Mrs. Kuntai exclaimed. Daryll gave her a confused expression, then looked down at my body; I was crumpled on the floor, teary eyed and breathing heavily.

"You want me to take it easy on a genocider? Don't make me laugh, Danielle Kuntai. This boy is a villain in the making, it's obvious!" Principal Lane cut him off by looming over him menacingly with his arms crossed. Principal Lane was a very tall, very muscular man, nearly seven feet tall and 280 pounds of pure muscle. Daryll's ego shrunk as he nodded then gingerly handcuffed me. He led me out of the hospital. The worst part: I had to walk past my classmates.

They watched with what I could only assume was disgust and fear. I couldn't look any of them in the eye—I was too guilty and shame-filled. I was placed in a police car and driven to the nearest police station.

Lucky for me, I guess, our state's official courtroom for Angel Criminal trials was in the next town. I wouldn't need to travel for now; I'd stay in Veena until my trial date, when I'd be driven half an hour to the courtroom. I dreaded that day. I didn't want to know what kind of questions would be asked and what kind of adjudication I would receive.

I hope I'm never let out; I don't deserve to be a hero anymore. I blew my chance, I'm a fraud. I'm Tyrant's son, and my whole life is already planned out for me. It doesn't matter what I do, I'll never escape it. I don't deserve to when I'm a family wrecker ...

Chapter 10
News

All the students except Kate and Hazel were released from the hospital that day. Principal Lane sent Vice Principal Kuntai with the students on the bus ride home, and he stayed in Veena until Hazel and Kate were released. The ride was sullen, very quiet. The energy died down when everyone saw me officially get arrested and sent away to prison.

Tonuko was still fuming, and his anger was building. Unlike me, he was able to control his anger and keep it to himself. He didn't want to share the information he knew, and he wanted to be there for Anya since her father had just passed. Tonuko comforted Anya on the bus, but her reaction surprised him.

"I'll be okay, it was for the best. I missed my dad so much, but he did so many bad things. I would take him back in a heartbeat, but he would have probably been p- put to death anyway by the Seven Influential." Tonuko was shocked by her acceptance. "I love him, he'll always be here no matter physical or not. I'll never be able to move on though if I worry about it 24/7."

"That is- really mature of you, Anya. I don't think I could react like that if my parent passed a few days ago." Anya tried to force a smile and nodded, then looked out the window as tears dripped down her face. Tonuko embraced her as she cried for the next few minutes.

"So, Alex, are you excited to go back home? I bet all our parents really miss us," Steven asked while looking out the window. Alex nodded happily and picked at the bandage on his left forearm.

"Yeah, I really hope we can stay home for a few days. Our parents must be so worried, I mean, how could they not be? We were just involved in a massive villain fight with Care-Givers and the most infamous kidnappers ever, a student was arrested for murder, our teacher was an undercover Care-Giver … the list goes on."

Alex looked up, but instead of sadness or anger, he looked determined. "But that doesn't matter. We're all gonna be heroes, and when we are, we'll have big fights like this where nobody will die. I just know it!" People in the surrounding seats smiled; it seemed Alex's mini-speech inspired some. Despite the students' feeling being lifted, most of the bus ride was silent. The trauma of the fight was too much to get over so soon.

A Few Days Later, a Couple of Cities Away:

BloodShot stepped out of the bus with a little boy at his side. Both wore the same type of mask, and the boy wore a black trench coat with a large collar and black cargo pants; his hair was pure white. Also, the tips of the boy's fingers were black all the way down to his second knuckles, but the cut off wasn't clean. Instead, the black spiked down farther and blended with his peach skin.

The two walked a few blocks, then made it to their destination: a small, one-story, faded yellow house with a gray roof. The roof had tiles falling off, and some of the windows in the house were shattered. BloodShot walked to the door as the boy hid behind him and knocked loudly. After a couple of seconds, they could hear shuffling in the house, then the knob slowly turned and the door opened.

"Ah, Sir BloodShot, I'm glad you made it. Please, come in," the man who answered the door said. He was gripping the white cross dangling from his chain, and along with the cross a white "12" pendant was attached to the gray chain. The man's hair was long, white, and patchy, and he stood with a hunch, shortening his already frail frame. BloodShot stepped in but kept his mask on and looked around.

"Where is King?" BloodShot sternly asked. The man turned around and waved his hand, signaling for BloodShot

166

to follow. They entered a doorway with a half-broken door and walked down the concrete stairs into the basement. When BloodShot turned the corner, he saw a man sitting on a large, burgundy wood chair with pink spurs of mist floating around his shoulders. One of the mist clumps flew out at BloodShot, making whispering noises as it did so. When it was closer, BloodShot could see that the mist had small, golden yellow dots for eyes. The mist flew around his head, then returned to the man. "King, a pleasure to see you again."

"BloodShot, why are you here? Did you come to steal another from my posse? We're already missing Stafer. We've started up business again, got a grand for possessing a hero-in-training's dad," the man, obviously King, ranted. King was fairly muscular and tall. His appearance was quite abnormal: his irises and sclerae were all the same shade of purple and his pupils were tiny, golden yellow dots, the same as his mists. Where his fingers should be were rich black claws, and his skin wasn't a normal human's color of skin, but instead gray with a hue of purple. BloodShot rolled his eyes, then leaned back on his right foot and put his hand behind the boy's head. The boy, who was about five-foot-eight (small in comparison to BloodShot, who was six-foot-seven), stepped from behind BloodShot but was still visibly timid. "Who's this?"

"This boy is the future of villainy; his name is Plague. Plague has an extremely powerful strength, and when activated by thought, he could very well kill anyone he touches. That being said, I know that you know many expert black-market crafters. I need a pair of strength-resistant gloves for Plague; you can take his measurements today," BloodShot explained in a condescending tone.

King snorted, then crossed his arms. "Oh, come to make demands, have you? You know I do nothing for free. Also, it seems the boy is touching you with no problems. If you had someone make you specialized clothing, why not have them make him specialized gloves?" King asked.

BloodShot crossed his arms to mimic King and glared into his eyes.

"You think I'm that stupid? Of course I would have had specialized gloves made for him, but my usual crafter was caught last week. You should know how seriously the idiotic heroes take the crafting of strength-enhancing and - restricting items." King nodded, then stood from his chair.

"I know, I'm just pulling your leg. I'll have the gloves soon-"

"I'm not finished. On top of the needing gloves, I've come to hire you for a job." King stopped moving to grab a cloth measuring tape and turned around to face BloodShot again. "As I've told you before, Tyrant has been struggling to find a healer to add to his Care-Givers for years. There is the famous Blavins' daughter in Tyrant's son's class. So, I need your group's help in kidnapping her. We might try to get Kyle as well."

"You expect me to risk my crew's life for Tyrant's personal needs? Get lost," King hissed. BloodShot opened his cloak and put his hand on the handle of his blade.

"Unless you want to end up dead, I suggest you comply. The payment I was talking about isn't little by any means. Getting a healer for Tyrant pays a hefty sum of cash." BloodShot and King stared each other down and, unlike others who crumble in the bloodlust of BloodShot, King stood his ground.

"You can steal Stafer from me, and make demands, but you will not threaten me in the presence of my kingdom." BloodShot raised an eyebrow and let out a small chuckle.

"You call this dirty cellar in a garbage house a kingdom?" BloodShot asked in a biting tone. King shook his head, then the yellow in his eyes lit up. He smirked and held his hands open and parallel at his sides.

"I wasn't talking about the cellar," King stated. The world around King, BloodShot, and Plague faded to pink. They were still standing on a concrete floor, but around them was a pink mist that went as far as the eye could see. Within the smoke, different vortexes opened and closed, and thousands upon thousands of the same smoke wisps were floating around. Plague gripped BloodShot's cloak tighter, then BloodShot took a deep breath and sighed.

"As much as I love to fight, that's not why I'm here today. I'm here to get an order for gloves for Plague and to inform you of the job opportunity and other recent news." When BloodShot let go of his blade handle, King blinked. His blink forced BloodShot and Plague to blink as well, and when they opened their eyes, they were back in the cellar.

"What other news do you speak of? I know you were in Veena, so is it about someone the Creature and Lokel managed to nab?"

BloodShot shook his head and grinned devilishly. "Better, they're *dead*." The cross man gasped and gripped his cross tighter.

"Dead, by who?" the cross man asked frantically. BloodShot smiled, a teethy, maniacal smile. He put his hands up, as if he was proud or if he was the person who killed the kidnappers.

"Our very own Kyle Straiter. Tyrant's son is growing into his own person, but his roots are still caging him in. His evil instincts are coming out in spurts. Even better, his evil instincts seem to be giving him power. A dark aura is living inside that boy, and when he unleashed it on the Creature, he killed it within seconds!" BloodShot exclaimed.

From behind King's chair, a rattling and hissing was heard. Then, a large woman—not fat or muscular, but overall just bigger than a normal human—crawled out and leaned on the back of the chair. Crawled was an accurate

169

description, as she didn't have human legs, but instead had large, cream–white, spider-like legs, eight of them to be exact. Her skin was the same cream–white color and protruding from her cheeks were large, brown centipede fangs. They repeatedly twitched and hit each other, creating the rattling noise. Her eyes were entirely red, her hair was black, and she had horns the same color as her fangs. Her teeth were razor sharp, and she had normal human arms that were proportionate to her body. In total, she was around fifteen to twenty feet long, and her head was two-hundred centimeters in circumference.

"I like the sssound of this boy. Kyle Sssstraiter ... maybe I'll add him to my lissst," she hissed. She smiled widely, and her fangs glimmered in the dim light from a hanging lightbulb that she was practically hitting her head on.

"And who might this be?" BloodShot asked while straightening his jacket. BloodShot's mood quickly changed, he was more on edge.

"This is our reaper, the White Reaper to be exact. Her strength is devastating," King boasted.

White Reaper, Strength: HellFlame—she can create white flames and creatures out of thin air. After burning for a while, the flames spawn the creatures, which look like beetles with the same fangs as her. She also can turn her bones into long claws that pierce her skin and shoot out like more limbs. She can control them as if they are arms or legs, depending on where they come out of her body.

"Interesting, I wasn't aware of this addition. I assume she is called the reaper because of her kill count?" White Reaper tilted her head and smiled eerily.

"5. 8. 7." BloodShot tensed his fist, and let out a small, quiet gasp.

"Five hundred and eighty-seven?!" BloodShot asked, completely appalled. She slowly nodded, and he cleared his throat.

"She's actually not a new addition. She is the pride of my squad, but we kept her hidden from you so you wouldn't steal her away from me. She's like the daughter I never had," King happily admitted while looking up at White Reaper.

"Oh, how gross. Anyway, Kyle will be going to court for his murders in less than a week, but I assume he will be set free as long as things go smoothly. If he is set free, we will begin planning on the ambush of E.H., but not strike for weeks. There is rumor spreading of the connection between Kyle and us, so we want to forbid any attacks until the rumors die down. If the connection of Tyrant and Kyle is released to the public, that could ruin our entire plan with him." King nodded, then BloodShot spun around on his heels, causing his cloak to swoop in the air.

Plague's measurements were quickly taken, then the two Care-Givers walked out, leaving King to ready his request for the gloves. As they walked out of the house, they noticed the day had turned to night. King could manipulate time within his dimension and caused several hours to pass.

"BloodShot, why were you afraid of that girl?" Plague asked while looking up at him nervously. BloodShot looked around, then sighed.

"Her kill count is five hundred and eighty-seven; she appears younger than me by at least a couple of years but has more than five hundred kills more than I do. She's deadly but," his frown turned to a mischievous smile, "that just means when we ambush E.H. there will be at least a few deaths at her hands." It was Friday, September 5th, only five days until my court trial.

Two Days Later: Madeline Jail, Cell 143:

I sat in silence against the wall in the back of my cell. Imagery of the dead bodies of police officers, the Nomeres, Blake, and the Creature haunted my mind. Blake's bloodied laceration and blank pupils, the Creature's caved-in face, my friends all hurt and partially dead while I could do nothing. It tortured me to think about it.

I don't deserve friends, I failed them. I'm in jail when I'm supposed to be training to be a hero. What the hell is wrong with me? Will I ever escape Tyrant's grasp?

I put my head in my hands and sat there, no crying or tears, but with the painful feeling of failure and despair. The man in the cell across from me sighed, then stood and walked to his cell bars.

"Kid, you got nothing to worry about. You had a reason to kill, it was villains in the process of hurting others. You'll be let outta here in no time." I looked up at him, then took a deep breath.

"I don't deserve to be let out. I went to jail in the first place, I'm just like him." The prisoner raised an eyebrow and scratched his head.

"Just like who? Your daddy?" The prisoner asked in a mocking tone.

"He's not my dad, he's a lunatic, an animal. I hate him, I hate him with every ounce of my being. I'll never be like him, never." The prisoner felt unease and nodded then laid back on his cot. A few minutes later, Daryll approached my cell and banged on the bars with his baton.

"Straiter, you have a couple of visitors. C'mon kid, let's go." I stood, confused, and followed Daryll. He led me to the usual room where prisoners communicated with their loved ones and told me which booth to go to. When I sat down and looked up, I saw Foul Odor through reinforced glass. He pointed at the phone to my left, so I picked it up and held it to my ear.

172

"Hey Kyle, I'm happy to see you've recovered well." I didn't say anything, just looked down at the table. I was too full of shame to look him in the eyes. "Well, I just wanted to say thank you for taking care of the kidnappers. Also, a couple of fighters and I have stepped down from fighting and agreed to help boost security at your school. I'll be working under Fox-Tails. Your principal said something about needing to beef up security until they can properly teach you students the proper mindset needed while a criminal is attacking. There's someone here to question you on personal relationships." Foul Odor looked at me one more time, then stood and handed the phone to another man who was wearing a black suit and a red tie. His greased back, black hair shined in the light.

"Hello Kyle Straiter, it's a pleasure to meet you. I'm George Johnson of the Villain Investigation Association. I questioned your principal the day of the attack on your personal relationships, and I have to say, you do have an uncanny resemblance of your father." I swiftly looked up wide-eyed at the man who just mentioned my dad. My heart beat faster, and I could feel sweat form on my back.

"How the fuck do you know I look like Tyrant? Just what the hell do you want?" George leaned back in the chair with a big, smug smirk.

"Actually, I didn't know. Your principal successfully avoided all questions about your family. But now I know! Now, there are a couple of questions I have for y-" I cut George off by slamming the phone into the concrete desk. The phone smashed in half, and bits of plastic flew everywhere. I glared menacingly at George as I was being handcuffed by Daryll. I continued to stare him down until I couldn't see him anymore. George looked at the papers in his hand and sighed. "Too much?"

"Of course that was too much! You didn't have to trick him like that when he's in a vulnerable state like this!"

Foul whisper–yelled with his fists tensed. George stopped smiling and looked at the broken phone in front of him.

"I am his lawyer; I need details about his family for the trial." George stood from his seat and stopped next to Foul. "Now that I know he's the," he covered his mouth with the papers and very quietly whispered, "son of Tyrant," then, he continued normally, "I can figure out alibis and ways for Kyle to get around or avoid completely personal questions at the trial. However, I need to get in touch with him again. I think he'd be more cooperative if he let me finish explaining what my purpose here was." Foul sighed and wiped his eyes, a common habit of stress, then reached into his short pocket. He pulled out his wallet, and from there, took out his Hero I.D. The two walked to the cells' entrance and Foul held up his I.D. for the guard.

"Hello, Mr. Odor," the big guard smiled while opening the door. The two walked in and saw Daryll locking me up again. As they walked toward the cells, they saw two tall, muscular, heavily armed men wearing ski masks and bullet-proof vests guarding my cell. Foul advanced to the cell bars and called out to me.

"Kyle, please listen, you got it all wrong!" I turned around and stomped up to the bars while huffing angrily.

"Got what all wrong?! This guy knows too much, he's gonna tell everyone! I'll never get out if everyone knows who my dad is!" I whisper–yelled. Foul shook his head, then George walked up next to Foul.

"Kyle, I'm a part of the V.I.A., but I'm also a graduated lawyer. I am defending you in the case under the Seven Influential. I need to know your family relationships, family life, connections, all of that. I need to plan strategies to avoid it during the trial, so the information won't get leaked everywhere. Please, allow us to take you to the organization and I promise you'll be more comfortable than here." I hesitated and looked over at Foul.

"I'll be staying there until you have to leave too. You won't be alone, I promise." I took a deep breath, then nodded. George smirked, then turned to face the two guards.

"We have permission and access as the V.I.A. to transfer Kyle Straiter to our facility here in this city." A dozen police officers made their way to my cage and one of them pulled out a large carabiner with dozens of keys. All the keys lit up, then the one that unlocked my cell door floated in the air. The officer unlocked my cell, and I was free to leave with George and Foul. They took me outside to a large, windowless black van that had the V.I.A. logo on the side. It was a gray circle with red details and "V.I.A." stretched across the middle. To my surprise, it was quite luxurious inside and we took off for the V.I.A. headquarters in Veena.

September 7th, the Day the Students Return to E.H.:

Alex walked to school, but without his usual smile plastered across his face. Students were relieved of living on campus until my trial, so everyone was able to see their families again. Alex's head hung low, and his hat covered his face. School didn't start for another thirty minutes, but he was meeting someone on campus. He walked through the bare halls and went to Iris's locker. Alex played on his phone, waiting, until she finally arrived.

"Why did you wanna meet so early?" Iris yawned, out of breath and her hair a mess. She finally looked at him, "Alex, why are you wearing a hat? I've known you for ten years and not once have you worn a brimmed hat like that." Alex looked down, and she still couldn't see his eyes. Water droplets fell to the floor, and his legs shook. He fell to his knees, so Iris did the same. Alex ripped the hat off, revealing a huge black eye, cuts, and bruises covering his face.

"Please," he murmured, "just heal me." Iris immediately began healing him.

After a bit of hesitation, she finally asked, "What happened? We've been at home the past few days, so why are you so beat up?" He looked away, stopping her healing. Iris had to lean in more and continued.

"Don't worry about it. Just keep healing me," Alex muttered. Iris did so, and when his bruises were gone, he shoved the hat into his bag and walked the opposite way he had come. Iris stood, worried, and walked toward the stairwell.

"Wait, Iris!" Alex yelled from across the hallway. She turned around as he continued, "Don't tell anyone about this! This stays between me and you!"

"O- Okay!" Iris nodded; he thanked her and turned the corner. Iris, still worried, walked down the stairs and out of the school. While making her way to the dorms, which were still open, so she could brush her hair and teeth, she ran into Tonuko, Devin, and Jon.

"Hey!" Jon waved while the three walked over to her.

"Why are you here so early?" Devin asked. Iris rubbed her arm and looked at the floor, not knowing how to answer.

"I was just," Iris saw her hairbrush in her pocket, so she took it out and smiled, "grabbing my hairbrush from my locker. I left it here before we left for Veena." The three obviously weren't buying it, but before any of them could ask anything, Alex walked up with his usual, big smile.

"It's true, I just saw her grabbing it!" He put his hands on Iris' shoulders and said hi to everyone. "We both got here a little early and talked by her locker!" Alex seemed overly happy today, making the trio even more suspicious. Tonuko looked down at Iris, whose face didn't match Alex's excitement by any means, then stuck his hands in his pockets.

"I get why Iris was here, but why were you, Alex?" Tonuko asked, trying to get Alex to break. Alex was smarter than that and had a quick-witted comeback.

"I had to get out of the house and clear my mind about the fight. It only happened nine days ago. I haven't really been able to relax yet."

Jon nodded and rubbed the back of his neck. "Yeah, it's been rough for everyone. Hazel and Kate still aren't back yet and Kyle's court trial is coming up in a couple of days. I think we'll all be able to start relaxing more now that we'll be together in school again," Jon ranted, trying to lift the mood.

"Yeah," Alex agreed. There was a silence among everyone, then Alex took his hands off Iris and said, "Well, I'm gonna take a walk around and grab a bite from the mall. See you two (Tonuko and Iris) in class, and you two (Jon and Devin) around." He walked away, and Iris' face faded to more worry.

Everyone could see the look, so Tonuko asked, "He's lying ... isn't he?" Iris looked up with puppy eyes and slowly nodded. Tonuko looked over at Jon and Devin, then ran his hand through his hair and took a deep breath. "We'll talk more about this later. He clearly wants to keep it a secret and we should respect that right now and not spread around an assumption." Tonuko watched Alex walk into the convenience store on campus, then turned and walked toward the school building. The others went their own separate ways and went on with their pre-school activities.

When the first bell rang, the freshman students, both advanced and honors' classes, were told to meet in the theatre. Tonuko walked to the auditorium but when he opened the door the atmosphere was completely different than usual. Instead of the joyful talking and laughing around the room, everyone was silent and solemn. One boy in particular was on the verge of tears. Daniel sat silently looking down at the ground, his hands plagued with a slight shake.

"You okay, Danny? Is it about Kyle?" Rose asked while rubbing his back. Daniel sniffled, then looked at her with agony lingering in his eyes.

"He's like a brother to me ... I can't stand the thought of his dream we've talked about for years just being ripped out of his grasp. What if he gets a life sentence?! He'll never be a hero!" Daniel sniffled again, then squeezed his arm. "Maybe, if I had known what was going on, I would have been able to help. I wouldn't have let him fight alone and lose his temper like that! I know him, I know how to calm him down!"

"Danny, it's alright," Rose comforted, "You can't focus on the negativity and the past. You couldn't be there, and you can't change that fact. Now, all we can do is hope and pray he doesn't receive any kind of sentence. I'm sure there will be plenty of leniency for him in the court trial since he did take out the most dangerous kidnapping duo in the country!"

After she said that, a man stepped into the doorway. He had bright, pink hair in a ponytail and wore a mischievous grin. "Nah, I hope that little asshole never gets outta jail. Maybe spending some time in the doghouse will fix that shit attitude of his!" the man mocked with a laugh. Tonuko stood from where he was seated and tensed his fist.

"You better chill with that old man. I don't know who the hell you think you are, but you aren't going to strut into this school and start laughing about a tragedy." The man stretched and cracked his back, then yawned.

"Well, I wouldn't say I'm old, nor did I 'strut' into this class. Also, it wasn't a tragedy for Kyle, so, three strikes, you're out!" Tonuko grew angrier by the man's hysterical comments.

"Who even are you anyway?!" Tonuko asked. The man pulled his ponytail to make sure it was tight enough, then cleared his throat.

"I am your new teacher, Fallen. The pleasure is all mine," Fallen smirked with a bow.

"Oh, fuck no, you can't be our teacher," Steven swore after also standing up. "You're barely even a hero, more like just an asshole that sometimes saves people." Fallen laughed out loud and wiped a fake tear from his eye.

"Aww, man, that's too funny. If I save people, I'm a hero! Gosh, you kiddos really do need teaching! I'm gonna be replacing that evil hag as the freshman honors' teacher. My way of fighting may be a little out of the ordinary for a hero, but, meh, don't fix what ain't broke."

Fallen, Strength: Distraught—he can read anyone's mind and use their insecurities as a power source. The power Fallen creates forms into beams of pure energy that can vaporize any matter at will. Depending on how strong the victim's insecurities are felt will range the power of the energy. For example, someone with little insecurity will cause the energy to leave burn marks and scratches, but someone who is very insecure will cause the energy to completely vaporize any matter, living or not.

"I don't care if you think it isn't broken; your strength may be strong, but that doesn't mean you can go around spewing insults to people about their insecurities!" Tonuko argued. He was getting very worked up and his face was turning red.

Fallen's eyes glowed as he stated, "I suggest you sit down boy, unless you want to end up like Kyle." The silence in the room was deafening. "You are the strongest freshman at this school now, that means you have a lot of power and influence over your peers. Based on how you're

179

acting now, that power might go to your fuckin' head and you'll end up rock bottom just like little criminal boy."

The last few words caused Daniel to snap. "Shut up! Just because you're a pro-hero and an adult doesn't mean you're any better than us! Stop belittling everyone and stop insulting the kid who just risked his life to save all of us and all the wrestlers! Kyle defeated the two strongest kidnappers in the nation, something you, as a pro, couldn't do!" Daniel shouted after standing. He glared at Fallen and Fallen held a stern look before chuckling.

"Ah, Daniel Onso. Of course you're getting worked up on Kyle's behalf. Listen kiddo, you might think of Kyle as this great, all-mighty hero, but heroes don't go to fuckin' jail ... do they? It does not matter in the least how you view me, how you view Kyle, how you view the event that just happened. All that matters is how the Seven Influential view Kyle, no more, no less." As much as it angered Daniel, he knew deep down Fallen was right. Tonuko did as well, but because of how angry he was his judgement was clouded. He swung his arm, creating a spike that shot out at Fallen.

"This is why we need the new class," Fallen sighed while putting his hand up. A small bit of orange energy spat out of his hand and covered the spike's sharp end. The sharp part of the spike evaporated, then the rest of the spike moved back into the spot it had been before Tonuko changed it.

"It's not worth it. Relax," Rake, who was sitting next to Tonuko, stated.

Fallen smiled at that, then put his arms behind his back and explained, "Now, as I was saying; I am replacing that villain's place as the freshman honors' teacher and adding in a new class, a very important class for you measles in fact. Clearly after this fiasco, Kyle's troubles ending him in prison, and countless other examples, we need a class to teach you young ins correct decision making—things like charging into a battle not knowing the enemy's strength taking on an unnecessary two-on-one battle," then, a little louder, he listed, "forming a spike at your teacher's head, leaving a half-dead boy to fight full-power enemies, stabbing your teammate, allowing a teammate to nearly drown, the list goes on and on." Tonuko became more uncomfortable and frustrated, and Alex blushed out of embarrassment.

"Alright, that's enough Fallen. Stop toying with the freshmen," Excalibur stated as he walked into the room. "This is a very serious class we need to teach." Both teachers walked down the aisle and stepped onto the stage in front of them. Excalibur elaborated, "I am the freshman advanced teacher: Excalibur. Fallen and I decided this class is a necessity because of the countless bad decisions we've seen lately. We urgently need to teach you how to act in real combat situations because, sad enough to say, with Kyle around, we'll be fighting many more villains, and more dangerous villains than ever expected."

"Again, some of these bad decisions include not utilizing your strengths to help others. Sorry to call you out, but I'm not sorry because you could have prevented so many injuries if you would have used your strength, Mr. Call," Fallen spoke while giving Jaxon a side eye. Jaxon looked down, disappointed in himself. "Another example is saving that pathetic boy Kyle without even considering using your strength, something an idiotic sophomore did."

"You shut your fucking mouth!" Hunter erupted as he practically jumped out of his seat. Daniel was furious with this statement as well.

He leapt and screamed, "What gives you the right to say Kyle deserved to die?! He saved the day by getting rid of the villainous scum! What the fuck did you do?! Huh?!" Though she knew it was true, Anya was saddened to hear her father called villainous scum.

"Silence, all of you! Fallen, knock it off with the patronizing! This is a very serious class, so let's all act like it!" Excalibur yelled after stomping his foot to get everyone's attention. Fallen couldn't help but chuckle.

"Alrighty, there are three students worthy of recognition because they made fantastic decisions in the previous encounter with villains. Iris Blavins, Zach Taling, and Steven Mallnen!" The three stood and their body languages were completely different. Zach was indifferent, Iris was embarrassed, and Steven was basking in the glory. "Iris utilized her strength to heal the injured, Zach stopped multiple people from being carelessly injured and almost successfully saved everyone from a collapsing building. Finally, Steven used his strength to rescue classmates and civilians from the rubble of the collapsed building instead of charging into battle like a lunatic." Fallen glanced at Daniel, then the three sat down.

"Now, let's get started. Say a villain with an unknown strength broke in and Fallen and I weren't here. What would you do ... Zayden?" Zayden thought for a couple of seconds, then smiled and flexed.

"I'd make my way to him underground and pop up behind him to get a clean hit and a chance at knocking him out!" Excalibur and Fallen looked at each other, then Fallen snorted.

"Uh, no. You should dig your way to a different classroom to get help for your classmates and have someone call the authorities depending on how dangerous the man is. Example, if it's David of the Care-Givers, call for immediate backup and have someone call the authorities. However, if it's just some random crook, no need for the authorities, we have enough heroes here to easily stop the scum." Zayden felt embarrassed and silently swore to himself, then Excalibur asked someone else.

"How about you Khloe? What would be the smart thing for you to do?"

"I should seek immediate cover, since my strength doesn't give me any kind of protection or way to escape to get help, and wait for one of my classmates to get help." Fallen clapped slowly and loudly while a big smile stretched across his face.

"You are now my favorite student. Well done, Carrie." Khloe looked confused and offended at the same time.

"Uh, you mean Khloe?"

"Yeah, yeah, whatever. How about uh, you Mr. Tough Guy? What should you do?" Fallen asked while pointing at Tonuko. Tonuko thought for a moment with his hand on his chin.

"My instincts tell me to fight him, since I can get him from a far distance, but-" Fallen made a loud buzzer noise.

"Wrong!" he shouted. "You should duck for cover and use your manipulation strength to try and trap him in a cement box with no windows!" Tonuko balled his fist and glared at Fallen, who in return gave him a big smirk.

"If you didn't cut me off, I was gonna say-"

"Hmm, don't care. How about you Danny-boy, since you wanna always add your opinion. What should you do if David the Care-Giver walked in right now?" Danny wiped his eyes and glared at Fallen.

"I should go invisible and take his gun from him," he muttered. Excalibur smiled and clapped for Daniel.

"Well done, Daniel, that's why you're the sharpest kid in advanced. You and Zach are the academic top advanced kids, so how about you Zach; what should you do?" Zach's expression didn't change, and he leaned back in his chair with his feet up on the chair in front of him.

183

"I should either create a box around the villain and make the lasers as close and as many as possible to minimize the bullets that can escape or make two large laser walls blocking his way to us and his way out so that 'Zayden' will have more time to fetch help." Zach blinked one eye at a time and ran his hand through his flowing hair.

"Excellent job, Zach, but look a little happier maybe?" Excalibur asked while crossing his arms and smiling.

"I'll try my best teach'." Fallen looked around the room for the last example of this scenario. He put his finger to his goatee and tapped it while scanning.

"What about you, what's your name?" Fallen asked while pointing at Jessica.

"My name is Jessica Alter, and I would hide and wait for help to arrive!" she answered.

Fallen looked at her weirdly, then questioned, "You wouldn't fight at all, or make an attempt to secure the criminal?" Jessica shrugged and thought for a second.

"Well, I could create flowers all around him to try and trap him and keep creating more if he tried to escape." Fallen smiled and clapped loudly again. He tapped his goatee again and looked out at the room.

"It seems the honors' class girls are smart, but surely not the boys! I need a smart boy to answer this next one!" The room was silent, then Cindy sighed.

"Kyle was the smartest boy in our class," she solemnly stated. The room was still silent, then Fallen stood still and clenched his jaw.

"Kyle this, Kyle that, is that all you kids talk about?! Kyle is just this amazing, flawless student, right?!" Everyone was shocked at the outburst, and Fallen continued, "Newsflash, no, he sure as hell isn't! Kyle was a loner,

184

worthless, no friends, no scholarships, no will, nothing! I would know because I mentored him this summer!"

"Will?" Alex asked. Fallen gave him a weird smile, his eyes wide, and nodded.

"Yes, sir, no will to live boy! Kyle wanted to give up, but Mr. Hated-Ol'-Me saved his ass! I helped him learn to love himself! Now that he decided to get arrested, who the hell knows if that will is there or not! The kid could tell the judges 'Mister and Misses Judges, just put me in jail! I don't want to be no hero' or he could up and tell em' 'Mister and Misses Judges, please just lemme go!' So, from now on, until he returns or doesn't, no more Kyle talk while in the classroom! Ya'll need to learn to focus on yourselves!"

Zach raised his hand, then Fallen asked, "What the hell do you want boy?"

"Why did your accent change from like, uptight, to more like a southern accent?" Fallen moved his body to face Zach.

"'Ion know, kid, it's just how weird I am!" Zach shrugged, and the class continued. "Now, miss Kyle lover over there, answer this for me! If Kyle became a villain and came to kill alla' us, what would you do?!"

Fallen was yelling to Cindy, but an advanced-class girl snarkily chimed, "I thought there was no more Kyle talk?" Fallen swatted at her as if she was a fly and continued looking at Cindy.

"I- uh, well, I would- um, I would ... I don't know." Fallen smiled and raised his hands while changing his expression from anger to a smile.

"That there is my very point! Hate me all you want kids, but I'm here to help! Any single one of you can become a villain, and the others would have no clue how to react! You need to be able to think on the spot about these things! Don't beat yourself up about them, but don't just think they're impossible. Everything is possible, but not everything is worth your time!"

Tonuko stood and looked Fallen in the eyes, then clapped. A couple of others joined, and eventually everyone was clapping. Fallen bowed and basked in the glory, then shouted, "Alright, that's all for today! I got your minds movin', and that's all I need. Time for the fun part of the day, trainin'!" The class cheered as Excalibur and Fallen walked down the aisle to lead the students to the Dome.

Chapter 11
Broken Boys

When the classes arrived at the Dome, the inside was changed. There were shooting ranges with dummies, combat areas with dummies, and different simulations of various environments. Before the classes separated, Fallen grabbed Jaxon's shoulder and whispered, "Activate your strength on the classes right now." Jaxon raised an eyebrow.

"You mean control everyone?" he whispered back.

"Exactly, now go," Fallen swiftly responded. Jaxon shrugged, then breathed in and out. When he breathed out, a pink smoke flooded the air and when people breathed in the smoke, their eyes faded to red. When the students and Excalibur were fully under Jaxon's control, Fallen smiled and crossed his arms. "If you get smarter, stronger, just think a little more, you can be extremely powerful. You aren't just a destined sidekick, Jaxon Call. Show me what you can do."

"Walk," Jaxon stated. The group walked, synchronized, then Jaxon commanded, "Stop." They stopped and Fallen clapped.

"With a little more confidence, you can do this in the field with a higher success rate! Call 'em off!" Jaxon slammed the door to the Dome behind him and left everyone uncontrolled. Excalibur fixed his sleeve while glaring at Fallen. "Just fixing up a student," Fallen smirked. Excalibur shook his head and told everyone to go to a station.

The students were assigned specific stations to work on what they needed. Fallen and Excalibur walked around, giving advice to the students. Excalibur complimented students and gave recommendations; Fallen, on the contrary, gave strict criticism and ridicule. Ironic for their looks.

Tonuko was pitted against a robot with big, heavy boxing gloves. He was supposed to take beatings from the robot, ranging from blocking to flat out being punched, to increase his strength and endurance. Iris was with him and would heal him after each beating. This would help increase her endurance with her healing.

"Tonuko, look over at Alex," Iris said softly while nudging her head to her right. Tonuko looked over and saw Alex put a bag down off to the side of the arena. Tonuko raised an eyebrow while panting, then Iris explained, "He has a hat hidden in that bag that he used to cover up his injuries. Maybe you could ask him about it to get more information?" Tonuko, who had been resting on his knees, stood up straight and put his hands on his hips while he thought.

Alex, who was waiting for a simulation in the dark, looked around nervously. Tonuko came up with a plan and executed it accordingly. He walked over to the bag Alex had placed on the floor, which caused Alex to scurry over and attempt to snag the bag. Tonuko grabbed it just as Alex did, and they started fighting over it.

"Hey, this is mine! What are you doing Tonuko?!" Alex yelled while gripping the bag with two hands. Alex pushed Tonuko, causing him to lose his handle on the bag, then Tonuko tackled Alex and they continued fighting over the bag. Eventually, students gathered around and the teachers attempted to step in. Tonuko gave the bag one more huge tug, causing the zipper to rip open. The contents of the bag spilled out, including a plain, white, curve-brim hat with a few blood stains on the brim. Cindy bent down and picked up the hat before Alex could get it, then looked at him with concern.

"Alex, you never wear hats ... why is there blood on it?" Alex looked at her, but the innocent, happy sparkle was gone from his eyes. His cheeks and nose were red, and tears brimmed his eyelids. Alex was shattered. For the first time ever, his classmates saw tears fall from the angel's eyes.

The Angel of the freshmen was broken.

Alex got to his knees and wiped tears from his cheeks, then Cindy knelt in front of him and gave him a tight hug. Others who Alex had known for a while joined in the hug, then Tonuko stood and dusted himself off. He wasn't pleased to have fought Alex for this, no one was happy seeing this scene.

"Everyone, leave the Dome, but stay outside the doors! None of you better leave campus. It is too dangerous on the streets for a bunch of tired students to be wandering!" Fallen commanded while pointing behind the large group of students at the door. The classes left, allowing Fallen and Excalibur to talk privately with Alex. Fallen had Alex stand and walked him to one of the benches; Alex didn't look up the entire time and he continued to cry. This made everyone more worried. Fallen sat next to Alex and leaned forward to look at his face.

"Alex, what's the matter? What happened?" Fallen asked. Although he hadn't known Alex for long, he knew something serious was wrong.

"M- My home has just been, not good l- lately," Alex stuttered through his tears. Excalibur and Fallen looked at each other and nonverbally agreed it must have been something serious.

"From what I've heard, you met with Iris this morning and had several injuries. What caused those injuries?" Alex stayed silent and wiped his eyes. "Alex, it's okay to tell us what happened. We're not going to get you in trouble or anything," Excalibur assured him. Alex remained quiet, leaving the teachers unsure of what to do next.

Outside:

The classmates stood around outside of the building; some peered into the Dome through a glass slit in the door to see what was happening. Cindy saw that Alex wasn't talking, then she wiped a tear from her eye. Jessica, an old classmate of Cindy's and Alex's, was fanning her eyes while attempting to not cry.

"Aww, Jess, c'mon, you're gonna make me cry," Cindy sniffled before hugging her.

Jessica sniffled as well, then cried out, "He's the Angel of our grade, and Angels aren't supposed to cry!" Her last words became incomprehensible through her tears. Tonuko, who stood nearby, tensed his fist.

"We need to figure out what the hell made him break down like that. Who gave him those injuries?" Everyone was silent, so Tonuko stated, "It's clearly something going on at his house."

"We should go pay a visit to see what's going on there. He lives a couple miles away, if we run we can make it there in under half an hour," Donte thought aloud; he was another of Alex's old classmates. The freshman honors' class had five Edith graduates: Alex, Cindy, Jessica, Donte, and Iris.

"Are you crazy?!" Steven asked loudly. "If we get caught leaving campus during the school day we'll get in huge trouble! We shouldn't be snooping in Alex's house either!" Tonuko turned to Steven with his fist balled.

"Yeah, well, Alex came to school today with cuts and bruises! He's crying in there because someone is hurting him! If you don't wanna get caught, fine by me, but I'm going!" Tonuko exclaimed in response. Steven backed down.

"Ever since Veena, you've been a real jerk to us," Steven quietly retorted. Tonuko ignored the remark, then looked at the rest of the group.

"Who's with me?!" he shouted. All but a select few were quiet and hesitant. Donte, Camilla, Jessica, Iris, Rake, and Cindy agreed to go; the others stayed silent.

"His parents work from home, so they should be there," Cindy informed the group. They agreed on the fastest route, then set off. Just as the seven students reached the gate and the last one walked through it, the teachers walked out of the Dome. Fallen saw Iris turn the corner and sighed.

"Call Fox-Tails, we need him to round up those kids. Can't have them wandering around unsupervised, especially with Kyle being gone. The target on our students' backs right now is too big for comfort," Fallen said to Excalibur. Excalibur nodded, then pulled out his phone and quick-dialed Fox-Tails' number. The remaining students were told to go to the theatre and wait. Alex was still inside the Dome.

Donte led the group to Alex's house, slowing down a few times so others could catch up. It was a standard two-story house and looked pretty peaceful. A mini-van was in the driveway, as well as an S.U.V.

"Let's ask these fuckers what they're doing to our Angel," Tonuko muttered through his teeth. He stomped up to the door and before he could knock, Fox-Tails leapt from a couple dozen feet away and tackled him. He flipped Tonuko over and knelt on his hands, then other guards caught up and restrained the six other students.

"We're got the runaways secured, we'll be bringing them back to campus now," Fox-Tails informed someone through an earpiece he was wearing.

"What the hell do you think you're doing?!" Rake shouted while trying to get free from the E.H. guard's grasp.

"You all should not be leaving campus during school hours," Fox-Tails said after helping Tonuko stand.

The guards forced the seven to start walking toward school but were interrupted by Tonuko shouting, "We're trying to figure out what is going on with our classmate! He could be getting abused; we should be going into that house and questioning Alex's parents!" He attempted to rip his hands out of Fox-Tails' grasp, but Fox-Tails' hands didn't budge.

"That's noble of you but leave it to us adults. Trust me, we aren't happy at all to see one of our students hurt, but we cannot investigate without a permit. Not only is that illegal, but you attempting to solve a crime is going to lead to your arrest!" Fox-Tails sighed. Tonuko didn't argue back, instead he quietly grumbled to himself the entire walk back to campus. When they arrived, the students were brought straight to Principal Lane's office where he, Mrs. Kuntai, Fallen, and Excalibur were waiting.

"Well look at what we have here," Fallen angrily stated while pacing back and forth in front of the seven who were being restrained by E.H. security guards. Fallen held his hands behind his back, then stopped in front of Tonuko and gave him a side-eye. "Maybe I'm just a little forgetful, but I thought I told my class to stay inside the campus because the streets around here are dangerous right now!"

"Why glare at just me? Six other kids left too, and I wasn't even the one to suggest leaving," Tonuko sneered, then angrily glanced at the guard holding him. The guard let go, and Tonuko rubbed his wrist, then looked back at Fallen and crossed his arms.

"Well Mr. Tough Guy, you are currently the leader of your class since Kyle-boy is, y'know, in jail and all. Anything you do, the others will follow. You need to be setting a good example and be more responsible so your classmates do the same!" Fallen reprimanded after crossing his arms to mock Tonuko.

"Oh, my bad; I didn't know I had to do your damn job for you! You're the teacher, you're supposed to set the example and lead the class to success! I'm just a student who needs guidance too!" It was clear Tonuko was getting very flustered and, since it wasn't Fallen's intent, he backed off with his biting tone.

"We at E.H. are teaching you to be self-sufficient future leaders. Everyone knows you will for certain be the leader of a future organization with many sidekicks and future generations looking up to you. Being able to do the same for your classmates is phenomenal practice; you should be thankful you have this opportunity," Fallen explained. He took a few steps back and stood next to Mrs. Kuntai, expecting Tonuko to relax and stop arguing. However, he was wrong.

"Well you know what, Kyle was supposed to be our leader, mine too, and look what happened to him! I looked up to him and tried following in his footsteps because at Veena with the kidnappers, Kyle put all of us first and nobody died! But when I put my trust in him and left him to fight like he said he could, he killed four people and got arrested! Now look at us! Our reputation has plummeted, and I have to be this big responsible adult with no problems or worries of my own!"

"Tonuko, that's not-" Fallen was swiftly cut off by Tonuko, who finished with an angry mutter.

"No, I understand perfectly what you're expecting. I won't disappoint again." With that, Tonuko stormed out of the room.

"Tonuko, don't just leave! That's very rude to turn your back on your teacher!" Mrs. Kuntai shouted while taking a step forward. Tonuko was already gone. The other six were reprimanded by the teachers and principals, then sent home along with the other freshman students. Alex was sent home as well and told to call the school if anything happened. He was reassured that someone would answer if he ever called. He was escorted home and, just like that, the first day back to school was over for the freshmen.

V.I.A. Headquarters, Veena:

I woke in the bed George provided me and yawned. I thought I was having trouble sleeping because I was in the cold prison, but it wasn't any better here. I still had nightmares.

I sat up and stretched for a minute, then stood and walked into the bathroom connected to my room. I saw myself for the first time in a week, and I looked horrible. My bright, blonde hair stuck up all over the place, bags upon bags were built up under my eyes, and my sky-blue eyes seemed dull. I scratched my head with another yawn, brushed my teeth, then showered. I changed into the clothes Foul had bought from a nearby thrift store. The shirt was too big and the shorts a little too short for my liking, but I quite honestly couldn't have given any less of a fuck about my clothes. I walked downstairs and sat on an uncomfortable leather couch. It was very stiff but fitting for an association's headquarters. Foul came in a few minutes later and grabbed a mug, then filled it with coffee.

"Do you want some?" he asked. I shook my head and turned on the news. My bloody, disoriented face while being arrested was plastered on the screen; I was the main story.

"The headstrong Eccentric High student Kyle Straiter has been arrested for the murder of four. Although the four that were killed were criminals, Kyle Straiter is only fourteen years old and is not a legal hero. The crazy boy apparently killed a man begging for his life, then caused a massive explosion while killing the other kidnappers, our eye-witnesses say." Foul quickly grabbed the remote and changed the channel, but the damage had been done.

Is this how everyone views me, even my classmates? I guess they have reason to. If I wasn't here, nobody would be getting attacked by villains. If I wasn't here, those at E.H. wouldn't live in fear wondering when they'd be attacked again. They have to rely on me to fix the problems I could never fix for myself. Why couldn't Tyrant have killed me instead of my mom?

"I thought I was a hero, I thought I saved people. Why are they making me sound like the villain?" I asked, staring blankly at the television. I looked down at my hands, then saw two black dots spiral onto my palms. It felt like a liquid was dripping down my face, but I didn't think I was crying. I put my hand to my face and felt my cheek, then pulled my fingers away. A thick, blood-like black liquid was oozing out of my eyes and mouth, but when I looked at Foul, he seemed to not see it.

"Listen Kyle, people make up stories to stir up controversy within the crowds. When you are deemed not guilty by the Seven Influential, this will all be forgotten and you'll be seen as a hero!" Foul explained trying to lighten my mood. I nodded, then saw George walk down the stairs.

"Morning gentlemen," George said loudly while smiling big. He poured himself a cup of coffee, then added a few sugar packets. He walked over beside the couch, picked up the remote, and shut off the T.V. "It's too early for that."

"George," I asked, "do you think I'll be let free?"

"I am one-hundred percent certain you will be found not guilty and sent home. It's not that I think you will be let free, it's a fact that you will." I nodded without looking at him. As George and Foul talked, I went back to my room. I laid on the bed, facing the ceiling, and analyzed the black dots on my hands. They were the same hue as my arm had been when I punched the Creature to kill it, and they weren't holes like I thought when I first saw them.

You know it's over when ... all your fears are gone ... because you don't care anymore if you die.

I put my hand on my head, then heard a deep, sharp whisper in my ears.

"*Kyle.*" I looked around, but no one was in the room. I rubbed my head, then my stomach made gargling noises and an immense pain exploded in it. I hunched over while hugging my stomach, then fell to my back and laid in fetal position. I laid like this for half an hour, unable to speak or move, then I heard a knock at my door.

"Kyle, we gotta discuss your family now. George said we should start planning so we can muster up as much information as possible to maximize what we can avoid," Foul said while walking into the room. I didn't move or respond, so he walked over to my bedside. "You alright?" When he touched my shoulder, the pain vanished. I turned around and nodded, acting like I just woke up. I followed Foul to a room in the back of the building. In there was a long, wooden table. I sat next to George, and Foul sat on the other side of him.

"Alright, Kyle," George started while neatly stacking his papers, "tell me about your home life as a kid. Was it fun and kind, or-?"

"It was horrible. I was forced into learning about the villain business by Tyrant, and," I stopped while staring down at the table. My eyes watered, then I finished, "and I had to watch my mother die in my arms after she was stabbed by him." I balled my fists and clenched my jaw. "I hate him, he killed her. He took her away from me."

"I'm sorry to hear that, Kyle; that's an awful tragedy to go through." George was writing vigorously, then clicked his pen and scanned the top sheet on the stack in front of him. "So, Kyle, who is this Daniel Onso I'm seeing? Is he a close friend, a cousin, what is he to you?"

"Daniel is the closest thing to a friend I've ever had. He was always there for me when I'd run away crying because Tyrant beat me up again or hit my mom, and he was the one who helped me train my new strengths whenever I manifested them," I weakly responded. George nodded, then Foul looked over at the sheet of questions.

"What did Tyrant think of Daniel?"

I swiftly responded, "Hated him, very much hated him. His parents were well-known heroes on the rise when we were children, so Tyrant always shunned me for spending time with a 'hero's kid.' My mom always let me play with Daniel though."

George continued writing while he asked, "Here's a big question: How do you feel about Tyrant now? Also, how do you feel about villains in general?" I looked down at the palms of my hands again while thinking.

How do I feel about villains? That should be an obvious question ... do they still not trust me?

"I hate Tyrant with every ounce of my being. He's the reason I'm here, and *I'll be the reason he goes. I have to* avenge my mom and kill Tyrant, I have to." I squeezed my fist tight, causing veins in my forearms to pulsate. "And I will *never* be a villain. They are corrupt people who want to hurt others. I could never do the things villains do."

"Thank the Lord. Considering you are the strongest teenager this society has ever seen, it's nice to have the reassurance that you will always be on our side!" Foul smiled as he leaned back in his chair.

I'm not the strongest ... Plague ... if Tyrant is afraid of him, just how strong is he?

"Yeah, thankfully I'll stay a hero." I felt the ooze pour from my eyes again, and it felt as though something was ripping through my stomach. I just stayed still, not moving a muscle.

"Good to hear, good to hear," George said while flipping the page on his notepad. I gripped my shirt and hunched over.

"Kyle, are you okay?" Foul asked. He looked at me, confused, then George glanced over as well. I put my head down, and projectile vomited a black and red substance before running off. I bumped into the wall as I left the room, then ran straight into my bedroom, closing and locking the door behind me.

What's happening to me, what is this?

I laid in my bed, curled into the fetus position, hoping and praying the pain would go away.

George knelt down and poked his pen into the odd substance I just threw up. Foul could hear a sizzling, and when he rounded the table, he saw George's pen had melted in half. George looked up at Foul with both confusion and concern.

Kyle Straiter, Strength One

Chapter 12
Two-Faced

I groaned in agony on my bed. Even after a day the pain wouldn't go away. The court case was tomorrow and I could barely think or walk.

BANG! BANG! BANG!

"Kyle, we need answers! If you lose this court case, your entire future is gone! Please, open up! Are you in pain, are you alright?! Please, answer me!" Foul shouted while banging his fist on my door. I ignored him and slipped out of consciousness. I could hear Tyrant calling my name; I woke when someone slapped me across the face.

"Kyle, wake up, dammit!" Tyrant shouted while shaking me. I blinked a few times and saw Tyrant in front of me. We were floating in the void again, but this time I heard a loud thumping that pained my stomach every time it thumped. "You called me here yesterday, why haven't you said anything?!" I looked around in a daze and flinched after every thump. "Kyle?!"

"The thumping ... do you hear it?"

"What thumping, what are you talking about?!" I groaned and held my head. Tyrant looked concerned, but before he could say anything, a presence loomed over me.

"*Tyrant.*" It was the same voice as the whisper from before, but this time it was an inhumanely deep, heart-quaking rumble of a voice. I swiftly looked up and around, but nothing was there. Tyrant's face was paler than usual, and he tensed his fists.

"Kyle, what the hell was that?!" I didn't answer, just kept looking around in circles. The pounding continued and grew louder. "Kyle, what are you doing?!"

"I don't know how I'm calling you here, but next time I do, don't respond," I snapped at Tyrant. He rolled his

eyes, then a loud noise resembling someone scratching their nails on a chalkboard filled our ears. A light beamed above me, then I woke in my room and was thrown into the ceiling. I fell back onto my bed, rolled over, and fell onto the ground. The loud noises caused Foul and George to run to my room, and eventually they broke in. I was laying on the ground, not unconscious but breathing heavily. My arms were pitch black and eyes were glowing a bright white.

"Kyle, what the hell?! Are you alright?!" Foul asked, clearly worried. I blinked and the light vanished. The darkness was sucked from my arms back into the black dots on my palms, and I got up onto my knees and elbows. Foul knelt beside me and tried to get me to talk. I was too weak to speak and simply continued panting.

After a few minutes, George pulled out his phone and said, "I'm calling an ambulance. Something is clearly wrong with him." Out of my palm, a black tentacle-like object flew at George and hit the phone out of his hand. The tentacle was sucked back into the dot.

"No, don't, I'm fine." George nodded, bent down and picked up his phone, then slowly walked out of the room. Foul was as shocked as George. He left the room as well and closed the door behind him. I fell over to my side, and laid lifeless ...

Kyle Straiter, Strength One

That Same Morning, at E.H.:

Alex ran to school, but he couldn't run straight and he had a slight limp. His right eye was swollen shut, he had bruises on his arms and legs and a shallow gash across his chest. He finally made it to campus and ran straight to the Dome. He burst through the doors but collapsed immediately after.

"Holy shit, is that Alex?!" Jon shouted while running over along with his teacher, Mrs. Davidson. Mrs. Davidson commanded for one of the sophomore girls to go get the freshman teachers, then she checked Alex's pulse. It was there, and thankfully he was still breathing. "Alex, what happened?!" Jon asked.

"D- Demon, he's a demon!" Alex cried through his gasps for air. Mrs. Davidson and Jon looked at each other, both very confused.

The sophomore girl threw open the theatre doors and shouted, "Mr. Fallen, Mr. Excalibur, it's that Alex kid! He's collapsed at the Dome doors!" Fallen nodded and ran out of the theatre with the girl. Excalibur and the classes followed closely behind, and when they arrived at the Dome, Alex was still on the ground, breathing heavily.

"I have to go control my class, but he was saying something about a man being a demon," Mrs. Davidson frantically informed Fallen. He nodded and knelt beside Alex, as did Excalibur. Iris joined them and began healing Alex. Some of the first years covered their mouths, others couldn't even look.

"Can we confront his parents now?!" Tonuko asked Fallen. Fallen looked down at Alex's body, then punched the ground.

His fist dug into the concrete, and when he pulled it out, he muttered, "Let's go."

It was the most serious they'd heard Fallen, and it scared them. Excalibur and Iris stayed with Alex, as did most of the freshmen. The group of six who'd left school the previous day went with Fallen and Fox-Tails; Donte led the group to Alex's house. Fallen was silent the entire time, and his strength was activated during the walk. His hair was floating, his fists were glowing a bright pink, and orange streaks ran up his arms. Fox-Tails' claws were out and sharp, and his legs and forearms were visibly more defined than usual. His fangs were so long that they hung out his mouth and one fang pierced his bottom lip.

When they arrived at the house, everyone stopped and looked at the heroes. "What are you going to say?" Rake asked.

"I'm gonna do a lot more than talk," Fallen sinisterly stated as he marched to the front door. He banged loudly on the door, causing Cindy to jump.

"He almost broke it down," she whispered to Rake. The students were now afraid of Fallen. As the door slowly opened, an unfamiliar man peered out. Donte took a step forward, but Tonuko grabbed his arm. Donte looked back and saw the terror in Tonuko's eyes.

"Who the fuck are you?! Where are Alex's parents?!" Camilla shouted while tensing her fists.

"Camilla, I am Mr. Galeger. Shouldn't you know?" the man eerily responded.

Jessica cringed and said, "No you aren't." The man reached out his purple hand but Fallen swiftly raised his own and gripped the man's wrist. The wind from Fallen lifting his hand shattered a window, and a very loud crack was heard all the way at the end of the driveway where Fox-Tails and the students stood.

"You clearly aren't Alex Galeger's father, so who the hell are you?" Fallen snarled. "What are you doing to him?" Fallen let go of the man's wrist and the man rubbed it.

"Why, yes I am, I always have been his dad. And I thought I told that goody-two-shoes ..." A purple flame spiraled in his hands as he continued, "to keep his damn mouth shut!"

Mr. Galeger blasted a large burst of flames, completely covering Fallen's body. Smoke floated into the sky and when the flames died down Fallen was holding his hands out at opposite shoulders. He was not burned. Scaly wings ripped from Mr. Galeger's shirt, and he tackled Fallen into the air, then threw him onto the grass. Tonuko used the opportunity of the fight to run toward the house to try and find Mrs. Galeger. As he was running, Mr. Galeger pounced at him. Fox-Tails speared Mr. Galeger, and Tonuko rolled under the attack from Fox-Tails, then made it through the front door.

"Mrs. Galeger, where are you?! I'm Tonuko Kuntai, I'm here to help you!" He heard commotion in a door to his right, and he hesitated before opening it. Mrs. Galeger was tied up at her hands, ankles, and mouth. As Tonuko tried to untie her, he was blinded by a pink and orange light.

Outside, Fallen had his hands raised in the air, palms to the sky. He clenched his fist and a pink laser shot out of a cloud, piercing and melting one of Mr. Galeger's wings. Mr. Galeger spun in the air, then crashed in the middle of the street. Fox-Tails moved quickly, using rope he had brought to restrain Mr. Galeger.

Fallen floated into the air and clenched his fists, which were still raised above his head. A beam of pink shot from the sky onto Mr. Galeger. The beam was translucent and inside the circle of pink, Mr. Galeger's demon features were sucked out of his body. The beam flew into the sky, then exploded like a firework. Fallen fell, landed in a crouched position, then looked up at Mr. Galeger. He looked completely different and was unconscious in Fox-Tails' hands.

Fallen, Real Strength: Transformation—he can conform anything caught within his pink and orange essence into whatever he pleases. Although he is powered by insecurity, he can control the power of the conformation. As well as this, he can store the power he's gained from an individual's insecurity, but he will slowly start to feel insecure about the same thing the person was if he contains it for too long.

Outside, the students were in awe; inside, Tonuko swiftly snapped out of it and untied Mrs. Galeger. Cindy ran into the house to help Tonuko then asked, "Mrs. Galeger, what happened?!" Mrs. Galeger was breathing heavily and struggling to stay conscious.

"Th- There was a man, a d- demon. He posses-sed Alex's f- father," Mrs. Galeger stuttered. Before they could ask anything else, she passed out. Twenty or so E.H. security guards ran to the scene; while half aided Fox-Tails, the others aided Fallen.

"Fallen, are you alright?" A woman with long, purple hair asked. Fallen nodded while panting, then looked down.

"I-I'll be fine. Un-possessing someone takes a crap ton of energy, and the thoughts the demons give ... they're horrifying." The woman nodded, then helped Fallen stand.

Tonuko ran out of the house carrying Mrs. Galeger and pushed her into one of the guard's hands. "Bring her and Mr. Galeger to Nurse Blavins A.S.A.P.!" Tonuko commanded. The guard was shocked and turned to Fox-Tails. Fox-Tails smirked and nodded to the guard. Two guards ran off with the Galegers, then Fallen walked over to the students.

"Tonuko," Fallen started weakly. Tonuko thought he would be scolded so he looked down and closed his eyes tightly. "Thank you; you took charge and found Mrs. Galeger, then immediately got her medical attention. Heroic choice, Tonuko, heroic choice." Tonuko smiled and nodded proudly.

"Thanks, and good job taking down Alex's dad without killing him. Can't say Kyle would've done the same." Everyone was shocked by the insensitive statement, but Tonuko wasn't laughing as if it was a joke. His face turned stern, then he walked away in the direction of the school. Fallen looked over at Fox-Tails, who just shrugged with a completely lost expression on his face. The rest of the group followed distantly behind Tonuko, and they returned to campus.

In the Nurse's Office:

Alex looked over at his mom and un-possessed dad, then smiled. His dad was finally back, he could be the Angel again.

After the dangerous fiasco, Principal Lane issued for all students to immediately return to living in the dorms. It was sudden, so students were sent home early to pack, then return. The last of the freshmen returned at 9:30 p.m. Some students sat around in the lobby, including Tonuko, Jessica, Khloe, and Zayden.

"So, Kyle's trial is tomorrow, huh?" Zayden asked while leaning on the counter. Everyone nodded, then Jessica sighed dramatically.

"The older kids seem certain he'll come back, so we have nothing to worry about. I wonder if it will be broadcasted ... maybe we'll be allowed to watch it during class." Tonuko, whose arms were crossed, squeezed his biceps.

He stood and loudly murmured, "He could go rot in prison for all I care." The others were confused but assumed Tonuko was talking out of his ass because he was shaken about what happened earlier.

The Next Day, 9:00 a.m.:

I woke on the floor again, but the room was pitch black. I rubbed my eyes and tried to stand. It took me a second to build the strength to get up, and when I did I had a massive headrush. My head hurt and felt staticky. I reached for the light switch, but my knees felt wobbly and I fell into the wall. I used the wall to stay standing, then the static grew more aggressive. It sounded as though someone was speaking ... yelling ... to me. Then, when I flicked the light on, it was gone.

205

I slowly walked down the stairs and saw George sitting on the couch. He was bouncing his leg anxiously. When he heard a stair creak, he looked over with a big frown. "There're clean clothes on the counter over there. Put them on so you look less dead. We're leaving in ten minutes, it's a thirty-minute drive and the trial is at ten," George informed me. I nodded, grabbed the clothes, then went back upstairs. I changed and brushed my teeth, then walked downstairs and joined Foul and George in loading into the car.

"To no one's surprise, your trial is going to be broadcast nationally. This means your friends, school, family, and dad can all view it. Also meaning that if they ask any questions about your relationships that we just cannot avoid, we must plead the fifth," George explained to me and Foul.

"How much can I plead the fifth?" I asked quietly. George scratched his arm while driving and looked at me through the rear-view mirror.

"We don't need to avoid any questions about the actual criminal case, we know we can win that, but if there are any questions about your family that you cannot vaguely answer and satisfy the Seven Influential, then you must use it. Everyone is gonna see this Kyle, if it gets out that you are related to Tyrant, it's over." I gulped and nodded, then looked out the window.

I could never be a hero; my career should end because of these murders. Maybe I should just join Tyrant, maybe it is my unavoidable destiny. Everyone has a destiny, right? Even if it's to be a villain, or to die. Everyone dies, there's no real purpose in saving others who will just die at some other point, right? No ... that's not true. The happiness I felt when that cop told me I saved his son's life, that was worth every second I suffered in that fight. I can't lose, I can't let people know my relations, I have to save myself. I can dig myself out of this grave, it's what Mom would've wanted!

Angel Criminal court cases worked much differently than a usual trial. The defense could present their evidence to the Seven Influential in the form of a paper copy, but only the Seven Influential could question the suspect. They knew best the difference between a criminal and hero. In addition, there was no jury; it was only the Seven Influential. They'd vote whether the suspect would be released or not ... essentially my career was in the hands of the seven strongest heroes.

When we arrived at the courthouse, it was a luxurious marble building with stone pillars and statues. There were paparazzi everywhere; their camera flashes blinded me as I walked into the courthouse. When we entered, I saw a long pathway with hundreds of seats on either side. In the back of the building were the seven luxurious seats where the Seven Influential sat. They had a long desk in front of them, and beside them was one lone seat, where I would sit for questioning. Additionally, there were two seats with desks in front of the Seven Influential; those were the lawyers' seats. I gulped as I sat in the lone seat, and my stomach dropped at the massive number of people that poured into the building. Cameras were set up all around, all aimed directly at me.

I wonder what my classmates are doing right now.

At E.H.:

All of the freshmen sat in the theatre and Fallen and Excalibur announced they would be watching the court trial. They deemed it would be a good learning experience for the students. Fallen wheeled in a large T.V., then turned it on. I was visible, sitting in my seat; there was no sound and at the bottom of the screen a message looped: KYLE STRAITER, ANGEL CRIMINAL COURT TRIAL IN FRONT OF THE SEVEN INFLUENTIAL.

Those last words stuck with Daniel. "Being tried for murder, I still can't believe it was him," he said while biting his nail. Rose rubbed his back as she looked at the screen.

"It's not as serious as it sounds. Heroes have to kill all the time, especially when the villains don't care enough about their lives to quit. Kyle must have had to do it. None of us know but him," Rose sighed.

Anya, who was sitting in the front row with Tonuko and Rake, looked down while twiddling her fingers. "*He took the blame for the person I killed, and if my dad wasn't a villain, Kyle might have not been tried at all. Why did he take the blame?*" she thought to herself.

Out of the corner of his eye, Tonuko glanced over at Anya. He put his arm around her, and whispered, "Don't worry, Anya, we'll find out why he did it." Anya nodded, then looked up.

"Kyle got a 100% on his entrance exam, he's super smart. It doesn't make sense why he would just randomly lose it and kill someone," Anya quietly said while squeezing her hands together.

Court Room, 10:00 a.m., Start of the Trial:

I looked up at George, who gave me a small smile and nodded. I could tell he was trying to reassure me, but my nerves wouldn't go away. I was terrified. Suddenly, a horn blasted and someone walked into the room from a dark doorway behind the Seven Influential. The man was short, very muscular with thick arms. He wore a cloak with short sleeves and lining the hood down to his feet was a tube full of a green and yellow liquid.

C.J. Dane, #7 Hero, Strength: Leak—he can leak acid from all parts of his body and uses a special cloak to prevent it from spilling. When he takes off the cloak, his

entire body is surrounded by acid and gives him superhuman abilities such as the ability to slide on the acid-like ice and the ability to latch a string of acid onto any surface and swing on it. Also, he can form solid structures and items out of acid.

He sat at the seat farthest from me, then a girl with pink, straight hair, lime-green skin, and a very bright and colorful jumpsuit walked in and sat next to him.

Aubrey Tato, #6 Hero, Strength: Color Bomb—she can shoot out bombs of multi-colored molten fluids, and the more colors the hotter the fluid. She has two types of bombs, ones that shoot out her left hand and ones that shoot out her right. The left-hand bombs are more pastel colors and rapidly cool at any temperature outside her body. She uses these to capture villains or seal holes. Her right-hand bombs are rainbow colored and heat up over time. This liquid can heat to 500 degrees Fahrenheit.

The next girl to walk in sat next to Aubrey. She looked holographic, was completely see-through, paper thin, and a light blue, almost gray color.

Eleanor Dainey, #5 Hero, Strength: Hologram— she is a holographic person that can make clones of herself. The clones cannot be hurt by physical attacks. They carry the weapons Eleanor carries and have the same martial skill as her. The most clones she can make without overworking herself is ten.

It was clear by now that the strongest heroes would sit next to me, making my nerves skyrocket. The next man to walk in was fit—not super muscular or scrawny—and wearing a long, black cape, goggles on the top of his head, and overly large metallic blue gloves.

Maverick Case, #4 Hero, Strength: Lightning Bug—harnessing the power of electricity that he can create out of his hands or feet, he can unleash powerful bolts of lightning or bursts of electricity that are like waves of power. Through training, he's mastered his electricity control to such an extreme that his lightning has turned from yellow to black and the electricity potency is particularly destructive and powerful.

I was shocked at the pure power sitting near me. All four heroes were lightyears ahead of me in strength. Why don't the Care-Givers focus on them instead of me? They've stopped so many villains and saved so many people.

"Everyone, please rise for the three strongest heroes in our country," a guard standing in front of me stated. We all stood, and in walked the third hero. He had a light dangling from his head, fangs, and fins sticking out of his cheeks; he looked like an Angler Fish.

Dame Qualin, #3 Hero, Strength: Angler Fish—he has a light dangling from his head that can shine as bright as the sun and he can breathe and swim quickly underwater. The strength gives the user a thirst for blood, but Dame counters this by drinking animals' blood daily and building up a resistance over time.

"This is always so overdramatic! Please, we're just people too, nothing special!" Dame yelled to the guard before sitting. Next, the hero I feared most walked in. The person's gender was unknown, but they were the second-strongest hero. They wore a walnut wood mask with native symbols painted in black. The symbols were worn down but still recognizable. I could see their eye stare me down as they sat.

Kaliska, #2 Hero, Strength: Native—they can use dead cells from the ground to summon zombified animals that are much larger and stronger than the animal was before it passed. Kaliska can also use the power of a Native Bible to unleash beams of pure power, eradicating anything within twenty feet of the book.

Kaliska said nothing and sat next to Dame. They were known as the coolest hero and Kaliska was barely the second-most powerful hero.

In walked the strongest, and his force shook the room. He was a very skinny, lanky, extremely tall man. He wore a long trench coat with a popped collar, steel-toed boots, and a fedora. He bowed after entering the room, and something compelled me to bow back.

Zane Kinder (Puppeteer), #1 Hero, Strength: Puppet—he can turn his soul into a transparent puppet that is controlled through his fingers by a very, very slim black rope. The puppet's mouth is always open and can mimic the strength of multiple people within a mile each direction. The puppet cannot be harmed by physical attacks, but any attack that lands on Zane or damages the puppet's strings affects both Zane and his puppet.

As Zane sat down, he stared into my soul. I was completely terrified, so terrified in fact, that I couldn't return his gaze.

"Bring forth the evidence," Zane stated while holding his hand out in front of the desk. The defense lawyer walked over and handed Zane a thin paper packet, then walked back to George and sat down.

"Not much evidence, huh?" George whispered to the defending lawyer.

"The ones I'm defending are damn dead, so I have no evidence to use," the lawyer whispered back. Zane looked at the two, and they quickly shut up. Zane flipped through the packet, then handed it to Kaliska and leaned on his desk while looking at me.

"Kyle Straiter, why don't you tell us how you feel about the event that occurred," Zane suggested, although it felt more like a command. I gulped, then tried to speak. The mic screeched loudly, so I apologized then began.

"Well, I was fighting to protect my friends a- and the kidnapped people. We fought the Nomeres and Spike in a tunnel underneath the wrestling complex, then-"

"Who's this Spike you speak of? Is he alive?" Kaliska asked, swiftly cutting me off. My eyes slightly widened, and I looked down while shaking my head. George sweated and couldn't help but slightly facepalm. "Who killed Spike?"

"I- I did. Spike was attacking me while I was trying to get past to retrieve my two kidnapped friends, so I needed to get him out of the way. I didn't try to kill him; I just threw him into the wall and-"

"Didn't try to kill him? Kyle, is this a joke to you?" Kaliska asked, cutting me off again. I felt sick when they asked that and shook my head again. Kaliska rolled their eyes and waved their hand at me. "Someone else ask him a question. We'll never get anywhere hearing him try and describe the events."

I've barely been able to describe them because you keep cutting me off.

"I'll take a question. What led to you murdering the two kidnappers?" Eleanor asked. Her tone was much nicer than Kaliska's.

"W- Well, I tried to reason with Lokel, since he is the father of one of my classmates. I kept telling him to join me and take down the Creature so he could go home and see his daughter." I teared up and squeezed the ends of my shorts. "He loved his daughter; you have to believe! He loved his family; it was the Creature's fault!" Everyone was silent, so I wiped my eyes and continued. "I'm sorry for my outburst ... After Lokel was bleeding out on the ground, I told him I would bring him to the surface to get medical attention. The Creature was going to attack again, though, so Lokel gave me a sword and told me to fight for him.

That's what I did, and I attacked the Creature. That led to his death, and that was the end of the fight."

A couple of pictures were taken, then Eleanor asked, "You just attacked the Creature and fully caved in his skull? There was a stab wound in his abdominal area, but where did this other injury come from?" I opened my mouth to answer, but I saw George shaking his head out of the corner of my eye. I stayed silent, making Eleanor ask, "Well?"

"I plead the fifth."

"Very well," Eleanor sighed, clearly annoyed. Dame took the next question and flipped through the packet in front of him.

"So, Kyle, what about the deaths of the Nomeres and Spike? How did those occur?" Dame asked with a more laid-back tone than the rest.

"Well, Spike was the first to go and as I said before, I hit him into the wall. My intention was to knock him out, but a giant mound of dirt fell from the ceiling and crushed him. Then, the girl expanded and blocked my flames, so I punched her, but I guess I punched her a bit too hard. Finally-"

Kaliska slammed their fist down and stood. "Punched her a bit too hard?! There was a gaping hole in her stomach along with blood spilled all over the tunnel! That seems like just a little too hard to you?!" I gulped.

"Her strength made her body like rubber, and when I punched her, my fist stretched in her stomach then pierced through. This caused her to spew blood through the hole as the excess air escaped the hole. I thought she would simply deflate, but I should have thought harder about how strengths are just an extended part of our bodies." Kaliska took a deep breath then sat down.

At E.H.:

Anya looked up at the screen and her eyes watered.

"He really covered for me, and he really cared about my dad ..." she thought.

In the Courtroom:

"What else happened during this long fight that pushed you into violence?" C.J. asked. I thought for a moment and had flashbacks of all the horrid things that happened.

"W- Well, I had to fight my own classmates because the Creature took over their minds, and Anya Lokel was hurting because of her dad. They took a junior who I look up to, Hazel Sparks, and intended to use her like they do their other kidnapped children. But the worst part was when I was being drowned ... and Kate saved me ... then, the Creature ... he stabbed her." I couldn't contain myself, and I cried out, "And now, she'll never be a hero!"

E.H.:

Hunter looked at the screen, shocked. "He really-, cares about my sister?" Zach nudged his arm.

"Duh, of course he does. I heard he started going ballistic only after she got hurt." Hunter looked over at Zach, then back to me on the screen.

Courtroom:

"I am very sorry for the trauma this experience has brought you," C.J. stated while holding his hand near his heart. I nodded.

"How about we talk about you, since you're here and all," Aubrey smiled while leaning back in her chair.

"Objection, that is irrelevant to the case!" George shouted while standing up. Zane waved him off, then glared at me again.

"Overruled. Aubrey, continue." My stomach dropped, and I felt like I was gonna throw up. George repeatedly tapped his pen, then wiped sweat from his forehead. This part of the trial, would decide everything ...

"How does your mother feel about this trial? Speaking of her, can we get any information on her?" I looked over at George, who shook his head again.

"I plead the fifth." Aubrey looked at the papers in front of her while mumbling, then Maverick spoke up.

"Well, how about your life as a child? Any reoccurring problems there that would have caused you to lose control during this fight?" George shook his head again, so I knew what to do.

"I- I plead the fifth." Although frustrated, Maverick nodded.

The judges were looking at their papers, then Zane asked, "How many strengths do you have? The world now knows of your three, since you were hiding one, but are there more that you are hiding? Seems pretty odd that the number went up, no?"

"U- Uh, yes. It is pretty odd," I started while glancing at George. He obviously was shaking his head, so I stated once again, "I plead the fifth." My leg began bouncing, and I was starting to sweat. Foul was extremely nervous as well, and he was seated closest to George.

"George, they're getting angry! He can't keep this up!" Foul whisper–yelled. George leaned back in his chair and moved his head toward Foul without taking his eyes off me.

"It is Kyle's Constitutional Right to plead the fifth. There's nothing they can say about it," George confirmed.

"Very well," Dame angrily said. "How about your father? That is someone we have no information on; care to elaborate on who he is and what kind of influence he's had on-"

"I hate him," I stated, cutting Dame off. There was a loud gasp throughout the building, and I could tell that greatly angered the heroes.

E.H.:

"Wait, so Kyle does have a dad? I thought his parents were unknown," Steven asked. Many others joined in his confusion, but Tonuko was just furious. He squeezed his chair's armrest, and his eyes were locked on me.

"You fucking lied to me, you scumbag."

Courtroom:

"First, you will not cut off a member of the Seven Influential while he is speaking. Second, we were told you have not only never met your father, but nobody knew who the father was when you were born. Last, if you don't straighten up your attitude, I will personally teach you a lesson!" Kaliska erupted while rising. Kaliska jumped over the desk, landed on the ground, then stomped in front of my stand. Kaliska pulled me off the chair, then asked loudly, "Who the hell are your mother and father?!" Kaliska held me by my collar, and I could hear their breathing through their mask.

"Kyle Straiter, we do not have all day. Answer. The. Question," Zane stated a minute later. I closed my eyes tight and tensed my fist. Flashbacks of all my beatings, my mother on the floor after Tyrant stabbed her, the Care-Givers attacking me and my classmates, it all rushed back to me at once.

"You cannot deny his right to deny any information he does not want to answer! You cannot deny his rights!" Kaliska stomped their foot, shutting George up.

I grabbed Kaliska's hands, then erupted, "SAMUEL STRAITER, MY FATHER IS SAMUEL STRAITER,

OTHERWISE KNOWN AS TYRANT! MY MOTHER IS
GEM STRAITER, AND SHE WAS MURDERED BY HIM
AND DIED IN MY FUCKING HANDS SIX-AND-A-
HALF YEARS AGO!"

Chapter 13
The Vows I Take, The Promises I Make

Kaliska gently put me down and took a step back. Tears streamed down my cheeks, I clenched my jaw, and my face was red. Zane stepped down from the podium in front of the Seven Influential and stood in front of me. I was filled with rage before, but when he loomed over me, I was just scared. I knew it was over, I broke. Zane lifted his arms up ... then hugged me. I was shocked and overwhelmed with emotion.

Everyone knows now, everyone. I'm Kyle Straiter, the son of Samuel Straiter, the man on top of the crime world.

E.H.:

Nobody knew what to say and Fallen shook his head.

"He ... lied to all of us," Cindy weakly said while looking at the screen.

"His father is the world's most infamous, most powerful villain," Camilla stuttered, her voice shaking.

"So what?!" Daniel shouted as he stood. "He's still Kyle Straiter, and clearly, he's trying to become a hero even if his family tried to decide otherwise!"

"Daniel, *did you know?!*" Tonuko screamed while standing and slowly turning around. His face was filled with fury. Daniel was frightened and didn't respond. His silence was enough of an answer.

"Daniel and I were there for Kyle when he was younger. He had it rough, his dad was crazy and would beat him and his mom every damn day! You think he'd follow in the footsteps of a monster like that?!" Jaxon argued while staring right at Tonuko. "C'mon, man, you've been getting close with him; you must have heard his declarations of killing that bastard. It's all the kid lives for!"

"I mean, we were there for Alex when his dad got possessed. Now that I think about it, during all the times Kyle had an emotional outburst, everyone just shunned him and ridiculed him. Why shouldn't we be there for him like we were for Alex, because Alex had some visible wound while Kyle's are inside?" Zach added while laying back in his seat.

"Did any of us make an effort to help him when he was hurting, or did we just think he was so strong and cocky he didn't need any of our help?" Anya asked while standing next to Tonuko. Tonuko looked down at her with a mixture of confusion and anger.

"He murdered your dad a little over a week ago and now you're defending him?!" Tonuko shouted to Anya.

"He did it to save us, Tonuko! We left him in that pit to die and he came out on top! How can we blame him for risking his life to save ours?!" Anya argued, standing her ground as usual. Tonuko was speechless, completely dumbfounded. He tensed his fist, then stormed out of the theatre.

"Where the hell is he going?! Listen, all of you supporting Kyle, from the bottom of my heart, thank you. I worked with him all summer, listened to his silent cries and pleas, and helped him overcome what his father did! He needs our help just as much as we need his, so those who are opposing him, grow the hell up!" Fallen yelled. He ran to the door, looked back at Excalibur and nodded, then chased after Tonuko. Excalibur snapped out of his shock and nodded back.

"Yes, his past does not define his future. Nothing his father did had anything to do with him. We cannot hate him for something he can't control!" Camilla looked down, and softly apologized.

219

"Sorry, it's just shocking that part of the reason we've been attacked so many times is because Tyrant is going after his son."

"Part of the reason?! It's all his fault we've been attacked so much and all his fault we've been hurt! We wouldn't be dealing with Care-Givers if Kyle didn't exist!" Zayden yelled at her.

"Don't talk about him like that! Sure, he may be the reason we were attacked in the first place, but our bad decision making got us hurt! Kyle can't control what we do, only what he does. And you know what he's done? Risked his life and nearly got killed protecting us!" Alex retorted. The class started arguing, destroying the progress they'd made building friendships.

Courtroom:

Zane and Kaliska returned to their seats, and I returned to mine. The black tears oozed out of my eyes, but I ignored them and looked at Zane.

"Mr. Straiter," Kaliska started. I flinched, assuming I was about to either be arrested or yelled at. Instead, Kaliska continued, "Thank you for being honest with us and revealing your trauma. The fact that you saved all those kidnapped people, even if it meant murdering five criminals, and that you acted like a hero instead of your scum of a father, is inspiring." I smiled at Kaliska and nodded my head.

"Thank you. I'll never end up like him," I softly responded. Kaliska nodded and gave me a thumbs up.

"It is not what you are given, or the road others pave for you, that dictates your future. It is you, the work and dedication you put in, and your accomplishments that make you succeed," Maverick profoundly spoke. Foul stood and clapped, then another person joined, and another, and

220

eventually the entire crowd was cheering for me, for Maverick, for heroes.

"Kyle, I am willing to drop any charges of murder on one, and only one, condition," Zane smiled while standing from his seat. I nodded, then Zane said, "As long as you promise to live up to the ceiling that you are given, prove the world wrong, and make it a better place in your later years, then I will be confident in my decision." I looked up at Zane, my eyes twinkling, and I nodded.

"Yes, I promise!"

"Promise me we will never see you here again, Kyle Straiter," Kaliska said after standing.

"I promise!"

"Promise me you'll be a hardworking, kind hero I can brag to my grandchildren about!" Dame yelled cheerfully.

"I promise!"

"Promise all of us that you will not commit an unprovoked murder ever again," Maverick smiled.

"I promise!"

"Promise me that when I next hear Kyle Straiter on the news, it will be for stopping another disgusting criminal in this world!" Eleanor shouted before standing.

"I promise!"

"Promise me that you will raise your own child to be just like you: a fine young hero who will accomplish more than anyone in this courtroom could imagine!" Aubrey yelled.

"I promise!"

"Promise that someday any of us will be able to fight by your side to vanquish the Care-Givers and Tyrant once and for all!" C.J. boldly stated.

"I promise!"

"And one more thing, Kyle," Zane said while reaching his hand out to me. "Promise me that one day you will compete with my son to take my spot. You will fight to be the best hero in history." With that final promise, I shook Zane's hand and was filled with glee. My black tears were gone, as well as the pain in my stomach. It was as if nobody even remembered I was Tyrant's son. "Very well, then, you are dismissed and free to return to your studies. Be a good student, and an even better hero," Zane smiled, waving me off.

"I will, and I hope to see you again, but for a good reason next time!" They laughed, then the Seven Influential returned to the back room. George, Foul, and I walked out of the courthouse first. There were nearly twice as many paparazzi as before. When we reached the van and got in, Foul turned around and poked at me while wearing a massive smile.

"Look at that Kyle, I told you we'd be fine!" Foul shouted before giving me a high-five.

"You did well up there kid, really well. I'm sorry the information had to get leaked, but it seems as though it was for the better. Everyone knows whose side you are on!" George said as he left the parking lot. There was a moment of silence, then Foul sighed.

"As happy as we are, the world does officially know who your father is. It's best we get you back to Eccentric High as quickly as possible." I nodded, and George sped toward the highway. I was delivered home around 7:00 p.m. When I stepped out of the car, Foul joined me, since he also would be living at E.H. I took a deep breath, then stretched my back and jumped into the air.

"The number-one hero said I would be the best hero in history! How freaking awesome is that?!" I exclaimed while punching the air. I pranced down the walkway and made my way to the freshman dorms. I'd been so happy the past couple of hours, I'd forgotten that the trial was nationally broadcast. My nerves caught up to me when I reached the front of the dorms, but I took a deep breath and opened the door.

It's my first time seeing my classmates in over a week. I wonder what's happened ...

The building was dead quiet, not a soul was in the main area. It was peculiar. Usually at least a few people would be down here eating or watching T.V.

I guess it is a school night, maybe the new teacher is stricter on bedtimes and crap. There's no way everyone follows the rules though.

I walked to the couch and jumped over the back of it. I laid there, sinking into the cushions, and smiled to myself. I heard someone walking down the stairs, and saw Khloe turn the corner. She saw me laying there, crossed her arms and rolled her eyes.

"I'm gonna guess you guys watched the trial?" I asked nervously. Khloe leaned back on her right foot and nodded. I gulped but didn't know what to say.

"I can't believe you didn't tell any of us. I mean, seriously?!" Khloe snapped before turning.

"It's a sensitive topic, I didn't know how to bring it up!" I yelled to her as she walked away. There was no response. I rested my head. Knowing people were mad worried me. Then I heard the door open and heard several footsteps walk into the room. I lifted my head and saw Alex, Tonuko, and Anya. I smiled and waved. "Hey guys, been a hot minute, eh?" Alex gave me the same energy, a big smile and wave, but Tonuko walked over with his fists tensed. He took another step toward me, then groaned and looked up.

"Fuck, it's taking all my might to not beat your ass right now!" Tonuko didn't give me a second glance before stomping away and up the stairs. My hand was just hanging in the air, and my confused smile was still smeared across my face. I slowly put down my hand, and my smile faded as I looked at Anya and Alex.

"He's uh- not taking the news well. He keeps calling you a liar," Anya sighed before sitting down across the couch.

"How are you holding up though? I mean, getting that off your chest must have been a relief, but it had to have been scary!" Alex asked as he sat next to me. I sat up straight and ran my hand through my hair while looking down.

"I'm fine, it was just a huge relief to finally not have to hide it anymore. It's been ... haunting me my entire life." Alex looked startled, so I asked, "You alright?" The black liquid poured out of my eyes and mouth, but I didn't know why.

"Yeah, yeah, I'm good. It was just a big shock to hear about how the Tyrant is your dad." I nodded and leaned back.

"I understand, it is a big shocker. That's why I kept it a secret, but Kaliska shook it right out of me. Kaliska was just too scary, I had to say it," I slightly chuckled while remembering how much they yelled at me.

"Some people can't seem to understand that. They think you were lying because you are still connected with your dad or something, not that you were lying because, you know, it's a pretty big deal!" Anya sighed.

"Yeah, we were arguing a lot after you came clean. I mean, class had to be canceled because there was so much fighting going on. People couldn't accept you for you," Alex added while glancing over at me. The liquid oozed again, and Alex looked startled like before. "And you're sure you're okay, right? You don't need to talk about anything?"

"Yeah, I already said I'm fine." He nodded, then they told me about what happened with Alex's father. It made me mad knowing that a villain would do something like that to a family as nice as Alex's. "I'm so sorry to hear that. Is your dad okay now?"

"Thanks, and yeah, he's doing much better. My mom is recovering swiftly too, all thanks to Nurse Blavins!" I nodded, relieved to hear the news. We all were silent again, but my snickers interrupted us.

"Sorry, I just can't believe Fallen is our teacher. I mean, what a guy he is!" We laughed while thinking about our Fallen interactions.

"Yeah, Fallen started out a complete ass! He was poking fun at the kidnappers fight and how you went to jail, but now I just see him as a total badass!" Alex smiled. After a few seconds, I stood and cracked my back.

"I'm gonna go make sure all my stuff is in my room and try to talk with some of the others. I guess, wish me luck?" Alex gave me a thumbs up, and Anya shook her head.

"You're gonna need it. I mean, I think your entire floor is P.O.'d." I let out an overexaggerated dreadful groan, making the two giggle, then I started up the stairs. When I reached my floor, it was dead quiet. All the doors were closed, except one. I walked over and saw Cindy doing her homework. I knocked twice on the door, then she looked over and her smile faded.

"What are you doing here, liar?" Cindy asked before standing.

Shit, she's mad at me too. I was kinda hoping she and Alex would be on the same side.

"I was just uh ... wondering how you were. I haven't seen any of you guys since the fight and even then we couldn't necessarily talk." There was a silence, then she walked toward me. She was wearing a blue tank top, big, fuzzy pajama pants, and slippers. "What were you doing over there?"

"Homework," she swiftly responded. I gave her a confused look and scratched my head.

"Homework? Normal school ended in middle school; what homework are you doing?"

"Oh, right, you've been gone. Our teachers started a new class about decision making and stuff on the battlefield. Y'know, since some of us don't know how to act when we're under attack."

Unnecessary attack, lowkey hurt ...

"Can I see what this homework looks like?" I asked while taking a step forward. Cindy put her hand on my stomach, stopping me from approaching.

"I think it's best you leave. I don't want you to mess up my homework with your lying and horrible decision making!"

She just keeps them coming, huh?

"Don't forget who was the one who saved everyone from the kidnappers. I didn't make bad decisions, I was in a bad situation and had to act to make sure we didn't lose anyone," I defended myself calmly; raising my voice would only make people angrier.

"You weren't the only one fighting to save people, so stop acting like it! Fighting isn't the only way of being a hero! Tonuko escorted everyone from the pit, Zach tried to save countless people by holding up an entire building, the police and heroes fought off Care-Givers, so don't sit there and act like you were the only person doing something!" Cindy shouted, her cheeks turning red as she gave me a death-stare.

"How am I supposed to beat the kidnappers, escort people, and fight off the Care-Givers? There's only one of me," I responded, now a little annoyed by her ignorance.

Cindy huffed, and muttered as she turned around, "Of course, what else should I expect?"

I was going to walk away as well, but I stopped when I heard that. "Excuse me?" I asked, looking back at her. She swiveled on her heels and crossed her arms while still glaring at me.

"What else should I expect from the son of Tyrant other than selfish cockiness?" I was speechless, in fact, and heard a crack in my heart.

"W- Wow, so after everything that's all you think of me?" With hurt in my voice, I continued, "After I busted my ass to make sure you would be okay, after I risked my life protecting your friends, after I took all the blame of everything, this is what I get in return? One confession just ruins everything, right?" She looked away and stared at her desk. I couldn't tell if she was still mad, sad, or felt guilty, so I walked out and quietly shut the door behind me.

So, that's all that I'm viewed as now? Even after the Seven Influential forgave me, after I was recognized for saving lives and being a hero, I'm treated like garbage? I'm just Tyrant's son now ... aren't I?

With that heartbreaking conversation, I went straight to bed, although I didn't sleep a lot. Throughout the night, the static returned in waves ...

I woke and turned off my alarm, then laid there for couple minutes. I took a deep breath, then sat up and held my head.

227

Nasty headrush, probably because I can't remember the last time I ate a full meal.

I got up off my bed, showered, dressed, and brushed my teeth. I couldn't even look at myself in the mirror, I had to brush my teeth in the shower. After I finished my morning routine, I threw on a plain, black sweatshirt and headed downstairs.

Ever since the confession, it seems as if people aren't very social. I get that it's early in the morning, but usually people are out and about. Tonuko is mad at me, like fuming, but he was still talking with Alex and Anya even though they support me. Why isn't anyone else like that?

Instead of going on my usual morning run, something I hadn't done in over a week, I decided to get something to eat at the little strip mall, mentioned in the invitation letter sent out, on campus.

I've never been to the strip mall; I wonder what kind of stuff it has.

There were four stores next to each other, each a little bigger than a classroom. Two of the stores were clothing stores, one for warm weather and the other for the cold, and all the clothes were branded with E.H.'s logo. The other two stores were for food. One was a convenience store with pre-packaged food as well as fresh foods, and the other had two chefs who made whatever dishes were on the menu for the day—one breakfast item, one lunch item, and one dinner item. I considered getting a cooked meal but decided instead to just grab a packaged muffin from the convenience store. I continued down the path while opening the wrapper, then noticed there were swimsuits in the warm-weather store.

Is there a pool here? Come to think of it, I've never actually been on the other side of the school. What's over there?

I made my way down the path, past the school, then saw a huge pool gated off behind the school. I was pretty surprised I'd never noticed it considering its size. Half the pool had separators for lanes of swimming, and the other was open water.

Maybe we could all go swimming together one day. Well, I guess that's if all the sour emotions go away ...

I continued touring around campus and walked past the sophomore and junior dorms; they looked the same as ours. The senior dorms were very bare and dark. I continued walking and eventually reached the front gate. Before I actually walked in front of it, I heard a ton of yelling, talking, and general commotion.

What the hell? Who's here so early?

I walked past the wall and looked through the metal gate, then my stomach dropped. There were countless guards trying to contain the hundreds of newscasters, cameramen, people in general. After I made my presence known, the commotion halted for a quick second, then everyone erupted with questions and yelling. The cameras were now on me and people were reaching their mics past the guards.

"Kyle Straiter, how is life back at school with everyone knowing you are the infamous Tyrant's son?!"

"Are you being accepted by your peers, or have you lost all your friends?!"

"Are you the reason for all the attacks on your class by Care-Givers?!"

"Will there be another attack in the close future?!"

I walked to the trash can next to the gate, threw out my muffin wrapper, then walked away. I could hear the screaming getting louder and the barrage of questions continued, but I ignored it and headed for the school's front doors. I wanted to pay Fallen a visit before class started. I went up the stairs and strolled down the hall until I reached my classroom. When I looked in through the door, I saw Fallen sitting at his desk correcting papers. I knocked before I turned the knob and Fallen looked up then grinned.

"There's the criminal! How ya been, Kyle?" I couldn't help but smile, and when we walked toward each other, we grabbed the other's hand and pulled in for a one-arm hug.

"I mean, you can probably guess I've been better," I responded after pulling off the hug. He took a step back, then sighed.

"Yeah, yeah. I can only imagine the kinda stress you've had on you this past week and a half. It must be tough knowing your class relied on you and trusted you, but now half the country hates you after only a day." I sat at the first desk by the door, and he leaned on his podium at the front of the room.

"Yep, I barely thought about the fact that my class probably saw the trial because I was so happy to be found not guilty. So far, it seems like most everyone here hates me now." He shook his head, frustrated.

"I don't know what others told you, but it was an ugly scene in that theatre. Everyone was pointing, shouting, swearing, insulting, just being total a-holes to each other. Unnecessary info was being spewed; it was just ... horrible. People were flat-out upset that Tyrant's son, son of a villain who's hurt so many people they know, is at this school. On top of that, knowing that not only you've been lying about how many strengths you have, but also the fact that it's probably because of you that we've been targeted by the Care-Givers, it just ignited more flames." I rested my arms on my desk and slouched in the chair while nodding my head.

"I think some of them were just jealous of my two strengths at first, but during the kidnapper fight, I had no choice but to use more to beat my mind-controlled teammates and the kidnappers. Kidnappings, torture, abuse—they were ... no; the Creature was just pleasuring his insanities." Fallen stood and grabbed a piece of chalk, then walked over to the chalk board and started to write. The school didn't have the funding for white boards, so every class had chalkboards. Fallen wrote in big letters:

Honesty

Bravery

Trustworthy

Respectful

Caring

Understanding

"These are the six qualities society expects heroes to retain. At first, HotSauce was known as the perfect hero, he had everything people wanted to see in someone who saves lives. He took the bare minimum a hero could make, worked overtime, travelled to help every city he could. He was amazing. However, since his death," Fallen raised his hand, then drew a large, thick "X" over the words, "the faith and trust in heroes has plummeted. The most selfless man alive died because he acted selfishly and tried to gain more power. That fact broke all heroes' images. Knowing that someone you respected and trusted died because of their selfish desires, whether they were good or bad, breaks people. It makes them hate that person and the concept of what they fought for." My eyes widened, and I tensed my body.

"Th- The faith in heroes, is- going down? But we fight to protect everyone! If they don't trust us, who will they trust?"

On top of that, what Fallen just said kinda sounds like what happened with me. I lost their trust and respect.

231

Fallen nodded and sighed, then elaborated, "Look, we're not supposed to tell any students, for fear of creating panic, but it has to be said. Riots are starting all over the country demanding rights for civilians and banning heroes from cities. Society everywhere does not trust heroes to take care of them, and believes they are only looking out for themselves and their money. The riots exploded in our state after your confession ..."

"Don't they realize we're fighting for them? Heroes surfaced to protect people from criminals!" Fallen shook his head and waved his finger.

"No, heroes surfaced to protect people from villains. Criminals have always been a thing and that's what cops were for, but villains, they're 'super criminals'. They abuse their powers, to—well, to put it plainly, to kill. Criminals either looked for money, or just weren't very strong and could be contained by police. However, villains were too powerful for the police to handle, and that's when people stood and fought back against these power-hungry villains. Heroes were cherished and loved by the people at first, but now, people are arguing that we cause more damage and put more lives at risk than we save. It's a hard and weird subject to understand if you aren't in their shoes." I looked down at the desk and thought back to the destroyed building, the innocent people scattered around crying, the hole in the street caused by David's grenades, then looked back up.

"Yeah, that makes sense. We do destroy a lot of property during battles. Who even paid for the damages at Veena?" Fallen put down his chalk and erased the board.

"I have no idea; they were paid for before I was hired as a teacher. Anyway, you should get going to the theatre. Excalibur and I will be talking to your class about something important." Fallen was extremely serious after he said that, so I figured it was best not to mention that I had no clue where the hell the theatre was. I scooted out of the classroom and walked to my locker, then looked down both ends of the hall. I saw many bare classrooms; some that were previously off limits were now open since construction was finished.

I wonder why there are so many classrooms here. What other classes besides homeroom, training, and I guess decision making are possible at a hero school?

I made my way back down the stairs, and saw Alex walk in through the front door.

"Alex, thank God you're here!" I shouted running up to him.

He looked confused, then asked, "What, is something wrong?" I shook my head and rubbed my neck, a little embarrassed.

"Well, not really. It's just ... where in the world is this so-called theatre?" He chuckled and closed his umbrella—I could now see it had started to rain.

"Just follow me." We went to his locker first so he could put his umbrella away, then he showed me where the theatre was. In the far back of the building, on the first floor, there was a huge room with multiple rows of comfy-enough looking chairs. Excalibur was seated on the stage, not responding to anyone who talked to him, and a couple of other students were seated already.

"Are there assigned seats in here or-?"

"No, you can sit wherever," he quickly responded. Alex sat next to Jessica and Scarlett so I followed. I assumed those two weren't mad at me since they were friendly with Alex when he said hi to them. However, when I sat next to Alex, Jessica scoffed, stood, and walked toward the other side of the aisle.

"Jess, c'mon!" Scarlett begged, to no avail. She sighed and apologized.

"Sorry Kyle, she isn't taking the news very well. I don't understand why people are so mad about it." I shrugged, but Alex leaned on his knees and looked at Jessica.

"Her cousin was killed in a building explosion caused by Tyrant a year ago. I have a feeling seeing Tyrant's son isn't making her feel any better." I looked down, full of guilt. Even though I had nothing to do with her cousin's death, I felt fully responsible.

"Fuck man, that's horrible," I said.

"Yeah, it is! Maybe we'll be next since the Care-Givers are attacking us because of you!" Jessica angrily screamed. I knew it would be best to stay quiet. When she reached the end of the aisle she sat next to Donte. Our classmates started piling in, and everyone who opposed me sat away from me, while the people who accepted me sat near me. Out of the thirty-two students, only twelve sat near me.

Wow, so this really has ruined friendships? Donte and Steven, Jessica and Scarlett, Alex and Cindy, Tonuko and Anya, Zayden and Rake, these people who were all good friends are now glaring and seething at each other. What do I do?

While everyone yelled and argued, Excalibur stayed quiet. Then Fallen kicked open the doors. The loud bang made everyone shut up. He walked in with his hands in his pockets, scanned the room, then clenched his jaw.

"Look at all of ya, letting these petty emotions get in the way of your growth as a grade. This is absolutely fucking ridiculous!" Fallen ridiculed while making his way down the aisle. Excalibur hopped off the stage and punched his hand against the wooden stage.

"All you've been doing is bickering about something that shouldn't matter! This is immature and wrong, and you should be punished! Yesterday was absolutely unacceptable!" Excalibur shouted. I could see guilt grow on my classmates' faces.

Woah, how bad was it yesterday?

"Since more than half of you have decided you cannot accept the student who you praised not too long ago—merely because he spoke up and got something off his chest—Excalibur and I have decided to issue a lockdown on all freshmen!" Fallen revealed while holding his hands up and grinning evilly.

"We aren't supposed to leave campus either way, so what will a lockdown do?" Tonuko asked, obviously being a smartass. Fallen shook his head and pointed behind him.

"The campus? More like your dorm building," Fallen retorted. Everyone shouted, "What?!"

"Isn't this a little extreme?! We have a lot of training to do, and the shadowing is coming up soon!" Steven argued after standing.

"Sit down boy!" Fallen snapped. Steven complied. "You all have the shadowing in a little over a month and you will be missing out on training during this lockdown. That's why you shouldn't be yelling at us but should be utterly disappointed in yourselves! We could be working on power-ups and all that bull crap, but since you are being childish and immature, we have no choice but to amend your trust in each other." Fallen paced back and forth in front of Excalibur. "Trust is the most important part of being a hero because you must work with sidekicks as well as other heroes and trust that they will have your back. If you can't even trust yourselves, the future of heroes, then how can we have trust that you will be able to go out and shadow hero organizations?" Fallen explained.

"Shadowing is one of the most important events of freshman year! If we can't train and get stronger, then how are we supposed to be able to train under a pro-hero and be ready?!" Cindy asked. Fallen shrugged and looked as though he was trying to hold back laughter.

"That's a great question Cindy, but I do not have the answer. This lockdown isn't just because of the hatred that's developed since the trial. We've noticed the freshman class is relying heavily on the chefs and they aren't doing many activities as a grade or even as classes! Every other class has gone shopping, used the pool, or at least damn trained on their own time with each other! The laziness and social distancing in this grade is sickening considering you should be working as hard as you can to become the best heroes you can be! You will not be allowed to buy food, since you won't be leaving the dorm, and we will provide groceries once a day. You will have enough food for breakfast, lunch, dinner, and minimal snacks."

Everyone mumbled and grumbled to each other, then Excalibur marched up the aisle and opened the doors. He kicked the doorstop down, then smugly grinned and made big swoops with his arms before pointing his hands out the door.

"Go on, get back to your dorms. You may want to open some windows, it can get stuffy in there," Excalibur snickered. Fallen couldn't help but chuckle, and the teachers followed us as we trudged to our dorms. I was the last to enter the building, but before I made it through the door Fallen put his hand on my shoulder.

"Fix up your friendships, and don't forget what I taught you: friendships save lives," he whispered. I didn't turn around; I watched as Tonuko turned the corner and went up the stairs.

"Don't worry, I'm gonna fix this," I gave him a thumbs up as I turned around and smiled, "It's what I owe to the people who respected me." He smirked and after I had entered, he closed and locked the doors. Jon walked by with Devin and the two burst out laughing.

Jon was holding his stomach as he wheezed, "Wow, the freshies are getting put in lockdown?! That is priceless! They need to just get along already!" Fallen and Excalibur joined in the laughter.

"That's what we're saying! Now that they are stuck in the building with each other, with a shared common space, they'll have to finally start damn socializing with each other!" Fallen snickered.

Chapter 14
Tension

A little more than half of the students immediately went to their rooms. The others stayed in the common area and made an effort to talk to each other.

"Well, I guess this is our life for a while," Rose sighed while sitting at a barstool and resting her head in her arms on the counter.

Daniel chuckled and responded, "I mean, it could be worse. We could be out fighting more villains or something!" They all agreed, but I didn't respond.

Iris walked up to the counter and looked afraid to talk. "U- Um, does anyone actually know how to cook?" she blurted out, then blushed in embarrassment. Nobody mentioned her shyness, but instead we looked at each other and no one answered.

After a few seconds, Scarlett grabbed Jess and wrapped her arm around Jess's shoulder. "We can do it! We took cooking lessons when we were younger!" Scarlett announced gleefully.

"Really?" Alex asked. "I've known Jessica for like eight years and I've never known she knew how to cook and never knew she's known you."

"Yeah, we're neighbors and my aunt used to give us cooking lessons on the weekends. It's been a while, but I think we can do it," Jessica clarified quietly. We heard a knock at the door, so I walked over and answered it. To our surprise, Hazel walked in along with Jon and Devin, and they were carrying bags of food.

"We got your food haul, freshies!" Hazel laughed while putting down the food.

She and I hugged, then I exclaimed, "I didn't know you were back already! You're okay, right?!" Hazel nodded, then wiped a tear from her eye. She pulled me back in and hugged me again.

"Kyle, just so you know, I will always accept you. Nothing about your past will change how I view you now," she reassured me.

Once we stopped, Jon leaned on my shoulder and waved his hand in front of his nose. "You freshmen sure are stinky; want me to pick up some air fresheners?" I rolled my eyes, while shaking my head. Jon snickered, then reached his other hand into one of the plastic bags and pulled out a carton of eggs. "Two bags are breakfast, two are lunch, two are dinner, and one is snacks and shit. There're recipe sheets, written by yours truly, in each bag for the meals today, but you're only getting them today!"

"Thanks guys. We're definitely gonna follow these recipes to the letter," Scarlett said while rifling through the first two bags. Devin backed up and peered out the door and saw his and Hazel's class leaving the school.

"Well, we're gonna get going. Get over this social hump fast so you can get back to training. Also, Fallen and Excalibur made a rule that you aren't allowed to close your doors before 10:00 p.m. It'll force you to be more social during the day," Devin informed us before walking out. Hazel and Jon said bye to us, then left. We groaned about the new rule and gathered around the counter.

"Let's go to our own floors and tell everyone about the door rule. Jessica and Scarlett, you can stay down here and start unpacking the groceries if you want," Camilla directed. I hesitated, then took a deep breath and exhaled quietly.

"Alex and Khloe, you stay and help Jessica and Scarlett. Iris and I will tell Tonuko and Cindy." I turned and looked at the stairs, but Khloe and Alex were confused. Alex just stood and shrugged.

"Alright, it's good to not leave all the work with Jessica and Scarlett anyway," Alex smiled while picking up the gallon of milk from one of the bags. Khloe was a little more hesitant.

"Are you sure it's smart for you to go near Tonuko right now? He's pretty mad," Khloe asked.

I shrugged and shook my head. "We're never gonna get out of here if we can't get along. Tonuko and I were gonna have to talk it out eventually." With that, Iris and I left for our floor. When we made it up the stairs, Iris scurried into Cindy's room.

When I walked past Cindy's open door, Iris poked her head out and asked, "Are you sure this is a good idea?"

I thought for a moment, then yawned and blinked a few times. I put my hands on my head and nodded. "Tonuko can't stay mad forever. If he does, then he's just a little baby," I snickered while walking away.

I made it to Tonuko's door and stood in front of it for a few minutes. I took a very deep breath, in through my nose, out through my mouth. I found myself more nervous than when I'd confronted Cindy, but after all that had happened my nerves were incomparable. I knocked on the door, then stated, "Tonuko, it's Kyle. We need to talk."

"Get the hell away from my room, lying-ass criminal," Tonuko hatefully remarked. I put my hand on the knob, then opened the door. In the room to my right, Iris and Cindy were hiding, yet listening. In his room, Tonuko was seated on his bed, the only light coming from the window that he was looking out.

He turned to look at me as I argued, "I'm not a criminal, you know that! When someone I'm related to, but not close to, turns out to be evil, that makes me the same?! What kind of stupid logic is that?"

Tonuko stood and marched over to me, then poked me in the chest, hard. "You lied to me; you hid your connection with Tyrant. You think this is all just a big game, *huh?!* You can't just lie straight to my face, act all heroic and mighty, then when everything you've said turns out wrong, act like nothing ever happened! You've got that villain blood surging through your veins. It's going to rise up and takeover eventually and when it does, I'll be there to *take you down!*" He shoved me back and I stumbled into the hall. He stepped out of his room, then I ran and grabbed his shirt collar.

"Just because my dirtbag father is a criminal doesn't mean I'm one! I just beat down two powerful villains with direct connections with my dad!" Tonuko's icy stare didn't ease up; he glared into my eyes and clenched his jaw.

"That event proved more that you're just a villain hiding with us. You're in denial, but you can't control your animalistic instincts! *You killed five people! You weren't any kind of damn hero!*" he snapped at me.

"You and I both know I killed three people, not five. We know who killed the Nomeres. I took the blame for you and Anya so you wouldn't have to deal with the backlash of being good people with wrong actions," I responded immediately in a quiet seethe.

Tonuko grabbed the collar of my shirt. "Stop being so fucking cocky! You didn't have to do shit! Don't act like we owe you anything, or like you saved our asses!" he erupted. I heard footsteps on the stairs, and people were gathering at the end of the hall.

Why the hell is everyone saying I'm being selfish and cocky?! I saved them from the villains! Is this what heroes get for saving the day: being shunned and yelled at?!

"Don't you understand?! I almost died trying to stop the kidnappers from getting anyone else! They tortured Hazel, paralyzed Kate, possessed you; I risked my life to

241

make sure you got to safety! Don't you dare forget what the hell I told you during the fight!" Tonuko's eyes slightly widened as he remembered.

"Tonuko, my life is worth so much less than all of yours! I don't have a real reason to keep going, but you all do! Don't let me be the reason you die, get out of here with yours and everyone else's lives, dammit!"

"Stop trying to make me feel guilty, asshole!" Tonuko screamed, shaking me back and forth then throwing me down the hall. I got up and tackled him onto the ground. "You've never cared about anyone; all you've done is be violent and put us in danger! You have no self-control!" He punched me in the face, so I retaliated with a punch of my own.

"I haven't cared because I don't know how to care about people! Why are you so closed-minded that you can't understand that I've never in my life had anyone care for me? Everyone acting as if there's a reason to protect each other ... it makes no sense!"

He tackled me and put me in a headlock, then a girl ran at us and speared me out of his grasp. She and I rolled on the ground for a couple of feet, then she sat up and held my arms behind my back.

"Would you two knock it off?! It's been like fifteen minutes and you're already fighting!" the girl shouted after rolling her eyes.

Tonuko charged at me again, but I kicked him in the stomach before he could reach me. I heated my arms so the girl holding me would let go and dove at Tonuko. After a few more seconds of us fighting, Rake managed to contain Tonuko, and the girl got a hold of me again.

"Chill out man. Why are you so against him?" Rake asked Tonuko. Tonuko wiped blood from his nose, then sighed instead of answering the question.

"Everyone, just go downstairs. Steven and I will help. Having more people who aren't biased will aid in settling this," Cora commanded. The students reluctantly followed, then Cora and Steven walked over between Tonuko and me.

"C'mon Tonuko, fighting him won't solve anything. I don't wanna make you madder or anything, but he's kinda like beaten you twice and you two have caused massive damage both times. We can't destroy these dorms, it's the place we sleep and eat!" Steven shouted at Tonuko.

Cora crossed her arms while looking down at me, then asked, "What gave you the idea that it was smart to confront him only a day after your announcement?" I shrugged, and the girl behind me shook her head and sighed.

"I can't believe you two babies are the top students in our grade! Come on and make up already!" the girl complained while gripping my arms tighter.

"Who even are you?" Tonuko patronized.

Her tough attitude fell, and she whined, "Aww man, you don't know my name?! That's so embarrassing! I'm Skye Harlem, the queen of the advanced class!" I finally calmed down enough to get a good look at her. Skye had big, red horns, red hair in a braided ponytail, large wings folded on her back, and her skin was a bright orange.

Skye Harlem, Strength: Demon—contrary to Alex, she can create a substance made of pure darkness that is freezing to the touch. She grew demonic-looking wings when she developed her strength. On top of that, Skye can grow her nails out at will and she has four fangs.

Finally, Skye let go of me, and Rake did the same for Tonuko.

"Could you guys, like, maybe just talk it out instead of fighting?" Rake asked as he wiped sweat from his forehead.

"I guess so, but you guys get out of here," Tonuko grumbled, still glaring at me. Cora, Steven, and Rake cautiously left, but Skye didn't budge.

"I'm gonna help you guys through this! You can't fight over something as silly as Kyle's family! If he's here, you have to realize it's for a reason, right?" Skye walked over then sat, forming a triangle between us.

"I know he's here for a reason, but what the hell is that reason? You've told me before how much you want to kill Tyrant, but when I offer peace and common ground, you get all angry and argue that you have to do it on your own! What are you, why are you so set on killing him?! Everything I hear you talk about with villains is how you hate Tyrant and how you want to kill Tyrant ... How am I supposed to believe you will be a consistent teammate on my side, not an outlier on your own side?" Tonuko ranted while running his hand through his hair.

"I didn't lie about what I said to you after the training tournament. I'm here to train, to get strong, to be a hero and to kill Tyrant. Plain and simple," I stated sternly.

"But then what?! That's the thing, what are you going to do after that?!" Tonuko shouted as he stood. I looked to my right and took a deep breath. Tonuko looked down at me in disbelief, then tensed his fist. He stomped over to me and grabbed the collar of my shirt again. "That's going to be it, right?! You want to kill Tyrant, then kill yourself! That's why you told me your life isn't worth the same as ours, you don't think of your life as worth anything! You were born to be the end of Tyrant and his bloodline!"

Skye quickly stood and grabbed Tonuko's arm, but she couldn't move it. "Tonuko, please! There's no need to get violent!" she pleaded while pulling his arm. Tonuko stared me dead in the eyes and clenched his jaw.

"Kyle," he seethed, "promise me you aren't going to die at your own hands." Tonuko's statement stunned me. I was at a loss for words and could only stutter. "You have to promise me, dammit!" He slightly shook me as he yelled.

Why? Why does he care whether I die or not? We were just arguing, not even ten minutes ago, about how I should die because I'm a lying criminal. Is he lying now, or was he lying before?

"Uh- I-"

"Kyle, you have to promise me!" Tonuko's eyes shimmered in the light, and I couldn't tell at this point if he was angry, sad, or something else.

Why are you adamant on this Tonuko? What's going on in your mind? Why do you care if I'm alive or not? I don't understand.

"Why do you care if I promise you?" I asked bluntly. I wasn't used to all these emotions, I only knew anger, sadness, happiness ... and disappointment.

"I care because you're my friend, you dumbass!" Tonuko shouted while shaking me back and forth another time. I stared up at him, utterly befuddled. "People here care about you! We aren't just classmates to go to school with, we're your friends that you will spend at least the next four years with. Stop talking about your life having no worth and saying Tyrant this and Tyrant that! I don't care about how horrible and dark your murkiest secrets are, I'll still be your friend and your ally! Forget the fact that you're Tyrant's son, when you lie to me about important things that you need help with, you make me feel like you can't trust me! On top of that, when you always imply you don't care about your life, it makes me feel sick! You're going to stick around for a while Kyle, promise me you will!"

I didn't know what to say, I was so ... happy that someone cared whether I was here or not.

All my life, I've just been Tyrant's son, a curse on the world. I thought everyone would think that too if they

245

ever found out, so I convinced myself it was the truth.
Maybe ... it's not ... Maybe I do deserve happiness ...

"I- I promise!" I shouted. Tonuko didn't smile, nor did I; he simply dropped me and turned to walk away. He stopped after a couple of steps but didn't look back at me.

He looked straight ahead as he said, "You and I have a lot of pressure from other people. We're two very strong first years, and the future of heroes as we know it. So, until we're both at the top, and I'm ahead of you, you're not allowed to leave." With that, Tonuko walked down the stairs to talk with those gathered on the first floor.

I stood dumbfounded, staring at the stairs. Skye put her hand on my shoulder and gave me a smile. "Well, that was pretty intense! But hey, I'd say you two are a-okay!" I slowly nodded.

"Y- Yeah, I guess we are." I didn't look at her. I continued staring wide-eyed straight ahead. We stood there for a few more seconds then I declared, "I think I'm going to go downstairs and talk to some people. You, uh, have fun doing whatever you do." I stood and walked toward the stairs and Skye followed me. I didn't care though, maybe we would be friends.

Caraline City, Thursday Morning; 3:33 a.m.:

The mist thickened as hail mixed with sleet rained down harder. A whooping gust of cold blew over the countless, scattered corpses. Thunder boomed in the sky as a man walked through the streets while wailing. His navy-blue cloak was stained red at the bottoms as it dragged on the ground, and his loud steps made by thick boots echoed throughout the streets. His honey-colored eyes practically glowed and his brown hair was messy and long, bangs hanging in his face. Trash was littered everywhere, drenched from the weather, and blood soaked the streets, washed around by the rain. The man's cries were almost loud enough to overtake the noise of the rain.

Lightning struck the ground and exploded a part of the street in front of him as he yelled, "Why must society follow these *disgusting* habits of battle?! Hero and villain, it's just segregating and separating-" Another bolt struck and strong winds took down a building, causing a massive crash. *"our beautiful lives!"* he concluded.

A dead woman's face was stuck in a shocked expression. Barely held in her hand was a large sign attached to a wooden pole that read:

CIVILIAN LIVES MATTER

YOU'RE HARMING US NOT HELPING

STOP SOCIETY CRUELTY

The crying man was the hero of the protest. He defeated those objecting to the large, record-breaking protest that stemmed from other states. In the process, he killed every last protestor. Was this man truly a hero of the people, or a villain hidden in the mist?

In King's Cellar:

"You can't just switch the plan on us! We had prepared to make an attack next week!" King roared furiously at BloodShot. "We have specifically laid low and lost thousands of dollars to not build suspicions about our attack on Eccentric High!"

BloodShot put his mask on, and scoffed, "Shut your mouth, will you? I'll do whatever the hell I want, whenever I want, and however I want it done! I'm the leader of this operation, so I control when it happens. Kyle snitched about Tyrant; we can't get into the city without being caught. Heroes, citizens, news reporters, they're all pouring into Camby to see the school with Tyrant's son and the top-ranked student of the freshman class, Tonuko Kuntai!"

The man with the white cross walked down the stairs and kept his distance from BloodShot. "When can we attack?" the cross man asked. BloodShot sighed and looked at his watch.

"I'll let you know when I know, dumbass! You're all just so useless! I have to go, but I'll return soon to collect Plague's gloves from you, King!" BloodShot pointed at King before turning and walking away as he waved them off.

"You're going to let that mutt boss us around?" White Reaper seethed after she heard the door close. One of her beetles crawled out of her mouth and into her robe, then white flames spiraled into existence on one of her legs. King swerved around, letting his cape flow in the air, then walked away. "I could kill him if I wanted. He shouldn't be able to tell us what we can and can't do!" King stopped and looked at White Reaper over his shoulder.

"I know, but he's right. The city's population is going to skyrocket, and their school is going to be the center of attention for television across the world. Considering the rumor of the education system changing drastically, people are also going to be moving closer to public schools they can afford. With more people comes more crime, which equates to more pros, and that means a higher chance of us all being arrested and put to death. We don't want that, do we?" King's pupils glowed with that last sentence, then he walked into the back room of his cellar.

After Plague and BloodShot left, they walked toward the train station. Plague looked down and fiddled with his fingers, then glanced up at BloodShot. "Why do we have to wait so long to bring Kyle to Tyrant? I wanna see this high school!" Plague suddenly blurted.

BloodShot looked at Plague out of the corner of his eye, then sighed, "Time will tell; don't forget that, young one," BloodShot told Plague. He looked both ways before crossing the street, then Plague held on to BloodShot's cloak as they crossed.

"What about with Mr. Tyrant?" Plague asked. "What will happen with him and the others if time will tell? Haven't they been doing this kind of stuff for a long time?"

"There's no need to worry about him. Tyrant was the most powerful villain and made an even stronger son. Throughout his time at the top, Tyrant broke down people's faith in heroes. He's had the biggest impact anyone has ever had on society since strengths first surfaced back in the early 2000s. Sure, it's only been a couple of hundred years, but strengths have had a stronger impact than the first types of technology."

Plague took this all in while staring at the ground trying to think of more questions. "Why are strengths such a big deal if they've only been around a couple hundred years?" BloodShot led Plague over to a bench outside a luscious park, and the two sat down.

"Before strengths surfaced, technology was the biggest focus in the human race. However, since strengths—then known as powers—started appearing in children, the focus immediately shifted. There have only been four generations older than 20: mine, Tyrants, and the two before his. Tyrant is a third-generation strength user, and I am a part of the fourth generation. You are a part of the fourth generation, as are Kyle and other children of two third-generation parents. Around sixty percent of people in the world have strengths, and thirty percent are heroes or villains/criminals. Therefore, strengths are advanced, but not very advanced. You need certain DNA to be able to control or hold a strength, and those who don't have it live lives like people in the early 2000s did. Those who can control their strengths either use their powers to their advantage or to stop others they feel abuse their powers." Plague swung his legs back and forth and rested his hands on the bench underneath his thighs.

"Will others be able to hold more than one power like Kyle can?" BloodShot looked around at the people walking, then grinned.

"Certainly, someone will try, and that someone will succeed. It's clearly very possible, but it might just be a very rare mutation, like a disease." Plague nodded his head, then looked at his fingertips. He wiggled his fingers, and his eyes slightly sparkled.

"A disease, like mine." BloodShot smirked, then stood from the bench.

"We'll master that strength, my child, then you will truly shine."

E.H. Freshman Dormitory, 9:30 a.m.:

After I made it down the stairs, I looked around at some of the unknown faces. I wasn't sure who to talk to because I didn't want to get into another big argument with someone who was mad at me. I looked around, feeling pretty anxious, then Skye leaned on my shoulder while standing on the last stair and pointed across the room.

"Those two over there are my best friends here. Go say hi to them, they're really nice!" Skye suggested with a big smile. She pointed at two girls who were talking. One of them had dark green skin; shiny, light blue goggles on her head; a big, green turtle shell on her back; and a few scales on her cheeks. The other was just as showy: blue hair with small, red streaks and her face was pale with the same color red patches all around her body and face. I nodded while taking a deep breath, then, after some hesitation, made my way over to the two advanced students.

"Uh, hi," I said, slightly interrupting their conversation, "I'm Kyle from honors. What are your names?" They looked over at me, then the girl with blue hair smiled and introduced herself and her friend.

"Trust me, we know who you are Kyle! I'm Emma, and this is my friend Violet!" I smiled because of her enthusiasm and shook her hand, then held my hand out to Violet.

"Nice to meet you both. I see you have an animalistic strength; that's pretty awesome," I stated trying to be kind. I figured I should try to sway conversations away from me and my life at this point.

"Oh, yes, my strength is quite fantastic!" Violet shouted while aggressively shaking my hand. Her goggles shined in the light as she grinned widely.

Violet Dedge, Strength: Turtle—because she developed an animalistic strength from spending so much time with her pet turtle, she has a large shell that attaches to her back and can be pulled off by only her hand. It is impenetrable by most attacks, having the ability to nullify fire, water, winds, etc. She also can swim abnormally fast and breathe underwater.

"I bet you'd be great in the pool behind the school!" I thought aloud. Her ocean-blue eyes lit up with glee, and her smile seemed to grow bigger.

"I know, right?!" Violet agreed. "I was hoping we would all be able to go sometime, have a little advanced and honors competition in the pool! I'm happy about this lockdown because it means we'll get close enough to all go together!" I nodded.

Wow, she's so positive. Honestly, it's a nice change of pace.

Suddenly, I felt someone's arm around my shoulder, and when I glanced over I saw Zayden standing next to me with a big smirk across his face.

"Did I hear there's another person with an animalistic strength?! I'm Zayden Attack from Honors, and you are?" Zayden held his other hand out to Violet, who in return shook it just as violently as she shook mine.

"You heard correctly Zayden, I'm a turtle! I'm Violet Dedge, and this is my friend Emma Lance! Pleasure to meet you shark boy!" Zayden and I both chuckled, then Zayden let go of her hand and stopped leaning on me.

"Wow, you sure are energetic! It's a nice change of pace from all the anger that's been going around." The two agreed, then Zayden turned to me and put his hands on my shoulders. I was confused, especially since he was looking straight down. "Kyle, I just gotta say ... I'm sorry. I was one of the people against you when you first confessed and I argued it was all your fault that villains attacked us. I shouldn't have said that, it's not-"

"Listen, if you really think about it, I'm the reason the Care-Givers have been obsessed with us. That's why I fought so hard to try and make sure no one around me would get hurt. Next time, I promise I'll fight my own fight without killing anyone," I declared to not only Zayden, but also to the two advanced girls.

Zayden looked up with a smile, then pulled me in for a quick hug. "I bet you will," he stated while pulling off.

The other two smiled, and Violet said, "You don't need to fight alone though." My eyes widened as I looked at her. "Us advanced kids, other than Daniel and Zach, haven't done much. Next time a villain attacks, you can at least count on Emma and me to fight right alongside you! No fight is just your own, we're all here to support you! That's what heroes do, right?"

I don't understand ... first Tonuko, and now these three ... why is everyone so adamant on helping me? I'm Tyrant's son, I deserve pain, suffering, torment, for all my life. I thought everyone hated me because of my family, so why are they being- so nice? It's ... so comforting ...

"W- Wow, I don't know what to say. Th- Thank you," I stuttered as my eyes slightly watered.

"No problem, we're all gonna be heroes, so we'll all be working together for decades to come!" Emma smiled.

"So, does this mean ... we're allies?" Violet and Emma looked at each other, then chuckled.

Why are they laughing? Am I wrong, are they faking, do they not actually care? Is that how Tonuko felt too, did he not actually-

"No, Kyle, it means we're friends!" Violet clarified. My smile grew wider, and I beamed with joy.

"O- Oh, right, that's what I meant!" They giggled and said goodbye, then walked toward the stairs. Zayden also left, so I made my way over to the counter and leaned on it. Scarlett finished cleaning up the table, then walked over and stood next to me while facing the rest of the room. There were students scattered around talking, but I noticed it was mostly honors' kids talking with honors' kids, advanced kids talking with advanced kids, or students who went to the same middle school.

"Do you think we'll be let out sooner rather than later? I mean, there are already a lot of people socializing," Scarlett asked before crossing her arms. I turned around and shook my head.

"You're not wrong that there are quite a few people talking, but don't you notice how anti-social the talking is? People are only talking to those they already know, so it's not much progress. No offense, but honestly, how many advanced kids do you even know?" She thought, then threw the small towel in her hand on the counter and sighed.

"Yeah, you're right. I don't really know any I guess."

Daniel and I made eye contact, then he headed toward me, along with Rose and Skye. "I hear you don't know any advanced kids ... well I guess it's time to meet some!" Daniel smiled while reaching his hand out to Scarlett. Daniel and Rose started talking to Scarlett, but Skye just stood wide-eyed next to me.

"O.M.G., is that Iris?!" Skye blurted out while pointing at Iris. Iris turned around, and her face lit up with glee. Skye jumped over the counter, surprising me by her sudden outburst of athleticism, and hugged Iris tightly. "I haven't seen you in, like, a year! How have you been?"

"Hey Skye, I've been pretty good. How about you?" Iris softly responded while returning Skye's hug.

"I've been good, good, great! Sorry, I just missed you so much!" They stopped hugging, and everyone either stood or sat around the counter.

"Aren't you the queen of the advanced? I feel like I remember hearing that earlier," Scarlett asked Skye.

"Oh yeah, I am the Queen of the advanced! Second ranked in our class, in fact!" Skye boldly announced loud enough for everyone in the room to hear. Daniel and Rose looked at each other, then snickered. "What's so funny?" Skye interjected.

"Sorry about how cocky she is everyone. Skye just loves attention!" Daniel laughed. Skye scrunched her nose and crossed her arms while retorting,

"I am not cocky! I am the most humble, gorgeous, outstanding student in our grade! How dare you say otherwise!" There was a short silence, then the three burst out laughing. I looked over at Scarlett and we made eye contact, then both shrugged.

"So, what are you two ranked in your class?" I asked looking at Daniel and Rose.

"Well, I'm the tenth-ranked student, and Daniel over here is the big, bad fifth-!" Rose answered while nudging Daniel with her elbow. I smirked while looking at Daniel, and he looked back with a mixture of confusion and annoyance.

"Wow, only fifth? Man, I thought you were stronger!" I teased. He rolled his eyes, then let out a chuckle.

"Aww, shut up hot shot, fifth is pretty good I'd say!" I nodded with a small smile.

"Yeah, I know, I was just joking. With how much you complain about your strength, I thought you would be lower!" Daniel cracked his shoulder and walked toward me, then fake punched me. Everyone else laughed, then Khloe and Jax came downstairs. I'd been downstairs long enough, so I went to sit in my room. I laid on my bed, pulled a blanket over me, and closed my eyes.

Maybe I just really need a nap.

I drifted off, then a couple of minutes later Alex walked by my room. Fear filled his eyes as he saw me lying in bed with an enormous pitch-black arm reaching out from my chest. He stood there, utterly horrified.

"Wh- What the hell is that?!" he whispered to himself. The hand wound up, then slammed my bed. A large, disgusting creature crawled out of my body. Alex hid behind the wall, breathing heavily and sweating. "It's the same color as those tears from yesterday ... what is that?!" After a couple of seconds, Alex heard footsteps marching toward my door.

They stopped when Cindy asked, "Alex, what are you doing?" Alex turned to Cindy with terror in his eyes and he said nothing. Cindy walked from her room to mine and looked in. She saw me sleeping, then chuckled, "C'mon, let him sleep! Let's go downstairs!" Alex saw the creature looming over Cindy.

It was as tall as the ceiling, had tentacles sticking out all over the place, and was inhumanely muscular. The creature's face had almost no identifiable features, except a large mouth with razor-sharp teeth. Cindy grabbed Alex's hand, then led him to the stairs. He looked back one last time, and saw it stare into what felt like his soul. They walked down the stairs, leaving the creature standing outside my door, seemingly guarding my sleeping body.

Flashback:

"We've only just started, why the hell are you crying already?! Get up boy!" Tyrant shouted with his fists balled. I wiped the tears and blood from my face and weakly stood while coughing.

"Papa, it hurts! I wanna go inside, please!" Tyrant stomped toward me and scoffed.

"Shut up, you cannot go in yet! We need to train you so you're ready!" I closed my eyes and tensed my fists, then went into another coughing fit.

"Ready for what?! I just want to play with Daniel!" Tyrant tensed his body then sped at me and kicked my side so fast that I couldn't react. I flew through a window and landed a few feet away from my mom. I stood, coughing even more, and ran to her. "Momma, he keeps hitting me again!"

Mom hugged and shushed me gently. "It's okay, sweetheart, you know he loses his temper sometimes. He just wants to see you succeed! Don't worry, we'll power through this, together," she said.

Tyrant threw open the sliding glass door and stomped inside to where we were. "Kyle, go on and go play with that disgusting hero's child. Your mother and I need to talk." I nodded as I fearfully ran through the house and out the front door. Before I fully closed it, I could hear my parents arguing loudly. I looked back and saw Tyrant backhand slap my mom across the face. When she fell to the ground, I closed the door and ran through the streets. I made my way into cat alley, running as fast as I could while crying profusely.

He is not my dad.

I made it to a busy street, then turned and sprinted into the big park (where E.H. is now built) that separated Daniel's house from mine.

He is not a real man.

Once I was across the park, my tears slowed. My jaw was clenched and my fists were tensed. My eyebrows were furrowed and I could barely focus my eyes because I was so furious.

He's just a strength-stealing demon.

Chapter 15
Class Competition

I woke abruptly to the sound of someone knocking on my door; it was Camilla. She stretched her back as I yawned, then informed me, "Sorry to wake you, but dinner's ready. I'd assume you're pretty hungry since you slept through breakfast and lunch." I blinked a few times, then glanced at my alarm clock. It was 6:00 p.m., which honestly surprised me. I sniffed and smelled meat cooking, then my stomach growled loudly. "Yeah, seems I'm right."

"It smells so good, wow!" I said before standing from my bed. Camilla looked around my room, then flicked the light switch on and turned.

"You should really clean up in there and turn on a light for once!" I rolled my eyes as she left, then walked to my desk and grabbed a pack of mints from the drawer. I popped two in my mouth while rubbing my eyes, trying to adjust to the light.

Nap breath is nasty, and did she really have to turn the light on?

I yawned again as I walked downstairs and saw everyone else sitting at the table. Scarlett and Jessica were bringing the food to the table and, out of the corner of my eye, I saw Daniel waving me over. When I sat down, Daniel was on my right, Skye was on my left, and Alex, Khloe, and Tonuko were across from me. Everyone dug into the large trays of boneless barbeque chicken wings and Cajun French fries. Once everyone had a plate of food, Steven asked, "How did you guys manage to make this?" Jessica smacked him on the head as she walked by and rolled her eyes. "Ow, that was a compliment!" We all laughed and began eating.

"So, I've been thinking about it all day: when is the Angel vs. Demon fight gonna happen?" Tonuko asked. I smirked and nudged Skye in the arm.

"Yeah, who would win?" I asked, trying to instigate the two. Alex and Skye chuckled, then Skye puffed out her chest and flipped a bang of her hair.

"I don't wanna crush the poor little Angel too hard, so it'll probably never happen!" she cockily boasted. Alex looked up with a confused expression and pointed at her, then at himself.

"Wait a minute, Advanced versus Honors?" Alex and Tonuko snickered, but Skye just rolled her eyes and crossed her arms.

"Oh whatever, that doesn't even matter!" Skye argued.

"I mean, it kinda means everything about strength!" Donte chimed in with barbeque sauce all over his hands.

"Okay dead last, I could probably take your spot in Honors if they gave me the chance!" Skye mocked while playfully glaring at him.

"Hey, I got put up against the Queen of Honors in the first round!" Donte yelled back.

Across the table, Rake shouted through his chuckles, "Yeah, and your strategy to defeat a wind user was to create wind, you dumbass!" Rake flipped hair out of his face, then Donte shook his fist at Rake.

"I'll kick your ass Rake!" he retorted. There was a quick silence, then countless people burst out laughing.

"Sure Donte, maybe if you beat him, you'll be fifteenth instead of sixteenth!" Cora taunted.

"Cora, you aren't in single digits either!" Anya giggled, nudging her. Tonuko and I stayed quiet during the argument. Alex and Camilla didn't say anything either. Hunter leaned back in his chair and grinned.

"Notice how all the lower numbers are the ones arguing? Meanwhile, all the top people don't care about their rank!" Zach snickered at him as he put down his glass of water.

"Hunter, Skye was the first to say something about rankings," Zach nonchalantly said.

"And are you even in honors, buddy?" Steven asked in between shoveling fries into his mouth.

Hunter's cheeks turned red as he stuttered, "W-Well, I'm the best- I mean the top of-"

"Exactly," Steven interrupted. He went back to stuffing his face, then a few eyes turned to Tonuko and me.

"How exactly are the two cockiest kids in our grade not saying anything?" Cindy asked. Tonuko and I simultaneously looked up and around to see everyone staring at us.

"Hey, we- I am not the cockiest kid in our grade!" Tonuko yelled in response.

"Woah, woah, woah, what the hell does that mean?" I asked, putting down the half-eaten wing in my hand. Tonuko grinned and put down the food in his hand as well.

"I mean, you know what I'm saying."

"Aren't you the one who came here so you would be top of the class with no competition?" I asked before laughing.

"Whatever!" he angrily shouted, "I mean, it kinda worked!" We all said "Mehhh" at the same time, signaling it clearly didn't. After that, we continued talking while we finished our food then cleaned our dishes and loaded the dishwasher.

While some waited to clean their plates, Violet leapt onto the countertop, clearly against Emma's pleas. "Everyone, I have a fantastic idea!" Violet excitedly squealed. We looked at her, then she suggested, "Why don't we ask tomorrow if we can go to the pool? We'll still be together, and doing a class activity like they suggested, so I'll bet Mr. Excalibur and Mr. Fallen would definitely let us!"

Tonuko put his plate in the sink and shrugged. "I mean, that's not a bad idea at all," Tonuko thought aloud.

"Yeah, I agree. We can ask them tomorrow when they deliver the groceries, or if it's Hazel, Jon, and Devin again, we can ask them to get our teachers," Alex added from the couch.

"I knew you would eventually say something about it," I said to Violet as she got down from the counter. I yawned for a few seconds, then rubbed the top of my head and looked over at the stairs.

Gosh, I've been sleeping all day, but I'm still so exhausted ... maybe I really need to catch up on sleep since I had such a tough time getting any last week.

"I think I'm gonna head to bed," I told Tonuko, Violet, and Emma, who stood near me. Tonuko raised an eyebrow and looked at me weirdly.

"You've been strangely tired the past two days. I mean, you just took a nap for almost ten hours," he observed. I shrugged while rubbing my eye.

"I didn't sleep a whole lot last week, so I think my sleep schedule is heavily off," I said. I wished them a good night and, as I walked by the couch, Alex waved to me.

"I'll close your door for you since you're not allowed to for another couple hours," Alex smiled. I nodded and waved to him, then trudged up to my room and passed out as soon as my head hit the pillow.

A few hours later, Alex turned the corner on the stairs and looked up at my door. It was a half hour past ten, so Alex decided he would close my door and go to bed himself. When he reached my room, he saw the creature walking around again. Alex covered his mouth, thought for a moment, then ran back toward the stairs and made his way up to Daniel's floor. He knocked frantically on Daniel's door.

Daniel answered a few seconds later. "Oh, hey Alex." Daniel saw the worry on Alex's face, so he asked, "Something wrong?"

"Just, come with me," Alex commanded while grabbing Daniel's forearm. The two went back down the stairs, and Alex cautiously approached my door, confusing Daniel even more. Alex took a deep breath, then peered into my room. The creature was standing over me—back to the door—just watching me. "You see that thing?" Alex whispered. Daniel looked around the room with a raised eyebrow and shook his head.

"Uh, what thing am I supposed to be looking for?"

The creature walked to the door and bent over, sticking its horrifying face only a few inches from Alex's. A tentacle raised from its chest and pressed on Alex's lips, then the creature shushed him. The tentacle retracted and the creature slowly marched back to me and continued his watch. Alex looked absolutely horrified, and he shook. "What's wrong? Is there something I'm missing?"

Alex shook his head while wiping his lips, then turned to Daniel. "No, never mind. I think I'm just hallucinating; I didn't sleep all that well last night," Alex sighed. Daniel put his hands on Alex's shoulders, then turned him around.

"Then you should probably go to bed now. I don't think anyone is gonna be hanging around downstairs tonight; we're all already getting sick of each other!" Daniel joked trying to lighten up Alex's mood. Alex couldn't help but smile and nod.

"Alright, well, I'll see you tomorrow. Hopefully we can go swimming." Daniel nodded and said bye to Alex, then looked into my room one more time. Nothing was there, so he shrugged and went back to his room.

Maroline City, 10 Miles from the State Capitol: Takorain; Thursday Night, 8:35 p.m.:

The crowd of protestors roared with anger, and a few news helicopters gathered in the sky.

"These heroes are destroying our cities!"

"Why do we have to fight?!"

"Strengths are not weapons!" the famous protestor chuckled and smirked as he stepped out from the crowd. His honey eyes were glowing, and the hood of his cloak rested on his head.

"Yes, why must we settle our differences through petty, destructive violence? Shouldn't strengths be used to better the future? To protect our children?" The riot police moved forward in a line with their riot shields braced in front of them. "Why do you have heavy artillery, officers? Why do you feel so threatened by us? Are you ... afraid?" The protestor held out his hands, palms facing the sky, and stood boldly.

"Back up, all of you! You have opinions and the right to express them, but you cannot use them to attack us!" an officer shouted, pushing the protestor with his shield. The man stumbled over but caught himself with his right foot. He clenched his fist and looked up at the officer with ferocious eyes that struck a life-threatening fear through the officer's body.

"Do not ignore me, and *do not* touch me!" The protestor swung his arm across the line of officers. Rain poured down and lighting shot from the sky and created a massive explosion. Mist seeped from what seemed like nothing, while winds picked up speed. "I am The Upriser and *I will be heard!*" The Upriser roared. Officers were stationed behind the crater explosion The Upriser had caused. They unloaded their guns at him, but with a swoop of his hand, a tornado spiraled into existence and sucked up all of the bullets. It moved toward the officers, ripping up the streets as it moved. A brave man from the crowd of protestors ran and grabbed The Upriser's shoulder.

"What are you doing?! We are peacefully protesting, not rioting! What is your problem man?!" the man shouted. The Upriser grabbed the man by the neck, then ripped his hand off. The Upriser turned around as he lifted his fist to the sky. A bolt of lightning shot down and was absorbed by a large ring on The Upriser's right ring finger. The Upriser then moved his arm and pressed the ring onto the man's forehead. The man freaked out and frantically kicked his feet.

"I'm sorry, sir, but sacrifices must be made to birth a new, perfect world," The Upriser spoke. His deep, booming voice shook the crowd to the bone. The man began screaming, and as quickly as his screaming had started, he stopped moving. Electricity poured out of his openings, then he exploded in The Upriser's hand. All that was left when the smoke cleared was a thick puddle of blood. The crowd of protestors screamed and ran, leaving some of them in tears. "Where are you going, why are you running?! I'm with you, I'm helping you make your cause heard!"

"You're a monster, a villain," a civilian lady shouted from the fearful crowd. The Upriser's eyebrows furrowed, and he clenched his fists.

"Villains are a part of the *disgusting* thing we are fighting against!" His screams brought more powerful winds, and he swiveled on his heels and walked away. Behind him, a thick building had been sliced in half by the powerful winds and fell onto the sprinting crowd, crushing those in its path. "You all do not understand, *you are the villains!* I will cleanse the world of you, you pathetic sheep! Tyrant, Puppeteer, BloodShot, Kaliska ... you will all be *purged!* I will create the *perfect, peaceful world!*"

A giant lightning bolt struck the debris of the fallen building, creating an enormous explosion and gruesomely killing any who had escaped its collapse. All helicopters had been taken out of the sky and all police force and heroes who were at the scene were dead. Blood ran the streets under The Upriser's feet again as he marched while crying. He made his way toward the train station, to find the next city of protestors.

E.H., Friday Morning, 9:30 a.m.:

After finishing my morning run, I showered then dressed and fixed my hair. I hung up the towel I'd used, walked out of the bathroom, grabbed my phone, and made my way downstairs. I nabbed an apple from the wooden bowl on the countertop then jumped over the back of the couch and sat down. I looked around, found the remote, and turned on the news.

"There are still no leads as to who the bloodthirsty rioter who has been wreaking havoc on protests is. This is the fifth protest he has attended; all have been left with no survivors. He has killed twenty-five heroes, along with hundreds of police officers and protestors. No one knows whose side he is on, but the Seven Influential have declared him as a national threat to civilization. The man, who calls himself 'The Upriser,' is still on the loose, so be cautious of any protests you had planned to attend if you are in this circle," the news castor explained. The screen changed to a map showing a large circle in our state. Camby and Takorain, the capitol, were included.

"Jeez, that doesn't sound good," Camilla said while on the last step of the stairs. She walked over while watching the T.V. and sat next to me.

"I know, this guy is weird. I've seen a little coverage on him before, and in the video I saw, he gave a speech about creating a new world or something before he commits the homicide," I explained with my eyes fixated on the T.V. A video was played, and it was a person showing a street in the first city The Upriser had attacked. There were people laying on the ground dead and bleeding, and The Upriser was seen strolling down the street while crying.

"Why must we fight when I'm on your side?! I want to free you from the shackles heroes and villains put on us! We can rise up together and create a purified, perfect world!" The Upriser wailed. I listened, and Camilla flinched at the visible corpses on the streets.

"This guy," I started, leaning forward and watching as lighting struck the street and exploded, "he's not trying to take down heroes or villains by himself ... he's trying to band the people against us, against heroes and villains. He's going to collect followers." We looked at each other, both wide-eyed.

"If he collects enough people toward his cause, there might be a new kind of social group—not a hero or a villain but an uprise of people wanting change." I stated, then leaned back in my chair and sighed.

"I mean, it probably won't ever happen. What kind of people want to work together with a leader who kills people on his side?" I asked rhetorically.

I wish I was right, and in that moment, I thought nobody would ever support the cause of The Upriser. Little did I realize he wasn't the only psycho in the world.

We sat in silence for a moment, then heard commotion coming from the stairs. Suddenly, Violet was flying through the air and landed in front of the stairs, then she swerved around the corner.

"Are the teachers here?! Did they come yet?!" Violet screamed. Camilla raised an eyebrow, confused because she hadn't been downstairs when Violet made the announcement the previous night.

"Violet has been going on and on about asking the teachers if our grade could go to the pool. She's been talking Emma's ear off apparently. You're a little excited, I assume?" I asked with a chortle.

"A little?! I'm so ecstatic I couldn't even sleep last night! I can't wait to get back in the water!" Violet shouted with pure joy. Camilla and I couldn't help but chuckle, then there was a knock at the door. We heard keys jingle, and Violet bolted toward the door, then excitedly hopped as the door slowly opened.

"Heyo'!" Fallen announced while stepping into the dormitory.

"Teacher, I have a question!" Violet shouted practically in his face. Hazel walked in behind Fallen, who had flinched from the loud Violet. I stood and walked to them, then put my hand on Violet's shoulder and pulled her back a few steps.

"I'll ask for you, Violet; you're a little too excited right now," I chuckled quietly. Excalibur walked in carrying some of the groceries and smiled when he heard what I said.

"Nice to hear you two know each other's names. I assume there has been some talking going on in here then?"

I grinned and nodded. "Yeah, yesterday was surprisingly social. I think the pressure of the shadowing has opened all of our eyes." The teachers were happy with that response, then Violet elbowed me hard in the side, signifying for me to ask the question. "Oh yeah, we've decided on an activity that would help us get even closer!"

"I'm listening," Fallen said in a monotone voice.

"Well, you would have to let us leave the dorm ... but we were wondering if everyone could go to the pool?" Fallen looked back at Excalibur, who shrugged.

"Alright, we'll let you go, but on two conditions." Fallen held up two fingers as he explained, "First, everyone in the dorm has to go, no exceptions. Second, you have to figure out a sport, activity, training workout, or something of the matter to do together. You cannot just relax there; you must be doing something. Also, I'm pretty sure the sophomore honors' class is using the pool to train later today, so you might get kicked out earlier than you want." We thanked him and they left.

I sighed out of relief, then turned and announced happily, "I guess we're all going swimming today!" Violet exploded with excitement and sprinted upstairs to tell Emma. Camilla and I looked at each other, then laughed. "Should we wake up Jessica and Scarlett for breakfast first? The four of us could probably crank out a meal for everyone within the hour."

"I think Violet might actually explode if we make her wait any longer," Camilla giggled while shaking her head, "We can just have an extra-big lunch today." I agreed, and we went to all the floors to tell everyone about the pool situation. We decided to leave at 10:15 a.m., a half hour after everyone knew we were going. I went back to my room to try and find my swimsuit.

"I know it's in here somewhere. I just ... don't know where." I searched my entire room, practically flipping it upside–down, but for the life of me I could not find that swimsuit anywhere. Tonuko and Alex walked past then laughed as they peered into my room.

"Kyle, what in the world happened in here? Was there a tornado?!" Alex asked. I frantically looked around, then sighed.

"I uh, can't find my suit anywhere."

I looked at the two and noticed their summer-festive outfits. Alex was wearing a loose, white-collared shirt with a black bucket hat and black-and-white polka-dot swim trunks. Tonuko was wearing a collared shirt with watermelons scattered all over it; his swim trunks had a large watermelon with a slice taken out of it on the side.

"Just go buy one at the store," Tonuko suggested and pointed out my window. I looked behind me at the clothing store, then picked up my wallet.

"I can spot you some money if you're running low," Alex added with a heartwarming smile. I shook my head.

"You might be late, so you better start running!" Tonuko snickered. I rolled my eyes with a grin, then ran past them and made my way down the stairs and out the door as fast as I could.

I'll be damned if I'm late.

I grabbed the first pair of swim trunks I saw, put them on the counter, and took out my wallet. The elderly lady scanned the tag on the shorts, then gave me a smile as she looked up.

"That will be twenty-five dollars," she said. I opened my wallet but saw only a ten dollar bill and two singles. I gulped, then looked back at the dorm.

I saw some students leaving for the pool already, so I asked, "Do you have any cheaper ones?" I asked while pulling out the three bills.

The lady looked at the money in my hand, then back up at me and shook her head. I looked down, knowing I would disappoint my class if I was the reason we were kicked out of the pool—without a swimsuit I wouldn't be able to get in the water.

"It's on me, Kyle Straiter," the lady smiled with a wink. My eyes twinkled, and I smiled brightly.

"W- Wow, thank you so much!" I glanced back and saw people leaving the dorm, so I hurriedly put my money back into my wallet, grabbed the trunks, then sprinted out of the store.

I passed Violet, who angrily yelled, "You better not be late Kyle! Pool time is important!"

"I know, I'm going as fast as I can!" I spun around to shout, then spun back around and ran faster to get into the dorms. I made it inside and up to my room, then finally changed into the trunks and walked down the stairs.

Honestly, there's no point in running. Pool time might be very important to Violet, a literal turtle, but I can wait. I'll only be late by a minute or two.

I walked out the door and was on my way to a fun day in the sun.

I stepped through the front doors of the school and navigated the bare halls trying to find the pool entrance. I had my towel draped over my shoulder, goggles on my head, and I was wearing a white tank top. I reached the back of the school and heard splashing on the other side of large, wooden doors I had just passed. I backtracked, then turned and opened the doors. The sunlight blinded me as I stepped outside onto the hot cement.

"Kyle!" Violet shouted, marching up to me. She was in her suit, and her shell was glimmering in the sunlight. She grabbed it and smacked me on the top of the head. "You're so late! Come on and get in the pool!"

"Jeez Violet, calm down a little! Unwind and have some fun!" Anya shouted from across the pool. She was about to jump in the water, but Tonuko ran up behind her and full on tackled her into the pool.

"Oh my," I quietly whispered, covering my mouth and looking as the two surfaced.

Violet gave me a side-eye, then she grumbled, "That'll be you next if you don't hurry up and get in!"

"Alright, I've just gotta put my stuff down and throw on some sunscreen!" I told her, then walked over to one of the tables and placed my towel on it. I realized something very important: I don't even own sunscreen.

"Kyle!" Alex yelled from the pool, "You can use my sunscreen! It's the spray bottle on your right!" I thanked him, then grabbed the bottle and sprayed my body. I put down the sunscreen, then took a step toward the pool. A pit formed in my stomach.

Shit, I thought I got over this!

"Kyle, what's wrong?" Anya questioned, swimming over to Alex. I took a few more steps toward the edge, then stretched my arm.

"Oh, psh, it's nothing. I'm just feeling, uh, tight right now."

I still can't get over my fear ... not since Caden ...

Daniel got out of the pool and shuffled over to me. Since he'd known me for so long, he could tell I was stretching because it was my nervous habit.

"Wait a minute, don't tell me-!" I quickly shushed Daniel, then turned him around so we were both facing away from the pool.

"Yes, I'm still afraid of water! It's just- ever since-just no!" I heard a snicker behind me, then I looked back and saw Tonuko laughing.

"What the hell are you gigglin' at Moody Earth?!"

"I said don't call me that!" he shouted while holding up his fist. Anya jumped up and pushed his head underwater, then gave me a taunting smirk.

"What's wrong Kyle? You afraid of the: 'scawy' water'?" she mocked.

"What the hell?! Of course I'm not afraid of some dumb water!" I argued.

"Alright, then jump in," Alex suggested, joining in the mockery. I stopped stretching and puffed out my chest.

"Alright, maybe I will!" I walked over and dipped my toe in the water. A shiver went up my spine and I backed up. Everyone started laughing at me, and I blushed out of embarrassment, then took a deep breath.

Come on, Kyle ... if you can beat two powerful villains, you can jump in a damn pool! It's just water, nothing more!

"Quit stalling you loser!" Tonuko yelled, acting bored. I gave him a sneering expression in response, then quietly hyped myself up and ran toward the edge. I skidded to a stop and didn't jump though, causing everyone to continue laughing.

"Oh come on Kyle, it's just some water! Violet practically lives in it!" Emma shouted. Tonuko and Alex looked behind me then grinned at each other. Alex got out of the pool and ran over to Violet, who was standing behind me with a mischievous grin.

"What are you two doing?" I asked anxiously while backing up. I felt Tonuko grab my legs, then gulped. Violet and Alex ran at me, then speared me into the pool. I fell back first into the water, then opened my eyes and looked at the surface. I had flashbacks of Caden trapping my head in his bubbles, practically trying to drown me, then of Lokel nearly drowning me. After I closed my eyes, I felt someone grab my hand. I opened my eyes slowly and saw Violet smiling at me while pulling me to the surface. I took a deep breath and looked around. Everyone was laughing and having fun, splashing one another and doing cannon balls.

Maybe this isn't so bad ...

Violet jumped on me while giggling.

"See, it's just water! It's not gonna hurt you!" she shouted.

"Yeah, I guess you're right!" I admitted with a smile. She sped around in the water. After a couple of minutes everyone was in the water but we couldn't agree on an activity.

"What about that? Isn't that water polo?" Zach asked while pointing at two goals and a ball in a corner of the fence. He got out of the pool and grabbed the supplies, then threw them into the pool. Violet caught the ball, then grinned.

"I freaking love water polo! How about a little class competition, ay? Advanced verses honors'?" Violet suggested.

"Bring it on fishy!" Steven mocked as the classes separated. We lined up at our respective goals and assigned goalies. We chose Rake and they chose a boy I'd never seen. He was very tan, a little lighter than Alex, and had frosted tips on his black, curly hair. After getting things sorted, we counted down, then swam at the ball in the middle of the pool. Donte activated his super speed and bolted toward the ball. He grabbed it, creating a huge wave in the process. The wave swept most of the advanced kids off their feet, including the goalie, so Donte had an easy throw in to make the score 1-0.

"Looks like you'll have to try a little harder than that, Violet!" I boasted. She grabbed the ball and started swimming the length of the pool. She dodged honors' kids left and right then, instead of going straight for the goal, she grabbed her shell and threw it at Rake. It smacked him in the head, then spun around and flew right back to her. Violet whipped the ball into our goal, tying the score at 1-1.

"Looks like you'll have to try a little harder, Kyle Straiter!" Violet smirked. After a few more points, commotion, and yelling, we heard someone shout from the fence closest to the school.

"Wow, you freshmen sure are competitive!" We stopped playing and looked over. Foul was patrolling and he was wearing his wrestling outfit.

"Woah, Foul?! What are you doing here?!" Daniel asked, astonished.

"A few wrestlers and I were asked to patrol the school. I couldn't say no, thinking about your grade, so we started patrol yesterday after you were put on lockdown!" Foul clarified with a chuckle.

"Wait, so does that mean you aren't a wrestler anymore?" Alex questioned sounding a little disappointed. Considering Foul Odor was the rising star wrestler of the nation, knowing he had to quit because of us would make everyone feel guilty.

"No, I'm still a wrestler; we all are. We're just taking a break for this school year until the villain activity calms down. As much as I love wrestling, your safety is a priority for the other patrollers and me. We're gonna be working under Fox-Tails for the time being," Foul explained. Catastrophe turned the corner with a raised eyebrow just as Foul finished his explanation.

"Hey kiddos, I thought you were on lockdown. What happened?" Catastrophe asked, walking up to Foul.

"We were allowed to go to the pool together!" Violet gleefully screamed. Catastrophe acted like his ear was hurting from her screaming and rubbed it.

"Golly girl, I'm right here!"

"Sorry, I'm just super excited to be in the water!" Violet apologized.

"Her strength is Turtle," Emma explained, "so she gets very excited when it comes to swimming and water."

"Unlike baby boy Kyle over here! This tough guy is scared of water!" Tonuko snickered while nudging me. I pushed him, then heard Foul laughing.

"Scared of water?! Kyle, c'mon man!" Foul and Catastrophe continued laughing as they walked away, but I angrily blushed. We continued playing for another hour, then spent a half hour doing other competitions. The honors' class swept the advanced, winning all battles. After the last one, Jon burst through the door with a towel on his head and his shirt off.

"Time to beat it, freshies! We've got training to do!" Jon cackled while standing with his legs spread wide and fists pressed on his hips. There was disappointment all around and everyone got out of the water. After we'd dried off, we made our way to the front of the school.

"Man, why can't we be in the pool for just a little longer?" Skye complained, crossing her arms and pouting. It was a group of Skye, Alex, Tonuko, and me, and Emma and Violet were a couple of feet ahead of us.

"I'm surprised you're so upset about this. I mean, not as upset as her though. Violet might be depressed now," Tonuko snickered, pointing at Violet. She trudged forward with her head held low, then she shook her fist behind her at us.

"You just shut your mouth," she muttered.

"It was so much fun competing with you guys. I guess I can't say that advanced doesn't get enough credit, because neither class is really getting any credit at all," Skye sighed. I looked at her, confused.

Alex thought aloud, "Oh yeah, when you think about it, we fought two super-powerful, infamous kidnappers but we've had almost no news coverage. There've been crowds of news people here, but they were for Kyle's trial." We stopped walking and stood in a half-circle.

"There definitely should be more hype about this school, all things considered. Who knows, maybe there actually is, and we just don't watch the news enough. When was the last time anyone checked the national rankings?" Tonuko asked.

"All I know is Kyle is gonna come to light and go from unranked to top ten, and Alex is top one-hundred, although, maybe a bunch of B.E.G. (Bade's Exceptionally Gifted) kids moved up in the rankings. Who knows," Skye pondered. Tonuko scoffed when Skye mentioned B.E.G. and crossed his arms.

"Ugh, B.E.G.; I hate that school. They gave me a full ride, but I didn't accept. From what I've heard from heroes connected with my mom and dad, it's a bunch of strict, stuck-up teachers." My mouth gaped and I clenched my fists.

He had a full ride to the top school in the nation ... and declined? Are you fucking joking?

"You dumbass, why in the world would you decline an offer like that?! You know how many people dream of going to B.E.G.?! Who cares if a few teachers are stuck-up, it's a dream school!" I yelled in disbelief. I expected an argument, but instead just heard giggles and chuckles. "What's so funny?"

"Wow, Kyle, just wow! How do you know how many people dream of going to B.E.G.?' It's obvious you're talking about yourself!" Alex laughed while patting my shoulder. I quickly calmed down and couldn't help but join in the laughter.

"Who cares anymore, I mean, I'm happy I went here instead. I've met some pretty cool people," Tonuko smiled and looked toward the dorm.

"I can't believe how smart and calm you honors' kids actually are!" Skye blurted out through her giggles. We looked at her, confused. "Well, not to be mean, but us advanced students always thought you honors' kids were dumb and loud. I mean, that robot kid is always the first to talk, so can you blame us?" Skye asked. We agreed and sighed, thinking about loudmouth Steven.

"Y'know, after seeing Fallen save Alex's dad, I realized something ..." Tonuko spoke. "None of us act like real heroes." Those words silenced the group. "And don't even try to argue it Ky-"

"No," I interrupted, "you're right. Just because I beat villains, doesn't mean I acted like a hero. A great hero recently taught me that heroes should portray these traits: honesty, bravery, and trustworthiness; they also need to be respectable, caring, and understanding. However, most importantly, a hero is someone who people can look at and feel safe with," I explained to the group.

"Yeah," Alex agreed, "honestly, all we've done is fight so far. That's it, just fought villains. We haven't saved anybody, or made others feel safe, just attacked anyone who's against us." Tonuko beamed with joy, then took a step forward and stuck his hand out between us.

"Let's all promise, as some of the strongest in our classes, to be real heroes in the next villain attack. Who knows when that'll be, but we have to change our ways, and change them quickly," Tonuko suggested with a smirk.

"Since when were you so mature?" I mocked. Tonuko rolled his eyes.

"Just agree, dammit!" he yelled. We all put our hands in and agreed, then finished the walk back to the dorm. I took another shower, and as I dried off, I wrapped the towel around my waist and looked around at my dark, dirty room.

Y'know, for how annoying Tonuko gets ... he's right. We're at a hero school, so it doesn't matter what villains want to attack us or why, we just need to protect those around us. That's why we train, to be strong enough to make others feel safe when we're around.

"Kyle, Scarlett and Jess said lunch will be ready soon!" Alex informed me, walking by my room and waving. I nodded and looked at the pile of clothes at my feet.

Maybe I should clean up.

Even though the smell of the food downstairs was amazing, I decided to take Camilla's ridicule and clean my room. After a couple of minutes, all the clothes were picked up off my floor, and I was changed and ready for lunch. I headed downstairs, and after turning the corner, saw everyone waiting for me. The table was loaded with burgers, potato chips, watermelon, apples, and even a bowl of pudding. I licked my lips as I walked to the table and grabbed a chip off my plate.

Fallen and Excalibur stepped into the dorm before I could sit down. They looked impressed by everyone sitting together and the delicious-looking food.

"See," Excalibur nudged Fallen, "I told you the long table was the right choice." Fallen snickered, then took a step forward.

"Everyone, we've decided to end the lockdown tomorrow, because although your socializing is very important, this shadowing event will most definitely be the biggest one in Eccentric High history!" Fallen announced, making us very happy.

"So, um, how will this shadowing work?" Skye asked with her hand raised.

"Basically, you have been getting requests to go and visit a Hero Organization from countless heroes over the past day and a half. For example, Kyle, you have gotten more than one hundred requests," Excalibur pronounced.

"Over a hundred, in one day?!" Steven angrily shouted, almost pouting.

"And Tonuko," Excalibur started with a big smile, "you have amazingly gotten nearly two hundred!" The room went silent. Even though I'd beaten Tonuko twice, even though I basically single-handedly defeated the infamous kidnappers, even though the Seven Influential put their trust in me, Tonuko ... had more than me?

Chapter 16
The Almighty Sons

"I mean, I guess he is ranked number one in the nation for freshmen, so it's not too surprising," Alex said while picking at his food. Fallen nudged his head forward, telling Excalibur to put the packet he was holding on the table.

"This packet shows all the people who've gotten offers and what offers they received. The top three are Tonuko, Kyle, and Iris," Fallen explained. Iris looked shocked and pointed at herself with wide eyes.

"M- Me?! Why am I higher than the others?!" Iris exclaimed.

"Well, it's quite simple Iris; you have one of the strongest healing strengths known, meaning heroes will want you at their organizations to have a powerful healing sidekick," Excalibur explained. Alex walked over and flipped through the packet, looking for his name.

"Aww man, only one offer? That's so embarrassing!" he nervously chuckled while rubbing the back of his head. Fallen put his hand on Alex's shoulder and gave him a reassuring smile.

"Also," Fallen announced, "when you decide who you want to shadow—it does not necessarily matter whether or not they chose you—you will call their organization. After that, they will state if they want just you, or if they want you to bring a couple of classmates. Some heroes will choose the top students of their classes simply to have them bring their top prospect buddies as well. Also, Kyle and Tonuko, we have fantastic news about who's requested you!" We looked curious and listened intently.

"It will not be hard for you two to choose, I imagine, as almost all of the Seven Influential have requested you! Kyle, you got requests from all but Kaliska; Tonuko, you got requests from all but Puppeteer," Excalibur informed us. The room went silent again.

"K- Kyle got a request from the number-one hero, but I didn't?" Tonuko asked in a scarily monotone voice.

"T- Tonuko, c'mon man! You got twice as many offers as me, so does it even matter?" I stuttered while holding up my hands. A nervous drop of sweat rolled down the side of my head as Tonuko turned toward me.

"I'm supposed to be the number one in the nation, right?! If that's the case, how come he keeps getting more credit than me?! He's not even ranked!" Tonuko shouted while pointing at me and looking at Fallen. Fallen crossed his arms, then shook his head.

"Listen kid, the rankings honestly don't matter until the Hero Olympics. We'll be informed about the official rankings of the freshman class a month before the Hero Olympics, and they could have changed drastically, no one knows. So until then, get off your high horse!" Fallen ridiculed.

"Yeah, it's alright Tonu! Even though Kyle got an offer from Puppeteer, you got one from the coolest hero, Kaliska!" Anya said, trying to encourage Tonuko. He took a deep breath and apologized, then the teachers walked out. Tonuko didn't talk to me for the rest of lunch, and after I was finished and my plate was cleaned, I called Puppeteer's Organization.

"Kyle, are you calling Puppeteer right now?!" Daniel asked excitedly. He sat next to me at the counter as I nodded.

"Here goes nothing!" I sighed while looking at the number I had found online. I hesitated, then clicked the number and put the phone to my ear. As it rang, a bunch of people gathered around to listen in. After a few more seconds of ringing, someone answered.

"Hello, this is Puppeteer's Organization. You are speaking to his assistant, Lady Antress. What is the problem in your area?" I gulped, then took a deep breath.

"I'm not calling for a problem, actually. This is Kyle Straiter, from Eccentric High, and I was calling to accept the offer to shadow at Puppeteer's Organization." Lady Antress sounded surprised, then she profusely apologized.

"That is my fault for not realizing it's you! So sorry to be rude, I'll get Puppeteer! He just came back from a meeting with Kaliska, so he may not be the happiest," Lady Antress warned me. I was put on hold, then moved the phone away from my mouth and smiled anxiously.

"She's getting him now!" I softly told everyone. Daniel looked as if he was about to explode with excitement.

Rake asked, "Which of his sidekicks was on the phone?" Before I could respond, I heard Puppeteer on the other end of the line. I put a finger up to Rake, and focused.

"Hello, am I speaking to Kyle?" Puppeteer asked. I took another deep breath, then sat up in my seat.

"Yes, this is him. I'm calling to tell you that I accept your offer and will be shadowing at your organization." I heard him chuckle, then it sounded as though he was flipping through papers.

"Ah yes, I'm glad you accepted. Just to go over a few minor details: I will not need you to bring any of your friends, just you, and I'll provide housing for you in my organization," Puppeteer explained. Daniel could hear him through the phone and looked disappointed when Puppeteer said I will go alone.

Damn, I was hoping I could bring at least one other person. That would've taken away a lot of my nerves ...

"That's not an issue, is it?" he asked, sounding suspicious.

"Oh no, that's perfectly fine! It might be a letdown to some of my friends, but that doesn't matter too much. Heroes can't always work with others; they'll work alone most of the time anyway!" I answered quickly. There was a long pause, which worried me.

Did I say something wrong? I didn't sound passive-aggressive, did I?

"Yeah, sure; we work alone sometimes. You won't be alone, though, because my son, Xavier, and hopefully one of our family friends, will also be shadowing here. Only seems right he does!" Puppeteer chuckled again, and I joined with a nervous laugh. "Anyway, I'll let you go, but I can't wait to see you again!"

"Bye," I nervously stated, slightly elongating the word. When I heard the beeping of the call ending, I put my phone on the table and looked straight ahead, wide-eyed. The others looked confused so I anxiously told them, "H-His son, Xavier from B.E.G., is going to be there, along with one of their family friends. It's just going to be me, the number-one hero, the number-one hero's son, and their close friend." Everyone erupted with excitement and happiness.

"Woah," Alex said as his eyes lit up.

"That's so cool Kyle! Gosh, you're so lucky!" Skye screamed, obviously jealous.

"Too bad you can't bring anyone else," Rake sighed, "I was kinda secretly hoping you could and would bring me. I don't wanna have to research for some animalistic hero!"

"You'll be fine, Rake. Maybe you'd learn more if you went to an animalistic hero's agency anyway!" I laughed. We all agreed, yet there was one student who hadn't joined in the excitement. Tonuko was standing by the staircase, glaring at the group.

He took out his phone and searched "Kaliska's Organization." He stared at the screen for a few moments, then dialed the phone number and put the phone to his ear. Anya stood close by, intrigued. She held his hand as Kaliska answered.

"Greetings, Kaliska from Kaliska's Organization here. How may I be of assistance?" Tonuko took a deep breath, just as I had.

"Hello Kaliska, it is Tonuko Kuntai calling. I wanted to call to tell you that I accept your offer to shadow at your organization," Tonuko stated. He bit his lip as the phone went silent, then Kaliska answered surprisingly gleefully.

"Oh, Tonuko! I'm happy you decided on my organization! There's not too much to talk about right now, other than the fact that housing will be provided, you will be joined by a student from Bade's Exceptionally Gifted and I am allowing you to bring two classmates! Don't be shy though, bring one honors' student and one advanced from your grade! I want to see for myself if there is a difference between skill level in those classes!" Tonuko smiled and breathed out, obviously relieved.

"Well, alright! I'll be sure to bring one of each! Do you have a preference of what ranking they should be in our classes?" Tonuko asked while looking at Anya.

"Oh no, not at all. Unlike some other pitiful heroes, I couldn't give a damn about rankings or whatever. I've heard about how heroic you've acted since a young age, and that's the reason I requested you! Bring others who you feel embody what being a hero truly means. Thanks for calling, but I'm getting another call and it might be urgent. No need to call back about who you've chosen, I know you'll choose wisely!" With that, Kaliska hung up.

"Kaliska wants me to bring two others that embody what a hero is. They also said they want me to bring one advanced student and one honors' student!" Anya smiled and rubbed the back of his hand with her finger.

"That's great! Congrats!" she complimented. Tonuko looked around the room, clearly thinking.

"I wonder what advanced kid I should take. I mean, I already know the honors' one I'm bringing is you-"

"No," Anya quickly interrupted, "don't choose me just because we're close. Even though I'd love to shadow Kaliska's Organization and learn from them ..." Anya looked down, and softly muttered, "I know I don't embody a hero yet. Ever since I killed that girl, I've been realizing how far behind I am from you and the others." Tonuko looked shocked and hugged her tightly.

"Are you sure? This could be a once-in-a-lifetime opportunity! Kaliska would probably adore you!" He said trying to convince Anya to change her mind. However, her decision was made.

"That doesn't matter Tonuko!" She raised her voice, then calmed down quickly. "Think about everything that has happened so far. Fallen and you even noticed it: we aren't really acting like heroes. I saw on the news that two B.E.G. students fought off two Care-Givers recently with zero casualties. Puppeteer's son, Xavier Kinder, and a girl named Rachel took the Care-Givers down almost effortlessly and saved all the civilians around them! That's what heroes do Tonuko!" she quietly explained. Tonuko thought about arguing, but he knew she was right.

"I guess you're right. Even though the school just opened, our class is probably one of the strongest around. We have, most likely, two kids in the top one hundred in the nation, and apparently at least one in the top ten. Yet, when we fought those kidnappers, all we did was focus on fighting and we caused countless avoidable casualties. I was talking to my mom about the experience, and the damage was in the hundreds of thousands of dollars. Hell, an entire building collapsed!" Tonuko agreed while running his hand through his hair.

"We all need a reality check. This isn't a comic book where heroes fight villains with no consequence and if the hero wins the day is saved. This is real life with consequences to our actions! We all need to smarten up and act more like how HotSauce was!" Anya finished for him. Tonuko squeezed his phone while looking down at it, then nodded.

"I will show this grade what it means to be a real hero, I promise! The next time a villain strikes, I'll take into consideration all that we've learned and act accordingly. I'll prevent the casualties of my friends and the nearby civilians and show the media who we are! I could have gone to B.E.G. and been in that fight, but I'm here. We technically have more experience than those B.E.G. kids, so I'll start acting like it!" Anya smiled and hugged him again.

"I'm sure you'll do great whenever another battle happens. Either way, I've had a couple of other heroes in mind that I wanna shadow. I saw some heroes on my list that suit me really well!" She pulled away, then ran up the stairs and waved. He watched as she turned the corner, then looked down at his phone again, then up at me.

"I'll make sure you don't die, Kyle. No more deaths will happen on my watch," he thought.

Tonuko walked to the couch and sat next to Alex. Alex looked over and smiled, then asked, "How did your call go?" Tonuko nodded while looking at his turned-off phone.

"It went pretty well. I get to bring a kid from honors and one from advanced." Tonuko looked directly into Alex's eyes. "With that being said, would you care to join me in shadowing Kaliska?"

286

Skye listened in as Alex gleefully accepted the offer. "No way, of course I'll go! Thank you so much, this means the world to me! The only offer I had was from a family friend!" Alex shouted as his eyes sparkled. Tonuko chuckled, then leaned back on the couch.

"Kaliska said I need to bring people who embody what a hero is. In all honesty, Kaliska was hyping me up as some natural-born hero, but I'm not. I may have a few of the qualities Kyle talked about, but you have the real important ones," Tonuko admitted with a sigh.

"What do you mean?" Alex asked.

"Well, it doesn't matter how many people or villains I beat, what matters is being someone who lightens the mood of the traumatized victims and can save them while bringing a smile to their faces. You're someone who everyone looks up to for joy; that's why when we found out you were being hurt, everyone got super angry and heartbroken. You have what I need to work on: being the sunshine people need in their life."

Alex grasped his shirt where his heart was and his eyes watered. "Wow, you'll never know how much that means to me Tonuko! Th- Thank you!" Tonuko smiled and looked up.

"Well, when you're the Angel of our grade, people can forget that you need some reassurance too!" Slowly, a pair of horns and red hair crawled into Tonuko's view. He raised an eyebrow as Skye's beaming face appeared.

"So, Tonuko; I hear you need a heroic advanced student?" Skye asked mischievously. Tonuko rolled his eyes and crossed his arms.

"How are you heroic?" Tonuko questioned. Skye scooted over and rested her arms on Alex's head.

"Well, I did run into yours and Kyle's fight without hesitation to break you two up! Also, I stayed with you and helped you get over your argument!" Skye pondered as she tapped her cheek. Tonuko thought with her, then nodded.

"Yeah, that's true. We aren't here to play games though. Do you truly think that you can represent our advanced class well?" she swiftly shouted.

"Don't worry earthy-boy! I won't let you or my class down!" He smirked, confident with his decisions.

"Alright, I'll let you come. However, you better work your ass off while training this month, you too Alex! I don't want Kaliska thinking we're all slackers who are only there because we're in the top of our classes!" Tonuko sat up and glared at the two, mostly at Skye.

"You've got nothing to worry about," she reassured him, "Even if I seem like a bubble-head, I do work hard! I'm the queen of my class for a reason!" They continued talking, and I couldn't help but eavesdrop, considering they were talking so loudly.

"Man, Tonuko sounds so mature when he's talking about that stuff. I just sat there dumbfounded when talking to the number-one hero," I sighed to Daniel.

"Hey, Kyle!" Tonuko yelled, startling me.

"Y- Yeah?! What do you want Moody Earth?!" I asked, looking back at him. He smirked, quite annoyed, but tried to ignore my nickname.

"You're shadowing the number-one hero with the number-one student from B.E.G.'s freshman class ... don't let us down, alright? Be mature, respectful, smart, and a hero," Tonuko seethed. I waved him off as I spun around in the swivel barstool.

"Duh, no need to tell me twice! We're here to be the strongest heroes we can be, so of course I'll be a hero when I'm at Puppeteer's Organization!" I mocked, clearly annoying Tonuko.

"Yeah, whatever! Just think about what we've all been saying recently after taking our decision-making class!" I raised my eyebrow but didn't respond.

The hell is that supposed to mean. Is he saying I don't know how to act like a real hero? And did he really have to add smart into that, as if I'm not always smart?!

"What does he mean by that?" Daniel asked while shaking his head. I shrugged and rested my head on my hand. Camilla took a deep breath.

"Something's changing with him. He's been talking really mature lately," she observed while looking over at the couch. After a few seconds, she looked back at Daniel with a smile. "So, did you get any offers Daniel?" He picked up the packet and scanned it for his name. When Daniel found his name, there were three hero organizations under it.

"Ugh, my parents requested me." He rolled his eyes and tossed the packet onto the counter in front of him.

"Hey, that's good for the long run. You'll be able to learn from them on how they use their strength in the battlefield," I said while patting his shoulder.

Daniel Onso, Strength: Hidden—he can become invisible at will, but when he's invisible he can only see people by their skeletons. His vision is like an x-ray when he's in his invisible state, and he becomes two times stronger. An advantage to his x-ray vision is he can see through walls on command.

"I guess, but while doing that they'll just get upset about how I don't have a good grasp on my strength," Daniel sighed.

"You'll only get better at it by training with people who have the same strength!" Violet shouted while slapping Daniel on the back of the head. Scarlett, who was washing plates, began scrubbing more aggressively. Suddenly, she swiveled around and huffed.

"I just don't understand how Fallen and Excalibur expect us to learn power-ups in one month! That's absolutely ludicrous!" Scarlett complained. Camilla walked over and took the plate out of her hand while wearing a comforting smile.

"Don't hold the plates when you're all flustered. I'm sure the teachers will help us figure it out!" Camilla reassured her. Scarlett grabbed a towel and wiped her hands after putting down the sponge.

"Yeah, you're probably right. It's just all so stressful, y'know?" We agreed, then everyone discussed power-ups. Most of my day was spent hanging around the lobby area or in my room. During dinner, people were excited to talk about what heroes they were thinking of shadowing. All the others were dreaming of the different heroes that would request them. Tonuko, Alex, Skye, and I were going to be living our dreams ... or so we thought ...

Parane, a Suburb Just Outside Takorain; Friday Evening:

Drenched from the rain outside, The Upriser walked into a broken-down motel and put his I.D. on the front desk. A suspicious-looking man in a white and purple tuxedo looked at it then grinned and gave The Upriser a room key.

"Take all the time you need here, Lawrence," he said. The Upriser nodded, took the key, and found his room. He opened the door and locked it behind him as he took off his navy-blue bowler hat and placed it on the small desk. He walked over and looked out the window.

"There will be very large protests soon. The annual freshman shadowing is happening in a month and the people will want to fight back. Takorain is home to Kaliska and Puppeteer ..." The Upriser looked down at the busy street as the clouds cleared, and hissed, "Perfect." He closed the drapes and spun around. "I'll show those strong heroes-in-training the corrupt world they're trying to succeed in."

I slowly opened my eyes and blinked a couple of times. I yawned as I looked at my clock, then my stomach dropped.

Fuck! Since it's Saturday, I forgot to set my alarm!

I swiftly showered, brushed my teeth and dressed, then ran out my door and down the stairs. To my surprise, Tonuko was sitting at the counter casually talking with Skye. They looked over at me, confused.

"Why the hell are you running around like a crazy person?" Tonuko asked. I looked around, confused as well, then pointed at the door.

"We're late for school ... right?" Skye and Tonuko looked at each other, then laughed. Now, I was even more confused.

"It's Saturday! The packet said any weekend classes will start an hour later!" I sighed out of relief as I made my way over to them.

"So class doesn't start for another thirty minutes?" They nodded, then I sat at the counter with Tonuko. He was staring down at his cup of water, hesitating.

"Listen, Kyle, about what I told you yesterday," he started. I looked over at him and he continued, "I wasn't trying to be an ass, but I was being serious. Have you seen the story all over the news right now?" I shook my head. I couldn't think of any kind of connection between The Upriser and me representing our school while shadowing at Puppeteer's Organization.

"Two B.E.G. students, Xavier Kinder and Rachel Carson, fought off two Care-Givers. However, unlike us, they fought the Care-Givers off without any casualties to civilians, and the fight caused very minimal damage to the city," Skye explained for Tonuko.

I get that it sounds super heroic and stuff, but why are they telling me this?

"Don't you understand?!" Tonuko suddenly shouted while squeezing his cup. It felt like he could read my mind. "We've fought many villains and somebody has gotten seriously hurt every single time! The one big battle that we had a chance to prove ourselves in we caused five enemy deaths and countless casualties. That's not even mentioning the thousands of dollars of damage we caused!" I was going to say something but nothing would come out of my mouth, so I looked down at the counter instead.

We beat the villains ... but at what cost?

"Kyle, when Tonuko said that to you yesterday, he just meant that we need to represent ourselves and our school better. It's obvious E.H. students have strength, but during our villain interactions, we failed and B.E.G.'s students passed. We have more experience with the Care-Givers, but we were completely humiliated by B.E.G.'s top students!" Skye sighed. I nodded in agreement, then stood and put my hand between the two.

"Let's all promise to be better in the next villain fight then! Sure, it's E.H.'s first year being open, but we can skyrocket its reputation! What do ya say?!" They looked at each other, then nodded and put their hands on top of mine.

We agreed on the promise then walked out the door toward the school. Through the front gate, we could see there were more newscasters than before. They were yelling to us, asking countless questions.

"How do you feel about other schools also dealing with the Care-Givers?!"

"Do you feel you could have handled your battle with the kidnappers better?!"

"Kyle Straiter, do you think you are the reason students your age are being preyed upon?!"

"Do you think going to shadow the hero organizations is a good idea considering the activity of the Care-Givers and the appearance of The Upriser?!"

Like usual, we ignored them and continued walking until we made it to the school. We strolled into the theatre, where Fallen and Excalibur were talking. We were the first students to arrive so we sat together. We discussed power-ups while waiting for the others to arrive.

Takorain, Capitol City Where B.E.G. is Located; Thursday (Two Days Ago) Afternoon:

Xavier Kinder led his class out of the infamous B.E.G. training grounds, known as the Junction One, and into the city. Their teacher stayed back to download the video of their hostage rescue simulation and told the students to go back to their classroom. Xavier laughed with a girl who had short, greasy black hair and huge eye bags as the class walked down the main street. Cars zoomed past and people scattered on the sidewalks, walking in and out of stores and restaurants.

"That fake hostage-thingy was easy-peasy! No need to thank me for carrying by the way!" said a girl with long, white hair sprinkled with light blue snowflakes. Xavier laughed out loud as he stretched his arms above his head.

"You really believe you carried?! I guess I'll let you have your fun!" He rested his hands on top of his head and continued leading the group toward their school. Seconds later, screams filled the air and people ran from the end of the block where the B.E.G. students were. Xavier grabbed the arm of a woman who was running away, then asked in a serious, comforting tone, "What's wrong, what happened?"

"Th- There're Care-Givers ... down the street!" she screamed through her gasps. Xavier looked down the street as he let go of the woman and squinted. At the end of the block was a large blue and purple portal.

He looked back at his class, and commanded, "Rachel, come on! Everyone else, protect the civilians and split into groups to cover more ground and make sure everyone is safe!"

The group agreed then Xavier and Rachel bolted down the street toward the portal as the rest of the class split into a few groups. When Rachel and Xavier were about fifteen feet away from the portal, a man stepped out. He wore a fuzzy black headband under his white hair and spun a diamond-encrusted stopwatch around his fingers. He tossed it into the air, then caught it with the same hand. Another man also floated out of the portal. He was sitting on air with his legs crossed, and the coat-tails of his jacket dragged on the ground. He had very long, purple hair up in a spiky ponytail, and all over his hair were small, yellow outlines of stars. He floated about two feet above the ground and kept his eyes closed. Xavier tensed his fists and stood in a defensive stance.

In contrast, Rachel slouched, looking very tired. "Who are you again?" Rachel yawned. The white-haired man smirked and held up his hands.

"That should be pretty obvious! We are followers of Tyrant, two of his Care-Givers!" The man opened the stopwatch, then suddenly Xavier's head smashed into the ground. "I am Kaci Clockwork, the master of time!"

Xavier's Point of View, Slowed-Down Time:

I couldn't move and saw the man, who I knew was Kaci Clockwork, slowly walk toward me. He stood next to me and leaned over to my ear as he put his palm on my forehead.

"I can see that you can see," Kaci whispered. After that, he pushed my head toward the ground and kicked my feet out from underneath me. As much as I tried, I couldn't move any part of my body except my eyes. Kaci stood straight up after positioning me and snapped. My head smashed into the ground, and he said, "I am Kaci Clockwork, the master of time!"

Normal Point of View:

Kaci stepped onto Xavier's cheek and snickered as he applied more weight.

"You two must be from that gifted school. Pity; such bright futures going to be taken away at my hands. Oh well, we have to make a statement, don't we, Favian?" Favian nodded slightly but did not open his eyes or move a muscle.

"We must follow orders, that is our job," Favian spoke. The portal behind him sucked in on itself and he finally opened his eyes. Rachel got lost in them—there was no pupil or anything, just pure galaxy inside his eye sockets. Then, Favian blinked and his eyes changed to normal white with red pupils. Rachel's eyelids sagged, giving her eyes the appearance of being barely open, and she yawned again.

"What kind of a name is Favian?" Rachel mocked nonchalantly. All of a sudden, instead of being calm Favian looked irked and he clenched his fists.

"What kind of name is Rachel?! It's not nice to make fun of others!" Favian argued while glaring at her. A white silhouette of Xavier jumped out of his body, then Xavier wiggled his fingers. The silhouette swung and punched Kaci in the face, causing him to step off Xavier and stumble back. A stream of black liquid, which appeared to be blood in its veins, flowed throughout the ghost. It swiftly grabbed and lifted Kaci. It hugged him and squeezed tightly. Xavier stared at Kaci, slowly moving his fingers closer to each other. As his fingers moved, the ghost squeezed tighter.

Xavier Kinder, Strength: Puppet—like his father, he can turn his soul into a transparent puppet that is controlled through his fingers by a very, very slim black rope. The puppet's mouth is always opened and can mimic the strengths of people within a two-mile radius. The

puppet cannot be harmed by physical attacks, but any attack that lands on Xavier or damages the strings affects both Xavier and his puppet.

"Favian," Kaci gasped, "portal!" Favian pointed at Kaci, then one of the same purple and blue portals sucked Kaci out of the ghost's grip. A new portal was created in the same spot behind Favian. Kaci stepped out again and straightened his jacket.

"Seems as though we are in a brawl against the number-one hero's son. How enticing," Favian stated while looking at Xavier. Xavier didn't respond, but instead swung his ghost, via the rope, at Kaci. The ghost clotheslined Kaci, causing him to fall back toward the portal. Before he fell, Kaci stopped time again.

Xavier's Point of View:

Kaci stopped himself from falling and grimaced at me.

What a nuisance. I can barely move again. As long as my ghost is out though, I can win.

"How purely pitiful; heroes-in-training, eh? Why train to be someone who fights outcasts and leaves others to rot at the bottom?!" Kaci shouted while walking toward me. He wound up a punch, but before he made contact my spirit turned around and socked him in the back of the head. Kaci fell onto me, and when his stopwatch touched me I could move again. I swung my hands behind me, pulling my spirit toward us as it tackled Kaci to the ground. I jumped back when the two landed and looked around. No one was moving, birds were still in the sky, my classmates, who were helping others, were frozen ... time had simply stopped.

"What the hell is this strength?! Turn it off!" I yelled at Kaci, who was standing. He cracked his jaw, then looked up at me with furious eyes.

"You are strong, but naïve. You're the perfect weakness to my strength, so it's not smart for me to stay," Kaci thought aloud. He snapped, causing time to resume, then looked back at Favian, "Let's go."

"Already? How horrid to think we were bested by two teenagers. Oh well, just an unlucky matchup," Favian sighed, creating a portal behind them. Kaci swiftly walked through it before Favian could float through, Rachel ran extremely fast, jumped into the air, spun in a circle, and kicked Favian in the side of the head. He flew into the wall of the building they were in front of, and Rachel landed gracefully.

"We can't let them get away Xavier!" Rachel shouted sleepily. By the time she finished her sentence, Favian had already created a new portal under where he landed and the two Care-Givers were gone.

Normal Point of View:

The snow-flake hair girl turned the corner, skating on ice that was radiating from her feet.

"Hey, are you two alright?! The area has been evacuated!" Xavier's spirit walked into him, then the two melded together and he put his hands in his pockets.

"We're fine, but they escaped. For being two Care-Givers, it wasn't much of a challenge, right Rachel?" No response. Xavier looked over, confused, but wasn't shocked to find her sleeping on the ground. He scooped her up in his arms like a baby, then the three caught up with their classmates at the front of the school.

"Woah, you fought them off with barely any scratches?!" a boy with light brown and blonde hair shouted at Xavier. Xavier wiggled his finger around in his ear, pretending to muffle the noise.

"No need to holler, I'm right here. It was a bad match up for those guys; anyone without a spirit strength

297

would have most likely been killed by Kaci Clockwork," Xavier stated. A breeze blew through his hair as he looked back at the now-peaceful city, and he sighed while shaking his head.

"Turn the lights off!" Rachel muttered as she slowly opened her eyes. She stood, out of Xavier's arms, and rubbed her eyes. She said, "Who cares if somebody else wouldn't have survived. We fought them, not someone else, and we survived." Xavier smiled and nodded. They heard running and panting behind them, so Xavier turned and saw his teacher gasping for air.

"A- Are you kids okay?! I he- heard what happened from the p- police!" the teacher nervously stuttered.

"We're alright; Rachel and I took those villains down like they were nothing!" Xavier boasted with a big smirk across his face.

"B- But what if you got hurt?! Gosh, I- I should have been there with you; I'm the pro!" the teacher yelled while rubbing his bald head. Snowflake girl wrapped her arm around the teacher's shoulder and gave him a big smile.

"Man, you are such a nervous wreck. Your hero name fits you perfectly!" she exclaimed.

Nervous Hero: Gladiator/Gerald Hatkins, Strength: Warrior—he can immediately sharpen any item he holds in his right hand and any shield he holds cancels out all strengths that attack it. Though he's a nervous wreck, he has unbelievable swordsmanship and martial arts skills.

"A- Anyway, Xavier, your father contacted the school about you going to h- his organization to shadow!" Gladiator informed Xavier.

"Alright, I'll give him a call when we get inside." The class headed back to their classroom and took their seats. Xavier took out his phone and called his dad. The phone rang then Puppeteer answered.

"Hey buddy, shouldn't you be in class right now?" Puppeteer asked.

Xavier chuckled as he heard Puppeteer flipping a few papers. "I am in class. Teacher just told me about the shadowing. I heard I'm going to your organization."

"Well, of course you are. Where else would you be going?" Xavier smirked and leaned back in his seat.

"I can't think of any better place! Is it going to be just you and me for the week?" Xavier questioned, sounding slightly hopeful.

"Well," Puppeteer responded, "I did invite this other kid from another school. Before I tell you about that, I want to let you know I just talked with Ashlyn's mom—such a nice woman—and I was thinking you could bring Ashlyn with you if she doesn't already have a place in mind!" Xavier looked over at Ashlyn, the snowflake haired girl, then shrugged.

"Yo, Ash, you wanna come with me to shadow my dad's organization?" Ashlyn's eyes lit up as she sped over to his desk. She leaned on it while looking at Xavier with gleaming eyes.

"Of course I do!" She stood straight up, twirled a piece of her hair then asked, "Is anyone from another school going?" Xavier nodded, then put the phone back to his ear.

"So who's that other kid you said was going? What school do they go to?" The phone went silent, Puppeteer was hesitating and was clearly anxious to tell Xavier.

"W- Well, he's from Eccentric High ..." Xavier's face turned from intrigue to disgust.

"Why the hell did you invite a kid from that problem school? Who is it: Tonuko Kuntai, Alex Galeger? You said he! Wait ... don't tell me ..."

"It's that strong fella', Kyle Straiter!" Puppeteer admitted, trying to sound happy and hoping to lift Xavier's mood. It didn't work.

"You invited a damn criminal to your organization?!" Xavier seethed angrily.

"He's not a criminal Xavier! If he was, he'd be in jail by my decision! I pardoned him, so I know if he's a hero or not! You know what, he might be stronger than you!" Puppeteer retorted. Xavier hung up, then rested his chin on his hand and sighed. Ashlyn was confused but interested.

"A criminal? Who did he invite?" Ashlyn asked, leaning on Xavier's desk again.

"That killer Kyle Straiter, from E.H." Xavier grunted. Ashlyn was bursting with excitement.

"Oh my gosh, no way! Kyle is such a hottie!" she squealed and blushed. "Just imagine if he and I hit it off! Maybe by the end of the shadowing, we'll be super close!" A girl with long, green curly hair looked over at Ashlyn and giggled.

"Look at you fan-girling, Ashy! What's up with you liking Kyle Straiter so much?" the girl teased. Ashlyn spun around and flung little snowflakes throughout the room.

"He's just so dreamy!" she sang, giggling and blushing even more. Xavier rolled his eyes and looked out the window.

"You're unbearable, just like that kid," he grumbled. "At least the kid ain't weak ..."

E.H.:

300

Approximately twenty-five minutes later, everyone was finally in the theatre. Fallen shushed our talking, then stood on the stage with his hands behind his back.

"I know it's only been a day since we told you about the shadowing, but has anyone chosen where they will be going?" Fallen asked while looking directly at Tonuko and me. We raised our hands, along with a few others including Alex, Skye, Scarlett, Camilla, and Jessica.

"No surprise for some of you. Tonuko, is anyone in a group with you?" Tonuko nodded, then pointed at Alex then Skye.

"Yep, Kaliska told me to bring one honors' and one advanced student." Fallen nodded his head, not surprised by Kaliska's request.

"As expected of Kaliska. How about you Kyle? Safe to assume your choice wasn't very hard," Fallen smirked. I chuckled as I leaned back in my chair.

"Yeah, it was pretty easy to choose. Too bad I can't bring anyone though." Fallen and Excalibur were again not surprised.

"That's Zane for ya. I'm sure he's having his son go, though," Fallen stated, expecting a response from me. I nodded.

Excalibur stood from the stage and announced, "Today, the classes will be separated. The power-up training takes longer than usual training, so we're going to have the honors' class go to the Dome first and the advanced students will stay in decision-making class. Then, we'll switch. That's how classes will go all month." There was a wave of disappointment among all the freshmen. As he stood, Tonuko looked at Skye and gave her a stern glare.

"I'm trusting that you'll work hard all month." She shrugged and nodded.

"You don't gotta worry about me, I always work hard! You better not let me outwork you!" Skye mocked. Tonuko chuckled while shaking his head, then all us honors' kids left for the Dome.

When we arrived, Rake questioned, "Shouldn't we go to a more open area if we're all doing power-ups? They can get pretty crazy."

Fallen smirked and flicked a switch by the door. The roof above us retracted and moved down the sides of the walls. "Now, let's begin, shall we?" Fallen asked with his grin still plastered on his face. "Who here has already practiced with power-ups? If you have, step forward." Tonuko, Anya, Rake, Steven, and I stepped forward.

"Rake, since when have you had experience with power-ups?" Jessica asked while petting a sunflower in her hand.

"Rake and I went to the same school, and at the end of the year we had basic training with power-ups," Steven answered for Rake. Jessica rolled her eyes and looked away, leaving Steven confused for a moment.

"I'm impressed with how many of you have had experience with power-ups! Now, Kyle, how about you demonstrate your power-up first since I know the level you're at!" I walked toward the middle of the stage and heard a scoff from Tonuko behind me. I grinned a little, then took a deep breath to focus. I threw my hand into the air and held it high above my head. A sword made entirely of flames spiraled into existence from my palm.

"Ember," I started. The flame sword's blade expanded, growing higher and wider until it was shaped like a lion, "Roar!" I swung the blade down, and the lion roared as it pounced and bit down into the ground. When it made contact, a mini explosion went off, launching me back a couple feet due to the air pressure. The explosion blinded everyone and when the smoke cleared, a very small mushroom cloud was left, similar to the one left after my attack on the Creature. People clapped, so I bowed then brushed the dust off my shorts.

"Lame!" Tonuko mocked while walking toward me. I chuckled and gave him a slight push, then he got settled and cracked his knuckles. "My turn!" He walked to the center of the stage, the same place I stood before, and stretched out his arms. He crouched low as he swung his hands onto the ground. A large wave glided through the ground at the same time that a cement ball was created a dozen feet away from him. "Wave of," he started loudly. The ball was thrown into the air when the wave reached it, then a hand rose from the ground and soared at the ball, "Demise!" The hand, being controlled by Tonuko, smacked down upon the ball. The ball flew at high speeds into the ground and was demolished. All the creation crumpled down as Tonuko cracked his right shoulder.

"Wow, that was spectacular! I expected nothing less than flashy from the number-one freshman in the nation!" Fallen complimented while softly clapping.

"Boring!" I teased while fake-yawning. Tonuko rolled his eyes and slightly smiled as he walked back to the group. Steven was eager to go next and ran to the front of the class.

"Mine's more of a classic power-up! Y'know, maxing out my strength!" Steven shouted. He looked at the ground and closed his eyes, focusing hard. His body morphed to metal, and red and blue wires sprouted out the sides of his arms and legs. Steven super-jumped into the air and landed in a crouched, heroic position. "Robotic Takeover!" he yelled with a smile. The class began clapping, then he turned back to human while panting. "I can't stay in that form for long 'cause it drains a lot of stamina, and I can't make my organs robotic just yet," Steven explained.

"That exceeded my expectations! I'm surprised you're so advanced with maxing out your strength; well done!" Fallen said, seeming actually impressed. Steven strutted back to the line then patted Rake on the back. Rake was clearly more nervous than the rest of us and didn't say anything as he walked out onto the stage. He flung his hands out, throwing all his fingers off his knuckles and onto the ground. They morphed into one massive snake that was about two dozen feet long and had large wings. He jumped onto the snake's back, then the two soared into the air. Rake crouched, flipped off of the snake, and swung a punch at the air.

"Airstrike Defeat!" he screeched as the snake flew by him and bit the air. Honestly, it was pretty awkward.

"It, uh, would've been a lot cooler if someone was ... y'know ... there," Rake sighed. Fallen shrugged and clapped.

"We all get the idea, and it's pretty neat! It could use some touching up though, but well done nonetheless!" Rake trudged back to the line, and all that was left was Anya. She smirked as she trotted out to the stage, then she stomped her foot.

"Armor of," she blurted while rocks crawled up her body. When she took a step forward, the rocks already on her body smoothed out. "Destruction!" she exclaimed as she threw up her hands. Then two red lasers—the same kind she'd used in weapons in her fight with Tonuko during the training tournament—charged up and blasted out from her palms at a specific spot a few feet in front of her. Countless lasers blasted the ground, then an explosion came out of nowhere. Debris flew everywhere, then her armor fell off her body and she flipped her hair.

"Very impressive!" Fallen shouted while clapping. We rejoined the rest of our class then Fallen said, "I'm very impressed with those of you who've had experience. Now, time for the rest of ya to get started!" We all split into groups of four and spread out on the stage, which was now larger than it had been during our training tournament. My group included Camilla, Alex, Cindy, and me.

"I think I've got an idea. I've tried out this kinda stuff before, and this move might be the one!" Alex smiled before taking a step forward away from the other groups. We watched as a ball of light lit up in Alex's hand. "Light," he punched his hand into the ground, creating a hole, and sent a stream of light underground. It ripped through the surface of the cement as it traveled about two dozen feet. "Oracle!" he shouted. The light grew extremely bright and the explosion was heard across the Dome. When the light faded, there was a hole in the ground, and Alex panted, looking at the destruction.

"Nice one, Alex!" I complimented while clapping loudly. He gave me a thumbs up with a big smile, then, Camilla grabbed my left arm.

"Hey, Kyle, can we talk?" she asked, looking almost embarrassed. I was confused and nodded. She hesitated, then took a deep breath, "Look, I just think you're super cute, and cool, and smart, and I was wondering if you'd like to go out with me sometime?" Camilla explained, shocking us all.

That was- so damn random. What the hell?

"Uh ... sorry, but no thanks. I'm good," I responded, thinking I did a good job of letting her down easy.

Sorry Camilla, but I don't really understand all that dating stuff. Maybe in the future, but not right now. You get it, right?

Camilla's expression changed from happy to very angry and displeased. She swiveled around, then held her arms in an "X" formation in front of her face.

"Wind Breaker!" she roared as she swung her arms down. Two wind blades flew at the Dome's front door and obliterated it. Camilla stomped away and out of the building, leaving Cindy, Alex, me, and everyone else completely shellshocked.

"Not the damn door! Do you kids know how expensive this kinda stuff is?!" Fallen cried while running at the debris. I blinked a few times, standing with my mouth gaping, then heard a holler of laughter across the Dome.

"Nice one Kyle; you sure are good with the ladies, huh?" Tonuko shouted through his wheezes. I turned around and saw him practically on his knees from laughing so hard. I rolled my eyes, then walked back toward Cindy and Alex.

"I guess I didn't let her down too easy ..." I sighed. Alex and Cindy shook their heads, then we chuckled and helped Cindy think of a power-up for her strength.

I can't believe she felt that strongly about me. I didn't think it was possible for someone to like me so much. Sorry, Camilla, but I can't be that close to anyone, I can't risk losing them.

Chapter 17
The Start of New Terror
Two Days Before the Shadowing; Thursday, October 3rd, 8:00 a.m. at E.H.:

I woke to my alarm, then punched the off button hard, causing the alarm to fall off my nightstand. I opened my droopy eyes and turned onto my back to face the ceiling.

How the hell am I supposed to go shadow Puppeteer in two days? I can barely move my body 'cause of dumb Hell Month!

Flashback:

"Come on you lazy bums! Move it!" Fallen screeched as he watched us run at the border of the school walls. "Only five more laps, let's go!"

"Why," Alex wheezed, "do we have to run so much?!" Donte zoomed in front of the group, then slowed to our pace and laughed.

"Come on guys! This ain't even that bad!" he mocked while back peddling.

"Easy for you to say!" We gasped and slowed even more.

This campus is fucking huge, how are we supposed to do ten laps?! This is ridiculous Fallen! I know you're over there giggling to yourself!

I looked over and saw Fallen giggling.

Called it.

When we finally finished our laps, we lined up in front of Fallen in the same formation as we did in our classroom seats. Everyone, except Donte, collapsed onto the ground while trying to control their breathing.

"Not done yet! First off, *one hundred pushups!*" Fallen commanded. Everyone groaned and swore.

"Why do we have to do so many Fallen?!" Cora yelled, laying on her back.

"Because," Fallen started, "if your bodies are strong, your strengths will be strong! Strengths are a part of the body, children, so if you work at a strong, healthy body, you will have a strong, healthy strength!" After a minute, we got into pushup stance and Fallen yelled "Down!" every couple of seconds.

Present:

I held my lower back and groaned as I sat up.

"Everything hurts!" I yelled, slowly standing. I waddled over to my wardrobe and grabbed a change of clothes, then took a brief shower, brushed my teeth, put on my clothes, then left my room. I trudged down the stairs and saw a few people laying on the couch. Camilla was at the counter with Jessica and they left as soon as they saw me. I shrugged and walked over to the couch to see who didn't make it up the stairs today. "So this time it was Rake, Donte, Rose, and two other advanced kids! Yesterday wasn't even a leg day, how could you not make it up the stairs?!" I mocked with a laugh, leaning against the back of the couch near Donte.

"My legs are really strong," Donte started, grabbing his thighs, "but not my twiggy arms!" He shook his arms, then groaned in agony and let them drop onto his chest and head.

I chuckled, then smacked his bicep and yelled, "C'mon Donte, we're done for the month! Fallen said today he's just gonna explain some things then it's a free day, and tomorrow we're gonna be packing and prepping for the big leave day!" He yelped when I slapped him and acted like he was going to get up and hit me. When he moved to stand, he cried out and instead stayed seated.

"Y'know Kyle," Donte sighed, putting his hand on his forehead, "I hate ya'." I laughed and walked over to Rake, who was still sound asleep and snoring. I decided to give him a nice wake up call.

Don't want him to be late to class, y'know?

"Time for school, Rakey-Poo!" I screamed in his ear. He jumped and stood defensively next to me, then cramped and fell to the ground.

"Fuck off, Kyle! I'm too sore for your shit today!" he seethed while holding his left arm. I laughed again, then waddled over to the counter.

"You guys are such sissies! I made it up the stairs every day of Hell Month!" I bragged as I slowly sat.

I saw Tonuko turn the corner, and he was walking with a big smirk on his face and his chest puffed out. "Psh, that's nothing! I'm not even sore today!" I rolled my eyes as he sat next to me. I heard muffled chuckling to my right, so I looked over and Tonuko started, "Hey Kyle."

"What do you want Moody Earth?" I asked, already knowing he was going to make fun of me.

"Your relationship with Camilla really ... *burned up* ... didn't it?" His voice got higher as he finished, "It's like these *burning* emotions just took over!" Tonuko burst out laughing and smacked me on the back. I pushed him with my right hand, causing him to fall off the barstool. He yelped, "Ow, my fucking back!" when he landed.

"I thought Mr. Tough Guy wasn't sore today?" I countered. Tonuko rolled his eye while still chuckling, then I offered my hand to help him stand. We talked for another twenty minutes about transportation to Takorain, then trudged along with a few others to class. We said bye to the advanced kids, walked into class, and painfully sat. Camilla was already seated and refused to bat an eye at me.

"She's still really mad at me," I whispered to Cindy. She giggled, then stopped out of pain. Everyone arrived within the next few minutes. Fallen stood from his desk and leaned on the podium in the front of the classroom.

"Morning class! How did everyone sleep?" We responded with a dull moan, causing him to chuckle. "As expected. I'm sure you're very happy that today and tomorrow are off days before the shadowing!" We cheered, yet without energy. "Now is your last chance to ask me questions about the shadowing. Any questions at all?"

Scarlett raised her hand, so he pointed at her. "If some people are going to organizations near each other, are we supposed to travel together?" she asked.

"Yes," Fallen answered, "For example, Tonuko, Alex, Kyle, and Skye from advanced will travel together since Kaliska's and Puppeteer's Organizations are in the same city. Also, don't forget to pack all your necessities! You will sleep at your respective organization for a week— assuming you're not going to a family or family friend's organization, where you can sleep at their house. You'll be there from this Saturday to the next, so be sure you have clean clothes and stuff like that for all seven days! You will leave bright and early on the 5th and will be expected to return by 10:30 a.m. on the 12th."

Tonuko raised his hand, then asked before Fallen called on him, "What happens if we encounter villains? What is expected of us?" Fallen rubbed his chin and looked as though he was hesitating.

"As your teacher, I must tell you to not engage alone. If you, for example, are with Kaliska, proceed with caution. When do proceed, do not fight to injure but instead to protect. That is the best advice I can give you. Legally, you are not allowed to severely injure villains; you are only allowed to use self-defense to capture them. Say Alex hits a villain and knocks him unconscious, but that's it; that is perfectly okay and encouraged. However, if he attacks a villain, makes him bleed, breaks his bones, then knocks him out, that is not okay. That is what I mean when I say fight to protect, not injure."

Everyone nodded. His explanation made perfect sense. Fallen waved us off, "The Juniors set up some ice baths in the Dome, a tradition of Hell Month in hero schools, so go and ice yourselves. You don't have to, but I strongly recommend it. You're free for the rest of the day!" Most of us made our way to the Dome. Inside, there were over a dozen wooden barrels filled to the brim with water and ice.

"Freshies, how was your Hell Month?!" Hazel shouted with a mocking grin.

"You knew about this month and didn't warn us?" I sinisterly muttered while pointing at her. She smacked my finger away, then threw her arm around my shoulder and walked me toward a tub.

"You guys did great! Sure, the soreness of this month is brutal, but it's so worth how much stronger you get! Hop in a tub, it's great!" I shrugged and took off my shirt and socks, then dipped a toe into the bath. A shiver went down my spine. When I took my foot out and took a step back, Jon ran up and shoved me from behind, causing me to fall face first into the frigid water. I stood, freezing and shivering.

"Jon, you asshole!" I screamed. Jon was bent over wheezing because he was laughing so hard. A few feet behind him Kate was laughing as well. My teeth chattered as I stuttered, "Th- This shit is freezing!"

"Come on ya baby, it's not that bad!" Tonuko yelled, walking to the tub next to mine.

"Shut your mouth Moody Earth!" I retorted. "How about you get in one if it's not so bad?"

"I am, you impatient pig!" Tonuko yelled while taking his shirt off.

Wow, a pig? You dick.

He was slowly getting into the bath when Jon gave him the freshman treatment, pushing him in like he did to me. Tonuko jumped, already shaking and chattering, then splashed some water at Jon.

"Ay, watch it!" Jon chuckled, hopping backward. We all laughed. Tonuko and I continued our ice baths while talking to the sophomores and juniors about their shadowing experiences.

The next day was absolutely frantic.

"Dude, I'm freaking out! What if I make a bad impression and the whole world finds out?!" Alex asked while gripping my shoulders and staring into my eyes.

"I'm sure you'll be fine. Don't worry too much or you might actually mess up," I reassured, taking his hands off of me. He started biting his nails, then Tonuko put his hand on Alex's shoulder.

"You'll do great! There's a reason I chose you!" Tonuko said with a smile. Skye walked over and gave Alex a smack on the back of the head.

"Yeah, relax Angel Boy! I'm in advanced but I'm less worried about my strength than you!" Alex rubbed the back of his head and pouted.

"Kaliska is just such a cold-faced hero. You don't know what's going on under that mask. Did you see how much they yelled during Kyle's court trial?" Alex muttered. Tonuko shrugged before crossing his arms, then blew a dangling piece of hair out of his eye.

"She seemed pretty chill over the phone, so maybe that anger during the trial was just a front to intimidate Kyle," Tonuko pondered. Everyone looked at him, with no verbal response, confusing him. "What?"

"She? Did you not hear his voice? Kaliska is obviously a boy!" I argued. Tonuko raised his eyebrow, then put his hands on his chest.

"Have you seen her body? No guy can pull that off. The mask probably has a voice modifier attached!" Tonuko retorted.

Alex scratched his head, then sighed, "Honestly, it could go both ways. Let's make it easy and keep saying they and them while talking to Kaliska because that's what they want." We agreed.

"Everyone, the delivery for our outfits came!" Khloe shouted from downstairs. We swiftly made our way downstairs, eager to finally see our hero outfits.

Rake opened his box, but his face turned to disappointment. "Aww, man, really?" Rake complained while reading a piece of paper that was stuck in his box. I opened mine and saw the same note.

"Damn, so they didn't have enough materials for our outfits. We really have to wear these out?!" I asked while looking at the dark khaki-colored tank top and black shorts. The tank top had the cursive E.H. school logo in black across the chest, and the shorts had the E.H. logo in the same dark khaki color on the bottom of the right pantleg. I sighed, then took the box upstairs. I finished packing my suitcase, wheeled it outside and left it next to my door, then went downstairs to relax. I sat on the couch along with Cindy, Khloe, Donte, and Steven.

"There is no way I am wearing those shorts out in public. I have my own short shorts I could just bring; I had a

313

very similar pair in mind for my hero-fit!" Donte complained, rolling his eyes and crossing his arms.

"Short shorts?" Steven asked, trying not to laugh.

"I'm paying homage to the running sports of the past that were popular before strengths! They wore short shorts, so I wear short shorts!" Donte grumbled, glaring at Steven. We all chuckled, then Cindy turned to face me.

"So Kyle, are ya nervous?" she asked.

"Yeah," Khloe added, "shadowing the number-one hero is a really big deal. Isn't it stressful to think about?"

I thought for a few seconds, then confidently stated, "Nah, I'll be fine."

Cindy moved her hair behind her ear and looked down wide-eyed. "Watch out, your cockiness is showing!" she whispered loudly. I smiled and rolled my eyes, then put my hands behind my head and took a deep breath.

"Oh no, me being cocky? That's ridiculous!" I acted distraught, which made them laugh.

"Don't let Xavier Kinder see you being all cocky like usual! I heard he's super mature and stuff; doesn't deal with nonsense, y'know?" Khloe giggled.

"Whatever! If he's got a problem then he's got a problem! What's he gonna do, cry about it to his daddy?" I dragged my finger down my cheek, mimicking a tear, and stuck my bottom lip out, then laughed.

"Lunch is ready!" Scarlett sang, practically dancing the large bowl of noodles to the table.

"Well you're excited Scarlett!" Steven analyzed. He sat in his usual spot at the head of the table.

"I can't wait to go and shadow my auntie! Jess and Camilla are going with me; it's gonna be so much fun!"

Scarlett explained. I took a scoop of the noodles in a meaty red sauce and plopped in on my plate.

"That's exciting! Daniel's gonna be shadowing family too!" I commented. Daniel sighed as he sat next to me.

"Yeah, in the next city over actually. I live on the border between two suburbs, but my parents stick to patrolling in Parane." Scarlett gasped and pointed at herself.

"No way, we're going to Parane too! Wanna walk over there with us?" Daniel nodded and smiled, then I patted him on the back.

"You guys are lucky your places are within walking distance. We gotta take a train for half an hour!" I complained and looked over at Tonuko. He raised an eyebrow, looking pretty surprised.

"Takorain is only a half-hour train ride? I could have sworn it was longer. You know what that means?" Tonuko asked. I shook my head, so he answered himself, "We're not even that far from B.E.G. lowkey. If the kids are cool, and we hit it off, we could definitely hang out with them during breaks or something."

"You turned down your offer to B.E.G., so why do you want to hang out with them all of a sudden?" Skye asked in a mocking tone.

"*You turned down an offer to B.E.G.?!*" those who didn't already know shouted. Tonuko nodded with a shrug.

"Yep, I didn't wanna go to some stuck-up school. Notice I said the school was stuck-up, not the kids. Most of them are pretty chill from what I've heard." We continued talking and finished lunch. Most of the nervousness diminished after everyone got their worries off their chest and received some support. Kids finished packing, got some much-needed rest after Hell Month, and overall, we just relaxed. Tomorrow would be one of the biggest days of our lives.

Meanwhile, at B.E.G.:

Xavier rustled in his closet, trying to get his suitcase down from the top shelf in his walk-in closet.

"Dammit, how is it this stuck? I got it up there, didn't I?!" he shouted as he continued tugging on it.

Ashlyn sang loudly, "Xavier, are you almost done packing?!" Xavier jumped and fell backward onto his butt, then looked back at her. The suitcase slowly moved forward, then fell off the shelf and smacked him on the top of the head. "Oh man, that's gonna leave a mark."

"What do you want?" Xavier seethed, rubbing his head and standing. He grabbed the handle of his suitcase and threw it on his bed as Ashlyn walked into the room.

"I'm just so excited to see my love!" she sang. Xavier continued rubbing his head as he looked through his drawers and rolled his eyes when he heard that.

"He isn't your love, Ashy. We don't even know him; what if he's an asshole and hates us?" Xavier asked bluntly. Her face went front joyful to tearful, and tears brimmed from her eyes.

"Wh- Why would you say that?" Ashlyn stuttered, sounding as though she was about to cry. Xavier rolled his eyes again.

"I meant he'll love you." Ashlyn smiled and skipped out of the room while humming. Xavier had finally started to pack when Rachel walked into his room and laid down on his bed.

"Rachel, wrong room," Xavier said, not even batting an eye as he continued packing. He heard a snore, so he shouted, "Rachel!" She opened her eyes, then yawned.

"Oh, sorry. I came to tell you that teach said Ashlyn, you, and I have to walk together to the organizations. He said something about it being required even if the organizations are intercity," Rachel explained.

"I assumed, now get out," Xavier hissed. He looked down at his bag, heard another snore and clenched his jaw. He grabbed his blanket off the floor, threw it on Rachel, and moved her to the center of the bed. Xavier closed his suitcase then did some homework.

Saturday, SHADOW DAY; 11:30 a.m. at E.H.:

We were gathered at the front gate with our luggage per Fallen's and Excalibur's command.

"Alright, it's best that most of you get going. Be respectful, kind, brave, and make the right damn choices!" Fallen announced with a big grin. He signaled for us to leave. After everyone except me was outside the gate, Fallen grabbed my arm and whispered, "Listen kid, your decision making is pretty shitty but you're strong. Be wise out there big man."

"I won't let you down!" I responded with a smile. I waved goodbye, then ran and caught up with Tonuko, Alex, and Skye. We made our way down the street, took a left after a few blocks, and arrived at the train station.

"It looks like the train leaves in a few minutes. Let's get inside so we can get good seats!" Skye shouted while looking at the schedule. We made our way onto the train and sat near the door. We were silent for most of the ride, and after what felt like forever being in a dark tunnel, sunlight filled the train. I turned to look out the window and saw the beautiful city of Takorain. There were large skyscrapers and fat apartment buildings along with small corner stores, and people flooded the streets. I wasn't used to seeing so many people walking around. I'd always lived in Camby, where that wasn't common.

"Woah, look at this place guys!" I said with sparkling eyes while pointing out the window. Alex was next to me and Tonuko and Skye were across from us. Tonuko smirked and Skye smiled.

"It's definitely nicer here than back home. Look, you can see B.E.G. on that hill over there," Tonuko stated while pointing behind me. I squinted and saw the massive school.

"Oh wow, it looks amazing!" Alex shouted, wide-eyed. People stared so we apologized. The train screeched to a halt at the station, then we exited. I breathed in the fresh Takorain air, then swiveled around with my hands in the air to look at the others.

"This could be the biggest opportunity of our lives! Let's make it count!" They agreed as we headed into the busy street and scanned the area. I plugged Puppeteer's Organization into my phone, and Tonuko did the same for Kaliska's. We navigated through the streets, passing some really good-looking food places that made my stomach rumble, and made it to Kaliska's Organization after ten minutes. It was a huge building with the top floor made up entirely of glass. The others walked to the door as they said goodbye to me.

I walked away, but after a few turns got a little lost.

How fucking hard can this place be to find?! It's gotta be massive, right?!

I continued walking as I looked around. I accidentally bumped into a girl as we rounded a street corner at the same time. "Sorry, that's my bad," I apologized, picking up her luggage and handing it back to her. The girl looked extremely tired, abnormally tired in fact. "Are you uh, okay?"

"Yeah," she nodded, "Why?" I raised an eyebrow while observing her, then shrugged.

"You just look," I saw her very baggy clothes and finished, "tired. That's all." She rubbed her eye then looked me up and down.

"Aren't you that Kylie from E.H.?" she asked.

Kylie? Are you joking?

"Excuse me, but Kylie? It's Kyle, okay, I'm not a girl! I'm a boy!" She shrugged and pointed down the street behind where she had turned.

"Xavier's dad's organization is that way. Just walk down the block and take a right." I looked at the G.P.S. and saw it was stuck on the other side of the block.

"Oh okay, thank you," I said. I waved goodbye, then followed her directions. After a few minutes I turned the second corner and finally saw the big, white building with black-stained windows. I sped to the door while anxiously checking the time.

Shit, I'm a couple of minutes late. I hope he'll understand since it's a pretty big city.

I hesitated for a moment; my nerves were catching up to me. I rang the doorbell before I got lost in my thoughts. After a couple of seconds, the door opened and a small lady stood behind it. She had long, straight black hair, two antennas on her head and held a clipboard in her hand. She was extremely short, maybe three feet tall, and had on a ton of makeup. She looked at her clipboard, then up at me and jumped a little.

"Oh, you must be Kyle Straiter! It's a pleasure to meet you; I am one of Puppeteer's sidekicks, Lady Antress!" she said. She reached out her hand and I shook it. To my surprise, her grip was incredibly strong.

Kerry Teravan/Lady Antress, Strength: Ant—she can carry up to fifteen times her body weight and has antennas on her head that wiggle when she senses danger.

319

She can swiftly dig through any surface with ease and she is unusually shifty.

"I know you, you're always on the news! You're Puppeteer's most-trusted sidekick!" I fanboyed, looking at her with awe.

"Yep, that would be me! Let me lead you to Puppeteer's office, the other two are already here. It wasn't too far of a walk for them," Lady Antress explained as she turned to walk.

"Oh, right, that would be true," I said, falling in beside her.

So both of them go to B.E.G., huh? I wonder who this close family friend is.

Lady Antress led me to an elevator, then clicked the up button. We waited a moment and entered once the elevator arrived. She hit the fourth-floor button, which was the highest floor. The first floor was the main area, where most business took place; the second and third floors housed the lounge, the bedrooms, and the nursery. Once on the fourth floor, we walked down a long hallway until we came to a tall, wooden door. Lady Antress knocked on the door a few times, and I heard Puppeteer yell, "Come in!"

Lady Antress signaled for me to walk in, so I nodded and grabbed the doorknob. My stomach sank when I did so, but I just closed my eyes and opened the door. I opened my eyes and saw Puppeteer sitting behind his desk along with two kids, one boy and one girl, sitting in chairs with their backs to me. The girl had white hair with light blue snowflakes scattered throughout it and black walnut skin; the boy had messy, light-brown hair and very pale skin. Puppeteer pointed to the seat in front of him. The girl turned and looked as though she would explode with excitement.

"Oh my gosh, I can't believe you're actually here!" the girl screamed, jumping out of her seat and running up to me, hugging me tight.

"D- Do I know you?" I gasped. She didn't respond. She continued hugging me and rubbing her head into my chest.

"She's Ashlyn Gray, and she's from my school. I'm sure you know me," Xavier explained in a biting tone.

Doesn't sound too mature to me ...

"Little cocky, don't you think?" I asked with a wheeze.

And can this girl stop hugging me so tight? I can barely breathe!

"I've got the right to be. Being this guy's son makes me pretty strong, eh?" Xavier retorted with a grin. I patted Ashlyn's back and wore an awkward smile.

"Thanks for the hug, but- I can't really breathe!" I said, causing Ashlyn to let go. She gave me a big smile, then she walked back to Xavier. I raised an eyebrow, then sat in my chair and asked, "So, can I ask what's up with her?"

Xavier looked at the blushing Ashlyn, then chuckled. "She, uh, really likes you," Xavier sighed.

"Yeah," I nodded, "I can tell." Puppeteer cleared his throat, so we looked at him. Ashlyn was seated next to me, and I could see in my peripheral vision that she was staring at me googly-eyed.

"Listen, I love how social you are but this is serious business. This isn't as much a social event as it is an opportunity for you to train for the future. We will be patrolling the town, a basic deed that heroes and police do all the time. Basically, we survey a certain area for criminal activity and help those we see who need it. As heroes, we want to make others happy and help them feel safe when they see us, so don't bite your tongue out there. Communicate with the townspeople and be kind!" Puppeteer explained while looking at Xavier, who rolled his eyes.

"Uh, excuse me?" I asked, trying to not be too loud.

"Yes Kyle?" Puppeteer responded.

"When will we be patrolling?" Puppeteer closed his eyes and took a deep breath, then leaned back in his chair and smiled.

"Well, I'm glad someone here wants to get started. In one hour, Kyle and Ashlyn will patrol from here to Green Street, and Xavier and I will go the opposite way to Aviator Drive. Kaliska's shadows will be out as well, so don't be shy, talk to them when you see them. If civilians see heroes talking to each other, they'll feel safer knowing that heroes around town communicate well. You will also see pros around, so talk to them as well so you get a feel as to how professionals talk to each other in the field."

"Why are Kyle and Ashlyn together? Shouldn't I go with her since we know each other?" Xavier asked, giving me a side-eye.

What the hell is his problem?

"I trust Kyle enough to not need to have a pro with him. Plus, we'll get some quality time together!" Puppeteer answered with a big smile. Xavier rolled his eyes again. Ashlyn seemed excited and I sulked in my seat.

I have to spend the entire day with this girl who's obsessed with me? Really?!

"Now go on and get settled in your rooms. They're on the third floor. We've labeled them for you," Puppeteer commanded. We rose, then walked out the door with our luggage. We made our way to the elevator, went down to the third floor, then exited the elevator and looked at each room we passed. My room was first—it had a sign on the door with my name. I opened the door, walked in, and closed it behind me. I laid on my bed facing the ceiling.

Wow, this is already insane. That random girl really likes me for some reason and ... I mean she's pretty cute. Why would she like me though? And why does Xavier Kinder keep giving me dirty looks?

Kaliska's Organization:

"Kyle dipped right after we rang the doorbell, huh? You think he's scared of Kaliska after his court trial?" Tonuko asked with a snicker as they watched me walk down the block. Alex nodded, also chuckling, but before he could verbally respond, the door opened. Instead of a sidekick opening the door, Kaliska themself greeted them.

"Hello Tonuko, it is a pleasure to meet you! Who did you decide to bring from your advanced and honors' classes?" Kaliska asked, holding out their gloved hand. Tonuko shook it, then looked at Alex and Skye.

"The pleasure is all mine. This is Alex Galeger from honors' and Skye Harlem from advanced," Tonuko told Kaliska.

"Thank you for allowing us to come to your organization," Alex said with a smile.

"Of course! Now come inside! The other shadow should be here shortly." Kaliska looked around, presumably for the other shadow, then stepped aside and let Tonuko, Alex, and Skye into their organization.

"Wow, they're nothing like they were at the court trial!" Alex whispered to Skye as they followed Kaliska. Kaliska walked up the stairs, causing the three to groan.

"What's the problem?" Kaliska asked, turning toward them.

"Well, we just had Hell Month, a month of constant, tedious workouts, so we're very sore. It's fine though, we can take it!" Tonuko explained hesitantly. The three expected anger or disappointment from Kaliska, but instead they laughed.

"Your principal is Simon Lane, correct? He and I went to the same hero school, and that's where the Hell Month tradition originated. I completely understand if you take the elevator, trust me I don't mind at all," Kaliska explained, still chuckling. They continued up the stairs. The E.H. students walked into the elevator and Tonuko hit the button labeled "Kaliska M.O." (Kaliska's Main Office). When the elevator closed, Tonuko let out a breath of stress. The elevator ride was silent. Once they arrived on the third floor and the door opened, they saw Kaliska standing in the hallway.

"How did you get up here so fast?" Alex asked in awe.

"I had a little help!" Kaliska giggled, petting a resurrected deer behind them. The deer was translucent and mostly brown, yet had patches of furless green. The deer crumbled into the ground, and Skye and Alex clapped while Tonuko rolled his eyes at them.

"How about we go to my office so I can explain a few things? The other shadow just arrived so she'll be up here in no time." Kaliska turned and walked down the hall. Tonuko saw the elevator move down to the first floor, and his curiosity as to who the other shadow was grew. The three followed Kaliska into their office and took a seat on one of two stiff couches. After a couple of minutes, a figure loomed in front of the office's glass door, then Rachel walked in. Tonuko's eyes widened when he saw her.

"Guys," he quietly whispered to Alex and Skye, "that's Rachel, the one who fought with Xavier Kinder to beat the Care-Givers a month ago!" Kaliska crossed the room and gave Rachel a sturdy slap on the head with a rolled-up paper.

"Took you long enough! What, did you sleep in?!" Kaliska roared. Rachel sleepily nodded, rubbed her eyes, then looked at the other shadows.

"Who are they?" Rachel asked bluntly. Skye and Alex who were confused and Tonuko was irked by the question.

"Oh, I'm just the number-one ranked kid in the nation for our grade. No big deal to you I guess," Tonuko sneered. Alex shook his head at Tonuko's cockiness, knowing it would irritate Kaliska.

"You're right Tonuko, it is no big deal. That is not why you're here," Kaliska stated with menacing eyes. Tonuko gulped and nodded, then Rachel moved to sit on the other couch. Kaliska sat in their chair, then explained, "Alright kids, this is the plan for today: you will go to your rooms and unpack—they're on the second floor. There are two rooms with two beds so the boys will share one and the girls will share the other. We'll begin patrol in one hour. I'm sure you know what patrolling is, so no need for me to explain. I've assigned the duos of Tonuko and Rachel and Alex and Skye. I will go by myself." The E.H. kids nodded, listening intently, but Rachel just stared at Kaliska with a blank expression. "What Rachel?"

"Is Tonuko the green-armed kid?" Tonuko clenched his jaw and let out an annoyed noise as Kaliska facepalmed.

"Yes, Rachel, he is the green-armed kid. Just get out of my face, all of you. I'm already getting a headache," Kaliska sighed as they waved them off. They left the office and went back to the elevator, then made their way downstairs to find their rooms. While Alex was unpacking, Tonuko sat on his bed and sighed, wiping his eyes with two fingers.

"That Rachel girl is a nutjob. I thought she would be something special since she fought Care-Givers and won unscathed, but she's just dense. She was either messing with me, or genuinely knows nothing about any other school," Tonuko ranted. Alex shrugged as he made his bed.

"I don't know man, but don't let her bother you. We know she's strong, so that should be good enough. I'm kinda just nervous about patrolling right away; I feel like we're gonna run into villains. Maybe I'm just paranoid from Veena, I don't know," Alex ranted as well. Tonuko took a deep breath, then smiled.

"Don't worry Alex, we've got this! We have a better idea on how to act in the battlefield, and we have way more experience with our strengths! There're also way more heroes out and about in Takorain than Veena or Camby. I think we'll have it under control!" Tonuko reassured him. Alex smiled and nodded.

"Yeah, you're right. What's the worst that could happen?"

Chapter 18
When Two Worlds Collide

I snorted and woke, rushed and worried. I swiftly turned to check the time on my phone and fell out of bed when I grabbed the phone. I hit the ground hard and rubbed my head as I looked at the time: 11:57 a.m. I quickly stood and popped a few mints in my mouth, then scoured my bag for the uniform E.H. provided.

I hate nap breath so much. Also, why couldn't they have just made our suits? Mine looked so cool! It had a black arm sleeve with fire, two fuzzy red arm bands, all kinds of cool stuff! Man, I can't wait to get it!

I found and changed into the uniform but felt out of place.

These arm holes are massive. My entire side is practically showing. These shorts are kinda great, though, the perfect height: just above the knees. At least I have my boots that I planned to wear with my costume—some simple black boots, heavily padded with shock-absorbent soles. With these, I can kick super hard and not damage my foot.

I tied the boots tight, then smacked my right boot (the second one I tied) twice and hopped onto my feet. After that, I tied my headband on my head, walked to my door, took a deep breath, and opened it. I saw Xavier and Ashlyn walking past, both wearing their hero suits.

Xavier was wearing a navy-blue cloak, similar to his father's, but the bottom was ripped. He had a dark gray tank top underneath, black shorts, and thick-soled boots similar to mine. Nothing about his suit really stood out, unlike Ashlyn's. She wore a skin-tight bodysuit covered with a snowy mountain landscape, a snowflake choker around her neck, and bright cyan running shoes. Her hair was up in a high ponytail, held by a white scrunchie. I blushed and looked away.

What the fuck, she looks so hot!

"You guys are so lucky to have your suits! Our school didn't have enough materials yet, so we're stuck with these dumb uniforms," I said, trying to cover the blushing as embarrassment.

"Make sure to emphasize the dumb part," Xavier snickered. Ashlyn giggled with him, making me roll my eyes. We took the elevator down to the main floor to meet with Puppeteer. He was wearing his hero suit as well, and it was exactly as I remembered from the court trial.

"Alright guys, let's get going!" Puppeteer cheerfully smiled. When we walked outside, Puppeteer pointed behind Ashlyn and me. "You two will patrol that way and stick to that side of town. Xavier and I will go right and stay around there. Let's go team, be brave, kind, and charming!" Ashlyn and I waved goodbye to Puppeteer and Xavier, then were on our way. We walked in silence for a couple of minutes, then she abruptly broke the silence.

"I, for one, kinda like your uniform! It makes you look really good, really shows off your muscles, y'know?!" Ashlyn boldly complimented. She felt my arm, making me blush again.

"Th- Thanks! Your outfit l- looks good t- too!" I stuttered without looking at her.

"Aww, thank you! You're the sweetest Kyle! I feel like mine could use some more safety features, but a winter theme creates some awesome designs!" she said, smiling.

"Oh yeah, what exactly is your strength anyway? I get that it's about winter, but what part of winter?" I asked.

"It's basically all of winter! I can create compact snow that can hold a couple of tons and ice out of any part of my body. The ice is kinda tricky though. I really only can create spikes and waves or freeze surfaces; nothing too special right now," Ashlyn explained while looking at her hands. I noticed that specs of snowflakes, along with a mist, were seeping out of her hands. Quite honestly, it looked very cool.

Ashlyn Gray, Strength: Blizzard—she can create compact snow that can withstand weight up to that of a semi-truck. The snow can be broken with strong pressure or heat and will weaken over the course of just a few minutes. Ashlyn can also create snowflakes that have little to no effect, as more of a sight to see. Finally, she can create ice out of any part of her body and spread it on surfaces. She can control it as she pleases, like Tonuko's strength. The ice shatters quite easily and can melt in the sunlight, but at night it's at its strongest.

"Woah," I exclaimed in awe, "that's so strong! What are you ranked nationally?" She smirked and held up seven fingers in front of my face.

"I was seventh, but I may have dropped. I'm not growing in power as much as I used to; this ice is kinda holding me back. Plus, people like Xavier and you are apparently flourishing nationally. I think Xavier might be the new number one!" My mood dropped slightly, but I didn't let it show.

Seems like Xavier isn't the only one confident in his abilities, huh?

"You think so? What about Tonuko?" I asked with a raised eyebrow. Ashlyn looked forward and shrugged with a grin.

"Believe what you want, but Xavier beat two Care-Givers with little help and was barely scratched! All the news coverage says it was him and Rachel, but all Rachel really did was allow Xavier's puppet to copy her strength and she landed one kick on that Favian guy!" I rubbed my chin while thinking.

"The Care-Givers barely landed a scratch even though it was Kaci and Favian? If Kaci couldn't land a hit, even though he can stop time, then Xavier must have found a loophole to his strength. Maybe that means Kaci isn't as much of the 'untouchable sidekick' he's been publicized to be," I thought aloud. Ashlyn gave me a confused look with her eyes but smiled and nodded. We continued to walk, then a hero wearing a red cloak and white mask with one eye hole walked up to us.

"Hey there kids, are you two shadows?" the man asked.

I know that voice ...

"Oh my, is that you Kyle?!" he shouted. His one visible eye lit up while he stared at me. "Kyle, I don't believe you've met my son before! This is- Paul!" The little boy with white hair, black leather gloves, and the same cloak and mask as his father reached to shake my hand. My stomach dropped, and I hesitated before nervously shaking "Paul's" hand.

"Uh, Kyle, who is this?" Ashlyn asked before grabbing my arm.

I took a deep, shaky breath, then the man, while still staring down at me menacingly, asked, "Why don't you give us some alone time, little girl? Kyle and I have some catching up to do; some private things to talk about." Plague squeezed my hand, and a shiver crawled down my spine as I thought about his strength.

"O- Oh, okay! I'll, uh, wait up here Kyle!" Ashlyn stuttered. She walked away but looked back at me one last time. I gave her a nervous smile and nodded, but as soon as she turned around my eyes watered; I was absolutely terrified. BloodShot led me into the closed store, then pushed me so I stumbled and fell on my butt. He took one look behind him, then partially took off his mask and let it rest on his head. "Don't make it obvious Kyle. You know we can kill you as quickly as we want!" BloodShot smiled devilishly. Plague also took off his mask ... and one of his gloves.

"So you're Mr. Tyrant's son, huh? It's nice to meet you!" My heart beat faster and I felt a scratching in my stomach.

N- No, stay back. Don't touch me with those fingers.

It felt as though something was moving inside my body.

"I- I'm not going to let you control my life, BloodShot! I'll t- take you down!" I shakily yelled while standing up. BloodShot revealed his sheath, showing the handle of the blade he used on me when he attacked me. I got flashbacks of the attack, and my fear grew. I shook, causing Plague to snicker.

"You're supposed to act strong if you aren't scared of us! You're really bad at this!" Plague whispered. My fist tensed, and a flame roared around it. The flame turned black, and the darkness crept out from my palms, encasing my arms until it reached my forearms. BloodShot raised an eyebrow, then grinned again.

"That's the power we saw you use against the Creature and Lokel. Must be one of your strengths, but which one is it?" BloodShot gripped his blade's handle and inched it out of the sheath. Plague took a step forward while reaching his ungloved hand out to me.

Are they r- really going to kill me right now? Before I can even kill Tyrant? Why is BloodShot so obsessed with me? Stay back!

"Hey, what are you doing in here?! This building is closed, it's illegal to be inside!" Tonuko shouted from the entrance. BloodShot let go of his blade and flipped his mask back on, then flipped Plague's back onto his face.

"Oh wow, I didn't even notice! Sorry about that mister, my son and I will be on our way!" BloodShot laughed in a fake-happy voice. BloodShot rushed out of the building, holding Plague's now-gloved hand and leaving just me in the darkness.

"Is that the Kylie guy from your school?" Rachel asked sleepily. Tonuko squinted, then facepalmed.

"Dammit Kyle, what the hell do you think you're doing?!" Tonuko yelled. I hunched over, gripped my right arm, and stared into the darkness. Violent whispers attacked my ears, uttering horrid things about BloodShot and Plague. It felt as though something was crawling through my organs, scratching them as it did so. Tonuko noticed I was shaking, and saw my wide eyes, so he told Rachel, "Go make sure the other shadow is okay. I'll talk with Kyle." Rachel trudged away from the store, and Tonuko ran to my side. "It's alright Kyle, the guy is gone."

"Th- That was BloodShot ... He's here. Last time he was in the same city as us—something bad happened," I stuttered, still shaking. Tonuko's eyes widened as he looked back at the store entrance.

"Who the hell was his son?" Tonuko whisper– yelled. I was about to tell him, then remembered what Tyrant commanded.

Flashback:

"Don't you dare tell anyone a word about Plague or I'll have BloodShot eliminate you! I'm fucking warning you Kyle!"

Present:

"I- I can't say. I mean ... I don't know," I gulped. Tonuko gave me a look calling out my bullshit, then helped me sit up straight.

"Come on, Kyle! I don't give a fuck about what BloodShot may have threatened you with, who is that kid?"

he asked. I started shaking again and felt the black liquid dripping down my cheeks.

"I- I can't tell you. He'll kill me!" The darkness spread further up my arms, worrying Tonuko.

"Fuck the rivalry crap, I don't care about it. You need to tell me about this stuff, and I promise I won't tell anyone else. All we do is fight, but I think you know you can trust me with this Care-Giver stuff. No more secrets, right?" I wiped my eyes, though no liquid rubbed off, then took a deep breath.

"Plague," I stated, "His name is Plague, and Tyrant recently told me that he, too, was scared of him." Tonuko was visibly shocked by this.

"What?! Tyrant is scared of a kid?! He looks like he's younger than us!" Tonuko whisper–yelled.

"He's eleven years old. I don't know what his strength is exactly, but Tyrant said that Plague can kill all of humanity with one move. I think it has something to do with his black fingers, that's why he wears gloves. When he took his glove off his fingertips were pure black, down to the first or second knuckle," I explained. I held up my arms as I said, "Like this." The darkness faded, leaving Tonuko speechless.

"We'll talk more about this later but be on your guard. They're in this city, and that's very dangerous. We should ale-"

"No," I interrupted while standing, "If they're here, something bad is going to happen. They were in the city when the Kidnappers and Care-Givers struck, and they visited me after Tyrant told me about Plague. Now, they're here ... "

Tonuko thought about this as he ran his hand through his hair. "Yeah, this can't be good. Something big is going to happen, but what? Who could be attacking? They

333

already had two Care-Givers visit the city and they lost. Could they want revenge?" Tonuko thought aloud.

"BloodShot isn't really a pupil to Tyrant. He's only there because he's strong and works behind the scenes by taking down big names. Just because he's here doesn't necessarily mean the Care-Givers will be involved. This could be his own doing, so be weary," I told Tonuko as I walked past him. "And do not tell Kaliska or the others. If it gets out that Plague exists ... I'm a dead man." Tonuko nodded, then followed me out of the store. As soon as we exited, Ashlyn ran and threw herself at me, hugging me tightly, though not as tight as earlier.

"Are you okay Kyle?! I was worried sick! I'm sorry, I didn't know that guy and his kid were trouble!" Ashlyn apologized while looking up at me. I slightly smiled and patted her on the back.

"You don't have to say sorry, it's fine. I wasn't hurt or anything so it doesn't matter," I responded. I heard snickers to my left, and when I looked up I saw Tonuko trying to contain his laughter. "What the hell are you laughing about Moody Earth?!"

"So first you reject Camilla in a cold-hearted fashion and now you have a little girlfriend here?! That's too funny!" Tonuko sneered through his laughs.

"Girlfriend? I kinda like the sound of that!" Ashlyn said while blushing. I rolled my eyes, then glared at Tonuko.

"Did you have to say girlfriend?! She's already obsessed with me!" I snarled in a whisper. Rachel laughed sleepily, then pulled Ashlyn off me.

"Yeah, Ashlyn was talking nonstop about you when she found out you'd be at Puppeteer's place together." Ashlyn looked away and blushed again, then Rachel took a moment to look at all of us. "We have a pretty strong group here ... the first nationally, the seventh, then Kyle and me

334

who've taken down top-tier villains. I guess that's what's gonna happen when shadows of Kaliska and Puppeteer meet up."

"Wait a minute, that's Ashlyn Gray?!" Tonuko asked with a raised eyebrow, pointing at Ashlyn.

"Yep," she nodded, "that's me! You must be Tonuko Kuntai. Nice to meet you!" The two shook hands, and I took a good look at Rachel's face.

"Aren't you the one who gave me directions to Puppeteer's place? You're shadowing at Kaliska's?" I questioned with my hand on my chin. Rachel nodded and pointed at herself.

"Yeah, Kaliska called me immediately after Xavier and I took down the Care-Givers. They said they wanted me to shadow there because of how smart and heroic I am," Rachel explained.

"You mean ... when Xavier took down the Care-Givers with your strength?" I teased with a snicker.

Not even a second had passed when Rachel crossed her arms and retorted, "At least we didn't kill them."

That's a low blow.

Tonuko let out a shocked snicker and I pouted without responding. We decided to continue patrolling together and made our way around a couple of blocks before we ran into actual pro-heroes.

"Are you shadowing at hero organizations?" a man with course gray skin asked. His hair was black and spiky, and the texture of his skin resembled a rock.

"Yeah, two of us are at Puppeteer's Organization and two are at Kaliska's," I responded. The man nodded, looking impressed at my statement, and the girl he was with ruffled Tonuko's hair with a smile.

"Aww, that's adorable! You are working together?!" she questioned. The girl hero was very fit and muscular and about my height. She had long, red hair, tan skin, and full, red lips.

"I mean, I guess so. We ran into each other and Kaliska told us to work with other shadows if we see them. Kaliska wants us to show the townspeople that the heroes around the area communicate well," Tonuko answered before moving his head away from her hand. She softly poked his nose with a giggle, then swerved around on her heels.

"Good luck with your shadowing! It's the most important event for getting your name out there before the Hero Olympics!" she shouted while walking away. Tonuko rolled his eyes and fixed his hair, then heard a giggle behind him.

"Wow, even the pros see your school as a bunch of babies," Rachel quietly chuckled.

"Shouldn't you be sleeping right now or something, you bum?" Tonuko seethed before walking away. The rest of the patrol was relatively peaceful and quiet. We said hello to passing townspeople and maintained a smile most of the time. When we made it back to our starting point, the point where we all had met up originally, Ashlyn and I said goodbye to Rachel and Tonuko and, just like that, our first patrolling experience ended. As Ashlyn and I walked toward Puppeteer's Organization, all I could think about was the run-in with BloodShot and Plague.

Should I have told Tonuko about Plague? Maybe that was selfish; now he's into the mix of things. If any of the Care-Givers find out Tonuko knows, I'm dead. Fuck man.

"That was a lot of fun!" Ashlyn exclaimed with a smile, interrupting my thoughts. "Well, except for the first part. That was just weird."

"Yeah," I added, "I'm sure you can tell those two weren't my friends." Ashlyn nodded.

"I could see that; the adult was very pushy and demanding. At least you and Tonuko took care of him!" Ashlyn said, obviously trying to lighten my mood. I agreed with a smile, then looked up at the clouds.

Plague is the future of villains ... so maybe it is a good thing I told Tonuko. If we can take him down before he has a firm grasp on his strength—I'm hoping he doesn't already—we can plummet villain society's future.

"Listen, just don't tell anyone about that situation, okay?" I asked Ashlyn as we walked through the doors to Puppeteer's Organization.

"Tell anyone about what situation?" Xavier questioned in a biting tone as he and Puppeteer walked in behind us. Ashlyn opened her mouth to speak, but I swiftly cut her off.

"Oh, well, I guess the cat is out of the bag now. I had a run in with an old classmate and we had a little bit of an argument. I hope it's not too big of a deal to where it affects how the townspeople who were around view us," I lied. Xavier crossed his arms and raised an eyebrow, then looked at Puppeteer.

"It shouldn't be too much of a problem as long as you didn't get physical. Heroes are people too, and we will have arguments from time to time. That's perfectly normal," Puppeteer profoundly explained. I nodded, then he sighed, "Well, I have paperwork to get done. We can go out to dinner in an hour or two. I'll let you know when I'm free." We agreed and left for the elevator. After we entered, Xavier clicked his tongue with his arms crossed.

"Why did you stop Ashlyn from talking, criminal? What happened on your patrol?" he asked, not having the audacity to look at me.

"Like I said, there was just an argument with an old classmate. Right, Ashlyn?" I responded, not looking at Xavier. Ashlyn was surprised and blushed slightly.

"Yeah, that's all that happened. We patrolled with Rachel and Tonuko Kuntai most of the time," Ashlyn softly affirmed. Xavier chuckled, shook his head, then turned to face me.

"No, you're lying. Ashlyn is a terrible liar; she gets quiet and nervous. Y'know, for being a criminal, you're a terrible liar too," Xavier mocked.

"Stop calling me a criminal, asshole," I swiftly demanded, giving him an angry side-eye.

"Or else what? Are you gonna kill my sibling and me, like you did the Nomeres? Better yet, maybe you'll go and kill my dad, like you did your classmate's father!" Xavier jeered, uncrossing his arms and tensing his fists.

"Xavier, stop! Leave him alone! He did what he had to do to save the people around him!" Ashlyn pleaded while touching his arm.

Xavier smacked her hand away, then roared, "How is murdering people saving others?! Heroes don't kill people, but his sad sack of a dad does!" I shoved him, banging him against the side of the elevator. The elevator beeped and the doors opened as I clenched my fists.

"You don't know shit about me, yet you sit there and act like you're better?! I could beat your ass into the ground, so don't act tough with me! I'm not Tyrant, I'll never be like him!" I shouted, then stomped out toward my room. I felt a chill run down my spine; I was punched in the stomach by Xavier's spirit. I stumbled back as Xavier walked out of the elevator with small, black strings connecting his fingers to the spirit.

"You think you can beat me? Don't make me laugh, you're not a challenge in the slightest," Xavier belittled. I was huffing, out of air. I quickly turned around, took a step, and punched him in the face. Xavier pulled his puppet toward him, triggering it to fly forward and tackle me. While on the ground, I gripped both sets of strings and pulled hard, throwing Xavier face-first to the ground and his spirit flew off me as well.

"I don't think, I know I can! A cocky douchebag with no backbone like you could never beat me!" I argued as I stood. Xavier held his chest as he stood and stared at me with a scowl. A light blue liquid flowed through his puppet's body, then the puppet lifted its hands up and launched two pillars of snow at me. I soared down the hall, skidded on the ground, and crashed into the window, which cracked.

What the hell ... didn't Ashlyn say that's her strength? So his puppet can mimic strengths, just like Puppeteer?!

I coughed into my hand and wiped away the blood that dripped from my nose. I stood as Ashlyn screamed, "Stop fighting, we're working together as shadows! Xavier, stop using my power!" She ran toward Xavier and tried to stop him, but he pushed her with his right arm, causing her to trip over and fall.

"I'm not letting a criminal act as if he's better than me in my own dad's agency! He shouldn't even be here, he's a villain's son! Not just any villain, fucking Tyrant's son!" I stood there, not knowing what to do. I was furious but hesitant to fight.

We're inside Puppeteer's Organization, the infamous building of the number-one hero in the nation. Should I really be fighting his son? With my connections to Tyrant, I'll be seen as the bad guy! But I gotta humble this fucker. Alright, it's showtime ...

I activated Energy Conversion, causing the yellow mist to seep out of my pours and outline my body, then

339

looked up at Xavier. My scornful expression didn't faze him, so I decided my actions would. I charged at him, and before Xavier could react, I was behind him and punched his upper back. He spit with an agony-filled face, then swore and swung the puppet around, causing it to punch me in the cheek. I didn't move, but instead held out a hand in front of his face. Flames sprouted in my palm, dancing around in a circle, but before they could roar out at him, a yell shook my bones.

"What the hell are you two doing?!" Puppeteer screamed, running out of the elevator and grabbing me by the back of my neck. My eyes turned white and the darkness crept out of my hands.

"He wants to call me a criminal and a villain, but he can't back up his word!" I shouted.

Xavier joined in the yelling while still on the ground. "Truth hurts, criminal! Dad, I was putting the killer in his place and showing him that villains don't belong in this organization!" Xavier looked at Puppeteer for support. Instead, Puppeteer dropped me and pointed at Xavier.

"I don't care how the fuck you feel about him, don't you dare waltz around here acting like the toughest guy around and putting down others! He's not a criminal by my word, which is much more valuable than yours, so that's how it is! So, son, how about you shut your mouth and go to your room, now!" Puppeteer screamed.

"Wh- What, b- bu-" Xavier stuttered, his face pale.

"I said *now!*" Xavier jumped up, marched to his room, and slammed the door behind him. I had fallen onto my butt and my eyes returned to normal but the darkness didn't leave. Ashlyn crouched next to me and hugged me and I rested my head on her shoulder. Puppeteer yelled, "Just because I told him off doesn't mean you're innocent, Straiter! There's no fighting in here, especially with people you should be working with!" I nodded with a blank expression. He left, holding his head and swearing to himself. My breathing turned to hyperventilating and it felt as if something was crawling out of my head.

"Are you okay?" Ashlyn asked, sitting next to me. I didn't respond. I continued breathing heavily, then I passed out ...

Darkness in Kyle's Slumber:

I slowly opened my eyes but couldn't see anything. I could tell I was in the same abyss where I had talked to Tyrant, but it was much darker now.

"*Kyle.*" I turned around, and my eyes watered.

Th- That voice ...

Reality:

I swiftly sat up in my bed, scaring Ashlyn half to death. She had been sleeping in a chair in my room. "Kyle, you're awake!" she exclaimed, standing. I didn't respond. Instead, I looked around frantically.

"*Kyle.*" I heard it again and turned. I looked outside and saw the bright silhouette of a woman in the street.

It can't be ... th- that's not possible!

"Are you alright, Kyle?" Ashlyn asked, looking out the window. She saw nothing and gave me a concerned look. I jumped out of my bed, then ran out the door. Ashlyn followed closely behind, watching as I jumped down the staircases and ran out the front door. The silhouette was gone, but I heard the voice again.

"*Kyle.*" I looked up at the dark, rainy sky as tears mixed with rain poured down my cheeks. My lip quivered as I opened my mouth.

"Mom ...?"

Chapter 19
Make the Effort

I spun around a few times, looking for my mother. She was nowhere to be seen, then I heard the voice again:

*"**Kyle ... Why are you fighting?**"* That question broke me. I stopped moving and let my arms dangle at my sides.

"Kyle, what's going on?! What are you looking for?!" Ashlyn asked while slowly walking toward me. I looked over at her with dead, devastated eyes, causing her to gasp. "What's wrong?!"

"I'm sorry," I said, but not to Ashlyn. "I'm sorry I keep getting into fights." I looked up at the sky filled with dark clouds, then clenched my jaw. "I'm trying to get better, I really am. I want to be nicer, to care for others, to be affectionate, but I don't know how. I can barely remember you at this point, all I can remember is all the horrible things that fucking asshole did to you. Why would you stay with him?! *Why?!*"

The white silhouette walked out of the air in front of me and started walking toward me. My eyes grew wide and I started with a few steps, then ran toward the silhouette. I reached out to hug her, but I passed right through her invisible body and fell hard onto the street.

*"**Kyle, J hear you**,"* my mother said, looking down at me. I was too weak to stand and just stared up at the silhouette. I noticed out of the corner of my eye a looming presence that slowly circled the area. *"**You are enough. J love you.**"*

Y- You do?

"B- But I killed you! Tyrant said so. It's my fault you're gone! I'm a curse!" I yelled. Ashlyn began backing up toward Puppeteer's Organization, unsure what to do. To her, I was just yelling at the air and crying, but she could tell something was going on. My face was lit by a light that wasn't there, she could see that. Additionally, she could faintly hear a woman's voice when she got close to me.

"Kyle's mom was killed by his dad, so how could she be here? What's going on?" Ashlyn whispered to herself, standing under cover from the rain.

"You did not kill me, nor did Sam. My passing was a must, sad as it is, it had to occur. I love Sam with all my heart, as do I love you with all my heart. You are my two boys! Please, pick yourself up, keep fighting, and don't give in to any whispers you hear."

The silhouette reached down and I felt human skin as she picked up my right hand. She turned it over and saw the darkness in my palm, then looked directly behind her at the looming presence. The presence was very tall, completely pitch black. It had tentacles of varying sizes protruding from its body and no identifiable facial features except for a sharp, toothy smile. *"You do not need help from anything else, I promise you that. You will do great things on your own, I'm sure of it. Goodbye, my beautiful son."* The silhouette cracked into what appeared to be shards of glass, just as my mother had when she passed.

"No, don't leave me again! Please, I love you too! Don't leave me!" I screamed, watching the pieces float into the sky.

Gem Straiter, Strength: _____

I crumbled to the ground in tears, then felt a large hand on my back. I looked up and stared into the face of the demon. I flinched. I was terrified, yet the demon's presence wasn't evil or toxic; instead, it was comforting.

"I know ... that you are suffering. I know ... that your mother does not trust me. However ... I am here ... for you. I am here ... to help you," the demon spoke in a deep, raspy voice. I couldn't look away from its terrifying appearance, not because I was scared but because I was intrigued.

"How can you help me?" I asked as the tears washed away.

"I already have. I gave you power. Those whispers ... are mine. The darkness ... is mine. We ... are one. So what is mine ... can be yours." I nodded, then thought about what my mother said. I opened my mouth to reject the demon's offer and was hit with flashbacks of all the times my mother bared through what Tyrant did to her yet did nothing. *"Your mother was a lovely person ... but she failed you. Love can only do so much ... power must make up the rest of it. Let me help you fulfill ... your purpose."*

B- But, my mom. I can't.

"You can." Before I could respond, Ashlyn grabbed my arm and helped me to my feet.

"Kyle, you'll get sick if you stay out here any longer! C'mon, let's get inside!" Ashlyn yelled. I nodded and followed her back to the building. I looked back one last time and saw the demon staring at me. I gulped and went inside. Ashlyn and I sat in silence at a table on the first floor. After a few minutes, she asked, "So ... what happened out there?"

"I- I honestly don't know. I saw ... my mom," I responded. Ashlyn looked around, then stood and walked to a nearby table that held some food. She pulled a paper-wrapped sandwich and a cup of fries out of a bag, then walked back and offered them to me.

"It's been a day since you first passed out, you must be hungry." I hesitated, then nodded and took the food from her.

"Thank you." She smiled brightly, lifting my mood.

I can't tell her about that demon. Nobody can know. I don't know who it is or why it's here, but it can't be good for my image.

"What's B.E.G. like?" I asked in an attempt to change the subject. Lucky for me, I was successful.

"Well, as much as a dream school as B.E.G. is, it's really hard. Their expectations of us are very high, since B.E.G. is the number-one ranked hero school in the country, and we train a crap ton. It's a lot," Ashlyn explained while leaning back in her chair. I nodded as I finished the sandwich, then wiped my mouth with a napkin.

"That does make sense. People expect the top school to produce top heroes and the only way you can be a top hero is through training," I said. Ashlyn nodded in agreement, then, after I ate a few fries, I stood and scratched my head. "I'm gonna go shower; I feel gross."

"Alright, sounds good! We basically had an off day since you were asleep and Xavier hasn't left his room!" Ashlyn informed me. I walked away then Ashlyn said, "Kyle, you are enough." My eyes widened as I turned around. "I think you've looked really sad ever since your fight with Xavier ended. He's just sore about you being the son of Tyrant, but honestly, it doesn't matter. You are you, not Tyrant, and you are enough."

Th- That's what Mom said ...

"O- Oh, thank you. That means a lot," I responded, trying not to cry. Ashlyn gave me a heartwarming smile and held her hands behind her.

"Of course! Everyone deserves kindness!" I nodded, then made my way to the elevator. I took it up to the third floor, grabbed some clothes from my room, then went to the bathroom. While in the shower, I cried. The cry was not only about my mom, but about Ashlyn and her words.

That couldn't be a coincidence. It couldn't be.

Kaliska's Organization, 7:30 p.m. (Same Time as Kyle's Shower):

"I'm sure you can tell what the problem is. There has been a downpour since 3:00 a.m., along with spurts of thunder and lightning," Kaliska sinisterly stated as they looked out the glass wall. Tonuko, Alex, Skye, and Rachel sat in the stiff sofas and they were nervous. "He is here, and he will invade the upcoming protest. We must go out and patrol. I will cover half the city and you four will cover the other half. I expect you to leave within the hour."

"We understand. What should we do if we find The Upriser?" Tonuko asked. He felt a pit in his stomach.

"You must clear any civilians from the area. I do not want you to engage in combat without me, and I do not want you to argue with anything he says. The people, as of now, are on his side. We must be cautious about arguing with him too much in front of protestors. It could lead to the end of heroes as we know it," Kaliska explained without looking back at the four.

"Crap, that's a huge responsibility. I've got it though ... keep everyone safe," Tonuko thought. His fear faded as his determination grew. *"This could be the biggest fight in the history of heroes."*

In an Alley of Takorain:

The Upriser cried loudly as he sat in the alleyway. The rain grew more aggressive and hail began to fall.

"Why are the heroes brainwashing the children who shadow them? Why do they think they're fighting for good? Why do people deem others as villains? Why can't we all be equal?" Another man nervously walked up to The Upriser and stopped a few feet away.

"S- Sir, are you alright? You've been crying outside of my store for half an hour," the man asked. The Upriser's crying stopped abruptly, and he looked up at the storeowner, then stood. He towered over the man.

"Don't you understand?! The world is *cruel!* People who agree with heroes, people who agree with villains," the storeowner backed away from The Upriser, and put his hands up in self-defense, "*shall be purged to create a perfect world!*" The storeowner turned and ran from the alley. As soon as he was out in the open, lightning struck with a loud explosion. The Upriser walked away, weaving through the system of alleyways.

"Upriser, we finally found you!" a man with a similar booming voice happily announced. The Upriser stopped walking and turned to face the man. Three others joined him, including a very muscular, abnormally tall man; a man with a long, white and golden robe and a large, silver calligraphy pen; and a girl with a raggedy, red tank top, black tights, and large, white boots.

"Who might you be?" The Upriser asked with curiosity lingering in his tone. The man who made the announcement wore a dark gray trench coat, glasses, and a black beanie. Pieces of his brown hair stuck out the bottom of the beanie, and he was even taller than The Upriser, who stood at six-foot-eleven.

"We are the Metaphorical Uprisers. We were cast away because of our strengths, left to rot in this cruel world. Upon meeting, we scoured the nation looking for a cause.

We heard about you and your beautiful speeches and decided to join your cause. Please, let us follow in your footsteps and help you rid the world of this disgusting hero and villain society!" the man pleaded. He held out a hand and introduced himself, "I am Gravaton. It is a pleasure to meet you." Without hesitation, The Upriser grabbed Gravaton's hand and shook it.

"I will never reject those who wish to join me. I will be joining the protest tonight and will make my move on Puppeteer and Kaliska. Please, join me if you truly wish to publicize my cause," The Upriser stated before turning.

"Yes, we will. Thank you for the hospitality," Gravaton responded with a smile. The five wandered through the alleyways, preparing to make their move ...

Puppeteer's Organization, 7:45 p.m.:

I walked into my room and changed back into the E.H. provided uniform. I heard from Lady Antress, when I was walking toward the elevator, something about The Upriser, so I assumed we would go and patrol soon. I sat on my bed, thinking about all that had just occurred, when I heard a knock at my door.

"Come in," I softly responded. The door cracked open, then Xavier poked his head in.

"Let's go," he stated swiftly. I raised an eyebrow, confused.

"Go where? Did Puppeteer call for a meeting or something?" I asked earnestly while standing. I reached into my pocket, pulled out my headband, then tied it around my head.

"Just ... follow me," Xavier mysteriously said before leaving the doorway.

The hell? Something must be up.

I reluctantly followed Xavier, and he led me out of the organization's building and into the dark streets. The rain was still pouring down and a cold wind blew past us a few times. We walked a couple of blocks down the street, then took a right on Larmon Road. When we were halfway down the block, Xavier stopped. He stood a few feet in front of me and I saw his fists clench.

"Y'know, I don't have a cloak like yours! It's pretty damn cold in the rain!" I shouted, hoping for some kind of response. Xavier's body tensed, then his puppet ran out of his back and toward me. I ducked, dodging it, then grabbed the strings. Xavier coughed a few times and turned around with a furious expression smeared across his face.

"Stop grabbing my fucking strings!" Xavier shouted while making movements with his fingers. The puppet held out its hand then shot a burst of flames directly at my face. I was covered in them, forcing me to let go of the strings. Xavier pulled his puppet back to his side then explained, "It's about time we really fight, no one interrupting us! If you think you can come here and steal my dad away from me, just because yours is a piece of shit, then you're dead wrong!" The flames dissipated and I coughed into my right fist.

"What are you talking about? I'm not trying to steal your dad away from you!" I argued. Xavier stood ready to attack, then his puppet bolted at me. I punched at it, but the puppet ran through me, sending another chill through my body. It elbowed me in the back with a much greater punch than earlier. I crashed face first into the ground and slowly lifted my head to spit out blood.

"Alright, if this is what you want, then I'll fight back!" I roared before activating Energy Conversion. In a flash, I appeared in front of Xavier and wound up a punch, then socked him square on the nose. He crashed backward and into the side of an apartment building. He spat blood-mixed-saliva as he yelped. Xavier jumped onto his feet, then commanded his puppet. The puppet ran at me and swung a punch at my face, which I ducked underneath. When I tried to run away, the concrete beneath me wrapped around my ankles and slowly crawled up my legs.

Dammit, we're close enough to Kaliska's Organization that he can use Tonuko's power. Too bad I've already fought him multiple times!

I broke out of the ground and swung a kick at Xavier. The air pressure sent the debris flying at him, but he dodged all but one rock. That rock hit him on the head, causing blood to seep down his forehead and the side of his face. Xavier's face twisted with pain and anger, so I stood defensively, expecting an attack. The puppet swiped its hand at me, forming spikes that shot at me from the ground. I dodged them all, flipping around on the ground, then I threw my hand up and let fire roar at Xavier. He ran out of its path and moved his puppet to run toward me with a punch. With the punch, the liquid inside the puppet switched from brown to black. I quickly flew into a streetlight post. I rolled onto my torso as I coughed and groaned in agony.

My head ... it's pounding. He's too good with his strength. He can use any strength he wants and switch between them in milliseconds ... how the hell am I supposed to beat this kid?!

Before I could react, the streetlight bent around my body, trapping me, then a bright light covered me and the street. It felt as if my skin was melting and I screamed out in pain. When the light vanished, I had burn marks all over my body, and I was panting. Xavier smirked as he and his puppet approached, then he put his foot on the streetlight.

"Still feel like acting like a tough guy?! Face it, criminal, you're nothing compared to a hero like me!" Xavier's puppet walked up to me and punched me across the head. That blow unleashed something in me. Out of the spots on my palms, darkness shot out and covered my arms

351

up to my shoulders and my legs up to my waist. My eyes faded to white. The mist around my body was no longer yellow; instead, it was a rich purple. I swiftly ripped the streetlight off my waist and threw my arm at Xavier. Black flames danced around my forearm, forming a few circles, then I shot a devastating fire attack toward him. Xavier screeched and backed up.

As the flames dissipated I asked, "Does it look like I'm done yet? I'm not letting some cocky dick like you beat me!" I charged at Xavier before he could compose himself and punched him in the stomach. He hit the ground hard and skidded back a dozen feet until he hit the next streetlight. I stood with my hands at my sides, panting, and looked at Xavier. Blood gushed from his head, as it did from mine, then he weakly stood. "Stay down, I win!" I shouted. The winds picked up, blowing my hair around, and I felt hail hit my back.

"I- It just looks like ... I'll have to start trying!" Xavier screeched. His puppet bolted at me and charged up a punch. The liquid inside was a mixture of yellow and black, and the spirit looked more muscular than before. I grabbed my right forearm with my left hand and held it up so my palm faced Xavier. I blasted a large ember of flames but before either attack could land, a wall of cement shot up between the puppet and me, absorbing both blows.

The wall shattered, then I heard Tonuko yell, "What the fuck are you two doing?! Are you seriously fighting in the street while The Upriser is loose in the city?!" I looked to my left and saw Tonuko, Alex, Skye, and Rachel at the street intersection. Rachel ran to Xavier's side, and Alex did the same with me. I fell backward onto my butt and wiped blood off my forehead.

Dammit, this is embarrassing. I let my emotions get the better of me. Just ... the fact that it's the number-one hero's son against the number-one villain's ... I couldn't let myself lose and be embarrassed. I guess that happened anyway.

"Kyle, what in the world were you thinking?! You can't just fight all your problems away!" Alex yelled while looking around at the damage we caused.

"Xavier, what's gotten into you? You've never acted out like this before," Rachel asked, seeing the anger and hatred in his eyes. Xavier didn't respond; he just glared at me, and I glared back at him.

"Guys, we can't be fighting each other! Not only is it a bad look for the heroes we're shadowing, but it's a terrible look for heroes as a whole! We're the future of heroes, so why are we trying to kill each other instead of working together?! You're on the same team, you're at the same agency!" Skye shouted, standing next to Tonuko between us.

"He's not on the same team as any of us! He's just a criminal, a murderer who should be in jail!" Xavier interrupted, pointing at me. Before I could retort, Tonuko put a hand up toward me, nonverbally telling me to shut up.

"I know how you feel man ... because I felt that way too. After hearing who his dad was, I thought he was good-for-nothing and a destined villain. But, when I looked past that and saw who Kyle really was, I realized he's a determined hero and a good friend! I've seen his work ethic and commitment, and it's like no other! We have to be able to look past his family and see Kyle for who he really is!" Tonuko yelled to Xavier.

"Shut up, you're nothing like me! You've always been a privileged little bastard who's never worked a day in your life for what you have! You got a free ride into B.E.G. but denied it and went to a free school to ride the bandwagon to the top of your class! You're just some gifted, spoiled brat!" Xavier retorted while standing. Tonuko smiled and looked down, shaking his head.

"You really think I'm the top of my class. Nah man, I'm only second," Tonuko revealed, looking back at me. Xavier's eyes widened as he looked over at me.

"Wh- What?! But you're the number one in the nation! H- How is he-" Xavier stuttered.

"Yeah," Tonuko sadly admitted, cutting Xavier off, "Kyle has beaten me twice already. He destroyed me in ten seconds in the entrance exam and beat me in our ranking tournament championship. It felt awful, it still does! I'm supposed to be the best in our grade, but this nobody came in and destroyed me! None of that matters though, I've just gotta keep my head high and move on! You should too!" Rain dripped down Xavier's face and he clenched his jaw and tensed his body.

"Exactly like you said: he's a nobody! That criminal shouldn't even be here! He kills people and acts nothing like a hero, but he gets all the recognition! He guilt-tripped my dad and now he cares more about Kyle than he does for me, his own damn son!" Xavier screamed, taking a step forward. Rachel grabbed his arm but didn't say anything.

This is all just a misunderstanding. Xavier isn't mad at me, he's mad at the support I'm getting from his dad. Maybe Puppeteer doesn't support Xavier as much as he should. Well ... I'll assure him that I don't need it.

"Xavier, I promise you I'm not trying to steal your dad! I understand why you would think that, but I don't want a replacement for Tyrant! I don't see him as anything to me, just a bloodthirsty bastard that I'm going to kill!" Xavier's arms dangled at his side and his eyes turned from anger to surprise once again. "I know I don't act anything like a hero, but I'm trying to learn and improve! I made horrible mistakes in the past, but I also protected a ton of people! I know I fought the wrong way, but I'm learning from my mistakes! Isn't a big thing about training to be a hero learning from your mistakes?!" I yelled while also standing and holding a fist at my chest.

"We all have a lot to learn ... but we can do it together! Fighting isn't going to solve anything but talking like this will!" Skye added with a smile. Thunder roared in the sky as we stood in silence for a moment, then Xavier walked over to me, pulling his arm out of Rachel's grip. He took a deep breath, stared into my eyes, then held out his hand.

"I'm ... sorry," Xavier slowly apologized with a sigh. I couldn't help but smile and took his hand and shook it.

"Me too. How about we make the effort to talk more about things back at the organization?" I suggested. Xavier smiled back at me and nodded.

"Yeah, sounds good." Everyone was happy with the outcome. As lightning cracked in the sky, Xavier commanded, "Let's go guys, it's getting bad out here! It isn't safe for us to wander around without pros!" We grouped up, then heard a familiar voice yell to us.

"What are you shadows doing?! Did you cause all of this damage?!" the rock-skinned hero from yesterday shouted.

He was with his partner, and she ridiculed, "If you fought out here, that was very dangerous and immature! You shouldn't be fighting each other, and on top of that, you shouldn't be out on the streets alone this late when The Upriser could be anywhere!" We heard shouting from down the street and saw a march of protestors from where the heroes had just come.

"We want rights!"

"These kids are a living example of how little heroes care about our cities!" There were signs and fists held up throughout the large crowd, and the protestors wore angry

355

faces. The two pro-heroes attempted to calm the protestors, but a booming voice shushed everyone.

"These kids are shadows, correct? Why aren't the heroes-in-training acting heroic? It's almost as if ... heroes don't know what being a hero really means." The rain and winds picked up, and the man with a trench coat and bowler hat stepped out in front of the wave of protestors.

"Th- That's him," Skye stated with pure fear in her eyes as she covered her mouth.

"The Upriser," Tonuko clarified through his teeth, tensing his fists and clenching his jaw. Tonuko took initiative and created a wall separating The Upriser and the protestors. "Kyle and Xavier, go find Ashlyn and Puppeteer; Rachel, find Kaliska. The two heroes should be around here somewhere!" Tonuko ordered in a whisper. We nodded then ran back to Puppeteer's Organization. Xavier and Rachel bolted past the building, but I entered and sprinted up the stairs until I reached the third floor. I banged repeatedly on Ashlyn's door until she opened it.

"Kyle? What's up?" she sleepily asked, rubbing her eyes.

I wasted no time and told her, "The Upriser is here! People are fighting him on Larmon Road. We gotta go!" Ashlyn closed the door. I heard some rustling then she opened the door again, this time wearing her hero suit.

"Let's go!" We ran back down the stairs, and I frantically informed Lady Antress of the situation.

"Listen, Kyle, round up all the protestors and lead them to Brawner Street. There, I will help you evacuate them all to a safer location. I'm counting on you!" Lady Antress commanded. I nodded, then Ashlyn and I left for the fight scene. When we arrived, Kaliska and Xavier were there but Puppeteer was nowhere to be seen. We ran over to

Tonuko, Alex, and Skye, but before I could tell Tonuko what Lady Antress said, The Upriser was yelling again.

"What's the problem heroes?! Why separate me from my protestors when we're fighting for the same reason?!" Thunder boomed above us. Tonuko nervously ran a hand through his middle part.

"We need to get him away from the protestors, but how?!" he thought aloud. Kaliska stomped on the ground with their right foot, and three bulls rose from the street. They snorted and kicked the ground, then ran at The Upriser. A large bolt of lightning shot down and annihilated the bulls along with a section of the street.

"Why must you resort to violence?! *Are you that scared of me, Kaliska?!*" The Upriser roared. Kaliska grinned with annoyance and punched the ground. A pack of five wolves burst out of the street behind The Upriser and charged at him.

Luckily, the attack made him move forward, and that was all Tonuko needed. He had enough space to form a hand from the ground and throw The Upriser over our heads. He landed and skidded a couple dozen feet behind us. The Upriser hopped back onto his feet, and when Tonuko broke down the wall he had created earlier, the protestors screamed and stood in shock.

"Lady Antress said we need to bring the protestors to Brawner Street! I'll distract The Upriser while you-" I started.

"No, Kyle! You, Ashlyn, and Xavier need to bring the protestors to safety! Being a hero isn't all about fighting, it's about saving the innocent from the evil!" Tonuko interjected before he slightly pushed me back. I was shocked and stood there dumbfounded.

"Y- Yeah, you're right ... Xavier, Ashlyn, let's evacuate the protestors!" They nodded, then we ran over to the fearful crowd.

"Listen, I know you don't want to be controlled by us, but you need to evacuate! This is a dangerous area and that man is not on your side! He is using your cause for his benefit and he will kill you like he's done at all other protests he's attended!" Xavier shouted with earnest plea. The protestors argued at first then reluctantly agreed to leave. We guided them down the street and led them down the block and to the left. When most of the people had made their way down Brawner Street, a large man stepped out from an alleyway behind us.

"You heroes think you're saving them? All you're doing is making them leave against their will!" the man moaned with a booming voice. Ashlyn took the lead and held out her arm; she shot two snow pillars on either side of the man, trapping him.

"Go and get the citizens out of here! I'll hold Gravaton off! The people are the priority!" Ashlyn yelled.

So, that man is Gravaton? I've heard of him before, but I thought he was a criminal ... why would he be working with The Upriser?

Xavier and I nodded, then continued leading the people away. The protestors screamed and ran, and Gravaton glanced over at Ashlyn. His eyes narrowed as a smile crept from his lips.

"Your guilt is there; it is bursting out of your body!" Gravaton roared. Ashlyn stomped her foot, and dozens of ice spikes shot at the man. He punched, shattering the ice, then let his strength work. Ashlyn's knees wobbled, and her body felt very heavy. Suddenly, she fell face first into the ground and laid on her stomach, unable to move. She was positioned with her head looking up at Gravaton, who was holding up his hands and grinning widely. The gravity in a circle around Ashlyn was visibly smushing her, and as the ground continued to crack it exploded, creating a mini-crater around her. Xavier turned and his eyes widened.

"No, Ashlyn!" Xavier shouted, running up and flinging his puppet at Gravaton. Gravaton held out one hand and crushed Xavier. Xavier's gravity force was much more intense than Ashlyn's, and the crater that formed around him was bigger than the one around her. "You're the Guilt Controller: Gravaton! I know you, and I know how many people you've murdered!" Gravaton smirked and held a hand at his chest.

"Well, it looks like I'm popular! The people who defy us deserve to perish, they have too much guilt and regret!" Gravaton spoke while holding his hands up again. Once the last person fled down Brawner Street, my arms and legs turned black and the purple mist surrounded my body. An audible click echoed down the street. I stomped on the ground, making it rumble, then a crack soared toward Gravaton's feet; it just passed under his body.

"You won't hurt any of the protestors or my friends! I won't let you!" I shouted before jumping at Gravaton. Soon after, I regretted my move.

My body, it feels so heavy! Shit, I shouldn't have jumped, that was a horrible decision!

When I was about a dozen feet to the left of Xavier's hole, I was thrown into the ground. I sank into the concrete as the street beneath me exploded into a massive crater—one much bigger than Xavier's or Ashlyn's. I was crushed under the weight of my own guilt.

Chapter 20
A Message to the World

Tonuko stood behind Alex and Skye, who let light and darkness cover their bodies, as it gave them boosts of speed and power. Alex looked at Skye and nodded; their wings stretched out from slits in their shirts and they flew at The Upriser. Alex threw up his hand and shot a beam of light at The Upriser. At the same time, Skye swung her leg up, kicking out a razor-sharp, thin slit of pure darkness at him. Before the attacks could connect, powerful winds swooped from the sides and disbanded them. Tonuko used this opportunity of The Upriser's distraction to make a move. He stomped, bending a pillar of concrete toward The Upriser, then, just as The Upriser leapt into the air and above the pillar, three bolts of lightning struck and hit each of them.

"Why must you kids slave away for the heroes who put false hope into your minds?! Join me, join the side of *true justice!*" The Upriser roared as Skye and Alex fell out of the air. Tonuko stumbled back, but in the time before he fell he managed to bend a wave of concrete. It carried Alex and Skye back to the others and him. As the wave reached the ground and sunk back into it, Kaliska punched their fist into the concrete, causing three hounds to rise at their side. Kaliska stood and pointed at The Upriser, sending the hounds after him. While The Upriser was busy running from them, Kaliska ran toward The Upriser and pulled out their Native Bible.

It was a thick, black book with silver swirls around the spine and the corners of the covers. A few words were written in the center of the front cover. Kaliska threw the book into the sky, then charged in for a punch. The Native Bible lit up in a very bright pink, then shot down a beam of energy at The Upriser. He smirked and threw his fist toward the sky before a massive bolt of lightning struck. It was absorbed by the ring and the excess electricity evaporated the hounds. The Upriser leapt backward, narrowly dodging the energy attack, then pointed his fist at Kaliska and propelled an enormous lightning bolt directly at them.

"*Kaliska!*" the hero girl screamed in awe. The first explosion mangled and tore apart the ground between Tonuko and The Upriser. Another bolt struck, demolishing a huge chunk of the debris. Tonuko was swept from the ground and crashed into Alex, who stood a few feet behind him. Tonuko blinked a couple of times, attempting to look at the damage, and saw Kaliska laying on the ground on their stomach, panting as they faced The Upriser. Half of Kaliska's mask was destroyed, showing their real face.

"You are no longer the cold and mysterious hero you once portrayed yourself to be!" The Upriser laughed, "Let the world see ... *who you really are!*" His ring flashed a bright yellow in the grooves of the design, signaling it was ready for another attack. He charged up an electric blast, but before it could strike Kaliska the stone-skinned hero ran in front of them and took the blow. Smoke cleared the scene, and the hero emerged unscathed. His skin was more defined and cracked, and it looked as though he was struggling to move. He truly was made of stone.

Grey Anadam, Strength: Statue—he can turn his skin into stone. He can also increase his skin's durability. It takes more energy to make his skin harder, and the feeling of his strength being activated is that of tensing his entire body.

"Get to cover, Kaliska! You're badly injured!" Grey shouted, standing between Kaliska and The Upriser, acting as a shield.

"I will not leave a novice such as yourself to fight alone! You'll die!" Kaliska argued. Their voice was more feminine now, confirming Kaliska's gender to the surrounding heroes and shadows.

"I will gladly give my life to protect the shadows! They are only kids with a bright future ahead of them! *I'll fight until my last breath! Statue of Justice!*" Grey shouted heroically while flexing his arms at his sides. Large cracks developed down his arms, legs, and shirtless back, and his fingers sharpened. Grey's soaking wet hair stuck to his forehead, then, he pounced. He swiftly charged at The Upriser and swiped his claws. The Upriser covered his face with his arms, causing Grey to rip three deep gashes on The Upriser's left arm. The Upriser grimaced as he looked at his gushing arm, then looked up at Grey with ferocious, bloodcurdling eyes.

"How *dare* you touch me?! Haven't you been taught that violence is never the answer, *you rookie town-destroyer?!*" The Upriser screamed as he grabbed Grey's right arm. Grey swiped at him again, but he dodged the attack by leaning his body back. The Upriser stomped his right foot and used it to turn around and slam Grey into the street. Grey's body dug a few inches into the ground, and as he struggled to stand back up, the rain above him came down harder. Grey screeched as the rain burned through his rough exterior. As The Upriser turned around with an angry expression on his face, he was greeted with a fist of light. Alex punched him in the cheek, causing The Upriser to stumble back; his left arm got caught in the acid rain. Alex quickly flew at Grey, grabbed him, then flew high into the sky. A massive gust of wind swooped him up, but Alex was able to successfully steady his flight and glide down to the group of heroes.

"I got Grey, now get him, Skye!" Alex yelled. Skye swiped her right hand across her face and toward The Upriser, separating her fingers as she did so. Five thick strings of darkness flew at The Upriser, yet he managed to nimbly duck underneath them. He let out a wail as he stood back up.

"*Why can't you kids see you're in the wrong?!* You're being brainwashed into harming a citizen who merely wants to help the crowds you're supposed to be protecting! You're being taught *falsities* of what a hero truly is!" The Upriser cried as he looked up at the sky with his hands out, palms facing up. The rain picked up, and large chunks of hail poured down as cracks of thunder roared from the sky. Tonuko bent the street to cover them, and his hair was blown out of his face from the intense winds.

"We need to take him out quickly, before he creates a supercell! That'll put the others at a greater risk since they don't have you there!" the lady hero shouted.

Tonuko looked up at The Upriser and yelled, "Where the hell are the others, or Puppeteer?! The bystanders should have been evacuated by now, and Rachel should have found Puppeteer! What the fuck?!"

Down the Block:

The gravity around me increased to the point where I couldn't lift a finger and I struggled to breathe. Gravaton paced back and forth in front of our craters, smirking with his arms crossed.

"Look at all the guilt in Tyrant's son! So much hatred, regret, anger!" he roared. I tried to move, to no avail.

I closed my eyes as I shouted, "What do you mean guilt?! What the hell are you talking about?!"

"It's his power, like the metaphor about the crushing weight of guilt! He transforms people's guilt into an increase of the gravity they feel!" Xavier answered through his groans.

Adrian Ken/Gravaton, Strength: Guilt—like the metaphor "the crushing weight of guilt," he can convert one's guilt into an increase of the gravity they feel. This increase in weight affects the person's strength and physical body in a spherical shape around them. Others inside the sphere won't feel the effect of the gravity, only the person under Gravaton's control.

363

Xavier's puppet slowly stood from his body but was thrown back into him by the gravitational force. Gravaton took a deep breath through his nose and closed his eyes.

"A boy with hatred for another. He feels as though he's belittled by both his father and the one he despises, and as though his father forgets about him. Oh ... what's this? He feels like the boy he hates is trying to steal his father's love ... how interesting!" Gravaton announced after exhaling. The gravity increased on Xavier, and Gravaton turned to Ashlyn.

"Shut up, dammit!" Xavier screamed. He tried to get onto all fours but was smashed back into the ground.

Gravaton continued, "Ah, a girl who's in love with the other. She puts him on a pedestal, thinks of him as someone she can look up to ... but ... deep down ... she knows he is dangerous. She hesitates to act on her feelings because she is scared of how others will think of her being with him. She loathes his family, and perhaps a part of him as well." The gravity increased on Ashlyn, and I was crushed knowing it was about me.

"That's not true! I don't hate any part of Kyle, and I don't think he's dangerous!" Ashlyn yelled with agony portrayed on her face. Gravaton chuckled as he shrugged.

"Sorry, but it's not my opinion. I'm just telling them what guilt and sorrow you feel inside!" Gravaton then turned to me with an excited look. He announced, "Last, but certainly not least, the son of pure evil! You act so tough and cocky on the outside, but in reality you cannot stand to look at yourself in the mirror! You see a disappointment, a failure, a killer, and a burden for your friends to carry! You know you have your father to thank for that, Mr. King of Villains Tyrant! You see him as your father and feel terrible for defying him, but at the same time you wish he were dead! Oh ... what else is there? It seems as though something is inside your heart ... something big!" Gravaton's eyes lit up, then he closed them again. After a couple of seconds, his smile vanished and he grabbed his head. Gravaton screamed, then crouched. He continued screaming and the gravity around me lifted.

I jumped up and charged up a punch, shouting, "Now's my chance!" Before the punch could hit, I was thrown hard into the ground and the street beneath me exploded once more. I was stuck, laying on the side of the massive crater, right under Gravaton. He looked down at me with an expression mixed with shock and disgust.

"What is that young man?! What is living inside your heart?!" My face writhed with agony, and my chin dug into the harsh street surface, which punctured me directly beneath my jaw.

"I- I don't know what you're talking about!" I responded with a lie.

Living inside my heart? Is he talking about that demon from earlier? Is that thing actually attached to me?

Gravaton rubbed his head while mumbling to himself, then looked up and smiled again.

"You all have guilt creeping through your blood and you shall be punished for your actions! You can't prance around as though you wish to save others when you cannot even save yourselves! We will tear down this selfish, destructive society and build a new, better one—one that doesn't need false heroes to 'save' people from false villains, one where everyone is equal!" Gravaton preached.

Xavier tensed his fist and glared at him. "That sounds to me like a deluded child's dream! There will never be full equality, people will always abuse their strengths! That's why heroes surfaced, to save people like you from those who want to harm you!" Xavier argued, still attempting to move. Gravaton laughed out loud.

"Save me?! You heroes pick and choose who to save! Heroes never even tried to save me, let alone anyone else society deemed as outcasts or as not good enough! You shadows really are gullible!" Gravaton ridiculed. Although he was laughing, anger lingered in his voice.

"No, you're wrong!" Ashlyn interrupted. "We sacrifice ourselves to beat those who hurt others! We run into battle head first to make sure those who've been hurt can smile again one day! Heroes don't pick who to save, they save whoever they can!" Gravaton looked surprised and bowed as he took his hat off to Ashlyn.

"Your view of heroes sounds great, my dear, but sadly it is incorrect. Heroes of this day and age only care about fame, money, and being the best, and villains merely want to see the world suffer. We want to eradicate these ideals and create a new world where no one will be put over another born of the same Earth!" When Gravaton finished his speech, large chunks of hail rained from the sky. Every ice ball made me want to yell, and it didn't help that Gravaton had taken out an umbrella, so all the hail that would have hit him bounced off his umbrella and landed on me. "How long until you cannot bear the pain and beg for mercy? An hour, a minute, a couple of seconds? We can only wait and see!"

"K- Kyle!" Xavier yelled, his voice trembling from the pain he bore, "I'm sorry about fighting you twice, I wasn't thinking straight! I just couldn't understand why my dad took such a liking to you even though you're Tyrants son, but I get it now! Your family and your past aren't you!" I smiled and chuckled, ignoring the pain from the hail pellets hitting my head.

"Xavier, I'm sorry too! I didn't respect you, I thought of you as merely competition and Puppeteer's son. I've learned over the past few days ... that I'm not a hero ..." My smile faded as I continued, "I've never acted like a hero, nor have I ever really thought like one! I thought of being like a comic book hero, where I'm nonstop fighting crime and when I beat them it's over, but a hero is so much more than that!" Xavier smiled, then closed his eyes as a few tears fell. The gravity around him increased even more, and he yelped in pain.

"Guys, this might be it ... I'm not sure about you, but I don't know what to do-" Xavier started, but Ashlyn didn't feel the same.

"What the hell guys?! Don't give up! You're acting like we lost, but we can still win!" Ashlyn shouted before slowly standing. "He may have increased my gravity, and my body is screaming for me to lay down, but I'll never give in to a criminal! I don't care what your intentions are, if you hurt my friends ... I'll get payback!" A path of ice zoomed out of Ashlyn's sphere of gravity, then morphed into spikes once it was free. Gravaton dodged the spikes, then laughed.

"That's all you can think of, hurting me?! Shouldn't you be thinking about finding a way to save your friends, or maybe save those who are looking for protection?!" Gravaton marched toward Ashlyn and kicked away the ice spikes she'd formed. He swiftly ran at her, gripped her neck, and slowly lifted her. Gravaton deactivated his strength on Ashlyn. Then, as she was scraping at his hands, he threw her into the sky and increased her gravity once again. Ashlyn's body violently slammed into the ground and, after colliding into the street ... she stopped moving.

"Ash!" Xavier shouted in complete shock.

"Ashlyn!" I screamed as tears brimmed my eyes. Gravaton strutted in front of us and put his hands on his hips.

"One of you is down, leaving two more. Join our cause or suffer the same fate as Ashlyn," Gravaton stated as he released his strength from her. She laid unconscious with blood pouring out of her head and her body was scraped and bruised. I squeezed my fist and tried to get up while clenching my jaw as hard as I could.

"Kyle, there's no point! We can't escape gravity, it's impossible! You're just wasting energy!" Xavier yelled. His voice cracked a few times because he was crying. My tears made everything blurry so I closed my eyes.

"We have to try, dammit! We can't let Ashlyn die!" I slowly stood, then my knees buckled and I fell face first back into the ground. Out of nowhere, I thought of the demon and something unleashed in me. The darkness from my arms and legs spread up my torso until it covered my jawline and chin and my eyes glowed white. When the darkness spread, Gravaton screamed and he fell. I slowly stood, the gravity weakening as I did, and I was able to move freely again. I jumped out from the crater, landed harder than I would have liked, then swiftly glared at Gravaton. Because of the increased gravity, my foot made an indent as I stomped forward. "We have to take this guy down, so Ashlyn can smile again!"

At The Upriser Fight Scene:

Tonuko held Kaliska's upper back and looked into their eyes.

"Kaliska, y- you're a girl?!" Tonuko asked in shock. Kaliska nodded, then coughed. visible hair was short and blonde, and their face was smooth and clear.

"Yes ... I thought if people didn't know I'm a woman, they would respect me more. People would respect a mysterious masculine hero more than a feminine one, right?"

"Now isn't the time shadow! Look alive!" the lady hero shouted, tensing her fists. The Upriser continued crying as the hail poured down and the clouds in the sky swirled around each other.

"Dammit, what do we do?! We can barely land a solid hit on him, he's just too experienced with his strength!" Alex swore, clenching his jaw. The thunder roared louder, and another lightning bolt shot down onto the cover. Tonuko softly laid Kaliska down, then stood with his chest puffed out.

"We have to beat him ... we just have to. We're all heroes, right? This is our job: to take down those who hurt others!" The hero lady stood with Tonuko and smiled when he spoke.

"You're absolutely right! Distract him and make an opening, that way I can land a solid hit!" Her muscles became more defined, and an eight-pack showed through her tight shirt.

Annabelle Claire/Muscle Hero: Equal, Strength: Muscle Growth—she can transform white blood cells into muscle fibers, which has benefits and downfalls. She gains massive muscle mass based on how many white blood cells she uses, but over time she loses the ability to tell who is friend or foe. She is also more vulnerable to any kind of sickness.

Tonuko nodded, then swiped his hand at The Upriser. Towers of cement zoomed toward him and he made the ground raise underneath The Upriser. The towers destroyed the raised ground, making him fall. This fall gave Equal a chance to strike. She jumped at The Upriser and swung a punch. To her surprise, The Upriser deflected her punch, then hit her in the face. She responded with a left-handed punch, flinging him into one of the falling rocks. He fell along with the debris and crashed into the street. Numerous large rocks fell on top of The Upriser and Equal landed at the very top.

"Nice work newbie!" Equal smirked before leaping off of the debris tower. She landed next to Tonuko and fist bumped him as the hail stopped. It seemed as though the battle was won, yet cries came from the rubble. A tornado formed in the sky, sucking up all the rocks, then it faded, causing the rocks to fall all over Tonuko's cover. It withstood a couple of blows, but eventually collapsed. Alex and Skye saved Kaliska and Grey, moving them behind Tonuko and Equal.

"Why must you fight me?! Why can't you see the greater good in me?! You heroes are supposed to protect others, so *why don't you protect me?!*" The Upriser roared as he crawled out from the debris. He held his fist up high, then a massive lightning bolt struck him, encapsulating his body. Within seconds, it was absorbed by his ring and The Upriser pointed it directly at the group. Tonuko acted quickly, making a thick, tall wall between them and The Upriser, then he ran and put his hand on it, reinforcing the wall.

"Everyone, *get the fuck out of here!*" Tonuko screamed. He was using a plethora of energy to continue reinforcing the wall.

"*Are you crazy?!* We can't leave you!" Skye argued, standing with him. Tonuko raised the ground under the group then threw them back a couple of dozen feet.

He looked Alex in the eyes with a tearful, pleading stare and begged, "Please, get them out of here! We'll all die if we stay, he's just too strong! Get everyone to safety! *I'm not letting people die because I wasn't strong enough!*" Alex stood shocked and dumbfounded, not knowing what to do. What he saw in Tonuko was the same determination he'd seen in me back in Veena. Alex nodded, then picked up Grey.

"Kaliska, can you walk?!" Alex asked.

"*I'm not letting one of my shadows die! I'm the number-two hero. I should be the one risking my life to save you kids!*" Kaliska jumped to their feet, then summoned two deer to save Tonuko. As they ran, a large boom sounded as the ground rumbled beneath them and the deer were killed.

The Upriser launched his attack at the wall. When it hit, the lightning caused a massive crack through the wall;

Tonuko continued reinforcing it. The pressure continued as electricity crept through and around the wall.

"My life is worth so much less than all of yours! I don't have a real reason to keep going, but you do! Don't let me be the reason you die. Get out of here, save everybody's lives, dammit!" Tonuko cried as tears dripped down his cheek. "*Kyle ... thank you. You probably don't realize it, but you've helped open my eyes to things I didn't even think I needed to learn about. You've helped me grow more than anyone I've ever known. I'm sorry I'm breaking our promise, but please ... don't kill yourself. Go be the best hero and don't forget about me. I'm sorry, Mom, but you'll only have one 'son' to look after. And Dad, it looks like you might have more lonely dinners. Fuck ... I'm scared ... I don't wanna die.*"

Kaliska ran as fast as they could, which wasn't very fast due to a limp, and created animals. Unfortunately, they were being destroyed because of the electricity. Tonuko closed his eyes, then the lightning broke through. It completely encased the wall, destroying it. As debris fell, another huge lightning bolt struck and demolished everything.

"*Tonuko!*" Kaliska screamed, stopping in horror. Tonuko let out a bloodcurdling scream. A second explosion erupted. Rocks flew everywhere, and there was a massive crater in the ground.

"What a noble sacrifice! Tonuko Kuntai, you truly were a hero! I'm sorry you will not be a part of the perfect future!" The Upriser cried, gazing at the sky. Alex's mouth gaped and his arms dangled as Skye fell to her knees.

Tears dripped down their cheeks and they cried out, "*TONUKO!*"

Down the Block:

I stomped toward Gravaton, each step causing my body to ache more, and created a path of ripped-up concrete.

371

After a couple of steps, I stood over Gravaton, raised my arm as high as it would go, and swung a devastating blow. I used the gravity to my advantage and landed a hefty punch on Gravaton's right cheek. The ground beneath him cracked as his head hit the street, then I lifted my foot to kick his stomach.

"That thing inside you helps you fight," Gravaton started, cracking his jaw, "but it also helps me." My gravity increased, causing me to fall forward and smash head-first into the ground. My head was pounding at this point, and I heard a yell that nearly brought tears of joy.

"There you guys are! Christ, what is going on here?!" Puppeteer shouted, looking around at the destruction and us. Rachel stood with him. We heard another explosion followed by Skye's and Alex's cry about Tonuko. "Let's get rid of this guy quickly so we can go and help the others," Puppeteer muttered. My eyes widened when I heard the yell, and I clenched my teeth.

Tonuko ... is he okay?! You made me promise we'd stay alive, so don't you dare break it! I don't know what the hell I'll do if you don't keep your end of the promise, you asshole!

"D- Dad, it's Gravaton! He joined sides with The Upriser!" Xavier yelled through his tears. Puppeteer cracked his knuckles, then threw his puppet out of his body.

"I know all about you, Gravaton. Thirty reported crimes, five of which were *murders!*" Puppeteer growled through his teeth. Gravaton smirked as he stepped over my body and puffed out his chest.

"Looks like I'm famous to you and your son! It won't be hard to fight you, number one; after seeing what your son is made of," Gravaton held out both hands as he screamed, "*you'll be crushed instantly!*" Puppeteer's feet made cracks in the ground and Rachel was smushed.

Nothing else happened. "Wh- What?! Why is your guilt not weighing you down?!"

"As a hero, you can never let guilt affect you. There're always people you can't save, people you fight with, and people you lose. That's never a reason to get down on yourself!" Puppeteer shouted before jumping into my old crater.

He stared up at Gravaton, and the two stood in a silent standoff for a few moments before Gravaton shouted, "Everyone has guilt. You cannot resist it! I'll just have to dig a little deeper to find your true guilt, just like Tyrant's son back there!" Gravaton focused on Puppeteer with his eyes closed, but once again nothing happened.

"I told you, as a hero," Puppeteer's puppet swiped ice spikes at Gravaton, then shot a beam of snow behind him, trapping him, "I never let guilt get to me. I'll always push forward and make sure these kids can grow up smiling! *I'll make sure they can laugh, play, and grow up to live better lives than any of us were given!*" Gravaton flipped over the snow, then glared at Puppeteer furiously.

"It's such a shame your son feels the opposite way! It's such a shame your son thinks you love Tyrant's son more than him! It's such a shame you failed as a father and deep down you know you have! *It's such a damn shame you let your wife die and did nothing to save her!*" Gravaton screeched. Puppeteer stopped and stood still. He sank farther into the ground as his gravity increased.

"Dad," Xavier stuttered, "i- it's not your fault! I love you, a- and I moved on from it! Please, don't lose!" The clouds above us thickened as Puppeteer's puppet reached out its hand.

"As Puppeteer, the number-one hero, I won't let it get to me! I couldn't save her, but *I can save them!*" A large lightning bolt struck down at Gravaton, but before it could make contact, a sparkle spurred into existence in front of

Gravaton, followed by a massive explosion. My gravity returned to normal as a result. I was thrown a couple of dozen feet to my left and noticed painful burns on my back.

In the Air:

Gravaton opened his eyes, then asked, "I- I survived?" The girl in the tank top from before nodded, then the two landed on a building.

"I saved you; you're lucky we were watching. Puppeteer copied The Upriser's strength," the girl stated. "Let's get out of here with the others. The Upriser just killed a shadow. His supercell will form shortly so he should be done soon."

Back with Puppeteer:

Puppeteer swore, then walked over to Xavier. He helped Xavier up and gave him a hug.

"I'm so sorry for making you feel that way. I love you more than anything in the world," Puppeteer solemnly whispered. Xavier hugged him tightly and nodded.

"I know, Dad, I know." Before they'd stopped hugging, I sprinted over to Ashlyn and put her head in my lap. She was unconscious and blood gushed from her head.

"She should be okay. She's still breathing, and nothing looks broken. Her head has a cut and she's bruised," I analyzed. Rachel crouched next to me, then smiled.

"Yeah, she's strong. She'll get through this. I'll take her now. You go help the others," Rachel commanded while picking up Ashlyn. I nodded, then stood and activated Energy Conversion.

Tonuko, you better not have died on me. I don't care about any of that rivalry bullshit ... we're both getting out of this alive! You promised, dammit!

"I'm going with Rachel to get Ashlyn medical attention and make sure the other civilians are okay! You guys go on ahead!" Xavier yelled. I looked back at Xavier, who smirked and nodded. I nodded too, then put my left foot back, pivoted off it, and bolted straight ahead.

"I'll finish this quickly. Take Ashlyn to my organization," Puppeteer commanded before also running down the street. As he ran, he and his puppet morphed together, but unlike earlier. This time, his puppet was on the outside of his body.

The Upriser Fight Scene:

As the smoke cleared, Kaliska stood over the edge of the hole. Tonuko was laying on the side of the crater, unconscious. He had burn marks all over his body, and his left arm was visibly broken.

"I'm sorry, young man, but your sacrifice was in vain! As long as the heroes keep fighting, they will die!" The Upriser cried. I ran into the scene, leapt onto a building to my left, then jumped off it and soared toward The Upriser.

"Just shut the fuck up already!" I screamed, flying past Kaliska and punching The Upriser in the face. He hit the ground hard, then flipped back a few times and jumped onto his feet.

"Y- You're that man's child! Shame on you for thinking you'll be anything in this world but a worthless villain!" The Upriser screeched. Lightning struck and I narrowly avoided it while jumping backward. I landed in the pit, grabbed Tonuko, then leapt out of the hole and grabbed Kaliska before flying back toward the group. I laid the two down, then stood in front of the group and gave The Upriser a side-eye.

"Kyle, why-?" Skye started, looking at the darkness on my body.

"I don't know," I interrupted, "This power just came over me." Alex stepped forward, wiped his tears, and put his hand on my chest.

"Don't worry," he started in the angriest voice I'd ever heard him speak in. "We'll finish this guy off." Alex looked back and nodded at Skye. She nodded, determined. "Kyle and Kaliska, distract him please!"

"You need to have enough power to knock him out now!" Kaliska yelled, swooping their hands and forming a large horse. "Do not let me down!" They hopped onto the horse, then it started galloping toward The Upriser. I flew in too, using flames as boosters on the soles of my feet, and wound up a punch surrounded by gray flames. The clouds above us circled in the sky, and we were struck by lightning at the same time. After that, strong winds knocked us aside, throwing me through a store's window and Kaliska into a brick wall.

"I cannot stand this! *I'll purge you, you'll all perish!*" The Upriser's force overwhelmed us. Everyone stood in fear as he screamed, "*You all think you're doing good, when all you're doing is hurting everyone you've known! I'll kill you all, I'll form a society ...*" The storm above grew more aggressive, and The Upriser screeched, "*that will never abandon its people!*"

"Alex ... now!" Skye shouted, flapping her wings. Alex nodded, then punched his light-filled fist into the ground.

"*Light Oracle!*" Alex screamed. The street between Alex and The Upriser was ripped apart as light tunneled toward The Upriser, then a sphere around him exploded into a light mess.

As The Upriser screamed, Skye screeched, "*Burdened Anchor!*" A chain of darkness formed in her hand and as she dragged it above her head, an enormous anchor grew out of the chain. Skye swung it down at The Upriser.

"You will all perish under the power of the real society! The Metaphorical Uprisers will carry out my will!" The Upriser shouted as the anchor collided into him. The area was filled with light and darkness, then an explosion went off. A few seconds later, Alex saw Puppeteer rush past him. His body was covered by his translucent spirit; a thick, black liquid covered his arms, legs, body, and head except for his eyes. As The Upriser flew through the air, Puppeteer leapt at him while winding up a punch. Puppeteer's red eyes glowed in the smoke.

As he stopped in front of The Upriser, he muttered, "Have fun in the Abyss, dirty mutt." Puppeteer punched The Upriser as hard as he could and felt The Upriser's cheekbone shatter. Puppeteer followed through, sending The Upriser crashing into the street. He skidded a dozen feet, then he hit a streetlight back first and spun around it. The Upriser was unconscious and the rain cleared.

Puppeteer landed on the ground and slid down the street. He slowly stood from a knee, then clenched his fist. "The Upriser will be no more," Puppeteer concluded with a grim expression on his face.

"Yes," Equal answered, talking into the phone, "it is the man who's been infiltrating protests around the area. Okay, thank you." Equal ended the call, then announced, "An Abyssal Penitentiary Unit is on the way. The Upriser will be locked up for a very long time."

I laid on the floor of the store where I'd landed, breathing heavily. Glass shards had pierced my skin—a large one had gone through my right calf—and I was in a puddle of my blood. I looked at the dark ceiling as my vision began fading.

Come on Kyle, you have to get up. You can't give up, think about who you were fighting for. Tonuko wouldn't give up, why should you?

The last thing I heard was sirens ...

Parane, the Next Morning:

Daniel woke at 11:00 a.m. and yawned as he rose. He stretched, scratched his head, got out of bed, showered, and brushed his teeth and hair.

"Even though I wasn't gone that long, I missed my bed!" Daniel chuckled to himself as he entered the hallway. He threw his worn clothes back into his room then made his way down the stairs. When he reached the last step, he looked over and saw his father's distraught expression as he watched the T.V.

"Daniel!" his father shouted, "You might want to see this!" Daniel, confused, walked into the room and looked at the T.V.

"See wha-?" Daniel stared at the television and felt a mixture of awe and sickness.

"Just under twelve hours after the horrible fight between top heroes—Kaliska, Puppeteer, and their shadows—against The Upriser and another well-known criminal, the streets still exhibit the destruction. Heroes and the shadows received multiple injuries. Three students were left in critical condition; fortunately, one has awoken. The students are Kyle Straiter, Tonuko Kuntai, and Ashlyn Gray. Gray woke after receiving damage to her head. She has no other exponential injuries. Kyle Straiter has not woken up. He has countless deep cuts, substantial bruising, and broken bones. Tonuko Kuntai is in life-threatening condition after receiving a devastating attack from The Upriser. He has not shown signs of waking. Tonuko has numerous second-degree burns, a broken arm, and a broken rib. Doctors are unable to attend to those injuries as they fear his body too weak to handle the stress. Attempting any healing now could use too much of his energy and risk Tonuko never waking," the newscaster informed the audience.

Daniel covered his mouth as he stared wide-eyed at the T.V. "N- No way ... they fought The Upriser?" Daniel stuttered. Daniel's mom nodded, then crossed one leg over the other.

"You're lucky it was honors' kids fighting. Any of you advanced children would have probably died!" Daniel's mom commented. Daniel tensed his fist and furrowed his eyebrows.

"Skye was there too," Daniel muttered, glaring at the back of his mom's head.

"As well as the students," the newscaster continued, "number-two hero Kaliska sustained great injuries and is also in critical condition. During the battle, Kaliska's mask was destroyed, but their identity is still yet to be disclosed to the general public. They are being held in a private room not open to visitors, and all that were in the fight refuse to admit Kaliska's identity. Along with the four critically injured, three other students were hospitalized. Xavier Kinder, Alex Galeger, and Skye Harlem were injured during battle but none were seriously hurt. While most injuries were minor, Xavier sustained a broken nose and a punctured lung. Everyone except Tonuko is expected to make a full recovery. His prognosis is unknown."

Daniel's dad shook his head and looked down with sorrow. "That's awful. I pray he makes a full recovery," he sighed.

"Hey, if he's out of the running, maybe Daniel will be moved up to honors'!" Daniel's mom interjected.

"Mom, that's disgusting that you'd even think like that! Tonuko will be fine, you'd better hope he is!" Daniel retorted before turning and storming out of the room.

"We're going out on patrol soon, so be ready!" Daniel's mom shouted down the hallway. Daniel grumbled as he walked back up the stairs and to his room. He changed out of his casual clothes and into the E.H. uniform, then took a deep breath before walking back down the stairs.

An Alleyway in Parane (the City Daniel Is In):

The large man's hand twitched as his eyes filled with rage. "Come on, Gravaton, let me loose! We have to make a scene since The Upriser lost or no one will take us seriously! Let me wreak havoc for a bit!" The man roared at Gravaton, who had his back to him. Gravaton sighed and looked at the explosion girl who'd saved him last night. She shook her head.

"We can't afford any more injuries. We need to find a healer to patch up Gravaton," she stated with a sigh. The large man punched his arm into the brick wall next to them, creating a deep hole and causing neighboring bricks to crack.

"I'll get myself patched up; it's not like I'll take that much damage anyway! *Let me fight!*" The other man, who had long, white hair tied into a ponytail, closed the book in his hand and smiled.

"I'll watch over Crocodilian while you two find a healer. Let's let him have some fun. To climb the societal ranks and make a name for ourselves, we must strike," the man stated. Gravaton put his hand on his head and sighed with a stressed expression, then waved them off.

"I guess if you say it needs to happen, then it needs to happen. Go have your fun, Crocodilian," Gravaton reluctantly said. Crocodilian smirked, then marched forward. With each step, his body sizzled and grew more muscular. Scales flipped out of his skin, and his jaw morphed, growing until it was a long, toothy snout.

He smiled again, and in a raspy, monstrous voice muttered, "Showtime."

Two Blocks Away:

Daniel stared up at the cloudy sky as he walked with his parents. His dad looked down at him, then smiled and gave Daniel a nudge.

"Those outfits are something, aye?" Daniel looked down at his shirt and snorted. His mom let out a huff.

"They are unprofessional and gross. Heroes shouldn't be wearing- gym clothes," she scoffed.

Daniel rolled his eyes, then looked down the street to his right and saw Camilla, Jessica, and Scarlett. "Oh, hey, those kids are from my school!" Daniel shouted before running to meet them.

"Danny, you can't just run away while we're on patrol! Get back here this instant!" Daniel's mom yelled, stomping her foot. Before they could move, Daniel turned invisible.

"Just let him go. This town is pretty peaceful anyway, so he should be fine," Daniel's dad sighed. His mom stood straight and continued down the block. Once Daniel was away from his parents, he turned off his strength.

"Hey guys! I didn't think I'd run into you!" Daniel smiled and waved. Scarlett returned the smile and wave; Jessica and Camilla simply looked over at him. While he had their attention, Daniel asked, "So ... did you guys see the news?" The others momentarily fell silent.

"It's tough to know how much stress and pain they went through. Just a couple of days ago we were eating and laughing together. I can't even begin to imagine how they feel," Jessica solemnly said.

"It's worrisome knowing Tonuko might never wake. I don't want to think about how horrible it would be if he died," Camilla added with a sigh.

The group agreed, then Scarlett noted, "I saw on the news before we left that everyone except Kyle and Tonuko had awoken. Their injuries are serious enough that they have to leave their organizations and return to school."

"Really? That sucks that they have to go back early, there's so much to learn from our shadowing!" Daniel sighed. Scarlett looked down the block to their left and saw her aunt rounding the corner.

"We should get going. I don't want my auntie or your parents getting mad because we haven't patrolled our area!" They started walking, and Camilla looked around. As her stomach rumbled, she touched her chin with her pointer finger and pointed to a few restaurants.

"There're some really good-looking food places around here! After our patrolling today, we should go out to eat." They agreed, then turned the corner onto the busiest street in Parane.

CRASH!

"*What is that thing?!*" a woman screamed as she and others ran. A wave of smoke and wind blasted the area, sweeping Daniel off his feet. He flipped in the air, then landed on his feet, stumbled back, and fell again. He swiftly stood and joined the others in squinting down the street.

"Is that ... an alligator?" Camilla asked as her eyes widened with fear.

"It's a human mixed with a lizard; an animalistic strength!" Jessica responded with shaky hands. They stood, full of fear, and their facial expressions perfectly reflected their feelings. The girls looked sick. Daniel snapped out of his fear and ran in front of the group.

"Come on, we're heroes, right?!" Daniel shouted before starting to down the street.

"No, we aren't! We're heroes-in-training; we don't have any certification or anything!" Scarlett responded. Daniel stopped running, hesitated, then tensed his fist.

"We can't run away and let people get hurt! We have to stand and defend! We don't have to kill the villain or anything, just immobilize him! We can do that!" Daniel courageously yelled in response. They looked at each other, then Camilla followed Daniel. Scarlett joined them.

"Aww, you guys, this is so scary!" Jessica squealed and chased after them.

As they neared the villain, Crocodilian roared at them. Daniel turned invisible, ran at Crocodilian, and swung a punch. Crocodilian pivoted on his left foot, dodged the punch, and punched at the air in front of him. Daniel blocked with both arms, but the strength of The Upriser was too much. He flew backward and crashed into the side of a car, triggering the car's alarm system. Daniel's invisibility vanished, and blood poured from his head.

Crocodilian, Strength: Reptile—symbolizing the metaphor "Chaos is a friend of mine," he can morph his body into a large reptilian state at will. In this state, he has armored scales, claws, a long snout filled with sharp teeth, and extreme muscular strength.

"Cover Daniel, I'll distract him!" Camilla commanded, swiping her arms and throwing blades of wind at Crocodilian. He swiped at the air, causing air pressure that dissipated the blades.

"We will avenge The Upriser and bring about his new world! His new society and laws will be implemented all over!" he roared. The wind from Crocodilian's swipe knocked Camilla off of her feet. While midair, she created mini whirlwinds under her feet, which allowed her to stay afloat. She drifted down and stood defensively, then four massive venus fly traps sprouted around the beast and simultaneously bit at him.

"Camilla, I'm gonna go find some help! I'd assume pros should arrive any minute, but we need help fast!" Scarlett shouted before running down the block in search of her aunt.

"I can't let that girl get away and get backup," Crocodilian muttered, grabbing one of the venus fly trap's stems and ripping it off. He swung it around, taking out the other three plants, then leapt into the air and crashed in front of Scarlett. She backed up, trembling with fear, and Crocodilian snorted, blowing her hair around. Jessica stood, fearfully wondering what to do. Suddenly, Crocodilian flew to his left and crashed into a thrift store. Jessica looked down behind her and saw Daniel was gone.

"*Run, Scarlett!*" Daniel screeched, still in his invisible state. Parts of his body were invisible, and none of his clothes were. People who were in the store fearfully screamed. Crocodilian slowly stood. Daniel swung a punch at him but missed and sent a metal clothes hanger flying into the wall. Crocodilian nonchalantly elbowed Daniel's back, forcefully faceplanting him into the ground. Daniel coughed blood, then Crocodilian grabbed his leg and chucked him out the broken window. Daniel collided into the building across the street, then fell backward, unconscious. Crocodilian stepped out of the giant hole he had created and looked down the street at Scarlett, who was running with her aunt toward the scene.

"I should leave. There's no need to get involved with pros and get too hurt," Crocodilian scoffed. In an instant, he jumped up and flew over Camilla's and Jessica's heads. He looked back to see if anyone had followed. As he did so, a portal opened in front of him and a vine grabbed his face, pushing him into the street. Vines poured out of the portal and latched onto two adjacent buildings. Gabriella and Laci were carried out of the portal by a vine platform.

"The Care-Givers," Scarlett's aunt muttered with a grimace.

"Yours truly has arrived. The dazzling princesses of the Care-Givers are making their grand entrance!" Gabriella announced with a bow. They were lowered onto the street and stood next to Camilla. She shook with terror and didn't move. Gabriella glanced over at her without moving her head and waved ahead of her. "Move along, honey. A child shouldn't be around here." Without looking, Jessica waved her hand, searching for Camilla. Once she found her, Jessica grabbed Camilla's wrist and pulled her. They ran by Scarlett and stood behind her aunt. Other heroes ran from the opposite side of the block, surrounding the three villains.

The Alleyway From Which Crocodilian Came:

The man with the white hair watched the action from the shadows. When the Care-Givers made their grand entrance, his expression turned scornful.

"Those disgusting villains are interfering with our message to the world. They want to silence us. Crocodilian needs to get out of there before things get ugly," the man muttered. Crocodilian didn't attempt to stand, but instead stayed sprawled out on the ground. The man stayed in the alley, but screamed loudly, *"Chaos is a friend of mine!"* Crocodilian's eyes glowed white, and his muscles grew bigger, scales hardened.

"Chaos is a friend of mine," Crocodilian muttered. He lifted his arms and bashed his elbows into the ground, launching himself into the air and cutting cleanly through the vines that hung from one of the buildings. He flew off and started to fall just as he was out of their view.

"Woah! Where did that power come from?!" Laci questioned, fully turning around and looking in the distance where Crocodilian flew. Gabriella absorbed her vines back into her hands, then sighed.

"That yell from the alleyway clearly correlated to his power. Such a shame, we could have shown the world that these 'Uprisers' aren't even a challenge." Laci turned around and looked at the four girls. She held her closed hand in front of her stomach, then threw her arm out. With that movement, her mace crashed to the ground.

"Oh well, it just means we have more room for fun with these 'heroes'!" Laci cheerfully announced.

Chapter 21
Come Back

I slowly opened my eyes and blinked a few times trying to adjust to the bright light. I heard beeps from my heart monitor and sat up. I looked at my arms, which were thankfully back to their normal color, and a chill ran down my spine. I tried to remember all that had happened last night.

Xavier and I's fight, Gravaton, Ashlyn's fall, Puppeteer saving us ... Tonuko!

I looked around the bare room but saw no one.

Is he okay?! Where the hell is he?!

I scooted to the side of my bed and tried to stand. I felt a shooting pain in my right calf as I fell onto the cold floor and surveyed my calf. It was wrapped in blood-spattered bandages that went all the way up my leg. I grimaced as I stood, then limped toward the door. The heart monitor and IV machine moved with me, slowing me down. I ripped the tubes out of my body and kept going.

I saw Ashlyn walking down the hall, a quarter of her head wrapped in bandages. When she saw me limping toward her, she ran to me. "Kyle, what are you doing?! You're in no condition to be walking around!" she exclaimed, holding me so I wouldn't fall. I looked her in the eyes, a mixture of seriousness and sadness, then grabbed her hand.

"Where is Tonuko?" I asked in a stern plea. She looked worried but reluctantly helped me down the hall. When we reached his room, I stared at the closed door for a few seconds. I took a deep breath and opened the door. I heard beeping—a heart monitor—and saw a doctor and a few nurses around Tonuko's bed. One of the nurses turned and looked shocked when she saw me.

"Kyle Straiter, get back to your room! You are in no condition to be sitting up, let alone walking around!" she admonished. I gently pushed Ashlyn off me and limped past the nurse to Tonuko's bedside. My mouth gaped and my eyes watered as I looked down at him. The left side of his body was covered in bandages, a few tubes were stuck into his chest, his left arm had an immobilizer, and padding stuck out of the bandages covering his left ribs.

This can't be real. What the fuck?!

"Mr. Straiter, please have a seat. Mr. and Mrs. Kuntai should be here soon. We will discuss Tonuko's condition once they arrive," the male doctor stated, gently putting a hand on my shoulder. I slowly nodded, then limped into one of the chairs at the end of Tonuko's bed and held my head in my hands. I shook, the beeping of the heart monitor haunting me; Ashlyn sat next to me and rubbed my back. After what felt like hours—but was actually only ten minutes—Tonuko's parents burst into the room.

"No, my baby!" Mrs. Kuntai shouted through her tears. She cried into her hands, and Mr. Kuntai held her while tearing up. He was a relatively short man, shorter than Mrs. Kuntai, with a stocky build and light brown, long hair.

"Just give it to us straight. Is he going to make it?" Mr. Kuntai whimpered. The doctor took his glasses off and put them into his shirt pocket, then cleared his throat.

As Xavier and Puppeteer walked in, the doctor announced, "Tonuko woke a few minutes ago, but his chances don't look good. The explosion caused a heart attack, and there is permanent damage to his left arm. I'm not sure he'll live to see another day."

The world stopped spinning. We were all in shock. I squeezed my eyes shut and gripped my head.

"No, Tonuko, you have to fight through this!" I screamed. I jumped out of my seat and limped over to him. Tonuko slowly opened his eyes and looked up at me.

"K- Ky- le."

"You can't give up! You can't just leave us! You made a promise, dammit, you made a promise! You have to hold up your end of the deal, just like I will!" I shouted as tears dripped down my cheeks onto the metal bedpost. Tonuko coughed, then weakly clenched his jaw.

"I- I'm not giving up, I'll never g- give up! You know I w- would never stop fighting!" Tonuko stuttered, then his faced writhed with pain and his body twitched.

"You're just gonna leave Anya, leave your parents, leave all of us?! You can't go, you have to prove me wrong! You're supposed to take me down if I become a villain! You can't die this young, that's not how it works!"

Ashlyn and Xavier ran to me and grabbed my arms, then Xavier whispered, "Kyle, you shouldn't be yelling! We're in a hospital!" I looked around the room and saw the tearful, agony-filled faces. I stopped yelling, then Mr. and Mrs. Kuntai walked to Tonuko's bedside. Mrs. Kunti brushed her finger against his cheek and smiled. Her tears had slowed to sniffles.

"You've always been my amazing baby boy, you know that? You've always kept our household sane and been a light in our lives," her voice cracking as she spoke.

"I could always rely on you to encourage us to fight crime. You never stopped believing in us, even when the town did. You've always been a hero in our hearts, and we're both so proud of all you've done so far," Mr. Kuntai smiled. He gently took Tonuko's fingers, which were peeking out of the cast. Tears drenched Tonuko's cheeks, and he was clearly in great pain.

"M- Mom ... Dad ... I love you so much." The room went silent as he cried, "I don't wanna go, I wanna be a hero! I- I'm scared, please don't let me go! I'll fight and survive, I- I swear! I'm not leaving you; I promise!" Mr. and Mrs. Kuntai were now crying uncontrollably, as were the rest of us. Xavier and Ashlyn slowly let go of my arms, allowing me to limp back to Tonuko's bed side. Mrs. Kuntai put her hand on my shoulder, and when I looked over at her, she gave me a nod.

"Ever since day one at this school, even during the entrance exam, you've been pushing me. You've pushed me to limits I didn't even know I had. You forced me to be social. Every fight we've had has made me think and made me grow. Every piece of advice you've given me has made me a better person. You opened my eyes to what a hero really is ... n- now, you're just gonna leave?" I squeezed the bars, then Tonuko slowly moved his left arm to touch my finger.

His faced squeezed with pain, but he bared through it as he explained, "N- No, Kyle, you've done that f- for me. Y- You made me realize, be- being the strongest isn't b- being the best. Being the b- best is saving others, a- and always being there f- for others." I squeezed the bars harder and clenched my jaw.

"Being there for others means never making them feel alone! You can't just leave us alone, you can't!" I put my head down as my tears turned black.

Tonuko, even if I don't have the guts to admit it out loud, you are my best friend. Don't leave me, please. You help me control my temper and are always there for me whenever I lose it. You can't go. You can't.

"K- Kyle ... you're never alone," Tonuko spat out. His eyes fluttered, then ... the beeping turned into one long, painful sound.

I stopped gritting my teeth and stood there in awe. I heard Mr. and Mrs. Kuntai crying. When I turned around, I saw Puppeteer standing in the back of the room, covering his mouth as his tears dripped to the floor. Ashlyn hugged my arm and wiped her tears onto my hospital gown, then the doctor roared, "Dammit, we can still save this boy! I'm not letting him die! Nurse, get me a damn defibrillator!"

I couldn't move, it felt like I had just died. After the nurses rushed out, I saw Alex, Skye, and Rachel enter the room; they stood next to the door, absolutely shocked. The crying was overtaken by the constant beep of the machine.

Tonuko ... why are you giving up? You have to fight; you can't just leave. Get up ... wake up ... please ...

The nurses ran back into the room with a defibrillator kit, and the doctor assembled it, then rubbed the two devices together. "Clear!" he screamed, pounding them onto Tonuko's chest. Tonuko jolted, but nothing happened. Another "Clear!" and another jolt, but nothing. "Come on buddy, you gotta hold on! You can make it through, you have the fight! Clear!"

With that final jolt ... the long sound was interrupted with a beep, then another, and another. I fell to the floor and covered my eyes, wiping my never-ending tears. Ashlyn crouched and hugged me as she smiled.

"It's alright, Kyle; he made it," she whispered. I continued crying as the pain in my chest grew worse. Alex had left the room; his eyes filled with fright and shock.

Alex's P.O.V.:

Skye, Rachel, and I rushed down the hall, and as we neared Tonuko's room we heard crying. Nurses were rushing out the door. We got to the doorway and my arms dropped when I looked into the room. The heart monitor's constant noise made me tear up; a pit grew in my stomach when I looked at Kyle. Looming over him ... was the demon.

It stretched out of his back and hung over his head while looking down at Tonuko. The nurses rushed past me into the room, then positioned the defibrillator for the doctor. After assembling it, the doctor used it twice, to no avail. On the third try the demon looked down at Kyle then back up at Tonuko before launching a tentacle toward the ceiling. The tentacle went straight through the ceiling, as if it was intangible, then swooped down, carrying with it a bright light. The light blinded me. After blinking a few times, I saw relief on everyone's faces and heard the monitor's steady beeping.

H- He's alive ... he's alive.

I left the room and rested against the wall outside the door as I held my chest. I was sweating bullets and completely terrified.

But ... what just happened? Did that demon save Tonuko's life?

I slowly peered back into the room and saw the demon hugging Kyle's head as Kyle cried uncontrollably.

Did it save Tonuko ... for Kyle?

Kyle's P.O.V., One Hour Later:

I was back in my room and hooked back up to the I.V. bag and heart monitor. I laid on my bed, looking up at the ceiling. Ashlyn was lying next to me, sound asleep. After all the heartbreak and intense emotions from Tonuko's death and comeback, she was drained. She rolled over and her arm wrapped around my stomach, causing me to blush. Ashlyn was smiling in her sleep while also blushing. I hesitated, then put my arm around her and held her close.

She's different ... I don't get it, but she really cares for me. She's not like any girl I've met before.

I tried to keep my eyes open but everything went blurry and I eventually fell asleep.

E.H. Faculty Room, Monday Afternoon; 1:42 p.m.:

Fox-Tails tapped his claws on the big, circular table, a disgruntled look on his face. He tightened his right hand then smashed it onto the table.

"Two of our students are in critical condition ... two! Are we going to just mope around like pathetic failures or do something about it?!" Fox-Tails erupted, standing from his chair and yelling at Principal Lane.

"It is awful news, truly, however, there are still twenty-eight students out and about that could die at any moment. We're calling back Kyle, Tonuko, Skye, and Alex; that's the most we can do for them. Here, they can be healed by Nurse Blavins, and we can watch their conditions to make sure there is no lasting damage physically or, just as important, mentally," Principal Lane explained calmly. This slightly calmed Fox-Tails, and he sat back in his seat.

"That's a wise choice, and we should focus especially on the mental part. We know the news about Tonuko's death and revival, and it happened in front of the other students. That's absolutely crushing ... heartbreaking," Fallen added while rubbing his goatee.

"Seeing a close friend pass, especially witnessing first-hand their last breath, is one of the most traumatic experiences someone can experience. I'm sure those students are not handling the stress well, so we need to make an extra effort to tell our students to involve them more and make them feel better," Mrs. Davidson explained. The teachers nodded, each with their own death experiences as a result of being heroes.

Kyle's Hospital Room, 2:05 p.m.:

I slowly opened my eyes and blinked a couple of times. I heard a snapping noise, similar to a phone camera, then looked to my left. Xavier was snickering and taking a picture of Ashlyn and me. I jumped and pulled my arm away from her. In doing so, I slipped and fell off my bed, landing with a loud thud.

"What the hell are you doing?!" I shouted, waking Ashlyn. She rubbed her eye and sat up as Xavier burst out laughing.

"Just capturing a moment of the 'adorable couple'!" Xavier retorted through his laughs.

I slowly stood and seethed, "You better delete that picture, ya bastard." He shook his head as Puppeteer knocked on the door and walked in. He took a step into the room and closed the door behind him.

"Good, you're all here," Puppeteer stated in a solemn voice. I raised an eyebrow and stood next to my bed, putting all the pressure onto my left leg.

"Is something wrong, Dad?" Xavier asked after turning around and putting his phone in his pocket. Puppeteer took a deep breath, rubbed the back of his head, then sighed.

"Well, I got a call from your teachers, Fallen and Gladiator, and they have requested that you return to campus as soon as possible. This means ... your shadowing is over." I looked down with frustration and tensed my fist.

"Really? Aww, man, that sucks. We're supposed to have four more days!" Ashlyn said with a sad tone. "No!" Xavier and I shouted at the same time.

"We need training; heroes don't quit after one fight!" Xavier argued.

"Yeah, we can't just go home; that's like giving up! Please let us stay!" I added with pleading eyes. Puppeteer sighed, walked over to Xavier, and put his hand on Xavier's shoulder before letting out another sigh.

394

"I'm sorry, but you must listen to your schools and pack up. I want you to stay longer as well, I really do, but it's not an option," Puppeteer said. No one responded so he finished, "Xavier and Ashlyn, the doctor needs to talk to Kyle in private. Since you two are doing well, you can head back with me to start packing." Ashlyn nodded and waved to me, then Xavier reluctantly followed them out of the room.

After they left, the doctor came in and shut the door behind her. "Hey, Kyle. How are you feeling?" I sat back on my bed and looked down at my calf.

"I feel pretty good except for my calf. It really hurts to stand on," I explained, gently touching the area of the cut.

"Well, I'm going to give you crutches to use, and those should help relieve stress from your calf. Also, it appears there is a stress fracture near your heart. Have Nurse Blavins keep an eye on it."

I nodded then asked, "Are those crutches going to add to my medical bill?" The doctor stopped flipping through her notes and took a deep breath as she put down the clipboard.

"That is mainly what I needed to talk to you about. I-I'm sorry to inform you, but your father, Mr. Samuel Straiter, has refused to pay your medical bills." My eyes widened and I felt a pound in my head.

"Wh- What?! But ... how am I supposed t- to pay the bill?! I don't have nearly enough money!" I stuttered. The doctor sighed and shrugged.

"I'm not sure what I can tell you Kyle; the number provided under Samuel Straiter is out of service now." I sat on the bed, staring at the sheets in awe.

You stopped paying my medical bills now? You really hate me ... don't you? Fuck, I hate you so much. You shallow scumbag ...

395

Danielle Kuntai listened in through the door and held her hands close to her heart. She thought, "*Gem, this is for you. I may have not been able to take him in, but I'll do this.*" She opened the door without hesitation and stood tall in the doorway.

"There is no need for Samuel to be paying the bill anyway. I'll take care of Kyle's hospital fees," Danielle announced. My eyes lit up, and I looked her in the eyes with pure gratitude. "I made a promise that I broke, Kyle, so this is the least I can do."

"Th- Thank you so much! You have no idea how much this means to me!" I responded happily. The doctor handed me a pair of crutches, smiled, then picked up her clipboard again.

"Well, Kyle, you are free to leave! I'll need to talk with Mrs. Kuntai about the paperwork, but you should be all set to go back to Puppeteer's Organization," the doctor said. "Also," she added, "Thank you for all you did in the fight. Us non-heroes really appreciate all that you heroes do to protect us." I nodded and smiled brightly, then I hobbled over to Mrs. Kuntai, gave her a hug, and thanked her again. After that, I shakily used my crutches to walk to the elevators, where I ran into Ashlyn.

"You're still here?" I asked, confused. She smiled, holding a hand behind her back, then hit the down button.

"Yep! I couldn't just leave you to get out of here on your own with crutches. C'mon, I'll walk you back to Puppeteer's place!" Ashlyn responded, giving me a fuzzy feeling in my chest. I smiled and thanked her, then we stepped into the elevator. Ashlyn hummed to the music, and I stared off into space, lost in the melody of her humming. With each hum, I sunk deeper and deeper into the traumatic thoughts of the Gravaton fight and Tonuko's death. The elevator dinged, snapping me out of my daze. I took a deep breath before standing up from resting on the hand bars.

Ashlyn looked over at me and touched my arm. "You ready?"

"Y- Yeah; I guess so," I responded in a far-off voice. We slowly left the hospital. When we got outside I was blinded by the sun. The road was very busy and numerous people passed by. "So, where is Puppeteer's place from here anyway?" I yawned as I looked around. Ashlyn squinted and stared at the street sign, then pointed at the intersection in front of us.

"It's down that street, then we go left and straight for a couple of blocks, then it's a right and straight for a couple more blocks, then we should be there!" she spoke. I gave her a confused look, then shrugged.

"I'll just uh ... take your word for it," I responded in a chuckle. Ashlyn giggled, then we made our way over to the crosswalk. She pushed the button, and after a couple of minutes a sign lit up telling us we could walk. While we crossed the street, a few cars honked, confusing us.

"I wonder what that was about? We weren't holding up traffic or anything," Ashlyn thought aloud while looking back. I noticed a few people's angry expressions as they glared at me.

"Yeah," I commented, "that was weird." We continued down the street and after about half a block the reality hit me. People booed us and shouted vulgar insults from their homes and shops.

"You kids are what's wrong with society!"

"Yeah, get the fuck outta our city!"

"Nobody wants you here!"

We tried to ignore them—arguing might put us in a worse place—and kept walking, but a short old lady walked up to us and poked my chest with her bony finger.

397

"Don't sit there and act like you're too good to hear us! You aren't heroes!" she shouted, giving me a death glare. I raised an eyebrow but decided to let Ashlyn talk because she's much more restrained with her words.

"Pardon me, but what do you mean? We aren't trying to act better than you or anything like th-"

"You are two of the 'heroic' high schoolers that hurt an innocent protestor! He was peaceful until you picked a fight! *You can't waltz around like a bunch of bad asses when all you did was beat up an innocent civilian!*" the lady roared, cutting Ashlyn off swiftly and glaring at her. I softly grabbed the lady's hand and moved it away from my chest, then exhaled.

"The Upriser was not an innocent protestor; he was abusing the cause of the people to gain power. He's murdered hundreds of protestors, police forces, and heroes and has damaged cities to an extreme. We aren't claiming to be heroes, but we did stop a villain," I calmly explained. The lady crossed her arms and mumbled swears to herself.

"He was not abusing us; he was a powerful advocate! Shouldn't heroes save others?! I was there, in the protestor crowd, and you heroes did nothing for us!" the lady moaned. That made me angry, saying we did nothing, so I put my foot down and shut the spoiled old hag up.

"How can you stand there and say we did nothing for you? We suffered numerous injuries and risked our lives to make sure none of you were harmed! The only casualties suffered from The Uprisers were us heroes! Three of my classmates risked their lives to take down your 'advocate' so nobody else would get injured by his fury!" I argued in a raised voice.

This bitch is really ticking me off. She probably goes home without worry every day and lives easily! How can she seriously say that we did nothing when we literally escorted all of the protestors away from the dangerous fight scene? Why are the heroic acts that we E.H. students are doing not getting recognition?

"Oh, I heard about your classmates. I hope that son of a bitch Tonuko never wakes up! He damaged so much property, and so did you and Xavier Kinder!" the lady scoffed. That crossed the line by a mile.

I pointed directly between her eyes, right above her crooked nose, and shouted furiously, "That 'son of a bitch' Tonuko just died and was brought back to life! He nearly died to make sure others were safe! He risked his life to protect all of you and risked his life to ensure that you could go home to your family! *Do you know how awful it must have been for all of his friends and his parents to watch him die, watch him take his last breath?!* Oh yeah, I know because I was there when he passed!"

The lady didn't argue back and the harassment around us ceased, but I didn't. "He spoke his last words to me, took his last breath *in front of my eyes!* I heard the heart monitor stop beeping and the doctor pronounce him dead! You wouldn't know what that's like though, because your privileged, spoiled ass is able to go home every day to your family and not have to worry about being *abused, being abandoned and left for dead with your dead mother in your arms!*" A tear rolled down my cheek and hit the sidewalk. The lady stood dumbfounded in front of me, unable to form any words.

Ashlyn covered her mouth, then grabbed my arm and gave me a small tug. "Come on, Kyle," she started with a quivering voice, "let's go." I glared at the spoiled old lady as we walked away, then quickly stopped to wipe my eyes. As I turned around I glanced at Ashlyn, saw her puppy eyes, and looked down the street again. "Was that last part ... about your mom and dad?"

"Y- Yeah, yeah, it was. It was tough back then, but the past is the past," I sighed. She didn't look satisfied, but I didn't want to continue talking about my past to I tried to change the subject. "What happened during the fight your class had with the Care-Givers?"

"You asked that earlier," Ashlyn stated, cutting me off. "Kyle, I'm so sorry you had to go through so much trauma as a child. I'm always here if you need to talk about it." My eyes began watering again, and I looked down, unable to make eye contact with Ashlyn.

Fuck, I'm so embarrassed. I feel so weak right now. Everyone has to look out for me and reassure me ... I feel like such a burden ...

"Thank you, but I really h- have nothing to say right now. Truly, I'm okay," I lied in response. Ashlyn clearly didn't buy it, but she nodded and looked straight ahead. I continued following her through the city until we finally reached Puppeteer's Organization. Looking up at the building, I was hit with flashbacks of Gravaton, The Upriser, my fights with Xavier, Ashlyn getting hurt, Tonuko dying, Kaliska, the two pro-heroes-.

Ashlyn hugged me, burying her head into my chest.

"It's alright Kyle; it's all over. You can relax now, you're safe," she whispered. I snapped back to reality and wrapped one arm around her, letting my crutch fall to the ground.

"Yeah, you're right. I'm fine," I said. Ashlyn looked up at me with a soft, closed-mouth smile, then picked my crutch up for me. We entered the organization and made our way to the elevator. Before the door opened on the third floor we heard Puppeteer and Xavier arguing.

As the door dinged and slowly opened, Xavier shouted, "Dad, I'll take care of it! Stop babysitting me!" Puppeteer stood outside his doorway and facepalmed when Xavier yelled.

"Look at the mess you're making! I wouldn't have to babysit you if you just knew how to pack a damn suitcase!"

Puppeteer argued. He looked over and saw us walking down the hall, then smiled. "Hey, you guys are back! Gosh Kyle, not good to see you in crutches!"

"Yeah, shouldn't be in them for too long. Just need these until this cut on my calf heals enough to where I can put pressure on it without much pain," I chuckled. Puppeteer nodded, then put his hands on his hips.

"With Nurse Blavins at your school you should heal in no time! Well, you two should start packing and cleaning your rooms. You'll be leaving along with Kaliska's shadows in an hour or two," Puppeteer explained then walked away.

Xavier poked his head out of his room. "Welp, we're actually leaving, eh?" he asked with a sigh. I scratched the back of my head and nodded.

"Yeah ... I guess so," I answered. Xavier walked out of his room and over to me, then held out his hand.

"I'm, uh, sorry for fighting you ... twice. Friends?" I smirked and snorted, then grabbed his hand and shook it.

"Yeah, friends," I agreed. He smiled and turned to walk back to his room, but instead rolled his eyes and sighed when he saw Ashlyn's glee.

"Aww, you two are so cute! You're both so moody!" she giggled. I joined Xavier and rolled my eyes before hobbling into my room. I sat on the bed and laid my crutches beside me, then took a deep breath while looking at my bag.

I don't have much to pack since we weren't here for long. I don't know how the hell Xavier made such a big mess ... he wore like two outfits, including his hero suit.

I stood on one leg and hopped over to my bag, then struggled to bend down and pick up clothes off the ground. Ashlyn walked in and grabbed a shirt I'd been reaching for

401

then asked, "Need help?" I blushed and nodded, then rubbed the back of my head.

"Y- Yeah, thanks." Ashlyn picked up another shirt and a pair of shorts, folded them and stuck them in my bag. I looked over on my bed and saw the sweatshirt I wore the first day here, then hesitated. I grabbed it, then looked away and held it out to her.

"W- Wait ... really?!" she squealed, snatching it out of my hand.

"J- Just ... take it." My face was beet red and I couldn't look over at her because I was so embarrassed.

"Thank you! I'll- see you around!" Ashlyn awkwardly sung while skipping out of my room.

I've seen people do it before ... so I thought I'd give it a try!

"Gosh, I wonder what Daniel would think," I chuckled to myself while trying to pick up a sock off the ground.

Parane:

Daniel laid unconscious next to the building he was thrown into. A puddle of blood formed around his head, but that wasn't the only blood spilt. Laci giggled as she skipped past unconscious bodies. Camilla, Jessica, Daniel's parents, Scarlett's aunt, they were all unconscious on the ground, all bloodied and bruised. Scarlett laid face down, then slowly lifted her head. Her vision was blurred and hazy, and her right eye was caked in blood and swollen shut. Laci stopped hopping, then crouched next to Scarlett and lifted up her chin.

"Look at this little cutie!" Laci exclaimed, looking into Scarlett's green eye. Gabriella glanced over, smirked, and tapped her finger on her jawline.

402

"She kind of looks like you," Gabriella mused. Laci was shocked and stared wide-eyed at Scarlett . She became very angry, stood, and swung her mace down onto Scarlett. It smashed into her right arm, causing her bone to crack and blood to spew out everywhere as Scarlett screamed. Gabriella quietly giggled, then looked up and saw a portal form in the same spot as earlier. "Let's go crazy; our work here is done," Gabriella commanded. She wrapped vines around Laci and herself, then lifted them into the portal as news helicopters roared above them.

Puppeteer's Organization, Kyle's Room:

I stood in horror looking at the mini T.V. on a dresser in my room.

"This is a gruesome, terrible scene! The Care-Givers have left, leaving the heroes and shadows in shambles! Police and ambulances are on their way, just a couple of blocks away!" the news reporter yelled into her microphone. My mouth gaped as I read the words that flashed across the screen.

Daniel Onso, Scarlett Yalvo, Camilla Xavier, and Jessica Alter are the four brutally injured shadows! Pro duo Invisistrength and pro-hero Misty are unconscious as well!

Kaliska's Hospital Room:

Alex, Skye, Rachel, and Tonuko, who was covered in bandages and had crutches, stood over Kaliska's bed. They sighed as they analyzed the injured students then looked at their hands.

"Listen, I'm so sorry for all you had to go through. I should have been stronger and protected you better," Kaliska apologized. Rachel looked confused, then yawned.

"It's not your fault. We decided to fight The Upriser with you, so injuries were bound to happen," Rachel stated. Kaliska sighed again, then waved them off.

"Right now, I can't stand to see you so hurt, both physically and mentally. Leave the hospital. My sidekick is waiting outside to escort you," Kaliska commanded.

Tonuko bowed with gratitude and said, "Thank you for everything." Water formed in Kaliska's eyes, but they wiped it away and pointed at Tonuko angrily.

"I still don't know why the hell you're leaving! You literally died an hour ago and now you're gonna just waltz on outta here like there's no tomorrow?!" angrily yelled.

"Tonuko needs to see Nurse Blavins as soon as possible. The doctor told him to leave today because Nurse Blavins will be able to do more for him than this hospital could dream of doing," Alex quickly explained, slightly interrupting Kaliska. Kaliska nodded and sent them on their way. They left the hospital, found Kaliska's sidekick, and followed her across the street. Tonuko slowly hobbled across the street. After crossing, he was greeted with a gradual applause from those who earlier had booed Ashlyn and me. The old lady was sitting dumbfounded on a bench. When she looked up and saw Tonuko, she stood and approached him. She stopped in front of him and took a deep breath.

"Thank you ... for saving us." Alex and Skye smiled, and Tonuko was filled with glee.

"Of course. That's our job as heroes," Tonuko responded. Instead of being disgruntled, the old lady smiled back, then walked past them.

"What a nice lady," Kaliska's sidekick noted as they continued on.

Chapter 22
Return

After an hour of staring at my phone in silence, I heard commotion outside my room. I assumed it was Ashlyn and Xavier leaving, so I grabbed my crutches, then my suitcase, and slowly left my room. Luckily, my luggage had straps so I was able to carry it on my back. Although it was heavy, it was easier than trying to drag the suitcase around. Ashlyn and Xavier had already entered the elevator, so it took a minute for it to make its way down to the first floor then back up to me on the third floor. Once I reached the first floor, I saw Puppeteer hugging Xavier, who had an irked expression.

"I'm gonna miss you son! You be safe out there!" Puppeteer cried, hugging Xavier tighter. Xavier rolled his eyes, then wiggled out of Puppeteer's grasp.

"Dad, relax! I'll be fine!" Xavier sighed. He looked over at me and waved, "Hey Kyle." Ashlyn ran up to me wearing my sweatshirt and gave me a big smile.

"I'll miss you, Kyle! We should totally hang out soon!" she exclaimed, hinting for a response. I smiled and nodded.

"Yeah, for sure! Some kids from my school were thinking we should hang soon; maybe one of the next weekends?" I asked looking at Ashlyn, then at Xavier.

"Sounds like a plan. We'll see how things play out," Xavier responded. Puppeteer shook Ashlyn's hand, then mine, and sent us on our way. I hobbled down the street in the opposite direction Xavier and Ashlyn were heading and heard a yell behind me.

"Wait, Kyle!" Ashlyn shouted. I turned around and saw her running toward me. She hugged me tightly, which hurt a little, but I managed to hug her back. She looked down in hesitation and turned, then swung around and stood on her tiptoes while softly kissing me. My cheeks felt very hot. "I- I'm gonna miss you," Ashlyn whispered.

"Y- Yeah, me too," I stuttered, surprised. I looked up and saw Xavier snickering with his phone out. I gave him a dirty look as Ashlyn ran back over to him, then the two walked away. I was still in shock but turned around and made my way to Kaliska's Organization.

Kaliska's Organization's Front Door:

I saw Alex, Skye, Tonuko, and Rachel talking as I arrived. They snickered when they noticed me. I raised an eyebrow, then realized my face was still burning and red.

"I told you she kissed him," Rachel said in a monotone voice.

"Wh- What?! I didn't kiss anyone!" I stuttered in a fluster. Skye rolled her eyes and Alex giggled to himself.

"Of course you found another girl to flirt with! You're something else Kyle!" Alex mocked.

"Shut up!" I yelled back. Tonuko chuckled while looking at my crutches, then lifted his right crutch up.

"Looks like we're twinning, Kyle," he snickered. I couldn't help but let out a little laugh.

"Nah, I think you just copied me." Tonuko responded with an unamused look.

"Yeah, I wanted to copy being crippled," he grumbled.

The three said their goodbyes to Rachel. As she passed me she gave me a slight nudge. "I'll make sure to put in a good word to Ashlyn for you, Kylie," she teased.

"How many times have I told you it's Kyle! Where did you even get Kylie from?!" I retorted. Rachel shrugged then turned and trudged away.

"We should get going. Tonuko needs Nurse Blavin's healing as soon as possible," Alex said after letting out a big yawn. We hobbled on our crutches as fast as we could to the train station. As we boarded the train, some passengers gave us dirty looks while others kindly thanked us. After a long ride, we finally made it home.

We noticed there was an unusually large crowd exiting the train, so Alex asked, "Since when were people so eager to go to Camby?" I shrugged.

Ever since E.H. came to light, the population of Camby has been skyrocketing ... Maybe we are giving E.H. a good rep, and more people want their children to go there.

While walking back to school, I noticed new houses, hotels, apartments, and an overall greater number of people on the streets. After a long and somewhat painful walk, we were back "home," back at E.H.

"Oh man, it's such a relief to be back," Skye sighed while walking down the large cement pathway. We all agreed, then heard a cry from inside the front gate, which was no longer crowded by newscasters.

"What were you kids *thinking?!* Do you have any idea how worried I was about all of you?! You're like my children. I was worried sick!" Hazel screamed as she sprinted toward us. She hugged me tightly, slightly lifting me into the air and causing me to drop my crutches.

"Sorry Hazel, shit happens," Tonuko snickered.

Hazel glared at him, then seethed, "Hey, I don't wanna hear a peep out of you until you are safe in a bed in the nurse's office! Get going, *now!*" Tonuko jumped a bit, then scurried as fast as he could to the school's entrance. Devin walked over to us, then crossed his arms and leaned back on his right foot.

"We were all worried about you guys. Not only you but also the other kids who were attacked yesterday by the Care-Givers," Devin stated. I looked down and let out a small sigh.

"Yeah, I saw the news. They were all severely injured and left unconscious. It was just ... blood and bodies everywhere," I commented. Devin shook his head out of frustration, so Hazel put her hand on his shoulder.

"They also fought against one of the new Upriser groupies. They call themselves the Metaphorical Uprisers, and the one they fought did a number on Daniel Onso," Hazel added solemnly. Alex and Skye looked shocked.

"Are they gonna be okay?" Alex asked.

Hazel perked up a little and nodded. "Yeah, they'll make full recoveries. They should be coming back within the next couple of days, depending on whether or not they have healers at the Parane hospitals," Hazel responded. I yawned, which made Hazel glance my way. "Was that a yawn I heard? That's it, I'm taking you back to your dorm!" She grabbed me with her ghostly arm, then picked me up.

"I'm fine! Let me go!" I yelled, struggling to break free. My phone dinged on the ground, so Alex picked it up.

"Hey Kyle, you drop-" He saw the notification: a tag from Xavier. Alex took out his phone and scrolled through his feed until he saw what Xavier had posted: a picture of Ashlyn and me kissing. Alex and Skye burst out laughing, so Hazel glanced over at the phone, then looked up at me with fury.

"You have a girlfriend?! Kyle, why didn't you tell me?" she screamed, shaking me. My head swung back and forth, and my face was bright red again.

"It isn't like that! I swear!" I argued, feeling nauseous from the shaking.

"It better be like that! You better not be kissing random girls!" Devin scoffed with an evil stare. I rolled my eyes, then Hazel walked me to the dorms. She talked my ear off about Ashlyn. As she put me down at our dorm door, I noticed the buildings under construction at the back of campus.

"What are all of those for?" I asked.

"Oh, your grade will hear about it from your teachers after the shadowing ends!" Hazel answered. I shrugged and Alex, Skye, and I walked into the dorm. I hobbled over to the couch and laid down, letting my legs hang off the armrest. Alex and Skye sat at the counter, then Fallen, Excalibur, and Foul Odor arrived.

"Well ... how do you feel?" Fallen somberly asked. Alex leaned on the counter and shrugged. He had a sullen look on his face.

"It was ... a lot. Seeing all the blood and Tonuko almost die ... but it also felt good to actually act like heroes and take down the villain civilly," Alex explained. Excalibur crossed his arms and nodded.

He looked outside as he took a deep breath. "We're very proud of you. You fought off a powerhouse—one who has been murdering hundreds of people—without killing others or being killed. I know Tonuko had a traumatizing scare, but you're all here and alive," Excalibur exhaled with a smile. I kept a straight face and stared at my bandaged leg. I felt uncomfortable just thinking back on all that happened. Foul glanced over at me, then took a few side-steps and leaned on the back of the couch.

"Meet Fallen and me in the Dome in one hour. We saw the news coverage of the fight and a video showed that dark power that overtook your body," Foul whispered. I nodded without looking at him, then he rubbed my head and gave me a big, comforting smile. "Good job, champ, you fought well!" I slightly smiled, then softly pushed his hand away while chuckling.

"Thanks, Foul." The teachers and Foul made sure we were okay then left the dorm. I looked at the door as it closed and sighed. Alex stood, walked to the fridge, then opened it. It was filled with half fresh food and half from before we'd left. He grabbed the egg carton and put it on the counter, then turned around.

"How do ya'll like your eggs?" he asked sincerely.

Skye smiled, then responded, "Scrambled, thanks Alex." He gave her a heartwarming smile back, then looked at me.

"Kyle?" I looked at the two, then shook my head.

"Sorry, but I don't really want food right now. Eggs are too much," I politely declined. Alex raised an eyebrow, then crossed his arms like a mom you'd see in a cartoon.

"When's the last time you ate?! You have to be starving! At least eat something!" Alex argued before turning around and taking out a spatula from a drawer. After a few seconds of silence, I gave in.

"Scrambled too," I concisely stated. Alex smirked, then searched for a pan.

"Good thing you both want scrambled, cause that's uh ... all I know how to make." We laughed as Alex turned on the stove.

I wonder how the Parane kids are recovering ...

Parane Hospital:

Scarlett slowly opened her eyes, and the lights in her hospital room felt like the blinding sun. She blinked a few times, then glanced to her left. The doctor was reading medicine bottles while muttering to himself. He looked toward Scarlett and was surprised.

"Oh, you're awake! How are you feeling?" Scarlett grimaced after trying to sit up using her right elbow.

She stayed on her back and stuttered, "M- My right arm, i- it feels-"

"I know. You suffered severe puncture wounds to the muscles in your right forearm. Your arm from the elbow down it going to feel very stiff and will be immobile. If you apply too much pressure on it, you may experience shooting pains. As you may know, we aren't the most populated city. That being said, the best doctor we have has the strength of making amazing healing teas, though he cannot heal directly," the doctor explained. Scarlet looked straight at the ceiling and clenched her jaw.

"What about my auntie and Camilla and Jessica? What about Daniel and his parents?" The doctor looked at his clipboard, then picked it up while reading the papers on it.

"Everyone except Daniel has awoken. I'm sure you know he has severe head trauma, which caused a concussion. Fortunately, he has no permanent damage." Tears welled up in Scarlett's eyes. The doctor took a deep breath and headed toward the door. "I can only imagine how terrible this experience has been, so I'll leave you to collect yourself. One of my nurses will give you pain-relieving medicine shortly." Scarlett nodded and sat up after he left. She grabbed a cup of water from the nightstand next to her hospital bed and stared at the ripples in the water.

"She kind of looks like you, Laci."

A couple of tears dripped down Scarlett's cheeks. She took a sip of the water and swallowed, then closed her eyes.

"I- I had a sister."

A Town an Hour Away; Pro-Hero Gospel's Organization:

411

Cindy didn't smile like her usual self as she sat at the table on the main floor of Gospel's agency. Donte sighed seeing how sad she was. He opened his mouth but no words formed. Jax stared at the table with his hands folded, the same sullen expression painted across all their faces. Footsteps echoed behind them, then Gospel put his hands on Cindy's shoulders.

"Why the long faces? Are you still worried about your classmates?" Cindy nodded without looking at Gospel, then he added, "Together we prayed for them, then my sidekicks and I prayed separately as well." Cindy hesitated, then sighed.

"It's not that we don't trust in your prayer, we really do, but-"

"Just the thought that our classmates are fighting for their lives while we've done nothing," Jax uttered as he squeezed his hands. Gospel walked to the head of the table while looking at their distraught faces, then smiled.

"Well, I guess I have good news then. You will no longer be doing nothing because we have a vital rescue operation to take care of," Gospel informed them.

Their faces lit up and Donte excitedly asked, "When are we going?" Gospel looked at the clock on his wall, then out the stained-glass window in front of him.

"Within the hour we will invade the villain's hideout and save the hostages. We have to wait for the bomb team to disable a bomb just outside their hideout. They are monitoring my organization right now. They threatened that if we leave they will set off the bomb, killing the hostage," Gospel explained with his hands behind his back. Jax leaned on his left fist and raised an eyebrow.

"Why can't we sneak out or break the cameras?" Jax questioned.

"I do wish we could, but at any sign of distress they will set off that bomb. Villains like them are not afraid of death and do not care if the bomb catches them as well. We have to be patient; that is an important characteristic of a hero," Gospel answered. After they nodded, Gospel swerved around, his orange and amber cloak flipped in the air, and he looked out the windows as he walked away.

"We'll rescue that hostage. We can be heroes too," Cindy stated with determination. The boys nodded.

Jax stood and suggested, "Let's go get changed into that school uniform. Hero work requires 'hero costumes', if you can even call those things that." They headed up the stairs and to their own rooms.

"I'll save that hostage and be like you, Kyle," Jax whispered after closing his door.

E.H., An Hour Later:

I walked past all the construction and saw two men talking with each other while looking at a big blueprint. They were pointing and talking about different parts of the buildings.

"These dorms are damn hard work! They're way different than the other ones!" One of the men boisterously complained.

"The boss said this job will pay well, so it's worth it. Shit, I mean, not as well as that Hero Olympics will, eh?" The two began laughing then went back to discussing the blueprint. Eventually, I reached the Dome, which was quite a walk from the freshman dorm. I saw through the door that Foul and Fallen talking. When I opened the doors, Foul looked over then waved.

"Hey Kyle!" Foul shouted.

413

I waved back and walked up to them then Fallen muttered, "It's just as I thought this summer ..." It was a pretty sinister statement, which worried me.

"What do you mean?" I asked with intrigue. Fallen rubbed his goatee and took a deep breath, closing his eyes.

"Well, I'm sure you've noticed it by now too, but there's some kind of dark power living inside of you. I mean ... literally living inside you. I can't say I know exactly what it is or where it came from, but it's here for a reason," Fallen explained after exhaling. I gulped and started to sweat.

I can't tell them about the demon. I mean- I should, but what would it do to me if I did? It's literally living in me, maybe near my heart assuming it's related to the stress fracture, so what would it do to my body if I revealed its existence?

"I guessed it would be something weird, but I never thought something would be alive in me," I lied as I looked at the black dots on my palms. I needed to buy some time for better lies so I asked, "What's with the new dorms being built?" Fallen and Foul looked at each other and Foul shrugged.

"I guess it doesn't matter if you learn about it earlier than your classmates. There're new expectations being set on hero schools. Since there are so many kids who want to be heroes—not saying that's a bad thing—the normal high schools for regular jobs are closing down. In the past, kids had to go to another level of learning in college to be able to get jobs, but since we cram in all the knowledge at a young age, we eradicated colleges," Foul explained.

"Yeah, that happened during the second generation of strength users," I interrupted while rubbing the back of my head.

Fallen nodded and continued for Foul, "Yep, but now that many normal job high schools are closing, kids who don't want to be a hero don't have a place to go. The

Education Board decided that all hero schools must open to any student, hence why we need more dorms. Also, we are required to incorporate a lunch period with provided food and at least three regular classes for you hero students. It's gonna be a pretty drastic change, and the educational classes and students will be added at the beginning of November." I nodded but wasn't pleased with the news.

"Damn, I thought we were done with stupid learning!" I complained as I rolled my eyes.

"Dumb kids like you need to learn more," Fallen shrugged with a smug grin. I glared at him, causing him to chuckle, then he said, "Alright, let's get started with this power of yours. What happened when that darkness covered your body?" I thought for a moment, then glanced down at my hands again.

"Well, it first happened over the shadowing when I was fighting Xavier. My flames turned a gray color and it seemed as if my strengths and senses were boosted, like one big power-up," I explained.

"Wh- What if that's your first strength?! It would make sense as to how your body is strong enough to hold so many strengths!" Foul gasped. Fallen's and my eyes widened as we looked at each other.

"Oh, yeah, it's like it increases my body's strength at all times so I'm strong enough to contain all these different strengths. Aren't strengths environmental though? How would this strength have developed?" I questioned. Fallen and Foul tried to come up with a solution, then Fallen crossed his arms and looked up at me.

"Well, not all strengths are environmental. It's a little rare, but people's strengths can come from experience and, very rarely, from genetics. Most people who gain their strength from genetics develop one of their parents' strengths or a combination of both parents. However, it wouldn't make too much sense for you to develop your strength genetically," Fallen thought aloud. He rubbed his goatee again while Foul tried to think of a solution. Eventually, everyone shrugged.

"I don't know if we'll be able to figure out the root of this strength, but we surely can train it. Let's get started," Foul said. "Can you call upon that power?" I stared at the black dots on my hands, then squeezed them into fists and closed my eyes, tensing my whole body. After around fifteen seconds ... nothing happened. I opened my eyes, confused, then looked at the two.

"It- It's not working," I sighed. Fallen's eyes glowed as he stared at me, then he shook his head.

"No wonder your dad left. Such a disappointment," Foul sneered. I was caught off guard by the insult. I glared at him with disbelief in my eyes and my jaw clenched.

"What the hell did you say?" I seethed through my teeth. Foul looked over at Fallen and raised an eyebrow but let him continue.

"Yeah, you fuckin' heard me. Maybe if you weren't so weak and useless your mom wouldn't have died." Veins pulsated in my arms as I squeezed my fists harder, and my eyes fixated on Fallen's eyes.

I know he wants what's best for me, but he's still an ass. It wasn't my fault my mom died; it was Tyrant's. Everything has been his fault ... the fucking bastard ...

The darkness overtook my hand then exploded out in tentacles that covered my arms.

"And maybe if you were strong enough then Tonuko wouldn't have died. Such a shame you're so weak, and he's so weak that you were bested by that pathetic Upriser," Fallen continued. The blackness spread through my body, covering my torso, legs, and neck up to my jawline. The whiteness of my sclera glowed in my eyes and gray flames spiraled around each of my arms, similar to a rope. Foul's

416

and Fallen's eyes widened, then Fallen apologized before asking, "So, this is it?" After calming down, I looked down at my body and saw the darkness, then shrugged.

"Y- Yeah, this is it." Foul crossed his arms.

"Listen Kyle, this training is going to be very intense. To have such a strong power without control that it's very dangerous. You need to get control over that strength and fast. Are you sure you want to go through with this, training normally during school and this extra stuff?" I took a deep breath, thinking about the scale fights I'd been in then nodded, knowing my answer.

"I'll do whatever it takes," I firmly stated. Fallen smirked and held out a fist to me.

"Of course you will, that's you." I fist-bumped him, and just like that, the most intense training of my life started.

Gospel's Organization:

Cindy walked out of her room while rubbing her arm, feeling embarrassed, and saw Jax and Donte talking. They looked over and Donte gave her a comforting smile.

"You ready to be a hero?" She nodded, forgetting her embarrassment about the uniform.

"I've never been more ready in my life!" Cindy exclaimed. They smiled then were interrupted by a bell coming from downstairs. They swiftly ran toward the noise and saw Gospel standing with his two sidekicks on the first floor. Gospel looked over and nodded.

"The time has come. The bomb is defused, so now it's our turn!" He walked toward the front door, then held his fist to the sky. Everyone smirked then followed Gospel out of the organization. Gospel's sidekicks, HolyWater and Shard, stayed behind the trio of shadows in case an ambush occurred from behind. After running for about five minutes,

417

the group arrived at a large cargo factory. Cindy gulped; Jax nudged her and smiled.

"Don't be nervous, we got this!" he whispered. She closed her eyes and took a deep breath, then nodded and exhaled. Gospel walked to the brick wall in front of them and moved the Bible he was holding against the wall. A large, red outline glowed on the wall, then all the bricks inside the outline started steaming before evaporating seconds later.

"Let's go," Gospel stated, slowly walking into the building. They followed.

Shard looked around and quietly suggested, "We should split in two so we can cover more ground." The other heroes agreed. Shard pointed at Jax and Cindy with one hand then commanded, "You two, come with me. We'll go right and search that half of the factory. You three will go left and search that half. Everyone be very cautious; the villains could be hiding behind any of these crates." Gospel nodded and took his group left. The other group ran right, then Cindy grabbed her shotguns and jumped up onto a crate. She scanned the area, then swore to herself.

"I can't see anything between the crates from up here. I'll keep hopping around. I'll shoot to the sky if I find anything," Cindy informed Shard and Jax. Shard gave her a thumbs up.

"All you newbies, move it!" Cindy leapt to a higher crate and continued her search. "Jaxon, follow me. Your strength isn't cut out to fight alone just yet." Jax, although upset, nodded and ran with Shard around a large mountain of three metal crates. They searched around every crate, in every corner, every shadow, behind every box, but found nothing.

"Dammit, people are suffering and we can't even fucking find them," Jax swore, tensing his fists.

418

"Hey, watch the language and relax. We'll find them, that's for sure!" They turned a corner, then heard a gunshot. Jax jumped slightly.

Shard yelled, "That's the signal! She found them!" They ran in the direction of the shot. As they got closer to the gun's smoke, they heard a child crying.

Cindy looked down at the scene and covered her mouth in horror. There was a lady wrapped in chains, a child in one of the villain's arms, and a man lying on the ground. He had blood splattered under and around his head. One villain was a man with blonde hair down to his shoulders. He wore sunglasses, a white tank top, red shorts, sandals, and a whistle. The other was a woman with chains wrapping her arms and torso. She had long, black hair, a gray and black tank top, and a plaid skirt. The man looked around, then pointed at Cindy as he looked directly at her.

"I see you, big mistake!" Cindy hid behind one of the crates and covered her mouth. She felt nauseous and her eyes watered. A chain flew into the sky, past the box, then curved and smacked her across the jaw. She fell to her right as the male villain screeched, "Crack!" The crate Cindy was hiding behind was torn apart down the middle. Cindy leapt into the sky, changed her trajectory by grabbing a pipe hanging from the ceiling, then swung around and landed onto some rafters in front of a window. She heard the muffled screamed of the child, whose mouth was covered by the chain villain, then the crack villain shout, *"Shut up, you brat!"*

Other Side of the Building:

They heard the gunshot, so HolyWater turned and ran toward the smoke.

"They must have found the villains. We have to get over there quickly!" HolyWater exclaimed.

"Yeah, no time to waste! Let's go!" Donte agreed, charging up his legs then bolting ahead.

"Don't go alone Donte! We don't know what the situation- is ..." Gospel yelled before Donte rounded a crate mountain. HolyWater and Gospel continued running toward the scene. In no time, Donte swerved around the last corner, sliding on the ground, then jumped at the chain lady and kicked her in the head. She crashed into the crack villain, causing them to both fall over.

As the crack villain fell he shouted, "Crack!" Donte felt a numbing pain in his right foot, and he screamed out in agony. He landed on his left leg, then hopped back and around a crate.

"F- Fuck, what the hell was that?! My foot, it hurts so much!" Donte swore to himself. He saw Shard and Jax hiding behind another crate, then he heard a child's cry next to him. He felt the little boy hug his leg, then swiftly looked down and reached for the boy.

"Please, don't let them take me from my momma and papa!" the boy cried. Before Donte could grab him, a chain soared out from around the corner, wrapped around the child's waist, and pulled him back.

"More kidnappers?!" Jax yelled. He pressed his back against the crate, afraid to look around the corner and caught by the crack strength. Shard looked past the crate and saw the villains standing; then he glanced up and saw Cindy standing in front of windows. Shard smirked, then cracked her neck.

"Cindy, duck!" Shard screamed. Cindy fell to her stomach as the window panels were ripped from the wall, shattered in the air, and flew to Shard's side. Shard mocked, "It's best you two just give up now. We have more reinforcements on the way and the building is surrounded by police." The man frowned for just a moment, then grinned again.

"Oh no, we're just getting started." Again he shouted, "Crack!" and one of the glass pieces shattered.

"Don't let him see your body! He can crack anything he sees by yelling 'Crack!'" the woman who was tied by chains yelled. The chain villain whipped the hostage in the head, knocking her unconscious. The chain crawled back around the villain's arm, then she wrapped her arm around the child's neck.

"Make any move, come any closer, and the child dies," chain villain threatened.

"Tsch, of course you would," Shard grumbled, a scowl on her face. Another gunshot sounded then three bullets pierced the crack man's calf.

He yelled out, glanced up at Cindy with one furious eye, and screeched, "Crack!" The rafter Cindy was standing on cracked, then split in half longways. One half fell and balanced on the mountains of crates on either side of the villains. Cindy stood on her tiptoes on the other thin half, bracing for a crack. She was relieved when she felt a hand made of water grab her as she was pulled to HolyWater and Gospel.

"I've got you, Cindy. Are you okay?" HolyWater asked.

"Yeah, I'm fine. Thank you," Cindy nodded.

Adrian Cate/Faithful Hero: HolyWater, Strength: Aqua Hands—he can create large hands made out of water and extend them or grow them at will. The fingers on his water hands can shoot water like a hose, and the hands have abnormal strength.

"What are you planning to do with that child?" Gospel asked, standing nonchalantly next to the crate the others were hiding behind. The crack villain smirked and patted the boy on the head. The boy tried to move his head away from the villain's hand.

"We've been informed that this boy has quite the strength," the crack villain told Gospel. Shard raised an eyebrow.

"What kind of strength are you talking about?" she asked. The crack villain wore a large smile, and he shrugged.

"That is none of your concern. We're just here to guide him down the right path, away from you 'heroes'." The child continued crying, then threw up on the chain villain's shirt.

"Eww, you stupid brat!" She smacked him on the head, angering the heroes.

"Child abuse is not okay," Jax breathed. His pink smoke shot toward the three and clouded the villains' heads. "For the kid, it's like nothing is there; for the villains, I dare you to take a breath and see what happens," Jax grinned. The villains backed up, trying to escape the smoke, but it was as if it was stuck to their faces.

"Good job, Jaxon," Gospel said, patting him on the back. "That should be the end of these guys. Once they are under your control, we can take them in for questioning." Shard jumped up and landed on a piece of glass, then ran in the air toward the villains. With each step a new piece of glass formed under her feet.

Alyssa Vern/Shard, Strength: Glass Control—she can control any glass in the area and harden any air she touches to make it a glass-like substance. Whenever anything rests on the glass she creates, it's like a solid floor that can hold up to a ton in weight. However, if the glass is hit, it has the same sensitivity as regular glass.

As Shard swung a punch at the chain villain, a portal formed in front of her, sucking up Jax's smoke. A hand reached out and grabbed her face. Another hand came out and punched her in the stomach, causing her to fly back into Donte. As she flew, the crack villain screamed, "Crack!", which caused Shard's head to jerk backward. Donte caught her but had to put all his weight on his right foot, causing him excruciating pain that made him yelp.

"Care-Givers ... I should have known Tyrant was behind this," Gospel grumbled, still gripping his Bible in his right hand. BloodShot stepped out of the portal with a big smirk across his face, then he looked back at the kidnappers.

"We'll be escorting this child now. Thank you for entertaining these two, but they must carry on our work," BloodShot stated. The child frantically looked at the villains, then squeezed his eyes shut and tensed his fists. Crystal tear-drop shaped shields formed out of the back of his wrists. They extended down half of his forearms and over his knuckles. They were a translucent dark blue, with green ends. Rough spikes made of the same material came out of the boy's back, and he swiped one of his shields at the chain villain. She managed to dodge it. While she focused on dodging the spikes, the boy wiggled free from her grasp and he ran toward the group. Gospel raced to the boy but as he grabbed him, a chain flew out and hit Gospel in the face.

"Gospel!" HolyWater shouted, running to his side. He held Gospel and the child, but the same chain wrapped around the boy's waist and tugged him out of HolyWater's hand. HolyWater grabbed the boy out of the air with his aquatic hand; he and the chain villain pulled the boy in opposite directions as hard as they could.

"Crack!" the crack villain shouted, causing a numbing pain in HolyWater's ribcage. He fell to his knee and touched just beneath his heart, maintaining his hold on the boy.

"What a nuisance," BloodShot mumbled, drawing his blade. BloodShot bolted at HolyWater and Cindy tried to intercept his path by shooting at him twice. BloodShot dodged all of the bullets nimbly and swiped a cut across HolyWater's stomach and chest. "This child is a part of the future. How dare you try to take that away from him?!" BloodShot roared as HolyWater's aquatic hand faded.

BloodShot kicked him to the ground just as Jax breathed out more smoke. It rushed at BloodShot's head and he held his breath for a few seconds before charging at the three heroes-in-training. BloodShot leapt at Jax, leading with his knee, and kneed him in the chin. While still in the air, he swung his body and sword to his left at Cindy, cutting some of her hair. HolyWater's wound expanded, creating unbearable pain.

"Please, you have to hurry and get him back through the portal!" HolyWater cried out, blood spewing from his mouth. A chain soared at him from behind and smacked him on the head, causing him to fall and bang his head on the ground. Cindy shot a few rounds at BloodShot, who in return threw up his left arm to block. Five bullets embedded into his arm, and BloodShot looked at his arm as his blood covered the ground.

"Petty girl ..." BloodShot hissed before hitting Cindy on the head with the butt of his sword handle. The blow knocked her out. Donte stared in horror at the man who just single-handedly took out the heroes. BloodShot barely glanced at Donte, then stomped down on his right foot. Donte screeched and fell, then BloodShot threw his sword through Donte's stomach. He ripped it out, turned around, and walked toward the boy to claim his prize.

"Leave me alone! Don't take me away from my momma and papa!" the boy cried. He swung his shield at BloodShot, who had picked him up by the head, and cut him across the cheek. BloodShot dropped the boy, who fell, then felt the wound. He stepped onto the boy's face, pressing him to the ground, and smiled devilishly with an eerie look in his eyes.

"You're mine," BloodShot muttered, sounding almost hungry. "I'll make you into a new person, a better person." He grabbed the boy by the neck and raised him, then chains wrapped around the boy and squeezed him tight. The chain villain dragged him into the portal with her. As the cops arrived at the scene, the portal sucked in on itself.

"M- My bluff didn't work, we t- took too long. Now ... we f- failed," Shard stuttered solemnly, staring up at the ceiling. Everything went blurry, then she passed out.

The Child/Kidnapped Boy, Strength: Poison Shard—the boy can create rough, poisonous shards out of all parts of his body. The shards can be broken or pulled out of him but are not poisonous when they aren't attached to him. The poison flows through his blood—but only when at least one shard is connected to his body— and flows into the tip of the shards.

Jax leaned against the giant metal crate he was kneed into and stared into space. He thought, "*I was ... useless ... I didn't do anything.*"

Medics waved in front of his face, trying to get his attention. He slowly looked up at one of them and muttered, "The child. They took- the child." The medics glanced at each other, confused.

One asked, "Are you feeling okay? Did you hit your head?" Jax stared at them with a blank expression, then tears formed in his eyes and dripped down his face.

"W- We failed. They- stole him," he stuttered. The medics laid Jax on his back, then moved him onto a stretcher and carried him out of the building. Jax stared at the roof of the ambulance and thought, "*Sorry, Kyle, ... I couldn't ... be like you.*"

Chapter 23
Just a Child

I laid on my bed letting my feet dangle off the bottom and stared at the ceiling, a frown stretched across my face. I gripped my phone, which was opened to the news feed of the recent fight between Gospel and his shadows and the Care-Givers. Three heroes were in critical condition; HolyWater, Gospel's famous sidekick, was dead.

It all ends the same. No matter what I do, no matter how strong I get, Tyrant attacks my friends and hurts them. He always kills those I get close to ... always.

I sat up and looked out the window. It was very dark out, considering it was eleven at night, and the school had no lights on.

I don't have class today. The teachers said classes will resume when everyone returns.

I stared at the roof of the school for a few more seconds, then left my room to take a walk. Nurse Blavins had healed my calf enough that I could walk with little to no pain. I went through the dorm doors and was hit with the crisp night air. I wore only shorts and a t-shirt so I was pretty cold. I didn't care, though; that was the least of my worries. I strolled past the school toward the Dome, then looked to my right when I was between buildings. I saw the ladder to the roof and thought of my argument with Tyrant on the second day of school. I climbed the ladder and stood near the edge looking out at the campus. I took a deep breath, lost in thought.

The Care-Givers have gotten more aggressive toward teenagers my age over the past school year than in any other year in the history of the Tyrant Age. I wonder why ...

It's all my fault.

Tyrant wants me to join his group and will stop at nothing until he gets what he wants. He keeps sending his posse after people close to me to show his power. He killed his own wife, my mom, so he'll kill anyone.

I felt a buzz in my pocket, so I checked my phone. The notification was from Ashlyn, then a few seconds later I got a notification from Xavier. I checked the messages and saw pictures of the two and Rachel, still awake in what I assumed was their dorm. I stared at the picture with Ashlyn closest to the screen for a couple of minutes.

Anyone.

The screen faded, then turned off. I saw a boy in the black screen. He had faded blonde hair, large black rings around his eyes, bruises and scars on his face, and a large frown. He looked like a complete stranger, but the longer I stared the more I recognized him.

That boy ... is me. I'm broken, faded, beaten, and ... sad.

I continued staring but I didn't feel pity for myself; instead, I felt anger at the boy.

That boy ... is a curse to this world. That boy has caused so many deaths. That boy is the reason Tyrant has been so aggressive the past fourteen years. Tyrant said so himself—that boy is the reason people die at his hands.

I closed my eyes and took another deep breath that caused my throat to sting a little. I could see all the blood, the punches and cuts, burns and bruises, broken bones, crack, crack, crack ... I grabbed my head and squeezed, then crouched. Tears dripped from my chin to the grass below.

I can't do this anymore ... I hate it so much. So much blood, so much death.

I continued to silently cry, letting out a few muffled noises and gasps here and there, and squeezed my head harder. My thoughts became hazy, violent. Veins pulsated in my arms. My vision faded and darkness encircled my peripheral vision. Memories terrorized me. Then, the scenes in my head transitioned to my childhood.

Beatings ... fighting ... blood ... torture ... that was my childhood. Tyrant beat me every day, beat my mother every day, terrorized us both. We could never live in peace, we were always afraid of him coming home angry. He sent me to Daniel's house when he beat my mom. I was ... terrified of him. I never fought back, never protected my mom. I was ... a coward. I let him do whatever he pleased and never fought back. He's right ... I caused everything. He knew I had the power to stop him, yet I never did. I was just as bad as he was.

I looked down at my palms, at the small black dots, then heard my phone ring. I had dropped it when I had crouched, so I sat down, letting my feet dangle off the edge of the Dome roof, and stared at the caller I.D. Ashlyn Gray was stretched across the top of my screen; at the bottom were the "answer" and "decline" buttons. I stared at the decline button for a few seconds, then clicked answer and put the phone to my ear.

"Hey Kyle! We just wanted to check in on you and make sure you're doing okay. We saw the news about Jaxon Call, so I assume he was one of your close friends!" Ashlyn exclaimed. My eyes widened and my hands shook.

Jaxon Call ... and me ... close friends? Was he ... no ... he couldn't have been. It was always me ... and Daniel ... and ... and-

"What did the news say about him?" I asked weakly. There was a silence on the line, then Xavier spoke

"Apparently, he was muttering about you when he was in the ambulance. He was saying something about how he couldn't be like you and how he tried to be strong but failed. It's pretty sad stuff, so I'm sorry to hear about all that the Care-Givers and BloodShot are putting your class through. They're such assholes," Xavier spoke with a sigh.

Assholes. The person causing all this pain is an asshole ...

"You and those other two looked so cute as children! It's sad that all three of you ended up hospitalized!" Ashlyn interrupted, clearly a couple of feet away from the phone.

It's true ... I ... I forgot him. I forgot about one of my best friends. He didn't forget about me; he was probably happy to see me again like Daniel was, but I ignored him. What- have I done?

My hands quivered, and I dropped the phone onto the roof. It bounced, then fell backward away from the edge. I stood, and took another deep breath through my nose, then exhaled out my mouth. Tears continued pouring out of my eyes, but I made no noise.

"Kyle, what was that bang? Hello?!" Xavier asked worriedly. I stared straight ahead, ignoring their talking. I heard the beeping from the phone as they hung up, then looked up at the stars.

It's all Tyrant's fault.

I swiftly turned around and saw the demon standing a half-dozen feet behind me. He looked up at the stars, then down at me.

You can't give up yet. You have a destiny to fulfill. We have a plan for life; don't ruin it now. We will train to be stronger than that monster then we'll kill him. You have to kill Tyrant; it's why you were born.

I give up ... I quit.

You can't quit! You've been enough of a failure, but you can actually succeed at this! I can give you power to win; you know I can! Go now; find Tyrant and kill him! You can do it as long as you don't quit!

No ... I can't.

I turned back around and looked at the ground. I heard a high-pitched noise, then glanced behind me and was blinded by a light. The silhouette of my mom was back, but it was too late.

Kyle, please! Come to me now! Kyle!

I'll see you in person Mom. I've never made the right decisions, everyone tells me that, but this time ... I'll kill the one who's caused everyone pain and agony. I'll finally kill the biggest curse this world has ever seen.

Without hesitation, I fell forward ... and off the roof. I turned around in the air and saw the light looking down at me, then it broke into shards and faded into the sky. I closed my eyes and finally let out a real smile.

I'll finally see the one who loves me again. I'll free everyone ... from having Kyle Straiter in their life.

After what felt like an eternity, I hit something hard. Surprisingly, I was fine, perfectly unscathed. When I sat up and looked around, I saw I was not far from the roof and was sitting on a large, shadowy hand. I peered over the edge of the hand and saw Hazel panting as she let me down slowly. When I reached the ground and stood in front of her, she grabbed me and hugged me tightly

"*Kyle, what the fuck are you doing?!*" Tears streaked my face and after Hazel pulled off the hug, I could see her eyes were watering. I looked down to my right, not answering her question. "Kyle!"

"How did you- find me?" I asked.

"I saw a bright light through my window. By the time I made it outside I saw you falling. I ran over in few strides with my demon legs ... but that doesn't matter!"

I hesitated, then muttered, "Go away." Hazel stared at me with disbelief, then shook her head.

"No, I won't! You're like a little brother to me, I'm not leaving you alone until I know you're okay!" Hazel argued with a shaky voice. I slowly looked into her eyes, and my face didn't show sadness or anger anymore, but instead there was nothing—a blank expression with dead eyes.

"Tyrant keeps attacking everyone I know and hurting people. It's all my fault he does it. If I wasn't here ... he would stop attacking this school. The Care-Givers would leave you alone." Hazel took a deep breath, then, to my surprise, yelled at me.

"Don't you dare ever talk like that again! You were born into this world as a gift, nothing can change that! I don't care how other people view you, your friends see you as a loved one and somebody to be around! *Nothing that Tyrant does is your fault!"* Hazel screamed as tears streamed down her cheeks. Behind her, Devin marched up and grabbed the collar of my shirt.

"Stop being so narrow-minded and open your fucking eyes, Kyle! I don't get what goes through your head, but you just refuse to accept any kind of love. You throw yourself into dangerous situations every time there's a life-threatening attack! *What is wrong with you?!"* Devin's look of anger was his resting face to me, but for some reason this time I could see sadness as well.

431

"I'm trying to take out the threat! Every time we're attacked by Care-Givers it's my fault! Tyrant told me I'm the fault of his kills, my existence is the one that makes him so angry, so if I take out the common problem then you'll be okay! I'm trying to help everyone, like a hero should!" I argued loudly. Devin didn't hesitate to slap me across the face, then his hand returned to my shirt collar.

"Stop fucking talking like that in front of Hazel! Get it through your thick skull: *you are not the problem!* No one cares anymore that you're Tyrant's son. We just wanna make sure you grow past it! You always talk about how you aren't Tyrant, yet nobody sees you that way! You're the only one holding yourself back!" Devin screamed while shaking me slightly. He moved his hands to my shoulders and gave me the sincerest look I'd ever seen out of him. "Kyle, please let yourself live. *We want you to, so why don't you?!*" My eyes widened and my hands shook again. I stuttered for a response but could only muster noises.

"We all love you in our own way, never forget that. I can only imagine how you feel having no family to care for you growing up, but you have all of us now. Friends can be just as good as siblings, and you need a sibling," Hazel said while holding her hands at her heart. "I don't know what got into your mind while living alone for all those years, but let those bad feelings go. They're only hurting you."

"B- But how can I just let my hate go? I need to kill Tyrant; h- he killed my mom! He beat me throughout my childhood, didn't let me be a kid! All I wanted to do was play with toys and have playdates with my friends! I wanted to hug my mom and have a loving dad, but that could never happen! How can I just let that go?!" I asked, secretly hoping they would have an answer.

"It's true, you couldn't have a real childhood, but you can have the things you wanted now. You can go out and have fun with your friends, hug people who love you, and be you! It's okay if you want to kill Tyrant, but that's not what your hate is. Your biggest want isn't to kill Tyrant, it's to kill the person you hate, the person you despise," Devin answered after taking a step back. Instead of sincerity, his last sentence had a darker, sadder tone.

"Wh- What? Tyrant is the one I hate the most!" I responded while tensing my fist.

I hate Tyrant with all my heart. That man hurt me so much. Who else could I possibly hate more than him?!

"No, the person you hate most is- is the person you can't even look at while brushing your teeth. You can go ahead and waltz around acting like the cockiest guy in the world, but when you can't even bare to look at yourself during basic activities, it's obvious who you despise," Devin elaborated. That ... completely broke me. I fell to my knees and cried again, wailing.

I can't deny it anymore, I can't run from it. I can't ... run from me.

Hazel and Devin knelt beside me and hugged me tight. We sat there a few more minutes then I took a deep breath and collected myself. They stood in front of me again, giving me a chance to thank them.

"I- really needed this. Thank you for saving me ... from me." They nodded, both now smiling. Hazel still had wet streaks on her cheeks. Even though Devin never cried I swear I saw dampness in his eyes. Hazel retrieved my phone from the roof, then they walked me to the freshman dorm.

Before I went inside, Hazel suggested, "You should go to Nurse Blavins tomorrow for some therapy. I think it would do you good to have a professional give you affirmations on life." I nodded with a slight smile, then turned and walked into the dorm. I laid on the couch and stared at the dark ceiling. After a minute or two, my eyes fluttered and I fell asleep.

Next Afternoon, 12:34 p.m.:

I opened my eyes and blinked a few times, then sat up and looked around, confused. I stood after a couple of seconds and headed to my room to brush my teeth and shower. I threw on a black jacket and gray sweatpants, then walked back into the bathroom to brush my wavy hair.

My hair sucks ... so hard to brush.

I threw the brush onto the shelf and, after hesitating for a few seconds, looked at myself. There were still dark circles around my eyes and bruises on my face and arms. I lifted my jacket and saw the scar from when Alex stabbed me. It crossed over an older, much larger scar that stretched across my torso.

I walked out of my room and out the dorm. Once outside, a cold wisp blew through my hair. I looked around and saw two people standing at the food store. I walked over and as I got closer, I could tell it was Alex and Skye. Alex looked behind him at me, then waved.

"Hey Kyle, come on over!" Alex yelled. I picked up my pace to a jog as I made my way to them. Alex was wearing a white long-sleeved shirt with the E.H. logo and gray sweatpants. Skye was wearing a fuzzy purple turtleneck sweater with the E.H. logo and black yoga pants. The lady at the counter gave them their food, then offered me a Styrofoam package the same as theirs.

"You look hungry!" she smiled, hinting for me to take the food.

"Sorry, but I don't have-"

"On the house!" the lady exclaimed happily. I thanked her and took the food, then opened the package while following Alex and Skye. There were two hot muffins: one blueberry and one chocolate chip. As I ate the chocolate chip muffin I noticed we were heading toward the school.

"Why are we going to school? We don't have class until everyone gets back," I asked, confused.

Skye answered as we walked through the doors, "We're gonna go visit Tonuko! We weren't allowed to yesterday because Nurse Blavins needed to focus. Now that she's done healing him he's gonna be released to the dorms by tomorrow!" We opened the medical office door, which was conveniently next to the school entrance, and saw two people in separate cots. Tonuko was passed out, snoring, and Kate was scrolling on her phone. She looked up, then smiled.

"Hey freshies!" We said our hellos back, then Alex sat on her bed.

"S- So ... is it true?" Alex asked somberly. Kate looked down at herself, then sighed.

"Yeah ... it's irreversible. A portion of my spine was completely shattered and Nurse Blavins can't heal it. I'm gonna be paralyzed from the waist down for life." Kate glanced over at Tonuko, then looked me in the eyes. "But just because I can't go out and fight doesn't mean I can't help you youngins! I'm gonna help around the school with teaching and be in the Dome during training to give advice! I mean, I worked my way up to the top ten in my grade so I think I know a thing or two!"

We smiled, happy with her determination, then caught up with her, telling her all that had happened. When Tonuko finally woke we talked to him as well.

We spent the week training together (or, in my case, sometimes with Fallen and Foul) and helping Tonuko until finally Saturday rolled around.

Saturday, 10:30 a.m.; E.H. Training Facility "The Dome":

I stood in the arena and squeezed my fists while staring at Fallen. My sclerae glowed as the purple mist swooped around my body. Fallen smirked, then held up a hand and waved his fingers toward himself.

"Come at me, Kyle-boy!" I leapt into the air at him and swung a punch. A purple and yellow mist floated around his body. As he caught my fist, a whoosh of air flew behind him, then a massive crater exploded into the ground a couple of feet away. I kicked Fallen's stomach, forcing him to let go of my fists, then jumped back. I flipped in the air and landed on the ground in a crouched position, skidding a few feet. When I stopped sliding, I heard clapping in the doorway behind me, so I looked over, confused. Two people stood there, one with curly brown hair and the other with blue hair sticking out of bandages. The darkness faded off my body as I stood straight with a smile.

"Hey, Daniel and Jax!" I yelled as I took a few steps. I stopped in front of them, then sighed, "Gosh, you guys got it pretty good, huh?"

"Yeah, I guess so, but so did you!" Daniel laughed in response. We chuckled and I looked at Jax.

"H- Hey, I just wanted to apologize for forgetting you. It's been- a rough couple years ... really rough. With that new hairdo I just didn't recognize you," I apologized, reaching out my hand. Jax looked down, then grabbed my hand and slightly smiled.

"No hard feelings, I understand. It was just- rough too." We hugged, and after I felt a tear drop onto my shoulder, he mumbled, "I missed you, man." I pulled away and looked him in the eyes, then smiled a big, closed mouth smile.

"I missed you too; now stop your crying ya baby!" Jax chuckled and wiped his tears, then Fallen and Foul approached us.

"I think you've had enough training for today," Foul started as he put a hand on my shoulder, "Why don't you go meet with your other classmates? They should be returning about now." I nodded, and Daniel excitedly pointed out the door and smiled.

"Yeah, let's go!" Daniel yelled, basically already halfway out the door. We continued talking about our fights as we walked. We passed the school and looked out the gates.

"Oh, is that a group of kids from our class?" I asked Jax.

"Yeah, looks like a group of honors' kids. Sorry Daniel," Jax responded, squinting and smirking. Daniel shrugged then waved us off.

"Go on and say hi to them. I'm gonna go take it easy at the dorm, my head kinda hurts." We waved to him, then walked toward the gate. I could see Rake, Steven, Anya, and Cora leading the group. I joined Jax and waved to them.

"Hey, you're back!" I shouted. Rake smirked and strolled over to me. We pound-hugged, then he took a deep breath and smiled.

"Man, I kinda missed this place!" he chuckled. Rake glanced at me and sighed, "Could you not get into fights every time there's an event. You're worrying us! We need you around here, man!"

My smile dwindled but returned when Steven joked, "Yeah, what would we do without yours and Tonuko's fights?! It would be so boring!" I shrugged and blushed slightly, not able to stop smiling. "You both fought big villains while I was stuck being lectured by some random! So not fair!"

"Sorry, it's not like we planned on fighting Care-Givers or Uprisers," Jax apologized.

"I nearly had a heart attack hearing about all the people getting injured! Where's Tonuko? I need to yell at him!" Anya roared. She stormed past us toward the dorm,

437

dragging her luggage behind her. As she stomped away, I heard an antagonizing snicker from Cora.

"Well, with her gone to see her lover, what about you Kyle? Who's this girl we saw you smooching it up with?" Cora shoved her phone in my face with the picture of Ashlyn and me kissing. I blushed out of embarrassment.

"W- Well, she's just- y'know," I stuttered, making them laugh. I sulked as we walked toward the dorm. When we were close to the front door, we heard cries and whines coming from inside.

Oh, boy.

I opened the door and saw Anya hugging Tonuko as she cried, "You had me worried sick! I thought you died for good, *you dumbass!*" He hugged her back and tried to calm her.

"Sorry, I didn't plan on dying. I'm here right now, so it's okay!" She continued crying as we piled into the room and calmed a little after a few minutes.

"Man, it's great to be back!" Zayden exclaimed, standing in the middle of the room. He took a deep breath, then exhaled with a smile.

"Yeah, I'm glad to finally be back here. It was tiring being away," Iris softly added from her seat at the counter. Skye ran to her and hugged her tightly until they started to giggle.

"Iris, I missed you so much girly! You have to tell me all about your shadowing!" Skye shouted. They chatted as I walked past and I sat on the couch. After a few seconds, I felt a tap on my shoulder. When I turned I saw Cindy leaning on the couch.

"Hey little lovebird! How was your shadow experience?" she asked in a mocking tone. I rolled my eyes and shrugged.

"Based on what you just called me, do I even need to answer that?" Cindy hopped over the back of the couch and sat next to me.

She gave me an even more mischievous grin as she continued, "Everyone already knows about your girlfriend at B.E.G., but what about Xavier? What about Puppeteer and The Upriser? I wanna know!" Her tone was not as mocking and she seemed genuinely intrigued.

"She's not my girlfriend! Also, what if I wanna know about what happened with you guys and the Care-Givers?!" I retorted. Cindy tapped her chin and looked up for a moment before nodding.

"Fair point ... but I asked first!" she responded.

"Alright, alright, it was fine. Xavier and I didn't really get along at first," I started. Cindy raised an eyebrow.

"Why? Was it like the tension between you and Tonuko?" she asked.

"Yeah, kinda," I answered, "I'm not too positive, but either way we fought ... twice. The second time, we were interrupted by Tonuko, Alex, Skye, and Rachel and they stopped us. After that, the big fight started. It was absolute hell: rain was pouring, thunder and lightning were cracking, and hail was pummeling us. Xavier, Ashlyn, and I split off to escort the civilians and we ran into Gravaton, one of the Metaphorical Uprisers. He babbled about our guilt then absolutely demolished us with his gravity strength. If Puppeteer hadn't saved us, I don't know if we'd be here today." Cindy bit her nail and looked very into my story.

"Where did that Gravaton guy go? I think I saw The Upriser was taken to the Abyssal Penitentiary, right?" Cindy questioned.

I sighed with a nod, then admitted, "To be honest ... we have zero clue where Gravaton went. One of his allies saved him and they clearly made it to Parane by the next day. As for The Upriser, Xavier told me he's being questioned by Puppeteer and Kaliska."

Abyssal Penitentiary, Undisclosed Location:

Puppeteer and Kaliska sat on the other side of a steel table, which was nailed to the ground, from The Upriser. He was strapped in a jacket that was wrapped in chains. He sat in silence with a small smile on his face, giving Puppeteer and Kaliska an eerie feeling.

"Why did you ambush those protests and murder the protestors when you have said you are a part of the people upset with how society is currently run?" Puppeteer asked with a stern stare. The Upriser let out a soft chuckle, then smirked.

"I was simply making a stand. Heroes never listened to our cries. As soon as we used violence, all eyes were on us," The Upriser responded. Puppeteer grimaced at the response and furrowed his eyebrows.

"That is no excuse to violently murder hundreds of civilians, heroes, and police force. You stole the lives of countless innocents and manipulated the protests for your own selfish desires," Puppeteer retorted. The Upriser's smile slowly turned upside down, and his presence changed.

"If my killings are seen as violent and selfishly driven ... then why was Tyrant's son praised for his murders and forgiven?" The Upriser bluntly asked.

"We decided as a group that Kyle's killings were wrong but driven by the right reason. He was pardoned because the ones he killed were evil and in the process of trying to hurt others. You have no excuse for yours," Kaliska swiftly answered.

"Ah ... excuses ... So you think that the protests about the wrongs in society are not justified? You feel as though the people pointing out your misdoings are scoundrels and unqualified?" The Upriser asked, clearly

440

hinting for the heroes to say something inconsiderate and controversial.

"Putting words into our mouths and making us seem like the bad guys isn't helping your case. If you're going to sit here rhyming and talking like a lunatic, we'll be on our way and leave you locked up for good," Puppeteer argued with a snort. The Upriser laughed and looked at Puppeteer and Kaliska with just his eyes.

"That's fine by me. You're the ones losing information, not me. Right now, I have nothing to lose." Kaliska was half-frowning under their mask. Puppeteer scanned the sheet he held in his hand, took a deep breath.

On the exhale, asked, "Who are your followers?" The Upriser moved his head down and shrugged as best as he could.

"You'll have to be more specific. I have many." Puppeteer rolled his eyes and shook his head.

"Who are your followers?" Puppeteer repeated, "The ones present at the fight scenes in Takorain and Parane." The Upriser's eyes lit up, and he gave them a big, toothy smile.

"Ah, yes, my loyal Metaphors. They call themselves the Metaphorical Uprisers, a homage to the strengths they possess—the strengths that society deemed as 'unfit for equal treatment'. They were cast out; some wanted revenge and fought those who looked down on them and some wanted justice. At some point, they found each other, destiny is what I would call it, and they formed an unbreakable bond. They were inspired by my actions and felt that my movement would bring them the justice they longed for. They told me they were willing to sacrifice their lives for my cause, to allow equality to be spread throughout the world." Even with this heartfelt speech, The Upriser couldn't get a reaction out of Puppeteer and Kaliska.

"Sorry, you can't guilt trip us with your false fantasy. The ones that 'sought revenge' are cold-blooded killers, and the others joined the dark side of the equality protests. They chose to go down a path of violent crimes instead of peaceful protesting," Puppeteer snarled, standing and dropping the paper on the ground. "We're done here. All you're doing is justifying your ridiculous dreams." Puppeteer swiveled on his heels and walked out of the room, then Kaliska followed while holding her mask against her face. With no one else in the room, The Upriser silently cried.

"You two don't know what is coming for you, what a tragedy. My dreams won't be just fantasies for much longer. I know the Metaphorical Uprisers will carry out my legacy and put an end to the tyranny of heroes and villains. People will no longer need to live in fear." As Puppeteer and Kaliska rode in their helicopter away from the Abyssal Penitentiary, rain poured down, hitting the glass of the helicopter hard.

One Hour after Return, E.H. Dorms:

I laughed as Rake described the terrible story of his shadowing experience.

"I mean, the damn dude—who was literally a lizard—told me my strength was creepy. He had scales for crying out loud!" Rake complained while flailing his hand around.

"I mean, it's kinda the same with your hair. It's basically scales, right?" Daniel chuckled, causing Rake to sigh.

"No, it just looks like it. My hair is actually pretty damn soft if I do say so myself," Rake explained. We laughed and before he could defend himself, Fallen and Excalibur knocked on the door.

Camilla opened it and Fallen shouted, "Welcome back boys and girls! I'd love to hear about all of your experiences, but I really wouldn't!" The room filled with sarcastic responses, triggering Excalibur to chuckle.

"Very funny Fallen, but we do actually have an announcement, a couple in fact. While talking with Gladiator, a Bade's Exceptionally Gifted teacher, about returning some of our students after the Takorain situation, we reached a mutual agreement. First, we were informed that at Bade's Exceptionally Gifted, they host a welcome back party for their shadows, so we will do the same tonight in the Dome. In addition, we arranged a little class mixer event for the honors' students!" Excalibur informed us with excitement. The advanced kids let out a whine, counter to the honors' students happiness.

"Why can't the advanced kids do something too?" Skye complained. Fallen flat-out ignored her, not even batting her an eye.

"Half of the honors' students will pack their things and go live at B.E.G. for one week. It'll be the week of Halloween," Fallen continued for Excalibur. "Half of their students will do the same and come here. Halloween falls on a Thursday this year and, per usual, the next day will be an off day for all schools, so the students returning will not miss any class time. Each school is responsible for different kinds of training during the week, then a big, fun event will take place on Halloween. At the party tonight, we will announce who will be packing their bags and headin' over to the big, bad B.E.G. campus!" I closed my eyes and sighed out of annoyance, as did Tonuko.

"What's wrong?" Anya asked, looking at us with confusion.

"Better start packing my bags," I stated, frankly a little bothered.

"Yep, better get going already!" Tonuko added with equal annoyance.

"Why are you guys so confident you're going over to B.E.G.? You never know," Khloe questioned with a raised eyebrow. I looked at her like she was stupid, then rolled my eyes.

"Do you honestly think they're not going to have Tonuko, Xavier, and me in the same group at the top school in the nation? I'm not trying to boast, but it seems obvious," I responded.

"Yeah, he's got a point. Two spots are already taken, so that leaves six more—most likely four girls and two guys left. I wonder who will get chosen," Jax pondered. He was lying on his stomach on the floor next to the packed couch.

I leaned over, since he was right next to me, and whispered, "Between me and you, I hope to God that Camilla and Ashlyn aren't in the same group. Bonus if I'm not there, because I feel like that might cause-"

"Drama, hate, tension?" Jax interrupted with a chortle. I nodded my head and sighed.

"All of the above." I felt a buzz in my pocket and took out my phone. I saw a text from Xavier and Ashlyn in a group chat Ashlyn had made, so I opened it. The group consisted of Tonuko, Ashlyn, Xavier, and me.

"Looks like we'll be training here during Halloween. Sounds like a blast, eh?" Xavier texted. I rolled my eyes with a smirk.

"Sure, that's what we'll call it," I responded.

"It'll be fun Kyle!" Ashlyn typed. Tonuko sent a smirking face; I responded with a glare across the room. Everyone else looked confused. Cindy leaned over my lap, trying to nab my phone out of my hand.

"Sooo, what's going on here?" she asked. I smacked her hand away, then followed through by pushing her head back until she was sitting upright.

"Relax. I'll show you," I said. She looked at my phone as I unlocked it, then saw the group chat.

"Ohhh, it's your girlfriend and Xavier Kinder!" Cindy mocked with a grin.

"She's not ... my girlfriend," I grunted after rolling my eyes.

"Oh, really? Well, if I just pull out my phone right here ... I can pull up this picture!" Cindy teased. I glared at her and glanced at the staircase, ignoring her. She pouted, then wiggled my arm.

"Kyle, stop ignoring me! It was a joke, c'mon!" she whined. I continued ignoring her then felt my phone buzz in my hand. I looked at the message and was confused when I saw it was from an unknown number.

"Greetings, friend," the text read. I looked at my phone weirdly and stood, causing everyone to stop laughing.

"Kyle, you good?" Daniel asked in a joking tone, assuming it was something with Ashlyn.

Without looking up, I answered, "Yeah, it's nothing." I typed back, "Who is this?" and walked toward the stairs then up them. When I reached my room, I threw my phone onto my bed and sat down. I was on the end, next to the window, and opened the blinds. As I cracked open the window I took a deep breath as the crisp air circulated into my room. I heard another buzz and grabbed my phone. I looked at the message ... and my stomach dropped.

No ... no, this has to be a joke ...

"It's your good bud Plague! I just want to talk, friend."

Chapter 24
Ruined

I stared at the message with a sick feeling in my stomach. My eyes were wide and my hands shook as I typed back.

"How did you get this number?" I asked, then I closed my eyes and took a very deep breath to try and calm myself down.

Maybe, just maybe, he'll somehow think he has the wrong number ... I don't know ...

I felt a buzz in my hand, then sighed as I looked down.

"I want to talk," Plague responded. I shook my head before tossing my phone across the room, letting it land on the hardwood floor. I walked into the bathroom and splashed cold water on my face, then leaned my hands on the counter and looked myself in the eyes. I closed them again after hearing more buzzes, then sighed and walked back into my room and to my phone. I picked it up and viewed the new messages.

"Kyle, don't ignore me."

"I know everything."

"Let's talk, brother to brother."

My heart stopped and my mouth gaped as I read that last message. My fingers trembled as I slowly typed the question,

"What do you mean 'brother'?" The texting bubble appeared, went away, then his response popped up.

"I don't actually mean brother, just that we're very similar. Think about it: two people born into villainy with paths carved out for them, but only one of us chose to follow the right road. The other defied." I squeezed the phone in my hand and calmed myself knowing Plague and I weren't actually brothers.

"We're not similar at all, you just admitted it by saying only one of us chose the path we were given. I chose the right road. Don't text me anymore," I snapped back. I could hear chatter down the hall and steps coming up the stairs. I smiled and walked toward my door, but then I felt another buzz in my hand. Although I had no interest in texting Plague anymore, I sighed and checked the message.

"Don't make me send BloodShot out there to do some bad stuff. Answer my call, now." As soon as I finished reading the message, a call rang from Plague. I hesitated and thought about his threat.

Honestly ... it's better for something bad to happen to me during this call than for Plague to send BloodShot here. BloodShot would hurt my classmates, maybe even kill one. I can't let that happen.

I answered the phone but didn't speak.

"Kyle, my best friend! I have a couple of questions to ask you!" Plague cheerfully shouted. I rolled my eyes and before I could respond a few of my classmates passed in front of my door.

"Hey, Kyle," Iris waved to me as she passed. She was with Tonuko, Skye, Violet, and Zach. I pointed at my phone with a serious expression on my face then sped-walked past them, leaving them confused.

"He must be on a call with Xavier or Puppeteer or something. I'll talk with him in a couple of minutes," Tonuko said with a shrug. I practically jogged out the front door of the dorm, past the rest of my classmates, and slowed to a quick stroll when I was a good distance away from the dormitory.

"Alright, I can talk. What do you want?" I tiredly asked. I could hear a pen clicking and some shifting, then Plague sighed.

"Well, I'm having trouble with my homework and I thought why not ask you!" Plague explained. My face turned from worry to a cringe.

"Why the fuck would you call me about schoolwork? We aren't friends, I hope you know that. When I met you you threatened to kill me!" I rudely responded. Plague let out a very dramatic gasp, then I heard his pen click a few more times.

"But Kyle, you're like my best friend! Come on bro, just help me out!" Plague whined. I ignored his whine and thought about his odd question.

Then it dawned on me: "Wait a minute, did you say homework? What are you doing that requires homework as a villain?"

There was a long silence on the line; all I could hear was the static of the phone. "That's uh ... none of your concern! Anyway, care to help?" I hung up and angrily stuck my phone into my pocket, then sighed heavily. I heard steps behind me and turned to see Tonuko coming my way.

"Hey," he said after catching up to me.

"Yeah, hi," I responded, running my hand through my hair. There was an awkward silence.

Tonuko asked, "Was that an important call? Who was it with?" I hesitated then shook my head.

"Nah, it's nothing to worry about. Let's just relax until this party, eh?"

"Yeah, let's just enjoy ourselves," he said as we turned around and headed back to the dorm.

I didn't talk to my classmates and Plague texted and called nonstop. The only thing that plagued my mind that day was Plague.

Five Hours Later:

I stood from my bed and stretched my back, then scratched my head as I walked out of my room. I wore a sweatshirt and baggy pants. I was pretty confused when I saw Alex walking out of his room wearing a blue suit, black tie, and gym shoes.

"Did you not get the memo? We're supposed to dress up!" Alex informed me, clearly seeing my bewilderment. I looked back in my dark room, then over at him and shrugged.

"I, uh, don't own a suit."

"Follow me, I have a spare," he chuckled. I raised an eyebrow as I entered Alex's room and was actually shocked when I saw him grab a white suit with a black bowtie from his closet.

"Why on earth do you have a spare suit just lying around?" I asked.

Alex admitted, "Well, back at my old school I had a couple of forgetful friends. I always had an extra suit at my house so if they forgot theirs, I could give them one. I decided that bringing an extra suit here for events like this would maybe save someone who might not be able to afford one or just forgot theirs!" I looked at the suit then smiled.

"Thanks, Alex. Suits are pretty damn expensive, so I had hoped we wouldn't need one." Alex nodded with a smile, then checked his phone.

"You should probably go change; the party starts soon. By the way, keep the suit!" I thanked him again, then went back to my room. After I changed, I opened my door and saw Alex waiting for me. "You ready?" I nodded and we were on our way.

"Sorry for making us late. I guess everyone already left," I apologized.

"Oh well, it's not a big deal. I was gonna leave like ten minutes ago so it wouldn't have been much of a difference," Alex laughed. We continued walking and my phone blew up with messages. There was a buzz every couple of seconds and Alex clearly had the wrong idea about it.

I saw him grinning as he asked, "So, who's blowing up your phone?" Butterflies fluttered in my stomach. I took out my phone and checked the notifications: fifteen messages from an unknown number and four missed calls. I swiftly shoved my phone back into my pocket, then shrugged.

"Oh, it's just a couple of app notifications. Gotta hate how some spam you, huh?" I lied. Alex chuckled and nodded. When we finally reached the Dome entrance, he walked to the door, opened it, and signaled for me to enter, all the while snickering.

"Ladies first!" I rolled my eyes and held back a smile. Music was blasting from big speakers at the back of the building and there were a dozen tables with chairs on the arena stage. Underneath the overhead seating balcony, there was a long table filled with an array of foods and drinks. I saw that most of those in my grade were dancing in front of the DJ's stage. Fox-Tails was the DJ, and he was bopping his head to the beat. Fallen and Excalibur stood next to him.

"You guys finally made it! What took you so long?!" Cindy screamed.

"You wouldn't believe how long it took Kyle to put on his makeup!" Alex snickered before nudging my arm with his elbow. I rolled my eyes and chuckled, then looked down at my phone. The messages were now at twenty so I wanted to see what exactly he was texting me.

"Kyle."

"You better answer me."

"I'll tell BloodShot."

"Kyle, come on!"

I sighed and texted back, "Stop texting me." Cindy looked confused and raised an eyebrow. Her smile faded when she saw my stressed face.

"What's wrong, Kyle? Who're ya texting?" she asked. I didn't respond, so she tried for a reaction, "Is it ... you girlfriend?" I glared at her, then stuck my phone into my pocket and walked away. I could hear the two laughing. I stuck my hands into my pockets when I made it to the food and beverage table. I scanned the items and saw pizza, chips, punch, and all kinds of candies. I walked away, not grabbing anything, then ran into Tonuko. He looked me up and down, then smirked.

"You know you're not supposed to wrinkle a suit, right?" Tonuko asked in a mocking tone. He was wearing a gray suit with a pink tie, and his hair was neater than usual. I shrugged.

"This is supposed to be a party. I didn't know we were stuck up rich kids going to a public school." Tonuko chuckled, then Scarlett and Anya walked up to us. Anya was wearing a green dress with a short skirt that was covered with a light green veil. While Anya's was simple, Scarlett was wearing a lavish pink and purple dress with a frilly skirt. Her hair was curled and she had wings of eyeliner along with shiny pink lip gloss. Anya, on the other hand, had a braided bun and little to no makeup.

451

"Wow, you two look totally different!" Tonuko yelled over the music. Scarlett brushed her hair out of her face and giggled.

"I think we have different opinions on dressing up! I love it, but Anya on the other hand-"

"I don't care for it. Not my favorite thing in the world," Anya finished for Scarlett.

She blushed and Tonuko wrapped his arm around her and complimented, "Don't worry, you look great! You don't have to be flashy to look good!" Anya smiled while Scarlett and I stood awkwardly.

"Maybe we should leave them alone. They're getting ... flirty," Scarlett whispered to me. I looked at her and nodded, then we walked to one of the tables and sat down. I rubbed my forehead then pushed back my hair, again staring at my phone. The texts from Plague were haunting me. Scarlett looked over and asked, "Are you okay?" I looked up and gave her a fake smile.

"Yeah, I'm fine." She turned her body to face me.

"I know we don't talk much, but I'm worried about you. We all are. There's been a lot going on with you lately." Scarlett reached out her hand to my cheek. As she did, a pink mist flowed into the air. I unknowingly breathed in a sigh, inhaling the mist, and instead of slapping her hand away I let her hold me. Her eyes looked so ... captivating and beautiful. She leaned in and I did as well ...

"Scarlett, stop being such a hoe!" Jessica yelled, slapping her in the head. Rake walked up next to me and knocked once on my head like a door, snapping me out of Scarlett's power.

"Why the fuck did you do that?" I growled, glaring at Scarlett. She blushed and smiled, then shrugged.

"It's been so tense lately, I just wanted to have some fun!" Scarlett responded.

I scolded her, then Rake chuckled, "Well, anyway, how's the day been for you guys otherwise?" He was clearly trying to ease the argument that was sure to ensue, so I sighed and shrugged.

"I mean, it's been pretty normal," I answered. Scarlett and Jessica agreed, but Jessica seemed very antsy.

"I'm so excited for the announcement of who's going to B.E.G. and who's staying!" she squealed. Rake nodded in agreement.

"Yeah, it'd be great to be able to go to B.E.G. for a week. Everyone who goes will get vast recognition across the nation, maybe even the world!" Rake dreamt.

"True, but who cares honestly? We're just as good as them, maybe even better!" I snickered with confidence. They looked at me like I was crazy, but my eyes gleamed as I stated, "Once the Hero Olympics comes around, we're gonna win. We're gonna have the Robust Ten filled to the brim with E.H. students!" Rake smirked and Jessica and Scarlett smiled and nodded.

Tonuko walked over to us and added, "Hell yeah. We're gonna bring this new school to the top, no doubt!" He and I fist bumped and he sat across the table from me.

My phone buzzed a couple of times and I begrudgingly checked it. Plague had sent a few more texts. I couldn't let anyone see what he'd written. I shook my head, put down my phone, and looked toward the DJ area. Everyone left to go dance, though I stayed put, as did Tonuko. I then looked at Plague's texts.

"Listen to me, Kyle, it's a matter of time. I feel we can make a connection before you return to your roots." I clenched my jaw and squeezed my phone.

"There's no way in hell I'll return to my roots. You've clearly got the wrong impression of me. I don't quit, nor do I lose," I furiously texted back.

"Exactly. If you don't lose, why stay on the side that's bound to?" By now I was visually angry, and Tonuko glanced over at me. He raised his eyebrow, then pulled out his phone and started texting someone. I didn't even notice, it was as if I had tunnel vision.

"I've got faith in my classmates that we can take down whatever you throw at us," I texted back. The texting bubble popped up, and Plague's message pushed me over the limit.

"There's quite the issue I see with that statement. Your faith means nothing, especially to dead people." My hands were now purely black and the darkness slowly crept up my forearms.

No. No more death.

"Whenever you're involved, Kyle, there's death to anyone close to you. You're a curse, just like me."

A curse ... no ... it's not my fault. It can't be my fault. They all trust me, think highly of me. I can't be the reason they keep getting attacked ... but ... I know I am ...

I was so furious that I was shaking. I was completely lost in my own mind. Then I received a notification from another person.

"Can't wait to see you soon! Text me back, I miss you! xoxo." My face relaxed and my grip loosened. I clicked on the message.

"Yeah, can't wait to see you!" I looked up and saw Tonuko's big, antagonizing grin, then my face turned red out of embarrassment.

"The hell are you smiling about, Moody Earth?" I snapped. He chuckled, leaned back in his chair, and rested his hands on his head.

"It's just so funny how she can change your mood that quickly. Relax, don't let whoever you're texting get in your head," Tonuko pointed out with a small chortle. The darkness stayed on my hands so I took a deep breath and calmed myself.

"Yeah, you're right. This kid is just pissing me off," I exhaled. Tonuko thought for a moment, then the grin left his face.

"Plague, I assume?" Tonuko grumbled. I hesitated then nodded. He rolled his eyes then muttered, "Don't worry, we'll beat the shit out of that kid eventually. He can't hide behind BloodShot forever." I smirked and nodded. His words made me dream of the day we would defeat Plague.

The music dimmed as Alex, Cindy, Jax, and Camilla walked to our table. There was a tapping noise through the speakers, then Fallen cleared his throat.

"I hope you're all having a grand old time so far. Now some of you might get a lil' upset! I will announce the names of those who will be headin' on over to B.E.G. for one week: four boys, four girls!" Fallen announced. Cindy and Camilla squealed to each other, and Alex leaned over next to my ear.

"Let's hope they keep us three together, ay?" Alex whispered, making me chuckle and nod. Fallen pulled out a dirty notecard from his suitcoat pocket, then squinted at it.

"Alright youngins, after I announce your names, boys, Foul Odor will move a headlight onto you. Y'know, put ya in the spotlight!" We looked up and saw him sitting in the rafters. Foul smiled and waved then Fallen yelled, "Alrighty, the four boys are-" A light blinded me as he shouted, "Big, bad Kyle Straiter!" There was a round of applause, then another light shown in our direction and,

"Mr. Dead Boy, Tonuko Kuntai!" Tonuko shook his head and laughed as Fallen continued. "The creepy snake boy Rake Clause!"

Rake blushed, then yammered, "How many times do I have to say this? My strength isn't that creepy!" I couldn't help but laugh and Fallen even stopped for a moment to chuckle.

"Finally, the mist man himself, Jaxon Call!" There were disappointed noises from some of the other guys, most notably Alex.

"Man, that's embarrassing. I thought for sure I would get picked!" Alex mumbled. I shrugged as Cindy patted him on the back.

"Don't worry, you still get to meet B.E.G. kids and you get to sleep in your own bed!" Cindy successfully made Alex laugh.

Fallen took a deep breath and smiled again. "Alright, don't let all those cocky boys get too much of the spotlight! Next are the four girls, and first is the flirt of the grade, Scarlett Yalvo!" Scarlett flipped her hair and smirked.

"Well, I guess this means I can show off my beauty to some more boys. Maybe I'll be the talk of the school!" Jessica put an arm on Scarlett's shoulder.

"Please don't embarrass yourself!" she earnestly insisted. Scarlett and Jessica giggled before Fallen continued.

"Next is the shiest person I've ever known, Iris Blavins!" Iris jumped slightly after hearing her name and covered her eyes with her right forearm as the light that was shining on Scarlett moved over to her.

"We have another one of our troublemakers! One of the villain magnets, Cindy Theon!" Fallen shouted, shocking Cindy.

"Congrats Cindy; you get to go to B.E.G.," Alex sighed. Cindy smiled brightly and assured Alex he would still have fun.

"Last, but certainly not least, we have little ol' temper tantrum, Camilla Xavier!" Our eyes widened simultaneously as Jax and Tonuko hollered with laughter. I sunk in my chair, frustrated, and others looked at us with confused expressions.

"Looks like the love triangle continues!" Tonuko spat through his laugher. He pounded on the table and Jax leaned on my shoulder with a face red from his snickers. I felt my phone buzz a few times, clearly a call, so I stood and walked away.

"Don't think I wanted to end up with you either," Camilla sneered as I passed her. I ignored her and made my way through the front doors. I answered my phone as a crisp breeze blew in my face.

"What the hell do you want, Plague?" I asked with annoyance.

"Just checking in on my favorite anti-villain! I've heard about the big B.E.G. and E.H. event going on this mon-!" Plague snickered. I quickly cut him off.

"Don't you fucking dare even think about doing anything. You'll regret it if you do." Plague went silent, then his antagonizing laughter returned.

"I'll regret it ... oh really? Who will make BloodShot and me regret anything?" I squeezed my left fist, and the darkness on my hands slightly bubbled.

"The one you're talking to. I'll kill you with my bare hands when I get the chance, you fucking freak," I furiously remarked. Instead of laughter, Plague went silent again. After a couple of seconds I heard an inaudible yell, some shuffling, and a new person was on the phone.

457

"You'll make us regret it and kill us ... really Kyle? Likely story," BloodShot snarled. My body shook with fear, and I opened my mouth to respond but no noise came out. Before I could stammer a retort, someone took the phone out of my hand. I looked over and watched as Tonuko turned the call to speaker.

"We will make you regret ever messing with us. We're done feeding your pathetic ego; you aren't someone to be afraid of," Tonuko hissed. BloodShot snorted and made a mocking teeth-chattering noise.

"I'm shaking in my boots, Tonuko Kuntai. We weren't planning on invading your little petty playdate with Bade's Egotistical Goons," BloodShot retorted.

Tonuko smirked and shook his head, then muttered menacingly, "Stay in your hideout like a pussy, that's fine by us. Make any move and we'll be sure you regret it. I'll bury you in hell myself." BloodShot began hooting with laughter, but before he could muster another insult Tonuko hung up. Tonuko smacked the phone onto my chest and dropped it, giving me little time to narrowly catch it, then he walked back inside. I leaned against the wall and took a deep breath through my nose and out my mouth.

Why can't they just leave me alone? Why can't I be happy without Tyrant or the Care-Givers ruining everything?

I looked up at the sky, frowning, and watched as the clouds floated around. The sun shown at an angle, creating large shadows around me. I closed my eyes and took another breath, then walked back inside.

The texts and calls ruined my mood and night. I reverted to my anti-socialism from earlier in the year and sat away from everyone. Tonuko told people to leave me alone. After a few hours I was the first to leave the party and I didn't look back. I reached my room and locked the door behind me. I didn't get much sleep that night, or the next, or the next.

Monday:

I hadn't dreamt the past few days, or at least I couldn't remember my dreams. I normally remembered them because they were usually horrific nightmares ... it was hard to not have nightmares when you had a life like mine. I also hadn't eaten much, just a few pieces of fruit and water. I only left my dorm room to train with Fallen and Foul, though I barely talked to them, and I didn't talk to any of my classmates.

When I lifted my head from my pillow, I was hit with a massive head rush. My vision was hazy and my head felt staticky. The static sounded like a familiar aggressive whisper. I held the sides of my head and grimaced, then heard a knock on my door. The static stopped and I walked to the door.

"Kyle, let's go! Class is in five minutes! Don't slack off now, we leave in a week for B.E.G.!" Tonuko shouted through my door as he knocked.

"G- Go on without me! I woke up late!" I responded. I scratched the back of my head. I heard several sets of steps walk away, then the static from earlier returned. I stumbled back and fell on to my bed, then to my knees. I scrunched up on the floor and squeezed my head, sweating profusely and staring wide-eyed at the floor.

"*I can give you more power. Let me,*" it whispered.

N- No ... I can't give in!

I squeezed my eyes shut and gritted my teeth, trying to do whatever I could to resist the demon's presence, to no avail. I felt a warmth spill from my chest and cover my body. My childhood violently flashed before my eyes, then I blinked and everything disappeared. I wiped away a tear that tried to escape my eye, stood and swayed side to side. I felt dizzy. I managed to change and brush my teeth before leaving for school.

I trudged down the path and reached the school building, then made my way to the theatre. When I opened the doors, everyone looked back at me. I saw Fallen standing on the stage with crossed arms while tapping his left foot.

"So, Kyle gets to show up whenever he wants? Is this how you'll act at B.E.G.?" Fallen angrily asked.

I shook my head and answered, "N- No sir." Fallen rubbed his eyes with one hand, took a deep breath, shook his head, and pointed in front of him at some seats.

"Just sit down," he commanded. I sat in the last row behind some advanced students and rubbed my eyes with fists. Something about me felt off, abnormal. The presence of the demon and warm feeling around my body lingered for the next week, subsequently making everything a blur. The only thing I remembered was seeing my first attack with this new power bestowed upon me.

The Dome, Wednesday:

The honors' kids marched into the training facility behind Fallen and I saw a teacher I'd never seen before. His skin was earthy brown and cracked and he had a spiky, nappy afro. He was in good shape, not extremely muscular nor scrawny, and when we entered, he held up a fist.

"Hey there, freshies! Welcome ... to my domain!" the teacher announced, confusing us.

Tonuko asked what we were all thinking, "Uh, who are you?"

The guy smirked and looked up to his right. "I am the new training teacher at E.H.! My name's Monte but call me by my hero name, Loam! I'd say I'm very qualified for this job considering my strength is Measure!"

__Monte Anderson/Testing Hero: Loam, Strength: Measure—he can create highly durable clones out of any substance that show a number measurement at the spot of death. The number scale is one to one hundred, and one hundred has never been reached. Based on research of similar strengths, reaching a power level of one hundred would need a combination of all strength-enhancing powers, and amplifying strengths. The clones' athletic abilities are based on his own.__

"Is that the strength they use in the Hero Olympics?" Alex asked excitedly, clearly fanboying. Loam nodded, then put his hands on his hips and stood tall.

"That's correct! Now ... which one of you kids wants to go first? Who thinks they're strong enough to get double digits?!" Loam yelled in a provocative voice. I took a step forward, but Steven pushed past me and ran up to Loam.

"Easy, I got this!" Steven shouted with a big grin.

"Alright, but before you go, I want everyone to know how this will work. First, you will attack my clone using your strength normally. For example, an attack you would use to start off a battle. Then you will use your power-ups! Ready?!" Loam's enthusiasm matched Steven's, who nodded and hardened his arms. His veins faded to red and morphed into wires, then the wires popped out of his metal skin and swayed in the air.

Loam created a clone out of the concrete floor a dozen feet away, and the clone had an interesting look. Its eyes were small, red dots, its mouth was a zigzag made of darkness that wasn't even connected to its face, its skin was made of concrete, and it maintained the shape of Loam's hair. Steven cracked his shoulder, charged at the clone, and wound up his fists. He punched as hard as he could—Steven always bragged about being ambidextrous—and sent the clone crashing backward. After it hit the far wall, a red text above its head flashed random numbers, then it beeped when a "**2**" was above its head.

"Only a two?! How damn harsh is this thing?!" Steven complained as he turned off his strength.

"Considering this is the same strength as the one used in the Hero Olympics, it is difficult to score high. It's literally impossible to get a score of one hundred. I'd be pleasantly surprised if any of you get a ten, at the very most fifteen. By then end of your high school career, you should all be able to get a twenty. That's the norm for a common hero."

Steven grumbled to himself, then closed his eyes and took a deep breath as Loam's clone returned to its position a dozen feet from us. Steven raised his arms, then thrusted them down as his body transformed into his cyborg form. His red eye locked on the clone as Steven leapt into the air and flung thrusters out of the soles of his feet. His thrusters roared flames, sending Steven flying at the clone. When he was an arms-length away, Steven swung his right foot— using the boosters to pack an extra punch—and kicked the clone in the head, breaking clean through its head. The clone collapsed onto the ground as Steven landed. When he turned around his feet gave off smoke. The meter calculated, then read "**3**."

"Well done, Steven, you went up a number!" Loam clapped. Steven became human again. He walked back to us, unsure if he should be happy that he went up a number or disappointed that his highest score was three. Loam patted him on the back as he passed, then asked, "Where's the little hotshot, Kyle? I want him next!"

With layers of bags under my eyes and a fuzzy head, I trudged out from the group. Loam smiled boldly and shouted, "Got what it takes to beat Steven?" I responded with a shrug, clearly disappointing him. Loam created another clone, then I cracked my knuckles and furrowed my eyebrow.

"Let's just get this over with," I mumbled. When I cracked my last knuckle on my right hand, the yellow mist from my Energy Conversion seeped out of my pores and embers roared on the backs of my hands. I ran up to the clone in the blink of an eye and, while in a crouched position, I swung and punched the clone in the chest. My hand passed through its body and popped out behind its head, then the clone erupted in flames and crumpled to the ground. The meter calculated for a moment, then showed "**8**." Everyone's jaws dropped, including Loam's and Fallen's.

"He already almost tripled your best Steven!" Cora laughed. Steven rolled his eyes with anger.

"Bravo Kyle! If that's your norm, what's your maximum?!" Loam cheered with eagerness as he formed a new clone. I thought about the haunting whispers of the demon and chose not use its power.

"No, that's my best. I'm done," I sighed. I did not convince anyone. Alex raised an eyebrow.

He asked, "What about that darkness that covered your body at Takorain? That was like a power-up!" Others, including Fallen, added their agreement.

"Yeah, Daniel and I saw you training with it. That looked pretty intense!" Jax shouted.

I sighed again and muttered, "Yeah ... you're right." After I turned around, the whisper came back in my right ear.

"Demonstrate our power. Soon, you'll have all I can give you."

I frowned, took a deep breath, and squeezed my fists. I flicked out my fingers, allowing the darkness to erupt

463

from my palms and wrap around my body. It seeped into my skin, and this time, covered to just under my eyes. The sclerae in my eyes glowed once again, and my hair slightly floated. The mist around my body faded to a rich purple, and my flames looked inverted—instead of being mostly red and yellow with black accents, the flames were gray and black with red accents. My flames surrounded my arms in a rope-like shape and stopped about mid-bicep. The only noise heard was the blazing flames. Then, I pounced.

Let's see what kind of power this thing is talking about.

I leapt into the sky and grabbed at the air, making a tight fist. The fires on my right arm exploded into a burning mess as I landed on the ceiling, digging two indents into the roof with my feet. I jumped down at the clone. With a trail of gray fires following me, I soared at it and swung as hard as I could. I hit the clone in the head and followed through toward the ground. The clone's head exploded. I threw the rock that stuck to my fist into the floor, sending a large crack straight ahead from me. The crack exploded into a large crater, and as the debris fell it crushed the rest of the clone's body. I used the falling debris to jump out of the hole, then stood tall while looking down at my result.

Everyone was shocked as the meter from the bottom of the rubble pile glowed "**38**."

Chapter 25
Playdate

I slowly opened my eyes when I heard my alarm buzz for the third time. My stomach hurt and my head was pounding, whether because of how little I'd eaten over the past few weeks or because of my inability to sleep soundly at night was unknown. I unplugged my alarm clock and closed my eyes again.

I do not wanna go to this little meetup thing at B.E.G. Maybe if I just sleep in I'll be allowed to stay here.

However, my clock wasn't the thing that was going to keep me awake.

"Kyle, get your ass up! *I'm about to break this door!*" Fallen yelled, banging on my door and turning the knob. I closed my eyes one more time.

After a few seconds, I sat up and retorted, "Alright, I'm awake old man; *fucking relax!*" Fallen stopped banging, then punched the door one more time.

"You better be ... the train leaves in thirty minutes, Einstein!" Fallen stomped away. Tonuko snickered as he looked at my closed door.

"Aw, the little baby needs his babysitter to wake him up! That is priceless!" Tonuko laughed.

Cindy giggled too as she dragged her suitcase out of her room. Tonuko was already ready to leave. He had a suitcase and was wearing a blue flannel coat over his gray shirt and black joggers. Cindy was dressed for the weather with a sweater and pants topped with her matching fluffy hat and scarf. Alex walked out of his room with a fake smile across his face. "Alex, what's wrong?"

"Nothing, I'm just here to wish you good luck at the big and amazing B.E.G. school! You're just ... so lucky!" Alex clearly lied. Cindy walked over and hugged Alex.

"Aww, Alex, it's okay to be jealous; I would definitely be too! Listen, while we're gone, we need someone to hold down fort here, and that's you! So," she pulled off and looked him straight in the eyes with her confident stare, "we need you to be big and strong and show the B.E.G. kids that they can't walk all over our place!" Alex took a deep breath, stood confidently, and nodded with determination. Tonuko yawned then looked at his watch.

"Let's head downstairs to meet with the others. Kyle should be ready soon ... I hope," Tonuko stated, glancing at my door. Cindy nodded, then the two said their goodbyes to Alex and walked downstairs. Soon after, I walked out of my room with my hastily packed suitcase and disheveled hair. I trudged down the stairs, ruffling my hair with my right hand, then rolled my eyes when I reached the main floor and saw everyone at the counter.

"What took you so long princess?" Jax asked with a smirk on his face. I glared at him as I walked up to the counter, then took out my phone to check the messages I'd received. At the top of the notifications was a text from Ashlyn: "Can't wait to see you today! I'm so excited!"

I couldn't hold back my smile and Rake mocked, "Aww, little lovebird Kyle is gonna be with his girl! So happy for you man!" I put down my phone and groaned.

"The walk is about ten minutes, so we should probably leave now," Scarlett informed us, pointing at the clock hanging by the door. The time was 7:45 a.m., and the train left at 8:00 a.m. We said goodbye to those who were in the lobby, then left for the suburbs. While walking through the gate, Fallen stopped me and grabbed my arm just as he'd done when we'd gone shadowing.

"Listen Kyle, I know how hard you've been working lately, but go have some fun for once! I wanna see a smile on your face and hear about all the friends you made when you get back!" To my surprise, Fallen hugged me tight, then pulled off and looked me in the eyes. "Also, don't get into any more huge fights with villains and get yourself almost killed ... again! Promise me all'a'that?"

"Yeah, I promise. Thanks for everything," I responded with a genuine smile. He smiled too, then waved me off. I caught up with the group and as we walked we passed my house. I stopped and stared at the place. After all these years, I finally recognized how horrible it was. The top-floor windows were shattered and glass coated the porch's roof. There were crumbling tiles on the roof, a large gash down the middle of the front door, cracks in the walls, and holes in the porch floor.

Looking at my childhood home this close, in such detail, brought back so many memories. So many, in fact, that a tear welled in my right eye. I wiped it away with my hand, then felt a comforting touch on my shoulder. Jax gave me a sincere smile and reassured me, "You're past that life. C'mon man, look up! You've got all these friends now and even a girl!" I faked a smile and nodded, then slowly walked away. I wish I had stayed longer ...

We arrived at the train station just as the train pulled in from Takorain. It brought passengers from Takorain to Camby, then would loop around and return to Takorain. Camilla glanced in the train and leaned back on her right foot.

"Isn't this train carrying people from Takorain? Shouldn't the B.E.G. kids going to our school be on it?" she pondered. We agreed. When the doors opened and I saw the person who led the B.E.G. students, my stomach dropped.

He walked past me and purposefully bumped my shoulder, hard, sending me stumbling a couple of steps to the side. "W- Watch where you're walking!" I seethed with a glare. The boy stopped, his white and ocean blue hair glimmered in the light like an open sea, then he glanced at me with a smug grin across his face and shrugged.

"Oh, did I hit you? I didn't even notice ... freak," he snorted. He walked away, along with the rest of the group. I was furious but controlled myself so as to not cause problems.

"Caden," Jax grumbled with a furrowed eyebrow and angry scowl. I walked past him, sighed, then stopped and looked at the train.

"It's fine. He's not worth it," I said before heading toward the train's entrance. We boarded and sat in the seats closest to the doors. The train departed for Takorain a couple of minutes later, and as much as I tried to keep my eyes open, I eventually fell asleep.

When we arrived, I felt a pinch on my arm. I slowly opened my eyes and blinked a few times, then looked over and saw Cindy's worried expression.

"Why have you been so tired lately? Are you sleeping alright at night?" Cindy asked. I nodded, a lie, then stood and exited the train behind Tonuko. The familiar smell of Takorain hit me as soon as I stepped out of the station, and it clearly hit Tonuko as well because he took a deep breath then smiled.

"Back here again! Alright, let's hit it! Fallen told me training should start right away so we can't be late!" Tonuko shouted with his hands on his hips. We walked down the steps of the station and out into the street. We followed Tonuko's lead down the sidewalk, and after a couple of minutes we made it to the front of B.E.G.'s campus. Some of us were nervous and sweating while others beamed with confidence.

"Let's hurry! I can't wait to see the hotties we'll be training with!" Scarlett ordered before strutting up the hill of a pathway. Once I'd gone a few steps, I noticed Iris hadn't moved. I looked back and saw her nervous expression.

"Don't worry, Iris, you're the strongest healer in the nation. You've got nothing to be nervous about," I said trying to lift her mood. Iris nodded but was still hesitant.

"What if I make a bad impression? What if I fail to meet my expectations?" Iris asked. I could see the worry in her eyes, but also a fierce determination.

She's worried about her expectations, just like me ...

I gave Iris a big, closed-mouth smile, then a thumbs up.

"Impossible, that won't happen! Don't worry about the what ifs. Focus on what you'll do!" Iris closed her eyes and clenched her fists, then beamed as she nodded. We caught up to the others and followed them through the extravagant gate. Up ahead, I saw a bunch of kids grouped together.

Xavier turned around, then smirked when he saw Tonuko. "Well, look who we have here: the E.H. kids!" Xavier shouted. Tonuko waved before we reached them, then dapped up Xavier with a grin.

"We gotta deal with you stuck-ups for a week? Oh man!" Tonuko teased. They chuckled then Xavier looked around and pointed at me.

"Don't be hiding in the back of the group Kyle!"

I thought I would laugh or even smile, but I couldn't. Instead, I rolled my eyes and yawned. Then I saw her. Ashlyn pushed through the crowd and hugged me as tight as she could.

"Kyle!" she sang as she squeezed me tighter. She wore the gray sweatshirt I'd given her, which made me blush. As I leaned in to hug her back, I heard snickering from the group in front of me. I sighed and lowered my hand. "Hug. Me. Back," Ashlyn growled, looking at me with her scary eyes. I was shocked and reluctantly hugged her with one arm.

"Y'know I don't do hugs," I muttered with another sigh.

"Don't care! I do!" she argued as she pressed her face into my chest. I quickly stepped back and took a good look at the group of B.E.G. kids. A girl with pointy, fluffy ears and a big, golden tail caught my eye. She had tons of freckles, and the tip of her nose was black.

Is that girl ... a dog?

There was also a girl with a big witch hat, a boy rolling around on wheeled shoes, and a boy with big, wooden earrings and black painted nails. Before I could analyze the others, one of the B.E.G. girls strolled over to Ashlyn and me and sized me up.

"So, you're the one Ashlyn always talks about? Her boyfriend?" She was closer than I expected—considering her height, our noses were almost touching—so I took a step back.

I was surprised by my stutter when I jabbered, "I m-mean, we aren't o- official. Who the h- hell are you?!" The girl smirked, then crossed her arms and took a small step back.

"Oh me? I'm called the mom of the group, mostly by Ashlyn. I'll keep you in check," she declared. Although I'd stuttered, this random girl did not intimidate me whatsoever. I raised my eyebrow, then crossed my arms, mocking her, and rolled my eyes.

"Wow, I'm so scared," I sarcastically remarked. She swiftly took a step forward and reached for my arm. Her move was so predictable that I was able to dodge out of the way, then trip her as she passed me. She fell to the ground, stood back up, and glared at me again.

470

"Touche," she hissed.

"O- Okay kids, don't fight y- yet!" A man who was sweating profusely shouted as he ran to us.

"Teach, there you are," the kid on wheeled shoes said after skirting to a stop next to the man. The teacher nodded slightly, then took a deep breath.

"W- Welcome Eccentric High Students! I am th- the Nervous Hero: Gladiator, also kn- known as the f- freshman honors' teacher at Bade's Exception- ally Gifted!" Gladiator announced with a smile.

"He might be more nervous than me," Iris whispered to Scarlett.

The two giggled as Gladiator continued, "F- First, you will introduce y- yourselves, th- en I will show the Eccentric High students which room they will st- stay in at the freshman dorm!"

"Thank you, Mr. Gladiator," Tonuko said with a bow, expressing his gratitude. Gladiator smiled and looked over at Xavier. Xavier was staring off into space but he snapped out of his daze and nodded.

"R- Right! I'm Xavier Kinder, son of the number-one hero, Puppeteer, and I'm the number-one ranked student in my class," Xavier boasted with a puffed-out chest.

"Are you single?" Scarlett blurted out. This faltered Xavier's cockiness and made him blush.

"W- Well, I'm not looking for anything," Xavier stuttered. Scarlett smiled devilishly, put her hand on her chest, and closed her eyes.

"I'm Scarlett Yalvo, the eighth-ranked student of my class," she proclaimed loudly. The B.E.G. students clapped, then Tonuko spoke up.

"I'm sure you know me, I'm Tonuko Kuntai, the number-one ranked student in our grade. I'm number two in my class." Instead of applause, all the B.E.G. students except Xavier were silent.

"Wait, you're number two in your class? Who's number one?" the boy with wooden earrings asked. He had a slight Japanese accent. My classmates turned to me, so I took a quick breath then introduced myself.

"Uh, yeah, I'm number one. I'm sure you know me as well, I'm Kyle Straiter, and I went to Trinity Plus," I droned. The boy with earrings didn't look impressed. Instead, he whispered to the girl with the witch hat, then the two giggled. For some reason it offended me, so I asked, "Got something to say? Say it to my face then." Jax's eyes widened slightly, and he elbowed my arm as he glanced over at me.

"Kyle, shut up and put your ego away for a second," Jax seethed quietly.

"Oh nothing. It's just ... you know Caden, right?" the boy snorted. I remembered the sparkly haired guy at the station, then nodded with a stern stare.

"Yeah, of fucking course I do," I muttered, making them both laugh.

"Well, anyway, I'm Ryuu Kimura (Ree-ooh Kih-moor-uh). I'm the third strongest of my class, and my strength-" Gladiator looked panicked and swiftly shushed Ryuu.

"D- Don't say your strengths yet! Y- you'll find out wh- what everyone's strengths a- are during the training today!" Gladiator shouted. Ryuu nodded then the witch girl flicked her hat with her right hand, moving it up on her head.

"Hello E.H. kids, I'm Olivia Anders. I'm the fifth-ranked student of my class." Rake jumped a little when Olivia said her ranking, then he pointed at himself with a dumbfounded look.

"Oh hey, I'm the fifth too. I'm Rake Clause." The dog–girl smirked with crossed arms, then looked Rake up and down.

"Well, scale boy," Rake's cheeks turned pink as the girl yelled, "I am Amy Lay! I'm seventh of my class!" During her introduction, Amy maintained eye contact with Rake. Even after she finished, her icy, intimidating stare stayed locked on Rake's eyes, making him feel anxious. I couldn't help but snicker. Before I could tease Rake, Ashlyn introduced herself.

"I'm Ashlyn Gray, the seventh-ranked student of our grade and the second of my class! Nice to meet you!" Ashlyn exclaimed with a bright smile. The girl who'd started an argument with me earlier clapped softly, then stood tall.

"And I am Sophia Amberrose. I'm the sixth of my class!" Sophia announced, shocking me with her rank.

These kids are ranked so high in B.E.G.'s freshman honors' class. It's crazy that they have their number one, two, and three here. I guess we have our one, two, and four so it's not much different. I can't wait to fight them in training.

Jax hesitated, clearly a little embarrassed, then sighed.

"Uh, I'm Jaxon Call, but call me Jax, and my ranking in my class is ... uh ... fourteenth." He rubbed the back of his head and blushed, but then the boy on wheeled shoes skirted over to Jax's side and threw his arm around Jax's shoulder.

"It's all good man, no need to be embarrassed. No one is judging. I'm Tanner Raith and I'm tenth." Tanner's hospitality comforted Jax, who smiled and felt better about himself. All but one of the B.E.G. students had introduced himself; Cindy, Camilla, and Iris were left from the E.H. kids.

"Hello everyone, my name is Connor Bindge! I am the eleventh of my class, and it's a pleasure to meet all of you Eccentric High Students!" Connor shouted boldly while saluting at us. He was very muscular, seemingly natural, and wore a black cutoff, green cargo pants, and black boots.

"Aren't you cold?" Camilla asked, confused by his demeanor. Connor shook his head after lowering his arm.

"Not at all, ma'am. I'm never cold," Connor answered.

So, he has some kind of hot or cold strength that keeps him from being cold. Interesting.

"Anyway, I'm Camilla Xavier. I'm the fourth of my class." Camilla then nudged Cindy, who stood up straight.

"I'm Cindy ... Cindy Theon! I- I'm the sixth of my cl- cl- class!" Cindy stammered. She was clearly embarrassed, and to her gratitude nobody said anything about her stutters. Instead, everyone looked at Iris. Her face was bright red and she was almost frozen.

"U- Uh, I'm I- Iris Blavins. I- I'm," Iris stopped talking and held out a one and a two.

Olivia softly smiled as she said, "Aww, you have no need to be so nervous. You're twelfth?" Iris nodded, then Olivia walked over to Iris and put her arm around her. Olivia's presence reminded me of Skye, and maybe it reminded Iris of Skye as well because she seemed to calm down after Olivia spoke up.

"I- I'm glad that was fast. Now, l- let's head over to the dorms!" Gladiator announced. He turned and started down the path. Connor followed, marching swiftly, while the rest of us trailed. Ryuu stopped after a couple of seconds and waited for me. He stepped in line with Ashlyn and me, and I could see his smirk out of the corner of my eye.

"Caden talks about you sometimes," Ryuu whispered to me. I raised an eyebrow and gritted my teeth.

"What does he say?" I asked, annoyance lingering in my voice. Ryuu attempted to hold in a laugh.

"He talks about how he would put you in your place every day at Trinity!" Ryuu then walked ahead of us and Ashlyn looked at me with worry. I wasn't angry or upset; instead, I was filled with fierce determination.

"Hey, kid!" I yelled, causing Ryuu to turn and start walking backward. I grinned and cockily stated, "I'm gonna beat your ass into the ground during training. Be ready." This caught him off guard. Instead of giving another snarky comment, Ryuu's smile faded to an angry frown. He clenched his jaw, nodded, and turned. I smirked and glanced back at Ashlyn, who was now smiling.

"Of course you'd say that," she giggled. I shrugged and nodded. After a couple of minutes walking through the enormous campus, we made it to the freshman dorms. The outside of the building was a white marbled quartz, like the new dorms being built at E.H., and the inside looked very lavish. The inside smelled like lavender and there was a bigger kitchen, bigger T.V. … everything was bigger than in our dorm.

"This is the freshman dormitory. Y- You will live here for the week you're here. I have the dorm assignments. On the first floor, Iris and R- Rake will join Amy and Olivia! The second floor, T- Tonuko and Camilla will be with Xavier and T- Tanner. On the third, J- Jaxon and Cindy will join Ryuu and Connor. Finally, on the t- top floor, Kyle and Scarlett will be with Ashlyn and Sophia!" I gulped and very slowly looked over at Sophia, who gave me a death stare. I quickly turned back to face the front. "O- Okay students, there are two elevators around the corner, s- so go get settled in your rooms."

I followed Ashlyn into the first elevator, then Scarlett, Sophia, and kids from Jaxon's floor followed. Sophia stood between Ashlyn and me and glared at me out of the corner of her eye.

"I'm going to keep an eye on you. Don't even think about doing anything with her," Sophia whispered. I gulped and nodded; Ashlyn rolled her eyes and sighed loudly.

"I'm my own person Sophia! I want to stand next to Kyle!" Ashlyn yelled. She squeezed past Cindy and Sophia, then stood in the open space next to me. She looked at me with captivating eyes. After the third-floor kids exited the elevator on their floor, Ashlyn leaned in for a kiss. Unexpectedly, Sophia smacked her arm, making Ashlyn sulk as she rubbed where Sophia had slapped.

Soon the elevator dinged and the doors opened. Our floor was very clean and it was bright because of the giant window at the end of the hall. Sophia and Ashlyn strode to their rooms, which were across the hall from one another, then Sophia commanded, "Scarlett, take the room next to Ashlyn, and Kyle, take the one next to me." I strolled over and opened the door and was pleasantly surprised by the luxury of the room. There was a pretty big window, a neatly made bed, a giant bathroom, a walk-in closet, and a desk even bigger than what I had in my E.H. dorm. I closed the door behind me and unpacked. Halfway through emptying my suitcase, I heard the elevator ding. Footsteps came closer then someone knocked on my door. I put down the shirts I was holding, walked to the door, and opened it. Xavier stood in the hall with a serious expression. He stepped into the room without waiting for an invitation.

"Well just walk right in, why don't you?" I grumbled. Xavier leaned on the desk, looked down at the floor, then back at me.

"I have information about the Hero Olympics that I think you'll find pretty interesting." I raised an eyebrow, then waved my hand in a circle in the air, signifying for him to continue. He glanced at the door then stated, "I know how two of the events and the final are going to be set up." My eyes widened. I leaned on my knees, focused.

"Explain," I quickly said.

"The first event is going to be the national favorite Hide-and-Seek, the second event is simply a power measurement of the remaining competitors. I'm unaware of what the third will be, but it should be one to eliminate a lot of people." I nodded as he continued. "The finale is going to be a two's tournament where everyone gets to choose their partner and the final twelve will fight for national rankings. The duo that wins the championship will face off against each other for the top spot."

"That sounds like a challenge. You have to choose someone who's strong, but not so strong that they'll wipe you in a fight," I thought aloud.

Xavier nodded, then offered, "How about you and I partner up? We know we'll make it through all the events, and no one would beat the two of us. You beat Tonuko in ten seconds—it's well known around here—and I held my own against you, so we're easily the strongest here. Tonuko's the only other competitor I can think of, unless certain duos team up well. With my power-up and your strengths, we can make it to the championship and finally have a real fight with nobody interrupting or stopping us." I smirked, raised my arms into the sky, and stretched my back.

"So," I started after finishing my stretch, "that's what this is all about? You want to finally have a full-out battle with me?" Xavier smirked and simply shrugged. "Yeah, sure," I accepted. "I can finally put you in your place. I've been working pretty damn hard on my power-up—it increases my power calculation by thirty on the meter of Loam."

"Damn, increases by thirty? That's pretty good, but I scored thirty-nine several times so I think I'll be just fine," Xavier chuckled. My heart skipped a beat. I suppressed my shock so he wouldn't see it.

He got ... one higher than me? I already had an unheard-of score, so how the hell is Xavier stronger? What the fuck is his power-up?!

Xavier stood, walked to the door, and opened it.

"Train hard; we need to win to face each other. Also, get changed. Gladiator wants us downstairs in five," Xavier concluded as he shut the door. I took a breath, still shocked, but shook it off and walked over to my luggage. I grabbed the same box that I'd had during the shadowing and placed it on my bed. I opened it and smiled brightly.

Here it is: the uniform that describes my character so far.

The sunset on the cutoff and arm sleeve with roaring embers were the first notable pieces of clothing that stuck out.

Chapter 26
B.E.G. Versus E.H.

I opened my door and stood confidently with my chest puffed out and hands on my sides. The breeze coming from the open window at the end of the hall blew through my hair and the strands on my ninja headband. Ashlyn opened her door a couple of seconds after me, and her eyes widened as she stared at me. She blushed, then zoomed over and touched my arms.

"You always surprise me with how big your arms are! You look so hot right now!" Ashlyn exclaimed, causing me to blush.

"Y- Yeah, so do y- you," I stuttered softly. Sophia and Scarlett opened their doors shortly after us. They also had on their hero suits. Sophia wore a black-and-white long-sleeved zip-up jacket and red, tight joggers. Her long hair was tied in a ponytail that reached her lower back. Scarlett wore a pink, long-sleeved crop-top, black leggings, and sneakers. Her hair was in tight curls. Scarlett looked at me as she had Xavier earlier, causing me even more embarrassment.

"Lookin' good, Kyle," she complimented before licking her lips. I gulped and quietly thanked her. Ashlyn was clearly jealous and gave Scarlett an angry glare.

"Yes, my man looks great!" Ashlyn loudly stated. Scarlett giggled. We walked to the elevator and entered. I was hit with the obnoxious smell of three perfumes. Scarlett's was especially potent, and as she leaned closer to me my nostrils burned. Ashlyn was again irked with Scarlett. She grabbed my arm and hugged it tightly to make a statement. The tension in the elevator was thick and I was pretty uncomfortable.

This is literally the worst-case scenario, being on a floor with these three ... I guess at least it's Scarlett instead of Camilla. Scarlett gets a little crazy at times, but she can be chill.

When we reached the bottom floor, I exited first and saw everyone was gathered by the front door, all wearing their hero suits. We all looked like an actual group of heroes.

"We're going to head over to the J- Junction and have a little r- rivalry game! We will play capture the flag, but i- it will be school versus school! Bade's Exceptionally Gifted versus Eccentric High!" Gladiator explained with glee.

"Isn't this a bit unfair?" Ryuu asked. "I mean, we're the top school in the nation and have almost all of our top-ten kids here. They're from some random public school!" I gritted my teeth and opened my mouth to respond, but Tonuko put a hand on my chest and furrowed his eyebrows.

"Yeah, it is unfair. We're gonna beat your asses and you won't have Iris to heal you," Tonuko retorted angrily. Ryuu stopped laughing and gave Tonuko a side-eye, but Tonuko's icy stare didn't let up. The teacher rubbed the back of his bald head and chuckled anxiously.

"C- Come on guys, let's save it f- for the battlefield. Let's get over th- there!" Gladiator pleaded. He led us away from B.E.G.'s campus and into town. We walked past the block where we had fought The Upriser; rebuilding was happening. Seeing the street and stores brought back many horrible memories.

We finally arrived at one of B.E.G.'s famous training grounds: Junction One. The gateway was made of thick, gray concrete and was massive. We entered and followed Gladiator to the first building on the left. When we walked in, we saw a giant screen with many different camera angles that viewed every square inch of the grounds.

"So, where are the flags?" Tanner nonchalantly asked, looking up at one of the cameras that showed a large, blue flag.

"The Eccentric High flag is in the top left of the Junction, and the B.E.G. fl- flag is in the bottom right. I'm n- not going to give any specific advice, bu- but I will say this: it never hurts to d- defend. Also, all power-ups and a-abilities are allowed, just don't kill or cripple anyone," Gladiator responded. He clapped twice and turned around with a smile. "You have five minutes to find your flag, then the game will begin! *Good luck to all and get moving!*" Gladiator shouted, surprising us.

Wow, I didn't think that guy could yell that loud.

We quickly exited the building, and before the groups split I hollered to Ryuu, "Hey, Caden lover, come find me." Ryuu responded with an agitated grimace, then he turned and ran with his classmates. We followed Tonuko and stayed in a group as we ran through the fake city.

"Alright, we should have the most versatile and agile students go for their flag. I suggest we have two defenders. Do you guys agree?" Tonuko shouted.

"Yeah, sounds good! We should keep Iris by the flag along with the two defenders so we can go back to her if we need healing!" Cindy added.

Iris nodded in agreement, then Camilla suggested, "How about Jax and Rake stay back since their strengths are pretty good for defending. Rake's snakes can get multiple eyes around the building, and Jax's smoke can block the B.E.G. kids from getting to certain places!" Rake and Jax looked at each other and nodded, also agreeing.

"Sounds good! We won't let you guys down!" Rake yelled with confidence. We made it to the far corner building that touched the western and northern walls: a large, brick factory. Inside, the blue flag sat in a corner. It was about five or six feet tall. The three defenders ran to the flag and Jax gave us a thumbs up, indicating for us to leave. Once we were outside, a speaker above clicked on.

"The first day of training will now commence. Ready? Begin!"

Before we could run, Scarlett commanded, "Let's split up and avoid combat! We don't need to fight them, just take the flag and go! The more people we can get to their flag at once, the better!" We nodded, then split up and ran. I stayed beside the western wall and planned on following it until I was parallel with the B.E.G. factory.

We have to take out some of their attackers or else we'll be giving Rake and Jax a death sentence. If I use my power-up, I should be able to take out most anyone who challenges me. Xavier will be a struggle though. Should I even use the thing's power? I still can't trust it ...

I sprinted without using Energy Conversion, then I slowed and looked around. I was a bit lost, but I knew that as long as I followed the western wall I would eventually reach the southern wall. From there, I'd follow it to B.E.G.'s factory. I was about to pick up pace again when I heard footsteps to my left. I slowly tiptoed over to the adjacent building, pressed my back against it, and listened intently. The steps grew closer then suddenly stopped. I was confused—deafened by the eerie silence. Ryuu leapt out from behind the building and swung a punch at me with his abnormally large arm, which was covered in emerald-green scales. I threw my arms in front of my face and blocked his attack, but I was pushed back by his sheer strength and slid a few feet.

"Found you!" Ryuu proclaimed. I smirked, then clenched my hands into fists and slid my left foot back.

"You'll regret that for sure!" I retorted. I cracked my knuckles, activating Energy Conversion, and jumped around on the walls of the two buildings. I boosted myself off the building to Ryuu's right, then swung a punch. To my surprise, he grabbed my fist and squeezed hard. A loud crack echoed from my hand. I swung my right leg and kicked Ryuu's chest, sending him sliding until he let go of me. My hand throbbed with pain; I grimaced and held it.

Ryuu tossed a belittling grin my way, then opened his mouth and breathed out a giant cloud of fire. I was able to jump up and over the embers and respond with my own fire attack. I unleashed a powerful blaze on him, torching his body. When the smoke cleared, I saw that Ryuu had sustained little to no damage because he'd blocked my attack with his arms, which were abnormally muscular and covered in scales.

Ryuu Kimura, Strength: Dragon Spirit—with the powers of a dragon—including inhuman strength, scaly arms that act as armor, fire breathing, flight through wings, and a special power: vision increase—he can focus his eyes to such an extreme that he can see the power flowing through a person's blood and their next move. Dragon Spirit is the most sacred strength in Japan.

The skin around Ryuu's eyes visibly cracked, and his pupils morphed into one thick, vertical line, like a lizard. He scanned my body and dodged when I jumped at him. Before I could move again, Ryuu punched down onto my back. I crashed into the ground and let out a yelp. I pushed at the ground, successfully throwing myself into the air, then I used a powerful blast of flames to push myself back. I pummeled into the wall behind me, ignoring the pain in my hand. Ryuu backed off and I used the opportunity to convert more energy, yellow mist seeping out of my pores.

This is it: the finishing blow. I don't even need the demon's power to beat this weakling.

I jumped back and forth between the two buildings faster than the normal eye could see, attempting to thwart Ryuu's vision. His eyes zoomed from side to side, seemingly locked on me. I used his confusion to my advantage and pounced. I pretended to go for a direct punch and he dodged to the side. Then I pushed off the ground and landed a devastating kick to his stomach. He coughed blood onto my leg as he wheezed, he fell then bounced back up. I used his bounce to land another devastating blow. I interlocked my fingers and clobbered my fists into his stomach, sending him backward into a metal fence before he fell face first to the ground. Assuming I'd won, I tried to catch my breath and relax. My stomach dropped when I heard chuckling.

"I guess you are pretty good at combat, but you aren't good enough." Ryuu stood and wiped his mouth. I saw blood pouring from his arm; some of his scales had been torn off when he'd hit the fence. I was appalled.

Dammit, I put everything I had into those hits. How is he acting like he's unscathed? Look at him …! His blood is pouring onto the ground!

Before I could think of a new plan, Ryuu's wings ripped out of his back and he bolted at me faster than I could react. I tried to block his punch but I was too slow and Ryuu landed a blow on my left cheek. As I flew back, I tried to hold in a cough and ended up spitting blood through my teeth. I hit a wall and fell forward. I laid on my stomach, panting, then Ryuu strutted over to me and stepped on my face.

"Where'd that empty threat go?! I thought you were going to beat me to a pulp, you Straiter! I see now why Caden beat you every day; your family and ego put a big target on your back that you can't defend!" Ryuu mocked before putting more pressure on my face. This unleashed the beast within me.

Let's take care of this scum, eh?

The darkness shot out of my palms in countless tentacles. They wrapped around my body and were absorbed into my skin. My hair didn't float this time, but my sclerae glowed as bright as ever. I swiftly gripped Ryuu's ankle and squeezed hard, causing a crack in him similar to the one that occurred in my wrist. He screamed and stepped off my head, then swung a punch at me.

I rolled over and caught his punch with one hand then stood holding his fist. Ryuu's arm shook from the force of pushing my hand. I grabbed his forearm with my left hand and hurled him into the wall behind me. As he crashed, I leapt at his head and swung a powerful attack, but Ryuu managed to use his wings to push himself off his wall and dodge me. I punched the wall, sending a couple of deep cracks up the building, and it collapsed. As the debris fell around me, Ryuu's eyes conveyed true fear.

"Empty threat, eh?" I asked, cracking my right shoulder. The purple mist seeped off my body and gray flames encircled my arms. I held out a hand, letting the embers ignite out at him. By the time the flames dissipated, Ryuu was gone. I took a deep breath and, without disabling off my power-up, I walked to where he'd initially been.

Across the Junction:

Cindy slowly maneuvered through the alleys, trying to lay low and avoid conflict. She heard the collapsing building in the distance, then thought, "*Man, I hope one of the B.E.G. kids was on the receiving end of that.*" She held the handles of her shotguns, keeping them holstered, then heard a buzzing noise quickly approaching from down the block. Before she could react, Tanner swerved around the corner and skidded to a stop, leaving thick, black skid marks on the ground. He had his hands in his pocket, and the bottoms of his shoes were smoking.

"Hey, you're Cindy, right?" Tanner asked, looking her up and down. Cindy didn't respond. Instead, she took out her guns and held them with her fingers off the triggers. "Oh, guns? That's fine. You have to hit the target to do damage with those, right?" Tanner mocked.

"Yeah, and I don't plan on missing," Cindy remarked with a scornful expression. She jumped up and pushed her feet against the wall behind her, then quickly lunged at Tanner. He lifted his right foot, then swung it back and did a half flip into the air. Cindy flew underneath him. While in the air, Tanner grabbed the air and did a handstand on two clear discs the size of his palms. Cindy turned and shot a few rounds at Tanner, but he pushed off the discs, dodging the bullets. Tanner soared through the air, touched the air under his feet, and hardened it. This created two larger discs. When his feet touched them, he zoomed around in the sky.

Tanner Raith, Strength: Hard Zoom—with the touch of his hands, he can willingly harden the oxygen of the surface he imagines, creating discs. He can turn this effect on and off. The discs are as big as he can calculate the circumference or area of the shape. He also can control the speed of anything his hands or feet touch. This is like an on/off switch and the speeds increase or decrease according to how long he keeps the effect going.

Tanner grabbed at the air and created a circle the size of his hand, then he balanced the disc on his left middle finger. As soon as he let go, the disc spun rapidly. Tanner jumped off the disc he was riding, tossed the spinning disc into the air, then flipped over and kicked it toward Cindy. It soared at Cindy, slicing her cheek. Blood spewed out but Cindy ignored the pain and tried to intercept where Tanner was landing. She leapt onto the building and jumped where she expected Tanner to land. Tanner stopped himself by grabbing a disc, swinging around, and speeding up his wheelies.

He skidded across Cindy's arm, embedding deep burns and causing her arms to bleed. Without turning around, Cindy shot at him backward. Two bullets landed on his left calf. She looked back at Tanner, who was still hanging on a disc, then turned and crashed head first into the top of a concrete building. She was knocked out on impact and fell backward toward the ground. Tanner acted quickly, swinging himself up and hopping onto the disc, then soaring downward. He caught Cindy just before she reached the ground then flew to the sky. He slowed to a steady coast, glided back down and placed her on the ground.

"Well, I can't just leave her here. What if she has a concussion or memory loss? I'll bring her to Gladiator, then continue the training," Tanner thought as he looked at Cindy's bleeding head. He picked up Cindy, hopped onto the discs he'd created, and sped into the sky toward Gladiator. Tanner jumped off the discs, letting them fly away, scaled the wall, and hopped to the ground. He walked in through the front door to find Gladiator smiling and rested Cindy on the ground in front of him.

"G- Good job Tanner, a- acting like a true hero. I- I'll take care of her and m- make sure she is alright," Gladiator said. Tanner nodded and road his wheelies out of the building. He put his hands back into his pockets, then drove off back into the battlefield.

East Junction Wall:

Tonuko dragged his hand against the wall as he walked. He closed his eyes and focused on the ground beneath his feet.

Flashback:

"With your Earth powers, you should be able to sense disturbances and vibrations in the area around you, Tonuko. Even if you are number one nationally, you are nowhere near mastering your strength," Fallen scolded with his arms crossed.

Present:

Tonuko took a deep breath and tried thinking of the vibrations of a footstep, the commotion of running. Suddenly, he could feel in the hand he pressed against the wall someone walking. They weren't sneaking around or trying to be light on their feet, but instead strolling as if they didn't care about running into anybody. Tonuko turned to his right to hide behind a wall, then he heard the footsteps approaching. He also heard a humming, a woman's humming.

Olivia hummed softly as she walked between the buildings and the eastern wall. Her floppy, blue hat bounced with each step, and she carried a bizarre, wooden staff. The top of the staff cradled a neon pink crystal, which wasn't as bright or vibrant as Tonuko expected. He laid his foot flat and focused on the space behind Olivia. A few seconds later, a large wave of cement overtook her, causing her to fall backward. Tonuko jumped from behind the wall and slapped his hands on the ground. He formed large pillars of cement that shot out at Olivia, but she managed to stand and dodge them before they made contact.

"So, I get to meet the witch, eh?" Tonuko asked. Olivia grinned, flicked her hat, and shrugged.

"Yes, the witch herself. Seems like I have a chance to quarrel with the number one." As she lifted her left hand white, glowing wisps seeped out of it and floated toward Tonuko. He backed up and gulped.

"What the hell? What kind of power could that be?" Tonuko thought as sweat dripped down the side of his head. He proceeded with caution, taking a few steps to his right to avoid the flying wisps. "Stand down and turn yourself in. This is a fight you can't win," Tonuko threatened as he tensed his fist. Olivia covered her mouth and giggled, then shrugged again.

"Oh, we shall see, yes? Anything is possible," she retorted. Tonuko smirked and stomped his foot. A large wave of spikes charged at Olivia, but she didn't move, completely bewildering Tonuko. The spikes continued moving toward her, but she still stayed put. Tonuko stopped them inches before they reached her. Olivia smiled and looked over from the spikes. "Why stop the spikes? Aren't you trying to win?" she asked in a condescending tone. Tonuko hesitated, leaned forward, and shot the spikes again. Olivia side-stepped and watched as they passed her.

"Is she even taking this seriously? Why is she so calm?" Tonuko thought. Olivia tapped her staff on the ground a couple of times and grinned devilishly.

"Geh Schlafen," she stated as she swayed her hand in the air. Tonuko's body glowed pink. He was extremely tired and struggled to keep his eyelids open. His knees felt weak, then they shook and he fell to the ground. Olivia walked to him and held his face with her right hand, and smiled. "Rest." As Tonuko fell asleep, Olivia dropped his head and strolled away.

Three Blocks Away from B.E.G.'s Flag Factory:

I followed the southern wall until I finally saw B.E.G.'s factory. It was identical to ours, a large, brick building. As I crept forward—expecting Ryuu to jump out at any time—I heard battling to my left. Bricks crumbled and Scarlett screamed so I ran in her direction. Even though I was weary and weak, I pushed forward. After passing a few buildings I saw Camilla and Scarlett in a fight with Connor. His body was made of ice and his fingers were sharpened. He and Camilla flew at each other and he swiped three deep gashes on Camilla's waist.

"What the hell is going on?! Is he that strong that both of you can't beat him?!" I asked, pushing past my exhaustion and running to Scarlett. She looked frantic.

"You don't understand, he's mastered his strength! It's impossible to hit him, he just slides around!" she argued.

Connor slid down the side of a building. The force of his feet touching the ground gave him a boost of speed and he collided into me. We crashed into separate buildings,

489

and I stood before he did. Connor rubbed his head as he slowly stood; I tensed my fist and glared at him.

Alright asshole, I wasn't even fighting you.

I jumped against the broken wall, then lunged forward at Connor. Before I made contact he swiped at me. I pulled my feet out from under me and blasted high-powered flames at his face. They melted the ice on his head. I soared backward and gripped the roof of the nearly collapsed building I'd crashed into earlier. Connor's face was burned and the ice had melted, soaking his hair. He saluted me before skating away toward their factory.

Camilla complained, "The more you let go, the more we have to fight at once at their flag! Have you beaten anyone?!"

I rolled my eyes, lifted myself onto the rooftop, and crouched. "I nearly knocked out the Ryuu kid, but he ran away. They have no healer, so that's going to be two there that are basically crippled. The fuck have you done, huh?" I retorted, glaring back at her. Camilla crossed her arms and rolled her eyes, then huffed and walked toward their factory. I leapt from roof to roof and jumped onto the factory. There was a singular skylight, so I slowly tiptoed over to it and cautiously peered in. I saw Ashlyn and Sophia walking around and Ryuu sitting in a corner. His arms were bandaged and he angrily stared at the ground. I walked to the edge of the roof by Camilla and Scarlett and held up three fingers.

"So, Connor didn't go back to their flag. Does that mean there're going to be five of them at our flag?" Scarlett asked.

"We don't know. Hopefully Cindy and Tonuko took out a couple of them. Otherwise, we'll have to rely on Rake and Jax," Camilla responded with a shrug. The two looked at each other. I was confused but went back to the skyline to look in again. This time, I saw a set of gray eyes look back at me. Then a large pillar of snow shot up and broke through the window. It flew past my face, then crumbled. The pieces fell back into the building.

"Holy shit, that was too close," I whispered, taking a step back.

"Can't hide anymore, Kyle! We know you're there!" Ryuu appeared in front of me before I could respond. His huge, ripped up wings flapped a few times, then he roared a fire breath straight at my face. Though I couldn't dodge it, I was able to throw my arms up to protect myself . Before the fire cleared, I felt motion to my left as Ryuu kicked me hard in the hip. I stumbled to my right and nearly fell off of the building. I steadied myself and balanced on the ledge. Ryuu grabbed me by the neck and held me into the air, my feet hanging off the ledge. I couldn't breathe.

"That power of yours is dangerous, as expected from a monster's son. Maybe disposing of you is a good thing," Ryuu scolded as his eyes sharpened again and he squeezed my neck harder. My head pounded as I repeatedly punched down on his arms, but they didn't budge. "It's time to get rid of your sick bloodline." I wheezed and coughed, and my vision narrowed and became hazy. The light was fading rapidly ...

Suddenly, a pillar of cement came from the roof beneath Ryuu and smacked him in the head. The pillar pushed forward, pummeling Ryuu's body into the roof. He let go of me, but I managed to grab the edge just before I fell. Tonuko ran over and helped me up.

Moments Earlier, East Wall:

Tonuko slowly opened his eyes and looked around, blinking. Olivia was gone, and there were banging and crashing noises all around.

"Dammit ... I got beat so easily. I was too in my head," Tonuko swore as he stood. He raised the street beneath him to see over the towering buildings around him but saw no one. He saw smoke coming from what he assumed were the factories. "I'll head over to their flag. I'd assume we have to have both flags in possession. The more manpower we have getting theirs will be more manpower to stop them from winning." He bent the pillar he was standing on and sent it flying forward, using it for transportation.

After a minute, Tonuko saw B.E.G.'s factory and noticed Ryuu holding me by the neck. When he was close enough, Tonuko leapt onto the factory's roof and attacked Ryuu.

Present:

I caught my breath after a few seconds and thanked Tonuko.

"Thanks, that guy has it out for me." Tonuko looked at Ryuu angrily, then stood.

"Yeah, I can see that," Tonuko furiously muttered. After my breathing steadied, we nodded and hopped into the building. Tonuko scaled down the wall, jumped, and landed squatted. I took one hop off the wall, landed on the ground, stood up straight, and looked around. Scarlett was down, her head bleeding, and Camilla was dodging attacks from Ashlyn and Sophia. Tonuko ran ahead. He bent a large wave that swept Ashlyn from her feet. Before she landed, snow shot from her feet and latched onto the ceiling, allowing her to hang upside down. She swiped both hands at Tonuko, creating two clusters of ice spikes that sped at him. Without much movement, Tonuko created two thick walls that obliterated the ice clusters when they collided.

"Sorry Kyle's girl, but I'm not going easy on you like he would," Tonuko mocked with a grin.

"Don't worry, I didn't plan on going easy on you or him," Ashlyn taunted. She let herself fall from the snow and flipped mid-air, successfully landing on her feet. Behind her, Sophia lowered her shoulder and rammed Camilla into the wall. Camilla cut a flat hand across the air, creating two blades of air that flew at Sophia. Sophia jumped and turned her body horizontal and the blades zoomed past her.

"Dammit, why are you so fucking nimble?!" Camilla exclaimed as her head dripped blood. Sophia snickered.

"Sad thing is, I haven't even activated my strength yet," Sophia taunted. Camilla's eyes widened then filled with rage. Wind encircled her feet and she flew into the air. She swayed her hands in a circular motion, creating two enormous tornadoes beside Sophia and Ashlyn. They were sucked up then shot toward opposite walls.

Without thinking, I sprung up and caught Ashlyn, who was about to crash head first into the wall. I kicked my feet out under me and landed against it. I used my calves and leverage to hold myself up. As I surveyed the damage, I heard a giggle. I looked down and saw Ashlyn still in my arms. My cheeks turned red, then she suggested, "Maybe we shouldn't be gentle with each other. We're supposed to be fighting, y'know?" I dropped her and shrugged.

"Okay."

After landing, Ashlyn ran between Tonuko and Camilla to get Sophia. She had saved herself but was down on one knee. While they were preoccupied, Tonuko ran to get the flag. Before he could reach the flag, a large pillar of snow flew across the room. He ran into it, bent it, and coughed up blood. I used the distraction as an opportunity to soar toward the flag. As I was flying over Tonuko, Ryuu jammed me in the side and I crashed into the wall to my left. Before I could move Ryuu rammed me again, breaking through the wall.

"I'm not- letting you get away," he uttered as he stood over me while breathing heavily. Smoke came from his mouth, he took a deep breath, and exhaled fiercely. A flame roared at me, burning ferociously.

E.H.'s Factory:

Rake crouched and put his finger to the ground. A snake dug through the surface and latched onto his empty knuckle, replacing his missing finger. He looked over at Jax, then gulped.

"We're in big trouble. Four are heading our way," Rake informed Jax, who was equally worried. Jax then took a deep breath, and his expression changed.

"I guess we'll just have to push beyond our limits," Jax replied. Just then, the door flew open. The two turned and stood defensively. Amy peeked around from the side and winked.

"Hey, scaly boy!" she shouted before sticking out her dog tongue. Xavier walked in and sighed.

"Don't play love bird like Kyle and Ashlyn. Let's just get that flag and go," Xavier said with his hands in his pockets and an unbothered look on his face.

"Both schools now have students in the opponents' flag factories! It's a show of whose defense is stronger!" Gladiator announced over the intercoms. Xavier grinned, snorted, and threw out his hands. His soul puppet flew from his body and stood tall in front of him. Amy smiled, showing off her white pointy fangs, then Rake reached for his left hand and ripped off all five of his fingers. When he threw them forward, snakes burrowed into the ground. The entire sequence made Xavier cringe.

"The hell?" Xavier asked, scanning the ground. A dark green liquid flowed throughout Xavier's spirit. It swung its arms to its sides as they thickened and grew larger, and their texture changed to large scales like Ryuu's strength. Jax stepped back, tensed his fists, and looked at Rake. He was extremely focused and within seconds his snakes shot out of the ground and latched onto Xavier's arms and legs. Their fangs seeped deep into his skin, which irked him. He grabbed one of the snakes and squeezed its body, causing Rake severe pain in his knuckle. Rake held his stumpy hand and grimaced, then two others pranced to the doorway.

"Ladies and gentlemen, reinforcements have arrived!" Olivia boldly announced. She and Tanner entered the building just as Xavier shook off the last snake.

He pulled the ropes back then thought, *"This flag is for sure going to get captured, so might as well go all out while I can."* His soul puppet covered his body instead of being absorbed back into him and the ropes vanished.

A layer of ice covered the ghost's already scaly body, then Xavier yelled, *"Ghostly Takeover, Frozen Era!"* His fingers sharpened as Xavier skated at Jax and Rake. He jumped over Rake, stabbing him in the shoulder as he passed, then stopped himself from hitting the wall. Rake grabbed his left shoulder, jumped forward, and turned around. Jax breathed out his commanding air, sending a cloud toward Xavier. The smoke stuck to his face. Holding his breath, Xavier blindly swung. He eventually gasped for air and breathed in the smoke. His eyes tinted red, he slid backward and bumped into the wall.

"So, a controlling strength, hmm?" Olivia asked, touching her bottom lip with one finger and slightly smiling. She flipped her staff between her hands and stabbed it into the ground. The pink crystal on top glowed, and the same wisps from earlier flew from the crystal to her hand. Tanner kicked a high-speed spinning disc onto his finger and leaned back on his right foot.

"With three of us versus one Xavier, this will be a piece of cake," he nonchalantly stated.

"Yeah, cake!" Amy barked as her nails grew longer and sharper. She focused her eyes, got down on all fours, and swiftly ran at the trio. Xavier pushed past Jax and Rake, a small flame ignited in the transparent throat of his puppet, then he opened both mouths and roared the embers at Amy. She leapt over the flame, landed on Rake, and tackled him to the ground. They rolled around and, after a struggle, she sat on his stomach. "I got you, snake boy!" Rake swung one arm, but Amy counter attacked and held it down. He then swung his nub, but she did the same.

"She clearly has that one covered, so let's just take care of that controlling guy," Tanner observed. He created another disc and spun it on his finger as Olivia picked up her staff, giggled, and stepped forward. Meanwhile, Tanner sped up his wheelies and zoomed around the room so fast that Jax couldn't keep up. Jax looked around while Xavier stayed focused on one spot, then he randomly punched forward at the air. Before Jax could think about how stupid it looked, the end of Xavier's punch landed on Tanner's face.

"Oh, shit. Nice hit," Jax complimented, surprisingly impressed. "Get him out of here, why don't ya?" Jax put his hands in his pocket and watched as transparent, ripped up wings flapped out of Xavier's back. Xavier launched himself at Tanner and dragged him out of the building. Jax smirked watching them leave then focused on the witch heading toward him. She held out her hand, letting the wisps float around Jax's face. Each wisp had a small trail following it, leaving Jax in slight awe at the beauty of them.

"Sich Verlieben," Olivia spoke. The wisps sped up, so Jax covered his mouth.

"*I don't know what language this girl is speaking, but I'd assume her strength has something to do with these things. I can't breathe them in,*" Jax thought. He kept one hand over his mouth and jumped back, then grabbed an army switchblade from his costume's belt. He flicked the blade out, tossed it in the air, and caught it backward.

Olivia licked her lips and implored, "You're quite the little genius, aren't you? You're the first of your peers to discover the basics of my strength, little boy." Olivia dashed toward him with her staff in her right hand. She held the crystal in the sunlight, allowing the light to reflect off the crystal and into Jax's eye. He closed his eye, limiting his vision, and Olivia spun her staff in her hands then swung the butt of it at Jax. He stopped the attack using his knife, then squeezed his switchblade's handle harder.

"Crap, I can't hold my breath forever. Even if my strength expands my lungs, I'm still not strong enough to beat this girl without oxygen. I need to get a puff out. How can I without opening my mouth?" he thought. He ripped his knife from the staff and swung again. This time, Olivia stopped him at his forearm with her staff.

She grinned, "Seems like you're trying to strategize. I can't let that brain work; you might figure me out." She pushed against Jax's forearm and jumped over him, then pulled back. This shoved Jax's hand into his face, throwing off his focus, and he finally gasped for air.

"Nice one Livvy!" Amy cheered while still restraining Rake. He squirmed to get loose, to no avail. As the effects of Olivia's spell manifested, Jax's stare turned blank and he blushed. He stared into her eyes yet didn't say a word.

"Look at this adorable little perm. I'd assume it was done recently. Really suits you, Jaxy-boy," Olivia simpered while touching his hair.

"What is wrong with you horny bastards?!" Rake spat, continuing to squirm. Jax laid his head in Olivia's lap and they heard a loud bang outside.

"Dammit," Rake sulked as he thought, *"that's it. We're toast."* Xavier and Tanner raced back into the building and grinned at the scene. Tanner navigated on his wheelies and grabbed the flag from behind everyone. He spun it in his palm and gripped it tightly.

"Let's bring this back so we can end this, eh?" Tanner suggested, a smirk on his face. Olivia continued caressing Jax's hair and shook her head.

497

"Go on without me. I'll keep this one company," she smiled. Jax still had a love-filled expression, and Rake was shimmying under Amy.

"And I'll watch this guy!" Amy yelled. Rake sighed and stopped struggling. "Finally!" Amy nagged, "It seemed like you thought you still had a chance!" Her tail wagged and her big eyes stared into Rake's.

"How the hell are you so strong? Aren't you a dog?" he asked in a biting tone. Amy sat up straight and proudly pointed at her chest.

"Why, yes, I am! I'm quite the strong pup!" she shouted boldly.

Amy Lay, Strength: Domestic—with all abilities of a dog—including super speed while on all fours, sonic hearing, super sniffing, an advanced sense of direction even in unknown areas—she can increase strength in her legs and can gradually lift others' moods over a twenty-minute period.

"I can tell. Can you maybe get off me since there's no point in me fighting anymore?" Rake pleaded. Amy shook her head and crossed her arms.

"Nope! I'm not getting up until it's announced that we won!"

The snakes that Xavier had shaken off finally made their way to Rake's hand, crawled onto it, and morphed back into fingers. Amy watched the transformation and exclaimed, "Your strength is so cool! Does it hurt?" Rake's eyes slightly lit up as he shook his head.

"No, just gives me a sort of aching feeling after the snakes are detached for too long. You're actually- the first person to not say my strength is creepy," Rake answered. Amy looked at him with a raised eyebrow.

"Why would people think your strength is creepy? Have they seen some of the other ones?!" she questioned.

As they bonded, Olivia glanced at them and grinned. "Aww, look at those two cuties," she tittered. As she finished her sentence, a static noise came over the intercoms.

"X- Xavier and Tanner have acquired E- Eccentric High's Flag!" Gladiator announced proudly.

Chapter 27
The True Number One

I quickly rolled over and nearly dodged the flames, but my arm was caught in the embers. The burning pain was immeasurable. I tried to hop up onto my feet, but Ryuu punched me down again with a rage-filled expression on his face.

Why the hell is this kid so mad at me?!

"I'll make you pay; your bloodline will never see the future!" he screeched before stabbing at me with his sharp claws. I threw my left arm up and blocked the attack by taking puncture wounds to my forearm, then my left eye began to swell.

"Wh- What do you mean you'll make me pay?! I just met you ... what could I have done?!" I panted with slight anger. My fury dwindled when we locked eyes. His look softened, and I could see the pain in his eyes. He quickly shut his eyes and teardrops spilled out on me, then he swung another punch. I caught his fist with two hands but struggled to hold him back. Ryuu ripped his fist out of my grasp. I took the opportunity to use my last bit of energy to shoot myself onto the roof. Ryuu flapped his wings to bring himself to the roof then charged at me.

"*Why?!*" Ryuu flew at me and threw another punch. After I parried it, he kicked me in the side. I barely stayed on my feet. "*Why is she gone ... because of your monstrous family?!*" Tears flowed down his cheeks. When I looked at Ryuu, I saw the most painful, miserable, despondent expression I'd ever seen. He lowered his fists and let his arms drop to his sides, leaving me dumbfounded.

"Wh- What are yo-"

"If your devil father didn't exist," Ryuu interrupted, "she wouldn't be gone. I'd be studying with her all the time, like we planned." I was still confused and stared back at his agony-filled face. Ryuu looked down, creating a shadow over his eyes so I couldn't see them. I could tell his jaw was clenched and shaking and was at a loss of words. Ryuu finally erupted, "If your dumbass family never existed ... *my sister would still be alive!*" He looked even more miserable, and the pain in his eyes felt like a bullet straight to the heart.

Flashback in Kyle's Eyes, Eight Years Ago:

Ryuu rubbed his eye as he trudged downstairs, dragging a large, plush dragon in his other hand. He looked around the dark living room, then asked, "Mommy, Daddy, Akemi? Where are you?" Ryuu wandered around the main floor and noticed the T.V. was on. He excitedly scurried over to it and sat on the floor, watching the news channel.

"Reporting live from a horrible scene of pure violence! Hero duo Dragonair and their hero-in-training daughter, Akemi Kimura, are the last heroes standing in a faceoff with the man himself! Tyrant's disciples are down, leaving just him against the heroes!" The woman newscaster shouted into her microphone. Tyrant stood calmly, licked his blood off his lips, and smirked, then picked up one of David's handguns that had dropped. Tyrant cocked the pistol and pointed it at Ryuu's mother.

"Now, now, let's all take a moment to relax! No need for ... hasty decisions, eh?" Tyrant mocked as he shot a bullet at her. A butterfly zoomed in front of Ryuu's mother and caught the bullet in its wings. Akemi reached her hand out, creating more butterflies out of thin air, and sent them toward Tyrant. His expression changed from glee to annoyance, and he turned to face Akemi. Ryuu stood and punched the air, still holding his plushie in one hand.

"Yeah, come on, Akemi! Take him down!" Ryuu cheered happily. Ryuu's father and mother charged at Tyrant—his father had Dragon Spirit as well—and Ryuu's eyes lit up as he watched his family fight for others. Tyrant leapt over the two heroes and sped at Akemi. She stepped forward to punch him, but he ducked under her attack and led with his elbow straight into her stomach. She coughed and her eyes widened. Before she could react, Tyrant grabbed her arm and pulled her toward him, then wrapped his right arm around her throat.

"Tyrant has a hold on the young shadow, Akemi. Hopefully she can escape his grasp!" the newscaster screamed. Ryuu's sparkling smile faded. His eyes grew wider as he stared at the screen. The camera zoomed in on Tyrant and, as it did, he flexed his arm, effectively choking Akemi.

"Let go of my daughter!" Ryuu's father screamed before breathing out a large cloud of fire at Tyrant. Tyrant dragged Akemi by her throat and dodged the duo. Tyrant ran and shot at the duo. Unsurprisingly, his aim was scarily accurate and both were shot in their legs. Ryuu's father crumbled to a knee, and his mother fell backward, unconscious. Tears filled Ryuu's father's eyes and covered his cheeks as he clenched his jaw.

"Kill me, *I don't care!* Leave my daughter alone! Please, *let her go!"* Ryuu's father painfully pleaded. He joined the other crippled heroes in the area, forced to watch as Tyrant pressed the gun on Akemi's head. Ryuu's father's knee gave out, leaving him on the ground near HotSauce's dead body. Butterflies swarmed Tyrant's head. He moved the gun and angrily swatted at the insects. Tyrant changed his grip and, instead of using his arm, he grabbed Akemi's throat with his left hand and raised her toward the sky. She clawed and punched at his arm. She swung at his stomach but Tyrant's strong grasp on her remained. The butterflies vanished, most likely from her lack of oxygen, then Tyrant placed the barrel of the gun on her forehead. Fear was evident in her eyes as she stopped struggling.

"N- No, it can't end ... R-Ryuu," Akemi gasped. Tears streamed down Ryuu's face as he watched Tyrant smirk and stare into Akemi's eyes. Then ... Tyrant pulled the trigger. Ryuu covered his eyes and looked away but heard four more gunshots. Blood splattered over Tyrant's face and arm. He dropped Akemi's lifeless body onto the ground and cackled loudly.

"Tyrant has just brutally murdered the student shadow, Akemi Kimura! The monster himself has single-handedly murdered five heroes and countless civilians. This truly is the doomsday he warned us about! HotSauce is dead, Counter is dead, Dan-J is dead, Flint is dead!" the newscaster screeched with horror.

To Ryuu, the world was moving in slow motion.

He stared wide-eyed at the T.V. screen, his cheeks caked with tears.

His plush slipped out of his hand and fell to the ground as the newscaster screamed, "Akemi Kimura is dead!" The tears continued but Ryuu made no noise. Boogers dripped from his nose, mixing with his tears and sweat.

He was filled with agonizing astonishment, and he could only make slight gasping noises, but then he screeched, "*AKEMI!*"

Present:

I was now on all fours and held my head as I smashed it into the roof, crying uncontrollably.

"*AKEMI!*" I screamed in a distraught, heartbroken tone, similar to what seven-year-old Ryuu would have used. Tears and blood dripped from my face as I continued bawling. Ryuu looked up at the sky, dropped to his knees, and silently cried remembering his sister's brutal death.

Kyle Straiter, Strength Two: Attachment—along with being able to talk to others' consciousnesses in his mind dimension, he can experience a tight bond with somebody's past memories. If he feels enough overwhelming emotion and pain, physical or mental, he can feel and see morally distressing actions from the past, and feel every ounce of pain, anger, sadness, all emotions from the person's point of view.

After crying and feeling the pain that I'd felt while watching my mother's dead body disappear, I forced myself to stand and walk over to Ryuu. While he looked down at his knees, I reached a hand in front of his face. He didn't move for a moment but eventually took my hand and stood. Without hesitation I hugged him, letting the darkness fade from my body. He clenched his jaw, looked dishearteningly into the sky, and hugged me back.

"Tyrant will pay for all he's done. Don't worry, *I'm going to kill him,*" I sinisterly muttered. Ryuu's scales flipped back into his skin, and he sighed.

"Yeah," Ryuu agreed, "we'll take him down." We shared this tender moment for a few more seconds, then silently agreed to split ways. Ryuu walked to the edge of the building and sat down, looking over the city of Takorain. I went the opposite way and jumped off the side of the building. The fall was bigger than I expected. When I reached the ground, I collapsed onto my back. I panted as I looked into the sky. My head throbbed with pain and I passed out from exhaustion.

Inside the Flag Factory:

The message had just sounded that Xavier and Tanner acquired the flag, so Tonuko looked over at the entrance and walked up to Camilla.

"You have to take these two down on your own. I'll intercept Tanner and Xavier. We can't let them get that flag in here or else it's over for us," Tonuko informed Camilla, who responded with a look of disbelief.

"You think I can take these two on alone and you can solo those two?! We don't have nearly the advanced experience with our strengths as these B.E.G. kids do!" Camilla argued.

Tonuko quickly shouted back, "Yeah, well, it's all we've got! Jax and Rake are clearly down, Iris is hidden away—not that she would be good for fighting—Kyle is involved with Ryuu, Scarlett is down, and Cindy is M.I.A. We're the last ones left; this is all we can do!" Camilla's anger softened when she saw Tonuko's serious, frantic expression, and she nodded. Tonuko ran out of the building, leaving her to face the girls.

Once Tonuko reached outside, he used the ground to lift himself into the sky so he could get a better view of where Xavier and Tanner were. He squinted and looked around, then saw a spec coming toward him. As it grew bigger, he saw it was Xavier and Tanner riding one of Tanner's discs. They were moving so fast, though, that before Tonuko could react they collided into him, sending them all barreling to the ground. Xavier landed on his feet, Tanner used several discs to swing down safely, and Tonuko hit the ground hard but immediately jumped back to his feet. Tanner stood with his hands in his pockets while Xavier and Tonuko stood low with their arms out and ready.

"Looks like we have the pleasure of fighting the national number one," Tanner noted, barley lifting his eyelids past his pupils. Tonuko bawled his fists as Xavier glanced to his left and saw my unconscious body.

"Looks like Ryuu took him out, or he took himself out. Either way, that makes things a little easier for us," Xavier observed. He looked back at Tonuko and activated his power-up again. "*Ghostly Takeover, Snowy Absorption!*" Xavier's soul puppet had a mixture of red and snow-white flowing through its body, like a candy cane, and its fingertips were covered in cracks. Tanner sighed as he held out his hand, letting Xavier touch it with one finger. A red mist poured out of Tanner's hand and into Xavier, then Tanner's legs shook and gave out after a few seconds.

Tanner looked as if he was on the brink of unconsciousness, while Xavier looked as energetic as ever.

"This is it. Who's the real number one?" Tonuko asked. Xavier grinned in response, dropped the flag, and bolted at Tonuko. He retaliated by creating a wall and lifting sections of the street so he could hop over the wall. Tonuko punched down at Xavier's back. Xavier stopped running and a large pillar of snow shot out of his back and hit Tonuko in the stomach. Tonuko coughed as the pillar pushed into him, smashing him into the building behind Xavier. The snow crumpled apart. Tonuko leapt to the ground then swiped his hand, creating dozens of spikes around them. He reinforced his trap with extra walls and pushed our flag away in the process.

"You baited me into the middle of the intersection so you could create a cage around us. As expected from the number one: smart and strong," Xavier complimented with a smile. Tonuko smirked. To his surprise, Xavier seemed to teleport behind him and punched him in the back of the head. Xavier then teleported again and kicked Tonuko in the side, sending him flying into the first wall he had created.

"*What the hell, is this from that red mist? Dammit, if Kyle could almost beat him, then I sure as hell can!*" Tonuko thought. He raised cement from the ground and covered his hands with it. When Xavier disappeared again, Tonuko focused on the vibrations under his feet and grabbed to his right with both hands. He clasped onto Xavier's calf, spun around, and threw Xavier into the farthest wall. Xavier spat blood and yelped as he made contact, but Tonuko wasted no time and shot himself forward using a pillar as a boost. He swung two punches. Just before they hit Xavier, he teleported again. All of a sudden, Tonuko soared into the ground. His body bounced up as he wheezed. Xavier brushed a finger against Tonuko's arm, sucking up a large red mist that made Tonuko extremely tired. Xavier then punched Tonuko in the side, sending him soaring into the wall in front of the factory. Tonuko crashed through the cage wall and its spikes and through the factory wall.

"F- Finally ... that guy is tough. If Sophia wasn't around, there's no way I would have won," Xavier stuttered as he absorbed his puppet again. He stumbled to his left, then caught himself on a wall and stood up straight again. "My power takes so much out of me. Using three strengths at once ... it's so difficult." He looked over at me, then walked back to the blue flag and picked it up. Xavier trudge over to the hole in the cage he had just made using Tonuko's body and walked inside.

Move

I slowly opened my eyes and looked up. Everything was blurry, but I could see three massive walls, a hole in the factory, and Tonuko laying on the ground, unconscious. I glanced to my left and saw a broken window, then slowly got up and looked inside. Camilla was beaten and had passed out. Sophia rested face down, and Ashlyn panted, sitting against a wall near the B.E.G. flag. I saw Xavier limping toward the flag area, which was untouched, and my eyes widened. I quickly lifted my arm toward the window. A sharp pain shot down my arm, but I ignored it and rested my wrist on the windowsill. When Xavier trudged past, I shot out a massive burst of flames. Xavier looked over with shock in his eyes, then the flames engulfed him.

"G- Got ... Got him," I stuttered. My left eye was swollen shut at this point and I struggled to keep my right one open. I crawled through the broken window, cutting my arms and legs, then I fell onto the factory floor. I took a couple of seconds to stand then trudged toward Xavier. He was face down on the ground, burned and unconscious. I limped over to their flag, grabbed it, and picked up ours on the way out. I glanced back at Ashlyn and a small flame burned in my pupil. Ashlyn took a deep breath, exhaled, and looked down. I could tell she wouldn't fight.

I just ... need to get to Iris. If only there was a way I could talk to her.

After exiting the building, my ears filled with the sound of static. I stumbled to my right then fell on to the ground. After blinking, the environment changed to my mind space, and in front of me was Iris. She looked extremely scared and confused.

"Iris, you have to meet up with me! I have their flag and ours, so if you can heal me, we can win this!"

Iris closed her eyes, tensed her fist, and nodded.

"I'll try, but there're two girls guarding our factory!" she yelled. "The witch and the dog took out Jaxon and Rake with ease, and now they're sitting by our flag area!" I shrugged and smiled.

"I know you can escape successfully; I believe in you. We'll meet on the east wall of the Junction, maybe the north if I have enough energy."

Iris smiled back and nodded, then we faded. I blinked a couple of times, a bit more awake, and looked around to make sure nobody else was conscious. I remembered that Connor was M.I.A., which made me cautious. I converted the last bit of energy I had into speed and ran down the east wall.

I can afford to pass out as long as I'm against this wall. Iris can heal me when she finds me.

I sped down the wall and surprisingly reached the corner in no time. However, when I turned to run down the northern wall, I tripped over my own foot and fell to the ground. I hit my head when I landed, making my vision narrowed and hazy. I looked up then down the northern wall. Before I fell unconscious again I whispered, "C'mon Iris, you can do this." My eyes closed. Thankfully, they slowly opened after a couple of minutes, and I saw Iris, still very frightened and stressed, healing me.

"I snuck out and got here as quickly as I could. It looks like no one else got to you before me," Iris nervously informed. I smiled and took a deep breath.

"You're amazing, Iris, thank you for this healing." Once she finished, I slowly sat up and cracked the shoulder that had previously hurt. "Now that I'm all healed, this'll be a piece of cake." Iris and I both stood. I suggested, "Maybe you should make your way over to B.E.G.'s flag factory and start healing people. In case you get there before we win, I'd say heal our classmates first then help the others." Iris nodded in agreement, then ran down the east wall. I used my newfound energy as a boost and zapped down the wall. Moments later, I reached our factory, leapt onto the roof, and quietly tiptoed over to the skylight. I peaked in cautiously and saw Olivia stroking Jax's hair and Amy immobilizing Rake. I backed away and strategized.

As long as I make it into the flag zone, we win. I don't need to fight them, so if I break the wall next to the zone and jump in, it'll be super easy!

I walked to the edge of the roof, jumped down, and scaled the western wall. I made it to the ground, wound up a punch, and swung at the wall as hard as I could. I annihilated half the wall. It crumbled as I ran in toward the zone. I nearly reached it but, to my surprise, Amy was ready for me.

"Sorry Ashlyn's man, but you aren't winning that easily!" she shouted as she lunged at me. Amy jumped onto my shoulders and scratched my face with her long claws.

"Yes, the announcement made it clear you were coming toward us. Also, when your healer escaped, it was obvious what your plan was," Olivia added, sending her wisps and Jax's smoke toward my face. They swarmed my head and I was forced to hold my breath. I could barely see through the commanding smoke, so I closed my eyes and used my other senses. I reached up and grabbed Amy's face. She bit my hand but I ignored the pain and smashed her head into the ground, knocking her out. After that, I breathed out of my nose, making sure not to breathe in. I held out my hand in the direction where Olivia had been earlier. Embers danced in my fingers, then blazed out toward Olivia and Jax. She grabbed Jax's lifeless body and dodged, then threw him at me. I felt the wind of the oncoming body and caught him, then let Jax fall to the ground. He hit his head and fell unconscious, which caused his smoke to dissipate.

Olivia was visibly frustrated and cast, "Geh Schlafen." I raised an eyebrow, shrugged, and ran in the direction of her voice. She swung her staff. When I heard the swooping sound, I jumped, flipping over it and her. I then swung my foot and kicked her in the back of the head. As Olivia's hat flew off, I managed to grab her right arm and pull it back against her body. I opened one eye and saw the wisps were gone, so I gasped for air.

"Make a move- and I break your arm," I stated, pulling a little harder.

"Y- You win. I forfeit," Olivia stuttered. I let go of her arm, walked to where Amy had passed out, and picked up the flags. I tossed them into the zone—E.H. claimed the win.

"O- Oh my goodness, Kyle wins it f- for Eccentric High! What a deficit to come back from!" Gladiator announced, shocked. Even though I was happy to beat B.E.G. and show them who I was, I didn't smile. I walked past Olivia, stopped behind her, and looked out through the factory's large hole.

"I assume you and Ryuu are good friends since you were whispering about me. Was he close to his sister?" I asked. Olivia still looked shocked, but snapped out of her daze and glanced over at me.

"Y- Yeah, he was very close to her. They moved here from Japan when she was invited to attend B.E.G. She taught him English," Olivia responded. I grunted and walked out of the factory in the direction of the Junction entrance. Olivia looked down at her hat, stared at it, then picked it up. "He beat Amy and me while holding his breath and keeping his eyes closed." She watched me walking away and thought, *"Just what is he?"*

I maneuvered through the streets of the Junction. I was very upset as I thought of Ryuu's tragedy. It replayed in my head ... the image of her being shot imprinted into my brain. Even though I didn't know her, I felt like shit.

Imagine how Ryuu feels, watching his sister be brutally murdered ... then seeing the son of the man who did it.

I clenched my jaw and squeezed my fists hard, making the calluses on my hands burn. My eyes changed from upset to completely furious. I thought of my mother in my arms, Kate's back, Tonuko's last breath, Hazel chained to a wall, Ryuu's sister ... all people who were hurt because of Tyrant ruling the villain society. I walked next to one of the buildings and punched the wall as hard as I could. A deep crack shot up the bricks to the top but the building didn't collapse this time. It did cause the ground to rumble though. I put my hand down to my side and saw my knuckles split open and bleeding.

I'm gonna kill you ... for everything you've done to everyone.

I continued walking, ignoring the pain in my hand, and reached the Junction's entrance. Soon after, Rake and Olivia came from behind a building carrying Amy and Jax. Everyone else was already there, including Cindy and Connor, who the students had deemed M.I.A.

"C- Congrats Eccentric High on beating m- my students! The M- M.V.P. of this match is ... obviously M- Mr. Kyle Straiter!" Gladiator announced. Olivia looked down at my bleeding knuckles, confused, then joined everyone in clapping. My scornful expression didn't let up. As Gladiator stated, "We'll meet in the classroom to review film from this training session," I left the Junction. I marched down the street back to the school and passed civilians ridiculing me. I bumped into a girl about my age who had her back to the street while cleaning windows. As I stumbled, her face smushed into the glass. She turned, confused, yet I continued walking and didn't bother to apologize.

"Oh my gosh, I'm so sorry! I don't know why he's acting like this, but he's very angry right now!" Ashlyn, who'd been trailing behind me, apologized to the girl.

"Oh, don't worry about it! It was just an accident!" The girl smiled and looked at me as I stomped away. Her face grew concerned, "That's the son of Tyrant, isn't it?" Ashlyn was surprised by this question and merely nodded. The girl sighed and returned to cleaning the window.

After a short walk, I reached the front of the school. I stopped and waited for everyone else. I ignored Ashlyn when she asked what was wrong. After her, Ryuu arrived. He strolled past me, not glancing my way, and continued toward the school. The others came in a group, some of whom had already been healed.

Class went quickly since it was a brief review of the major fights. We discussed what decisions could have been made to alter the outcomes of fights, and Ryuu and I were scolded for our dangerous behavior. Although a couple of people asked him and me what we'd talked about, neither of us answered. While Olivia knew the basics, only we knew the true depths of our discussion—not verbally, but emotionally.

Three Hours Later, B.E.G. Dorms:

Since the event had been so successful and considering how many injuries had occurred, Gladiator gave us the rest of the day off. As soon as class was dismissed, I

512

went to the dorms and locked myself in my room. Sitting in the middle of my room, I meditated yet didn't feel relaxed. Every few minutes, I saw flashes of the bloodied bodies I'd seen over the past few months. It made me furious. My phone buzzed, then buzzed again, and again. I knew who was calling me, and at this point, I was happy he was.

"Kyle, so glad you can talk!" Plague shouted. I didn't respond, I just stared at my desk. I could sense his hesitation during my silence, then he said, "Well, uh ... how is your playdate going with those stuck-up brats? We know about your little girlfr-"

"Put Tyrant on the line," I stated swiftly.

I heard Plague stutter a couple of times, then he spat out, "What?! Why do you want me to get him? Can't you call him on your-"

"Did I fucking stutter? Put Tyrant on the line, now." I heard a small noise from Plague, then a lot of rustling.

"Mr. Tyrant, your son wants you!" Plague distantly yelled. I heard loud footsteps echoing throughout whatever building they were in, then someone picked up the phone.

"What do you want?" Tyrant asked in a low mutter. I squeezed my phone and clenched my jaw when I heard his voice, and the darkness slowly seeped out of the dots on my palms.

"Akemi. Akemi Kimura," I grumbled.

"Hmm? Did you ask for me to say a name? Quit wasting me ti-!"

"Do you know Akemi Kimura?" I interrupted. Tyrant's tone changed from annoyance to a slight glee as he chuckled.

"Of course I know Akemi. She was such a pretty and promising young lady; it's such a shame she is no longer with us though," Tyrant revealed, causing me great rage. I

513

squeezed my left hand, sending a sharp pain down my knuckles.

I growled, "You're the reason she's gone. You killed her in cold blood the same day you killed HotSauce. It was the same battle ... in front of her parents and Ryuu."

"Yes, it was quite the bloody scene that day. I had no idea you knew her brother. I guess it would make sense that you two would have met at some point since he now goes to Bade's. I had no choice but to kill her, she was getting in the way," Tyrant replied with a sigh. I couldn't believe he was taking it so lightly.

You truly are fucking heartless.

"You ruined his life ... all for your stupid ego! It's your fault Kate won't be able to be a hero, it's your fault Tonuko almost died because you caused people to rise up against our society, and it's your fault my mom is fucking dead!" I yelled in a whisper, trying to make sure no one else heard me.

I can only imagine the uproar it would cause if people knew I was on a phone call with Tyrant.

"Kyle, listen to yourself! For fucks sake ... none of that is my fault! The Kate girl was crippled by the infamous kidnapping duo, not by me! Tonuko was almost killed by a psychotic man who wanted to act out his weird ideals, not by me! Your mother was killed because your existence and selfishness caused an uproar in the villainy business! If I hadn't given her a painless death, she would've been kidnapped, tortured, and given the most brutal death imaginable! All I'm doing is acting accordingly in the business I am in! *Grow up and wake up!*" Tyrant roared back. I was ready to hang up, then he hissed, "Think about a common denominator of who was present for all of those events. You are the problem."

I threw my phone against the wall, causing a loud bang and cracking my screen. I stood in the middle of my room, shaking, as tears dripped down my face.

No.

I crouched and held my head in my knees.

It can't be my fault. I thought nobody blamed me. Nobody thinks it's my fault, right?

The darkness crawled up my arms, eventually reaching my collarbone.

Then how come every time I see Tyrant ... he's the one that's mad? How come every new person I meet ... wants to kill me?

He is such a nuisance, such a villain. He's the reason you have these problems in your life and the reason you can't fit into society like everyone else.

For the first time since it started speaking to me, I wasn't surprised by the demon's voice. It was on my side.

We must end that bastard ... to end all the wrongness in the world. When he's gone, you can pluck out the rest of his groupies. You will rid the world of those social rejects plaguing your life.

I nodded and heard a knocking at my door before I could respond. I wiped my eyes, slowly stood, and walked to the door. I looked through the peep hole and saw Ashlyn, Sophia, and Scarlett looking both curious and concerned.

"Kyle, are you alright in there? What was that noise?" Scarlett asked before knocking on the door again. She looked down and saw the shadow of my feet in the crack of the door, then backed up.

I can't let them see me like this.

"Y- Yeah, I'm fine. I just dropped my phone and it had a couple unlucky bounces on the desk," I responded. I turned away from the door and stared out the window across the room. I could see the city and a spec of the sun in the sky.

"Well, we were thinking of going out to eat. There's a really nice place down the street to get lunch; we just need Gladiator's permission," Ashlyn informed me. I gently put my head against the door and looked up at the ceiling, trying to hold back tears.

"Sounds great. I'll be out in a m- minute," I responded in a shaky voice. Apparently it was convincing enough because they headed for the elevator. I slid down my door and held my head in my hands.

They think of me as a problem that they have to check in with. They don't trust that I'm not doing anything suspicious when I'm alone. Do they ... see me the same as Tyrant does? Do they think of me ... as a villain trying to be a hero?

I changed out of my bloody hero suit and into comfy clothes: sweatpants, a plain, white t-shirt, and a gray, loose-bottom sweatshirt. I slipped on slides, then walked out of the door and toward the elevator. When I reached the bottom floor, the others were waiting. I walked out of the elevator and followed the crowd outside. Xavier and Amy ran to us from the direction of the school, both wearing large smiles.

"We got approval! Let's go!" Amy yelled excitedly. We headed down the path, out of campus, and into the streets of Takorain. After a short walk, we arrived. The glass was spotless, freshly cleaned, and a girl with tan skin and bright blonde hair welcomed us with a smile.

Chapter 28
Scapegoat

Tonuko stepped forward and opened the door for everyone. The bell on the door jingled and as I passed Tonuko, he gave me a concerned look. I stuck my hands in my pockets and ignored him as we were led by the blonde girl to a booth in the back. It included a large, circular table surrounded by a long, leather couch. I sat on the left end between Tonuko and Ashlyn. She sat very close to me while Sophia grumbled to herself and glared at me. Across the table, Olivia and Ryuu sat next to each other. Ryuu just stared down at the table and Olivia rubbed his back.

In my mind, I could hear the echo of his scream: "*AKEMI!*" A shiver went down my spine, and my hands shook. Just as I tensed my fists, I felt a soft hand on my right forearm. I glanced over and saw Ashlyn smile as she held my arm a little tighter. I took a deep breath, then grabbed her hand. We held each other's hands under the table just as our server came by. She was the same girl who had been cleaning the glass earlier, and her eyes sparkled.

"I can't believe I get to serve you! You're so famous, it's like having celebrities in here!" she squealed as she handed out menus. I took mine from her hand without looking and dropped it on the table. Her smile faltered for a second, then returned as she handed Tonuko his.

"I guess we are a little popular, but we're just students. Don't treat us any differently than your other customers," Tonuko chuckled with a grin.

"I'm Jennifer and I'll be your server this afternoon! May I start you off with some drinks?" She took our beverage orders then left us to look over the menu.

It was uncomfortably silent, so Cindy spoke up, "What's good here?"

"All of their lunch food is very excellent. My personal favorite is the burger!" Connor responded with a sharp smile.

"I love their steaks! They're so juicy!" Amy added.

"Of course the dog wants a steak!" Rake snickered in a mocking tone, angering Amy.

She snarled, "What, does the snake want a mouse?" Rake rolled his eyes and looked at the menu, giving Amy the last laugh.

Xavier took a big sip of his water, then placed the glass down and smiled as he swallowed. "So, how did the training go for everyone?" he asked. Olivia, Ryuu, and I still hadn't talked to anyone, clearly worrying a few.

"It was a pretty fun experience! I'm surprised I managed to beat you, Camilla!" Ashlyn answered. Camilla responded with a shrug and twirled her hair between her fingers.

"Yeah, it was a tough-" Before Camilla could finish, a loud crash sounded outside. Tonuko stood and walked toward the door, assuming it was a car accident. We looked confused. Our questions were answered when a cloaked man crashed through the front window of the restaurant and tackled Tonuko. They wrestled on the ground for a moment, then the man pinned Tonuko and grinned devilishly.

"So we meet again, ground boy! This time, I've got backup!" Bobby shouted as he wound up a punch. Connor rammed into Bobby's side, hitting him into the wall. Connor leapt over Tonuko and dug his claws into Bobby's left hip.

"Stand down, we outnumber you! Pros will be on their way to take down your backup shortly!" Connor commanded. Bobby grimaced in pain, then spat blood through his teeth.

"Foolish snob, don't you know who we are?! Some petty heroes won't be able to take down the Care-Givers!"

Bobby roared. BloodShot and Stafer came around the wall and walked to the broken window.

"Stay back Jennifer, we'll protect you and the rest of the staff!" Ryuu shouted. Tonuko and I gasped when we saw BloodShot. I stood in my seat, jumped over the table, and lunged at him.

"What the hell are you doing here?! Leave us alone!" I seethed as I wound up a punch, then swung at him. BloodShot parried my attack, grinning devilishly.

"Tyrant is not too pleased with you Kyle, so he sent us to, y'know, correct your errors!" BloodShot cackled. My eyes widened as I backed up a few steps and my hands shook.

They're going to hurt more people close to me ... because of me ... again?

As BloodShot took a step closer, a chair sped past me and broke over him. He backed up. Another chair flew in from the side, BloodShot caught it and licked his lips with a fiendish look in his eyes.

"Clever girl," BloodShot uttered as Jennifer walked up next to me. Ryuu looked behind him, then back at Jennifer and me, confused.

"Quit acting like a baby, Kyle Straiter! C'mon!" Jennifer whispered as she nudged my arm. This spurred something inside me. The darkness erupted out of my palms and covered my body.

"Let's stop this monster from hurting more of your peers," Demon muttered in my right ear. I held my hands at my waist and glared into BloodShot's eyes, then zoomed at him again. I tackled him onto the windowsill and Jennifer used a table to push us out of the store. We crashed onto the street, and I skidded a few feet farther than him. Cars screeched to a halt and the townspeople were petrified.

"Jennifer, get back! You don't have the training to face off against villains of this caliber!" Xavier demanded as he threw out his puppet. Stafer locked eyes with Jennifer and smirked. He used her power against her, sending two chairs covered in darkness flying at her from either side. She jumped backward, successfully dodging the chairs.

"Who said that just because I'm a waitress I haven't had training?" Jennifer retorted with a condescending grin. Xavier shook his head and threw out his puppet at Stafer. The puppet's arms were covered in scales as it punched Stafer. He unsuccessfully tried blocking but flew out of the restaurant.

"We'll hold down Bobby. Everyone else, go take care of those two!" Tonuko commanded with his foot on Bobby's face. The others ran out of the restaurant and were caught off guard by three, large shadow beasts.

"Little Tonuko, did you forget my strength?" Bobby asked. "As long as I'm breathing, I can keep em' coming!"

Across the street, BloodShot swiftly hopped onto his feet, then gripped his blade's handle. I stood as well but hesitated when I saw his sword.

"G- Get the fuck out of here ... now," I commanded with a stutter. He laughed at me and smirked provocatively.

"Why the hell would I listen to you? I could kill you right now if I wanted to!" he mocked. I looked around at the civilians and calmed myself a little.

"Why are you here?" I asked. BloodShot continued smiling and didn't respond. He ran at me, swiftly drawing his blade. I dodged his strike but he immediately kicked me in the stomach. Before I could fly back, BloodShot grabbed my arm and threw me into the ground.

Dammit ... he has too much combat experience. He's too strong!

BloodShot placed his hand on my face and held his sword at his waist. The blade faced away from us. I shook again and he snickered.

"Just like every other time we've met, you're terrified of me, Kyle," BloodShot stated. He glanced behind him with a focused look and stared at Iris. *"We could take them right now and not even need to plan an ambush."* BloodShot shook his head as he looked back at my frustrated face.

"I am going to kill you," I mumbled.

"Hmm, what was that?" BloodShot asked in an attempt to exasperate me.

"I'm going to fucking kill you!" I screeched as I used my arms to lift his hand off my face. I quickly let go and punched Bloodshot in the cheek with my right hand, causing him to fall from me. We stood at the same time, and as I stared at BloodShot he wiped a speck of blood from his lip and grinned inhumanely. He tossed his blade into the air and pounced at me so fast I couldn't react. BloodShot grabbed me by the neck and lifted me into the air, then caught his blade and held it up to the side of my head.

"Little Tyrant is already acting like his daddy. You've got a lot to learn. For example, you will never kill me," BloodShot pestered. I kicked my legs around, attempting to falter his grasp, to no avail. He looked me in the eye and smiled with pure joy. He let go of my neck, then yelled, "Favian, let's go! We're done here!" Favian floated out from the alleyway near us and summoned a portal behind me. BloodShot walked past me and I swiftly grabbed his forearm and squeezed tightly.

"N- No, you can't leave yet! I haven't beaten you; I need to destroy you!" I pleaded with slight franticness. BloodShot ripped his arm from my grasp.

"It's never going to happen; you will never beat me," he started, enraging me even more. "However, I will

521

be in Bade's Egotistical Goon's Junction One on the midnight after Halloween. If you are there before 12:05, I will fight you." My hands trembled but I tensed them and nodded, filled with determination. I thought that was it, but BloodShot added, "If you win, Tyrant and I will leave you and your classmates alone until after the Hero Olympics. If I win, I will take you back to Tyrant with me."

My eyes widened and a pit in my stomach grew. I wasn't able to respond before BloodShot vanished into Favian's portal. I turned and saw Xavier, Ryuu, and Ashlyn holding down Stafer while the others tried to fend off Bobby's Creatures.

"Stafer, it is time to leave. Stop playing around," Favian commanded from across the street. Stafer grinned, stood with no issues (using an amplified version of my enhanced strength), and spun around, throwing the three students off of him. He walked past me toward Favian and into the same portal as BloodShot. Favian sighed seeing Bobby under pressure, then he opened one eye and placed his left pointer and middle fingers on his left temple. He raised out his right hand and Bobby was sucked into a vortex from underneath Tonuko and Connor. Favian then floated through his own portal and, as it disappeared, all of Bobby's creatures dissipated.

"Kyle, what the hell?! You let them get away!" Xavier shouted as he ran up to me. I rubbed my neck—a bruise was forming from when BloodShot choked me—walked past Xavier, and bumped his shoulder.

"We couldn't stop them anyway. BloodShot could solo half of us if he wanted to," I lied in a sullen voice. Xavier gave me a disturbed look and tensed his fists.

"When the fuck would Kyle Straiter ever give up like that?!" he yelled. I ignored him and caught up with the rest of the group. Jennifer wiped sweat from her forehead as she panted.

Ashlyn complimented, "Wow, I didn't know a waitress could be that skilled! Why aren't you a hero?" Jennifer giggled as she put her hair back into a tight ponytail and shrugged.

"Thanks, but it just never appealed to me. On top of that, my family doesn't have nearly enough money to send me to a hero school," Jennifer admitted with a slight sigh.

"You do know E.H. is free, right?" Camilla asked as she walked over. Jennifer's eyes sparkled in the light, then she rubbed the back of her head.

"Psh, of course I knew that!" Jennifer lied in a high-pitched voice. We helped her clean up all the broken glass and damaged chairs, gave the staff a tip, and left once the police and nearby heroes took over. I went straight to my room and laid on my bed facing the ceiling. I felt my phone buzz in my hand and groaned when I read the message.

"Surprise," Plague taunted. I stared at the ceiling, lost in thought.

Of course it was my fault they were attacked again ... when is it not? Tyrant and the Care-Givers are the mob bosses of the villain industry right now. They're the leaders of the kidnappers, half the reason The Upriser rose, and now there are less-popular villains kidnapping children. What the hell is your plan, Tyrant and BloodShot?

Five Hours Later, 6:00 p.m.:

I woke to the sound of knocking at my door, then sat up once I heard Ashlyn's voice.

"Hey Kyle, are you gonna come to dinner?" I took a deep breath, stood from my bed, and answered the door. To my surprise, it was just Ashlyn. I nodded and she said, "Good, we better get going then! We want to be able to pick our seats in the cafeteria, right?"

"Yeah, I guess so. Let's go," I chuckled in response. We walked to the elevator and clicked the bottom floor button. Out of the corner of my eye, I saw Ashlyn move a little closer so I looked at her. She was blushing heavily, quickly leaned up and kissed me then looked back down. I was now blushing too as she rested her head on my arm.

"Since Sophia stopped us earlier, y'know?" Ashlyn whispered just as the elevator dinged. As we walked out of the dorm, I felt a gnawing feeling in my stomach, an itch to ask her a question. After much hesitation, I caved.

"Do you know anything about Akemi?" I spat out. Ashlyn was surprised by the sudden question and solemnly looked forward with drooped eyelids.

"I know of the incident, but not really any of the details. I don't talk to Ryuu that much, but if you ask Olivia or Xavier I'm sure they can tell you more. Olivia is Ryuu's best friend, and he and Xavier seem to have a connection. They have a lot in common," Ashlyn sighed. I raised an eyebrow and scratched my arm.

"How so?" I questioned. Ashlyn bit her lip and dithered.

"W- Well, I shouldn't be telling you this ... but you heard what Gravaton was yelling at Puppeteer about. Xavier's mom was killed in battle, in front of Puppeteer," Ashlyn quietly explained. I looked down at the grass to my left and sighed.

"Yeah, I figured. I still don't understand how that relates them so much?" Ashlyn held her left arm then stopped. I stopped walking a little farther than her and looked back. She stared at the ground and twirled a rock under her foot. When she looked up at me worry and sorrow filled her eyes.

"Kyle ... it was your dad. Xavier's mom, Laura Kinder, better known as the pro-hero Flint, was killed in the same battle against Tyrant that Akemi died in," Ashlyn revealed. My eyes widened and my mouth gaped. I thought back to the newscaster screaming the names of the defeated heroes ... and remembered.

*"HotSauce is dead, Counter is dead, Dan-J is dead, **Flint is dead!**"*

"N- No, no it can't be true," I whimpered. Ashlyn took a couple steps toward me while holding her hands close to her heart, and she stuttered before getting a word out.

"No one thinks it's your fault, Kyle! No one blames you, I promise!" Ashlyn implored with a quivering voice.

I clenched my jaw, shut my eyes, then opened them and screamed, "Are you joking?! Ryuu tried killing me because of what happened, Xavier and I fought during the shadowing because of his and my families ... *everyone thinks it's my fault!*" I retorted, tears dripping down my face. A couple of drops splashed onto the gravel road as I tensed my fist and clenched my jaw.

Apparently Jax was outside B.E.G.'s main entrance, and he ran over after hearing the commotion. "Kyle, what the hell is going on?! Why are you yelling and crying?!" Jax asked as he put his hands on my shoulders. I wiped my eyes and didn't answer, so Jax looked over at Ashlyn.

"Kyle thinks it's his fault for the things his dad did to ... other people's families," she sighed. Jax raised an eyebrow as he looked back at me. Ashlyn slightly shook my shoulders, making me look up.

"C'mon man, you know that's not true. Nobody blames you for something your dad did when you were a kid. How could that possibly be your fault?" Jax whispered. I smacked his arms away. I wiped away the rest of my tears, and the distraught look in my eyes had faded.

"Let's just go eat," I murmured and walked toward the school's front doors, leaving Jax and Ashlyn to follow. As I entered, I was hit with the enticing smell of beef. I had to wait for Ashlyn so she could lead Jax and me to the cafeteria. Once we arrived, I felt slightly overwhelmed. Almost all the tables were filled with students, the kitchen had three chefs racing around making food, and teachers were serving students.

Talk about a fancy ass school.

Jax and I followed Ashlyn to one of the back tables where the rest of the freshman honors' kids were seated. We sat down and a teacher ran over and served us heaping plates of fried rice, steak bits, and vegetables (peas, carrots, bean sprouts). Ashlyn and Jax dug in but I stared at my food for a moment. After a deep breath, I took my first bite.

I was pleasantly surprised by how delicious the food was, and that first bite made me realize just how hungry I was. Everyone else talked as we ate while I remained quiet. I scarfed down my food, stood, and walked out. I ignored the other kids' calls as I left the school building.

As I headed toward the dorms, I heard footsteps in the gravel behind me. I stopped under a lamppost, turned around, and saw two older kids who I assumed were juniors or seniors. One was a pale boy with dyed red and black hair, all spiky and messy, and the other was a girl with olive skin and a frizzy afro; she was taller than the boy. They stopped once they were close enough to offer a handshake.

"You're that first year Kyle Straiter, right?" the guy asked, nudging for a handshake. I nodded as I weakly shook his hand, then I turned to the girl. Her energy was the opposite of mine: loud and giddy. She aggressively shook my hand as her smile somehow grew wider.

"We heard you got the M.V.P. and carried your school's team to victory against our first years! You beat Olivia and Amy without opening your eyes; that's so crazy! Why aren't you attending here?!" she shouted. I blinked a few times then yawned as I pulled my hand away from hers.

"Money," I bluntly responded.

"Huh? You didn't come here because of money?" the guy asked genuinely.

"I don't have money to pay for this school and I didn't get a scholarship. If you know me, or of me, then you probably know the answer why for both of those," I elaborated with a nod. The guy shrugged, then looked over at the girl.

"Welp, I guess we all have our family issues," he intoned as he stretched his back. "Even if you are at E.H., keep going kid. You're gonna be a big deal one day." I shook my head, annoyed, and walked away without responding.

Did they really stop me just to berate my poorness and my school choice and to make me feel like a child? What dickheads.

Thankfully they didn't stop me again, so I was able to make it to the dorms without issue. I went straight to my room and collapsed on my bed. My head raced as I stared at the ceiling, but I only stayed awake a few minutes before I fell into a deep sleep.

The next day, my alarm didn't sound. Luckily, the sunlight shining through the window woke me. I arose at 7:45 a.m., early enough to get ready for school. Classes at B.E.G. start at 8:30, the same time as at E.H. I showered, brushed my teeth, and dressed, then opened my door. Sitting on the ground was a black, drawstring bag with the orange logo of the company that makes our hero costumes. A small note was stuck on the bag.

"Here is your fixed-hero costume. Enjoy!" it read. I crumpled the note and tossed it behind me, then threw on the bag and took the elevator down to the first floor. I grabbed an apple from the fruit basket on the counter and took a bite as I passed through the dorm entrance. Unlike E.H., there were a ton of people mingling about.

Why the hell are there so many kids? I get B.E.G. actually has a senior class, but this seems like a little too much.

Still perplexed, I threw away my apple core and continued down the pathway. I passed four students who looked my age and heard chattering. Once I was a couple of steps away, one of them spoke up.

"Hey, Kyle Straiter! We're huge fans!" one of the two girls shouted. I slowly turned around and, already a little aggravated, gave them a puzzled look.

"Eh? You're huge fans?" I questioned in a biting tone. One of the guys strolled up and threw his arm around my shoulder. He had spiky, ash-brown hair, olive skin, a gray headband, and was clearly Asian of some sorts.

"You hero kids are practically celebrities, especially you, Xavier, and Tonuko Kuntai! Haven't you noticed how many people recognize you? You're famous worldwide!" the guy explained. I grabbed his wrist, lifted it off my shoulder, then dropped it.

"What do you mean 'you hero kids'? Don't you go here?" I asked in response. They looked at each other, then a lightbulb went off for headband guy.

"Oh, right, E.H. hasn't incorporated it just yet. We're academic course kids! We started school on Monday!" he informed me. "We're super excited to meet people our age who are so strong!"

I don't feel like dealing with these kids' energy.

"Great, just what I needed," I grumbled as I stuck my hands in my pockets, turned, and walked away.

"Hmph, rude!" the girl who'd engaged with me pouted. She had luscious pink hair, a fuzzy, blue scarf, and was slender.

"I told you he doesn't like people! Saying hi to hero course kids will really show ya how full of themselves they are!" the other guy cackled. I stopped after he finished his sentence, and he gulped as I swiveled on my heels to face them once again.

"What did you say?" I sinisterly asked, causing him to sweat.

"Well, y- you see ... I- I uh, w- well ..." I closed my eyes and took a very deep breath.

These are just innocent students, not enemies. I can't go around acting like a piece of shit to everyone. That would make me the same as Tyrant.

"So, what did you guys want?" I asked in a calmer tone as I walked back over. Headband guy, who I could now see had a thick scar from his left temple to his jawline, rubbed the back of his head and looked down.

"Well, we just wanted to say hi to you! You're like an idol to us!" he explained.

An ... idol? Me?

"You really think of me as an idol?" My face softened as they assented, and I couldn't help but smile. "Oh, well, thanks. That means a lot." I expressed my gratitude and they looked happy.

The girl who hadn't yet spoken—she had short, black pigtails and a sweater with sleeves that had holes for her thumbs—nervously suggested, "H- How about we eat lunch together? I know people get mad when they are idolized and not treated like a person, so why don't we get to know each other?" I leaned back on my right foot while thinking, then nodded intently.

"Yeah, sounds good to me. C'ya then." When I walked away this time I heard excited gibberish. It put me in a jovial mood.

I navigated through the busy hallways, eventually reaching the freshman honors' classroom. After walking through the door, Xavier marched over to me and put his hands on my shoulders. "Dude, we're freaking famous! Did you get stopped too?" he asked excitedly. I nodded, then Connor walked over and stood tall.

"It's like we are famous! We should keep a good image of ourselves since we're known globally!" Connor suggested.

We agreed, and I added, "Kinda seems like everything we've done has been covered by the news and broadcast all over the world. That's crazy to think about." Xavier stared past me, so I glanced back and saw two older girls strutting in our direction. One winked and waved at Xavier, making him blush. "Looks like you're pretty popular with the chicks, huh?" I grinned.

"I guess you could say that," Xavier snickered. Just then, Gladiator cleared his throat as he stepped up to his podium.

"Today will b- be regular power-up training! T- To assist me in supervising today is n- none other than p- pro-hero: Identify!" Everyone clapped as the man entered the room. He was very muscular and tall, had one completely red eye (similar to Steven's), and a sharp handlebar mustache. Identify looked around the room, then clicked his heels together and saluted.

"Good morning students, and welcome to our school Eccentric High students! I am Identify. With the power to identify your strengths, I will be able to help you improve in ways you didn't know you could! For example," Identify looked around the room then stared at Tonuko. He closed his normal eye, then stated, "Tonuko Kuntai, strength: Earth

Control. Strength level: Ground Control!" There were gasps across the room, but Tonuko was the most shocked.

"Y- You mean, I haven't even been using my real power?" he asked. Identify nodded. His strict persona faltered slightly when he glanced at me.

"Hmm, Kyle Straiter ... you might be a challenge. I've never used my strength on someone with multiple strengths."

"Give it a shot, I guess. No harm in seeing what happens," I sighed with a shrug.

At this point, everyone knows I'm hiding strengths. The kids who were with me during the kidnapper battle saw me use other strengths, and I even used another one on Iris and Ryuu during Capture the Flag. There's no point in hiding it anymore; the more strengths I can publicly use, the easier it'll be to take down Tyrant and BloodShot.

Identify stared at me with his red eye then gasped. He opened his eyes, cleared his throat, and declared, "Kyle Straiter, strength ...: Tyrant." The classroom was silent and my eyes widened as I squeezed my desk. I clenched my jaw, then looked at my palms. The two small, black dots were on my palms.

It all makes sense.

Flashback of Kyle Running to Daniel's House as a Child:

<u>***He's just a strength-stealing demon.***</u>

Present:

"Wait, so what does that mean? What is his strength?" Cindy asked, first looking back at me, then at Identify. He coughed into his hand and scratched the back of his neck.

"It is not my decision to publicly state the details of Kyle's strength. If you wish, Kyle, I can explain to you what it exactly is in my office, then you can make the decision on whether or not to tell your classmates," Identify suggested. I nodded, stood, and followed him out of the classroom. After I shut the door behind us, Identify led me to a room down the hall. I sat in a seat in front of his desk as Identify closed the door, marched to his seat, and sat down. "I'm sure you already have a basic idea of this strength. It gives you an immense increase of pure strength, along with boosting all of your strengths," Identify explained.

I nodded, then asked, "It?" Identify scratched his head as he took a deep breath, then he folded his hands on his desk.

"Well, you have- a demon of sorts living inside you. Any kind of whispering, white noise, looming presences, or shadowy figures are ways this demon communicates with you." I squeezed my pants and clenched my jaw. I had one question I needed to get off my chest.

"Does this strength ... give me the power to steal strengths?" I asked. I secretly hoped he would say no, but I knew the answer.

"Yes ... it does. Well, sort of. The demon inside you has the ability to steal others' strengths without harming them, not you directly. However, since strengths are a part of our bodies, any strength the demon has stolen, you have the ability to wield. I cannot see how many strengths the demon has in its arsenal for you to use, but I can assure you that it must be more than however many you have told the public. I think you know that too," Identify responded sternly. I sighed then he asked, "What do you want to do? We can tell your classmates of the details of this strength or leave it between you and me and only explain part of it. I promise you that if you choose to leave it between us, my lips will stay sealed till death."

I can't let others know about the fact that there is a demon living inside me that can steal strengths. I will never be seen as a hero if I wield stolen strengths.

"Let's just tell them I have the ability to boost my strengths. It can't be wise to tell others that there's not only a demon inside me but that it has stolen strengths from others." Identify agreed, we shook hands, stood, and left the office. I took another deep breath before returning to the classroom.

Did Mom ... know about this strength? She keeps warning me about it now, assuming that is her, so did she know before?

The class was silent as Identify and I stood at the podium. Everyone was very curious and listened intently.

Fuck ... why couldn't it just be a strength booster?

"My strength, Tyrant, is a strength boosting power that increases my physical strength, athleticism, and all of my strengths. It also increases my reaction time and is activated when that darkness covers my body," I explained. The others let out curious, yet relieved noises.

Identify looked around as I sat in my seat and in his deep, raspy voice he commanded, "Now that that's over, let's go to the training center and work on your power-ups. We don't have any kind of competition planned, just normal training with Split." Everyone stood and followed the teachers, but before we made it to the training center Tonuko asked what we E.H. kids were wondering.

"Who's Split?" he asked, waiting for one of the B.E.G. kids to answer.

"Split has the same strength as Loam, the clone user at your school I believe. She creates clones for us to fight against, and they measure our strength potency," Olivia explained. "Basically, she helps us train our power-ups and signature moves."

533

"Signature moves and power-ups? Aren't those the same thing?" Tonuko asked with a raised eyebrow.

Olivia rolled her eyes before continuing, "Gosh, what on Earth are you learning at that public school? Signature moves are special attacks only you can perform based on your strength and body condition. On the other hand, power-ups are you using your strength at its current maximum. Say you are creating an Earth clone or something, or Kyle's full-body Tyrant strength."

Tonuko thanked her, but I couldn't help but notice how she sounded hesitant when she said my strength.

It's gonna take some time for people to get over that, isn't it?

Tonuko looked down at his hands, then formed fists. *"So, I'm not even using my real strength? All this time I've been boasting about being number one, but really, I've been holding back, I guess. Earth control is such a strong, rare strength ... did Fallen know I have it?"* Tonuko thought as we walked past different academic classrooms. It felt weird hearing actual classes in session.

"Sir, will the E.H. students join us in our academic classes?" Connor asked sternly. We E.H. kids dreaded the thought of that.

"Yes, they will join you in your regular schedule of training, mathematics, lunch, l- literature, then science," Gladiator responded and we groaned.

We changed in the locker rooms and once everyone was in their hero costumes, we left for the training area. It was a massive gymnasium with large windows across the top of the wall and, unlike the Dome, it had no seating for spectators. The walls were made of concrete, unlike the brick walls of the Dome.

"Hello students, I am Split! I will provide your training dummies to improve your scores!" she exclaimed happily. Her hero name was very fitting, as half of her hair was bleach blonde, half was brown. Her costume matched her eyes—the right half was blue, the left half metallic green. Split smiled then switched to an intimidating glare in an instant. "Get to it, freshies! We don't have all damn day!" I was very confused so Xavier leaned over and answered my silent question.

"She has spontaneous mood swings. One minute she's happy and respectful, and the next she's threatening us and swearing. It's pretty entertaining!" Xavier whispered, making me snicker.

"Oh boy, one of the public school kids thinks he's a big ol' tough guy who can laugh at me! You'll be training with me, hotshot!" Split yelled, pointing at me. I walked to the front of the room, crossed my arms, and stood in front of Split.

"Really, I'm training with you? I don't wanna hurt you," I remarked. Split didn't look amused and swiftly crouched and kicked my legs out from beneath me. I fell onto my butt as she stood and clapped the dirt off her hands.

"I'm not worried," she smirked. I rubbed my head and stood back up, feeling a little embarrassed, then Split commanded, "Everyone separate and give yourselves enough space so you have room to let it all out. Be careful and do not hurt each other!" The B.E.G. kids walked to specific spots and the rest of us followed by spacing equally in different areas. Everyone except me, that is. "Come on, Kyle, let's go!" Split exclaimed as she waived her finger at me.

Welp, she changed again.

Split stopped then crouched and placed both hands on the ground. Clones of herself morphed out of the cement floor in front of everyone and she grinned.

"Go on dumbasses, begin!" We fought our clones, who fought back, unlike when Loam's clones tested our power-ups. Split stood and stared at me, then waved her hand back and forth. "Hello?! Don't stand there all dazed, show me what you've got!" she shouted as the clone charged at me. It swung a punch, but I easily parried it then punched it in the stomach. Without using my Tyrant strength, I sent it soaring into the wall in front of us. At the place of death, the number "**6**" shone brightly. Split raised an eyebrow, stomped over to me, and poked my forehead. "Only a six?! How damn weak are ya'?! You can't act all tough, then get a measly six!"

"I only used my super strength!" I retorted as I closed my eyes and smacked her hand away.

Split snorted, "Well then, use all your power! I want to see a forty!" I looked at her as if she was stupid, then rolled my eyes and opened my hands. The darkness erupted out of my palms and wrapped my body up to my eyes. My hair didn't float this time, but my eyes glowed white. The flame ropes sprouted from my forearms, and purple mist swirled around my body. Split gave a big, toothy smile, then morphed a clone next to her. She took a couple of steps back and screamed, "*Let it rip baby!*"

What a nuisance.

I ignored the Tyrant Demon's voice and squeezed my fists, causing the veins in my arms to pulsate. As I glared at the clone, I thought, I need to beat BloodShot so I have to train like these clones are him.

The clone ran at me and slid under my legs, punching back and hitting my calves as it slid by. I flipped back, grabbed the clone's head as I was in the air over it, and threw it into the air as I landed. The clone flew about twenty feet into the air, then the ground cracked beneath my feet as I leapt at the clone. I collided into it, punched it in the body a few times, spun a full circle in the air, and kicked down on the clone's head. It crashed into the ground at extremely high speeds, creating a massive rock explosion

Everyone else stopped and stared in awe, and as I fell back down, the number read "**41**."

Split's clap echoed as I landed, then she strolled over to me.

"Well done, Kyle, I'm slightly impressed! A public school kid like you hitting the forties as a freshie?!" Split held out her fist and gave me a genuine smile while saying, "Good job." I smiled back and fist-bumped her just as the number vanished.

Xavier seethed and hit his clone with all he had. The clone scraped against the ground, then crashed into the wall—the same wall that stretched in front of me. Through the dirt and smoke mixture, Xavier saw his number read "**36**." He looked frustrated and looked down at his hands, which were covered by a layer of translucent matter.

On the other side of the building, Tonuko looked at the both of us with hot cheeks. As our numbers glowed in the high thirties and forties, his shone a mere "**29**." Tonuko was embarrassed and he swiftly looked away, over at me again. The sound of his clone's body crumbling into a rock pile filled his ears as he thought, "*How can I be bragging about being number one if these two are getting scores that are seven and twelve points higher than mine? This doesn't make any fucking sense. How have I gotten ... weaker?*"

One Hour Later, End of Training:

I wiped sweat from my forehead. My legs burned from jumping so much. I leaned on my knees, breathing deeply, then heard Gladiator clap once.

"T- Training is over fo- for today! G- Get washed up and ch- changed, then head over to mathematics!" he announced and we groaned again. We showered and dressed in the locker room, then followed Gladiator back to our classroom. I fell into my seat and yawned. I looked up at the clock, which read 10:15 a.m.

537

The training plus changing and homeroom lasted an hour and forty-five minutes, but the actual training itself was an hour and fifteen minutes. So, every class will most likely be an hour fifteen, meaning lunch will be at 11:30. Oh yeah, I'm gonna sit with those academic kids ... I probably should have asked their names, shouldn't I?

As we waited for our teacher to arrive, Rake leaned over and tapped my desk. "Bro, you got a forty today? That's actually insane!" he complimented with a big smile.

"Yeah," I chuckled, "I guess it was pretty good. I can do better though, I know it." Rake chuckled as he shook his head, then Amy spun around in her seat.

"You more than quintupled this weaklings score! Man, that's so embarrassing!" she mocked, causing Rake to blush.

"Yeah and what the hell did you get, mutt?" Rake snapped. Amy's face changed from giddy to offended.

"I got a nine, so he barely quadrupled my score!" Amy answered. To her surprise, Rake responded with an antagonizing laugh.

"You're actually so stupid; I got a nine too!" Rake mocked. Amy's cheeks turned red, then she turned around in her chair and sulked. I fist-bumped Rake while quietly chuckling, and that's when our math teacher sauntered in. The teacher walked to the podium. At this point, I was unsure of the teacher's gender.

"Hello students, I am Ms. Launder, also known as pro-hero Algorithm. Pleasure to meet you." Algorithm had numbers and equations tattooed all over her body, countless piercings, and a shaved head that was faintly purple. She grabbed a black marker from behind her and wrote on the board "Systematic Equations."

"Today, we will learn about systematic equations, something briefly taught in middle school." I rolled my eyes

538

and leaned on my head thinking, Man, this class just started and I'm already falling asleep. It doesn't help that she has literally zero emotion in her voice.

After the brutal math class, it was finally lunch time. Apparently eating only an apple for breakfast was a mistake because my stomach roared loudly as we headed to the cafeteria. Ashlyn skipped up next to me, grabbed my arm, and smiled brightly.

"Hey Kyle, wanna eat together?" she asked. I felt bad but I knew I couldn't.

"Sorry, but I already told some academic kids I'd eat with them. I was kinda an asshole to them at first, so I pretty much owe it to them," I responded. To my surprise, Ashlyn didn't look too upset.

She shrugged, "Aww alright, we can eat tomorrow. Promise to?" I half-smiled and nodded.

"Yeah, promise."

We continued talking as we walked and chatted with Tanner and Scarlett once in the lunch line, which was extremely long. When we finally had our food—steak tacos and tortilla chips—I looked around for the academic kids. I saw the girl with pink hair waving, so I made my way over to them. I wasn't expecting to see five of them, but the more the merrier, I guess.

"Hey Kyle!" the boy with gray hair exclaimed as he patted the seat next to him. I sat down on the end seat, with the girl in pink across from me.

"So, I never got any of your names. What are they?" I asked.

"The name's Ellie Dean!" the girl with pink hair yelled first.

"I'm Catherine Bale," the girl with black pigtails said next.

"Caleb Otto!" the guy who'd laughed at them earlier proclaimed boldly. The guy sitting next to me chuckled a bit, then he pointed at himself.

"I'm Hitoshi Makino. I was born in Japan but moved here with my family," the gray hair guy explained. As I ate a tortilla chip, I noted how his accent now made sense.

"Wow, that's pretty cool. Why'd you move here?" I questioned. Hitoshi smiled, then ran his hand through his hair.

"Well, I got a letter about B.E.G.'s academic courses opening up, and I just couldn't turn that down. My mom and I moved here. Since I was already bilingual, it wasn't much of a change." I nodded, impressed with how good his English was considering his short time here. I looked over at the fifth person, a girl whose hair was like space.

"So, who're you? I don't think I've seen you around campus." The girl's eyes were big and curious, but she seemed shy.

"I'm Nora Cate. Nice to meet you, Kyle."

"Nice to meet you too," I responded with a smile. "Now, I've got a question for you, but you don't have to answer it if you don't want to." They were intrigued so I continued, "Why didn't you guys want to be heroes? Most kids I knew growing up dreamed of being heroes." Hitoshi scratched his head, then shrugged.

"Oh, well I'm just not strong enough. My strength is Arsenal, and I can pretty much just put things in a pocket dimension and summon them at will. See." Hitoshi demonstrated by flinging out his hand. His phone warped over his hand and plopped into it.

I looked at him and complimented, "Are you kidding? That strength is awesome! With training, you could stop things from hitting you by putting them in your dimension or having rope or weapons in it so you could capture a villain!" Hitoshi looked at me and smiled widely.

"R- Really, you think so?!" he asked excitedly. I nodded and held up a fist with a big smirk on my face.

"Hell yeah, you could totally be a strong hero!" Hitoshi looked down at his hands, then Ellie cleared her throat loudly.

"Me next! My strength is Waterfall; I can absorb water, hold it in my body, then shoot it out!" Ellie explained as she put one finger over her cup and sprayed a bit of water into it.

"That could be pretty strong too. With training, you could probably increase the water pressure and amount you can hold in your body," I said, making Ellie feel good about herself. Caleb looked a little more embarrassed than the others, which I could already tell was abnormal for him.

"I'm honestly just too scared to fight villains. Knowing I could die at any moment during a fight is intimidating!" he admitted.

"Yeah, it is pretty scary getting attacked or fighting a villain; it hurts too. Honestly, I've always just forgotten that they're trying to kill me. It's easy to forget that these people aren't gonna hold back like we do in training battles," I agreed.

Caleb nodded and joked, "Makes sense. People are crazy."

"Yeah, it's the same reason for me," Catherine agreed, "That's why, in the academic course, I'm trying to major in technology so I can work behind the scenes as a sidekick, but I won't have to actually fight anyone." I gave her a thumbs up.

I quoted, "'Every kind of hero has a purpose, no matter if you fight in the front lines or help from the side!' You know who said that? HotSauce, the greatest hero ever!"

Catherine smiled, looked down, then back up with an embarrassed grin.

"He was my favorite. He gave me the courage to pursue my dreams of being a behind-the-scenes sidekick. My I.Q. strength gives me the intelligence to be one, so I'll work my hardest in school to make my dream a reality!" I smiled, but we were quickly cut off by Nora, who had been staring off into space.

"My strength is Future; it allows me to see what happens to a person in the next week. I don't want to be a hero, because I know the kinds of horrors I'll see happen to heroes, villains, Uprisers, civilians," Nora explained. I looked down at my food.

She categorized Uprisers separately from villains and heroes ... seems like they've already made their statement as a brute force of a new category of people bringing a change to society.

Before I could ask for their opinions on the Metaphorical Uprisers, I felt someone smack their hands onto my shoulders. I jumped a bit, then turned around curiously. My eyes grew wide then watery as I stood and hugged the person.

She hugged back then whispered, "Long time no see, little ol' Kyle."

Chapter 29

No Cessation

I hugged her tight and rested my head on her shoulder as I attempted to not tear up. Her dark blue and cyan hair shimmered in the light. As our hug loosened, she whispered, "How ya been?"

"Wh- what are you doing here?! You stopped sending letters so long ago ... Daniel thought you died!" I exclaimed. I got a good look at her face—she had a few new scars and a nasty bruise on the right side.

Just wait until Daniel and Jax see her. They're gonna be so fucking happy.

"I know, it was tough to lose contact with him," she sighed, "After I got sent on that mission across the country, it got very, very shaky. One of the Care-Givers, Otto Lavender, tormented the town where I was stationed for years. An Upriser killed him a month ago. My team and I were in a massive fight with The Upriser, but we managed to prevail and bring the woman to the Abyssal Penitentiary. That should get us a lot more information on what the movement is all about," she explained.

Abby was in a fight across the country with an Upriser? How did their movement spread so fast, and why would a person with the power to kill Otto Lavender ever join The Uprisers?

"Well, how's the little tough guy doing, eh? I hear about how much stronger you're getting!" Abby smiled as she roughed up my hair.

"Yeah, I guess I have been training a lot. So much has happened over the past ... months," I sighed. Abby glanced over my shoulder at the kids I was sitting with and smiled softly.

"How about we catch up after your school day? I don't wanna steal you from your friends!" she suggested. I looked at my new friends, half-smiled, and nodded.

"Yeah, sounds good," I agreed. We hugged once more and she left. I sat back down and took a big bite of one of my tacos, which was absolutely delicious.

Man, these chefs make some good ass food. I hope E.H. hires some people who can make food as good as this.

"So, who was that?" Hitoshi asked as he watched Abby search for Jax.

"That's one of my best friends' sister. She's a pro, and a damn good one." The academic kids expressed enthusiasm, then I asked, "Well, anyway, how have classes gone for you guys?"

Tyrant's Secret Base, A Broken-Down Factory in a Deserted Field:

BloodShot slammed his fist onto a large, metal table, grabbed a mesh paper tray, and whipped it across the room. The tray slammed and stuck into the cement wall, and BloodShot breathed heavily as he hunched over the table.

"What the fuck do you mean I'm not allowed to fight him?! We're about to get your son back, you dumbass!" BloodShot roared as he flung his hand into the air. Tyrant stood with a wide stance and crossed his arms, not backing down.

"You'll kill the boy, BloodShot. With all that has happened, Kyle is always under watchful eyes. Whether it is the heroes or The Uprisers, someone will see you two fighting and ambush you. The time will come when we will strike. You must be patient!" Tyrant boomed. The other Care-Givers sat against the wall, cringing as they watched the argument. They whispered amongst themselves but none dared to speak up.

BloodShot glared angrily at Tyrant, who responded with his own icy stare. The two stood in a standoff until Plague entered the room and walked up behind BloodShot. He held a piece of paper and pencil in his hand and scratched his head with the eraser of the pencil.

"Hey, BloodShot, how do I-?" BloodShot turned and back-hand slapped Plague across the head. Plague fell back and slid a few feet away, stopping in front of Laci and Gabriella.

544

"Can't you see I'm fucking busy?! Get the hell out of here!" BloodShot snarled. He turned back to Tyrant and the two continued bickering. Gabriella used a vine to help Plague stand, then he walked over and sat between her and Laci. Laci wrapped her arm around Plague and rubbed his head as it rested on her shoulder. A large bump formed on his head and tears streamed down his face.

"Why is he like this? He's hitting a child, basically all of the Care-Giver's child," Laci muttered to Gabriella, who responded with a sullen nod. Veins pulsated in BloodShot's arm as he continued punching the metal table.

He shouted, "Just because you're too much of a pussy to make a move, doesn't mean the rest of us can't! I'm going to fight Kyle, kick his ass, and drag him back to where the hell he belongs! I'm sick of you babying that boy and letting him do whatever the hell his ego desires!"

Tyrant shifted his foot forward and furrowed his eyebrows. "Kyle has killed our two fattest cash cows! The kidnappers made a large buck with each child they sold, and now that whole section of the industry is shut down! Uprisers are everywhere ... we are fucking falling apart! This move will take a stand, show the world that we aren't getting weaker, but immensely stronger! Just fucking listen to me!"

"I don't give a damn how strong you think you are; you will do as I say!" Tyrant snapped. "You will not fight Kyle, you will not disobey my order, and you will not disrespect the child of the future!"

"Your petty command is useless! All I need is Favian to teleport me, and I'll be there with or without your permission!" BloodShot yelled as he pointed at Favian, who opened one eye and looked at the two.

"Favian," Tyrant called out without batting an eye toward him, "You do not listen to him. He does not command you; I do."

"No, you listen to me, Favian! You'll do as I say, got it?! You know as well as I do that this is the move we need to make. Tyrant is being soft!" BloodShot roared. He looked back at Tyrant and seethed, "I'm going to bring your son back to where he fucking belongs."

"Quit acting all high and mighty, BloodShot. Know your place!" David commented from the steel box he was sitting on. "The number-one and two-heroes are in that city. Fighting Kyle in Takorain is not a smart decision in any sense of the term!" BloodShot clenched his jaw, picked up a stapler, and threw it at David. The stapler crashed into the metal box between David's legs and wedged itself into a dent it had made.

"Know my place? You're a weak little weaponsmith, stick to your job! The real villains are talking!" BloodShot snarled. David rolled his eyes and crossed his arms.

"You can't go around insulting us like you're our boss! We're all equal under the authority of Tyrant!" Laci argued.

"Yeah, stop acting like you're better than all of us!" Gabriella added. Their pleas made BloodShot giggle psychotically.

"Are the weak ass women really trying to say we're equal?" BloodShot asked hysterically. "Stick to the cleanups, girls, that's all women are useful for." BloodShot's statement made Stafer cackle, but all of the others, except Favian, grumbled to themselves.

"Get the hell out of my sight," Tyrant muttered sinisterly. BloodShot scoffed then stomped past him.

"I'm going to beat that runt, then bring him back for the purification," BloodShot angrily stated.

Tyrant closed his eyes, took a deep breath, sighed, and nodded. "If you won't listen to me, fine, but you better bring him back alive. If we can perform the purification then

Kyle will be trimmed to perfection," Tyrant said to BloodShot before he left the room. Once he was gone, the furious chatter grew louder.

"You're really going to let him insult you and us like that then walk off unscathed? You're getting soft for him, Tyrant," Kane questioned in an annoyed tone.

"I'm not getting soft for him," Tyrant clarified, "he's just getting to be too much to try and control. For now, let's let BloodShot have his fun." With that, Tyrant also left the room, then Stafer and Favian walked out to find BloodShot. Once the commotion ended, a little boy with metallic green hair with purple highlights ran into the room, over to Laci, and jumped into her arms.

"What happened in here? I heard a lot of yelling," he asked as he looked at Plague.

Laci smiled, hugged the boy, and sputtered, "W-Well, nothing really. There was just ... a disagreement, y-y'know?" The child smiled, sat down on the other side of Laci, and leaned on her arm. He closed his eyes, making Laci's smile grow, then she sighed and leaned her head against the wall. *"Ever since I started caring for these children, I couldn't help but wonder how Tyrant really felt about Kyle."* Laci's smile faltered as she looked up at the ceiling. *"And ... how is Scarlett doing?"*

Later that Night, 8:00 p.m. at B.E.G.:

Caleb wandered out of his room, over to the common area, and sat on the couch next to Nora, who hadn't acted her usual self since lunch. He stretched his arms and yawned, grabbed the remote, and turned on the news. Concerned, Caleb glanced at Nora and saw her holding both hands close to her chest, staring at the table. Her eyes gleamed in the light. He raised an eyebrow, hesitated, then sighed.

547

"Is, uh, everything okay?" Nora jumped a bit and looked over at him. She saw the worried expression on his face and shrugged.

"Y- Yeah ... everything's fine."

Caleb didn't necessarily believe her, yet he moved on. "Well, how's the homework treating ya? I'm struggling with math," Caleb randomly asked but Nora didn't respond. Hitoshi and Ellie walked in.

"Hey you two! Finished your homework?!" Hitoshi exclaimed as he waved. Caleb nodded; Nora didn't move. Caleb gave them a confused look.

Hitoshi glanced at Nora then nodded. "Hey, everything alright? You don't exactly look like yourself," Hitoshi questioned.

"Yeah, you look kinda pale," Ellie added. "Are you feeling okay?" Nora closed her eyes and hesitated, then looked at them.

"I know I shouldn't have, but I looked at Kyle Straiter's future!" Nora suddenly blurted.

"Woah, what?! Why would you do that?" Hitoshi interrogated, taking his hands out of his pockets and leaning on the chair in front of him.

Equally shocked, the others looked at Nora as she explained, "His eyes were telling a story of fury, sorrow, and bloodlust! I was worried, so I felt like I had to! Kyle's going to make a foolish move and fight a Care-Giver! He'll lose and face brutal torture!" Caleb stood and looked at the others. Even though Hitoshi and Ellie were both wearing pajama pants and tank tops, they nodded and ran out the door.

First-Year Hero Dorm:

I was shadow punching outside the dorm's front doors, getting in extra training. I wiped sweat from my forehead and looked up at the starry sky.

I have to beat BloodShot, to show I'm not afraid anymore. If I can beat him, then my classmates and I can finally have peace for a couple of months. I'll make up for what I've done to them, for the pain I've put everyone through.

Panting, I swung another punch then I heard footsteps behind me. I turned to see three of the five academic kids I'd sat with at lunch running toward me. They stopped and for a couple of seconds we just stared at each other. I picked up the hand towel I'd brought, wiped my face, and smirked.

"Hey, did you guys rush to find me or something? You look out of breath," I commented. To my surprise, none were smiling. Instead, they wore serious and worried expressions. I raised an eyebrow and Hitoshi answered.

"We know what you're planning," Hitoshi stated. I was caught off-guard but knew what he meant. I squeezed the towel in my hand as my smile faded, and I clenched my jaw.

"So, that's what this is about? Let me guess, Nora looked at my future?" I muttered. After some hesitation, Caleb nodded.

He exclaimed in a shaky voice, "W- We can't let you go and fight a Care-Giver on your own! You won't win!"

That last statement filled me with rage but I kept a calm persona. "I thought you were fans of mine. You should know I won't lose," I claimed boldly.

"Kyle, you're being blinded by your anger! We all know your past and why you want to fight, but that doesn't justify this kind of suicide!" Ellie argued swiftly. I gritted my teeth.

What the hell? They don't know my past. All they know is the tip of the iceberg: the murder of my mom. They don't know all the other trauma Tyrant put me through.

Seven Years Ago, Kyle's House:

While I sat on the floor playing with my dinosaur toys, my mom watched her favorite cooking show on the T.V. She often used it to get new recipes, to please Tyrant. Mom smiled as she simultaneously listened to my roaring noises and watched her show, then she crossed one leg over the other and picked up the remote. Suddenly, the front door burst open, scaring both of us. The doorknob crashed into the wall, cracking it, and Tyrant stomped over to the kitchen counter, leaned on it, and held his face.

"Honey, are you alright?" Mom asked, walking over and putting a hand on his shoulder. I couldn't see over the couch, but I heard a loud slap and a thud that I could feel in the floor.

"What the fuck does it look like, huh?! Ugh, dammit!" Tyrant roared. I stood, walked over, and saw my mom laying on the ground. A large, red mark graced her cheek. Tyrant glanced down at me with pure evil in his eyes, then turned to face me. He had a large cut from the center of his forehead to just under his right ear and bruises all over his face. He stomped past and gripped my upper arm. "Let's go. You're getting some endurance training," Tyrant commanded. I nodded and followed him out the back door.

Tyrant stood a couple of feet away, cracked his neck, then bolted at me. Although I was only eight years old, I reacted quickly and threw my hands up to block. Tyrant obviously overpowered me and uppercut me square in the nose. I skidded back a few feet, holding my nose, then he swept my feet from under me. I bashed the back of my head on the hard dirt and struggled to get back up.

"Stand up, you crybaby!" Tyrant shouted. I sniffled as I stood and held the back of my head. Before I could blink, he took a powerful step forward and kicked my ribs with his left foot. A loud crack vibrated throughout my body, I soared into our wooden fence and crashed through it. As I landed, a jagged piece of wood pierced through my back and stabbed my lung. Tyrant clapped dust off his hands, turned, and walked back into the house, leaving me to bleed until our neighbors noticed. They took me inside their home and called an ambulance.

Present:

I turned and lifted my shirt, showing the kids the large scar that stretched across the right side of my back.

"I had to have surgery because Tyrant went too far with my endurance training. He'd call it that, but in reality it was his way of taking out his anger on something. He would come home, hit my mom, then beat the shit out of me," I sternly explained as I turned back around. I saw their distraught expressions. "It's not that I'm blinded by anger, it's that Tyrant deserves all that's coming."

"Y- You aren't fighting Tyrant, are you?" Ellie spat out. I shook my head as I picked up my things and sighed.

"No, I'm fighting one of the Care-Givers that I've had a lot of quarrels with. I'm not telling you why because you'll just tattle on me," I responded. I grabbed my water bottle, looked back at them, and seethed, "And you better not tell anyone about my fight. It's happening my last day here ... stay the fuck out of my business."

Hitoshi's P.O.V.:

Kyle's glare was that of a psychopath, filled with determination and fury. Looking into his narrowed stare, I felt like my chest was being crushed. I couldn't move or look away. Those eyes ... were possessed.

Kyle P.O.V.:

I walked toward the dormitory entrance and suddenly felt ropes wrap around my waist, chest, and head. I glanced behind me and saw Caleb, shaking, constraining me with his strength.

"K- Kyle," he gulped, "we're going to tell people about this. We can't let you die." Ellie nodded in agreement and took a step forward.

"Nora is s- sick from looking into your future. If your f- fight is on Halloween, then that means all she saw was the aftermath of a d- day into your future," Ellie stuttered. I ignored their pleas and simply shrugged.

"She probably feels sick from seeing how badly I beat the guy I'm fighting. Now, let me go," I bragged. Caleb shook his head, then a lightbulb went off in Hitoshi's head.

"I saw Tonuko Kuntai walking past our dorms when we ran! I'll go get him!" Hitoshi yelled. As he started running, I activated Energy Conversion, jumped out of the ropes, and landed in front of him.

"I already made it clear earlier: I don't want to be mean to allies. However," I sighed as I grabbed Hitoshi's collar, then lifted him off the ground, "if you tell anyone, I'll personally beat the shit out of you. Don't make this mistake, please." I dropped him and looked at the others. "Do you two need a little lecture too? Get going!"

"R- Right!" Ellie responded. She grabbed Caleb's hand and ran. Hitoshi was still on the ground, panting, so I reached out my hand. He looked nervous and didn't take it; he stared at me with fear.

"Look, I'm not going to hurt you. I'm a hero, not a villain," I said, calming Hitoshi enough so he took my hand and stood. "This fight is over personal issues, so please don't get involved. I'll be fine, don't worry about me," I explained. I gently punched his arm and smiled. "Just focus on becoming a hero. E.H. is always an option if you change your mind and want to be one."

I walked past Hitoshi and heard him quietly stutter, "Th- Thanks."

As I entered the dorm, Tonuko walked by Hitoshi. Hitoshi hesitated before exclaiming, "Tonuko Kuntai!" Tonuko raised an eyebrow, then turned.

"Oh, you're one of the academic kids Kyle was hanging around with. What's your name again?"

"Hitoshi Makino," Hitoshi quietly answered. Tonuko nodded then looked Hitoshi up and down.

"Nice to meet you. Do you need something? You look like you just rolled around in the dirt," Tonuko observed. Hitoshi looked down at his pajama pants, which were mud stained, rubbed the back of his head, and shrugged.

"O- Oh, not really. I just wanted to say I'm a big fan of yours!" Tonuko smiled and held out his fist.

"Thanks man, means a lot." Hitoshi and Tonuko fist bumped before Tonuko walked inside. As Hitoshi made his way back to the academic dorm he thought, "What do I do? I can't let Kyle go and fight a Care-Giver on his own ... he's not gonna make it! I know I should trust in the heroes, but Kyle just isn't thinking straight. I- I want to save him!"

Next Day, Saturday:

I yawned as I woke naturally and scratched my lower back as I stood. I got a good stretch of my back, then opened the curtains. Unsurprisingly, I saw a ton of people talking and hanging around campus.

We were told we wouldn't have any classes or training on the weekends.

Aren't those just two wasted days? I can't afford to miss a day of training ... I can't lose.

I showered and dressed before heading to the training center to practice some special moves.

I did the same on Sunday, as well as after school every day until the day before Halloween—the second to last day at B.E.G. Unlike on Saturday, I woke abruptly and energized. I jumped out of bed, showered, and put on my hero costume.

Before I put on my tank top, I looked at myself in the mirror, at all my scars. The scars from the training tournament, the kidnappers, The Uprisers, and my childhood. I gripped my shirt in my hand as I looked at my drained face.

"Why ... can't I just be happy? Why can't I smile and laugh and have a truly good time every day like everyone else? What's it like to be truly happy with your life?" I asked myself.

Gladiator had said we'd have special events today and tomorrow, with today focused on team combat. The rumors existed that we were gonna fight some upperclassmen. When I reached the others outside, I saw Gladiator holding a clipboard. He cleared his throat and looked up at us.

"Good m- morning everyone! Today, w- we're doing a r- rescue mission! We wi- will travel to Jun-ction Three and e- elaborate from there!" We followed him across town, passing Jennifer's restaurant. It was empty this time, and the front window wasn't fixed yet. We reached the new junction, and I was pretty impressed. It was much smaller, one humongous apartment building surrounded by walls.

"So, we finally get to train here, eh?" Xavier rhetorically asked. Tanner skirted up next to him and threw his arm around Xavier's shoulder while observing the huge tower.

"Guess so. About time we train with the big dogs," Tanner nonchalantly stated.

"Today you will be trying to rescue four civilians from inside this building. The twist is that they are being held hostage by our top four seniors. You mustn't damage the building or harm the civilians in any way. Good luck!" Gladiator explained, then looked happy with himself that he didn't stutter. I took a few steps forward, expecting the others to follow, and I felt a hand grab my forearm.

"Wait Kyle," Ryuu said. I looked back, confused, then glanced at Olivia, who was walking toward us.

"We should split into four even groups to safely search the four floors for the hostages. Having groups should give us better odds for speed and beating the seniors," Olivia pronounced. The others agreed so I sighed and went along with it. We ensured Xavier, Tonuko, Ashlyn, and I were in separate groups. Mine included Jax, Olivia, Amy, and me. I led them into the building and to the stairs.

"Let's take the stairs up to the fourth floor. The elevator is an easy way to get ambushed," I commanded. After climbing one flight, we saw that the rest of the stairs had caved in.

"Well ... I guess we're taking the elevator!" Amy shouted. I reluctantly went with them into the elevator and to the top floor. As the doors opened, Amy leapt out and scanned the area. The lobby was pretty small, and there were hallways on either side. Amy closed her eyes and sniffed the air, then informed us, "Liam's scent is coming from the right."

"Oh shit, we got Liam?" Olivia asked in a panic. Jax and I looked at each other and shrugged.

"Uh, who's Liam?" he asked.

"Liam is the strongest senior, the number one in the nation. He has red and black spiky hair, and his strength numbs your senses according to which of his fingers touches you," Olivia explained as she gripped her staff.

Her description sounds like that ass from the other night. I can't wait to fight him.

"Okay, so just don't let him touch me. Easy," I boasted, then marched forth.

"Kyle, we can't just march in headfirst! We need a plan!" Jax yelled in a nervous tone. I stopped and shrugged without turning.

"This guy is nothing compared to Bl- to villains," I retorted. I continued walking and they followed. After we passed a few doors, Olivia let some of her wisps float out of her hand and into the wall.

"Stop, he's ahead!" she blurted, so we stopped. We heard footsteps echoing in the distance, getting closer, and I couldn't help but smirk. I activated Tyrant and Energy Conversion, and as the darkness crept up my body, Liam came into sight. He wore a long, gray jacket, black gloves, and a fuzzy black headband.

"Hey, it's the pouty kid from the public school! Glad I got to you first!" Liam antagonized with a grin. He bolted at me—much faster than I predicted he would be—and ripped off his glove. I dodged his hand and kicked him in the stomach. Liam flew toward the ceiling, stopped himself on it, then leapt at me and smacked my forehead with his pointer finger. I stood and looked around, completely dumbfounded. He smirked and walked backward to face us.

"Fuck, he got him!" Olivia yelled as she sucked back in her wisps.

"Kyle, you good?! Can you hear or see?!" Jax asked as he shook my shoulder. I glanced back at him with a blank stare, then nodded. However, I couldn't feel a thing.

Second Floor:

Tonuko cautiously walked around the shops, then motioned for his team to move forward. Connor was the first to march on and he crouched next to Tonuko.

"The hostage must be in a shop, most likely tied up. If we can distract the senior, one of us can sneak in and grab the hostage, and leave unscathed," Connor suggested in a whisper. Tonuko shushed him as he nodded and focused on the ground beneath his feet. Tonuko felt light footsteps on the soles of his feet.

"The senior is near," Sophia stated as she looked around, listening.

"Yeah, and sounds like a girl," Scarlett added. Tonuko slowly peered around the corner and saw the frizzy-haired senior—the one who was with Liam when they'd approached me—walking away from them. She was in a wide hallway, surrounded by different brandless stores. The senior wore rainbow leggings, a long-sleeved, black crop top, and a gold choker. She skipped down the hall, stopped suddenly, and turned.

"There you freshies are! Come fight me already!" she proclaimed with a bright smile. She held her fists in the air and her hair was up in two large buns, secured with pink scrunchies.

Tonuko ducked back behind the corner and formulated, "We can't charge in head on, we don't know her strength. Instead, we should split and try to entrap her. Two go around this section, and two go by her back. I'm assuming the hostage is somewhere in the hallways she's guarding, but still double check all the shops on your way.

If you find the hostage, immediately leave." Everyone nodded.

"We should keep the duos with people who go to the same school, that way we'll have better teamwork on both sides. Sophia and I will go around," Connor suggested. Tonuko nodded in agreement, then waved them off.

"Yeah, that makes the most sense. You two go and be sure to search for the hostage first. That should be our priority," Tonuko commanded. He took a deep breath as Connor and Sophia snuck away, then jumped out from the corner.

"Oh hey, you're the number-one freshie, aren't you? Great, I get to see how strong this year's freshies really are!" the senior exclaimed when she saw him. Tonuko cracked his neck as Scarlett walked out from around the corner.

"And I get to see how much better I am than a senior!" he mocked. As he held out his hands he thought, *"Come on, you are the number one. All that straining on your strength ... use it!"* Tonuko swiped his hands and clapped them, making dozens of pillars out of the walls and guiding them toward her. The senior leapt over the first two, causing them to crash into each other, then she sprinted toward Tonuko and Scarlett.

Scarlett let a green mist flow from her body and warned Tonuko, "Try to not breathe in too much. One sniff of this perfume and you'll be all kinds of nauseous!" Tonuko covered his nose and mouth with his sleeve, and the senior girl held her breath as she charged the two. Four pillars trailed her, but she was too fast, and managed to run between Tonuko and Scarlett and touch both of their arms.

First Floor:

Rake felt his hands, each missing two fingers, on the ground and closed his eyes. After a few seconds, three snakes burrowed out and reattached to his fingers, then he stood.

"There's one person on this floor, and he's on the other side of the building. He's guarding the hostage, who is tied to a chair by her arms and she has tape over her eyes and mouth. I'm keeping an eye on the senior," Rake informed the group.

Tanner nodded, looking impressed, then commented, "That's a pretty creepy but versatile strength dude." Rake thanked him, ignoring the creepy part, then Ashlyn took charge.

"Let's get this hostage and get out! What did the senior look like?" Rake closed his eyes again and took a deep breath.

"He's pretty short, heavy, has a shaved head, and looks pretty damn angry," Rake explained. Ashlyn rubbed the back of her head, then glanced over at Tanner, who sighed.

"Looks like we're up against the fourth strongest of the seniors. His strength is something about calories, but I'm not sure what. All I know is he's stronger than he looks," Tanner confirmed.

"Doesn't matter, we can beat him," Camilla shrugged." With the four of us, we just have to overwhelm him then bring the hostage outside." She walked in front of the group, leaving them to follow. "I'm the queen of E.H., and I sure as hell am not gonna let the queen of B.E.G. outdo me." Tanner wheeled circles around the group as they walked through the large, open lobby.

"This wall is a half-circle; so, this is the flat part, and it's curved in these two hallways," Rake described as he pointed at the corridors on the right and left. "We shouldn't split up, and it wouldn't be productive if we did. They're the same length and lead to the same place. The guy hasn't

moved out of the room, so I think he's waiting for us."
Ashlyn nodded, then she turned serious.

"Let's move quickly. If we can get the hostage fast, we can go and help the others, especially the groups facing the king or queen of B.E.G." Tanner nodded, then wheeled into the hall. The others followed close behind. Tanner stopped wheeling to make less noise. They slowly crept around the curve and saw the door that led into the hostage room. Rake put his finger to his lips and tip-toed next to the door.

"This guy knows we're here, but he's trying to act unbothered. His paced slowed and his breathing quickened slightly. I think he knows my snake is in there," Rake thought. Camilla held up her hand then counted down from three. They took a deep breath then burst into the room. They surrounded both the hostage and the senior and Tanner took charge.

"Give us the girl, or we're going to take her by force. You're outnumbered by some of the tops of our schools, so it would be wise to not resist," Tanner nonchalantly commanded. His threat only made the senior chuckle.

"Oh, those empty threats don't worry me. I'm one of the tops at the best school, so it seems that carries a heavier weight than the top of the freshies, right?" the senior sarcastically questioned. Tanner rolled his eyes and took his hands out of his pockets, created a disc, and dropped it onto his left foot. As it spun extremely fast, Tanner tossed it into the air, spun around, and kicked it at the senior. The disc narrowly missed, grazing the senior's ear.

"I tried to warn you." Tanner sped around the third year, getting faster by the second. Ashlyn created two snow barriers, trapping them.

"Get him Tanner!" Ashlyn cheered. Tanner threw another disc at the senior and jumped in to go for a kick. Suddenly, the senior swiftly side-hopped, dodging Tanner's attack, and swung a punch. Tanner created and grabbed onto an air disc, avoiding the punch, then he swung on the disc, going for another kick.

"Tanner, you should know my strength! I'm not going to get hit that easily!" the senior boasted. He grabbed Tanner's leg and punched him in the stomach. Tanner spat as the punch landed then soared into the wall behind the hostage. The impact created deep cracks in the bricks but didn't break the wall. A pit formed in Rake's stomach, and his eyes widened.

"Wh- What's your name anyway?!" Rake yelled. The third year smirked, watching Tanner fall to the ground, then he turned around and stood tall.

"Andy Clem, but I'm known as CC in the hero world!" CC responded. Camilla clenched her first and swiped her right hand across her body. Strong winds tripped CC and with a loud thud.

Camilla screeched, "I don't wanna hear your stupid bragging! We're getting the hostage out of here quickly and efficiently!" CC quickly jumped back to his feet and crossed his arms.

"Bragging? When did I brag? I was just answering your friend's question, that's all, hotshot," CC retorted, making Camilla scoff.

"Whatever, we're beating you and getting out. Simple as that."

Third Floor:

Ryuu walked ahead of the others, not saying a word. Xavier softly grabbed Cindy's arm, then sighed. "Listen, just stay a bit back. Ryuu has been acting strange since this whole combination event started, so I'm gonna go try to clear things up."

Cindy nodded, grabbed Iris's hand, and stood still. They let the two get a good distance ahead, then started walking again.

"Yo, Ryuu, everything good?" Xavier asked; Ryuu didn't look at him.

"Fine," he swiftly responded. Xavier looked around, trying to spot any suspicious activity in the empty room, but saw nothing.

"You sure? Ever since the E.H. kids came, you haven't really been talking to anyone, not even Olivia. You and Kyle clearly picked a fight with each other; what happened?" Xavier questioned, trying for a solid response. Ryuu took a deep breath, then stopped walking.

"We discussed something important, and it's all figured out now," he stated. Xavier raised an eyebrow, then suddenly Ryuu put his hand on Xavier's chest. He activated his dragon eyes and seethed, "She's lurking." Xavier looked around, then heard a loud grumble.

"Ugh, stupid little boys. So blind." They turned and saw a tall, fit girl with curly black hair that faded to blonde. Ryuu took a step back, seeing that she held Cindy and Iris by the backs of their collars. The girls were unconscious.

Chapter 30
Full Commitment

The sensation of nothing was very weird. I could see I was standing on the ground but felt nothing. All the soreness and pain in my body was gone. Whenever I blinked I couldn't feel it, I couldn't even feel myself breathe.

"What the hell do we do?" Jax asked worriedly. "Our strongest teammate is basically out of commission!" Amy dug her claws into the ground.

"Well, we obviously don't give up! Who the hell needs Kyle anyway?!" Amy shouted as she ran at Liam on all fours.

"Amy, don't just charge in!" Olivia pleaded, but it was too late. Amy leapt onto the wall and used her claws to run across it, then she leapt past Liam and swiped at him. He narrowly dodged and swiped his own hand at her. Amy spun around, dodging Liam's hand, and jumped onto the wall and back at him. She grabbed Liam's forehead, swung on it, landed on his shoulders, and pulled back on his eyes. Liam spun around, loosening Amy's grip, and threw her into the wall. In the process, he touched her arm with his ring finger, and after Amy landed, she rubbed her nose.

"Dammit, I can't smell a thing! I lost the hostage!" Amy complained. Jax glanced over at Olivia and took out his switchblade. She gripped her staff with both hands.

"Well, pretty boy, let's do this thing." Jax spun the blade in his hand, grabbed it backward, and grinned.

"Hell yeah!" Smoke seeped out of his mouth, down his arm, and covered his knife in a thick layer. "Just one cut and he's under my control." Liam pulled his glove out of his coat pocket and smirked.

"I don't even want to immobilize the rest of you. This'll be a bla-" Suddenly, he was met with a face full of black flames. I followed through, making him crash through the wall. I stood straight up and grinned.

"Just because I can't feel anything, doesn't mean I can't punch," I boasted. Liam chuckled as he walked back out of the hole in the wall.

"Should've let me put my glove back on." My eyes widened as my vision faded to darkness, and I fell backward, not knowing if I'd hit the ground yet.

What's happening? Where am I? I can't even tell if I'm still facing him. Did I move?

"C'mon, get him while he's distracted!" Amy commanded as she leapt at Liam. He used his forearm to block her claws, then punched her in the cheek.

"You freshmen have to learn to think a little! My glove is still off!" Liam sighed. Amy crashed into the ground and didn't move, clearly affected by nearly all of Liam's effects. Jax gulped and stood defensively, holding his knife at eye level.

"If we're gonna win, we have to outsmart him," Olivia quipped, letting her wisps float around her head. Liam walked out from the rubble, cracked his neck, suddenly lunged at Jax, and swung a punch with his gloved hand. Jax blocked with his left arm and swung his knife across Liam's body. He cut a hole in the shirt Liam wore under his Jacket, but made no skin contact, then Olivia discreetly sent five wisps at Liam. In response, he jumped back and chuckled.

"I know how your strength works, Olivia. We were given a packet detailing all of your strengths. As long as I don't let those things touch me or breathe them in, I'm safe!" Liam taunted and Olivia frowned. Her wisps moved faster so Jax took the opportunity to charge in and attack Liam. He swiped his knife several times but Liam dodged every swing. Next, he kicked Jax's feet out from under him. He fell, leapt back onto his feet, and hopped up next to

Olivia. Liam continued to dodge wisps and once he was near the two, Olivia swung her staff at him. However, Liam was ready. He grabbed the staff, pulled it toward him, and kicked Olivia in the stomach. She flew back into Jax and the two crashed into a wall. Jax held Olivia's arms, worried she was down for the count, and was pleasantly surprised when she glanced back at him with a mischievous, flirtatious smirk.

"We can continue this later," Olivia simpered, making Jax blush. She stood, spun her staff in her hands a couple of times, and smashed it into the ground. Liam grinned, spun in a circle while lifting his jacket and grinned.

"I'm clean, no wisps on me! What's that staff gonna do?!" he yelled. His cocky demeanor disappeared when he saw Olivia lick her lips.

"Star formation," Olivia stated. Liam's eyes widened and he frantically looked around the hall. The wisps clung to different parts of the floor, walls, and ceiling, creating a star. *"Purifying Ray!"* Olivia screeched. The wisps lit up and shot out extremely bright lasers onto Liam, blinding him. Jax stood, holding a bow and arrow made of pink smoke, lined up the shot, and let the arrow soar.

Flashback:

"Jaxon, I'm trying my hardest to help you succeed ... as of right now, you're a one trick pony," Fallen sighed as he put his hand on Jax's head, who was crouching and wheezing. "You need to be more versatile, more than just a promising sidekick."

Jax glanced up, only opening one eye, and asked, "But how? My strength is simply smoke coming out of my mouth. Any kind of strength-enhancing additions to our costumes are against the law. What more can my strength do?" Fallen smirked, patted his head, and ruffled his hair before starting to walk away.

"Use that brain of yours! You'll figure out something!" Fallen shouted. Jax looked down at his hands, then clenched them.

Present:

The mist arrow flew past Olivia's ear, narrowly missing it, then soared into the light mess. The commotion stopped and before the light faded, Jax strutted up to Olivia and slung his arm around her.

"It's over, he's under my command," Jax said as he fake-yawned. The light vanished, revealing Liam, who stood dumfounded with red eyes. Olivia grinned, looked over, and kissed Jax on the cheek.

"Fix it up, pretty boy," she commanded. Jax looked at Olivia with flirty eyes as he walked toward Liam, then he stuck his hands into his pockets and took a deep breath.

"Alright bud, fix up Kyle and Amy. Get rid of your effects on them," Jax nonchalantly demanded.

"Yes sir," Liam responded with a nod. He walked over and touched me with his pointer finger, thumb, and middle fingers. I instantly regained my sense of touch, sight, and hearing.

I sighed, "Man, I didn't do anything. Lame." Jax laughed as he helped me up. Once Amy was relieved of Liam's strength, we followed her to the hostage.

"So, what's with the lipstick mark on your cheek?" I teased Jax quietly. Jax blushed and pushed me, then rubbed his cheek.

"Nothing. Shut up," he muttered in response. I chuckled as I opened the door Amy stopped at and was surprised to see messy, spikey gray hair. I ripped the blindfold off the hostage and smirked.

"What's up Hitoshi?" I asked. Hitoshi looked up and grinned, then shuffled his hands.

"Could ya get these ropes off me? I'm starting to get rope burn!" he complained. I melted the knot in the rope, letting it fall off his body. Hitoshi stretched his arms and chest, stood, and sighed, "Alright, get me outta here. I have class to get to." I put my hands on my head and thought for a moment.

"Since Jax has control over Liam, we don't need everyone to escort Hitoshi. I'll go help people on the first floor and make my way up from there," I said. The others nodded and we made our way back to the elevator. Once on the first floor, the three took Liam and Hitoshi outside while I ran toward where I heard commotion.

Second Floor:

The senior slid on her feet past Scarlett and Tonuko, touching an arm of each as she sped by them. Tonuko braced for impact, expecting a big attack or pain, but nothing happened. He opened his eyes and blinked a couple of times then glanced to where Scarlett had been.

"Tonuko, where'd you go?" Scarlett asked, looking around, confused.

"What do you mean? Where'd you go?" Tonuko responded. The realization came and a pit grew in Tonuko's stomach as he looked back at the senior, who was beaming with joy and clapping her hands.

"Wow, you guys are so clueless! Classic freshies!" she giggled.

"We're invisible," Tonuko stated bluntly. The senior's laughing faltered, and after she nodded, Tonuko seethed, "Yeah, not so clueless, huh?" The senior shrugged and backed up a few feet.

"Who cares if we're invisible? It doesn't hurt us," Scarlett added with a giggle.

"If that's what you think," she sighed. Tonuko knew the truth and sweat dripped down his face as he clenched his fist.

"Scarlett, if we can't see each other, how are we going to fight together? Connor and Sophia don't know we're invisible, so they'll catch us in the crossfire or start searching for us. Our chemistry is fucked like this," Tonuko explained.

"Well then, we just have to beat this senior down before Connor gets here," Scarlett muttered as she slid her foot back. Tonuko took a deep breath, crouched, and placed his hands on the ground. The floor around the senior stretched all the way to the ceiling, essentially trapping her in a box.

"Let's keep her trapped until the others come!" Tonuko suggested.

"Yeah, good idea," Scarlett responded. They relaxed slightly but then a banging came from inside the box. With each pound a crack formed in the wall and Tonuko frowned. A giant hole broke through and there stood the third-year, her fists covered with large brass-knuckles.

"Since my strength isn't good for physical fights, I got some equipment!" Tonuko hopped back and shot pillars out from the sides at the senior. When they were about to make contact, something hit Tonuko, knocking him over and making him lose concentration.

"Oh my gosh, sorry! I didn't know you moved!" Scarlett yelled. She felt around for his arm and helped him up. Tonuko hesitated, grabbed a rock from his broken wall, and tossed it in his mouth. Scarlett, now grossed out, asked, "What did you just do?"

"Now you can see where I am, right?" Tonuko mumbled, cringing from the salty taste.

"Clever boy. Not surprising from the number-one freshie!" The senior dashed to Tonuko's right and kicked. She didn't connect with him. After a second Tonuko caught Scarlett and the two flew back. They skidded on the ground and slammed into a garage-type door.

"Damn, she's strong. I tried blocking, but-"

"It's fine," Tonuko swiftly interrupted as he stood. "We've got this." Pillars shot from around them, barreling toward the senior.

"By the way, you can call me Visible! That's my hero name after all!" Visible wound up and punched the middle point of all fight pillars. They shattered and Tonuko tensed up as the debris fell but nothing happened.

"Dammit," Tonuko mumbled, "I still can't do it." Scarlett stood next to him and brushed herself off.

"You gotta stop being so hard on yourself. You've got this!" Scarlett encouraged. She then let off a perfume of strength.

"Thanks, that'll help a lot," Tonuko said. When he took a deep breath, he felt the smoke rush through his blood and he felt physically stronger. He mocked, "That's it, you're defeated!"

"Oh really? You sure are confident!" Visible giggled. Tonuko formed more pillars at his side. Across the room, he morphed dozens of spikes. Simultaneously, both groups shot at Visible. Rolling noises echoed from down the hall. Tonuko glanced over and saw Connor barreling toward Visible. He crashed into her, essentially saving her from Tonuko's attack.

Sophia ran around the corner. "Tonuko, Scarlett?! Where are you guys?!" she yelled as she surveyed the room.

"Over here! Visible makes others invisible by a touch!" Scarlett responded. Sophia saw the floating rock in Tonuko's mouth and sprinted over.

"Fuckin' Connor. He just saved her," Tonuko grumbled. Watching Connor turn invisible made him even angrier.

"I told him not to just charge into battle but of course he ignored me," Sophia scolded. Tonuko started strategizing, then remembered his fight with Xavier during capture the flag.

"Wait, you absorb people's physical properties, right?" Tonuko asked.

"Yeah, if I touch somebody with at least two fingers, I can absorb their physical attack power and speed. The longer I touch someone, the more I absorb. However, getting your physical properties absorbed takes a lot out of you," Sophia explained. "Why?"

"Absorb my power," Tonuko swiftly commanded. "Then, during my next attack, shatter the spikes I create and get out of the way."

"No," Scarlett interrupted, "absorb mine. Tonuko needs his strength to help the other floors when we're done." Tonuko glanced over, obviously saw nothing, and sighed.

"Alright, I'll do it. You just need me to shatter your stuff?" Sophia asked, clarifying before committing. The floating rock moved up and down, so Sophia assumed Tonuko was nodding. She reached out blindly, eventually finding Scarlett's arm and touching it with two fingers. A red smoke poured out of Scarlett, into Sophia's fingers, and eventually lessened. Scarlett's legs shook and she collapsed onto the ground. "G- Go guys ..."

"Now that he's taken care of, time to finish the rest of ya!" Visible shouted. She turned and ran at the three but

Sophia reacted quickly, moving faster than the eye could see, and kicked Visible. Tonuko started the same attack he'd used earlier, this time bigger and faster. There were more spikes, more pillars. Visible giggled then taunted, "You've already tried this! I'm not stupid, y'know!"

"Yeah, of course I know!" Tonuko yelled, spitting out the rock in the process. Once the pillars and spikes were close, Sophia leapt up and went ballistic. She shattered the spikes in a flash, and, to Tonuko's advantage, Visible destroyed the pillars with one punch. As the debris fell, Sophia ran down the hall. Tonuko screamed, "Rock Trap!" The tiny pebbles closest to Visible expanded rapidly, creating a thick sphere around her, then the other pieces crashed onto the sphere and grew, expanding it. Eventually, the sphere was massive, touching the ceiling and stopping just a few inches in front of Tonuko and Scarlett. As he panted, Tonuko thought, "Dammit, I can't keep this up for long ... but it worked. I really do have Earth Control."

"T- Tonuko, I didn't know y- you could do that," Scarlett commented, barely keeping her eyes open.

"Yeah, I didn't either," Tonuko chuckled weakly as they faded back to visibility. "I guess I do have Earth Control." Connor and Sophia walked over to them and Connor apologized.

"Sorry about ruining your attack earlier. I was too excited about fighting and I acted foolishly." Tonuko shrugged. Sophia helped him up and as soon as she let go of his arm, Tonuko fell down again.

"You guys need to go, now. I'll keep her contained until you're off the floor," Tonuko wheezed.

After Connor helped Scarlett up, she shouted, "Are you crazy?! We're not leaving you!" Tonuko looked up at Sophia with one eye and gave her a silent command. She knew exactly what he wanted and nodded.

571

"Let's go, quickly. Connor, you help Scarlett get to the elevator, I'll get the hostage. Move!" Sophia demanded. Connor nodded, picked up Scarlett, turned his legs to ice, and skated toward the elevator. Sophia backed up a couple of steps and saluted Tonuko. He held up two fingers and saluted in response as Scarlett ran toward where she'd come. Tonuko sat on his butt and looked down.

"Fuck, I can't keep this up much longer. I feel like ... the world is spinning."

First Floor:

Camilla glared ferociously at CC, who stood in a defensive stance. Rake, Camilla, and Ashlyn surrounded him but CC was unworried.

"Don't be reckless! We have to take him down and immobilize him! Rake, do your snakes have any kind of venom that paralyzes people?!" Ashlyn asked.

"Yes, they actually do!" Rake responded as his eyes lit up. He gripped the fingers of his left hand and the veins faded to purple. He ripped his fingers off and tossed them out. They formed into snakes in the air and burrowed into the ground once they landed.

"Eww, creepy," CC cringed. Ashlyn formed ice spikes on all sides of him, then Camilla thickened the air inside the ice chamber. This impaired CC's vision but it didn't matter. With one stomp on the ground, the floor cracked on all sides and the ice shattered. A cold wind blew throughout the room, throwing the freshmen off their feet.

"Why are you so damn strong?" Camilla seethed. Rake swiftly stood back up and focused with one eye closed. Ashlyn glanced at the knocked-out Tanner then back at CC. Camilla cracked her fingers and muttered, "Time to get serious." Whirlwinds formed at her feet and hands, and she used them to boost forward. Camilla soared at CC. When he punched, she shot out winds from the whirlwinds to propel herself over him. She flipped in the air, pointed the soles of her feet at him, then shot out explosive, violent winds. He stumbled forward and swiped his right arm back, barely missing Camilla. The wind force from his swipe sent her flying into the wall.

"Good distraction Camilla!" Ashlyn cheered as she ran in at CC. Snow formed under her feet, lifting her up as if she was running on stairs, then she jumped and shot snow at CC's head. He dodged and swung another punch. The snow on Ashlyn's feet crumbled. After dodging the punch, she flipped and shot more snow using her hands. CC was ready, though, and he caught the pillars and used them to throw Ashlyn into the wall. Camilla was back in the fight, charging full speed at CC. At the same time, two snakes shot up from the ground. CC was nimble enough to dodge all three attackers. Camilla smirked; him dodging was a part of her plan.

"Simple minded," she sighed.

Now behind him, she swayed her hands out and swiped them across her chest. Large waves of wind flooded CC's head, creating an awful, extremely loud noise in his ears. CC yelped as he held his ears and closed his eyes. I soared into the room, past Rake, and punched CC in the cheek. He crashed into the same wall he'd punched Tanner into. Three snakes shot out of the ground and bit onto CC's calves, injecting him with the paralyzing venom. I backed up, glanced at Camilla, and smirked but she quickly looked away, annoyed.

"Woah, Kyle?! Where'd you come from?!" Rake asked in an excited tone as we fist-bumped.

"My floor beat the king, so I came to help. I couldn't be carried like I was and not give someone a good punch," I responded. Rake and I snickered, then I looked over at Ashlyn. She was still on the ground, so I walked over to her and held out my hand. "You're not done yet, are you?" Ashlyn smiled, took my hand, and stood.

"Of course not, I'm just getting started!" she confidently responded. I analyzed the room, saw Tanner, who was hurt, the hostage, and CC.

I commanded, "Alright, you guys take those three outside. If you need help, Jax, Olivia, and Amy are out there. I'm going to the next floor to help." Camilla rolled her eyes, crossed her arms, and let out a "Hmph!"

"Who put you in charge?!" she retorted.

"Go bring them outside, thanks," Ashlyn stated with a grin. Camilla stuttered, flustered, and grumbled as she untied the hostage. I nodded to Ashlyn and we ran out of the room. When we made it inside the elevator, she suggested, "How about I go to the second floor and you go to the third. One more person for each floor should be more than enough help."

"Yeah," I agreed, "Good idea." When we reached the second floor, Ashlyn sprinted out and I headed to the third.

Second Floor:

Ashlyn ran down the hallway, listening for any commotion. Instead, she found Sophia, Connor carrying Scarlett, and who she assumed was the hostage walking out from around a corner.

"Oh, Ashlyn, hey! Did your floor beat the senior?" Sophia asked with a big smile.

"Yep, looks like you guys did too. Where's Tonuko?" Ashlyn asked. The mood changed from happy to guilty.

Connor couldn't look Ashlyn in the eye as he informed her, "Tonuko is keeping Visible at bay so we can escape. He's going to collapse soon; I don't think we should have left him alone." Ashlyn nodded and ran past them, toward the corner from where they'd come.

"Where do you think you're going?!" Sophia shouted.

"To help Tonuko obviously! A hero doesn't leave people behind!" She let those words hang in the air as she sprinted away, and she continued to run until she reached the main hallway. Ashlyn looked in awe at the massive sphere and saw Tonuko collapsed onto the ground. "Tonuko!"

"Is that, A- Ashlyn?" he mumbled, looking up and seeing her running toward him. His vision was blurry and shaky, and he was sweating and panting heavily.

"Tonuko, you're in no shape to keep this up. The others should be at the elevator now, you can release Visible," Ashlyn implored.

"B- But what if she attacks us? I need to keep her here ... just a little longer," Tonuko wheezed. He looked down at his hands and thought, "Kyle and Xavier wouldn't give up. Why should I?" A deep, rumbling noise boomed from inside the sphere, then a crack shot down the middle of it. After a few more hits, a large hole burst out of the sphere, sending rocks flying down the hall. Once the hole was made, Tonuko released the rest of the sphere, which exploded into millions of tiny pebbles. Visible's face looked serious but quickly changed to gleeful when she turned to Ashlyn and Tonuko.

"Wow, what a fight!" Visible shouted, putting her hands behind her head. "What a shame I lost though, huh?" Her happiness surprised Ashlyn and Tonuko, and they relaxed. Ashlyn lowered her fists, and Tonuko sat up, trying his hardest to hold on to consciousness.

"So ... you aren't going to attack us?" Ashlyn asked. Visible grimaced and shook her head.

"I'm not a real villain, that would just be cruel. The other freshies got the hostage off the floor so I lost!"

Tonuko grinned as he fell to the ground facing up and lifted a fist into the air.

"We did it ... we did it." Ashlyn and Visible smiled at him and helped him up, then they headed toward the elevator.

Third Floor:

The elevator dinged as the doors opened. Through the crack I saw Xavier and Ryuu standing back-to-back, and Cindy and Iris laying on the ground. The boys were on high alert, constantly scanning the room around them.

"Yo, you guys need some help?!" I asked hysterically as I ran toward them.

"Kyle duck!" Ryuu screeched, jumping at my head. I crouched and watched as he flew over my head, colliding into a girl.

What the hell, I didn't even notice her. How did she sneak up on me without a trace?

"We think she has some kind of presence-nullifying strength," Xavier informed me. "Without Ryuu's dragon vision, she moves completely unnoticed, even if she's right in front of us." I nodded as I stood back up, then turned around. Ryuu slid on the ground a few feet away; the senior had fallen onto the ground. Blood dripped from her face as she swore.

"Fucking freshmen, always charging in head first without thinking of repercussions. How idiotic!" She leapt to her feet and walked to her right. As she did so, she vanished from sight. Her presence was concealed, but I noticed Ryuu's eyes wandering past us. With the jolt from his left arm, I swung my right fist up, uppercutting her in the jaw. She stumbled back and came into sight again, so I swiveled around and swung a kick with my left foot. The senior ducked, swiping my feet from under me in the process. As I fell back, I managed to create flames from my

576

left arm and launch them out at her. She bent her body back, narrowly dodging.

How the hell is she so nimble?

When I hit the ground, it looked like I kept falling. The room faded in the distance, leaving me in a familiar realm: my mind abyss. I laid there, floating around in silence while very confused.

"Why am I here?"

I could hear distant commotion, like fighting or talking, so I swam to where I heard the noise. After a couple of seconds, I saw a bright light in my peripheral vision to my right. I turned to face the familiar silhouette of my mother.

"Kyle, what are you doing?" I blinked a couple of times, completely lost at this point.

"What do you mean? I'm in the middle of a training fight, I have to get back."

I swam again, but her words made me stop in my tracks.

"I don't care about the training fight. You know what I'm talking about. Don't lie to your mother." Sweat dripped down the side of my head, then I took a deep breath.

"No, I don't know. All I'm doing is getting stronger so I can avenge you and everyone else Tyrant has hurt. What's so bad about that?"

"Why are you working with It? Why are you letting It control you, Kyle?"

"It? Letting what control me? Mom, what in the world are you talking about?"

"The demon, Kyle. You're letting that thing make decision for you, aren't you?" I thought about all the talks

577

I'd had with the Tyrant Demon, but nothing came to mind as to why my mother was so against It.

"It's my real strength, and it's helping me get strong. I don't understand what the issue is here."

Third Floor:

"Kyle, what the hell … Wake up!" Xavier yelled while shaking me. Ryuu stopped fighting and ran over to us, and the senior turned off her strength as well. Ryuu stood over me, looking down at my unconscious face. From under my right eye, small, black lines crept out from my closed eyelid.

"Let's get him outside," the senior commanded. "This is a training battle, not a real one. If he's seriously injured, we need to get him medical attention immediately." The boys nodded and Ryuu helped the senior carry Iris and Cindy as Xavier picked me up. They traveled down to the first floor where everyone was gathered. Gladiator and two school nurses ran over when Ryuu, Xavier, and the senior made it outside, asking what had happened. The senior informed them, "The kid hit the ground and passed out. I don't know much about him, but there're some weird black lines coming out of his eye."

"One of his strengths involves the same darkness covering his body and giving him some kind of power boost. It comes out of his hands from what I've seen in combat," Ryuu added swiftly. The nurses requested that I be laid down and they checked my vitals.

As they treated anything they could, Gladiator instructed the class, "F- Follow Liam back to campus. For now, cl- class is dismissed." Everyone nodded and followed Liam, who had already walked out of the Junction.

Kyle's Mind:

"*You know that strength is called Tyrant. It's what he and J are afraid of in you. That thing is a* physical manifestation of your view on your father, Kyle. Why on Earth would you ever trust it?"

"Wh- What do you mean? It's not how I view Tyrant, it's my hatred toward him. It has the same goals as me, gives me power in dangerous situations, and gives me advice when I'm fighting. Mom, this demon thing is helping me stay safe while staying strong!"

"Yes, Mrs. Gem Straiter. I am simply acting as a guardian to your dear son. You can trust me; all I wish to do is annihilate anything that is hurting Kyle. Our number-one priority, is killing that monster that tormented him for years."

"How should I trust something with that name, the Tyrant Demon? How should I trust something that is using your emotions to lead you into danger? Kyle, I know you're going to fight BloodShot; I won't allow it."

"Mom, I'm doing it with or without your permission. This is to protect my peers, who keep getting hurt because of me!"

I heard noises of what sounded like crying coming from the silhouette. Her next words destroyed me.

"Listen to yourself, Kyle. You can't even call anyone a friend." That sentence made my heart sink. For my entire life, I'd never been able to truly think of people as friends. I'd always thought they had a secret motive, a reason to use me for my power. I know it's just a side effect from my childhood ... but ...

"Wh- Why ... can't I? Why don't I trust anyone?"

"Kyle, you have a job to do. Do not back down on me now." When I looked up, I saw the demon floating in front of me. Its glaring smile was sharp and wide, and its overall presence gave me ... comfort.

"Y- Yeah, you're right. I should get back to training, so Mom, let me free."

"J'm not going to let you fight for a cause you don't have to be a part of! Don't do this to me Kyle. Don't make me watch you end up like me because you tried to fight against your father before you're ready!" For some reason, I felt anger. Hearing her talk like that, it sounded like hypocrisy to me.

The demon floated through me and put its hands on my shoulders as I roared, "What do you mean 'Don't do this to you?!' Don't you know what he did to me ... what you did to me?! Don't you know that you left me alone to be beaten and tortured every day?!"

"Kyle, J-"

"No, y'know what? I don't wanna hear about any of that shit from you. You left me; you took the easy way out. Don't you know ... how damn jealous I've been of you?! I didn't ask to live this life. I've been looking for a way to escape it for years now!"

"That's it; let it all out now. No need for emotional thoughts like this out on the battlefield. Thinking will only slow you down." I tensed my fist and squeezed my eyes shut. Finally, I let loose a thought that'd been lingering in the back of my mind for years.

"Mom, you left me all alone! You're just as bad as Tyrant, you just stood by and watched me get beat every day! He was gone half the day, and in those times, you could've told heroes, or police, or at least done something to try and stop him! But no, you did absolutely fucking nothing! You stood by and let me be abused, injured, traumatized! Yeah, maybe I am working with a demon that's

manifested from my pure rage, so what?! It's the only thing that has protected me my entire life!"

"**Stop it right now, you know that's not true! I loved you so much, I never wanted to leave you! I wish I could go back and redo all that's happened! I dream of being able to kiss you and hug you just one last time! Ever since I transferred myself into your head, all I've wanted to do is be able to hold you and tell you everything is going to be okay because I'm here for you! Don't you know how much torture it is seeing the light of my life get beat and nearly killed every day by the man I loved?! Kyle, every single day for the past eight years I've wished I could have been there for you more, loved you more, gotten you away from him. I would give my life a thousand times to see you smile just once!"**

"M- Mom ..."

"**Please Kyle, don't do this to yourself. Don't end up like me. There are people who are doing the job I wasn't strong enough to do for you. Hazel Sparks, Ashlyn Gray, Tonuko and Danielle Kuntai, Fallen ... they're all there for you. Don't leave them, don't put them through what I did to you. Please.**" Before I could respond, the abyss faded away around me.

I jolted awake in a hospital cot in B.E.G.'s infirmary, scaring the doctor. I sat up, looked around, and saw the doctor holding his chest while panting and chuckling.

"Wow, you scared me half to death! Good thing you're awake, you were out for a few hours." When I awoke, the lines from my eye sunk back into my pupils and were replaced with tears.

581

"D- Did Xavier and Ryuu win?" I asked as I wiped away the tears. "How did the battle go?" The doctor scanned his computer and clicked his tongue as he shook his head.

"Well, they stopped the fight when you mysteriously passed out. They were worried about your condition. So, I guess it was technically a draw." I laid back down and stared at the ceiling, resting my arms on my forehead.

So, my dumbass ruined another event? Fantastic.

I was free to leave since there was no physical damage and I was healed. I made my way out of the school and toward the dorm. As a crisp breeze blew, I took a deep breath and felt my lungs burn. I exhaled as I walked up to the freshman dorm, sighed, then entered the front doors. Some people were sitting around and talking, but it went silent when I cleared my throat.

"Sorry for ruining the event today," I apologized sadly. Scarlett giggled, stood and walked over to me.

"Kyle, no one thinks you ruined the event. We're just glad you're okay," she smiled.

After that, Xavier waddled over to me and leaned on my shoulder as he teased, "Yeah, we were just laughing about how weak you are! Gosh, I thought you were strong enough to handle one fall!" I stepped far to my left as Xavier cackled, causing him to stumble.

"Whatever. I'm going to my room," I muttered, confusing them all as I trudged away. I took the elevator to the top floor, walked over and entered my room, then laid onto my bed and stared at the ceiling. I held my hands up, scanning them front to back, and let them fall onto my chest. I closed my eyes and took a deep breath.

Does Mom just not have faith in my strength or is it something else? Why does she think I'll die if I fight back?

I stood, thinking about going down and hanging out with everyone. When I reached the door, I couldn't get my hand to turn the knob. I slowly looked back, feeling as if I was being watched, and saw the demon a few feet away, towering over me. It was the same height as the ten-foot ceiling.

You are wasting time trying to make friends. You have one purpose, don't lose sight of it.

"B- But you heard my mom: there're people out there who love me!" I whisper–yelled in response.

Bullshit!

That was the first time the demon had yelled at me.

You must train, get stronger, and kill Tyrant. That's all you need to do. You need to get out there and kill BloodShot first! Right now, BloodShot is the only person that should be on your mind!

"What about Ashlyn? She's ... she's amazing and helps me so much. Why can't I think about h-?"

The demon took one step forward, grabbed my neck, and lifted me. My feet dangled and my head touched the ceiling as It pressed me against the door.

ONE! GOAL! YOU MUST KILL TYRANT, KILL BLOODSHOT, AND FREE THE WORLD OF PURE EVIL! WE KNOW HOW THIS STORY ENDS, KYLE STRAITER! BE THE ONE WHO SAVES EVERYONE FROM WHAT WE'VE DONE!

"Kyle, what was that bang?" Ashlyn asked from outside the door. I struggled to breathe and couldn't respond.

"Sorry, I just tripped!" the Tyrant Demon responded with a laugh—its voice was identical to mine.

"Oh, well, do you wanna go get some lunch with me? There's something I want to talk ab-!"

"Nope, sorry! I'm super tired from being healed!" the Tyrant Demon swiftly answered.

"Oh ... maybe tomorrow then," Ashlyn sighed then walked away.

I tried to grab the Tyrant Demon's arm, wanting It to stop choking me so I could apologize to Ashlyn, but my hands went right through its translucent arms.

I will not let you go until you realize the goal.

My life flashed before my eyes, and I felt weaker by the second. I remembered all Tyrant had done to me, Mom sitting by watching, and BloodShot's ridicules. The kidnappers, Lokel dying, The Uprisers ... everything.

My eyebrows furrowed, then I screeched with all my heart, "I know my goal!" The Tyrant Demon smiled, then dropped me. I coughed and wheezed and slowly looked up. It was gone, vanished into thin air. I stood then looked down at my fist. I clenched it tight, making my palm bleed, looked up, and stared out the window.

One goal ... one purpose. Kill BloodShot, then kill Tyrant.

Chapter 31
Halloween

I woke on the floor at 10:00 a.m., which was much later than usual. I yawned as I sat up, then went through my usual morning routine. The soreness from the event was starting to kick in but it was nothing compared to hell month. I dressed in gray sweatpants and a white sweatshirt, then opened my door. Ashlyn stood by the elevator. She smiled cutely and waved. I waved back and entered the elevator with her. Once the elevator started moving, she stepped a little closer. Our hands were barely separate, and, after slight hesitation, I shifted my hand and grabbed hers. She softly held my hand. When the elevator opened, Xavier was on the other side, holding a bowl of cereal and a spoon in his mouth. A grin stretched across his face when he moved his eyes down; I rolled my eyes.

"Look at the little lovebirds holding hands! Aww!" Xavier teased in a muffled voice. We let go of each other's hands as we walked past him, heading toward the kitchen counter where Jax and Olivia were cooking. The three of us sat down, then Ashlyn turned to face me.

"So, are we partners for the event tonight?" she asked bluntly. I pretended to think for a moment, then nodded.

"I mean, yeah, I guess so," I responded smugly.

"You guess so?!" Ashlyn retorted with a fake-offended smile.

I heard giggling to my left, and without glancing over, I shouted, "I know the two lovers cooking together aren't laughing at us!" When I turned, I saw Jax and Olivia chuckling to each other, and Xavier eating.

"You guys are all so ... icky," he sighed. Everyone turned to look at him and Olivia flicked her wrist at him, spraying Xavier with salt. "You asshole, it's in my eyes!" Xavier yelped while looking up and wiping his eyes.

"Don't be talking bad about my Jaxy like that," Olivia tittered after grabbing Jax's waist. I let out a couple of chortles and burst out laughing.

"Jaxy?! You've gotta be kidding!" I cackled. Jax rolled his eyes in response and flipped the pancake on the griddle.

I didn't eat anything that morning; my appetite wasn't on my mind. My stomach felt sick and upside down, like butterflies were scattered within it, because tonight was the night.

We were instructed to go to class at 11:00 a.m. to get instructions on the final activity. Gladiator had informed us yesterday that we would need partners to do this "heroic work," hence why everyone had teamed up. The walk to the school was nice and brisk, with crisp air blowing in our faces. I greeted my academic friends as we walked past.

When we finally made it to class, Gladiator announced, "H- Hello everyone! P- Please, sit next t- to your partner!" Ashlyn and I sat in the front, next to Rake and Amy. A lady in a suit and tie walked into the room. She wore glasses, had a slick bun, carried a clipboard, and scanned the room with sharp eyes.

"Trick-or-treating is a fun tradition for kids yet stressful for parents. As heroes, your job is to help others, whether it is fighting criminals, rescuing hostages, helping in disaster areas, or simply doing good deeds around town. For your official Eccentric High and Bade's Exceptionally Gifted team-up event, you will be assigned to a child who you'll take trick-or-treating. We will send you a text message including a map of the area where you will take the child as well as the child's address. Pick up is at 3:00 p.m.," the woman sternly explained.

"This is so cute," Ashlyn excitedly jabbered as she grabbed my arm. I rolled my eyes yet couldn't help but smile.

"Two groups will be picking up neighbors, and you can go together if you'd like. I have a good feeling the kids will want to go together." As soon as the woman finished her sentence, everyone received a text message. When I looked at my phone, I saw two text messages from an unknown number. After opening them, I saw a screenshot from a map app and a text that read, "Savannah Greene, 127 Ally Road." Rake leaned over to look at my text, then sighed.

"Bummer, we aren't in a group together," he stated.

"Yeah, that's too bad. I wonder who is together."

"Who has Savannah Greene or Christopher Jacobs?" the woman asked. Ashlyn and I raised our hands, as did Jax and Olivia. I looked back and grinned as the woman stated the obvious. "You are the two groups going to get neighbors." I gave Jax a nod and he responded, signifying we would go together. After that, we were dismissed.

Skipping breakfast had caught up to me and I was starving so Ashlyn and I went to grab lunch. We walked around town until we found a sandwich shop, where Ashlyn dragged me inside. As we were seated, Ashlyn's eyes nervously scanned the room.

"So, today's the last day of this combined group," she suddenly spat out, staring at the table. I nodded and slightly snorted, then sighed.

"Yeah, I guess it is. At least it's been a lot of fun. We got some good-ass training and met new people," I responded with a shrug. Our eyes met after a couple of seconds and we blushed.

"It's been a lot of fun hanging out with you, Kyle."

"Yeah, it's been fun being with you, too. Looks like we get to hang out a lot more tonight." Ashlyn bit her lip, clearly thinking or hesitating, and she blurted out, startling everyone in the restaurant.

"Do you maybe wanna be my boyfriend or something?!" I glanced around, surprised, and saw people look at us, then back to their food or friends. I looked at the table and took a deep breath.

"I've never really had something like that, y'know?" I confessed, almost embarrassed.

"I mean, I haven't either," she admitted. "B- But we can learn about it together!" I thought about the shadowing, and all of our moments together.

I do ... like her. Maybe we could-

Remember. Your. Goal. Your. Purpose.

I jumped a little in my seat, surprising Ashlyn. I closed my eyes and sighed, "I'll have to think about it." Ashlyn nodded and leaned back in her chair.

"Of course, take the time you need! Why don't we order food?" She seemed embarrassed, which made me feel pretty bad. Deep down, I knew the answer I wanted to say ... but I had to focus. I have one purpose.

We ordered, ate, then headed back to the dorms. I waited in my room for a while, meditating and trying to hype myself up for the fight tonight. At 2:30 p.m. there was a knock on my door.

"Yeah, who is it?"

"It's me!" Ashlyn responded. "We should get going soon, the apartment is across town!"

"Alright, give me a minute!" I rushed to change into my hero costume, then glanced out the window. I took a deep breath, thinking about her question at the restaurant, and looked down at my hands.

Why does she like me so much? What does she see ... in a villain like me? I just- don't understand.

Ashlyn and I took the elevator to the lobby to meet up with Jax and Olivia. Once we reached them, Jax threw his arm over my shoulder and poked me in the chest a few times.

"Ready to go, big man?" he asked through our chuckles.

"Yeah, let's go trick-or-treating I guess," I sighed happily. We left campus and were on our way to Ally Road. The city didn't have many trick-or-treaters, hence why we were given the map. It showed us the suburb borders because the suburbs were the hotspots for Halloween. After a twenty-five-minute walk, we made it to the apartment complex. It was a big, brick building with tiny balconies off each room.

"Let's stick together during the trick-or-treating. Villains are more active on Halloween, so by being together we'll have better protection for the kids," Jax suggested as he opened the door for us. We agreed and followed the numbers down the hall until we reached the two addresses we'd been given. Both doors were decorated with papers skeletons and pumpkins, obviously colored by the kids, and two carved pumpkins rested against the wall between the rooms. I took charge and rang the Greene's door, and after a couple seconds, it opened. There stood a tall man with big muscles, a stern face, and a fuzzy white mustache. His arms were crossed and he looked me in the eyes, which was quite intimidating.

"Are you the heroes here for my daughter?" he asked in his raspy voice. Before I could answer, a small girl ran through his legs and stood between us, looking up at me. She looked different, but adorable. Her skin was brown, her hair was long and white, and she had curious, red eyes. The features that made her different were tiny black horns, long fangs, and a skinny tail that had a bit of fluff on the end. She wore a little which costume and held her big, floppy hat with both hands. After seeing us, she became embarrassed, looked down, and blushed. I crouched in front of her and gave her a big smile.

"Hi there, you must be Savannah Greene!" I exclaimed. She nodded but didn't look up. I pointed at myself while saying, "I'm Kyle Straiter, future number-one hero, at your service. I'll take care of you tonight and protect you. Sound good?" Savannah giggled and smiled, now looking up at me.

"Kyle Straiter! What is your hero name?!" she yelled, pointing at me like it was an interrogation. I looked at her and pretended to be nervous, using it as a disguise to think, then I nodded.

"My hero name? You can call me Sun, like the big bright ball in the sky." Savannah's dad grabbed her hand and walked her back inside.

"Wait here, I'll get her ready." After he closed the door, I turned and saw the others staring at me.

"Sun? What kind of a hero name is that?" Jax snickered.

"It's more symbolic than flashy. I don't want to be known as just the son of Tyrant, I wanna be something the world can rely on. What's something that everyone relies on? The sun," I explained.

Ashlyn smiled and hopped to my side. "I like it! Honestly, it's still pretty flashy and bold when you think about it! Aiming to be as bright and reliable as the sun is a big goal!" Ashlyn complimented. I flexed my arm and held my bicep, feeling a tender bruise from yesterday.

"I'm willing to take the risk of a big goal! It'll motivate me to work harder!" They smiled then Olivia grabbed Jax's hand and walked over to the Jacobs' door. She knocked and they answered almost instantly. Unlike Mr. Greene, Mrs. Jacobs greeted them with a bright smile.

"You must be the heroes taking my Chris out! Thank you so much for this. I wish I could be there for him and Savannah, but work is just so hectic right now with all of the Care-Giver action lately," Mrs. Jacobs sighed. She had brown hair that barely reached her shoulders and overall looked worn out.

"We heroes are here so you can trust your son can go out and still have fun while being safe. If you ever need help, don't be afraid to ask for it!" Jax said with a smile, giving Mrs. Jacobs peace. She nodded, then a little boy ran from behind her and tugged on Jax's pantleg. He looked down and saw the boy, who was wearing a little blue robe and a big wizard's hat.

"You're a real hero, right?! Wow, I can't wait to be like you some day!" the boy yelled with a bright smile. Jax crouched and patted Chris on the head.

"I can't wait to see you be a hero. It's the bravest thing a person can be!" Jax responded. The Greene's door opened and Savannah jumped out wearing her witch hat and holding a plastic pumpkin bucket. Chris ran past Jax and Olivia toward Savannah, and the two hugged while giggling. It was honestly one of the most adorable things I'd ever seen.

We said goodbye to their parents and left to go trick-or-treating. We students analyzed the map and determined the best, safest route to take the kids on. We set off and were about half-way through of our trip before we ran into trouble.

The kids got candy from a house that gave out huge chocolate bars, so Chris and Savannah compared theirs.

They wanted to take a little break to eat some of their candy, so we took them over to a park bench. Jax and I stood on lookout a few feet away from the bench, and the girls made sure the kids didn't choke or hurt themselves.

"Man, I love Halloween," Jax smiled, resting his hands on his head. "The smell of fall and the atmosphere are just- perfect!" I nodded in agreement and took a deep breath. The crisp air gave the inside of my nose the slightest burning sensation, and the wind was getting colder by the minute. It was 5:47 p.m. and other pro-heroes could be seen patrolling the area. I didn't care whether heroes were around or not. Tonight, I would duel with BloodShot. Since I was going to beat him, there was no criminal who could even scratch me.

"Mr. Sun!" Savannah exclaimed, walking up to me.

"Hmm, what's up?" I asked as I crouched. Savannah swayed back and forth, holding her hands behind her, and suddenly shoved a chocolate wafer bar in my face.

"Here's your pay for your hard work!"

I smiled brightly and chuckled. "Wow, thank you so much boss!" I responded as I took the candy. Savannah giggled, then gave me a big hug.

"I can't believe the next number-one hero is working for me!" she yelled as she pulled off the hug. I gave her a salute as she ran back to the bench. My smile faded as I looked at the sun peeking out from the clouds.

One purpose. One goal.

After the little break was over, we resumed trick-or-treating but crowds lined the busy street. Apparently, there was a scary attraction at one of the houses and it was the most popular attraction in Takorain.

"Man, we're backed up all down the block! We can't even go back!" Olivia complained as she squinted and looked behind us, where she saw people continuing to line up. I yawned as I stretched my arms above my head, then I glanced down at Savannah, who was smiling brightly.

"Mr. Sun, are we almost there?" she asked. I looked up and saw we were maybe halfway down the block. It would be another ten to twenty minutes before we arrived at the attraction.

"We're getting there," I stated, trying to be positive. She asked to be picked up so she could see, so I did. Savannah stared at the large crowd in front of us, then gave me a pretend-pouty face.

"You're lying," she stated before giggling. I chuckled. I heard a sinister mumble from a stranger next to me and out of the corner of my eye, I could see the person wore a cloak covering their face. I caught a glimpse of purple mist coming from the cloak's hood. The stranger was a few inches taller than me; next to them was a person wearing an identical cloak. The second person was about the same height as Ashlyn. I said something to Savannah as a distraction, then focused on the person next to me.

"He's right here, and that's the child." I tensed as I turned my head to face the tall figure. In a flash, the person reached their right arm out to my face and an explosion of dark matter erupted out of their skinny, pale palm. People around us screamed in horror and pushed each other to get away from the cloud of purple mist. I coughed a few times, as did Savannah, and as the mist faded, I ran to Jax and shoved Savannah into his arms.

"Get everyone out of here! Make sure the kids are safe, that's our top priority!" I turned to fight the attacker. Before I could run into battle Savannah grabbed the straps on my headband.

"You're not going to get hurt, are you?!" She had genuine concern in her voice, so I turned back around and put my hand on her head.

"Of course not. Did you already forget who you're talking to? The future number-one hero would never get hurt by some little bad guy like this!" I responded with a large smile. Savannah's eyes sparkled as she watched me sprint toward the cloaked villains. The cold wind slightly blew into the tall man's hood, revealing a sight that sent a chill down my spine. His face was extremely pale and skinny; he had black lines painted all over his face, dull, sunken red eyes, protruding cheekbones, and not a strand of hair anywhere. In one hand he carried a thick, brown book I'd never seen before. The person next to him carried the same book. "Who are you and why are you after the girl and me?!"

The second attacker sped past the tall man at an alarming speed and punched me in the chest. They tried to follow through but I didn't move. I swiftly grabbed the attacker's hood and removed it, then grabbed her shoulder and spun her around so she faced the man with me. I leaned on her and yawned.

"Listen, I'm just trying to let these kids have the best Halloween ever. I really don't have time to play around," I said smugly. The girl had the same skin tone as Ashlyn, long eyelashes, heavy makeup, and a long, braided, blonde ponytail. Instead of acting out or trying to hit me, she threw her arm around me and sighed.

"Well, we want to play so we're going to! Don't worry, we're not gonna hurt the kids; we actually want to protect the girl!" she informed me. I nodded and let go of her. A pillar of snow hit her in the head and Ashlyn walked up beside me with a stern face and crossed arms.

"I don't appreciate you being all touchy with my man," Ashlyn seethed at the girl. The girl attacker glared at Ashlyn then turned back to me.

"Listen, Kyle Straiter, it's important that you know you're making a big mistake. A message from The Uprisers:

you will fail, and you will cause the demise of all of us." I raised an eyebrow and tensed my fists.

Is she talking about my fight with BloodShot, or just me in general? What mistake could I be making right now?

"I am talking about your fight. It will end poorly for you, very poorly in fact," she responded as if I'd spoken out loud. The pale Upriser released another gas, but only a small amount this time. The rich red gas moved as if it was alive and wrapped itself around Ashlyn's body. She struggled to break free as The Upriser girl pranced up to me and threw her arms around my neck. She flicked my ninja headband and stared into my eyes. "If you don't agree to call off the fight, we'll have to take you ourselves. This can go the easy way or the hard way. Don't bother trying to lie either, I'll know."

I refuse to talk unless no one else can hear us.

The girl smirked and nodded, then lifted her right hand and snapped. The pale Upriser reached out his bony hand and released a blue smoke that surrounded us. She crossed her arms, leaned back on her left foot, and nodded her head once.

"Talk."

"I won't call off my fight, I'll win it," I boldly stated. The Upriser girl shook her head and sighed. I noticed a slight blush as well.

"That is you. Of course you won't back down." I didn't understand why she said that. How would she know what I'm like? "Zen and I have been following you for quite some time. Our leader assigned us to check in on you from a distance. We've been around a week and a half."

"So long story short, you've been stalking me for two weeks," I blurted. She became flustered and stuttered trying to retort an insult, to no avail. I rolled my eyes and put my hands on my hips as she cleared her throat.

"I suppose you could say it like that if you wish. You must understand how valuable you are to all sides. The heroes don't want you to turn to villainy and take over the world, the villains want you too, and we want you to be the leader that takes a stand against society. Since you're so powerful, people would listen," she explained.

I rubbed the back of my head, hesitating, and asked sincerely, "Well, with all due respect, why don't we get rid of one of those sides?"

She raised an eyebrow so I elaborated, "I'm a hero at the core, no matter who my father is. Why don't The Uprisers join the heroes? Hero society is going to change again with our generation. We're going to evolve and place saving people's lives over glory, power, or fame. Why don't The Uprisers help heroes take down the main problem—the Care-Givers—and then we can work together to create the right society?" The girl shook her head no but didn't seem angry at the suggestion.

"I hear what you're saying, I really do. It's not completely out of the question, but it won't happen any time soon. I know it's not just me who feels this way. Until I see a change, I won't follow you heroes." I nodded; I couldn't argue with that.

"I understand. In the future, I will show you that heroes aren't selfish assholes. My classmates and I will revive the faith in heroes. I promise." I reached out a hand and she just stared at it. It looked as though her eyes sparkled, then she reached for my hand and shook it.

"I hope you do show me." We smiled for a moment before she remembered why she was there. "Wait, don't try to soften me! You cannot go fight BloodShot. We will take you away right now if you keep refusing! You are going to lose, and you will be taken and brutally tortured! Is that really what you want?!" she suddenly erupted.

"But I won't lose!" I interrupted after taking a step forward. "I don't care what you say, or if you have a future reader or something, but no matter what future awaits, I'll change it! I will beat BloodShot, whether that's what the future holds or not." She looked down and gripped pieces of her cloak. Her face turned redder, her eyes were squeezed shut tightly, and she scrunched her nose.

The Upriser girl swiveled on her feet to face away from me, then uttered, "Hmph, fine! Go ahead and fight BloodShot, but we'll be there too! We'll be watching and when you lose, we'll save you! Deal?!"

"Uh, yeah. Deal." I was almost left speechless by her tenacity. The smoke dissipated and the two left just as heroes arrived. They questioned me about the strangers, but I limited the information to they were Uprisers. I could have told the heroes the pale man's name was Zen, but I felt since they were going to protect me if anything happened, I should protect their aliases.

The rest of the night was peaceful. We avoided any places where there were sketchy people and stayed on track with the map. Over time, I noticed more and more how adorable Savannah and Chris were. Their relationship was so cute and they absolutely adored us heroes.

Once we'd finished the route, we walked Savannah and Chris back to their apartments. My heart beat faster and my stomach did backflips; the time was coming. Ashlyn and I hugged Savannah, then said goodbye to her parents. As our group walked back, Ashlyn was clingier than usual.

"Man, I just love kids. Don't you, Kyle?" she flirtatiously asked. I blushed and looked away quickly without responding. Ashlyn giggled, as did Olivia and Jax, then she squeezed my hand tightly, causing me slight concern.

I really hope this isn't about what The Upriser girl said. It's going to be a problem if Ashlyn intervenes, or tells others like Tonuko and Xavier ...

"I can't wait to go lay in bed for the rest of the night, I'm exhausted! Aren't you, Kyle?" Ashlyn's tone was different. She seemed much pushier and more aggressive, suggesting quietly that I'd better not leave my room tonight.

"Yeah, can't wait. I'm beat," I responded with a nervous chuckle. We arrived back at B.E.G.'s campus and went straight to the dorms. Gladiator made sure everyone made it back safely, then congratulated us on our success during this combination event.

"Y- You all have grown so much in just a week. It's b- been an honor t- teaching you Eccentric High students! I h- hope to see you again at the Hero Olym-pics!" Gladiator stuttered. We cheered and after chatting for a few minutes, Gladiator left for the teacher's dorm. I watched through the glass door as he walked down the pathway.

Good, he's going to sleep. That's one less person to try and stop me.

"Man, I'm exhausted! Kids are no fuckin' joke, huh?!" Xavier sighed while nudging my arm. I smiled slightly and nodded my head, then scanned the room. Ashlyn wasn't talking seriously to people, and everyone seemed pretty calm. After about half an hour, everybody went to their rooms to change or relax. I stayed in mine instead of joining them for a going-away party. I knew what I needed to do.

One purpose. One goal.

Chapter 32
Tyranny

I glanced at my clock and saw it was fifteen minutes from midnight. I didn't want to arrive early and seem desperate, nor too late and miss him. Now would be the perfect time to leave. I was so nervous that I felt like I could throw up and so excited that I could jump through the roof. My palms were sweating and my knees were jelly. I thought of beating the life out of BloodShot, beating his head with blow after blow. At the same time, I thought of what would happen if I lost: torture, pain, suffering, death ...

Out of all my worries one was making my heart beat in my throat—I knew I needed to say goodbye to Ashlyn, in case I didn't come back. I walked to my door and took a deep breath, through my nose, out my mouth. A smile crept from my lips but I forced myself to conceal it. I turned the knob and opened the door.

The hallway was dark and silent, outside was the same. All of the partying had died down and, as far as I knew, everyone was asleep. I tiptoed over to Ashlyn's room, hesitated for a moment, and knocked on the door. After a minute, she opened the door and looked at me with serious eyes.

"Kyle, get back in your room. Now," she commanded. I could see the worry in her eyes and hear her voice breaking, though she tried to cover it with her stern attitude.

"Ashlyn." I couldn't think of any words to say, so I just hugged her. She hugged back tightly. I felt a liquid drop onto my shoulder, tears. To my surprise, my eyes also watered. I closed them and opened them as I stood up straight. "I'm about to do something ... really crazy. It's a matter of importance, a personal matter of importance, that I have to do. I just ... wanted to say goodbye in case-"

"Sleeping isn't a reason to say goodbye!" Ashlyn cried out. "Get back in your room, or else." It was scary how quickly Ashlyn's personality changed from gleeful and ditsy to depressed to serious and deadly all within a few words. "I'm not letting you go somewhere if you aren't guaranteed to come back."

"I already told you: I have to do this. If you won't stay out of my way ... then-" I looked her dead in the eyes, she could see my rage, bloodlust, determination. "I'm sorry." I pushed her back, causing her to stumble and fall onto the floor. I gripped the doorknob, slammed the door shut, and ripped the knob off it.

"Kyle, don't do this! Please come back to me! Kyle!" Her screams were very loud and definitely alerted at least someone on our floor. I decided the quickest way out was through the window to my right. I hopped a few times to build up courage, then ran and broke through it just as Scarlett's and Sophia's doors opened. The fall was long. Once it ended, Energy Conversion kept me from being harmed. As I bolted toward the front entrance, strong ropes made of a yellow light wrapped around my waist, stopping me. I looked back and saw Hitoshi, Caleb, Ellie, and Catherine standing there, panting.

"Kyle, you're fucking crazy man! You can't go, you'll die!" Hitoshi shouted as he pulled his phone from his pocket dimension. I blinked a few times, feeling a slight bit of regret.

No backing down. You know your purpose, they don't. They don't know what you've been through.

"You don't understand!" I screeched. I grabbed the rope and pulled hard to my right, throwing Caleb into the other three. They toppled over so I took the opportunity to leap out of Caleb's ropes and book it out the gate.

"Dammit, we need to call heroes and tell them!" Hitoshi yelled as he dialed 911. After a couple of seconds staring at the phone, he asked, "Where is he going?!"

"Nora didn't say!" Ellie responded as she helped Catherine up.

"Well, where the hell is Nora?!" Hitoshi shouted. The two girls stood in silence, almost seeming guilty or regretful. "Well?!"

"She wasn't in her room, but her window was open. She's gone," Catherine informed the boys, who wore shocked expressions.

Within a minute, I'd run the fifteen-minute walk to the Junction and saw a man sitting on top of a roof: Favian. On another rooftop, more hidden than Favian, were the Upriser girl and Zen. I walked into the Junction and made it to the middle where BloodShot stood. He smiled eerily once he saw me.

"You're early Straiter and wearing your pathetic costume!" he taunted. "I know about those Upriser pussies over on that building; they better not be your lackies!" Similar to when he first attacked me, BloodShot's presence was plainly off, full of bloodlust. It felt as if I was being choked when I looked at him, and I was extremely scared now. I calmed my fears with a deep breath, then glared at him.

"I'm going to kill you for all the things you've done! You can't scare me anymore! You're a monster, and you deserve to rot in hell!" BloodShot's smile slightly faded, and my fury and rage grew, blinding me. "I'll take you down to the devil, drag you by force if I have to. I'll murder you, whether that means I survive or not!" My body moved on its own as I jumped at him. I swung a punch with all my might, but BloodShot nonchalantly caught it and threw me aside into a building.

"Absolutely pathetic! I thought you had Enhanced Strength? I thought you were the hotshot around here?! Come on then, come at me!" BloodShot grew louder with every yell. I squeezed my fingers into the ground, then leapt at him again. A loud whisper echoed in my head,

Let me lend my power. You can kill him ... with me.

Yes, I accept all of your power.

The darkness exploded out of my palms after a couple missed hits on BloodShot and wrapped around my body. It stuck to my skin, sunk into my body, and changed the pigment of my skin to a marbling of my normal peach and pitch black. I led with gray flames powering my punch, but he caught my attack yet again. BloodShot slid back a few inches this time, then cackled in my face and threw me onto the ground. I felt an excruciating pain in my right shoulder, and it didn't help that BloodShot was now stepping on my head.

"You're so very angry, lost, confused. You're thinking: 'how the hell is he stopping me so easily? I have Enhanced Strength, I should be able to overpower him easily!'" BloodShot mocked. I blasted flames out of the hand he wasn't holding, stood, and flipped back to face him again. My nose bled. I was so enraged I couldn't focus my eyes. I gritted my teeth so hard that my jaw hurt and my breathing turned to a seethe.

"I'm going to fucking kill you," I sinisterly sneered in a deep, raspy voice. BloodShot fake shivered then cackled obnoxiously. I used fire to boost me toward him and released an entourage of attacks. I punched at his face; he dodged. I swung a kick at his stomach; he dodged. I flipped while floating and tried to land a devastating blow on the top of his head with my heel, but he grabbed my foot.

"Oh my, what is this? Your presence is changing, isn't it?! You aren't Kyle Straiter anymore, are you?!" BloodShot questioned with a near leer. "Come on out, Demon, you're already as clear as day!"

Kyle, let me take over your body. Please, trust me.

Without hesitation, I agreed.

Yes, I- I let you.

I stopped tensing my body and let loose, which allowed It to take full control. Dark tentacles shot out of me and one hit BloodShot in the cheek. He dropped me as more tentacles crawled from my back and lifted me high into the sky. Others gripped buildings around us and a few more shot out at BloodShot. I couldn't think straight; my body was controlled by the Tyrant Demon.

"Whatever that is really has a grip on you, huh?! Such power, such force, such *rage!* You're so blinded by your hatred and fury that you made a deal with a demon, Kyle! You are even crazier than I am, *but still weaker!*" BloodShot elegantly dodged all the tentacles soaring at him, then my body practically teleported in front of him. Purple mist covered BloodShot's face as I landed a devastating punch to his cheekbone. He skidded back a few feet and giggled. BloodShot licked the inside of his cheek and spat out a wad of blood.

How did he not suffer more damage?! I hit him with everything we had! That should have killed any normal man!

"I can see your dumbfounded expression, Demon! You're wondering how I'm so strong, both of you are! How can I easily deflect your Enhanced Strength punches?!" BloodShot taunted.

"Yeah, I am wondering," I stated. It felt weird being able to talk while the rest of my body was numb, but that was the least of my worries.

"I bet you thought I only had Inflation, just one strength! Everybody assumes I only have one strength. It's hilarious! You aren't the only anomaly, Kyle!" I felt my heart sink and heard the Tyrant Demon's growl as BloodShot revealed, "Inflation isn't my natural-born strength, Kyle! I wasn't born with this incredible power! I trained for this strength; I was gifted another at birth!"

"*Don't tell me ...*" Tyrant Demon stated through my vocal cords.

"Yes, it's exactly what you think, Demon! I am able to easily beat you down because I was born with Enhanced Strength! My adopted master taught me Inflation, then ... I fucking killed him with the power he taught me! Isn't that great?!" BloodShot's voice grew higher as he screeched, "I was free, free to kill everyone with the legacy he built! I'm too strong for you Kyle; I'm fucking amazing, aren't I?!" The Tyrant Demon's anger played like a rumbling in my ears. Gray ropes of flames crawled out of the bottom of my palms and wrapped around my arms, and my muscles grew a bit.

The mist around my body grew thicker as the Tyrant Demon stated, "*You aren't stronger than me.*"

My veins pulsated seeing BloodShot's antagonizing smirk. He still had yet to draw his blade. In an instant I was behind him, in front of him, behind him, then in front once again. After a second, BloodShot had received multiple blows that mangled him and threw him to the ground. He swiftly hopped to his feet and swung a punch at me. I boosted myself away with flames, scorching his body in the process. I skidded on the ground and landed in a crouched position, then smacked my hands on the ground, creating four clones.

"I've seen this before! Not intimidating," BloodShot mocked. When the clones and I charged in at him from all fronts, BloodShot waited until we were close, then stomped on the ground. He created a powerful air force that shattered my clones and threw me back. While I soared through the air, BloodShot leapt over me and matched my speed, then swiftly drew his blade. "Let's get rid of this nuisance, yeah?" He stabbed into my stomach, causing an eerie, high-pitch screech from my mouth. I crashed back first into a building and BloodShot landed beside me, then thrust his sword deeper into my stomach. My eyes widened when I saw his sword through my body. He ripped it out and flipped off the building. I fell onto the ground hard, leaving a blood trail on the wall behind me.

Is this it? Am I going to die?

I gained control of my body, so all the pain rushed me at once. My tailbone ached from the fall and my stomach had a numbing pain. My eyelids drooped and drool dribbled from the corner of my mouth.

"Shit, that's not good. Is he even alive?" the Upriser girl asked, biting her nail.

"I'm not sure, Kiesh, but it will be difficult to get to him," Zen calmly stated. He made eye contact with Favian and saw a portal form behind him. "They're waiting for someone to make a move."

B.E.G., 11:55 p.m.:

Sophia kicked at the door while Ashlyn cried inside her room. Luckily, someone came up the stairs. Ashlyn heard Sophia and Xavier chatting, then the door burst open after a loud booming noise.

"Ashlyn, are you alright?!" Xavier shouted frantically.

605

"Xavier, I couldn't stop him! Kyle's gone to fight someone! I don't know who, where, or why, but an Upriser girl told Kyle he'd lose if he went to the fight! We have to get him!" Ashlyn cried as she hugged Xavier.

"I know, Hitoshi from the academic course just told Tonuko and me. Tonuko ran, saying he'd be able to find Kyle and we should get the pros on the case. We'll get him and ensure he makes it home alive," Xavier reassured Ashlyn. They left the room and Xavier looked over at the broken window. *"Kyle, you damn idiot. Don't you dare die on us."*

Tonuko ran as fast as he could through the city, focusing on each step. He was extremely frustrated. Tonuko tensed his fists tight and closed his eyes, where tears had formed, as he sprinted.

"Fuck Kyle, why do you have to be so damn stupid?! You don't have to go and fight all these dangerous people alone. Why can't you see that?! We're all friends, right?! We're here to support you! If you die now, I swear I'll kick your ass!" News helicopters flew overhead to investigate the noises that had been reported. Tonuko felt a thump in his right foot. He stopped running for a few moments and his eyes lit up. "The Junction." He quickly made his way to it and booked it through the front gates just as some pros from around the area arrived. One was Abby Onso.

Favian floated down from the building where he'd been stationed and a few Care-Givers, including Stafer, Kaci, and Bobby, stepped out from the portal. Their job was to prevent any pros from entering the Junction.

"Sorry heroes, but only students and BloodShot are allowed in here. Better luck next time," Kaci smiled.

"You sick fucks," Abby muttered ferociously.

Tonuko made his way through the Junction buildings and ran in on the scene. I sat on the ground, staring blankly, and BloodShot wheezed because he was laughing so hard. BloodShot's laughing stopped suddenly, then he slowly turned his head while wearing an inhumanely large smile.

"Oh my, there's the Earth boy. Come to ... save you friend? My, my, it's too late, isn't it?" Tonuko felt sick to his stomach and he began to sweat. He bent a wall between BloodShot and me, then ran to my aid. He knelt down and shook my shoulder.

"Kyle, Kyle, are you there? Are you ... alive?!" Tonuko frantically yelled with a cracking voice. I felt something thick crawl up my throat, then, instead of vomit, I threw up blood. It was sticky and hot and left strings in my mouth. I swallowed, but it didn't do much. A banging sounded from the wall. When Tonuko glanced toward it, a large crack shot up the wall. "Kyle, you have to get up! We need to get out of here, now!" Tonuko screamed, continuing to shake me. I stared at him, still dazed, then BloodShot broke down Tonuko's wall and led with a knee to his head. My eyes grew wide as Tonuko smashed through the wall I'd been leaning on.

"No need for interruptions. Thanks, though," BloodShot hissed, standing over Tonuko. I exploded and punched BloodShot in the face. A tentacle whizzed out of my chest, grabbed his free-flying body, and pulled him back toward me. We headbutted, then I spun around and whipped BloodShot into the building across from us. Even with blood pouring down his face, BloodShot still grinned psychotically. "Yes, show me your anger!" As the words left his mouth, I body slammed into him, breaking through the wall of the building, as well as the next one.

"Holy- shit ..." Tonuko stuttered in awe. I launched myself into the air, grabbed some large debris with two tentacles, and chucked the boulders at BloodShot. He tried to lift his arms to block but was surprised when he couldn't. Black ice froze his forearms to his hips. BloodShot looked up and down frantically, then jumped up, spun around, and kicked the rocks. They shattered and flew past his body, making him grin again, but the moment was short lived. I'd picked up a shank and plunged it into his stomach.

"*I've got you now!*" I screeched. As the shank stabbed into the ice, BloodShot jumped up and kicked me in the side of the head. I soared left and crashed through another wall. I had led with my head and everything was getting dark. The tentacles moved on their own to help me stand, but with all my blood loss I was too weak to maintain them. The tentacles were sucked back into my body and darkness faded. My stab wound slowly expanded and the pain was unimaginable. I wobbled toward BloodShot and swung a weak fist at him; he didn't bother blocking, just let the punch poke his arm. BloodShot ripped his arms out of the ice and gripped my throat, lifting me high into the sky.

"I can see you approaching, trying to save this demon! Your attempts are futile!" BloodShot shouted at Tonuko, Ryuu, and Xavier. Ryuu and Xavier flew straight in at BloodShot, Ryuu using his wings and Xavier copying Ryuu's strength. BloodShot turned sideways and let them fly past. Ryuu landed and immediately turned to attack BloodShot, who parried all of his attacks with one hand, then he sliced a gash on his cheek. Xavier and Tonuko bent large pillars, attempting to squish BloodShot. He jumped high and over the pillars, causing them to crash into each other. Ryuu flew at BloodShot and swung another punch at his face but BloodShot swiftly moved his hand aside. A portal formed, sucked in Ryuu's hand, and another formed next to his face, making him punch himself. At this point, I was viciously scratching at BloodShot's hand while he continued choking me. Blood and spit from my face dripped onto his hand as I blacked out.

Three large creatures restrained my classmates as Bobby entered the scene. Looking at my unconscious body, he clapped and smiled brightly.

"Well done, BloodShot, very well done! Poor little almighty Kyle has fallen!" Bobby cheered. Ryuu, Xavier, and Tonuko struggled to break free of the beasts' grasps, then Stafer and Kaci walked up, dragging some of the paralyzed heroes behind them.

"Give him back! You can't take him!" Ryuu cried out. I slowly opened my eyes and blinked a few times. Some of my other classmates were dragged in by Stafer's replicas of Bobby's creatures, and Kaci had placed almost all of them under his control. They were unable to move. BloodShot's grip had loosened, which allowed me to breathe and regain consciousness.

"Kyle, you have to get away from them, please!" Ashlyn sobbed as she shuffled around in the grip of a creature. A large, purple and black smokescreen formed in the area, then Kiesh jumped in to try and nab me. BloodShot swung his sword at her, but she dodged effortlessly and ripped my body from his grasp. As she leapt high toward a building, BloodShot grabbed her leg and slammed her into the ground. She grimaced with pain and let go of me, then the smoke faded as Favian distracted Zen.

"That's the girl from earlier!" Jax shouted angrily. He was under Kaci's control, unable to move his limbs. I slowly looked up at Kiesh, who I was laying on, and saw her crying. BloodShot kicked me off her body and stood with his feet on either side of her thighs. She smiled at me, then Bloodshot mercilessly stabbed her multiple times. He killed her after a few more, leaving nothing but a mangled body and bloody mess in front of me.

"This is what happens to those you care for Kyle! Anybody you love, I'll kill right in front of your eyes! Anyone and Everyone!" BloodShot devilishly announced after kicking Kiesh's body aside. I couldn't believe my eyes, she actually died. After our talk in the smoke, how she'd promised to be more open about heroes if I could show her change, she died.

N- No ... she can't. Y- You. You MONSTER!

My fury was immeasurable as I lunged myself into BloodShot. A tentacle, not my doing, pushed us high into the air. He punched my face repeatedly, giving me a black eye, but I ignored the pain and went higher. When we were high enough, I spun around and chucked him down, then used flames to body slam him hard. We soared toward the ground then my fingers forcibly snapped. A large orb, which looked as if it was filled with space, formed at the ground. When BloodShot and I landed in the orb, it erupted and exploded. Everybody was swept off their feet, and almost all the buildings in the Junction were destroyed.

"A mysterious explosion just went off, causing mass damage to Junction One! Heroes are dead, students are injured! Did Kyle Straiter and BloodShot survive that direct attack?!" the newscaster screamed from the helicopter above us. The wind pressure from the explosion caused the helicopter to shake, but the pilot stabilized the control.

E.H. Dorms:

"Come on guys, get him away from there! Where are Puppeteer and Kaliska?!" Alex screamed at the T.V. screen. The others in the dorm lobby were stunned, unable to speak. Daniel couldn't believe his eyes, as one unconscious hero's outfit looked oddly familiar.

Junction:

Was that me? How did I do that?

BloodShot slowly stood, holding his head, and glared ferociously at me. There was more rage than I'd ever seen out of him. He was serious now. I felt true fear as I watched him stomp over to me. I put my shaky hands up to block my head, but he ripped through them and headbutted me hard. I fell back, then he picked me up by the collar and seethed.

"Favian, let's get out of here, now! I'm starting to get pissed off!" Favian floated next to us, then snapped. A portal exploded out of the air and BloodShot turned to look at it. I could see numerous scars over his face and a layer of skin on his cheek was completely burned off.

"No, Kyle! Fight back, come on!" Tonuko screamed as he ran toward us. He raised a platform underneath BloodShot and me. A pillar covered in darkness bent from the ground and smacked him in the jaw.

"Stay down boy," Stafer growled.

"Kyle, give up, you lost. We had a deal, and if you break it, I will kill every last person here," BloodShot threatened, locking eyes with me. I gulped and looked at everyone. The students and pros were down and injured. Only the low-level heroes were around; no Puppeteer, no Kaliska. There weren't even any well-known heroes other than Abby, who was lying face down halfway across the Junction. I took a deep breath, then nodded.

"I'll go with you, just don't hurt anyone else." BloodShot cackled, then dropped me. I fell onto my knees and looked around one more time. Tears plagued the crowd. I felt more like a wild animal than a human to the eyes.

"Kyle, please don't do this! Don't leave me!" Ashlyn screamed through her cries.

"This is it, guys, I'll finally be leaving you. You won't have to worry about being targeted anymore because the source is gone. I hope you become successful, I really do," I said as I slowly stood. Tonuko and I made eye contact, then my eyelids drooped. "Sorry, but I guess I will be breaking our promise." I looked at Ashlyn one last time and saw her mouth form the words "I love you." I didn't respond. Instead, I turned and trudged into the portal.

The other Care-Givers left just as Puppeteer and Kaliska arrived. Puppeteer tensed his fists then swore, "Dammit, we were too late! He's gone ... Kyle is gone!"

Puppeteer crouched and punched the ground. Kaci and Bobby's strengths were released, freeing everyone to move again. Tonuko stared at the spot where the portal was; he was in shock.

"So, does this mean- the son of Tyrant is back with him? Is Kyle Straiter a villain now?" a hero asked. Xavier clenched his jaw, swiftly stood, and pointed at the hero.

"Is that all you fucking people think of that kid?! That he's Tyrant's son, bound to end up a villain once he's brought back to his dad?! Are you fucking serious?!" He took another step forward, but felt a hand on his right shoulder. He glanced back and saw Ryuu, who had a stern stare.

"Kyle feels more guilt about his father's actions than he does happiness about his heroic deeds! Kyle feels sympathy for everyone affected by Tyrant and knows first-hand how horrible it is to have things you hold dearly stripped from your grasp! How dare you say since he was captured, he's now destined to be like Tyrant! We should be planning a rescue mission!" Ryuu added furiously. Kaliska nodded their head and took a deep breath.

"Alright, Puppeteer and I want any and all information on the location of Tyrant and his goons. Search teams will explore areas where Care-Givers have been seen recently," Kaliska commanded. They turned and glared at Zen, who was sitting upright a few feet behind Kaliska and Puppeteer. "As for you, take your friend's body ... and get going. I don't think that girl's life is savable, but medics in the area will be open for treatment. Now go." Zen was surprised to hear the kindness from Kaliska and nodded. He solemnly picked up Kiesh's body and fled the scene.

"We'll put those scumbag Care-Givers into custody. Mark my words, BloodShot: you will not live to see another year," Puppeteer stated before turning to walk away.

Tyrant's Factory:

BloodShot led me into the area where all the Care-Giver's sat. What happened after was a blur. I remember being harassed, punched, tripped, kicked, and pushed on my way to a different room. Tyrant and the Care-Givers watched as Laci strapped me to a cold, metal table. It was upright but leaned back slightly. From what I could see, her expression wasn't as prideful and happy as the others'; instead, there was a hint of sadness. I felt like an attraction for these sick people, just amusement to satisfy their depressions. According to Tyrant, though, this was my real family, closer than blood.

"I want his wounds treated immediately. Call in any black-market healers you need," Tyrant demanded with a frown. "Soon, very soon, we will start his purification." He glanced at me once more then walked away.

The world today is dark and grim. The world today feels they lost. The world today ... is under the foot of the man on top of the underworld, the man who is truly on top of the country.

Author's Note

This is a work of fiction, though several situations depicted are based on real-world problems and have been changed to fit the superpower-filled society. Issues such as the protesting for civilian right's, Kaliska's belief that they would not receive equal respect as a woman hero compared to a man hero, and some of the Care-Givers'—most notably BloodShot's and Stafer's—beliefs that others are inferior to them are very real in our society. They would not simply go away if superpowers became prevalent.

I wish to depict these issues and create a realistic society in this fictional world to which many can relate. My hope is for people to feel comforted seeing how characters react/actively change to get past these problems. A prime example is Kyle's evolution throughout the story. Of course, there is a fall in his self-esteem and his will to live toward the end of the story, but he undergoes countless changes—in his attitude and how he handles his emotions—that forge friendships with those who truly care about him. Kyle's development should serve as an exemplar to those struggling with mental issues. There is a way to dig yourself out of a hole you have been trapped in, especially when it's caused by someone else or something out of your control.

There's always a group for you and others who care for your life.

Never give up.